2018
PUSHCART PRIZE XLII
BEST OF THE
SMALL PRESSES

EDITED BY BILL HENDERSON
WITH THE PUSHCART PRIZE EDITORS

D0113620

Note: nominations for this series are invited from any small, independent, literary book press or magazine in the world, print or online. Up to six nominations—tear sheets or copies, selected from work published, or about to be published, in the calendar year—are accepted by our December 1 deadline each year. Write to Pushcart Fellowships, P.O. Box 380, Wainscott, N.Y. 11975 for more information or consult our website www.pushcartprize.com.

Acknowledgments
Selections for The Pushcart Prize are reprinted with the permission of authors and presses cited. Copyright reverts to authors and presses immediately after publication.

Distributed by W. W. Norton & Co.
500 Fifth Ave., New York, N.Y. 10110

Library of Congress Card Number: 76-58675
ISBN (hardcover): 978-1-888889-84-0
ISBN (paperback): 978-1-888889-85-7
ISSN: 0149-7863

for
Barack Obama, writer

INTRODUCTION

Over the past four decades these introductions have often lauded small press editors and authors. This year we honor Barack Obama, writer.

In his three books, *Dreams for My Father, The Audacity of Hope,* and *Of Thee I Sing,* he is honest, elegant and generous. In the White House he insisted on the dignity of the office and didn't waste time with flatulent opinions or ridiculous, and often dangerous, fantasies. He didn't "do stupid" and he didn't speak or write stupid either.

We miss him.

Obama's eight years seem like a distant dream, a memory of a better time that vanished in a snap. Up jumped a chameleon with no respect for words, facts or people, a poseur with the intellectual profundity of a coat of varnish.

And so we dedicate this Pushcart Prize to our writing friend Barack Obama. Not the politician, not the President—the writer, who respects what words mean and can do.

✻　✻　✻

Now that the yahoos are in charge of the government, we hear the familiar cry to abolish the National Endowment for the Arts, a major funder of small press writers and presses. Over the next few years I expect this will be a continuing theme song in yahoo land.

All this reminds me of the events that *The Paris Review*'s George Plimpton recorded in his guest Introduction to *Pushcart Prize* X. Plimpton's NEA-funded *American Literary Anthology* project had just been killed by a rabidly righteous Congressman.

Plimpton recalled the experience:

> "What led to the finish of the Anthology was a one word calligraphic poem by Aram Saroyan ("lighght") which was published in Volume II of the Anthology.
>
> "Its brevity caught (and held!) the eye of Congressman William Scherle of Iowa.
>
> "An arch-critic of the National Endowment and its programs. . . . He flailed away on the floor of the Congress. Editorials and letters had a field day. Among other things, the furor caused the Endowment to take a much closer look at the contents scheduled for Volume III. There, to their dismay, they discovered an essay by Ed Sanders on Peace-eye Bookstore in the East Village, an avant-garde establishment which had on its shelves a number of 'literary' artifacts. Among these Sanders had described a half used Vaseline jar, which had once belonged to Allen Ginsberg with a legend affixed describing what it had been used for.
>
> "Eyes popping, the Endowment people read this, and decided that if the description ever fell into the hands of Congressman William Scherle he could very well use it to bring down the entire National Endowment for the Arts."

The poem was removed and the terrified NEA canceled the Anthology project.

❊   ❊   ❊

My own experiences with the NEA have been more pleasant. Back in the 1980's I ran *Writer's Choice*, an advertising project for small press authors backed by the Endowment. I asked participants to endorse our endeavor. Nobody said it better than Raymond Carver, poet and short story writer and author of books that include: *Will You Please Be Quiet, Please?*; *What We Talk About When We Talk About Love* and *Cathedral*. Carver wrote to me:

6

"I don't think the value of the small presses can be over-estimated in any degree. In truth, I feel they are the backbone of the national literature.

"Speaking for myself, I don't believe I would have had a literary life, or not much of one anyway, had it not been for small press publishers and the little magazines. My first three books were poems and they were published by Kayak Press and Capra Press. And my first fiction that was ever published in book form was a chapbook from Capra . . . Small presses and little magazines sustained me for more than a decade, when none of the larger magazines would publish my work . . . the mere fact that someone was publishing my work in whatever form was an indication to me that somebody cared. . . . The best of the small presses are doing work that is every bit the equal, if not superior to, the literature being issued by the larger better know and certainly more financially sound presses."

*　　*　　*

The tradition of presses supporting new, and established, writers continues in the Pushcart Prize which, by the way, receives no government or institutional funding.

Of particular excitement to me was the nomination that Charles Baxter sent to Pushcart in November, 2016. You may recall his unforgettable short story "Avarice" in last year's prize—and his 12 Pushcart Prize stories and essays starting with PPVI. He is the winner of the Rea Award for the Short Story and the author most recently of *There's Something I Want You To Do: Stories.*

Baxter's nomination letter reads:

"The Pushcart Prize has changed the face of American literary publishing and has given untold numbers of young writers a boost. In light of that, I want to nominate a great story by a young writer just out of the box: the story is 'Catacombs,' which appeared in *One Story* April 7, 2016, and its author is Jason Zencka. According to the author's note it is his first published story. It will knock you out."

7

We agreed with Baxter. You will find Jason Zencka's story as the lead in this edition.

As George Plimpton, Ray Carver and Charles Baxter remind us, small presses give hope to new writers and support veterans. Their spirit keeps us all alive in the age of chameleons and yahoos.

❋   ❋   ❋

Over the years we have lost writers who were close to my heart and I have remembered many of them in these introductions. This year Brian Doyle died far too young of brain cancer as we were going to press. He was the author of several prize-winning books but I will always remember his brief essays that appeared in previous Pushcart Prize volumes especially "Joyas Voladoras" (PPXX). Read it again if you want to feel again the miracle of all life—including your own. His most recent Pushcart Prize essay appears on page 83.

❋   ❋   ❋

So many people to thank for assembling the 71 stories, poems, essays and memoirs from 53 presses in PPXLII—first our Guest Editors: the distinguished poets Stephen Dunn, Sally Wen Mao, and Robert Wrigley (poetry) and Dominica Phetteplace, Douglas Milliken, and Kalpana Narayanan (prose). We thank also our more than 200 Contributing Editors for this volume and Phil Schultz and Cedering Fox for celebratory efforts. And we welcome two new staff members—Jackie Krass, who has just finished graduate work at Pembroke College, Cambridge, UK, and Giulia Mascali, just out of Bard College.

As I said last year, while we move into the next decade my only worry is that so much truly terrific work will overwhelm the PP. We simply have no room in our limited volume for all that is wonderful and new. Please consult the Special Mention section: each of these poems, stories, essays and memoirs deserves to be widely read.

And while we are appreciating our writers, please honor our donors to the Pushcart Prize Fellowships and perhaps consider joining them. You will find their names listed in all editions. We wouldn't be here unless they cared. Your donation too will be noted in all future volumes.

8

As always, thanks to you, dear reader. Without you we would perish. You remind us of this every year. This frantic world needs you more than ever. Keep the faith.

Bill Henderson

THE PEOPLE WHO HELPED

FOUNDING EDITORS—Anaïs Nin (1903-1977), Buckminster Fuller (1895-1983), Charles Newman (1938-2006), Daniel Halpern, Gordon Lish, Harry Smith (1936-2012), Hugh Fox (1932-2011), Ishmael Reed, Joyce Carol Oates, Len Fulton (1934-2011), Leonard Randolph, Leslie Fiedler (1917-2003), Nona Balakian (1918-1991), Paul Bowles (1910-1999), Paul Engle (1908-1991), Ralph Ellison (1913-1994), Reynolds Price (1933-2011), Rhoda Schwartz, Richard Morris, Ted Wilentz (1915-2001), Tom Montag, William Phillips (1907-2002). Poetry editor: H. L. Van Brunt

CONTRIBUTING EDITORS FOR THIS EDITION—Steve Adams, Dan Albergotti, Dick Allen, John Allman, Idris Anderson, Antler, Tony Ardizzone, Reneé Ashley, David Baker, Kim Barnes, Steven Barthelme, Ellen Bass, Rick Bass, Claire Bateman, Bruce Beasley, Marvin Bell, Molly Bendall, Pinckney Benedict, Bruce Bennett, Marie-Helene Bertino, Linda Bierds, Marianne Boruch, Michael Bowden, Krista Bremer, Fleda Brown, Rosellen Brown, Michael Dennis Browne, Ayse Papatya Bucak, Christopher Buckley, E. Shaskan Bumas, Richard Burgin, Kathy Callaway, Richard Cecil, Kim Chinquee, Suzanne Cleary, Billy Collins, Martha Collins, Lydia Conklin, Stephen Corey, Lisa Couturier, Paul Crenshaw, Claire Davis, Chard deNiord, Jaquira Diaz, Stuart Dischell, Stephen Dixon, Daniel L. Dolgin, Chris Drangle, Jack Driscoll, John Drury, Emma Duffy-Comparone, Karl Elder, Elizabeth Ellen, Martín Espada, Ed Falco, Beth Ann Fennelly, Gary Fincke, Maribeth Fischer, April L. Ford, Robert Long Foreman, Ben Fountain, H. E. Francis, Alice Friman, Sarah Frisch, John Fulton, Richard Garcia, Frank X. Gaspar, Christine Gelineau, David Gessner, Nancy Geyer, Gary Gildner, Elton Glaser, Mark Halliday, Jeffrey Hammond, James Harms, Jeffrey Harrison, Timothy Hedges, Daniel Lee Henry, David Hernandez,

11

DeWitt Henry, Bob Hicok, Edward Hirsch, Jane Hirshfield, Jen Hirt, Edward Hoagland, Charles Holdefer, Andrea Hollander, Chloe Honum, David Hornibrook, Maria Hummel, Karla Huston, Colette Inez, Mark Irwin, Catherine Jagoe, David Jauss, Leslie Johnson, Bret Anthony Johnston, Jeff P. Jones, Michael Kardos, Laura Kasischke, George Keithley, Thomas E. Kennedy, James Kimbrell, David Kirby, John Kistner, Richard Kostelanetz, Mary Kuryla, Wally Lamb, Don Lee, Lisa Lee, Fred Leebron, Sandra Leong, Kate Levin, E. J. Levy, Gerald Locklin, Jennifer Lunden, Margaret Luongo, William Lychack, Clarence Major, Alexander Maksik, Paul Maliszewski, Michael Marberry, Matt Mason, Dan Masterson, Adrian Matejka, Lou Matthews, Alice Mattison, Tracy Mayor, Robert McBrearty, Rebecca McClanahan, Davis McCombs, Elizabeth McKenzie, Edward McPherson, Lincoln Michel, Douglas W. Milliken, Nancy Mitchell, Jim Moore, Joan Murray, Kent Nelson, Michael Newirth, Aimee Nezhukumatathil, Meghan O'Gieblyn, Joyce Carol Oates, William Olsen, Dzvinia Orlowsky, Peter Orner, Kathleen Ossip, Alicia Ostriker, Tom Paine, Alan Michael Parker, Dominica Phetteplace, C. E. Poverman, D. A. Powell, Melissa Pritchard, Kevin Prufer, Lia Purpura, James Reiss, Donald Revell, Nancy Richard, Laura Rodley, Jessica Roeder, Jay Rogoff, Rachel Rose, Mary Ruefle, Maxine Scates, Alice Schell, Grace Schulman, Philip Schultz, Lloyd Schwartz, Maureen Seaton, Asako Serizawa, Diane Seuss, Anis Shivani, Gary Short, Taije Silverman, Floyd Skloot, Arthur Smith, David St. John, Maura Stanton, Maureen Stanton, Pamela Stewart, Patricia Strachan, Terese Svoboda, Barrett Swanson, Ron Tanner, Katherine Taylor, Elaine Terranova, Susan Terris, Joni Tevis, Robert Thomas, Melanie Rae Thon, William Trowbridge, Frederic Tuten, David J. Unger, Lee Upton, Nance Van Winckel, G. C. Waldrep, Anthony Wallace, BJ Ward, Don Waters, Michael Waters, LaToya Watkins, Marc Watkins, Charles Harper Webb, Roger Weingarten, William Wenthe, Allison Benis White, Philip White, Jessica Wilbanks, Joe Wilkins, Kirby Williams, Eleanor Wilner, Sandi Wisenberg, Mark Wisniewski, David Wojahn, Shelley Wong, Angela Woodward, Carolyne Wright, Robert Wrigley, Christina Zawadiwsky, Liz Ziemska, Paul Zimmer

PAST POETRY EDITORS—H.L. Van Brunt, Naomi Lazard, Lynne Spaulding, Herb Leibowitz, Jon Galassi, Grace Schulman, Carolyn Forché, Gerald Stern, Stanley Plumly, William Stafford, Philip Levine, David Wojahn, Jorie Graham, Robert Hass, Philip Booth, Jay Meek, Sandra McPherson, Laura Jensen, William Heyen, Elizabeth Spires,

CONTENTS

CATACOMBS

fiction by JASON ZENCKA

from ONE STORY

Take another look at her: the woman at the bar.

Sitting alone atop a barstool, fingers tracing the stem of a margarita. Blue dress, full, rounded shoulders, tall. She's a paradox: You'll remember her for her singularity, and yet her singularity cries out for metaphor, bows to the truth of things that are other things. The tension of her figure against the blue fabric is a suspended orchestral note—rich, dissonant, ever-hovering above resolution. Her smile—teeth, winningly disheveled, free of the eugenic tyranny of orthodontia—is a stand of birches, castle ruins.

Her name is Rosalina. And she has come here on vacation: *Las Olas Místicas* seaside resort bar in Acapulco, Mexico, January, 1980: the first scene of this story.

When this kid strolls up to the bar and sits down next to her.

An American. Mousey pageboy hair, tight jeans and a red softball jersey hugging his torso, which is narrow and suggests the constricted airways of an asthmatic. His head looks small behind his overlarge glasses. He can't be older than fourteen.

Settling onto his barstool, he signals the bartender before he turns to her.

He smiles.

On the far side of this kid is another, smaller kid, clambering noisily onto a stool. If it weren't for his platinum blond pageboy hair and the gap between his two front teeth, the second kid would be a dead ringer for the first.

"How are you?" the first boy says, allowing a beat to pass while the woman looks him over. He leans toward her, extends his right hand. "My name is Winnie Budzinski. Lovely to meet you."

"And I'm George."

The woman leans back so she can see the younger child, whose smile is, like the older boy's, gigantic, and, unlike the older boy's, age-appropriate.

Winnie keeps his gaze on Rosalina, his grin unflinching.

"I love to travel," he says, breaking eye contact for a moment to look around the bar. "May I ask your name?"

The woman smiles, barely. "Rosalina," she says.

The boy nods, as if confirming for himself that the two of them share knowledge of some difficult and wearying truth.

The bartender arrives. "Vodka tonic, please," the boy says, pulling a fifty *peso* mark from his jeans and putting it on the counter.

"How old are you?" Rosalina asks.

"Eighteen."

"He's—" George begins, then stops himself. "*I'm* eight," he says.

Winnie plugs his hand into his jeans and pulls out another fifty *pesos*. "Could you get him a Shirley Temple? With a cherry," he says. The bartender shrugs and walks away. "I'm sorry, I didn't catch your last name."

"Martín," Rosalina says. "This is your brother?"

"That's right. I like to take him on some of my trips, since his mother doesn't travel with children. She's a famous scientist. In the jungle for years at a clip and my brother here has barely left San Diego. Of course, California isn't so much for me. I live in Dallas."

George's mouth has fallen open.

"And you, Rosalina? Where are you from? If I might ask." Winnie brings the glass the bartender has brought him to his lips—he blinks furiously for a moment after taking a sip.

"Uruguay. I'm here on vacation." Rosalina speaks loudly so George can hear. "I'm a secretary at—*cómo se dice?* A law firm. In Montevideo."

Winnie nods. "Vacation. Lovely. Me, it's my first time in Acapulco." He lifts the drink back to his lips. "I must say," he says, but then he lowers the drink and sets it gingerly on the counter in front of him without finishing his sentence.

The bartender returns and sets a Collins glass on the counter. The drink is radioactively blue. George cradles the tumbler between both hands and sips, letting the paper umbrella spear his eyebrow. He rests the glass against his tiny chest and looks at Winnie.

"It's sweet."

Winnie turns back to the woman at the bar. "Rosalina, I'd like to not beat around the bush here if I could." As the boy speaks, he trains his eye on the assortment of bottles on the back wall of the bar. "You're a very beautiful woman. I've seen my share, of course, traveling as I do. And I think that—and forgive me for being blunt—I think I'm sensing a connection between two people here. Between the two of us. An instinctual connection, right? At the—" he moves his drink to his lips for a moment before setting it back down, "—glandular level. A kind of glandular instinctual connection between two people, if that makes sense."

He fumbles with his glasses, taking them off and putting them on again.

"Believe it or not, I'm not all that experienced, in terms of—well, terms you might call carnal. But I think I could give you pleasure, Rosalina. I think I could do this. If you'd allow me the pleasure of— of doing this."

Rosalina looks past Winnie to the end of the bar, where the bartender has removed a maroon pouch from the inside of his leather jacket. Wetting his fingers on his tongue, the man begins to roll a cigarette.

"Winnie, I think you are what—thirteen, fourteen?"

Instead of speaking, Winnie casts his hand out and places it on top of Rosalina's. He meets her eye. She looks at their intertwined fingers. Their hands are the same size. Rosalina draws her hand from his grasp and brings it to the back of Winnie's head, where she slides her fingers through the nest of his hair. She then draws Winnie's head gently to her mouth, as if he were a bridled horse. She whispers in his ear.

George watches, his drink still cradled with both hands against his chest. Rosalina's lips, painted red, contract wildly, like some flexing sea anemone. Her dress makes a taut blue band around her thighs, which have parted slightly, and look thick and sturdy. She holds Winnie, ear to mouth, for a good ten seconds, her words spilling in a thin white stream. Then she lets go of the boy and stands up.

"You have kind eyes," she says. "Like my daughter."

She steps to George and puts her hand on his head. "And you, young George. In Spanish they would call you *Jorge*."

George looks up at her, his mouth stained blue. He watches as she leaves the bar. Eventually, Winnie turns to George and slides the blue drink from George's hands. He sips thoughtfully.

* * *

This all happened some thirty-five years ago. Is it strange to wonder: In the intervening years, does Rosalina Martín, secretary of Montevideo, ever think of these boys? And if so, how? Does she remember what they said? What their faces looked like? Does she remember them with bemusement? With regret?

Is it possible she remembers them with regret?

One thing about the eight-year-old boy in this story: He's me. In 1980, my family went on vacation to Acapulco. Which was strange since we weren't wealthy and weren't much for destination holidays. No Disneyland, no Grand Canyon. If we went anywhere at all it was to my uncle's potato farm, about two hours from our home in central Wisconsin, where my mom was a secretary at the public junior high school and my dad made manhole covers at the Neenah Foundry. Winnie had pretty well made up his mind that going to Acapulco was just another of the many worthless ideas my parents were churning out in those days until it occurred to him that it might be the site of his deflowering. Winnie was thirteen, but he was lively and precocious, especially in his eccentricity. At St. Ignatius Catholic, where we went to school, he handed out the opening pages of self-authored, unfinished stories to his teachers and peers like valentines—tales of hobos and space pirates that ranged from the cryptic to the cornball; they could often be found in a splatter pattern around St. Ignatius's garbage cans. Winnie had a few champions—particularly Mrs. Kohlhagen, his freckled and willowy Language Arts teacher—but Winnie's peers, mostly sons of men from the foundry or one of the nearby paper mills, viewed him with suspicion on their most charitable days, and Winnie yearned for wider realms.

The night we met Rosalina, Winnie and I returned to our room, where I watched *Laverne and Shirley*—dubbed in Spanish—while Winnie sat on the bed and paged through *Hellstrom's Hive*. He'd already read it twice. He put the book down and looked at me.

"Of course, she had a daughter so I don't know where we would have done it anyway. That's a problem unique to Rosalina, but I hadn't thought of it. It'll be harder trying for women with daughters. Or young daughters, anyway. What'd you think of her?"

"Well," I said. I was accustomed to holding forth on topics about which I had no actual opinions. "I liked her dress. But I didn't like her hair."

Winnie had a habit of taking the arm of his glasses and placing its tip between his teeth, then looking at you for long stretches before speaking. Our mother often made the same gesture on the nights she sat us down and interrogated us on our opinions of God and the universe, which she did every few weeks, reading to us from *A Wrinkle in Time* or *The Wind in the Willows*. As a onetime Quaker hippie from Philadelphia, she consented to our parochial education, but felt the need to temper it. Winnie and I tolerated these dreamy, ruminative conversations, and sometimes even liked them.

"You wanna get ice?" Winnie finally said.

We had discovered the ice machine earlier in the week. It was a form of insanity, my brother and I felt, to not have a teeming, frosty bucket propped nearby most times, since the ice was free and plentiful. We had not been in a hotel before. Early in our trip, we had invented a game where we would each stuff a fist into the ice bucket and see which one of us could hold it there longer. We called it Ice Bowl. The winner got to give the loser a charley horse. Naturally, Winnie always won. But by that time, his hand was so reddened and glassy with cold, punching me in the thigh was probably more painful for him than it was for me, so it was an act of machismo and an act of charity both.

When we passed the laundry room Winnie pulled me inside and put his hand over my mouth. The melodrama of this didn't faze me—I had grown used to my brother summarily rewriting the rules to whatever project he'd laid out for us and looked forward to these flourishes.

"Look," my brother said, reaching into his pocket. When he unfurled his palm he held a giant tooth, its base sheathed in knotty brown plastic and attached to a leather string.

"Whoa," I said, reaching for it. Winnie slid both index fingers up the leather tie, lifting the whole apparatus over his neck so the tooth eased to rest just below his clavicle.

"It's a shark's tooth," he said.

I nodded solemnly. It wasn't a shark's tooth. At eight years old, I had already worked my way through the staple boy obsessions—dinosaurs, trucks, sharks, space travel—the niceties of shark dentistry were definitely in my wheelhouse. Winnie's tooth had the slightly curved peapod shape of a feline tooth—a puma's, maybe, or a jaguar's.

"Guess where I got it."

"Dad?"

My brother laughed.

"Gizmo, where would dad get a shark's tooth?"

"I dunno. Milwaukee?"

My brother smacked his hand against his forehead and stomped his feet.

"Where'd you get it?" I asked.

Winnie did a dramatic pan of the laundry room, even though it was barely big enough to hold the two of us. "Acapulco." He gave me a minute to let this sink in. "*The city*. I went into town while mom took you to look at that cathedral. I told mom I would read in our room while dad took a nap, and then I hopped on a bus."

I scratched my face, not wanting to appear any more hopeless than usual. "Like a *bus* bus?"

"There's a stop just down the street. The lady who cleans our room takes it."

"Did you—"

"I don't think she recognized me."

"Why did you take a bus to the city?"

My brother rolled his eyes. He grabbed my shoulders, turned me around and marched me out of the laundry room. "The city's where all the action is, Gizmo. Women, for instance."

"There are women here. What about Rosalina?"

"This place is played out. It's all mothers with daughters. That won't work."

To my knowledge, Rosalina was the only woman Winnie had propositioned. Instead of saying so, I craned my head behind me. We were walking further and further away from the ice machine.

"Rosalina just had one daughter."

"Mothers, plural. Each mother has one daughter."

We were back at our door. I nodded, having received my wisdom for the day.

"Listen. I'd take you. I'd like to. But it's just not safe for a kid. And I need you to cover for me tomorrow. I'll tell mom I wanna read for the day and then I'm gonna grab the morning bus. Can you say that you checked in on me every few hours—'Winnie says he's not hungry,' 'Winnie's taking a nap'—that kind of thing?"

I nodded. Winnie could have told me to meet him at daybreak a hundred feet under the surface of the ocean and I would have nodded.

"Are we gonna play Ice Bowl?" I asked.

"How we gonna do that, Gizmo?" my brother said, throwing the door open and belly-flopping onto the bed. "You forgot the ice."

The next morning Winnie reviewed the plan with me before we joined my parents in the dining room. The resort staff had laid out a buffet of powdered eggs, tortillas, and a tray of ancient-looking breakfast meats. My family lowered their heads while my mom extemporized a lengthy blessing—she spurned the rote *BlessusohLords* my Polish Catholic father muttered when called upon to say grace. When she'd finished, Winnie took to talking incessantly about the book he was reading, interrupting my parents to narrate convoluted subplots and summarize backstories of fictional characters.

"I'm just really into this book," he said, waving his fork, the tines of which held a raisiny sausage. "I think maybe I'll stay in for a few hours this morning and finish this book I'm so into it."

My dad reached across the table and pinched my brother's cheek until Winnie flinched.

"Your son's in an ocean paradise, and wants to read a book all day," he said, the Bloody Mary in his other hand angling dangerously toward the table. At home, my dad was brooding and quick to anger. He worked tirelessly at the foundry, a job he did not love, and he spent much of his free time in his makeshift office in our unfinished basement, fretting over bills. His willingness to go on an extravagant vacation had surprised us all, but his attitude during the first days of that vacation—relaxed and jokey—was so unusual as to unsettle me.

My mother smirked, despite herself. "Honey, haven't you already read this book?" she asked.

Winnie looked at me for a moment, then crammed the entire sausage into his mouth.

"When I was George's age. I hardly even understood it."

My father looked to my mother and shrugged. As my parents balled up their napkins and drained their coffees, Winnie stayed in his chair, spearing his fork across the table to nab a strip of bacon I'd left idling.

"Wellsoprobably I'll read for a few hours and hit the beach around dinnertime."

Have I said how I loved this boy? Of course, I didn't realize he was a boy then, and it'd be years and years before I did. But I loved him terribly. I would have waged wars for him, committed numberless atrocities. Surely goodness and mercy would follow such a child all the days of his life, would fill whatever house he dwelled in, light it up like the gaudiest of Christmas trees.

That morning at the resort after breakfast, Winnie gave me a wink and a salute before leaving for the bus. I waved to him from the door to our room, where I was supposed to be changing into my swimsuit. Then Winnie walked around the corner, toward the concierge's desk and the front door and out of sight, and when my parents asked, I said he was reading in our room, and Winnie didn't come back at all that afternoon, or that evening either, or the next day, or the next.

In the days following Winnie's disappearance, our family received many visitors. Hotel detectives, Mexican police, embassy folk. Official men with stony, unknowing faces. The first night Winnie did not return, I'd told my parents what I knew of my brother's plan, surprised to see pain in their faces where I expected anger; now I told the men who searched for Winnie the same story with resignation: I knew they would not find him.

How could they? When I was the one who had lost him?

I alone was present when Winnie conceived of his mission. I alone helped him to embark upon it by covering for him. Not only that—I alone knew the name of the bildungsroman Winnie was writing about a teenaged Chewbacca. I alone knew he'd had a dream in which he kissed Mrs. Kohlhagen's inner thighs. I alone knew the smell of the inside of his baseball mitt. Who were these interlopers, to whom Winnie was a wallet-sized sixth-grade portrait pulled from my mother's purse? As the search expanded then stalled, expanded then stalled, I retreated deeper and deeper into myself, tormented by the idea that only I could bring Winnie back. My love for my brother writhed and howled in me like a roomful of bloodhounds.

"Winnie is okay. They'll find him," my father would tell us, over and over again, night after night. He had taken to standing vigil in the dark of my hotel room while my mother lay awake with me in the bed Winnie and I had shared.

I'd better tell you now that my brother never returns to us. At the end of my story he won't show up naked at the door to our hotel room, leaves and twigs stuck to him, his head evacuated of all memory of his travels. Fifteen years later on a Ute Indian Reservation in Colorado, I won't see him with a rain stick and a big beard, wandering behind the dumpsters at a gas station. I don't want to create a false sense of suspense here. And anyway, that's not what the story's about—whether or not my brother made it—because he didn't, and it seems crummy to string anyone along on the promise that maybe he'll come back some-day, as if it's a big mystery, and he's still out there banging his way through Central America and down to Antarctica, and we're all waiting for his next postcard. My family has acknowledged that he almost cer-tainly died in Mexico, and we've moved on more or less, and while this story is about Winnie, my brother, it's also about where I went and what I found when I broke from my family and went looking for him myself.

It wasn't hard, believe it or not.

Here's what I did: I waited until my mother went around the corner . . . then I walked out the door.

I'd collected *pesos* from her purse and my father's wallet throughout the week, and when I'd gotten two hundred *pesos* I stuffed them in my jeans, put on one of my brother's shirts and walked out of the resort and down the street until I found the bus my brother had told me about. Then I rode into town. I wrote down the name of the street where I got off and I made a note every time I turned after that and I walked and walked and walked around the city, looking in the sea of strange faces for the person that looked most like me. After I'd walked for a good hour or two, I was hungry, and I wandered into a *taquería*.

It was a sweaty place. Everything looked wet. Even the walls, which were two-tone, concrete painted royal blue on the bottom half and white on the top. At a single table, two men played dominoes, both of them wizened and leathery. Behind the cash register, a man danced silently in place, one hand on top of his head and one flat against his abdomen. I couldn't hear any music, except for a whispery, fragmentary melody he would hum every few seconds, over and over again, like the brass line in a salsa tune.

He could have been anywhere from seventeen to thirty-five. He was compact and muscular, with the incongruous bulge of a pot belly peek-ing from under his striped tanktop. His hair was long and messy, deep brown with a copper glint, and as he moved it fell across his nose, which was broad and misshapen, as if from repeated breakings. Also, he wore a necklace—a single feline tooth, clasped in brown plastic, strung with a leather strap.

My brother's necklace. Or one exactly like it. The man stopped danc-ing and looked at me.

"What do you want?" he said. "You want *enchilada*? Number three? *Quieres el tres*?"

I looked around the room. There were no pictures on the walls, only a handwritten sign taped to the counter written in Spanish. In Wisconsin, my parents had signed me up for an after-school Spanish class at St. Ignatius School, where I was a third-grader, and from which I retained a few basic numbers and phrases. But there was nothing in the room I could read.

I nodded.

"You have money?"

I pulled a fifty *peso* mark out of my pocket and handed it to the man, who took it and walked into the kitchen where I couldn't see him.

I waited for minutes. When I glanced at the old men playing dominoes, one of them looked at me and shook his head. It seemed as if the motion had required a great effort. If only to avoid his gaze, I scurried around the counter and into the kitchen, which was narrow and mostly empty. Only a single frying pan, caked with egg, balanced on the range of an oven, as if thrown there. At the back of the building, I found a door that led to a small concrete lot behind the *taquería*. It was there I found the man with my brother's necklace.

The concrete lot was a bustling miniature city of wooden milk crates and empty coffee cans, crowded under a makeshift ceiling of corrugated tin sheets. It was a small area, teeming with bric-a-brac. A spray of aluminum rods was bundled upright against the *taquería* wall. A tower of sagging cardboard boxes vomited old clothes onto teetering stacks of eight millimeter film cannisters piled up like totem poles, their surfaces pocked and scarred. Two children's bicycles, each missing a wheel, were balanced between the building wall and the boxes of clothes. The place had the look of a lair, the site of some terrible private labor, its execution both obsessive and slapdash.

On the top of a milk crate in the center of the lot sat the man who had taken my order, his legs spread wide in a V. In his lap, he stripped an orange with his fingers and was throwing ribbons of peel to a dog, a grayish, spidery mutt who dropped whatever was in its mouth and chased after each new piece as it was tossed. Sitting on the concrete near the man's feet was a child, a thin boy between my age and my brother's. He had a wide scab above one eye and wore a ragged tank top and athletic shorts. His head had been recently shaved. As I stepped into the lot, the man was whispering in Spanish—to himself or to the boy I couldn't tell. He looked up at me, then returned to his orange.

"No number three."

He snickered, laughing at his own joke. Juice pulsed down his fingers as he tore wedges of flesh from the fruit. Next to him, the boy used the detached blade of a pocketknife to carve something onto a cardboard box, and the blade kept slipping from his grasp.

When I tried to speak, my voice broke, as if I hadn't spoken in days. "Where'd you get that necklace?"

The man sniffed fiercely, and I flinched when he spat onto the concrete.

"I'm looking for my brother," I said. "Winnie Budzinski."

There was a tug on the corner of the man's mouth—an aborted smile or a grimace or an itch.

"What does this Winnie look like?"

"Like me. But he's thirteen."

The man raised his head and scratched the corner of his mouth with his middle finger as he looked me up and down.

"All boys look like you."

"He has brown hair."

The man smiled.

"Brown like me?"

He splayed his fingers and fanned them through the hair that fell along his right shoulder.

"More light than that."

"I see. Yes. *Claro*," he said, nodding.

"And glasses."

"*Por supuesto*, with the glasses."

"And," I said, fidgeting, tugging at my jeans. "He has—he has kind eyes."

The man watched me as he peeled off a wedge of orange. He brought it to his lips then stopped and offered it to the boy, who took it and folded it into his mouth. Then the man peeled off another piece and ate it himself. He put the ravaged orange down on the concrete between his feet and wiped his hands on his thighs. The dog crouched, eyeing the fruit, but didn't approach.

"*Cigarro*," the man said, turning his head slightly to the boy. The boy nodded and climbed to his feet, pulling a plastic bag from the elastic band of his shorts. He loosened a piece of rolling paper and cradled it in his palm. The man looked back at me.

"Your brother is gone. Stop looking."

I took a small step forward. "You've seen him?"

"I do not need to see him to know he is gone."

"Did he come in your shop?"

31

"No, that would not happen."

I clenched and unclenched my fists. Whenever the man met my eye, something in me jangled like ice-glazed branches clacking under a heavy wind.

"I can bring money," I said. "Or go somewhere else. I can go anywhere in the city on the bus, or my parents can—"

"*Oyeme*." The man met my eye. "Listen to me. Every year this happens. Every year. The boy comes to town. The child—the boy, see? He is lost. Far away. Foolish, this boy, to be so far away, you understand? So the men come. They take him. They take him to the—what is this called? The thing—the thing that is under the ground?" He looked at the boy, who was dabbing pinches of tobacco into the rolling paper in his palm. "*Cómo se dice*, do you know this? The place, the underground place?"

The boy tilted his head, as if he were thinking. "*Las catacumbas*?"

The man looked at me and raised his eyebrows. "*Las catacumbas*? Do you know this?"

I shrugged, shook my head. The man turned his upper body to the boy, pulled back his right hand and struck the boy hard across his face with his palm. The sound rattled through the lot. The boy, pulled off his feet and spun onto the concrete, hit the ground with a doughy smack, tobacco raining around him in clumps. The dog froze, its ears back, then scuttled past me out of the lot and down the alley.

"*Rola otro cigarro*," the man said, running his hand through his hair.

The boy picked the contents of his plastic bag off the ground. While he worked, he glowered at me.

"You speak Spanish?" the man said.

I nodded without thinking. The man spoke in Spanish for the better part of a minute—quickly, almost feverishly, with a bullying, groping intensity, as if he were reprimanding a lover. There was a wild, shimmering quality to his words, like the scales of a fast-moving fish, or the flash of a knife. I understood exactly none of them.

"*Entiendes*?" the man finished. The man's voice was softer now, as if he pitied me. He snapped his fingers several times at me. "*Entiendes*?"

"Poor Sue Presto," I said.

"*Bueno*," he said. "*Por favor*, go home now. You will not find him. Do you understand? No one finds."

I nodded furiously. "Claire-Oh," I said. Then I turned around and walked back through the building, through the kitchen and the front room where the men had not finished their game, and past the dog, its eyes open and bored-looking, its body curled up like an apostrophe near the front door frame.

In Paris, *l'Ossuaire Municipal* sprawls for miles, a spindly network of tombs fanning north across the city like the tendrils of an underground mushroom colony. More than six million Parisians are in the catacombs. They grin at you from the walls. In the passageways, their breath is damp and cool. When you emerge, your shoes trail bone dust for blocks, soft and chalky.

In the catacombs beneath the *Convento de San Francisco* in Lima, there is a famous room which houses a broad embroidery of bones, the skulls arranged in tidy concentric rings, doily-like, as if to make a huge Mandela. A wheel. Or an unblinking eye. I like it there. I've spent a lot of time looking at it.

In the summer of ninety-eight, I got lost in the catacombs at St. Paul's in Malta for thirty-seven hours. Afterward, I stayed on in Malta for another four months and spent a lot of that time underground. I find it very hard to become lost there now.

And in the *Cementerio de La Recoleta* in Buenos Aires, there's a man who built his tomb practically on top of his wife's, but the bust of his head is facing away from her because they were in a fight when she died. I love that place, and I often corral passersby to tell them the story. *Un monumento a la vida*, I say. But a cemetery is not a catacombs.

Same with the labyrinthine underground village in Znojmo, and the boarded-up passageways under the City Market in Indianapolis. Not catacombs, really. Just tunnels.

Still. Tunnels have their charms. Cemeteries, too. I lived with a woman in a shanty made from trash near the Freedom Tunnel in New York one winter in the mid-nineties. And later, I spent a winter in the lattice of steam pits and cement conduits that undergird St. Olaf College, where a cousin of mine worked as a janitor. It was a dank, cheerless place, and in the spring, I often came across the corpses of solitary baby ducks, a paddling of which must have wandered into the wrong hole and then dispersed, before starving.

I cherish these places; I keep many such tunnels in my mind. I find a kind of hope underground—if hope can feel like an itch, or like fear. It's not as if I think I'll find Winnie, living this way. But I do hope that in the cool dark of these chambers, I might preserve what remains of him in my memory, that what I know of him won't be bleached white by the sun, or cast to oblivion by the wind. Already, so many of my memories of him have eroded, or have been polluted through contact with the life and dreams that came after him. I've lost much.

There are no catacombs in Acapulco, of course. It's a coastal town. The shale is too soft.

I'd like to say what happened next, when I returned from the *taquería*. How I found my way back to the resort, and what fuss greeted me there—shrieking and crying and hysterical laughing—all the usual outbursts you get when people have all the feeling beaten out of them and then, suddenly, are made to feel something again. But I don't remember any of this. After the *taquería*, I don't remember anything at all, although I've been told that three weeks after Winnie walked away from breakfast and out of our lives, my family packed up and returned to Wisconsin, where we waited and waited, my dad flying down to Acapulco every four or five months, and then all of us finally having a memorial service the following summer.

Actually, for a long time, I didn't remember the *taquería* either. Then, when I'd gotten expelled from my high school at seventeen and had to see Ms. Olson, a therapist, for a while, the memory of my solo trip into the city of Acapulco came back to me. I'd forgotten it for almost a decade, or buried it—this strange, comfortless vision of the world into which my brother sank. And then I stumbled onto the memory inadvertently, in conversation with Ms. Olson—came across it like a pair of car keys I'd lost years ago and found when I was moving out of an apartment after I'd already gotten rid of the car.

I told my mother about this memory three years later, when I was twenty. This was just after my father died of cirrhosis of the liver, and she had joined the Sisters of St. Joseph. When I told her about the *taquería*, my mother told me what I said was impossible: I'd never left the hotel on my own. After my brother went missing she kept me at her side until we'd boarded the plane for home—kept me pretty much handcuffed to her side until she could tuck me into my bed in our home in Wisconsin.

Probably, she told me—still tells me—what I call a "memory" is something I made up. Not maliciously, but as a way of coping with the loss of the brother I loved so much. She says this, over and over: I loved him so, so much.

And I understand that. I understand that my mother wouldn't lie to me, that she has no reason to, that everything she says is verifiable. All the same. At an intuitive level—a bone-deep, subterranean level—I have trouble believing what she insists upon is true.

A lot of the time, in fact, it seems as if what I remember seeing that day at the *taquería* is the story of my whole life, the story that keeps telling itself over and over and over again, growing in richness and detail, in every little thing I do—in every argument I have with a lover, or train ticket I buy, or job I lose—moments in which this whole story rushes back through me like a gust through a wind sock, and I steady myself against the wall with my hand and I think: *Of course.* I think: *Claro.*

Here's the last piece of this story: I have a distinct, vivid memory of playing catch with Winnie on the beach next to our hotel. We were tossing a ball back and forth in the waves in our swimsuits. But for some reason, the way the memory is arranged in my mind, it comes *after* Winnie ran away or got lost or killed. Naturally, this is impossible. It's not like Winnie came back to play catch with me and then disappeared again and nobody noticed. But this is where the memory seems to fit in my mind, in the chronological slot marked After Winnie Left, and I've given up trying to maneuver it elsewhere. I remember this moment and in the remembering it feels like something that came *after*. And when I'm done remembering it, I remind myself of how and where I got it wrong.

We're standing in the waves, Winnie and I, and they're big. Way bigger than the waves in Lake Michigan, where our parents sometimes took us in the summer. Massive, terrific waves. We stand there, the tide smashing us every few seconds, while we hurl this rubber ball back and forth—this bright blue, cantaloupe-sized ball with red stars on it. I'll never forget that ball. We're throwing the ball for close to an hour, as if it's the first fun we've ever had, talking now and then, but mostly just throwing the ball to each other and bouncing up and down in the big water.

And every once in a while when one of us throws the ball he'll ask a question like: *Do you think seaweed knows it's alive? And is it better to be seaweed than nothing at all?*

Or: *Is it possible God has had any of the same exact thoughts we've had?*

Or: *How do you know you're the person you think you are, that God didn't send your soul to take over for the real Winnie or George a few seconds ago? And God just gave you all of George's or Winnie's memories and feelings so it feels like it was you that was George or Winnie yesterday or last month or last year, but really somebody else was, and you got here this very second, just started existing right now as we speak?*

Or now?

Or now?

And I remember at one point Winnie asks me, "You know how you laughed at Dad's joke at lunch even though he forgot he told it already in the pool yesterday?"

"I did?" I say, though I remember exactly.

"Why do you do that shit?"

Winnie is throwing the ball harder now.

"Are you a nutjob?" he says.

"No," I say, lunging into the water after the ball, though at this time I'm not even sure I know what a nutjob is, except that I don't want to be it, at least not with Winnie saying it.

"You're such a fuckwad," Winnie says.

"*You're* a fuckwad," I say.

"You're a *culero*," he says. "*Eres un pinche culero.*"

What's weird about this is I know my brother doesn't speak any Spanish, and never did. My parents had enrolled me in the after-school Spanish class, but they'd let Winnie sign up for band instead, where he played the French Horn. But in my mind when I remember, he's saying this sentence in Spanish, probably because of where I live now, thirty-five years later, and the fact that I think and even dream in Spanish mostly.

"*Tú lo eres!*" I scream, and I throw the ball as hard as I can, but the throw is wide—or maybe he throws it as hard as he can and it bounces flat off my palms. It flies into the ocean in a soundless, autumn-leaf arc, smacks against the water far enough that we don't feel we can reach it, we can see it's already moving out to sea, cresting up and down on the big waves. We move closer together and stand next to each other in the water.

"Goodbye, ball," Winnie says, laughing.

"Goodbye, ball," I say.

"I wonder who'll find it," he says.

We can see the ball so clearly, even as it sails further and further out.

It's this bright little blue speck against a huge blue ocean, but the blues are different enough that we can follow it, riding the ripples and hillocks and dark, dark blue mountains as it glides toward the horizon. We can still see it, small as it is, as it zooms out for miles and miles and miles and miles.

Nominated by Charles Baxter,
Nancy Richard,
One Story

THANKS FOR COMING IN

by RON KOERTGE

from NERVE COWBOY

We just want to talk about your excursion on the 27th.
Sunday before last. Isn't that right? You wore that thrift
store sombrero. Move a little closer to the machine, please.
There's nothing to be afraid of. Excursions are allowed.
It isn't as if you tried to escape. We're only looking for
clarification. You and your companion began by
chatting about radioactive waste management. Excellent.
Then you put your hand on her leg. And by "her" we mean
your not-wife, she of the lavender underthings. Stay seated,
please. We are measuring electro-dermal activity. Nod if
you understand. No, wait. Blink twice. This new machine
is very sensitive. Try and relax. We have only another question
or two. Remember pulling over at the Scenic Viewpoint?
Good. Now before you got into the back seat and
mussed up your uniforms, you read to your not-wife from
a book. None of what was recorded made sense to our data
banks, so we were wondering what exactly were you reading?
Poetry. Really. Well. Would you like some water? We're
going to be here awhile.

Nominated by Charles Harper Webb

THE WORK OF ART IN THE AGE OF MECHANICAL REPRODUCTION

fiction by ANTHONY WALLACE

from THE SOUTHERN REVIEW

A well-dressed couple entered the lobby of the Hôtel Saint-Dominique, the young woman first, pushing an expensive-looking pram, the muscles in her slender arms and legs taut with purpose. When they came to the hostess's desk just outside the bar, the young woman recited their family name and the time of the reservation. She looked at her wristwatch to show that they were exactly on time. The hostess smiled and then the young woman added, "A corner table, private but with a view of the dining room. I don't want to wake her."

The hostess held up two long menus and asked that they follow her through the barroom and into the dining room. A corner table had indeed been reserved for them, one usually given to parties of four, and the hostess asked if this table was satisfactory. Without saying anything the young woman tucked the pram safely into the corner and then adjusted her chair so that the pram was behind her and angled a little to her right.

"That will be all," said the young woman.

The hostess smiled artificially and went away.

The pram was navy blue, with chrome trim and white rubber wheels, an updated version of the kind of carriage English nannies push along the streets of Mayfair, or used to, anyway. The husband and wife themselves were dressed as if to complement it: the man in a blue blazer, jaunty rep tie, and white ducks (it was high summer); the young woman in a tailored white linen suit set off by a topaz-colored silk blouse. The man was a professor at Boston University, a "University Professor," and the woman was the wife of a University Professor.

The professor had a meticulously groomed beard such as real, tenured professors usually wear. His wife was younger than he by some fifteen years, and very beautiful. She had sensuous lips, a fine full figure of which she was in complete control, and lustrous black hair, but it was her eyes that one was irresistibly drawn to with their finely reticulated gray irises and luminous, overlarge pupils. Her appearance was so striking that she could not go anywhere without attracting attention. The professor liked this and disliked it at the same time; he understood that it was the price one paid for beauty, or at least it was part of the price.

The waiter, arriving breathless, began to tell them how the brunch would proceed—buffet selections for the first two courses, followed by entrees prepared to order—but the young woman indicated by a slight turn of her wrist that they knew all that, they'd been here many times, how was it they'd never seen him before? The waiter, in an effort not to stare, became a bit abrupt, and this happens frequently, that the disguised reaction is in direct proportion to the emotion being disguised. The waiter could not look the professor's wife in the face. For just a moment he put both palms to his eyes in a way that the professor considered oedipal. Beauty of this magnitude is the greatest agony, thought the professor, ordering two glasses of Taittinger Brut. Beauty is no antidote to suffering. Quite the reverse.

The waiter was glad to take the order and get away. The young woman beamed complacently, as if she had not noticed any of this (and there was a good chance she hadn't), or as if she was quite accustomed to putting out men's eyes.

"I'll get something for us to start while he fetches the drinks," said the professor, standing, walking toward the buffet table, beaming sideways at his wife's brilliant beaming. There is something cruel in that, in the very nature of things, that beauty kills, and likes to kill—the tiger, the most beautiful land animal in the world, and the deadliest, though he knew such thinking was clichéd or worse. Beauty destroys and devours so that the world may live on. That seemed less trite, but not by much.

The professor returned bearing two small plates, then silence descended on the table as husband and wife sat staring at the carved Scottish smoked salmon draped over grilled slices of brioche cut into quatrefoils, the name of the restaurant and also its logo. They were waiting for their champagne.

"I can have just one," the young wife told the waiter as he set down the bubbling saucers. "The price of motherhood." She wasn't happy that she'd had to wait for the champagne in order to begin her first course, and she was even less happy that the champagne had arrived in saucers instead of flutes—hadn't she mentioned that to them the last time?—but she was working on being less critical.

"I understand," said the waiter. "My wife is due in September."

"I hate it when they get personal," she remarked after the waiter had gone. "They try to erase the proper boundaries, so unprofessional. And arriving late with the wine. I should report him."

There was a time when the professor would have pointed out that it was she who had initiated the conversation, and it was merely the waiter's job to provide a response of some kind. Not only that, but the champagne had been brought to them as quickly as anybody would be able to open the bottle and pour it. But he had long ago stopped pointing out this kind of thing. It would do no good, and it would spoil her fun, which was to be haughty and capricious. Maria was from the Czech Republic and had grown up in Prague, where her own father had been a professor of comparative literature at Charles University. In this way she proceeded through life from the standpoint of not only financial but also cultural superiority. She was not an American and did not understand the democratization of roles that was an important aspect of American life, that a gas station attendant, for example, would not think anything of initiating a personal conversation with anyone who might pull up. The professor had seen his wife on more than one occasion tell such a man to go away and tend to his gasoline pump. "Go and look after your *hose*," she'd said one time, and it was all he could do not to laugh out loud. He saw no real harm in that, and she wasn't even too far wrong. It was the imagined slights and impertinences that worried him, although she was not shrewish to him personally. She merely became angry when her position was not understood and when, worst of all, her husband's position was not understood. In the world in which she had grown up, everybody's position was always understood, or at least that was how she'd explained it to him. So he humored her on these small matters, and with the constant show that needed to be acted out, the too-expensive meals, her voice on the phone when she made the reservations and insisted on the best table, and her tantrums when occasionally she arrived to find that she didn't have the best table, or, even more disappointing, when she'd been given some stooge's idea of what the best table was.

And it surprised her also, on this day when she'd been so happy, so ready to enjoy life, so full of energy and vitality, that in this place where they dined so often, and were known so well, that they should be sent a waiter who did not know them, their likes and dislikes, that she should have to explain what she had explained all too often, that there must be a responsible person to stand next to the baby when they both went up to select the next course, which she was now ready to do, and she would have to call him over, *wherever he was*, and explain all this, and how could you explain all this and not lose the timing—in her view that was the whole experience of dining, the timing—and now it would be ruined, there was no saving it, they should go, why didn't they just stay at home if this was going to be the result. She stopped herself short, admitting her own foolishness, that she sought perfection but the world would not yield it, she understood that, she was not a child, only it was disappointing, after all this time, when you thought you had arrived at a certain place in your life, worked for and earned, that what you believed was yours was still just a little out of reach. She rested her forehead for a moment on the cuff of his jacket, at the place where the edge of blue shirtsleeve peeped out, as if to implore forgiveness, which of course was granted in advance of anything she did or might do, for he loved her, as he explained time and again—that was the one thing she should never lose sight of.

Now she went off to fix her face, and after she had passed the bar the waiter once more came back to the table to clear the plates, to offer another round, standing by the wife's chair and looking, as chance would have it, at the baby that had been sleeping quietly the entire time.

"Your first?" the waiter asked, glancing into the carriage.

"Yes," said the professor, "a girl," suddenly spilling a glass of water. "Oh my," said the professor, and at once uniformed men appeared to blot the spilled water, to pick up the ice cubes, to change the linen on the table and replace the entire setting, including the centerpiece, before the lady returned.

In a few moments everything was as it had been. The professor was presented with a wine list even as the waiter apologized for his clumsiness. The professor waved away the list; he knew what he wanted. The professor's wife meanwhile returned to her place and smiled bravely, as if to show that she could buck up, there were things one had no control over, and that was a simple fact of life. She took his hand, squeezed it meaningfully, then turned her attention to the reclining figure in the pram.

"Why don't you just wait here and I'll choose the next course," said the professor as he stood up. He paused at the end of a table where a variety of cold seafood was set out on blocks of ice carved to resemble the fish and shellfish on display. Beside this table was a low wooden archway that led back into the sparsely lit barroom and adjoining wine cellar called Vespers (the building had once been a convent for Dominican nuns). There the waiter who had been assigned their table was talking to the hostess. The professor couldn't see them, but he could hear their voices.

"A life-size doll!" said the waiter's voice. "All dressed up in a little paisley pinafore! Unbelievable! Fantastic!"

The hostess, seeing the professor stand back from the buffet table, stepped on the waiter's foot. The professor paused for a moment just outside the bar. Both employees froze in place. He did not see anyone behind the bar. It was a slow time of year because the colleges and universities were not in session. Anybody could have gotten that corner table; it didn't prove anything. He turned without a word and went back to the buffet table, where he filled two salad plates with cold lobster and king crab.

"But I'm telling you, it's just a doll," the waiter said in a low voice when the professor was again out of earshot. "A plastic replica. A simulacrum."

The waiter had recognized the professor, had a few months before attended one of his lectures on the theory and practice of translation, a field in which he was an eminent authority—the man who some people said was the next Walter Benjamin in that he frequently discussed literary translation not in terms of what it got right but, more importantly, what it got wrong: the misreading or misinterpretation that led, strangely, to greater fidelity to living art and the possibilities for interpretation that implies.

"It's your job," the hostess pointed out. She rolled her eyes. "Just do what they tell you to do. Come when they bloody well tell you to come, and leave when they bloody well tell you to leave. It's really very simple."

The waiter shrugged, adjusted his tie, which was patterned with identical blue and red bug-eyed carp, and went back into the dining room.

The couple sat together in silence, picking over their second course. The waiter arrived with a bottle of Chablis, that green-eyed goddess, uncorked the bottle in front of them, and poured a small amount for the professor to taste, but he only waved his hand in the air to suggest that the waiter should not bother with this formality. When the wine had been poured (the lady would have a second glass after all), the waiter asked the couple if they'd decided on the main course. First he turned to the young woman, who stared back at him with gray, guileless eyes. She would have the Dover sole. She picked up her wineglass and continued to stare at him over the rim. He looked back at her and was determined not to be the first one to look away. The sight of her, though, was extraordinarily powerful, like something he'd heard about but had never actually experienced firsthand. While this was going on the husband mumbled that he'd have the same thing as his wife.

"Yes, of course," said the waiter. "Certainly, sir."

The professor toyed with the middle button of his sport coat, stroked his beard pensively, then emptied his glass just as the waiter was bringing over the sole, which was artfully arranged on two oversize plates and set off against an outer circle of tiny, truffled potatoes.

The professor, without acknowledging the originality of the presentation, signaled for the waiter to refill his glass.

The professor's wife had the baby out of the pram and was rocking it slowly in her arms, whispering unintelligible things and cooing into its ear. She clutched the baby to her breast and stared meaningfully into her husband's eyes. He returned her gaze and spoke his wife's name, once, quietly, and in a way that sounded like a question.

"Can I bring you two anything else?" asked the waiter, but neither one responded.

The waiter came back to the hostess's desk and said, for no apparent reason, "Her name is Maria. And I've seen him before, attended his lectures. In my field he's a celebrity. He's written what some critics are calling the most definitive translation of *Madame Bovary* in fifty years. It's funny, he says he did it by disregarding or in some sense not considering Flaubert's intentions, including the mot juste, a version of the novel not identical or 'faithful' to the original, but a version that can have a life of its own in the world *alongside* the original."

"Every Eurotrash female east of Dubrovnik is named Maria," remarked the hostess. "Do they have a name shortage along with all the other shortages? Like with the long lines just to get a roll of toilet paper.

Do you suppose the young mothers stand in a long line, and some guy with metal-tipped shoelaces says, 'Sorry, ladies, only Maria is left today, all the other names are taken. Please name your daughters Maria until further notice. That is all, comrades.'"

She pronounced these last few sentences in a heavy, archly fake Eastern European accent that was intended to convey bemused cynicism, which included an ironic disregard of the fact that Soviet Communism and its influence in Eastern Europe had been dead for a couple of decades. Dealing with the public can make one terribly cynical. The hostess, who had an MFA in screenwriting and who'd written two screenplays she was unable to sell, was just such a cynical product of the service industry. To her way of thinking, there were only two kinds of people in the world: those who'd had their screenplays optioned, and those who hadn't. In fact, her second screenplay was called "The Optioned." In the first group were the people who stayed at the Hôtel Saint-Dominique and took their meals in the restaurant where she worked. In the second group were the people waiting for their screenplays to be optioned and who, in the meanwhile, put in time serving the first group. For her, the important distinction was that the optioned got to live in the historical moment, and hence live real lives, while those not optioned were consigned to live at the end of history, like orphans stranded at the end of a dirt road. The hostess had remained in the second group far longer than she'd expected, and she was in the process of adjusting herself to that fact.

The waiter, though, still believed he was tied to this job for only a short while, that he was on his way elsewhere. But what would be so terrible if he wasn't? Some of what went on here—the people you met, what they said and did, the unusual and complicated lives they led—was really very interesting. While the hostess went on ridiculing the couple in her archly fake Eastern European accent, the waiter gazed wistfully toward the dining room, sighed, and looked forward to the moment when he could return to clear the plates, offer coffee and tea, and wheel in the dessert cart.

Today he had flourless chocolate torte served with whipped cream and freshly minted strawberries macerated in Grand Marnier. He had blueberry and Meyer lemon crème brûlée with house-made lavender gelato. He had warm praline and chocolate chip bread pudding with a bourbon hard sauce, also served with whipped cream, upon which he would shave additional chocolate from a brick of Teuscher dark. He had ricotta cheesecake served straight up, no fruit, no whipped cream, no cinnamon or nutmeg, no graham cracker crust, just the real deal, brought in daily from a farm in the Champlain Islands, grass-fed Holsteins of historically important lineage, magnificent. He also had the restaurant's own individually baked Boston cream pies, a signature item he often took home to his girlfriend, Susan Anselm Parker, an architect who was growing weary of him not finishing his dissertation even as he was growing weary of his dissertation and Susan Anselm Parker.

After dinner they would take their secondhand pies into the living room and he would tell her the story of the couple and their unusual baby girl. But what he would not tell her, what she would find out or not, as time went on, is that he had seen true beauty and originality and had been forever changed by his encounter with them, though in the near term, as is always the case, it was not possible to say precisely how. It was like Paul on his way to Damascus: you got hit in the eyes by the thing you had been missing but that you had not known you'd been missing until it came down and knocked you off your horse. The thing you'd suspected was possible while not believing for a second that it really was possible. The thing that, having once experienced it, there is nothing left to do but throw away everything and follow after it like a helpless child, and be near to it, or as near to it as mortal man can be.

These musings occupied the waiter while he waited to go back into the dining room, to wheel in the dessert cart, to offer the gray-eyed goddess what was in his power to offer her. The gray-eyed goddess, the trim-coifed goddess—

"Jesus H. Fuck," gasped the hostess, then drove her slender screenwriter's elbow into the waiter's ribs.

He emerged from his reverie just in time to witness man, woman, and pram moving procession-like through the darkened barroom. The man pushed the pram with one hand and ushered the woman forward with the other; the woman held the doll by one leg and fixed her eyes straight ahead.

"Just put it on my tab," the man called to them in a febrile bray.

"Oh, let us once and for all escape this stinking toilet!" shrieked the young woman with sensuous lips and lustrous black hair and fine full figure barely contained in white linen suit, then shifted into a language that made her tantrum all the more mysterious and beautiful, made the spectacle of her dismembering the doll in its paisley pinafore and scattering its limbs to the four corners of the room all the more terrible, profound, like Aeschylus, like Milton, like the object that had dropped with such languid grace from the Enola Gay—like the veil of the tem-

46

ple that was rent in twain and the earth shook and the rocks were split, and the tombs were opened, and the bodies of the saints that had fallen asleep were raised.

Close by the waiter's ear the hostess's breath caught sharp in her throat.

"Wow," said the waiter in a low voice. "Wow wow wow." He whistled through his teeth.

The professor and his wife passed by the hostess's desk on their way to the front door. "Tip yourself fifteen percent on the food, but not the alcohol," the professor called back to the waiter. "I'll send someone for the carriage later today." His wife clutched his right arm; she stumbled along beside him as if she'd broken a heel. They passed through the doorway and disappeared into the sunny summer afternoon.

The pram lay on its side in the barroom, the back wheel slowly turning. Pieces of the doll lay scattered about in a way that suggested an important human truth without revealing it.

"Kubrick would probably have optioned that concept," said the hostess. "Or even Polanski." She walked toward the doll's head as if she were about to kick it, then did kick it, once only, but deftly, and with finality, to the other end of the bar, followed by peals of girlish laughter and a cleanup crew of three busboys from Nicaragua.

Nominated by Gary Gildner

IMPERATIVES FOR CARRYING ON IN THE AFTERMATH

by NATASHA TRETHEWEY

from POEM-A-DAY

Do not hang your head or clench your fists
when even your friend, after hearing the story,
says: *My mother would never put up with that.*

Fight the urge to rattle off statistics: that,
more often, a woman who chooses to leave
is then murdered. The hundredth time

your father says, *But she hated violence,*
why would she marry a guy like that?—
don't waste your breath explaining, again,

how abusers wait, are patient, that they
don't beat you on the first date, sometimes
not even the first few years of a marriage.

Keep an impassive face whenever you hear
Stand by Your Man, and let go your rage
when you recall those words were advice

given your mother. Try to forget the first
trial, before she was dead, when the charge
was only *attempted murder*, don't belabor

the thinking or the sentence that allowed
her ex-husband's release a year later, or
the juror who said, *It's a domestic issue—*

they should work it out themselves. Just
breathe when, after you read your poems
about grief, a woman asks: *Do you think*

your mother was weak for men? Learn
to ignore subtext. Imagine a thought-
cloud above your head, dark and heavy

with the words you cannot say; let silence
rain down. Remember you were told
by your famous professor, that you should

write about something else, *unburden
yourself of the death of your mother* and
just pour your heart out in the poems.

Ask yourself what's in your heart, that
reliquary—blood locket and seed-bed—and
contend with what it means, the folk-saying

you learned from a Korean poet in Seoul:
*that one does not bury the mother's body
in the ground but in the chest, or—like you—*

you carry her corpse on your back.

Nominated by Dan Albergotti, Rachel Rose,
Taije Silverman, Michael Waters

BAJADAS

by FRANCISCO CANTÚ

from PLOUGHSHARES

ba·ja·da noun
1: a steep curved descending road or trail
2: an alluvial plain formed at the base of a mountain by the
coalescing of several alluvial fans
Origin 1865–70, Americanism: from the Spanish feminine past participle
of bajar: to descend

December 20

Santiago quit the academy yesterday. We were on our way into town when I heard the news, speeding across the cold and brittle grasslands of New Mexico. Morales must have told me, or maybe it was Hart. I called Santiago as soon as I found out. You don't have to quit, I told him, you can still finish, you should stay. I can't, he said, it's not the work for me. I have to go back to Puerto Rico; I have to be with my family. I wished him luck and told him I was sorry to see him go. He thanked me and said to finish for the both of us, and I promised that I would.

Of all my classmates, it was Santiago I most wanted to see graduate. He marched out of step, his gear was a mess, he couldn't handle his weapon, and it took him over fifteen minutes to run the mile and a half. But he tried harder than any of us. He sweat the most, yelled the loudest. He was thirty-eight, an accountant from Puerto Rico, a husband and a father. Yesterday, he left the firing range with a pocket full of live rounds, and the instructors ordered him to sing "I'm a Little Teapot" in front of the class. He didn't know the song, so they suggested "God Bless America." He belted out the chorus at the top of his lungs, his chest heaving after each line. We laughed, all of us, at his thick accent, at the misremembered verses, at his voice, off-key and quaking.

In town, over drinks, Hart went on about the winters in Detroit. I can't go back there, he said, not like Santiago. Fuck that. He asked Morales and me about winter in Arizona. Morales laughed. You don't have to worry about snow where we're going, *vato*, that's for sure. Hart thought it sounded nice. Nice, I asked? Just wait until the summer. Have you ever felt 115 degrees? Hell no, he said. Well, I told him, we'll be out in the heat, fetching dead bodies from the desert. Who the fuck walks in the desert when it's 115, he asked? I drank my way through another beer and went rambling on about how everyone used to cross in the city, in San Diego and El Paso, until they shut it all down in the '90s with fences and newly hired Border Patrol agents like us. If they sealed the cities, they thought, people wouldn't risk crossing in the mountains and the deserts. But they were wrong, I said, and now we're the ones who get to deal with it. Morales looked at me, his eyes dark and buried beneath his brow. I'm sorry, I told them, I can't help it—I studied this shit in school.

On our way back to the academy, I sat in the backseat of Morales' truck. In the front, Morales told Hart about growing up on the border in Douglas, about uncles and cousins on the south side, and I sat with my head against the cold glass of the window, staring at the darkened plain, slipping in and out of sleep.

3 January

Last week, my mother flew in from Arizona to see me, because—she said—we've never missed a Christmas together. She picked me up at the academy on Christmas Eve and we drove through the straw-colored hills, leaving behind the trembling Chihuahuan grasslands as we climbed into the evergreen mountains of southern New Mexico. We stayed the night in a two-room cabin, warm and bright with pinewood. We set up a miniature tree on the living room table, decorating it with tiny glass bulbs. Then, wrapped in blankets, we laughed and drank eggnog and brandy until the conversation deteriorated into discussion of my impending work.

Look, my mother said, I spent most of my adult life working for the government as a park ranger, so don't take this the wrong way—but don't you think it's below you, earning a degree just to become a border-cop? Look, I said, I spent four years away from home, studying this place through facts, policy, and history. I'm tired of reading. I want to exist outside, to know the reality of this border, day in and day out. Are you crazy, she said? You grew up with me, living in deserts and national parks. We've never been far from the border. Sure, I said, but I don't truly understand the landscape, I don't know how to handle myself in the face of ugliness or danger. My mother balked. There are ways to learn that don't place you at risk, she said, ways that let you help people. I fumed. I can still help people, I told her—I speak Spanish, I've lived in Mexico, I've been to the places where people are coming from. And don't worry, I told her, I won't place myself at risk—I'm not too proud to back away from danger.

Good, she said. We hugged, and she told me she was happy I'd soon be back home in Arizona, closer to her. Before bed, we each opened a single present, as we have done every Christmas Eve since I can remember.

In the morning, we ate brunch at the town's historic hotel, feasting on pot roast by a crackling fire. Afterward we climbed the stairs to a narrow lookout tower where people crowded and huddled together in jackets, walking in slow circles to take in the view. Below us, an expanse of sunlit plain stretched westward from the base of the mountain. I watched as the landscape shifted under the winter light. Behind me, my mother placed her hand on my shoulder and pointed to a cloud of gypsum sand in the distance, impossibly small, swirling across the basin desert.

24 February

We caught our first dope load today, only our second day after arriving at the station from the academy. We were east of the port of entry when the sensor hit at Sykes trail. At the trailhead, Cole, our supervisor, found foot sign for eight and had us pile out of the vehicles. For four miles we made our way toward the mountains following toe digs and kicked-over rocks. Cole went in front and called us up one by one to watch us cut sign. We found the first bundle discarded among the boulders at the base of the pass. We spread out to comb the hillsides and after about ten minutes we had recovered two backpacks filled with food and clothes and four more fifty-pound bundles wrapped in sugar sacks spray-painted black. Cole had us dump the packs, and I watched as several of my classmates ripped and tore at the clothing, scattering it among the tangled branches of mesquite and paloverde. In one of the backpacks, I found a laminated prayer card depicting Saint Jude, a tongue of flames hovering above his head. Morales found a pack of cigarettes and sat smoking on a rock as others laughed loudly and stepped on a heap of food. Nearby, Hart giggled and shouted to us as he pissed on a pile of ransacked belongings. As we hiked with the bundles back to our vehicles the February sun grew low in the sky and cast

52

a warm light over the desert. At the edge of the trail, in the pink shade of a paloverde, a desert tortoise raised itself up on its front legs to watch us pass.

2 April

Tonight we stood for hours in the darkness along the pole line. After we had tired of the cold and the buzzing of the power lines, Cole had us lay a spike strip across the dirt road and return to wait in our vehicles parked in a nearby wash. We sat with the engines on and the heat blasting, and after a few minutes of silence, Morales asked Cole why some of the agents at the station called him "Black Death." He laughed and pulled a can of Copenhagen from his shirt pocket. You have to be careful, he said, the Indians out here, when they're drunk and walking at night between the villages, they fall asleep on the fucking road. He packed the can as he spoke, swinging his right arm and thumping his forefinger across the lid. When it's cold out, he explained, the asphalt holds warmth from the sun, even at night. A few years ago, I was working the midnight shift, driving down IR- 9, and I saw this fucking Indian asleep in the middle of the road. I stopped the truck and woke his ass up. His brother was there with him, sleeping in the bushes. They were drunk as hell. Cole pinched a wad of dip into his mouth. His lower lip bulged, catching the green light from the control panel. I gave the guys a ride into the next village, he said, dropped them off at their cousin's place. Told them not to sleep on the goddamn road. Cole grabbed an empty Pepsi cup from the center console and spit. Maybe nine or ten months later, he continued, same fucking spot, I ran over the guy, killed him right there. Same fucking guy, asleep on the damn road. I never even saw him. After that, they started calling me Black Death. Cole laughed and spat into his cup and a few of us laughed with him, not knowing exactly what kind of laugh it was.

Just after midnight, a blacked-out truck roared across the spikes and three of its tires went. We tore after it, speeding blindly through a cloud of dust until we realized the vehicle had turned. We doubled back to where the tire sign left the road and followed it until we found the truck abandoned at the foot of a hill. In the back of the truck we found two marijuana bundles and a .22 rifle. Cole sent us to scour the hillside with our flashlights, but we only found one other bundle. It's a fucking gimme load, Cole said. I asked what he meant. It's a goddamn distraction, that's what. They're waiting us out. But my classmates and I didn't care, we were high from the chase. We drove the truck into a wash until it became stuck, and slashed the unpopped tire, leaving it there with the lights on and the engine running. On the way back to the station, I asked Cole what would happen to the truck. He told me he'd call the tribal police to seize the vehicle, but I knew he wouldn't. Even if he did, they wouldn't come for it, they wouldn't want the paperwork either. They, too, would leave it here to be ransacked, picked over, and lit on fire—evidence of a swirling disorder.

4 April

After sundown, Cole sent Morales up a hill near the highway with a thermal reconnaissance camera. Let me borrow your beanie, *vato*, he said to me, it's cold out. I handed it to him and stayed inside the vehicle, waiting with the others. An hour later, he spotted a group of ten just east of mile marker five. We rushed out of the car and set out on foot as he guided us in on the radio, but by the time we reached the group, they had already scattered. We found them one by one, huddled in the brush and curled up around the trunks of paloverde trees and cholla cactus. Not one of them ran. We made them take off their shoelaces and empty their backpacks, and we walked all ten of them single file back to the road. For a while I walked next to an older man who told me they were all from Michoacán. It's beautiful there, I said. Yes, he replied, but there's no work. You've been to Michoacán, he asked? I told him I had. Then you must have seen what it is to live in Mexico, he said. And now you see what it is like for us at the border. *Pues sí*, I said, we're out here every day. For a while we walked silently next to each other and then, after several minutes, he sighed deeply. *Hay mucha desesperación*, he told me, almost whispering. I tried to look at his face, but it was too dark.

At the station, I processed the man for deportation, and he asked me after I had taken his fingerprints if there was any work at the station for him. You don't understand, I said, you've just got to wait here until the bus comes. They'll take you to Tucson and then to Nogales and then you'll be back in Mexico. I understand, he assured me, I just want to know if there is something I can do while I wait, something to help. I can take out the trash or clean out the cells. I want to show you that I'm here to work, that I'm not a bad person, that I'm not here to bring in drugs, I'm not here to do anything illegal. I want to work. I looked at him. I know that, I said.

7 April

Sunday night, Cole showed us the layup spot where he had almost been run over by smugglers. He led us to a wide wash full of old blankets and discarded clothes and pieces of twine and empty cans of tuna and crushed water bottles. We climbed out of the wash and walked to a nearby cactus, a tall and sprawling chain-fruit cholla, and Cole asked if any of us had hand sanitizer. Someone tossed him a small bottle and he emptied the gel on the black trunk of the cactus. Cole asked for a lighter and with it, he lit the gel and stepped back to watch the flames crawl up the trunk, crackling and popping as they engulfed the plant's spiny arms. In the light from the fire, Cole packed his can of dip and took a pinch into his mouth. His bottom lip shone taut and smooth, his shaved black skin reflecting the flames. He spit into the fire and the rest of us stood with him in a circle around the cholla as it burned, laughing loudly, taking pictures and video with our phones, watching as thick smoke billowed into the night, filling the air with the burnt smell of tar and resin, like freshly laid asphalt.

9 April

Cole was ahead scouting the trail in the darkness when he radioed about the mountain lion. Come with your sidearms drawn, he said. We figured he was full of shit. We had been talking loudly, walking with our flashlights on—surely a mountain lion would shy away. We continued down the trail until the ground leveled off, and it was then that a grave hiss issued up from the darkness beside us, a sound like hot wind escaping the depths of the earth. Holy fucking shit, we said. We drew our sidearms and shuffled down the path back-to-back, casting light in all directions around us. In that moment, I felt a profound and immediate fear—not of the danger posed to us by the animal, but rather, the idea that it would show itself to us, so many men armed and heedless, that it would be shot down and lit on fire and left here beside the trail, another relic of a desert unspooling.

7 June

There are days when I feel I am becoming good at what I do. And then I wonder, what does it mean to be good at this? I wonder sometimes how I might explain certain things, the sense in what we do when they run from us, scattering into the brush, leaving behind their water jugs and their backpacks full of food and clothes, how to explain what we do when we discover their layup spots stocked with water and stashed rations. Of course, what you do depends on who you're with, depends on what kind of agent you are, what kind of agent you want to become, but it's true that we slash their bottles and drain their water into the dry earth, that we dump their backpacks and pile their food and clothes to be crushed and pissed on and stepped over, strewn across the desert and set ablaze, and Christ, it sounds terrible, and maybe it is, but the idea is that when they come out from their hiding places, when they regroup and return to find their stockpiles ransacked and stripped, they'll realize then their situation, that they're fucked, that it's hopeless to continue on, and they'll quit right then and there, they'll save themselves, they'll struggle toward the nearest highway or dirt road to flag down some passing agent or they'll head for the nearest parched village to knock on someone's door, someone who will give them food and water and call us to take them in—that's the idea, the sense in it all. But still I have nightmares, visions of them staggering through the desert, men from Michoacán, from places I've known, men lost and wandering without food or water, dying slowly as they look for some road, some village, some way out. In my dreams I seek them, searching in vain until finally I am met by their bodies lying face-down on the ground before me, dead and stinking on the desert floor, human waypoints in a vast and smoldering expanse.

23 June

Last month, we were released from the training unit and dispersed into rotating shifts to work under journeymen agents. For the past week, I've been partnered with Mortenson, a four-year veteran and the Mormon son of a Salt Lake City cop. This morning, at dawn, we sat together in the port of entry and watched from the camera room as two men and a woman cut a hole in the pedestrian fence. Mortenson and I bolted from the room and ran to the site of the breach, rounding the corner just in time to see the two men already scrambling back through the hole to Mexico. The woman stood motionless beside the fence, too scared to run. As Mortenson inspected the breach, the girl wept, telling me it was her birthday, that she was turning twenty-three, and she pleaded for me to let her go, swearing she would never cross again. Mortenson turned and took a long look at the woman and then laughed. I booked her last week, he said.

She spoke hurriedly to us as we walked back to the port of entry, and while Mortenson went inside to gather our things, I stood with her in the parking lot. She told me she was from Guadalajara, that she had some problems there, that she had already tried four times to cross. She swore to me that she would stay in Mexico for good this time, that she would finally go back to finish music school. *Te lo juro*, she said. She looked at me and smiled. Someday I'm going to be a singer, you know. I believe it, I said, smiling back. She told me that she thought I was nice, and before Mortenson returned from the port, she snuck her counterfeit green card into my hand, telling me she didn't want to get in trouble if they found it on her at the processing center. When Mortenson came back, we helped her into the patrol vehicle and drove north toward the station, laughing and applauding as she sang to us from the backseat. She's going to be a singer, I told Mortenson. The woman beamed. She already is, he said.

27 July

Last night, finally allowed to patrol on my own, I sat watching storms roll across the moonlit desert. There were three of them: the first due south in Mexico; the second in the east, creeping down from the mountains; the third hovering just behind me, close enough for me to feel smatterings of rain and gusts of warm wind. In the distance, hot lightning appeared like a line of neon, illuminating the desert in a shuddering white light.

30 July

Agents found Martin Ubalde de la Vega and his three companions on the bombing range ten miles west of the highway. At the time of rescue, the four men had been in the desert for six days and had wandered in the July heat for more than forty-eight hours without food or water. By the time they were found, one of the men had already met his death. Of the survivors, one was quickly treated and discharged from the hospital, while another remained in intensive care, recently awoken from a coma, unable to remember his own name. When I arrived at the hospital asking for the third survivor, nurses explained that he was recovering from kidney failure and they guided me to his room, where he lay hidden like a dark stone in white sheets.

I had been charged with watching over de la Vega until his condition was stable, at which point I would transport him to the station to be processed for deportation. I settled in a chair next to him, and after several moments of silence, I asked him to tell me about himself. He answered timidly, as if unsure of what to say or even how to speak.

57

He began by apologizing for his Spanish, explaining that he only knew what they had taught him in school. He told me he came from the jungles of Guerrero, that in his village they spoke Mixtec and farmed the green earth. He was the father of seven children, he said, five girls and two boys. His elder daughter lived in California and he had crossed the border with plans to go there, to live with her and find work.

We spent the following hours watching *telenovelas* and occasionally de la Vega would turn to ask me about the women in America, wondering if they were like the ones on TV. Then, smiling, he began to tell me about his youngest daughter, still in Mexico. She's just turned eighteen, he said. You could marry her.

Later that afternoon, de la Vega was cleared for release. The nurse brought in his belongings—a pair of blue jeans and sneakers with holes worn through the soles. I asked what had happened to his shirt. I don't know, he told me. I looked at the nurse and she shrugged, telling me he had come that way. We've got no clothes here, she added, only hospital gowns. As we exited the building, I imagined de la Vega's embarrassment, the fear he must have at remaining bare-chested as he was to be ferried through alien territory, booked and transferred between government processing centers and bussed to the border to enter his country alone and half naked.

At the patrol vehicle, I placed de la Vega in the passenger seat and popped the trunk. At the back of the cruiser, I undid my gun belt, unbuttoned my uniform shirt, and removed my white v-neck. Then I reassembled my uniform and returned to the passenger door and offered de la Vega my undershirt. Before leaving town, I asked de la Vega if he was hungry. You should eat something now, I told him, at the station there's only juice and crackers. De la Vega agreed and I asked what he was hungry for. What do Americans eat, he asked? I laughed. Here we eat mostly Mexican food. He looked at me unbelievingly. But we also eat hamburgers, I said. As we pulled into the drive-thru window at McDonald's, de la Vega told me he didn't have any money. *Yo te invito*, I said.

As we drove south along the open highway, I tuned into a Mexican radio station and we listened to the sounds of norteño as de la Vega finished his meal. After he had eaten, de la Vega sat silently next to me, watching the passing desert. Then, quietly, as if whispering to me or to someone else, he began to speak of the rains in Guerrero, about the wet and green jungle, and I wondered if he could have ever been made to imagine a place like this—a place where one of his companions would meet his death and another would be made to forget his own name, a landscape where the earth still burned with volcanic heat.

4 August

This evening as I cut for sign along the border road, I watched a Sonoran coachwhip snake try to find its way into Mexico through the pedestrian fence. The animal slithered along the length of the mesh looking for a way south, hitting its head against the rusted metal again and again until finally I guided it over to the wide opening of a wash grate. After the snake made its way across the adjacent road, I stood for a while looking through the mesh, staring at the undulating tracks it left in the dirt.

7 August

Yesterday, on the border road, a woman on the south side of the pedestrian fence flagged me down as I passed. I stopped my vehicle and went over to her. With panic in her voice she asked me if I knew about her son—he had crossed days ago, she said, or maybe it was a week ago, she wasn't sure. She hadn't heard anything from him, no one had, and she didn't know if he had been caught or if he was lost somewhere in the desert or if he was even still alive. *Estamos desesperados*, she told me, her voice quivering, with one hand clawing at her chest and the other pressed trembling against the border fence. I don't remember what I told her, if I took down the man's name or if I gave her the phone number to some faraway office or remote hotline, but I remember thinking later about de la Vega, about his dead and delirious companions, about all the questions I should have asked the woman. I arrived home that evening and threw my gun belt and uniform across the couch, standing alone in my cavernous living room. I called my mother. I'm safe, I told her, I'm at home.

29 August

At the end of the night, Mortenson called me into the processing room and asked me to translate for two girls who had just been brought in, nine- and ten-year-old sisters who were picked up with two women at the checkpoint. He told me to ask them basic questions: Where is your mother? In California. Who are the women who brought you here? Friends. Where are you from? Sinaloa. The girls peppered me with nervous questions in return: When could they go home? Where were the women who drove them, when were they coming back? Could they call their mother? I tried to explain things to them, but they were too young, too bewildered, too distraught at being surrounded by men in uniform. One of the agents brought the girls a bag of Skittles, but even then they couldn't smile, they couldn't say thank you, they just stood there, looking at the candy with horror.

After the girls were placed in a holding cell, I told Mortenson I had to leave. My shift's over, I said. He told me they still needed to interview the women who were picked up with the girls and asked me to stay and translate. I can't help anymore, I told him, I have to go home. As I drove away from the station, I tried not to think of the girls and my hands shook at the wheel. I wanted to call my mother, but it was too late, it was the middle of the night.

30 August

Last night I dreamed I was grinding my teeth out, spitting the crumbled pieces into my palms and holding them in my cupped hands, searching for someone to show them to, someone who could see what was happening.

12 September

Morales was the first to hear him, screaming in the distance from one of the spider roads. He hiked for a mile or two and found the kid lying on the ground, hysterical. For more than twenty-four hours he had been lost in a vast mesquite thicket. The coyote who left him there told him he was holding back the group and handed him half a liter of water, pointing to some hills in the distance, telling him to walk at them until he found a road. When I arrived with the water, the kid was on the ground next to Morales, lurching in the shade and crying like a child. The kid was fat—his pants hung from his ass and his fly was half open, his zipper broken, his shirt hanging loosely from his shoulders, inside out and torn and soaked in sweat. Morales looked at me and smiled and then turned to the kid. Your water's here, *Gordo*. I kneeled next to him and handed him the gallon jug. He took a sip and began to pant and groan. Drink more, I said, but drink slowly. I can't, he moaned, I'm going to die. No you're not, I told him, you're still sweating.

After the kid drank some water, we helped him up and tried walking him through the thicket toward the road. He lagged and staggered, crying out behind us. *Ay oficial*, he would moan, *no puedo*. As we crouched and barged through tangled branches, I slowly became overwhelmed by his panic until finally we broke out of the thicket and spotted the dirt road. You see the trucks, *Gordo*? Can you make it that far? Maybe we should just leave you here, *no puedes, verdad*?

On the ride back to the station, the kid regained some composure. He was nineteen years old, he told me, and had planned to go to Oregon to sell heroine, *un puño a la vez*. You can make a lot of money that way, he told me. For several minutes the kid was silent. You know, he finally said, I really thought I was going to die in that thicket. I prayed to God that I would get out, I prayed to the Virgin and to all the saints, to every saint I could think of. It's strange, he said, I've never done that before. I've never believed in God.

30 September

Today I went to the hospital to see Morales. He was in a motorcycle accident two weeks ago and wasn't wearing his helmet. For a while we had been hearing at the station that he might not make it. I was too afraid to see him a week ago when he was in a coma and I was afraid, still, to see him a few days later after he had come out of it, when he would wake up cursing and pulling his tubes out, when he still didn't recognize anybody. When I finally saw him, I was surprised how thin he was, how frail. He had bruises under his deep-set eyes, a feeding tube in his nose, an IV line in his arm, and a huge gash across the left side of his skull where half his hair had been shaved off. *Ey vato*, he said to me quietly. I smiled at him. I like your haircut, I said. As Morales spoke to me he seemed far away, his eyes scanning the room as if searching for some landmark, something to suggest the nature of the place he had come to. His childhood friend from Douglas was there. He told me Morales couldn't see out of his left eye, but that doctors thought the sight would come back eventually. His mother and father were there too, speaking quietly to each other in Spanish. A little while after I arrived, Cole and Hart came, and as they stood talking at his bedside, I could see a wet glaze in Cole's eyes. I excused myself from the room, telling everyone I'd come back, but I didn't.

13 October

Last week I took the border road out to the lava flow, driving for more than an hour across rocky hills and long valleys. The earth became darker as I neared the flow, devoid of plants and cactus. To the south a pale band of sand dunes underlined the base of a nameless cordillera, shifting at the horizon in shades of purple and dark clay. I drove across the lava flow and looked over black rocks glistening as if wet under the afternoon sun, rocks pockmarked from a time when the earth melted and simmered between erupting volcanoes, a molten crust cracking and shifting as it cooled.

25 December

At midnight on Christmas Eve, just before the end of my shift, I heard gunshots ring out in Mexico. I stopped my vehicle at the top of a small hill and stood on the roof to watch the sparkling of fireworks along the southern horizon. After returning home, I woke my mother who had come to visit for the holiday, her eyes bleary with worry and sleep. We sat in my empty living room in the night-weary hours of the morning, drinking eggnog and stringing popcorn around an artificial tree. My mother asked about my shift. It was fine, I said. She asked me if I liked my work, if I was learning what I wanted. It's not something to like, I said, it's not a classroom. It's a job, and I'm getting used to it, and I'm getting good at it. I can make sense of what that means later.

You know, my mother said, it's not just your safety I worry about. I know how the soul can be placed at hazard fighting impossible battles. I spent my whole career working for the government, slowly losing a sense of purpose even though I remained close to the outdoors, close to my passion. I don't want that for you.

I cut her off—I didn't want to tell about my dreams of dead bodies, about the fires burning in the desert, about my hands shaking at the wheel. Mom—I said—let's open a present.

30 December

Tonight the scope truck spotted a group of twenty just north of the line. The operator said they were moving slowly, that it looked as if there might be women and children in the group. He guided us in, and we quickly located their sign and then lost it again across a stretch of hard-packed desert pavement. We split up and combed the hillside, hunting for toe digs and kicked-over rocks. On the walk back to the car, I became furious. There were supposed to be twenty of them, they were supposed to be slow, but still I couldn't catch up, I couldn't stay on the sign, I couldn't even get close enough to hear them in the distance, and so now they remained out there in the desert: men, women, and children, entire families invisible and unheard, and I was powerless to help them, powerless to keep them from straying through the night and the cold.

Nominated by Ploughshares

THE PLATE-SPINNER

fiction by STEVE STERN

from AGNI

There used to be thirty-six. You should have seen them in their glory days, what a spectacle! Silhouetted in amber spotlights on a muggy August evening, the saints were truly the carnival's main attraction. No spring chickens even then, they were still remarkably spry, their stamina inexhaustible as they galloped night and day, each on his own spinning plate the size of a barrel lid, their beards and earlocks flying, the tails of their caftans streaming horizontally behind them. The prayers they chanted could drown out the tinny country music piped all over the lot. Back then you had almost as many spinners as there were poles to shake. Me and the other carnics, we took shifts: nobody was ever assigned to the task full-time. We volunteered gladly—it was a hoot just to be part of their act. I'd knock off operating a hanky-pank or grab-stand to take a turn. Sometimes we'd do-si-do from pole to pole like in a square dance, really hamming it up, though the marks never paid us much mind. They were too busy ogling the rabbis hotfooting it overhead.

Still, folks would stuff our pockets with coins as we jigged past them. The act depended on donations, since it was mounted out of doors, running as it did 24/7 with no blow-off, and the crowds were always generous. Naturally we were made to empty our pockets at the end of the day. It didn't pay to resist, since Abednego the Albino Giant grabbed our ankles for an ass-over-elbows shakedown, but usually enough bills stayed stuck in our pockets to make the job more than worthwhile.

In those days I hardly even knew their names, the saints, or "stylites," as Old Man Rothstein called them, nor did I set much store by the pitch he'd worked up for their act:

"Ladies and gents, please to observe the Lamed Vovniks—which is Hebrew for Thirty-Sixers, count 'em—holy men from the legendary city of Sfat. See how they got to keep steppin' lively on them magic plates or else the good Lord'll remove His grace from the world. In other words, my feller mishpookies, if ever they stop their centrifugatin', or them plates cease their gyroscopic whirligiggery, it's all she wrote for the rest of us . . ."

Did anybody believe him? I wouldn't have put it past those families of slack-jawed yokels, judging from the way they stood there mesmerized, oblivious to the bally all around them. The Lamed Vovniks' act was not so much a single-o as the midway's centerpiece. Even when we caravanned from town to town, they kept at it—or we kept them at it, in any case, loading them still mounted atop their poles onto a flatbed truck. They humped it even during the off-months, when the show wintered in a trailer park down in the Everglades. They were high-maintenance, all right, and needed as much looking after as the sideshow freaks and reptiles, but it was an article of faith in our outfit that the luck of the carnival somehow depended on the rabbis treading those whirling zinc discs.

Even Mr. Saul Rothstein, their manager, couldn't say how long they'd been running, so obscure were their origins and so patchy was the old man's memory. Sure, they might slow to a canter from time to time, when they ate the stuffed chicken necks and noodle puddings that Rothstein had specially imported from Yankee delicatessens; they slept standing up but still jogging, and did their business while in motion in bags fastened under their caftans, which they let drop for quick disposal by grumbling roughies. Occasionally, for no discernible reason—neither inclement weather nor blistering sunshine—they might come to a halt, which left them riding their discs in circles like a Tilt-a-Whirl, but this was a rare occurrence. So when they did begin to stop trotting, or anyway a goodly portion of them, it took the carnival by surprise. Rabbi I-forget-his-name—the one with half a halo of wooly hair—was the first: he had his heart attack and plummeted like a sandbag in front of the horrified crowd. His plate wobbled a few ticks on its own before it too toppled from the pole and crashed with a dinging *dong* into the front-end lot. Women shrieked and covered the eyes of their children.

Not long after that, another one, Rabbi Yosi the Nose (distinctive for a schnoz like a dorsal fin), complained of spasms in his spine before losing his balance and plunging headlong to his reward. Others followed in fairly regular succession over the next couple of seasons, felled by strokes, blind staggers, falling sickness, or just plain decrepitude, until their number was reduced to a ragged ten survivors. "A minyan," said Old Man Rothstein, who had a fund of secret mystical words he used to lend color to the act. A minyan was the minimum number needed for their prayers to be effective, he explained. Ten saints were enough to keep the world from teetering off its axis into oblivion—this despite his having insisted for years that nothing short of the original thirty-six were required. Then Rothstein himself, who seemed to actually believe his own patter, was retired to a community for antiquated carnies in Florida, where I heard he soon died of acute nostalgia.

Of course, the planet had already begun to come apart, give or take the rabbis on their gyrating plates. It may have been mere coincidence that the international cyberwars started around the time the Lamed Vovniks began to drop out of the air. Computers the world over shut down, and what was left of the staggering global economy collapsed. The revolutions and anarchy that followed in the wake of universal bankruptcy hastened the unraveling of nations; even the armed citadels of the super-rich weren't safe. Add to that the flight of whole populations from coastlines inundated by the melting of the polar ice caps, and you're left with a planet in a state of mortal disarray. Needless to say, conditions were less than optimum for business, and traveling carnivals were no exception. Fiscally kaput, the Cavalcade of Fun began to disband by degrees: little by little the barkers and concessionaires, the kootch-dancers, weight-guessers, sword-swallowers, fire-eaters, roughies, and boxing chimpanzees went their separate ways. The dismantled rides were repossessed by their manufacturers, who sold them for scrap, and the human oddities drifted into quarters where they were least conspicuous, which wasn't hard, given the unsightly countenance of so much of humanity:

The remaining rabbis, however, maintained their perpetual motion, thanks largely to the efforts of yours truly. My carnival brethren seemed content to abandon the stylites to their fate; they would have allowed their wavering poles to come to a standstill, the zinc plates to wobble and drop off with their brittle-boned burdens. But I thought I'd exploit the act a little longer—though I don't know what devil put that notion in my head. Was it just some misplaced allegiance to Mr. Rothstein, who'd shown me the ropes in the early days of my apprenticeship? Whatever the case, I couldn't quite grasp that current events had taken such a toll on the Cavalcade of Fun. I'd always believed we were proof against the intrusions of history.

When I was a green kid, a few of us orphans played truant from the asylum, biking down to the Memphis Cotton Carnival midway, where we crawled under the flap of the grind show tent. I got an eyeful of Madame Vivien's G-String Revue and, later, the jam auction, the Dark Ride, the Barrel of Joy, and all the grifters in their blazing mug joints, and never looked back. The carnival was pure freedom then. Sure, society was coming undone all around us, but we managed to steer clear of that mishegoss. In the towns and cities, people would unglue themselves from their gadgets and screens to greet us, often providing attractions of their own. For me it was always the girls, and I was some champion fornicator, I can tell you. I'd give the tattoo on my bicep a little twitch as I tucked some cutie into the Tickler; I'd give her a sly wink even as I handed a trio of balls to her escort at the bottle pitch. Then, after the ride or the game of skill, when I awarded her some choice item of slum merchandise, she'd thank me with a smile and her tacit consent to meet me after hours. I did a lot of shtupping, as Old Man Rothstein would say. I also tangled with no end of boyfriends, sometimes stomped them and sometimes got my scrawny ass stomped. I had my share of broken teeth, crotch critters, and the drip, but what did I care? That was living, and it was ace-high being young. I had the six-toed cats for pets, Delmar the Wall-of-Death rider and Meatball the Missing Link for my pals; I ate fried pies and barbecued ribs in Iuka, crawfish gumbo and bread pudding in Baton Rouge, drank branch water and bourbon with Carl the Cyclops in the ten-in-one tent, and smoked muggles with Kongo the gorilla in the Jungle of Dread. We knew as well as the tip what was in the headlines, but the carnival wasn't about studying headlines. We set up our midway on the outskirts of recorded time, and the townspeople met us there to ride the Wild Chipmunk and play pokerino, see Olga the Headless Teuton and watch Pristine the Dixie Pixie rotate her pasties, one clockwise and one counter but always in sync.

Then the crowds stopped coming, though whether from poverty or fear (for it was dangerous to leave your house anymore) I couldn't say. Maybe it was just that fun had gone out of fashion. As it happened, we finally ran aground in Memphis, which was as close to a hometown as I'd ever known. We could have fetched up anywhere, but it was at the bottom of the Bluff City levee that the Cavalcade of Fun called it quits. There was no more money for fuel, scarcely any fuel to be had in any case, no credit left for tying rusty cables to power lines, which were for the most part defunct. So we finished in the city where it had all begun for me. Me and the remaining roughnecks, we rolled those mounted poles with their millstone anchors (always a tricky business) off the ramp from the foundered flatbed and set up the Lamed Vovniks on their spinning plates. That's when we realized it was over: there were no other attractions left. We were a broke-down ragbag relic and nobody in that skeleton crew thought twice about taking off.

Nobody but me. Did I really think I could make a go of it alone, or was it the ghost of old Rothstein, who'd fished me out of the bozo tank and taught me to assimilate fancy words (like "assimilate") into my hustles—was it his kindly ghost pricking my conscience? At any rate, I found myself lunging like a fool from pole to pole, shaking those tapered spars—worn smooth from generations of spinners—for all I was worth.

*　*　*

After I'd been at it a while, some street kids of no identifiable gender showed up, the kind of marauding pack you saw everywhere lately, menacing despite their pint size. Up to my knees in leftover hanky-pank prizes, I offered them penny whistles and stuffed pandas—at first to appease them, and then in exchange for taking my place just long enough for me to nip up the bluff and forage for food. It was a risk I had to take, and I half expected to return and find my hired help vanished and the stylites tumbled from their pillars. That might have been, frankly, a relief. But when I came back with a sack of sandwiches (which I'd also purchased with tchotchkes—it had become largely a barter economy), I discovered the urchins gleefully spinning the plates, skipping in time to the rabbis' chanted devotions. I shared the food with them, some of which they gobbled on the run while delivering the rest to the saints with the aluminum reacher.

The one called Rabbi Ashlag of Vishnitz, him with his beard like a singed horse's mane, spoke first. "I can't eat this treyf!" he shouted, and flung the sandwich at me. Others followed suit. It seemed that the sandwiches I'd brought from the quick-lunch stand, practically the only going concern on that desolate downtown street, weren't kosher. The ham was forbidden and the addition of cheese slathered in mayonnaise made the whole production trebly reprehensible.

"Then starve!" I replied.

Their silence suggested they were happy to do just that, having long incorporated starvation into their act. They were forever commemorating some abomination perpetrated against the Jews with a fast. *Luftmenschen* was one of the names Rothstein had for them: the men who lived in air could also live *on* air. Nevertheless, the next time the urchins—who came and went at irregular intervals—appeared, I conscripted them to take my place again, then managed to locate a flyblown delicatessen at the blighted north end of Main Street. Its menu wasn't strictly kosher, but the cold cuts and blintzes were kosher-style and the saints condescended to eat.

"Don't do me no favors," I muttered, though I shooed the kids away and began once more to agitate the poles myself.

It wasn't long before I realized I'd taken on more than I could handle—and for what? Where was the audience, unless you included my feral helpers? I suppose you could call their sporadic plate-spinning a kind of audience participation; it was, anyway, as close to civilized behavior as I ever observed in them. But while their part-time assistance let me tend to my own meager needs and catch the odd catnap in the cab of the truck, all they really did was help to perpetuate a losing proposition. There was no profit in exhibiting the Lamed Vovniks anymore. Every so often a drifter or unemployed loiterer, or maybe a dispossessed family, would pause a bit on the cobbles, but unlike the awestruck carnival crowds, these passersby appeared merely confused, even a little frightened, since almost everything on Earth seemed lately to inspire fear. Moreover, they hadn't a dime between them to leave as an offering. And truth be told, I shared their bewilderment, though mine had more to do with being no longer young, or fortified with strong drink, and yet continuing to lurch from pole to pole to keep the pirouetting discs in motion.

Not to mention all the extracurricular efforts their maintenance involved. There was the toilet issue, about which the less said the better, and the fact that I was running out of kitsch items to exchange for food and the urchins' employment. Up on North Main, Mr. Rosen had taken in so much slum that his deli was practically converted to a souvenir shop; it was only the occasional sale of a pinwheel or the plastic bust of a movie star that kept him amenable to trading for more potato pancakes and gefilte fish. Meanwhile the weird children, who looked more like hungry ghosts with each visitation, appareled as they were in the outsize Elvis T-shirts I'd swapped for their services, had lost interest in my stock of worthless prizes. What they preferred was a portion of the rabbis' victuals, of which Rosen's Deli was becoming an increasingly stingy provider. If they hadn't regarded the spinning as a species of hoopla, they might not have turned up at all. Myself, I was a wreck from trying to keep everyone satisfied: my job was at least as demanding as that of the rabbis, who got a boost from their alleged beatitude. I say "alleged," since aside from their constant prayers, which may have been gibberish for all I knew, I couldn't see what was so holy about them. For my own troubles they seemed to have no consideration at all, even mocking me when they were so inclined.

"Give a look!" This from Rabbi Kitsl of Takhshitz, his naked knees like dimpled spuds. "He runs around like an Abraham that just got circumcised."

"Like an Adam looking for his lost rib," from Rabbi Ponim Zvi of Vorkl, a man so thin as to seem composed of twin profiles.

And if I complained of being unappreciated, Elimelekh, the so-called Seer of Zhldscz, peering from beneath the fur boa of his monobrow, would weigh in: "If you act like an ass, don't get insulted when people ride you."

For a time I protested in disbelief: how could they be so insensitive to my exertions? "If I should stop shaking your poles," I reminded them, "you'll drop to the cobbles and shatter like Humpty Dumpties."

"Threats he makes, the shmegegge," said Rabbi Zusya the Lublin Angel. "Careful or I'll make your teeth to mutiny and chew off your head!"

"I'll turn your blood to whiskey," said the pop-eyed Shmelke of Ger, not to be outdone, "so a hundred bedbugs get drunk on it and dance in your pupik a mazurka." They were a competitive lot, those Yid sky pilots.

"*I'm* supposed to be scared?" said the Seer of Zhldscz in delayed response to my warning. "I been dead already before. In heaven they told me, Come back again when they're finished, your good deeds." And with smug self-righteousness, "Do your worst, paskudnyak, my dues are paid."

"Oh holy Elimelekh," chided Meshullam Shloyme, the Genius of Medzibozh, pushing his pince-nez up the slope of his parrot beak, "his fortzes that they smell from frankincense. Now my own humble soul hid in the chaos before man was created, which it's why it never had to share in his sin."

Upon which Elimelekh countered with a discourse on the prominence of his placement among the saints, how his pole somehow corresponded to Jacob's pillar, which corresponded in turn to the hallowed middle finger of the right hand, and so on. "You mean this one?" queried the Genius, raising the finger in question.

I didn't know what was worse: their rivalries, insults, or terrible jokes.

Meanwhile the rabbis Baruch and Yitzkhok, of Poupko and Otwock respectively, bided their time atop their pinnacles, rehearsing an interminable repertoire of groaners.

Baruch the straight man, gangling and earnest: "Reb Yitz, did you ever, when you were married, make love with your wife?"

Yitzkhok, stumpy and brash: "Just once."

Baruch: "And what did she say to you in the morning?"

Yitzkhok: "Don't stop!"

Baruch: "Reb Yitz, that's a nice pocket watch you got."

Yitzkhok, sentimental: "My zayde sold me on his deathbed."

Nor were they above lampooning their fellows, like Simcha Bunam the Flagellant, who sported in his ecstasies a frequent pride below the belt of his kapote.

Baruch: "Reb Yitz, what happens when with his stiff shvantz Simcha Bunam walks into a wall?"

Yitzkhok, innocent now: "He breaks his nose?"

If I hadn't been busy wringing the necks of their cedar pedestals, I'd have clapped my hands over my ears.

While I was never sure exactly what day it was—each was like any other but for the weather—the Lamed Vovniks now chose to sit out one day of every week. From dusk till dusk they refused to run and sat idly revolving on their plates, repeating their everlasting prayers: "Sh'ma yisroayl yitgadol veyitkaddash yahdah yahdah tarara boom . . ."

"What's a matter you should take a day off?" I asked—sometimes even I sounded like them.

"It's Shabbos," announced Rabbi Ashlag. "the day of rest," as if any ninny would know.

I reminded him there were also Shabboses all those years on Rothstein's watch and nobody took a break then.

"That man," chimed in the eroded Pomm Zvi, "a slave driver."

"No longer are we slaves but are led out of bondage!" declared Elimelekh the Seer to a chorus of hearty huzzahs.

I glanced at the cobblestones curving like an alligator's back along the river, iron mooring rings attached as if the levee might be portable. A gutted houseboat wallowed in its mucky berth, and the shore was awash in refuse: tin cans, dead rats, a still-gasping, torpedo-sized garfish. "So this would be what, the Promised Land?" I asked.

"Didn't we cease our wandering?" responded Rabbi Kitsl of the dimpled knees.

It galled me how these Yids always answered questions with questions, but couldn't I also play their game? "So why I don't get a day of rest too?"

A beat before bug-eyed Shmelke asserted, "You're the Shabbos goy."

That triggered a spate of speculations to the effect that there might in fact be some Jew in me. "Perhaps of the red-headed tribe," observed Rabbi Zusya (though my hair was tobacco brown), "they that dwell across the River Sambatyon." He looked wistfully beyond the sluggish Mississippi toward the Arkansas floodplain.

"If that's the case," cautioned the hidebound Ashlag, "then he's in violation of the Sabbath and cannot be expiated, his sins."

Such a headache I got from listening to their nonsense that I released the pole I'd been stirring. "I'm on strike!" I declared. The plate on which Rabbi Simcha Bunam sat—lashing himself with his phylacteries—wobbled, and I grabbed it again in the nick of time.

"Why on earth, am I killing myself for this bunch of nudniks?" I muttered.

"Because we're such good company?" said Baruch and Yitzkhok in unison.

At that point I was overtaken by an exhaustion so complete that I feared I couldn't go on, and I wondered at the saints' relentless endurance. "Why do *you* do it?"

I anticipated, if anything, the usual pabulum that Rothstein had fed the rubes all those years, even after the complement of Lamed Vovniks had shrunk to ten: how if they fell off their poles, the Earth would cease its own spinning and the sorrows of mankind poison even the souls of newborn babes—that old saw. So it surprised me when my question was met with utter silence. Did they think it was none of my business? Then one of them, Meshullam Shloyme I believe it was, said, "*I* don't remember. Zusya, do you remember?" The Angel of Lublin screwed up his face of a bearded carp and replied, "Not me; ask Kitsl, I think he knows." If he did, Kitsl was disinclined to answer; twirling an earlock with a crooked forefinger, he passed the buck to the Seer of Zhldscz, so reliably fluent in esoteric hokum. "It's something to do with if we don't want to go backwards, we got to run?" Elimelekh tendered uncertainly. This moved Rabbi Simcha Bunam, universally acknowledged as simpleminded, to cry out as he flogged himself about the temples, "When that he climbs, the just man, the Phallus of Divinity, desire is aroused in the Earth, and is perfected the connection between the upper and lower worlds. Then is having intercourse the Highest with His bride and the voice of the Beloved will knock in your mouth, the lyre sing of itself, and the sun release to quiver in your blood its yellow butterflies"—which was pure claptrap, of course, though also kind of picturesque. Reeling beneath them, I heard the runty Yitzkhok of Otwock ask his stilt-legged opposite Rabbi Baruch what he thought about sex. Baruch said he liked to have it infrequently, upon which Yitzkhok inquired was that one word or two.

As I was just about to collapse in a heap, the kids showed up in their filthy T-shirts and hoodies. They no longer demanded compensation but took over the spinning voluntarily, like they were frolicking around a grove of maypoles. You wouldn't have thought those grim-faced castaways had it in them to abandon themselves to play. I dragged my sorry self to the truck and passed out in the cab, which I'd converted over the weeks into a relatively cozy nest. In my dreams I continued the spinning.

Though I never knew when the kids would come and go, I began to count on their shifts, which always seemed to commence around the time I was close to giving out from overwork. So the days took on a kind of fitful rhythm. There was also a new development: shadowy folk lurking on the periphery of the lot started to leave what I guess you'd call gifts—some of it rabbi food, like twisty breads and beet soup. I recalled how the busloads of synagogue congregants, brought in to view the saints back in the day, had left similar donations, and figured Mr. Rosen from the deli must have put in a word with the faithful. (Were there still faithful?) But I wondered why they only ventured in under the cover of darkness, as if they were ashamed.

Despite the barbarity that lay beyond it, the atmosphere by the river at night had a certain charm. For one thing, it was cooler after dusk, the mosquito-dense humidity having dissipated, and while there were gunshots and other inhuman noises to remind you that the city above the levee was a perilous place, there were also stretches of serenity. In the absence of spotlights I couldn't see the saints hoofing it above me, but I could hear the hum of their whirling discs, the tattoo of their footfalls, and the singsong murmur of their evening prayers. It was like their poles became the throttles of some great musical instrument I was playing by ear. I won't pretend I didn't still worry, mainly from nightfall to around midnight, when the rabbis claimed the demons were most active. (I imagined them attacking with chainsaws.) But after midnight, when the dam between the celestial and the terrestrial was said to spring a leak, evil receded from the air and the dew of Eden mingled with the Mississippi mud. The moon tugged at the river like a bride lifting the fabric of a luminous veil, its folds stitched with gold thread, and even the stench and the slop of dirty water against the stones raised my spirits. Then sometimes, especially on Sabbath nights when the rabbis told me a Jew was granted an extra soul—the *neshamah yeterah* that gave him a vigor he lacked during the working week—I felt mighty, like I alone was responsible for sustaining the equilibrium of the world.

❊   ❊   ❊

It was a mild winter—what winter wasn't anymore? There was a whole generation now for whom snow was a myth—but in my apprehension I thought I detected signs that some of the saints might be running down. For a start, they'd ceased bickering so much: Rabbi Shmelke actually conceding to Ponim Zvi that the soul garment of the Baal Shem Tov was made from the seminal emission of the Holy Ari rather than from that of Moses, and old Elimelekh allowing as how the stylites might not be the reincarnation of the Ten Martyrs after all. One morning a groggy Rabbi Zusya skipped three of the Eighteen Benedictions, which I'd taken to counting. Then April arrived with its rains as soft as thistledown, crape myrtles blossoming along the bluff like candelabras with purple flames, and the rebbes did appear a little friskier. While they continued to take my labors for granted, I no longer resented their entitled attitude, and god help me, I couldn't seem to get enough of their gab. Over the months, something in my temperament had changed, though you probably couldn't have told it from looking at me. Maybe the calluses on my hands were more hornified, my stringy muscles more case-hardened from the strenuous grind; okay, so I was worn to the bone, but I was otherwise the same flinty refugee from the Cavalcade of Fun. Still, even if nobody else recognized it, I knew how indispensable I'd become. Wasn't I an honorary Lamed Vovnik in my own right, doing what I was born to do? Nothing could quicken my pulse more than when one of the rabbis addressed me directly, such as when the broad-billed Genius of Medzibozh called down in the wee hours before dawn, "Watchman, what of the night?"

I don't know when she first appeared or when I first noticed her; she might have been among the families of scavengers that combed the bluff, or even among the gangs that preyed on the scavengers, little though they had to steal. Barge traffic on the river was next to nonexistent, but the spring thaw had dislodged rafts of detritus that floated downstream from up north, on some of which rode humans. Disembarked at the levee, these transients paused only briefly to regard the saints, having, I guess, seen stranger things in their travels. A few of the rougher sort might catcall, some even interfering out of mischief with the oscillating poles, but I was quick to correct any imbalance they caused. Naturally they stole the food left by nocturnal visitors, which meant we had to integrate more fasting into our routine. Otherwise they left us alone. Sometimes I wondered why, while the whole planet was being ransacked, they left us so alone.

It was during those hours when the urchins spelled me that I realized she was lingering. I was slouching toward the cab of the truck, which was stripped now of all but my flea-bitten pallet, when I thought I saw her wink at me. She had coal-black hair, half gathered in a topknot like a ball of yarn, half cascading across her face, her eyes (as blue as lapis) peering from behind the strands. Rake-thin, she was wearing an old floral housedress, threadbare where the points of her hips and shoulder blades gouged through. A hound as herring-gutted as its mistress, its head like an inverted brogan with a lolling tongue, emitted a phlegmy growl as I passed. When I emerged again from my nap, she was gone, though sometime in the night she reappeared with a basket of plums, one of which she offered and I snatched on the run. (It was ambrosially sweet.) The others she tossed up to the saints.

"Keep 'em regular," she said, as I worked the pole nearest to her.

Funny that the first thing I felt when she spoke was offended. *I* was in charge of the care and feeding of the Lamed Vovniks, and, dog-weariness aside, I didn't welcome anyone's meddling.

On my next pass I asked her, suspiciously, "Where'd you get the plums?" It was my first exchange with a stranger in recent memory.

"Off a plum tree," she answered, stating the obvious as if it was uncommon knowledge. "Name's Lily."

I didn't offer my own. What business was it of hers? Besides, I hadn't spoken my name, nor heard it spoken, in an age. The holy men called me everything from *golem* to *shtik goy* to *Amalekite* and never bothered to inquire after my Christian. "Corliss," I finally let out on my second or third pass in her vicinity. I never knew who gave me the stupid handle or what it meant.

"Pleased to meet you," I believe she said, but I was too involved with tending to my duties to pay her much heed.

She stuck around nonetheless, though her comings and goings were as erratic as those of the kids. She always returned with her basket filled with fruits and vegetables, which she filched from who knew what orchard or garden. They were luscious despite being curiously deformed—

74

the berries that Rabbi Yitzkhok said "like rectal polyps, they look," the potatoes Ponim Zvi took to be sprouting tentacles. It amazed me that, while civilization had ground to a halt, nature persisted and even flourished, as if it had been liberated at last.

After a while she and her churlish dog ("Get down, Belzebub!") were more or less fixtures on the levee. Continuing to accept her fruit as tribute, me and the rabbis had grown accustomed to her presence— that is, until the afternoon she found the gumption to ask me, "Can I have a go?"

I was spinning the plate on top of which bounded the doctrinaire Rabbi Ashlag, who was as usual reciting a catalog of caveats from the Code of Jewish Law: "It is forbidden to remove from the armpits or genital organ the hair; it is forbidden to urinate before sacred books, to spit in a place where it will scatter your saliva, the wind . . ." My impulse was to tell her I didn't need any help, though I had to admit I couldn't have managed without the aid of the urchins. I was explaining that the spinning required an expert skill when her toothless dog locked its gums on my pants cuff and began to tug. I let go of the pole to pry him loose, and when I did she grabbed hold of it herself and gave it a shake.

"Gevalt!" cried Rabbi Ashlag, stumbling in mid-stride.

I made to take over again, but she was determined to hang on. Reluctantly, I advised her that manning the pole was less about shaking than rocking it, "like you'd do a cradle."

She modulated her wagging to a circular motion that was oddly provocative. The pole began to undulate, the disc that crowned it to spin smoothly, and the rabbi—leisurely loping on his plate—to chant a verse from the Song of Songs.

"Does this make me a spinster?" she quipped, squinching up her face, stippled with either freckles or dirt. She was clearly satisfied with herself.

Then it seemed that for better or worse I'd acquired an assistant, capricious though she was. Like the stray children, she appeared and departed at random hours, and like them she addressed the poles as a variety of play. Sometimes she kicked off her clunky shoes and joined the kids in their capers, the whole company scampering from pillar to post while I caught some winks in the truck. (I even took to trimming my beard and nose hairs in the cracked rearview mirror.) It was a little strange, the effect her spinning seemed to have on the rabbis, who fairly crooned their prayers when she handled their poles—which she did with a measured movement that resembled massage. Apparently influenced by her manipulation, the Seer of Zhldscz pronounced that the custom of davening was meant to duplicate the act of coition, and the dogmatic Ashlag included, among the list of things you're permitted to think about during intercourse, the wife herself. Simcha Bunam, in his blissed-out transports, was heard to cry, "Is like the narrow sex of the gazelle, the Torah, for whose husband every time is like the first!"

Occasionally our spinning overlapped like we were partners in a dance, and once, as we lurched past one another, I asked her, while shaking her ugly mutt from my heels, "Why are you doing this?"

"Why're *you*?" she replied, with that infernal tit-for-tat I was used to from the rabbis. It was particularly aggravating coming from her.

"I asked you first," I snapped, but had to wait till we'd done a complete tour of the poles again before I got her answer.

"It's fun," she said.

"Huh?" I was supposed to be the professional where fun was concerned, having served my veteran hitch in the Cavalcade of, but never once had I thought of my duties toward the saints as *fun*. At the next opportunity I began to rehearse, for her edification, the supreme significance of the Lamed Vovniks, borrowing the words of Rothstein's spiel. "In every generation there are righteous men for whose sake—"

"And bladdy blah blah blah . . ."

After that our conversations settled into a casual chitchat, during which I confess I was somewhat sullen, while Lily was quite forthcoming. "I was always the independent type," she assured me, this side of boastful. "I seen a lot of life." She'd waitressed at Phaedra's Chocolate Log in Mobile until the city was under water—"The floods dried up the work: get it?"—and she headed north. She tended bar a while at the Tequila Mockingbird in Selma, which was an anarchist watering hole until the police shut it down. ("In Selma you still had cops.") Then she came to Memphis, where the only work she could find was as a cashier at a Piggly Wiggly that was employing humans since all the robot checkouts were on the fritz. "They was making do with a antique cash register the manager had bought from a museum auction, but business was in the toilet anyway since the banks went bust and folks had no money. When they let us go, we et up the store."

What perplexed me was that she could speak of such terrible fortune as if it was simple bad luck and not apocalypse itself. "Weren't you scared, a young girl alone in the world?" I asked her.

"Scared of what?"

I itemized a host of dangers one might do well to be afraid of, but she dismissed them with a shrug.

"I got the Bub here to protect me," she said, letting go of the pole long enough to give her mangy dog a stroke, which elicited its signature snarl. "Besides, what makes you think I was always alone?"

For some reason that didn't sit well with me. "Lily," I said, "don't you know this planet's a train wreck?"

She grinned, like she found the idea amusing.

I worried about her whenever she was out of my sight, but when she was around, things were fine again. And the saints, no less cranky and prone to backbiting, showed a renewed gusto in their disputes. Even Baruch and Yitzkhok would drop their running burlesque in favor of engaging in thorny Talmudic logic.

Baruch: "'And the Lord saw everything He had made and, behold, it was good'—Genesis, 1:31; that's what we call the good desire."

Yitzkhok, reaching out to tug Baruch's goatish beard like a bell-pull: "'Behold, it was very good'—ibid; and that's the evil desire."

Baruch, indignant: "What are you saying, that the evil desire is good?"

Yitzkhok, with eyebrows hopping: "I'm saying it's *very* good."

Then the swell-headed Meshullam Shloyme threw in his two cents: "Him that's greater than his fellow, his desire that it's greater too."

When they intoned their prayers, their poles ticktocking like metronomes, they revived the harmony that had once so delighted the side-show mobs.

I guess she was pretty, Lily, in a rangy, unbroken-colt sort of way. She was restless and herky-jerky in her movements, her loose limbs always about to wriggle free of her flimsy dress—except when she was spinning. Then she was practically a ballerina. She gave the impression that, for her, the business of survival was one big adventure, and sometimes her attitude was contagious. Just brushing past her on the way to shake the next pole could remind me of when my own life was equally bracing, back when I was wild with energy all the time. I remembered the charge I got from every whistle-stop the Cavalcade set up in, the fresh promise of every girl I met. It seemed the whole world was a carnival, and our midway a tidal pool refilled daily by a great sea of fun. But that sea was a desert now, swarming with hostile tribes—which made the rabbis (I reckoned) some version of desert saints.

There came a stormy night. We'd had a deal of rain that spring, and when it began, this night was not so different from others—there was considerable thunder and lightning, and the saints and I got royally pelted, but it was nothing we hadn't endured before. Personally I enjoyed the drama of a good downpour. It was a change from the monotony of our days. But at some point the wind picked up and the rain built to a sweeping intensity, passing over us in waves like the strokes of some fiendish broom. The cobbles had become so slippery I had a hard time maintaining my cadence with the poles, so I was relieved when Lily showed up and offered support. It felt natural now to accept her help, and I could hardly remember why I'd ever hesitated. The storm was a real gully-washer now, the sky an ebony shell cracked open to reveal a fiery yolk beneath. It was some brilliant pyrotechnic display, the forked lightning like X-rays of God's own nervous system.

The lightning made firefly lanterns of the clouds, illuminating Lily as well, her dress soaked clean through, the fabric clinging to her body like tissue. Between the blinding flashes and my effort to concentrate, I had few opportunities to get my fill of looking at her, but a moment's radiance was enough to leave an indelible print on my brain: the dark medallions where her small breasts showed through the material; the shadow between her thighs that the kootch-dancers called their "fur scutch." Strewn across her face like seaweed, her inky hair lent her a kind of mermaid aspect, and as we lunged from pole to pole, I had the sense she was enticing me, as in a game of hide-and-seek. My mouth became too dry for swallowing and I began to ache, every clap of thunder unseating some new awareness in my head. It came to me that I wasn't so awfully old, that I still had a heart full of wanting and most of my hair, that it wasn't for the sake of the saints that the girl stuck around but for me—I was the reason for her lingering presence on the levee.

Then Rabbi Simcha Bunam, coattails whipped by the wind like a serpent's tongue, cried out in his exultation, "He who at Mount Moriah answered Abraham our father—" to which the others responded as one, "He shall answer us!"

"He who at the Red Sea answered Moses—" his throaty voice risen above the squall.

"He shall answer us!"

Lightning flared around us, branching in streamers that traveled earthward and struck each of the rabbis' heads. Their skull-capped noggins received those electrical bolts like an experiment in some

Frankenstein's laboratory, their bones glowing incandescently through their clothes; but still they persisted in their call-and-response.

"He who answered Joshua at Gilgal—" belted out the crazy flagellant, beating his brow with the heel of his hand, and the rest in raucous discord: "He shall answer us!"

Their illumination left me breathless, and Lily, enchanted by it all, yipped and pranced, posing so saucily beside the poles that I found myself wanting desperately to capture her and hold her still. As she hugged the pillar supporting the fish-faced Angel of Lublin, I let go of old Shmelke's spar and grabbed her about the waist. She attempted to wriggle out of my grasp, giggling—but I held on tight, nailing her in place with an urgent kiss, and this she returned with equal fervor. She wrapped her arms around me like the "cleaving to the sublime" the rabbis claimed to practice at their prayers. As I lifted her in my arms and carried her to the cab of the truck, Belzebub barked and snapped his gums at the seat of my pants, but I paid him no mind.

"He who answered Samuel at Mizpah—" warbled Rabbi Simcha Bunam.

"He shall answer us!"

"He who answered Elijah at—"

"—."

Under the bug-infested blanket in that rusted-out flatbed, with rain slanting through the smashed windshield and clattering outside, I tasted the sweetness that surpasses understanding. When I finally came back to myself, it was too late.

❊   ❊   ❊

There was no way I could've dug their graves beneath those granite cobbles, across which they lay scattered in the early sunlight like more of the flotsam the storm had blown in. At first you might have taken their banged-up plates for the shields of fallen warriors, but this was no battlefield. The papery corpses in their sable garments looked more like cast-off chrysalises than human beings. Maybe by abandoning their bodies I'd set free their souls. It would have been nice to think so, but in their absence—broken bodies notwithstanding—I'd never felt so alone.

Stumbling mechanically about that doleful scene, I stepped onto the half-sunken houseboat at the river's edge and began to pull down one of its wall panels. I kicked at the soggy baseboards, wrestled the wood from its frame, and tossed it from the deck into the shallows. The girl must

have fled before dawn, and had her disagreeable dog not remained be-
hind, probably to gloat, I might have doubted she ever existed. Amid
the debris I found a length of nylon barge rope with three slime-coated
pontoons attached. These I lashed to the panel now bobbing at the foot
of the levee and made a serviceable raft, then loaded the Lamed Vovniks
onto it. They weighed little more than their torn knickers and caftans,
and while the raft sank a few inches below the surface of the river, it
stayed relatively afloat. With a calcified piece of rubber hose and a leaky
watering can—if you weren't particular you could find what you needed
in the muck—I siphoned off the residue from the gas tank of the truck
and sprinkled it over the bodies as the sun hid behind a bank of sulfur-
green clouds. The humidity was soup, the stillness of the morning air
something unnatural; nothing was as it ought to be. I struck a match on
my zipper and tossed it onto the raft, which instantly combusted. Who
would have thought a load of old Jews would make such good kindling?

"May the memory of the righteous be a blessing," I started, then
suddenly left off, though not because I didn't know the prayer. I knew
them all: the prayer for martyrs, the one you say upon seeing a rainbow,
before taking a dump, the prayer over spilled milk, a dropped stitch,
new shoes, but I'd forfeited the right to pronounce them. Wading into
the shoals, I shoved the flaming raft out into the current and watched
the river carry it swirling rudderless downstream. Only when it was a
feather of smoke beneath the railroad bridge, did I realize I was flanked
by a contingent of urchins watching alongside me.

After that I didn't know what. Turning toward those dead-calm poles,
all of which had stayed upright, I waited to be struck dumb or blind. In
the wake of last night's washout there wasn't even the whisper of a
wind, and it occurred to me I'd never seen the poles in repose. What
power, I wondered, had set them swaying in the first place? For the
plates had needed some original "gyroscopic effect," as Old Man Roth-
stein liked to inform the crowds, or how else could the saints have
begun their immemorial sprint?

The river had crept up the levee during the turbulence, but had since
retreated, leaving the millstones that supported the poles in pools of
standing water. All of the tips of those slender timbers were bare of
their zinc discs except one, a battered plate dangling from it like a hel-
met on a lance. It was Rabbi Simcha Bunam's, from whose spire the old
loon had declared it was easier to speak with the birds and trees. A
pug-faced little monkey in a duffel coat spilling its lining ambled over

and knelt without ceremony beside the pole. Another kid, sheepdog bangs concealing his or her eyes, knelt beside the first, then another beside that one, and so forth, the lot of them crouching on all fours across the swampy stones. Then several more of that ragtag company climbed on top of the first row and crouched on their backs, while more scrambled up to stoop on top of those. In short order they'd erected a pyramid that came close to reaching the height of the cedar pole.

The color of the sky now matched the bile of the river so perfectly that only the sliver of Arkansas Delta on the other side marked the division between them. Flinging a curse at that heap of motherless brats for challenging me, I stepped onto the raised buttocks of the bottom row and proceeded to clamber up to the second and then the third tier. The kids' pliant backs and shoulders settled under me as I climbed, but held firm, and having scaled them to their summit, I was reaching for the metal disc when a scuttling sensation crept over my spine. I would have discounted it as nerves if the mongrel Belzebub hadn't leapt in front of me, evincing his irritable growl. He managed, after much slipping and joggling, to tilt the plate back into a horizontal position, which made it possible for me to kick off from the head of the top-mounted urchin and haul myself onto the plate, where I lay some moments on my belly before endeavoring to stand.

The plate wobbled a bit, but the dog's tremulous posture stabilized it and helped me—along with all the years I'd observed the rabbis' techniques—to strike my own giddy balance. Meanwhile the firmament had intensified its dark verdigris, eclipsing the light of day, and the breeze acquired a chilly edge. Dollops of rain slapped my cheeks. Below me the pyramid collapsed, and the kids beat it in their several directions; the winds came up and a driving rain commenced that soon surpassed the fury of the previous night's storm. This caused the supple pole to whip back and forth like a pendulum, at which point Belzebub, starting to trot in place, accelerated our spinning. Clumsily, until I found my footing, I attempted—having no choice—to follow his lead.

We gathered momentum, the dog and I, charging ahead while the tempest raged and a different order of weather was taking shape in the river—you could glimpse the waters of heaven pouring down into the waters of Earth, which were rising up to meet them. The river swelled, its broad expanse swiftly increasing, fanning out until it overflowed its banks and began to swallow the levee. I was running to beat the devil now, wondering, as I did, if the spinning had prompted the deluge or vice versa. Had the saints been saving the world from disaster or propelling it toward its destruction? Had the revolving plates mattered at all? What I do know for sure, however, I can't let on; because if I told you all I could see from that lofty perch, before the approaching waterspout lifted me and the Bub up into its black funnel, you would rip your garments to the navel in grief for having lost that wisdom.

Nominated by Jay Rogoff

MEMORIAL DAY

by BRIAN DOYLE

from THE SUN

We are at a parade. It is Memorial Day. I am sitting on the curb in front
of the church with my brother, reserving our family's spot. The rest of
the family is coming along slowly, our father carrying the baby, but my
brother and I have run ahead because we don't want to miss a single
soldier in uniform or girl twirling a baton or bespectacled beaming che-
rubic man wearing a fez. We might see an elephant. We will see horses
and firetrucks. We will see politicians in convertibles. We will see men
older than our dad wearing their Army uniforms. Army is green and the
others are blue. Our dad will not walk in the parade wearing his uni-
form. He declines politely every year when he is asked. He says he no
longer has his uniform. He says he does not know where it went, al-
though we think he does know where it went. He says he wore it only
because the job had to be done, and now that the war is over, there is
no reason to have a uniform. He says uniforms are dangerous state-
ments, if you think about it. He says uniforms can easily confer false
authority, and encourage hollow bravado, and augment unfortunate in-
clinations, and exacerbate violent predilections. This is how he talks. He
says uniforms are public pronouncements, like parades, and we should
be careful about what we say in public. He says we should be leery of
men marching in uniforms. He says no one has more respect for mem-
bers of the armed forces than he does, but that it would be a better
world if no one ever had to take up arms, and that is a fact. He says in
his experience it is the man who has been in a war who understands that
war is cruel and foolish and sinful, and anyone who defends war as
natural to the human condition is a person of stunted imagination. He

83

says a study of history shows not only that we are a savage species but that we are a species capable of extraordinary imaginative leaps. He says that someday we might devise ways to *outwit* violence, as Mr. Mohandas Gandhi tried to do. He says most wars, maybe all wars, are about money in the end, and that when we hear the beating of war drums, we should suspect that it is really a call for market expansion. He says war is a virus and imagination is the cure.

Our father does not have his uniform anymore, but he does have a wooden box in a drawer in his bureau at home. There are medals and service bars and ribbons in the box. We have secretly opened the box, my brother and I, and handled its contents, and put them back exactly the way we found them, so that he would not know, but he knows. His photographs are in another drawer. In them he is tall and thin and shockingly young. He is a private, a sergeant, a lieutenant. He is on Bougainville Island in the South Pacific. Then he is in the Philippines. He is preparing for the invasion of Japan. He is preparing to die.

Today he is standing next to us at the Memorial Day parade as the soldiers and sailors pass by. Some men in the crowd salute, but he does not. He keeps his eyes locked on the soldiers, though, even as we are pulling at his hands and pant legs and the baby is crying and wriggling. The one time he hands off the baby and applauds quietly is when the firemen pass by in their trucks. After the firemen come the Girl Scouts and Boy Scouts, and the Little League baseball players, and the Knights of Columbus, and the Rotary Club, and finally a visiting fife-and-drum corps from Ireland, and then we walk home, our dad carrying the baby, who fell asleep just after the Girl Scouts walked by.

Nominated by Daniel Henry,
Joan Murray

CREATIVE TYPES

fiction by TOM BISSELL

from THE PARIS REVIEW

The night before their appointment, they sent Haley one final e-mail in which they reaffirmed the when and where and tastefully restated their excitement. But Reuben managed to smuggle in a request: Would Haley mind wearing "normal clothes"? He was about to hit send when Brenna, proofreading over his shoulder, announced that his use of "normal" was, in this context, "problematic."

"Problematic," he said. Their son had been asleep for an hour.

Bren, looking at the laptop's screen, only nodded.

Reuben poised his e-mail-sending finger above the enter key like a scientist about to launch something toward Pluto. "Bren, come on. I'm sending it."

Bren paid this no attention at all, probably because she knew he wouldn't send it, not without her go-ahead. "'Normal.' It just seems like a very classist thing to write. Normal to *whom*?"

For as long as he'd known her, Bren had worried about classism. These days, of course, he and Bren were doing well, perhaps even embarrassingly well. However, their many years of doing less well had made Bren afraid of succumbing to the thoughtless consumption patterns of their friends, such as Annabelle and Isaac, who recently built a thirteen-thousand-dollar outdoor pizza oven with imported Umbrian stone. To Bren's way of thinking, success, particularly Hollywood success, was mostly an accident; she never wanted to condescend to those who hadn't been as lucky as she. But this meant that virtually everything Reuben said to servers and valets was later subjected to Bren's undergrad-Marxist rhetorical analysis. He didn't mind. If anything, he admired her for it. When Annabelle and Isaac whipped up their first batch of pizzas, everyone politely chewed and smiled on their sunlit patio. Bren was the first person to actually say, "Is it me or is this not very good?"

Reuben kicked back in his chair. "Well," he said, "you know what you're assuming, right?"

Bren looked at him. "What am I assuming?"

"You're assuming a woman in her line of work is automatically of a lower class."

"I am not." But as Bren thought about it, as he knew she would, her face fell. "Oh God. I am."

"And given her rates, I'd say that's a pretty dubious assumption, frankly."

Bren nevertheless convinced Reuben to put *normal clothes* in scare quotes, so "We'd appreciate it if you wore normal clothes (neighbors!)" became "We'd appreciate it if you wore 'normal clothes' (neighbors!)" Minutes after his no longer—or at least somewhat less—problematic e-mail finally went out, Bren was rereading it on her phone. (She'd been cc'd.) "A *lot* going on in that sentence," she said unhappily. Haley's response came ten minutes later: emoticon thumbs-up, emoticon rose, emoticon kiss.

Haley arrived the next night in a plain black circle skirt and kimonoish green blouse. She looked like the hostess of the type of sushi bar that had Mexican sushi chefs, so the outfit was normal enough, and already Reuben had a good feeling about how the night was going to go. This good feeling grew apace when Haley wrapped him up in a big tight hug. "It's so nice to see you again!" Haley said, her neck warm with spice and citrus, her hair a cascade of coconut, her clothes all powdered lavender. Reuben's hands were on Haley's back. They felt good there. They fit. Her blouse was satin, gem green, smooth and slick and glossy. Hugging Haley was like lying in a strange bed you didn't want to get out of. Then, beneath his hands, Haley's shoulder blades flexed; their hug was ending. Reuben stepped away, closed the door, and turned to see Bren standing in the long entryway hall, clasping her enormous wine glass by its stem. Haley moved toward her.

"Oh!" Bren said, as though Haley were a dirty-pawed puppy about to jump into her lap. "Okay! Hello!" While they embraced, Bren held her wine glass—a festive red orb of Malbec—up above her and Haley's heads, which somehow made Reuben think of mistletoe. His hands had been respectfully stationary on Haley's body, but Bren's free hand moved familiarly up and down Haley's back. That was one great socio-cultural advantage of women's hands, wasn't it. They could go where they wanted to go. They had free rein.

Haley released Bren, after which she took up a position in the front hall that allowed her to look at both Bren and him simultaneously. She obviously wasn't in the habit of putting her back to people she didn't know well, and for that he blamed her not a bit. No one said anything for a moment. They were all smiling like naughty children.

"It's nice to see *you* again," Reuben said finally.

Haley laughed. "Ah. That. So when I arrive, I always say, 'Nice to see you again,' even if it's my first time somewhere." At this point Reuben realized that Haley was subtly chewing gum. She had nice lips, and nice everything else, at least as far as he could tell. He wondered if he'd get to kiss her tonight. He and Bren had worked out some ground rules for what he could and couldn't do to Haley, but when it came to kissing, Bren was conflicted. It depended, she said, on how everything felt in the moment. What doesn't?

"Hey," Haley said brightly, "can I use your bathroom?"

Bren showed Haley the way. Reuben went to the kitchen and gulped down a swallow of red wine so large he was able to track precisely its journey from pharynx to gullet to gut. Around the corner from the kitchen area he heard the dull closing *thunk* of their half-bathroom door. Bren came back into view and mouthed, *She's pretty!* As though this were surprising. As though they had literally not gone shopping for Haley together. What surprised her, he guessed, because it surprised him, was how closely Haley resembled the lingerie'd human they'd seen in the JPEGs on the escort website. Despite the check of authentication next to Haley's profile, they'd been preparing for the absolute worst on that front. Now he wanted to know: How did the site authenticate? Was there a lab-coated team driving around Los Angeles right now, skillfully authenticating escorts?

Bren approached and kissed him with warm parted lips. The Malbec and the Listerine breath strips they'd both been popping for the last two hours had not paired well, concocting a vaguely mephitine compound in their mouths. They'd agreed that the only way to do this was at least a little drunk, which was convenient. Since their son's birth fourteen months ago, they'd been spending a couple hours of almost every night at least a little drunk. Reuben couldn't remember the last time he and Bren had kissed like this, slow and tonguey and in no particular hurry. From the bathroom they could hear the compressed gush of their sink at half blast. Beneath the sound, Haley's voice maintained its steady murmur.

Bren pulled away. "Who do you think she's talking to?" She was rubbing Reuben through his gray wool trousers the same slow way she'd been kissing him.

His hands were under her skirt, rubbing her through her underwear, which felt like lacy Braille stretched over warm moss. "I think they have check-in policies. Like, I'm here. If you don't hear from me again in an hour, call the cops."

Bren inhaled sharply; he was touching her just right. "Probably not the cops."

"Okay, not the cops."

Brenna stopped rubbing him, stilled his hand, and looked back at the bathroom. "I wonder if she's talking to her boyfriend."

Before Reuben could say anything, the bathroom door opened with its quick efficient pop, and here was Haley, smiling, walking back into the kitchen area. *Please*, he wanted to tell her, *make yourself at home while I finger my wife.* Yet Haley somehow didn't notice he was fingering his wife. Instead, she set her carry-on-size Hermès bag atop their granite-topped kitchen island and looked over the crackers, cheese, and olives they'd set out there. She smiled at the spread in a sadly amused way, like a woman who'd been proposed to by a man she'd just met. "Snacks," she said. "That's so *nice.*" (The snacks were Bren's idea. *It's not like we're hosting a dinner party*, he'd said, watching her lay them out. Bren's retort: *Company's coming. That means fucking snacks.*)

Bren began to rub Reuben through his trousers once again, but with faster, more performative gusto. This Haley noticed, saying, "Hel-*lo,*" and putting an affectedly scandalized hand to her cheek. Interesting: he'd never been "watched" by a stranger doing anything like this before. In fact, the one prerequisite for doing anything like this was that a stranger *wasn't* watching. Being watched by this particular stranger turned out to be a lot more arousing than he'd anticipated. Haley seemed to think so, too. She actually steadied herself, for a moment, against their kitchen island. The snack tray was within reach, and for no reason Reuben could explain—maybe decadence was reason enough, for all of this—he reached out, secured a fat, green olive, and popped it into his mouth. Salt, oil, brine: these were sex tastes. Probably why Bren put them out in the first place. Yet again, she was smarter than he was.

"Sooooo," Bren said, stopping to retrieve her wine glass, "do you need to ask us if we're cops or something?"

Haley crossed her arms and gave them a mock stern look of appraisal. "Pretty sure you're not cops. Also, it's a myth that cops need to tell you they're cops."

"Oh really? I didn't know that." Bren sipped her wine.

"I have a friend, a good friend, who met a client in his hotel room. This was like five years ago. In Hollywood. She sits down with the guy—good-looking, nice looking—and asks him, Are you a cop? No, he says. No way. So she goes down on him. And he comes. And he arrests her anyway."

Bren, after a nearly literal spit take, said "Wow" in a loud, flat voice.

"Obviously my friend is upset—"

Bren: "Well *yeah.*"

"—and says she'll narc him out. Who are they gonna believe? he says. You or me?"

"Not cool," Bren said. Meanwhile Reuben was thinking, What happened to my hand job? But Bren was locked into this conversation now. Processes of all kinds—and from all realms of legality—were of cardinal interest to her, and no wonder: Bren worked in unscripted television. She said to Haley, "So how do you deal with the cops? If you don't mind me asking."

Haley plucked from its dish a pitted black olive so wizened and oily it resembled the liver of a vampire bat. "Not at all! So what I do is I have a friend. She sleeps with a vice detective pretty regularly. He tips her off where the cops are gonna be that week. Which hotels. Like maybe it's 'Stay away from the W' on Saturday and 'Avoid the Roosevelt' on Tuesday." Thoughtfully, she ate her olive. "I prefer homes anyway. I really don't do that much hotel work. A lot of the entrapment rules were relaxed."

Bren: "Entrapment rules?"

"So yeah. Cops can get naked now. They can arrest you even if you just walk into the room in some places. Obviously certain states are better than others. California's actually okay. But if you have to get arrested, Hawaii's the place. They can't search your stuff without permission in Hawaii. Which is amazing. I got picked up in Maui once with three grams of pure Molly in my purse, and when I got out and got my purse back, I looked inside. Still there." She reached into her vaguely squarish Hermès bag, which really was a stunner, resembling an unusually elegant picnic basket. "Speaking of which." Now a white pill was pinned between Haley's thumb and forefinger; she showed it to them. "Do you mind?"

"That's Molly?" he asked.

"Yeah. I'll warn you, though—once I get rolling, I'm *very* friendly."

"Go ahead," Bren said encouragingly.

Haley stepped toward them. Actually, no. She was ducking under Reuben's arm, getting between them, squirreling herself right in there. Haley placed the pill on her tongue and closed her fingers around the stem of Bren's wine glass, just below Bren's fingers. She asked Bren, "Do you mind?" Bren shook her head. Haley guided Bren's glass to her lips and washed down the pill with a tiny first-communion sip.

And then Haley's hand was in Bren's underwear with his. "Do you have any more?" Reuben asked her, meaning the Molly.

"Sorry," Haley said. It sort of felt as if their fingers were oil wrestling inside Bren.

Bren was breathing hard; her hand was taloned around the knob of Reuben's shoulder. "We used to do coke," she said, between breaths.

Haley kissed Bren on the neck while the blood in Reuben's body began its vascular stampede. "Why'd you stop?" Haley asked her.

Reuben knew the answer: they quit doing coke because they'd had a baby, but Bren couldn't say that because they'd agreed they wouldn't tell Haley they had a baby. (The baby was staying with their nanny overnight, under the nearly accurate auspices of their need for "couple time".) They also wouldn't tell Haley that the whole point of this evening was to forget things like babies. They wouldn't tell Haley that, until they began seriously considering a night like this, with someone like her, they'd gone eight full months without having sex to completion, "to completion" being the operative term here, one or both of them having fallen asleep in the middle of the act on three different occasions. After they'd booked time with Haley, late last week, they'd had sex four times in five nights, though they wouldn't tell her that either. What else? They wouldn't tell Haley about the many times, before the birth of their son, that they'd privately mocked those couples with children who succumbed to literally knee-slapping laughter when asked if having kids had adversely affected their sex life. They wouldn't tell Haley about how confidently they'd reassured each other that their sex lives wouldn't be so easily assassinated. They wouldn't tell Haley about the night, five years ago, when one of Brenna's on-set friends, Gemma, who was actually sort of Bren's subordinate (which: cue future problems) and going through a messy divorce, stayed late after a dinner party and somehow started kissing Bren, whose record of staunch heterosexuality had gone hitherto unblemished, which ultimately led to the three of them—Reuben, Bren, Gemma—groping on the couch and then retiring to the bedroom, and how this unsought but nevertheless astounding arrangement went on for a few weeks until Bren realized that Gemma, whose messy divorce involved drug use (hers) and infidelity (her husband's), was actually in love with Bren, or at least thought she was, and how after a couple weird incidents Bren told Gemma she felt obliged to report the whole sordid affair to their supervising producer, after which a duly mortified Gemma apologized and left the project, and how as upsetting as the whole thing was in the aggregate (the weird incidents included Gemma's seeming threat—feigned, thank Christ—that she'd recorded their ménages), what did Reuben and Bren go back to, what did they talk about and relive in so much of their sex that followed, including that which, he was pretty sure, conceived their one and only son? Of course, they talked about and relived those strange, silvery nights with loony Gemma and how utterly crazy they'd been for what they did to her separately and together. The very last thing they wouldn't tell Haley was that they now understood why people with small children stopped having sex. It wasn't because they were tired or no longer attracted to each other, though that's what it often felt like. Intimacy between men and women begins as a hungry, prickly current that recharges itself by moving back and forth along a straight line. It was an *exchange.* But when you add a child to this line, it bends until it's no longer a line but a circle that goes past, through, and around you both, self-replenishing and internally regenerating. And this was a *process.* Once you've intimately bathed and dried and kissed your baby's knees and belly before bed and held your spouse afterward, perfectly and sexlessly content, the other, former, carnal intimacy—once so overridingly important—felt like nothing more than a low, disreputable road traveled in the dark.

Or: It wasn't possible for Reuben to read *Hippos Go Berserk!* twice in a row to their son and then go fuck Bren. Bren couldn't breast-feed and then return to bed and spread her legs for Reuben. Thus, Haley. Thus, this one night to walk again along the low, disreputable road.

"Drugs are fun," Bren said, in answer to Haley's question about cocaine. "For a while. Then you get old and discover Netflix." She leaned toward Haley to kiss her.

But Haley pulled away. "Let's take a little break," she said, removing her hand from Bren's underwear. "We've got plenty of time." This was true: they'd booked her for four hours. Haley walked over to the couch, removing her green satin blouse as she went and dropping it like a big shimmery lily pad on their fake hardwood floor. Tattooed on the small of Haley's back, in so-called tramp-stamp territory, were the words CLA$$Y LADY. Haley sat down, unhooked her bra, and patted the couch cushion next to her. "Come. Join me."

On her way to Haley, Bren took off her blouse, too, but left her bra on, so Reuben untucked and unbuttoned his shirt. They sat on either side of Haley, who gently took their hands and placed them on her breasts, which were small and warm. "Sometimes," Haley said, "it's nice to get to know each other a little first."

"Totally," Bren said. She looked at Haley's breast in her hand and quickly burst out laughing. "I'm sorry, but this is just too funny." She extended to Haley the hand that did not have a breast in it for a quick shake. "I'm Bren, by the way."

"Haley," Haley said, shaking.

"So! What do you like, breast-wise? Should I squeeze or pinch or—?"

Haley put her hands on both their thighs and rubbed and kneaded. "Do whatever you like, so long as it's not too rough." Bren began to touch Haley with teasing lightness, which was the way she liked to be touched, at least initially; Reuben followed her lead. Haley, enjoying herself, or at the very least convincingly pretending to enjoy herself, made a vaguely feline sound and fell back against the couch cushion. "So tell me. What do you guys do for work?"

Bren and Reuben looked at each other. They'd talked about this, too—what to say, and what not to say, in case Haley asked. They'd decided they'd just tell her the truth. She had their e-mail, after all, and now their home address. That said, they couldn't imagine Haley actually would ask. But here she was, asking.

"I work in TV," Bren said, after which she started to kiss Haley's breast.

Haley smiled. "You and everyone."

"I know, right? We're everywhere." With that, Bren gave her a big wide-tongued lick.

Haley responded with a pleased shudder. "Oh really? Which show?"

"It's unscripted. A reality thing."

Haley's head swiveled over to him, "Let me guess what you do."

"Please don't."

"Okay." Haley was beginning to undo his trousers. Bren reached over to help: she knew the small, covered button on this pair of trousers was notoriously tricky. Unfortunately, Reuben was no longer hard. The culprit, he suspected, was Haley's CLA$$Y LADY tattoo, however small of him that seemed, and it did seem small of him. He knew it did. Reuben scooted away from their reaching hands. His hope was that if he stalled and watched them go at it a little more, his erection might return.

"Actually," he said to Haley, "now I'm genuinely curious. Go ahead. Guess what I do."

Bren stopped licking Haley's breast and looked at Reuben with smiling neutrality. He knew this look. It was her "Exactly what are you trying to accomplish here?" look. She did not unleash this look very often, and the times she did it was invariably justified. Take now, for instance. Reuben in fact had no idea exactly what he was trying to accomplish here. Haley's arm was around Bren. But for the fact that Haley was naked from the waist up, one of Bren's pendulous breasts had escaped her bra, and Bren's mouth had recently been suctioned around Haley's nipple, they looked like tousled old friends spontaneously posing for a photo.

Haley carefully studied Reuben while playing with a strand of Bren's hair. "I'd say . . . you direct." Then, she cunningly refined her guess: "Industrials."

"Ouch," Reuben said. "Also: no. Nice try, though."

But Haley had another guess in her chamber: "Then I'd say you're probably a writer of some kind." Bren laughed too hard too quickly. Haley turned to her for affirmation. "I'm right, aren't I?" Bren buried her nodding face in Haley's neck. She asked Haley how she knew. Again Haley looked at Reuben, her eyes less judgmental now, softer. "I don't know. He just looks like a creative type. You both do."

Reuben had published his first book, a short-story collection, at twenty-seven, three months after he'd finished his M.F.A. at Columbia, where he was widely loathed by his fellow fiction writers. Columbia was also where he'd met Bren, who was getting a master's in social work. Six months later, in December 2001, armed with fifty pages of prose and a febrile outline, Reuben sold a high-concept novel, a retelling of *Henry IV* set during the Soviet invasion of Afghanistan, in which a young Saudi fighter named Hassan has to contend with the influence of his stern, bin Laden-like father while an irreligious and overweight Afghan fighter named Fahad urges him toward a less violent life. The following spring, a PEN prize and a Whiting Award rolled in, after which Reuben set forth on the residency and fellowship tour—Bread Loaf,

Yaddo, MacDowell, assorted European castles and estates—and occasionally worked on his Afghanistan novel. He never published his Afghanistan novel or, indeed, anything else. He taught briefly in Alabama and Virginia and finally moved to Los Angeles, at Bren's suggestion, to try his hand in the notoriously friendly and uncompetitive world of professional screenwriting. That didn't work out either. His longest-held job in Los Angeles was as a security guard for Barneys, which he told himself was research for a short story he never wrote. Happily, and totally accidentally, Bren found her calling in Los Angeles, lucking into a PA job on *Fear Factor*. From there she forged an actual career, working her way up from a noted Hollywood sociopath's assistant to becoming one of three executive producers on *For Richer, For Poorer*, which took married couples of disparate financial circumstances and forced them to trade places for a week. In the landscape of unscripted, it was a show with an unbudgeable vision of civic morality, of *fairness*, a lot of which was directly traceable to Bren's influence. Still, three days a week, Reuben went to an office in West Hollywood ostensibly to write, and sometimes he actually did—sometimes he actually sat there and gave shape to airy nothings. He wasn't sure if Bren would be relieved or horrified to know that all he'd written for the last three years was poetry. Was it good poetry? Unclear. Really, how was he supposed to even know? Like any sensible person, he disliked poetry.

All of which meant Bren was the winner of bread in this particular household, Bren was the wearer of pants. Reuben didn't find the largesse of his generous, supportive partner emasculating or depressing—at least, it was no more emasculating or depressing than his failures as a writer. Often he thought back to the young writers whose careers launched simultaneous to his. He'd read with them at City Lights, had dinner with them at the American Academy in Berlin, did lines of pitiful coke with them at *n*+1 parties in Brooklyn, and walked along the sea with them in Saint-Malo. These days almost all of them were utterly and completely absent from what his former agent used to refer to as "the conversation," their sole published books selling for a penny on Amazon and their Wikipedia pages cruelly flagged for "notability." For a young writer, the most humiliating fate imaginable was to end up middle-aged and unnoted. As it turned out, this fate wasn't humiliating in the least. On the contrary, it was distressingly endurable. It didn't even hurt.

Maybe if Haley had asked Reuben what he did fourteen months ago, before the birth of their son, he might have said, with that familiar combination of pride and embarrassment, Who me? Oh, I'm a writer. But his son was his world now, a living story he had all to himself, because Bren routinely worked seventy-hour weeks, whereas he was lucky if he worked a seventy-hour *year*. Reuben wondered, suddenly, what he and Bren were doing here with Haley when they could have been watching their son sleep, or talking about him, or sleeping and dreaming about him. Which is when Reuben knew. His boner had indeed been killed stone-dead by Haley's CLA$$Y LADY tattoo.

"My turn to ask you something," Reuben said.

Haley and Bren were making out and touching each other, and so her response was half spoken into Bren's mouth: "Go ahead."

"Your tattoo."

Haley stopped kissing Bren. They both looked over at him. "My tattoo," she said.

"Where'd it come from?"

She shrugged. "It's a tattoo. Where do you think it came from?"

"A tattoo parlor?"

Haley laughed and went back to kissing Bren. Bren's hand played along Haley's inner thigh before finally going for it. Haley's back went as straight as an icicle and she pulled Bren toward her. It was curious, how unbothered he was watching Bren's intimacy with another person. Earlier in his life, he'd been what was politely known as the possessive type. The older he'd grown, the more absurd behavioral ownership of any kind seemed to him. Fidelity was an insurance company, and roughly as reliable. Better to see the person you loved enjoying herself. He wondered if it would make any difference if Haley were a man. He didn't wonder long: of course it would. Which meant what? He was sure Bren could have explained it to him. "It just doesn't seem very you, is all," he said to Haley, after a while. Her tattoo, he meant.

At this, Bren backed away from Haley and fixed upon Reuben a more burningly interrogative version of her "Exactly what are you trying to accomplish here?" look. That's when Bren noticed her boob was hanging out of her bra. Almost shyly, she tucked it back in.

"Okay," Haley said. Although her voice was playful, her eyes had the flat, eerie calm of a storm-dark lake. "How is my tattoo not me?"

Over Haley's shoulder, Bren was making an urgent new face, a face Reuben had never seen before. If he were forced to translate what this face was trying to communicate, he would have essayed something along the lines of "Fix this situation you've created now immediately, you blundering fucking dolt."

95

Reuben, taking Bren's point, put his hands up. "Haley, forgive me. If I've offended you—"

"You haven't offended me," she said quickly. "I'm—what did you say before?—I'm genuinely curious."

"I *like* your tattoo," Bren said with such obvious condescension she winced immediately after saying it. Haley didn't even bother to acknowledge her.

Reuben concentrated on holding Haley's gaze, which had grown colder by several centigrade. He tried to speak carefully: "It's just that your Hermès bag is, I think, ten thousand dollars"—the cost of women's luxury goods had always baffled and impressed him while he was working at Barneys—"and your tattoo, meanwhile, your tattoo seems . . ." Haley stared at him with a sniper's malevolent patience while Reuben struggled with a respectful conclusion to his negative analogy.

"Seems like *what?* Bren finally said when the silence became unbearable.

Reuben just shook his head. "I don't know."

Haley removed her arm from around Bren's shoulder. "Maybe," she said, "it seems like the opposite of a ten-thousand-dollar Hermès bag. Is that it?"

"Yeah," Reuben said. "Maybe." He watched as Bren's face tipped forth into the waiting platter of her hands.

For a moment, Haley said nothing. Then she rose from the couch and walked over to the notorious Hermès bag itself. In went her fishing hand and out came an LG Vio phone, which she efficiently swiped awake. The startled light emitted by its oversize screen was so radiant the room instantly went from crepuscular monastery to lurid discotheque. After tapping in her code, Haley came back to the couch and sat. On her home screen was a picture of a younger Haley and another equally young woman. This other woman was brown haired and less conventionally pretty than Haley, but taller, bustier, thicker, more sexually weaponized. The photo had been taken during or immediately after a night of vigorous partying: they both had greasy we've-been-dancing-for-hours hair and were throwing up fake gang signs. It seemed like a photo whose documentary survival absolutely depended on something terrible happening to the person in the photo shortly after it was taken.

"This is Vanessa," Haley said. "We ran away from home together and came to LA ten years ago, which is—God—kind of amazing."

"Why'd you run away?" Bren asked her.

"You've obviously never been to Moon Lake, Florida." Haley began cycling through other curated photos of her and Vanessa. Most had been snapped in nightclubs or bars. Compositionally, they were all the same photo. With every swipe, though, Haley and Vanessa grew thinner, blonder, harder, colder, while the backgrounds became darker and more frenetic. He could almost hear the ventricular music of these douche-bag pandaemoniums. After a dozen swipes, Haley said, "I found a place for us in Studio City, and we did the whole amateur-porn-circuit thing for like six months. Vanessa convinced me porn was a good way to get a modeling and acting career going. I was so stupid I believed her. See, I'm kind of a creative type myself. We made decent money for a while but spent it as fast as we got it. I really hated doing porn. The day I finally quit I had two scenes. First this guy comes in my eyes when I was promised he wouldn't. Then, what was supposed to be a girl-girl had the director trying to get in on it. He offered me twenty-five hundred dollars to go bareback with him, and that was enough for me. I walked away, discovered escorting, took some classes—"

At this, Reuben couldn't help but interject: "Wait. Classes?"

"Courtesan classes. Led by an 'intimacy coach' who lived in Venice and made us refer to her as Goddess. She taught me about posture, which is all in the shoulders, and about diction, and how to eat well, how to take care of my skin. I also took some personal-finance classes."

"From the Goddess?"

"No. Not from the Goddess. See, there's two kinds of escorts. The ones who do it because they choose to, and the ones who do it because they have to."

Bren: "And you're a Choose To."

"I am."

"Okay. Good."

"I tried to get Vanessa into escorting, but she liked porn better. It was faster, and she didn't have to take care of herself. It didn't really matter if she looked and sounded like a Moon Lake hick because she was doing this gonzo, hillbilly porn, so it worked for her. Some of it was really disturbing—incest, daddy's-girl stuff." Here Haley paused. "Which wasn't exactly healthy for her."

To this, Reuben and Bren said nothing. The screen of Haley's phone had become some kind of reverse Medusa: look away now and turn to stone.

Haley came to a photo of Vanessa wearing a spectacularly feathered white wedding dress. "Here she is getting married. Now that's a story.

I was her bridesmaid. Check out her ring. Sixty-five grand." Haley slid the photo down and reverse pinched the screen to enlarge Vanessa's $65,000 ring, but all her enlargement did was exaggerate the pixilation: what was Vanessa's recognizable hand and ring at one moment became a smashed digital sculpture the next. "Her husband was an eighty-year-old widower from Vegas. They met on Facebook. His kids managed to block Vanessa with a prenup, and she wound up cashing out with something like a hundred grand. Of course, she didn't put it in a bank account because she didn't trust banks—don't even ask—and almost everyone she knew socially was a porn person or a crack dealer, so she couldn't ask them. I offered to introduce her to my financial adviser, but by that point she didn't trust me either. She was all messed up: meth, pills, coke. I do Molly, but that's pretty much it—other than weed, and only edibles. But drugs pushed Vanessa into some *crazy* situations. Like this one time, she goes to a party in Vegas and meets this guy, this rich Arab guy. At the end of the night, he asks her if she wants to go with him to Gabon, which is in, like, West Africa. Private jet. But there's a stopover first, in London. Vanessa thinks, Great. I'll go shopping. She gets twenty grand out of a hole she's dug in her backyard and flies to London with the Arab. When she arrives, she changes her twenty grand into pounds. But after eight hours in London, the Arab decides they're going to Paris instead. Vanessa's like, Great, okay, and changes her twelve thousand pounds into sixteen thousand Euros. But they don't stay long in Paris either, and by this point the Arab is making her fuck every other Arab they meet. Eventually they get to Gabon. Vanessa's never been to Africa, obviously. It's not like I have, but even I'd know *not* to change sixteen thousand euros into six point eight million African francs. The Arab guy does whatever he does in Gabon—she's back at the hotel, fucking his friends—and they leave after three days. Vanessa lands back in JFK with six and a half million African francs, which no one—literally no one—in New York will convert back into dollars for her. The only way for her to get her money back is to fly to Gabon, change it, and come back to New York again. Which she does. She *still* doesn't know what she's doing in Gabon, so she gets ripped off, but to make a long story short, she makes it back to JFK with a little under four thousand dollars—and she never even got to go shopping. The rest of her money she eventually spent on a new nose and boobs. My best friend—even when she stopped thinking of me as *her* friend, she was always my best friend. Before her head got all twisted, she'd do anything for anyone, if she could. Once, right after we first got here, I watched her give her last twenty dollars to a homeless lady. I asked her why—I was actually really pissed about it—and she said because the lady needed it more than she did. Which, you know what, was true. Last year, Vanessa finally wound up OD'ing on roxy, though I'm pretty sure it was suicide. There were only three people at her funeral." Reuben and Bren were now looking at a photo of Haley and Vanessa as teenagers on what he gathered was a street in Moon Lake. Haley was wearing an °NSYNC T-shirt. Vanessa had braces.

"As for my tattoo," Haley said, "I got it on Hollywood Boulevard with Vanessa three days after I turned eighteen. I had other tattoos, a bunch of them, actually, but I got rid of them all. Lasers, followed by microdermabrasion. But I couldn't get rid of that first one, because it was Vanessa's idea. Her design, even. It's a stupid tattoo and I hate it, believe me, but I couldn't do it. I couldn't burn it off. So I kept it, and when people ask—*really* ask, like you did—I decided I'd always tell the truth."

"Why?" This was Bren.

Haley turned off her phone. "Vanessa's family failed Vanessa and Vanessa's friends failed Vanessa and Vanessa obviously failed Vanessa. She let people rip her up and throw her away. So I use that. I use her memory to remind me why I'll never let anyone rip me up or disrespect me or make me feel shame. Okay? Like I said, I'm here with you because I choose to be. And I'll give you a great time. But I won't be shamed and I won't be pitied, so if you have any more comments about my body or who you think I am, I'd like to hear them now before this goes any further." That's when Reuben noticed that Haley's pupils resembled beads of dilated black oil floating atop her eyeballs. "And holy shit did I just start rolling."

"Would you like a glass of water?" Bren asked her.

"Absolutely," Haley said.

While Bren was fetching the water, Haley got Reuben's pants open, reached between his legs, and closed her hand around the formless squish there. She looked at him. "Everything okay?"

"I kinda lost it," he said.

"Well," she said, smiling, "let's find it."

Bren came back with Haley's glass of water. She sat down on the couch, still holding the glass, and watched while Haley went down on Reuben. Bren had the trapped look of a secretary with unpleasant news waiting for her boss to finish a trivial personal call. As for Haley's blow-job, it felt no more or less erotic than being rinsed with a warm hand towel. When Haley finally stopped and looked up at Reuben, he could only shrug.

"Is there anything I can do?" Haley asked.

"I don't think so," he said.

Haley looked back at Bren, who handed Haley her water. She drank half the glass in one gulp. Bren, with a sad smile, said, "Incest porn—that's pretty much where you lost me."

Haley finished her water and set the glass on the floor. Her eyes were flicking everywhere, two water bugs trapped in the tiny ponds of her face. Thoughts seemed to tumble around in her skull's unwashing machine of drug logic, mismatched and unassociated. Finally, she stood. "All right. I've got an idea. Let's go to your bedroom. We can make this right." When Reuben and Bren didn't move, she grabbed their hands and pulled them up from the couch.

"Okay," Bren said. "Sure." As they walked Haley to their bedroom, Bren held Reuben's hand tight. Reuben was wondering at which of Haley's courtesan classes dead-friend etiquette had been so calamitously addressed. The three of them took off their clothes next to the bed in the sputtering light of lilac-scented candles, which Bren had set out earlier in the evening, right after she'd prepared the snacks, on the assumption they'd wind up here, doing exactly what they were doing. Haley began to kiss Reuben while Bren stood behind her with her hands on Haley's waist, but Reuben felt immaterial, like a shadow, or a puppet. No, the shadows they cast on their bedroom wall were the puppets and they were the masters. Watch the black shapes move and intersect: they'd done this a thousand times. Above the stage, the puppet masters worked their puppets with one hand and read the obituaries and sipped coffee with the other. Meanwhile, their audience clapped and gawked below. By this point, Haley was rolling so hard that at times Reuben and Bren seemed only incidentally involved. Still, they tried any number of Modern Standard Porno positions: Reuben behind Bren on top of Haley, Haley on top of Bren while Reuben watched, Reuben on top of Bren while Haley watched, Reuben under Haley and Bren while they did whatever they were doing. Bren's moans were affectless, almost androidal: *Pressure applied and acknowledged, human*. Haley pursued her orgasm like a high-value bounty. She finally achieved it squatting over Bren's face while Reuben played with her breasts. When she was

100

done, Bren crawled out from underneath Haley and went to the bathroom to wash up. Apparently, squirting was a thing Haley was capable of. Haley lay there on the bed next to Reuben, breathing and gorgeous and sweaty and glistening, a dessert he was simply too full to finish.

"I feel like you guys aren't having much fun," she said.

"Oh," Reuben said with an inflection that promised more words. There were no more words.

"We still have two and a half hours. Maybe it would help if you guys told me why you were doing this."

He could hear Bren peeing with the force of a garden hose in the bathroom and wondered how long she'd politely held it while waiting for Haley to climax. It was so like her, to do something like that. "We had a baby last year, and things since haven't been great, sexually. We thought this might help."

"Spice things up."

"Yeah. That was pretty much the plan."

"I get that a lot from the couples I see."

"I bet."

"Boy or a girl?"

"Boy."

"Name?"

"Theodore."

"That's a really nice name."

"We thought so. Classic, but not too common. We didn't want one of those LA baby names."

Haley breathed. Then: "I have a daughter."

Reuben bipodded onto his elbows to look at her. "Really?"

"Yeah. She's two. As of last week."

"What's her name?"

"Garland."

Bren was coming out of the bathroom and wiping her hands on a towel. "Haley has a daughter," Reuben said. "Named Garland." Even in the dim light he could see Bren's what-the-fuck face. Quickly, he clarified: "I told her about Theo."

"Well," Bren said, climbing into bed, "I guess *that* cat's been de-bagged."

"I pretty much knew anyway," Haley said.

Bren spooned up against Reuben. "Really? How?"

"In the bathroom. Saw baby wipes on the shelf above the toilet."

Bren's small, appalled laugh was not without mirth. "Fuck. I remember thinking, *I have to move those.* Then I forgot."

"It's not a big deal," Haley said. "Is there anything else you guys want to do?"

Around the bed, strewn clothes, end tables, lamps and cords and phones. Beyond their bedroom window, Hollywood streetlights burned as bright as a forest fire. Even in the dark, all their things were illuminated and revealed. Bren rolled over and grabbed her phone from the end table. Then Haley did the same. Each already knew what the other was thinking. "That's him," Bren said, handing Haley her phone. "And that's her," Haley said, handing Bren her phone. They said other things while Reuben watched one of Bren's scented candles burn down to the wick. Almost there. Wait for it. And there it was, the flame surging with a final valiant attempt at ignition. Then it went out. Then it waved its farewell banner of smoke.

Nominated by Ben Fountain

FLOAT

fiction by REGINALD McKNIGHT

from THE GEORGIA REVIEW

Walk into my room and come to find one of my Jordan Air Max 360s floating about five foot off the ground. Soon as I see it, my heart kinda go pie-yow! and my neck get hot. Then I smile at my foolish, foolish dumb-ass ass, and I say to myself my brother Ricky had done strung it up from the ceiling. I grab the thing, but it don't budge. It's like it's glued up there in the air, and much as I tug and pull on it, that bad boy ain't coming down. It ain't hanging from nothing I can see, just up there where it don't belong. Feel my neck start to warm up again, and my hands tremble a little. I tug, a couple more times, then give up. Turn back to my door like I'm fenda go ask somebody to come have a look, but I don't know who in this house gonna explain this. I can hear Mama banging pots and pans in the kitchen, and *Maury* on the TV, meaning Daiziah home from school. She got that bad boy up loud, too, so I can hear people talking about, "Now hold on, Wayne, if she's the mother of your son, the least you can do . . ." and "Face facts, Dontrell, DNA doesn't lie," and, "McDonald's DOUBLE filet of Fish, when you want one, you *gotta* have one.

Girl been supposed to be doing her homework—just like me. But hear me on this—every day's a new day. Some days TV and floating shoes trumps homework. You don't be studying no studying, if you see what I mean.

I grab on to the shoe, and pull hard, my breath chugging. Forehead so tight it got to be shining like a eight ball. Pretty soon I'm hanging from the damn thing. Hanging basically in midair.

I know what you thinking. That I'm too young and too dumb to see

103

I was like a reverse Michael Jordan up there, floating, and all that so-and-so. Sheee-it. So, like, after I had done pulled and yanked on that damn shoe for two, three minutes, I sit down on Ricky's bed, and think till my forehead get hot, and my skinny-ass arms stop trembling. Whom I gonna tell? Daiziah's a kid and Mama'll just say she ain't got the time for practical jokes and childish bullshit. Ricky ain't gonna be home for a couple hours and, well, the boy ain't stupid but he ain't into "seeing" shit. What he'd do is put a M-80 in that shoe, and blow it the fuck out the sky. Ricky one pragmatic Negro. He get pissed at things that don't make sense. He'll quote Papa every Friday before the rest of us head off to mosque, talking 'bout, "If you believe in things you don't understand, you suffer." And he'll look at the old man like he saying, "What you got say, Sergeant Cooper?"

You ask me, I think Papa's proud of him. If he wanted to say something back, he would.

Papa's out in the yard, right now, working on that purple Fiesta belong to Mr. Hearn. He got at least ten more lined up, which means he three days behind on them repairs. Papa cain't fix electric, but too proud to say so. "We'll get that old son to work, Mr. Hearn. Ain't a broke thing cain't be fixed, you keep digging at it." I done already said "Hey" to him, like I always do when I get home, and like always, he didn't say boo back. The old man say even though he basically around here 24/7, to treat him like he on the other side of town till dinner, and that's three hours away. Funny thing is, if I don't say hi to him when I get home, I'm gonna hear about it at dinner.

So I sit down right under that shoe, and I just stop thinking for a minute or two. What else I'm gonna do?

Take my homework outta my pack, and read four pages of social studies. It's usually my favorite subject, but I cain't focus on nothing 'cause the shoe 'bout as hot as the sun up there, staring down at me. I put my stuff away, and smooth my ass marks off Ricky's bed. Go into the kitchen and tell Mama I'm going to the library for a minute. All she say is "Mm hm," and don't even turn to look at me. Before I leave the house, I roll on back to the bedroom for one more good look at the shoe. Perfect black sole, perfect gray sides, perfect yellow laces. Ain't a damn thing not right about that shoe, except what it's doing. I take some paper and a pen out my backpack, and write Ricky a note. All I can think to say is, "How you do this, man?"

Papa walk into the room. The grease rag in his hands, cold cigar between them hard yellow teeth of his. Mama don't let him smoke indoors, but he can still reekify the whole house with them cold stogies. He finish wiping his big hands, and bunch the rag in his back pocket. He tip his Ravens cap up off his brow and say, "You left my crescent wrench next to your bike again, boy. Whad I tell you about that? Whad I say I'd do if you left my tools out?" He looking right at me, but for a split second I see his eyes glance at the Air Jordan, then his eyes click right back on me, then he reach up and slide the stogie out his teeth and take a step deeper into the room.

"Whadn't me," I told him, said, "I mean . . . I did leave it out there, but it ain't your wrench, Papa."

Old Man standing right next to the shoe, and he glance at the thing and rest his elbow on it like that's what it's there for. I feel sweat spring out of my forehead quick as tears. "Whose is it then?" he say back.

"Mines."

His brow folds up. "Yours."

"Yeah, I bought my own 'cause I got tired a having to give up my iPod every time I messed up."

"So what you done learned is that instead of tearing up my possessions, you can mess up your own." He smiling at me now, but it ain't no smile. "Look like to me you ain't learning too good."

"I guess not."

"You *guess* not? Boy—"

"You want my 'Pod?"

"Well, you too big to beat."

I mean, he just got his arm all crooked up on that 360, and I feel like I got to say something, but I ain't got idea-the-first how to start. I wanna say, "Hey, Papa, how you think that shoe got up there?" or maybe, "Uh, do you notice anything strange?" or, "I spy something floating in the air that shouldn't be." But Papa got his elbow up on the thing like it ain't nothing. All he do is switch the cigar from the right side of his mouth to the left side, and say, "My hands is all greasy, just leave the thing on the dresser in my bedroom," and he turn and leave. I sit there, head all hot, and like to cry. Godmothafuckindammit, I'm going, Godmothafuckindammit. Must be, I'm thinking, that I'm seeing it all wrong. It ain't my shoe, it's something else and my mind insist on seeing it all wrong, like it is when your belt look like a corn snake, or a piece a ravel is a spider until your mind turn around and you see what a thing really is. Papa say he heard about people who taste sound and hear colors. They wires is all switched around. And they tend to stay that way.

All right, so I'm at the library, now. I read all this stuff online and from the stacks on unexplained phenomena. The kind of shit you ain't supposed to talk about at school or mosque. At school they call you crazy and at mosque they say you courting the devil. But if that's the case, well, they ain't gonna be enough room in Hell on Judgment Day, and way too many crazy people walking around free and naked-brained as they wanna be. Must be three hundred books on them shelves, and they too many websites to count. Some of the books good, and the online stuff, too, but only thing I learn from the online stuff is a whole lotta people cain't spell no better than me. Grown people. White people. Motherfuckers from England.

You got your stories about ghosts, UFOs, weird animals, and whatnot, but I'm looking for things like a floating Air Jordan. A whole buncha online people get too excited about shit that don't matter, like people who know what time it is without looking at clocks and watches, and people who take a picture and see little blue balls floating around after they develop it, and people who hear soft music coming out a turned off radio, and more stories than you can count about people who went on long trips that should have taken like five hours, but ended up being two hours. Please.

But there is some pretty tight stuff like this lady who grows feathers out her arms, and another lady who seen a little girl and her daddy who had cats' eyes, and two dudes who tore some linoleum off a kitchen floor and seen this silver liquid that was under it that moved on its own through cracks in the wood floor beneath, and a lady who gave a cab ride to some cat who breathed fire. Lotta weird things going on in this world, but it look like I'm on my own with this shoe bidness. I think about getting a book or two about people with brain damage, but to tell you the truth, I cain't deal with that. Plain and simple, don't want this to be about *my* disconnect.

Get back home just about an hour after dinner. Mama done left me a plate wrapped in foil in the oven. I'm hungry, but cain't eat till I get back to my room for another look-see. When I get there I see a damp towel hanging off the shoe, and Ricky's school clothes dropped on the floor like some kinda maid supposed to come by and clean up behind him. I go to the living room, and Mama and Papa sitting watching *American Idol*.

"Ricky gone?" I ask Mama, 'cause Papa wouldn't know or care half the time.

Mama say, "Um hm," but she don't look at me.

"Mama, you been in my room today?"

"Put your laundry away 'bout three. Whycome?"

"You see anything weird?"

"Them mice back?"

"No'm. Ain't seen no mice."

Papa say, "I tell you what *I* ain't seen. Ain't seen no iPod on my dresser."

"No, no mice. You know when Ricky be back?"

Mama don't say nothing. Papa say, "On my dresser, son."

I tell Papa, "Yes sir," and turn away, and then turn back. I think to myself, Mama been in my room, Papa been in there and looked right at the shoe, Ricky come, used the shoe for a towel rack, and gone. And ain't nobody said nothing about the shoe, which mean either they playing me, or I done lost my mind. I stand there for about a minute, looking at some fat white cat on the tube tear up a Wilson Pickett song. He sing good, but he need to shave that fat face of his. That leather coat he got on make him look more like a bouncer than a singer.

Mama say, "You finish your homework?" but she ain't looking at me, just at the white boy singing "Knock on Wood." I'm looking at him, too. He singing like it ain't no yesterday, today, or tomorrow. I stand there, and it's like I cain't move. "Yes'm, I done my homework." And then I turn to go, but I turn back, and I say, "Naw, I ain't done no homework 'cause there's a gotdamn Air Jordan 360 floating in my room, and ya'll don't seem to notice."

"I tell you what," Mama says, and she still ain't took her eyes off the TV. "You don't get that homework done, I'll take them shoes right on back to the store. Them things cost me a week's pay."

And Papa nods, "And I'll tell you something else, boy: you leave any more tools—yours or mines—out to rust and ruin? Next time you see that iPod? You'll need a hearing aid to listen to that ungodly noise you call music."

I go back to my room, and first thing I see is the other shoe up in the air just about six inches below the first one. Feel like both them shoes done kicked me in the chest. I walk round both shoes, and fall face-down on my bed. I fall asleep for what seem like a second or two and feel Ricky shaking me to get up, talking 'bout it's morning. It cain't be.

"Yo, 'Trey, man, get up. Showtime, man."

Time is it?

"Six-forty. Mama said you ain't up in five seconds, you get a Power Bar and box-juice for breakfast."

"Whatever."

"She making waffles, grits, and turkey bacon, nigger."

"Waffles. What the fuck I care 'bout waffles? You *have* seen them shoes, I reckon."

The big negro jump onto my bed and start tap-tapping my head like bongos, till I'm up on my knees with my, "Shit nigro, get off me," and naturally he clamp a headlock on me, pull me out the bed, and smack me with my pillow one hard time. When my brother play, he's never playing. When he let go, feels like a waffle iron had done hit my face and neck. Used to it.

"Ricardo. What about them shoes?"

"You got about five minutes to knock out them kinks, wash the funk off your neck and dress. If not, them waffles belongs to yours truly."

So I eat my Power Bar on the walk to school, walked to school cause I missed the bus, missed first period, too, and in second period got a F for the homework I didn't do. In third forgot to bring my workbook out my locker, and got licks from Mr. Salib, who tole me, "It's either me or Allah, and he hits a whole lot harder than I do, son." Had me some double detention at 2:15, which meant I prob'ly wouldn't see my 'Pod for a couple more weeks on top of the month I was sure to get for forgetting to put the damn thing on Papa's dresser last night. When I get off the bus, I walk by the Ancient One without saying a word. Trying to draw me some fire, you see.

"I know you ain't trying to step past me without my respect, boy."

"No sir."

"iPod on my dresser?"

"No sir."

He put down his sprayer, and shut off the valve. Mr. Hearn deathtrap still sitting there, off to the side, where Papa ain't got to think about it. He ain't wearing no gloves, so his fingers are purple like that pointless car he trying to patch up. Dude got some big-ass hands. Knuckles like wood. He crook a finger at me, "'M' over here, little spook."

He ain't called me that word in so long, I'm like to bust a spring in my gut, hearing it now.

108

"Mr. Salib called me today."

"Figured he would."

"Well." He wasn't asking no question. I breathe deep before I answer. I figure that if my voice start to tremble, I'll just walk the fuck away.

"I was late."

"Maybe that iPod don't mean nothing to you, like your tools and mines, like your bike and whatnot."

I swear I'm like to bust open if I just don't say what I worked out in detention. Ain't nothing else to do up in that bad boy but think, and that's all I did, for three straight hours. So blah-dee-blah, I go, "Oh, I left you the 'Pod. Left it up in one of them shoes floating in my room."

At first his nod's all natural, like he hearing what he expecting to hear, but then the nod break for just a nanoblip, and his eyes widget so fast from left to right you can almost hear them niggers click.

Old Man is back to smooth so fast ain't nothing but dust behind him, and all he say back is, "I ast you to put it on my dresser."

Go on into the house, and on my way to the kitchen, drop the 'Pod on the old man's dresser. I find Daiziah at the kitchen table, reading a book with a white boy in a black leather jacket on the cover. The boy got one hand in his jean pockets, and one hanging like ape knuckles below his hip. He leaning on a invisible wall. Old son looked like he could handle things. "Yo, Dee Dee," I say, "hold up on the gang-related activities, I need to ast you something." She squint at me and say, "Nigro, did you dime on me?"

"Could have. About what?"

"I'm serious." And so when she look up at me, I see she got a purple mark on her neck, couple inches below her ear. About the size of a quarter. It ain't ink. It ain't paint. It ain't cancer. "Dag, Smurf, what you do to yourself?"

She stand up and fold the book to her chest like she all grow up. And she do look grown up, kinda. She all long and smooth. Move more like Mama do than something on four uneven legs like she used to do. She used to be fat, used to chunk around this house like a fat pony. Now she straight as a sunbeam, like Granmamma used to say. Skin bright and tight as new change, them lashes. You cain't be hitting something so pretty. Or choking or whatever the fuck happened.

"Please, 'Trey, don't *even* front."

"All right, okay—'What you done *did*? is the question."

She do what Old Man done, froze up then thawed back so quick it's like it didn't happen and then, well, shit, it came to me maybe it didn't happen. My thing, not hers, I mean. Maybe the fact I'm nosing around without being straight up about the shoe is why people ain't acting right. Or let's say they is up there. Maybe they thinking, 'Trey's room, 'Trey's shoes. Why ain't he said nothing? Or maybe they just plain scared. My shoes, see, must mean God is talking to me. Or some ghost. Or Darth Vader, or whatever. Either I'm seeing things, or I'm the one got some explaining to do.

Excuse me, a cab fare breathing fire? Come again?—People with what kinda eyes? Now what's all this? Floating shoes, and feathered women? I see. Well, next time you come by, Mr. 'Trey S. Porter, help your self to the Doritos and shit, but just stay the fuck away from me.

I reach over and touch her bruise with my finger. Gentle. "Papa do it?"

"Mama did."

"What you do?"

She look at me and look at the book. She put the book down, say, "Forgot to close the window in my room." She sat back down, opened the book. "You can go now."

Now, when she said that she looked down—at the book—but she was all eyebrows up and looking bored like she twenty-three and I'm in diapers.

"What you mean I can go now'? Who you, Cleo-gotdamn-patra?"

"I got homework, Dontrell."

I spin on one foot, and throw a shoulder. "You wanna study something? Come to my room, Cleo-gotdamn-patra. Got a book you ain't read yet. Genius."

"Ricky told me to stay out y'all's room . . ."

Way she say it make me jerk my head back to her. Her voice kinda broke, kinda made ice-tea all down her own chest.

So, you know what? I turn and I look at her. Give her one of them Muslim school looks: one part God, three parts hitman.

"You been already seen them shoes, ain't you, girl?"

Cocks her head. "I seen em."

I look at her eyes, and then at that neck. Like some kinda ugly grape, that thing on there. Thumb couldn't do that. Rolling pin? Poker? Knuckle sweeping by? Sheee-it, you tell me.

I say. "Daddy know, too. Act like they there, but ain't no big deal.

Looked right at one. Dropped his elbow on it like that's what it was there for."

"Mm."

"Ricky hung his towel on one."

"Typical."

"Don't know if it mean he actually seen it or not."

"True."

"Still . . ."

"Um-hm."

"You see what I'm saying?"

"Oh, yes, I see all right."

"But they there, all right."

"Truly."

"Yeah, they up there."

I don't and she don't say nothing for, like, a whole minute. Then she say, "You know I cain't say nothing about it, right?"

"Oh, I know that."

"I mean—"

"No, no, I know."

"You see what *I'm* saying."

"Yeah, yeah, yeah, I see. I see."

And that's about it. Smurf sat down, opened her book.

Went on down the hallway toward my room, but stopped in front the doorway to Mama's and Papa's room. Stood there for a second, but then just went on in, grabbed my iPod, put the headphones on and cranked that bad boy up, and before I got into my room and on my bed, High Priest was testifying "They Will Never See," which is my least favorite track on *Born Identity*. But I put it on repeat, and played it over and over until my room got dark, and I could barely see them shoes, but if you looked hard, you could see em. They was still up there.

Nominated by The Georgia Review,
Rebecca McClanahan

MICHAUX STATE FOREST, NEW YEAR'S

by CHRISTOPHER KEMPF

from THE GETTYSBURG REVIEW

We run the *kókúku* trail (translation—
snow owl, in late-American) alone
this morning, its strict, midwinter alders
dark against the snowfall, its flocks of crows
shrieking as we pass. & as for the river—
there is a river. & as for those vast
accumulations of gasses—& as,
too, for the Fords & Hyundais, & the flows
of copper from Chile to Santa Cruz
& the migrant workers of Sri Lanka
scaling their towers in Dubai—that will,
some evening, rear up & expunge us,
yes, we can almost imagine ourselves
last here, our species' sole surviving pair
of scavengers ventured forth for water
& shelter, as surely it will be, we
accept now, those new years the planet—poor
rock—is at last absolved of us. Except,
of course, someone, we notice, has just this
morning cleared the fallen mulberry tree
from the trail, & someone, we know, has worked
all month at the little plaque-like nameplates
for *oak* & *honeysuckle*, has rendered, we
can see, their intricate arboreal
branch-work with all the gaudy reverence

112

of an amateur. & aren't we? It was
the French who began such labor. Who came
south with their fur trade, & who carried here
the sextants & compasses & their bug
for the new science, with which, I was taught
in the sixth grade, they lopped & divided
& named & measured & mapped the atlas
of the marvelous world. It must have been
a kind of paradise then, no? Its crows
would eat from your hand. Its hickory trees
bore such fruit, reports say, Stéphane Michaux
lived all winter on their plenty. The French
imagined their future—children laughing,
democracy, et cetera. Our trail
turns west, & we follow, now, through the sedge
& crusted snow, to a bluff beyond which,
we observe, the stubbled fields fall away
toward Pittsburgh & Cleveland. & we can see
our breath as it pools & vanishes. Deer
flee. From the highest location for miles,
Milton says, he is shown, Adam, the wide
& lavishly manifold history
that will follow him. & it is glorious,
partly. How the banners ripple cleanly
from their turrets. With what refinéd grace
the courtesans attend their farandoles
& coronations. Paintings. Waltzes. Also,
however, in the teeming congeries
of men & animals, influenza
racing like a terror. Diphtheria
lifting its lurid flag, & back of this,
Milton describes, the emergent money
systems of sixteenth-century Europe
carried forth in the rolling cannon smoke
of capital. He would have, Michaux, heard
often of their savagery. He would have
called it that, & been properly appalled
when four Lenape entered a schoolhouse
here, winter 1764, & peeled
their blades across the skulls of the children

113

as they practiced their numbers. He would have
wept probably, though for the Lenape
it seemed simply the extravagant end
of a whole history of sicknesses
& ruin. & we could understand this,
could we not? When finally the earth—or
"this goodly frame, a spot," Milton says—starves
us from its forests & riversides, it
will not be merciful. It will finish
us slowly. We know this. We make our way
back, together, through the honeysuckle
& alders, our garden's great beasts shifting
in their warrens, the river's ice floes
slipping, like us, out to that fallen world
where, today, we will watch the recordings
of some marvelous ball dropping, again,
through the old year's last seconds. Its smallness—
that's what gets him. How for Adam the vast
globes rolling in their sky lanes, & comets
& stars & "space incomprehensible"
between the moon & Sirius exist
merely—oh, & here he is particularly
brilliant, listen—to "officiate light"
round this meager atom, the world. & round
its lemon trees & robins. Round his wife's
hair in its evening coruscations. Her hand
in his hand. & the lush & ample breast
of the new world laid before them. For that,
he thinks, my God, what wouldn't we butcher?

Nominated by Fred Leebron

TOLSTOY AND GOD

by BRIAN MORTON

from AGNI

Saul Bellow had been my favorite living writer for almost twenty years, but I'd never even thought about trying to meet him. I was so much in awe of him, he seemed so firmly fixed in literary history that I'm not sure it ever occurred to me that you *could* meet him. It would be like trying to get together with Milton or Wordsworth or Blake.

But now it looked like I was going to meet him after all. He had entered my life in an unusual way.

At that point I'd been writing fiction for fifteen years, and I'd never published a word. Three different novels had come close, but in each case the editors who liked them had been overruled by their all-powerful marketing departments. Now, though, an editor who knew Bellow had read and liked my fourth attempt, and it looked as though good things were about to happen for me.

The editor, Ted Solotaroff, had recently put out a collection of essays by a dear friend of Bellow's who had died too young, and Bellow was inclined to do him a favor. So Bellow was blurbing my book. Solotaroff had told me frankly that he wouldn't be able to publish my novel without a blurb from Bellow—but *with* a blurb from Bellow, the marketing department would be willing, as he put it, to promote the crap out of the thing.

It felt really big to me, and it also felt really weird. Bellow was not only *blurbing* it, he was going to blurb it without having read it. And he was not only blurbing it without having read it, he was going to say that "Morton may well prove to be the most distinguished moral intelligence of his generation."

"I don't get it," I said to Solotaroff. "How can he call me that? How can he call me that without reading the thing?"

"Honestly," Solotaroff said, "he did read a few pages and thinks your writing is 'workmanlike and uninspired.' So he's not willing to say anything about your prose. But I pleaded your case. Told him what a good guy you are, how long you've been writing without getting any breaks. And finally he came up with the line about your . . . moral intelligence."

"But . . . the most distinguished moral intelligence of my generation?"

"It says you 'may well prove to be.' Not that you *are*. When you turn out, inevitably, *not* to be the most distinguished moral intelligence of your generation, Saul's in the clear."

"But why would he say it about a writer he doesn't even like?"

"Look. Saul knows it's his novels that will live, not his blurbs. I think it's all a joke to him."

There was something humiliating about being the beneficiary of a great man's sense of humor in this way, but I was too desperate for recognition to think about it much.

"The only thing he wants you to do before he sends in the blurb," Solotaroff said, "is go to one of his dinner parties. You can bring your girlfriend if you want."

"He wants me to come to a dinner party?"

"That's what he said. If you turn out to be a maniac years from now, that's your privilege, but . . . I guess he just wants to make sure you're not a maniac now."

When I told my girlfriend, she wasn't as happy as I would have wished.

"Aren't you even a little ashamed of yourself?" she said. "Groveling for a blurb from someone who hasn't even read you?"

"I'll have the luxury of being ashamed of myself after the book gets published."

"And . . . Saul Bellow? Really?"

"What's wrong with Saul Bellow? You know I love Saul Bellow."

"It's something I've tried to overlook," she said.

"What does that even mean?"

"Saul Bellow," she said. "Have you noticed how the main characters in his books are always a lot like him? And have you noticed how they're always a little more *real* than anybody else in the books? It's like the worldview of a ten-year-old boy, who thinks that everybody else is a robot. And have you noticed how his main characters always have these spiritual yearnings that we're supposed to regard lovingly, and their ex-wives have these spiritual yearnings that we're supposed to laugh at?"

"Ah," I said. "The feminist critique."

"Yes, the feminist critique. I'm serious."

"Look," I said. "This is important to me. Just promise me that you're not going to fuck things up."

"Of course I'm not. I only fuck things up when you tell me to."

This was a reference to one of our first dates, when I'd started to get a sense of what she was capable of. For my birthday she'd bought tickets to an Arthur Miller play starring Patrick Stewart, whom I loved from his role as Jean-Luc Picard on *Star Trek*. It was Miller's last play, and it was pretty bad. The plot hinged on a tragically ill-timed busy signal, Miller evidently having failed to get the news that there really weren't busy signals anymore. And Stewart wasn't in top form. His American accent was not convincing, and his toupee was even less so. At one particularly boring moment I took out my notepad and wrote, "I'll give you five hundred dollars if you yell out something *Star Trek* related." She smiled and closed her eyes for a moment, and before I could stop her she called out, "Beam me up, Jean-Luc!" After that, the biggest surprise of the evening was how gently we were escorted out of the theater.

That was why I was concerned that she not screw things up at the Bellow dinner. One of the many delightful things about her is that I don't always know what to expect.

On the night of the dinner party, I waited in the living room while she dressed.

"How's this?" she said.

She was wearing a T-shirt that said "Fuck the patriarchy."

"Oh, come on, Heather," I said.

"These are my beliefs," she said.

"First of all: really? Second of all—"

"Just kidding," she said.

She went back into the bedroom and came out wearing a short shimmering silver sleeveless dress. She had a theory that the primate core of the male brain is very easily activated and that no man can think straight in the presence of a woman in a sparkly dress.

"How's this?"

"Thank you," I said.

"There's no way he can fail to consider you the most distinguished moral intelligence of your generation now," she said.

117

Bellow had an apartment near the UN. When we got there, he greeted us in a courtly way, but then glanced at me a second time and said, "Nice of you to dress."

I was wearing my usual: a button-down shirt and a jacket that I'd bought at Men's Wearhouse. I'd thought it would be appropriate, but if I'd been a little more tuned in to literary gossip, I would have known how clothes-conscious Bellow was.

Shiny dresses aside, I hardly ever notice what people are wearing. But it was impossible not to notice what Bellow was wearing, and impossible not to be impressed. It must have been a thousand-dollar suit. Maybe it was a ten-thousand-dollar suit. The fabric was so rich you wanted to touch it. You wanted to eat it. You wanted to nominate it for president, then let it declare martial law and cancel all further elections so it could be president for life. It was that kind of suit.

Bellow's apartment was a penthouse with a wraparound terrace. From the living room you could see all of Manhattan. Five or ten people were already there, including Solotaroff.

"What are you drinking?" Bellow said.

I asked for a scotch, because I thought it would seem masculine and 1950s. Heather said she was fine.

"You must," Bellow said.

"I'm sorry," Heather said. "When I drink I get loopy."

"Loopy's not bad," he said. "One drink."

"I wish I could."

Bellow turned to me. "A minute ago," he said, "I envied you. Now I'm not sure. You know what they say about honey in the ice box."

I didn't, and didn't want to. I gave him a vague smile and hoped that would be enough of a response.

At the dinner table, Bellow told stories. We learned what a hypocrite Norman Mailer was; we learned what an opportunist Susan Sontag was; we learned what a bore Irving Howe was. That last one was hard to take, because I'd worked with Irving at *Dissent* until his death the year before. I loved his socialist politics; I loved his seriousness; I loved his surprising playfulness. I loved *him*.

Bellow was also trying out first drafts of remarks he'd eventually make in public.

"I keep hearing people say we need to open up the literary canon to new voices," he said at one point. "And I'm perfectly fine with that, once we discover some new voices worth listening to. If they find the

118

Tolstoy of the Tutsis or the Hemingway of the Hutus, I'd be happy to read them."

Heather was getting irritated.

"Maybe I will have some wine," she said.

"Are you sure it's a good idea?" I said.

"Oh, I think it's a very good idea."

Bellow returned to the subject of Irving Howe.

"Lionel Trilling once told me that he used to give away his old suits to the Salvation Army on West 110th Street. After a while he noticed that he'd eventually see them on Irving. And the funny thing is, Irving was vain about his clothes. That's the story of Irving. He was vain about his ideas too, but every single one of them was secondhand."

Bellow's assistant had called a few weeks earlier to ask if we had any special dietary requirements, and I'd told her I was a vegetarian. The soup I was served was rich and delicious, and I said it was hard to believe it was vegetarian.

"That's because it's not," Bellow said. "I told the cook he could use beef stock. A novelist shouldn't be a vegetarian. A novelist has to want to devour everything. Thought I could teach you something. Hope you don't mind."

After dinner, Heather and I had a moment to ourselves.

"Why is this man important to you again?"

"He's important to me because of his books."

And this was true. On the one hand, I agreed with everything she'd said about his writing. Given his gifts, if Bellow had been fascinated by other people—the way Chekhov was, the way George Eliot was—he might have been the greatest fiction writer who ever lived. He had gifts that no one else had, but most of his fiction was subtly marred by what seemed to be his disdain for other people.

But on the other hand, there was his genius. I knew many writers who were hardworking and talented and generous to the bone, but their work wouldn't outlive them, and his work would outlive us all. No one could make a moment come alive like Bellow. When Bellow described walking down Broadway, it put you there more vividly than when you were walking down Broadway yourself.

And I didn't know of any other living fiction writer who thought as persistently as Bellow did about the life of the spirit. I'd once read the transcript of a conversation he'd had with some writing students: one of them had asked a question about literary technique, and he'd answered that technique was unimportant; what was important for a writer was to find and follow the promptings of one's soul. You could feel, all through his work, that he was a writer who *had* followed the promptings of his soul. In another place he'd written that "The name of the game is give all," and the line had stayed with me for years. You can love a writer's work without loving everything about it, and you can love a writer's work without loving the writer. Nothing Bellow could do or say at this party would make me love his work any less.

"I'm glad you're behaving yourself," Solotaroff said to me later. "Saul does like to put people through a trial by fire. Just grin and bear it, he'll give us the blurb, and we'll all live happily ever after."

Later we were given a tour of the apartment. Bellow was a collector of rare things.

He showed us an ancient silver bowl that a wealthy admirer from Brazil had given him, in honor of his story "A Silver Dish."

He showed us a miniature landscape painting by a Russian master whose name I can't remember. It was one of the few works by that painter that had survived the Russian Revolution.

"When the Winter Palace was overrun," Bellow said, "the Czar had time to warn his servants in one wing or to rescue a few works of art in the other. When you look at this, you have to admit he made the right choice."

"Do you?" Heather said.

"Life is short, art is long," Bellow said. "The servants would be gone by now in any case."

He opened the door of another room.

"And these," he said, "are my newest trophies."

There were two small, indescribably beautiful birds, in one wide cage.

"I call them Tolstoy and God," he said.

I understood the reference, only because it was something Bellow had written about. Maxim Gorky had once said that Tolstoy seemed to regard God as a rival, as if they were two bears in the same cave.

"Which one's Tolstoy?" Heather said.

"The bigger one," Bellow answered.

"What are they?" I asked.

"They're kestrels. Tiny hawks. An old friend of mine procured them for me," he said. "More than that I can't say."

"Why not?"

"Let's just say that owning them is not quite legal. Every once in a

120

while I think about setting them free, but I can't quite bring myself to do it."

"Would they be able to survive?"

"Anywhere. They're incredibly hardy creatures."

We all went out on the terrace. It was a clear summer night; the lights of Manhattan were all around us.

Bellow was explaining that Mary McCarthy had never really understood America.

"Forgive me, my love," Heather said to me. "But this is too much." And she walked away.

I thought she meant she didn't want to listen to him anymore, but a minute later, through the glass panels of the living room, I saw her reemerge on another wing of the terrace, holding the birdcage.

Bellow and the others went after her. I was surprised at how quickly he could move.

Solotaroff stopped me before I could follow.

"If she gives them back, Saul might still do this for you," he said. "He's familiar with impulsive spouses. If this doesn't go any further, he'll probably just be amused by it all."

Heather was leaning against the balcony, holding the cage in one hand with the other resting on the cage door.

"Talk some sense into your lady friend," Bellow said.

Heather looked over at me.

"What'll it be?" she said.

Maybe it was the shimmery dress, but I don't think so.

You have to follow the promptings of your soul. And the name of the game is give all.

"Open it up," I said. "Let 'em go."

Nominated by Rosellen Brown

THE HOME FOR BUDDHIST WIDOWS

fiction by BLAIR HURLEY

from WEST BRANCH

Before light has come and the little birds whose names we don't know are fluttering and darting out of the eaves of the temple, one of the monks is hitting the ancient cast-iron bell.

We are lying in the warm casings of our bedrolls and it feels like we are children again staying over at someone's house for a sleepover and there are girls all around us: Bonnie curled in a ball, refusing to rise without her slippers and fuzzy robe from home, Sandy looking bleakly about her, trying to make a to-do list for the day the way she has every day for forty years. Elizabeth nudging them both, forever the half-panicked kid late for the bus. I run a hand through my hair, and feel that bald scabby expanse instead. We still feel that loss. That moment is the hardest of the day, when we feel like prisoners of a futuristic war.

We are novices and so we must hurry in everything. Now we race to brush our teeth, to pee, to pull on our navy blue day robes. At first we bumped into each other but now we dart and maneuver like bees in a hive. We must dash across the compound to the dining hall, and be seated in silent rows by the time the *roshi*, the master and teacher of the monastery, appears. There are prayers to be said, and rice and powerfully vegetal green tea to drink. The morning ritual is conducted in silence. Quiet mouths make quiet thoughts, the *roshi* tells us. The oldest among us think, loose lips sink ships. The long dining hall is full of monks, monks and us, the widows. But the only sound is the slurping of tea. We make eyes at each other over our ceramic bowls. *Shizuka ni,* barks the monk we all hate, Shiro, the one charged with policing unruly us. *Be quiet.* We stick out our tongues at his retreating back.

We are not exactly sure why we are here.

*   *   *

We are not nuns. But we are here to pretend we are nuns for a time. We don't speak Japanese beyond a few simple greetings, the many ways that apologies can be offered for incorrect behavior. And we are far from the major cities, where English is commonly spoken. We panicked, at first.

So much of the day can be conducted in gesture and silence, though. There is the morning meditation to attend, seated on our ankles at the back of the great hall, behind all of the monks. The floor is a beautiful polished cedar but it kills our arthritic ankles and knees. To get a special cushion we have to take a long humiliating walk of shame to the front of the room and pluck it from a pile under the *roshi's* disappointed gaze. Most of us tough it out. We came here with worse than sore tailbones. We are all damaged goods, women dried up and whittled hollow. What is a little pain to people like us, we think, and dig our nails into our wrinkled palms.

*   *   *

Some of the monks despise us. Out of the *roshi's* sight they glare. We all learn the Japanese word for foreigner *(gaijin),* for tourist *(kankōkyaku).*

*   *   *

It is traditional in many Asian countries to withdraw from the world for a time after the loss of the husband, to rest, to recover from one's grief through contemplation. Indian women might join an ashram. Here in Japan, medieval noblewomen would visit a monastery to live as nuns, to purify and replenish themselves. Now the notion has fallen out of fashion; there are few Buddhist nuns in Japan anymore. But word has spread among the Americans. There's something beautiful about the idea of pulling back into the high snowy mountains, drinking tea, ringing bells, whatever it is that nuns are supposed to do.

In Akron, in São Paolo, a pamphlet is pushed across the table by a friend. Or late-night browsing on the internet for "how do widows" and letting Google autofill "how do widows cope, how do widows recover" leads us to a Buddhist website.

After all the grief, the panic of it, the savage emptiness of the house still cluttered with things, the tightening knot of friends and relatives who won't leave us alone with their relentless buzzing concern—suddenly it is late and I am still up, prowling the house like an intruder in my own former life, and the idea comes: an image of elegant architecture, a raked garden, a line of monks with bent heads, the deep gong of a bell, the clean, chilly, minimalist promise of Japan. Why not? It has to be better than *THIS*, I think.

*   *   *

We are fractious, cranky, and spoiled. We are too old for outhouses, there is no romance left in roughing it. We are always hungry. We want tempura shrimp and hot oily pots of ramen. We want sushi but get rice with a cold cube of tofu quivering in the center. At night the cold wind off the sea creeps in the cracks of our wooden dormitory and we must huddle together for warmth. We think of the medieval haiku that we are studying:

> weathered bones
> just thinking of the wind
> it pierces my body

The monks scowl at us when they think the *roshi* isn't looking. The *roshi* speaks an elegant, stilted sort of English that doesn't leave room for subtleties. We are indignant at every turn. We use our daily meeting with the *roshi* to complain. The floors are hard, the work is hard. Aren't you supposed to respect your elders in this country? He shrugs and smiles, putting up his hands. He has learned this very American gesture of absolving oneself of responsibility. You can always leave, he says. It sounds like he doesn't know why we are here anymore than we do. This is not what we want to hear.

*   *   *

In the afternoons we sweep the temple. This is something our bodies understand. We move back and forth with the broom, some like we're dancing, some in vicious stabs across the floor. All women, the rich and poor among us, know how to sweep. And as it turns out, monks do too. They run at a steep tilt with their wet rags swiping the floorboards. We race with them, but we can't keep up. They laugh, watching our stuttering efforts, not unkindly. They are mostly young. In Japan, to be a monk is an acceptable vocation. They call us *sobo,* the grandmothers, though only some of us are grandmothers. Most treat us with a cold respect. But in truth, as female novices, we are lowly. No one is beneath us. We must bow and scrape when a senior monk enters a room. It rankles for those of us who were activists, who marched and burned bras. Some of us told ourselves we would never bow and fawn to a man again.

* * *

Danielle, one of the youngest, a widow at thirty-five, gets in an argument with the monks. It's our turn to rake the stone garden, she insists, holding on to the steel rake. We're always mopping. Let us rake today. Danielle has been here long enough for her hair, blond fuzz, to have started growing back. She looks like a boy with a buzz cut, tough and militant. We hear her arguing with the *roshi* sometimes in their private meetings, in a way the rest of us wouldn't dare.

The monk named Haruto shakes his head. That is not a job for novices, he says. And never women. The raking is a spiritual practice.

How is that an answer? Aren't we spiritual too? Danielle retorts.

It's tradition, says Haruto, tight-lipped and angry.

We've all gazed out on the pristine sand garden, admiring the concentric circles around stones, the monochrome beauty of it. Only a religion like Buddhism can bear to be so abstract in its art forms. It's an unanswered question, an elegant void. But we've never been allowed to rake. Some of us take Danielle's side. Why can't we rake? Soon there's a yelling match going on in the yard. The *roshi* has to come out with his arms raised. Women don't rake, he says.

There's a lot we're doing at this monastery that isn't traditional, says Danielle. She has chosen her line in the sand, as it were. Her big tough jaw is clenched. She clings to the rake.

Go sweep the floors. No arguing, the *roshi* says, and bows his head. He is ashamed for us, for our shrill vulgarity.

The worst part is seeing the monks, smirking at us. We sweep and mop in an angry silence. But late that night, I wake to a rasping sound and rise. I go to the window; it's like my dream, the one where I see my husband off on a trip, and he wants me to run out and kiss him goodbye, but we've just fought and I won't. I'm always going to the window and watching him leave, and I don't know why I won't bend, why I can't make the cold center of myself soften.

In the real world, I see Danielle standing in the sand garden. She is

right in the middle, ruining the pattern with her footsteps. She's stand-
ing lit by moonlight.

What is *THIS*?

   This is watching the light creep into the window of a house that we
know holds no warm breath but our own. *This* was waiting for an ex-
cuse to speak all day, to the bank teller, to the neighbor who is just
trying to get a car seat into his minivan and doesn't have time for you,
standing on your lawn in your robe or in your Sunday best, hoping for
just a little conversation. *This* is inviting the Jehovah's Witnesses in
and serving them cookies just to listen. *This* is going to the dentist
more than you need to just to feel those warm latex fingers in your
mouth, massaging your gums. It is looking at art or listening to your
favorite songs and feeling puzzled by them, those things you loved
suddenly bereft of meaning. *This* is looking down the long dark sub-
way tunnel of your life and thinking, all right, I can do this, even if it
is alone, if I just keep walking, keep rising and eating and sleeping and
waking . . .

❁   ❁   ❁

Oh, Danielle. We look over at her meditating there at the end of the
hall, and we feel for her, we mourn her life, we mourn the lovely blond
hair we have seen in photographs the way a mother would mourn it.
She won't talk about her husband, what brought her here. But one day
some of us are sweeping up in the dormitory and her box of personal
effects falls from a shelf and we are on it like black-robed vultures,
pushing and pecking and prying. She has brought the same rubber-
banded stack of travel documents we all have, and almost nothing else.
A pair of fuzzy dice, a half-finished pack of gum, and three photo-
graphs. Here on the beach in the arms of who we imagine is her hus-
band. A good-looking bearded guy, as is the fashion for the young. Then
another photo of the two perched on an outcropping of rock, tiny and
far away. The third photo is of him almost unrecognizable in a hospital
bed. When our husbands were dying, some of us had this impulse to
take one more picture, to freeze him in time. And all of us regret it. It
is like a death mask, like that ghoulish Victorian fad of photographing
the dead propped up as if they were still alive, still drinking tea or about
to get up out of the favorite chair. Yet now that the picture exists, we
can't let it go. We stare and stare.

* * *

Grief, the *roshi* tells us, is like a fire that is licking at our bodies from the inside. Like anger, it stems from a kind of greed. We are clinging to our loved ones, to our former lives, like children cling to toys. We are desperate not to let go. This desperation is slowly eating us alive. It is a hungry and relentless fire.

Bullshit, Sandy says that night when we are tucking under our comforters. To say that grief is greedy? That's shit. Like I should feel bad for grieving?

I don't think that's what he meant, says Frieda. She's forty, and lost her husband to ALS. Much as we want to respect that, honor her surely harrowing experience, most of us can't stand her. She is always trying to explain the *roshi's* sermons to us. One of the few luxury items she brought is a book of Buddhist philosophy. She reads it at night while the rest of us are trying to sleep. When we meditate, she looks trustingly up at the master the entire time, like a good dog. She is ahead of all of us by three koans and we. hate. her.

It's not good or bad that we grieve, she says. It's that either way, it's an expression of clinging and grasping. And it's like anger because it's an expression of rage that we can't hold on to the person.

Sandy sits up on her blanket; she can't let this comment go, be the last thing anyone says for the night. We expect some sort of fight. But Sandy's voice is quiet, low under her smoker's rasp.

Anger has always helped me survive, she says. Anger kept me alive when my husband was slamming my head in drawers. Anger sets you free.

Why did you even come here, if that's the way you think about it? Frieda says, and we feel a small triumph that there is scorn and annoyance in her voice; we've broken her just a little.

But that is the question none of us can really answer, and we go to bed uneasy, our hearts knocking hard against the wooden floor.

* * *

For some of us, widowhood was like waking from a long sleep, mouth sticky and head banging, still hungover from the forty-year party of the night before. And now?

* * *

Have we joined a cult? Are we victims of some insidious criminal enterprise, some game of manipulation and spiritual theft? This is what

127

our friends want to know. On our weekly phone calls some of us call our children and some of us call the friends left back at home, and spend our time reassuring them. No, we are not victims. We are Okay.

If the people back home got a look at us, though, they would be harder to convince. Here we are, flapping down the corridor in our matching oversized robes like a flock of ungainly cranes. Our wrinkled white scalps look like the tops of mushrooms; we're a fairy circle, trooping through the forest in our robes. It's not a good look on old white ladies.

Our friends back home are a little horrified, we know, by what we've done to ourselves. But the moment someone becomes a widow, the world wants her to stop in time, to freeze exactly as she was. She must stay in the same house, read the same books, sit in the same chair. There's something dangerous about a widow who continues to change and grow, who grabs out at the world, demanding something, instead of wilting quietly from it. We are looking to become. At night we can feel it in our bones. They groan like the skeletons of teenagers, changing their shape too fast for our flesh to keep up.

What were the Buddha's last words?

All things are changeable. Nothing is lasting.

＊　＊　＊

To our academic friends we say, we are exploring the possibility of becoming theosophists. We are exploring the existential possibility and esoteric nature of the divine.

To our children we say, we need some alone time.

To our parents, if they are still alive, we say, It's about damned time I got some time for myself. Isn't that what you said when you kicked me out of the house and sold my record collection?

God, records! How old are we? Too old!

＊　＊　＊

In Hokkaido, the first snows often come in October. We walk along the beach with our warmest robes wrapped around us, watching the gray tide pull seaweed into its foaming mouth. Our robes flap and tug in the wind. We are thinking lofty thoughts of infinity, of ceaseless cyclical change. Or we are thinking about waking slowly as young newlywed women, our husbands heavy and solid beside us, their warmth, their smell, their weight like a frame that will encase the whole of the rest of our lives.

Somewhere far across the dark sea is our home; but we don't really know if it exists anymore. Then Sandy is running, robes flying behind her. Caw! Caw! she's crying like one of the seagulls that swoop and dive around our heads. And before we know it, we're all running with her, flapping our arms and croaking our hoarse cries. We screech and keen and fly over the water.

*　*　*

For me, *this* was seeing off the last guest the afternoon of the funeral and wondering who I was, something I hadn't really paused to wonder for a long time. I married young, and marriage was a benevolent monster, eating me gently from the inside. I never had to be anyone at all, as long as there was the monster there to care and feed. Some of the women around me are the same. But now that the monster is gone, where does that leave us? Who shall we feed?

*　*　*

During the day there is a steady influx of people to the temple. They come to make offerings to relatives at the cemetery, which is a building lined wall to wall with apothecary drawers. The locals light a stick of incense and drop a coin in a slotted wooden box. They bow to the relative's little drawer and say a quiet, clipped prayer. They stay sometimes for a sermon, but most Japanese people these days are not religious. Buddhism has become what the monks call "the religion of funerals." When someone dies, people observe the Buddhist rites, but that's pretty much it.

The locals don't know what to make of us. They don't get tourists that often, this far north. They bow and we bow, but we are not asked for blessings the way the monks are. Once a few of us stumble into a group of mourners returning from the cemetery. The women are in black kimonos, the men in black suits. An older woman, the widow we imagine, is leaning heavily on her son's arm, exhausted. Or so we think. Elizabeth pauses to bow and the tiny old lady draws herself up, releasing a stream of hot language. We don't know what is said, but we can hear the vitriol. She hates us; we are unexpected tourists to her suffering. Elizabeth bows deeper, her face reddening. She doesn't like outsiders, the son says, and he is not apologetic. We retreat.

In the dormitory that night, we argue about whether to make ourselves scarce. We don't want to be a burden. Nothing worse than an uninvited guest at a wake. A few of us have experienced just that, have had lovers show up, or distant relatives demanding money. A death can bring all the assholes out of the woodwork.

But we don't want to disappear.

We start attending the funerals and the one-year ceremonies and the seven-year ceremonies. We sit at the back of the hall while our *roshi* chants a prayer from the sutras. His voice is a lovely, dark brown baritone and the chant is hypnotic and warm, buzzing with energy. We bring legitimacy in our numbers. The whole somber flock of us, bowing low, makes it seem that the departed is mourned by crowds.

We start to find packets of rice balls and toasted seaweed outside the sliding door of our dormitory. They are offerings for us: little slices of dried fish, bricks of tofu, red-wrapped candies with the faces of cats.

*   *   *

Relax, relax, the *roshi* tells us during meditation, but we cannot relax. We do not know what the word means. Relaxation is what happens to other people. We have spent the past year caring for our husbands. It has involved rigorous schedules of medications and various embarrassing apparatuses and panicked late-night drives to the ER. We have held the hand of someone we loved and wept. How can we not be angry, how can we not be furious at the hand we have been dealt? Death has required us to be steely in our attentions, in our resolve. Now when meditating our spines are straight and stiff and there is a fine trembling in every muscle that has been there forever and only someone as close as a lover can see. But the *roshi* walks by us, his robes brushing our knees. And he sees.

Now we chant, the *roshi* tells us. This will be the afternoon, every afternoon: chanting. We barely understand the words. The monks recite in a deep, thrumming bass. It is like the repeated creaking of old floorboards. We join them, humming our best alto notes. The sound is gutteral, atonal. We are chanting for clarity, insight, rebirth.

It is exhausting to maintain this continuous prayer. It reminds some of us of sitting in ICU's late at night alone, when no matter how old we were, we were not old enough to handle this, when our thoughts were one frantic stream, *helpplease pleasehelp,* over and over.

But somewhere into the second hour, we realize that we have all at last found the same rhythm, that we are all chanting at the same tempo and breathing at the same time. We wait for it, and there is the collective intake of breath; we are all organs of a larger body, all saying *helpplease* together.

* * *

"This will be my last body," the nuns in the old scrolls say, when they sing of achieving enlightenment. It's a triumph, the highest of accomplishments. No more wheel of samsara, no more vicious cycling of birth and death. But in typical Buddhist fashion, there's something mournful about the pronouncement. Now the dizzy whirling of life has ended; now this body is all that remains to me. My last inheritance. *So . . . this is it?* At night after the evening sermon we curl up like children under our quilts and hug our knees to our chests. Some of us get in their quilts together and cling to each other, and maybe we do more than cling. We are hungry and cold, after all. And a body has a right to be curious.

* * *

We are not supposed to mingle with the monks outside of the shrine room. But on some nights after kitchen duty, when we have all been scrubbing the big rice pots, the monks sit at the half-lit table and smoke, and we sit with them. Too many people in Japan still smoke, and they must be allowed a pack a week or there would be a revolt. It amuses us, this vice. And the former smokers among us suck in the smoke greedily.

Have you heard of the suicide priest? someone asks.

We are learning that suicide is a big problem here. In Japan, there are books and pamphlets and printed guides for how to do it without inconveniencing everybody. You can electrocute yourself or hang. The books don't recommend pills because it is too easy for people to revive you. Bonnie's husband shot himself, but guns are very difficult to obtain here.

I was studying to be an engineer, but I was very depressed, Kuro tells us. His English is shaky and we make it through the story step by step, with detours and hand gestures. A friend told me about a priest who works with suicidal people. I studied with him a year. Now I want to do what he does. I transferred here to study for my ordination.

How do you feel? Sandy asks, always blunt. Are you happy?

He puffs on his cigarette, then takes it out of his mouth and looks at it. For a moment the kitchen is quiet and the light draws close around us.

I want to live, he says.

The monks teach us *hanafuda*, a complex card game with little palm-sized cards whose suits are different varieties of flowers. We can't tell the maple from the magnolia; we're hopelessly lost. The monks

131

grin and shuffle the deck with crisp thwacks. *Sobo, we got you again,* they say.

Danielle is missing. She said she was too sick for morning meditation and we left her bundled in the blankets like a caterpillar in its cocoon. It isn't until after the midday meal that Bonnie goes back to get her warmer robe and finds her gone. She reports this quietly to us. We do not tell the *roshi,* not right away. We have to think.

During afternoon time we return to the dormitory. There is her comforter, rolled tightly in a ball and stacked with the others. But her civilian clothes are gone. She is AWOL.

We argue in low voices what to do. Maybe she has had enough. We understand this impulse. Maybe she has called a taxi and finally ridden away. In eighteen hours she could be in San Francisco. I stop to picture her there, biting into a hamburger. Juice all over her hands. Wearing sweatpants. In the morning she could rise at ten, watch television, check her email, go to the movies and shove popcorn mechanically into her mouth.

But she wouldn't really leave without saying goodbye, would she? She needs our help. She's alone and afraid, maybe. We have to find her and bring her back.

We all put our civilian clothes on to go to the village. It's strange, walking beside the ocean road in our sneakers and jeans. The wind whips across our fuzzy crew cut heads. The jeans are too big on our leaner bodies. We're exposed for the first time in weeks, not wrapped in fabric, women (albeit, strange-looking women) walking to town.

We drift through the streets of the fishing village, not sure where to look. Dogs bark at us and townspeople come to their doors, crossing their arms under their coats. Have you seen a woman go by? we ask. We use the Japanese word, *nisou,* meaning nun. The *nisou* with the blond hair? The people who come to the door—mothers and old women, mostly—shake their heads.

We go to the local pub, the beer and noodles place where fishermen and solitary workers come for fast drinks and dinner. It's past the lunch rush and half-empty; only old men sitting by the windows here, their hands gnarled by years on fishing boats. We sit at the bar, feeling every eye on us. Have you seen a woman go by? we ask the bartender. A *nisou?* American?

The bartender speaks a little English. He confirms that Danielle was here a few hours ago. She had a beer and left, he says. Very good tip.

Did she say where she was going? asks Sandy, our unofficial leader.

He half-smiles. Very good tip, he says again.

We walk on. It's getting dark. The weather here is unpredictable and it has begun to snow. Our steps are more urgent now. We ask strangers on the street but are brushed away. We are not welcome here, either in our robes or our jeans. Either way, we are oddities. All we can do is keep walking along the beach, looking out at the gray little houses in the dimming light. She can't disappear. She is one of us. She wouldn't leave us.

Snow is falling along the beach. We start walking back. We'll be missed soon, and we'll have to tell the *roshi* our sister is missing. We hug each other, stumbling through the damp sand. We're thinking about Sandy's husband, who said a prayer every time he went out on his fishing boat. It worked. It was lung cancer that got him.

The villagers do not trust us and we don't know them. What must they think of us, strange silly Americans, fumbling out there in the cold, looking for something they scarcely understand. It's an insult to their faith.

There's a light on in the fisherman's hut down close to the shore. This is the building owned communally by the town; it's a shelter for fishermen coming back from days at sea. It's prone to flooding and has structural problems from past earthquakes, a monk told us. But for people who need shelter, it's better than nothing.

We're cold and hungry. We know there are supplies in there, lamp oil and packs of ramen. We cluster close to the lit window to see who's taking shelter tonight. We're hardly surprised, really, to see the blond back of Danielle's head in the window. She's there, of course; she's safe, taking a breather from the monastery. She's in a big oversized sweater, and a bowl of something steaming is in her hands. The scene is a small miracle of normalcy.

Then the monk Haruto emerges in the window. He looks so normal, too, with a blue nylon anorak, a collared shirt. His shaved head gleams in the low light. And he sits beside Danielle and they embrace, long and silently. The scene is so innocent, so purely intimate, that we don't think for a moment they're doing something wrong.

I am thinking instead of reading books on Sunday afternoons, of the day at the concert when we met. I'm thinking about coming home late, stuck in traffic, flight delayed, and knowing that someone is worried. I'm thinking of sex. I'm thinking of children. I'm thinking of waking up in the morning, again and again, never knowing which one will be the last.

We walk back in silence, heads down, concentrating on our footing in the shifting sand. Late at night, Danielle returns, crawling into her blanket, pressing close to me. I hold her and hold her.

Nominated by West Branch,
Ron Tanner

THE LEASH

by ADA LIMÓN

from POEM-A-DAY

After the birthing of bombs of forks and fear,
the frantic automatic weapons unleashed,
the spray of bullets into a crowd holding hands,
that brute sky opening in a slate metal maw
that swallows only the unsayable in each of us, what's
left? Even the hidden nowhere river is poisoned
orange and acidic by a coal mine. How can
you not fear humanity, want to lick the creek
bottom dry to suck the deadly water up into
your own lungs, like venom? Reader, I want to
say, *Don't die.* Even when silvery fish after fish
comes back belly up, and the country plummets
into a crepitating crater of hatred, isn't there still
something singing? The truth is: I don't know.
But sometimes, I swear I hear it, the wound closing
like a rusted-over garage door, and I can still move
my living limbs into the world without too much
pain, can still marvel at how the dog runs straight
toward the pickup trucks break-necking down
the road, because she thinks she loves them,
because she's sure, without a doubt, that the loud
roaring things will love her back, her soft small self
alive with desire to share her goddamn enthusiasm,
until I yank the leash back to save her because
I want her to survive forever. *Don't die,* I say,

and we decide to walk for a bit longer, starlings
high and fevered above us, winter coming to lay
her cold corpse down upon this little plot of earth.
Perhaps, we are always hurtling our body towards
the thing that will obliterate us, begging for love
from the speeding passage of time, and so maybe
like the dog obedient at my heels, we can walk together
peacefully, at least until the next truck comes.

Nominated by Jim Moore

PRAYING MANTIS IN MY HUSBAND'S SALAD

by LAURA KASISCHKE

from LAKE EFFECT

Once, he found one
among the lettuce leaves and
cabbage shreds a former
girlfriend had

arranged on a plate for him. If

it was still alive, I can't
remember what my husband said that
he and the girlfriend did with it. But
so it is, this

remembrance of the stories of the days of love
with another love of the one you love. She had

blue eyes. He told me that. And
long black hair. She
may or may not have worn glasses. If
she did she would have looked like a scholar in them, and
then the whole sexy scholar thing when she took them off
to lie down beside him on the bed. This

was long before I met him. So
why should I be jealous, or even sad? Even

stranger is
how can I remember it?
And remember it so well?

But I can—having
seen some praying mantises myself.
Their switchblade limbs. The precision
of their folding insectness.

And their Martian faces, of course, with
such innocent expressions.
But all-knowing.
And all business.
And the lettuce-green of them. This

bitch, I looked her up
on the internet. She's
still alive, in California, where she teaches something
pointless, like linguistics. But

here's the thing: He's never, my
husband, been
a salad-eater. Was he then? Was
the praying mantis he found once in his lettuce
the reason he has eaten
no salad since I met him?

Or was he just in love? Was

he trying to please this salad-tossing girlfriend
from the past, who
offered up to him the last pale-green thing
he'd ever eat again?

Maybe they were brown, her eyes.
Now, I can't remember that, but I'd

bet you any amount of money that her legs were
long, and that she shaved them in his bathtub
with his razor. Her

neck, elegant as a swan's, blah blah.
But then, imagine

it, their surprise, and just
try not to laugh out loud:

My tiny, triangular head, swiveling
from side to side. My
dead expression, while
my arms (sharpened swords, in fact—for I've
been seen to slice and eat a hummingbird
on National Geographic) seemed

folded up in supplication, or in praise, or in
solemn meditation, just

as they were spreading out their napkins
on their laps, and
raising, perhaps, their glasses in a toast
to the meal she'd made for him, and which
they were about to share, beginning

with that salad, and
also ending there.

Nominated by Lake Effect,
Pinckney Benedict, James Harms,
David Hernandez, Mark Irwin

TIDAL WAVE

fiction by VALERIE SAYERS

from IMAGE

In the early days of integration, when only white girls tried out for cheerleader, our elections were a cross between small-town participatory democracy, Soviet-style anointment of the chosen, and the Miss America Pageant. We sat rapt in the bleachers while the candidates cartwheeled in front of the whole school, flashing their white panties. Then we trooped back to homeroom to cast our votes.

We were chatterers, smarty-pants, A-track girls who raised our hands on one beat and never let the boys get a word in edgewise. We would never be cheerleaders, but we knew what it took: a cheerleader didn't need to be pretty, though most of ours were pretty, as a matter of fact, and a cheerleader didn't need to be athletic, though some of ours weren't too shabby in the handstand department. A cheerleader only needed to exude unshakable self-confidence and, maybe as a corollary, to beam bubbly friendliness and make it look like it wasn't fake—we knew all about fake friendliness. We were growing up in South Carolina, for God's sake.

All our stories are unresolved high school stories. We were the Tidal Wave, the class of '69 at Due East High School, our school years punctuated by assassinations and riots, by the Tet Offensive, by flower children in San Francisco whose very existence suggested that we were living in some remote outpost of civilization that didn't get updates on a regular basis. The Due East boys who couldn't get a word in edgewise volunteered to go to war while the rest of America burned its draft cards. We heard that Bo Channing, who'd just moved to Due East from Twenty-Nine Palms, smoked pot, but we couldn't imagine where he got hold of it or what would happen if the MPs caught him with it on base. We couldn't imagine what we would do if Bo Channing cast his icy-hot gaze on us.

We were a chorus that sang with one voice, and now in every Facebook post we hear one of those voices standing close. We spend all our waking hours online, poring over photos, but the only face we really care about seeing again is Vonda Freeman's. She was our homecoming queen, our sweetheart of Due East High, and once upon a time we A-track girls were her court. She was—yes—our head cheerleader. She was also the most self-contained girl we ever knew, so we're not surprised she boycotts Facebook, but that doesn't stop us from looking for her night and day. That doesn't stop us from craving her love.

The minute we saw Vonda Freeman, freshman year when she stepped off the bus from Saint Elizabeth's Island, we were stunned by her eyes, a strange light green. Would she mesmerize us. We weren't entirely sure she was beautiful, because redheads were not supposed to be beautiful, and the auburn brows framing her cat eyes drew too thick a line. She wasn't even tanned, which was a challenge to everything we knew about the attributes of beautiful girls. Mr. Thigsby said we were ignorant little yahoos the way we lathered on baby oil and roasted ourselves at the beach, when for centuries poets had known the most beautiful skin was alabaster. *Look at Botticelli's Venus, look at Vonda Freeman, for goodness sake.*

So we all did. We twisted in our seats toward the back of the room where Vonda's face had turned one of those fiery shades that is certainly not alabaster. She wore an expression we had never seen on each other's faces, a combination of pain and shame and sweetness, and she stared down at her desk so assiduously that Mr. Thigsby said: *Vonda, sugar, I most certainly did not mean to put you on the spot, but now you have perfectly illustrated feminine grace .*

Later, we all agreed that when she finally allowed herself to look up that day with her slow-breaking smile, her eyes darted toward Margaret Washington and Marcus Toomer, who stared out the window as assiduously as Vonda has stared down at her desk while the white folk discussed the perfect shade of pale.

We were a pod of porpoises swooping and diving through tidal creeks, and we had to have Vonda swimming among us. We worshipped Mr. Thigsby, but we resolved to take Vonda to the beach, to slather baby oil

141

all down her while sloping back. We crammed in one car and headed to Saint Elizabeth's, to the ends of the earth.

Bouncing down Vonda's dirt drive, lined with crushed shells, we remembered the oyster beds dying, the canning factory shuttered. The Freemans' yard was encased in chain link and covered by a tattered rug of brittle brown leaves. Beyond, their squat house was concrete block, its windows small enough for prison cells, because enlisted families always had to live like that. But pines rose up like spires, the live oaks dangled dappled moss, the light was dream light. We smelled the marsh, somewhere close. Maybe the Freemans knew something we didn't know, something about what to do if the waters rose or the world came to its close.

A shadow passed the prison window and we exited the car as one pulsing heart. We knew that Vonda had brothers and sisters, six or seven, which meant they must be Catholic, our mothers said. It made us ashamed to look at Vonda's mother who came to the door with a wan smile, her long thin hair a sickly yellow.

Our eyes trained above on a pileated woodpecker, rat-tat-tatting, mocking us. A preening bluebird perched below. Those birds never perched in our well-pruned trees. We never heard that low clear hum.

We were bad as buzzards, scavengers, pickers at the dead meat of gossip. But what could we say about sweet Vonda? She looked like a candidate for all kinds of loving—hadn't Mr. Thigsby called her a goddess?—but her only dates were with Elliott Schwartzman, who was so far off in his math-and-science world that he and Herb, the Schwartzman twins, spoke a language nobody else understood. Yet somehow Elliott knew the words to ask her out, and Vonda, for some reason nobody understood either, said yes.

One Wednesday night, cruising through town, we saw Vonda standing in front of the Church of God. Vonda: the holy rollers. Did Elliott know about this? We turned our faces so she wouldn't see us gaping, but our screeches might have reached the moon. The church was asbestos shingle, raised off the ground, with big red doors the rollers threw open when they got to rolling. We'd spent our whole lives staring at that church every time we drove by, hoping to see someone cavorting with the Spirit or shouting out in tongues, and sometimes we did see lumpy white folks pounding out the Jericho march, speaking a language stranger than the Schwartzman twins', a language that came from some place so far beyond Due East it was beyond our powers of imagination to conjure it. Our mothers said the way the Church of God carried on, they ought to call it *Church of the Holy Fools*.

Vonda could not possibly believe what holy rollers believed. When we craned our necks, we saw a scraggle of yellow hair swaying on the front steps, and Vonda yanking her mother so hard it looked as if she herself, our priestess, was on fire with the Spirit.

Our screeching calmed. Would we tell? Or would we swallow her shame and make it our own?

A few years back, we heard her name on the radio: *Vonda Freeman-Toomer*. Within the hour, Mindy Bottom, who'd always claimed to be Vonda's closest friend, posted the NPR link. Our aging giggles rippled out across the Southeast as we played it again and again: Vonda at an Occupy demonstration in Oakland, our Vonda in California among the latter-day hippies. She said something sweet about idealistic young folks, and we pictured her casting her green eyes down. Then she led a chant into the people's mike, and Mindy posted: *She certainly is putting those old cheerleading skills to use.*

We couldn't make out a word of her chant. Over and over, the segment came to an end, till Mindy sent the link to Vonda's faculty page at Berkeley, where she taught physics: Vonda, a professor of quantum mechanics. Elliott Schwartzman was already instructing his Facebook friends in the mysteries of wave-particle duality and the concept of entangled twins.

Vonda was nothing like her mother and nothing like us: her hair was short, thick, pure white. We didn't know a single woman our age who even let the gray show. She wore old movie star glasses, rhinestone studded, and behind the lenses her eyes looked like they were lit up by the Due East sun. She was just starting on that slow-breaking smile, beautiful as ever.

Vonda's father was due to ship out to Vietnam, the way so many fathers did, but what could we do? We were the women's auxiliary, the USO girls. The war beamed at us day and night, from the *Today* show and Walter Cronkite and even WAPE, the Big Ape out of Jacksonville, but we knew when to hold our tongues.

The Monday Vonda didn't get off the bus, Mindy Bottom reported that she had seen the military police kick up white dust as they departed, speeding down the oyster shell drive. Vonda's father hadn't shown up for the transport, so the MPs came to fetch him and when they got there—

He hid from them *under the bed.*

We were agog. According to Mindy, Sergeant Freeman didn't want blood on his hands. After they took him away, Vonda locked herself in her room, which as we all knew wasn't a room at all but a large closet, and wouldn't answer a knock except to say; *Mindy, you are my closest friend but I don't know that I'll ever come out.*

The truth was, Vonda wasn't anybody's closest friend: she was our porcelain doll, and we fussed over her, but did any of us ever get close? We imagined her on her knees, losing track of day and night, mumbling strange holy roller syllables no one could understand. After he heard the story, Elliott Schwartzman yanked his curls and paced the lunch-room. He stopped in front of our table to keen: *What if they hand-cuffed him?*

We had not pictured that, but now we did, and more: what if they shackled him and took him to Vietnam a prisoner in chains? A father who didn't do his duty shook us like nothing our parents had ever done, not tomcatting fathers or mothers with sherry-breath. Mindy's mother had swallowed all her sleeping pills once, but this was different: this was shoving your finger in the whole country's eye. Hiding under the bed, drunk or sober, wasn't something we would call manly.

The longer Vonda stayed away from school, the more we shivered at the memory of the down on her cheek when the light dappled through the moss. We pictured Vonda's father smoking pot and dressed in wom-en's underwear. Where had we picked up such notions? He could get killed in Vietnam!

We even said it aloud. Not a month after Vonda came back to school, they called her to the office to get the news. When she walked back into A-track trig, the sight of her was hard to take in: Mr. Thigsby said beauty required a flaw, but surely he didn't mean a glob of snot stuck to her upper lip. She didn't look beautiful—she didn't even look pretty—but she did look like someone who would mow us all down if we said so much as a word. The student-teacher stood slack-jawed, helpless, while the rest of us stared down at our desks assiduously, which Vonda had taught us to do. She gathered up her things.

Vonda's father, who hadn't wanted to go to war, who'd done some-thing you just didn't do, was dead, dead, dead. Now everything was wrong, upside down and inside out, every truth we'd ever breathed in with the salt air that blew through these islands. If there was a God, why did he make Vonda for such suffering? Oh God, why did you make us for such suffering? We couldn't find out about the funeral: no one knew, not even Elliott Schwartzman. We called and we called, but not one of the Freeman children ever picked up the phone. Our mothers said: *Stop calling, why don't you. They've gone to bury whatever's left of him.*

We snuck our extensions into our closets. We were as bad as B-track boys who knew they were going to get turned down but had to keep asking for the date. She was the most elusive girl at Due East High School and we knew we couldn't have her but we just couldn't stop.

Vonda's father dying turned the very tide. When she came back to school, Elliott had already lost her to her grief. She walked dazed and unearthly through the halls, and Mr. Thigsby whispered "Ophelia" when she passed. The whole football team tripped over each other to save her from other boys on the team who might take advantage of her sorrow, and she latched onto a halfback as her protector. We heard that Vonda Freeman put out for her halfback, because that was what boys said about girls. It wasn't enough, though, not in that place, not in that time. Soon enough we heard that Vonda put out for Marcus Toomer, too.

Marcus Toomer. *Miscegenation* was a word our teachers hissed, as if the very concept were obscene. In the spring of '68, the spring Martin Luther King was killed, it did not matter that Mr. Thigsby had marched for voting rights. Marcus and Vonda could have been killed, too.

Our mothers said they were asking for trouble, letting Marcus run for student council president. The three candidates sat in folding chairs on the gym floor in front of the stage and we sat before them, docile lambs craving a shepherd. One by one they went to the podium to deliver their speeches. First Calhoun Booth stumbled and forgot the jokes he'd practiced. We remember Herb Schwartzman next, droning on while Elliott, his campaign manager, mouthed the whole boring speech in unison from high in the bleachers.

Marcus sat in his folding chair with some of that self-possession we'd seen in Vonda, as if he knew perfectly well that it was his turn to speak but declined the opportunity, thank you kindly. Then the curtains on the stage above parted to reveal a band: two hulking guitarists, a sleepy-eyed drummer, a bassist with an Angela-Davis Afro. We'd never seen such a thing. We'd certainly never seen a girl bassist. Marcus had enlisted the officers' sons with the longest hair, the hair they grew to spite their father's high-and-tights: that was Bo Channing on drums, probably stoned out of his mind. The band struck a chord, and we all swallowed little strangled cries when they launched into a soul version of "Revolution."

That song acted as a drug on us: we were bedazzled, ecstatic, released. Bo Channing slurred the words but we didn't need the words. We saw Vonda's mother swaying outside the church, Vonda kneeling by the bedside where her father was rolled up like a rug, hiding from the military police. His hand reached out to grab her white leg and then—poof, presto-change-o—the song was over. The assistant principal pulled the switch to draw the curtains and Marcus Toomer walked to the podium, the slightest smile playing on his lips.

We tensed as the band marched down the side stage steps (remember, this was the spring of James Earl Ray). Marcus reached the microphone and nonchalantly spoke a line we'd only heard on Walter Cronkite: *Power to the people.*

Bo Channing, halfway down the steps, raised a drumstick high, and the gymnatorium erupted. From that moment, we knew Marcus would pull it off. We ached for whatever he could see so clearly. We were his acolytes now, in our bleacher row, his fan club, his groupies. We felt Vonda's body heat radiating. Who was to say that Mr. Thigsby wasn't right? Who was to say our churches weren't crazy too, blessing fighter jets?

It was as if she could hear my thoughts: Vonda looked at me—not at us, at me. It was the longest gaze anyone had ever directed my way, her smile full-throttle for once. We were alone. I was alone. My eyes locked with hers. She knew the thoughts I thought. She knew who'd called and called. She knew I loved her, and now I loved Marcus, too, and I didn't even know what I meant by *love*. She knew I'd never speak my thoughts, not now, not on Facebook, not ever.

After the NPR story, that picture of Vonda adorned a dozen Facebook walls. Did Marcus shoot it? There was no Marcus Toomer we could positively ID as our Marcus in the first twelve Google pages, though both the pastor and the political consultant looked like possibilities. Mindy tweeted them out into the void.

For weeks, we played the interview. We could make out the words by then: Vonda was chanting *Power to the people*, of course. It echoed through the internet, enough to make us want to drive downtown in the middle of the night to occupy Atlanta and Charleston and Charlotte. But we were not the occupying sort, so we occupied Facebook instead. While we were trying to locate Marcus, scanned black-and-white snapshots from the Tidal Wave days crowded our walls: Marcus underexposed, Vonda too pale and perfect to keep onscreen for long. She made our eyes sting.

Our nostalgia weighed down the cloud, and eventually the others moved on, even Mindy. Grandchildren replaced the old high school pictures just as the Occupy tents started to disappear, like that tide: turning, then turning back.

For a brief while we were upstarts. We stuck our fingers in our parents' eyes and voted for Marcus Toomer: he was Marvin Gaye and we were his backup singers. We said things we'd never dreamed of saying—*Keep the faith, baby; fight the power*—but the rumors were carpet bombs, exploding all around us. Vonda never told us she was seeing Marcus. She told us she was going out for cheerleader.

For cheerleader, we repeated, uncomprehending as our mothers.

The concrete-block house and the dead father and the holy rollers? And now Marcus? We even thought, for one split second, that she might not win—the gossip was sticky as napalm, adhering to her perfect skin—but Vonda did fine at the audition. What could we say about whooping and shaking a pompom? Everyone she'd been kind to voted for her, and of course all the boys were mesmerized, and we voted for her, too. We were loyal, we were faithful, and that was that. Vonda was an actual cheerleader: our friend Vonda Freeman.

Of course the other cheerleaders took her under their shapely wings, whereas we were just boring A-track girls, some of us a little plump. The cheerleaders were certainly super-friendly. Vonda never acted like she was too good for us. She never let on what she knew about me, and I never let on what I knew about her. And maybe we were both wrong. Maybe I didn't love her, and maybe she didn't disappear into the ranks of the girls beaming self-confidence to protect him, to protect them both.

Even before Facebook, we thought of her over the years. Mr. Thigsby was wrong about the flaw: we never saw Vonda's. But when the assistant principal announced the scholarships, we didn't know why Vonda would want to go to hoity-toity Bryn Mawr, so far away. And *Marcus Toomer*,

Haverford—we'd never heard of Haverford. What was a pair of Quaker schools, or geography for that matter, to the Tidal Wave? We heard that they were married and year after year we looked for them at our reunions. We had three interracial couples by our twentieth, and by our thirtieth we wouldn't have been surprised to see somebody walk in with a gay partner—though they haven't, not yet. Vonda and Marcus could certainly have come to a reunion, but they never did. They just simply did not.

With husband number three, I moved to the Atlanta burbs like everybody else, but I miss the lowcountry like a limb that's been taken from me. The prelapsarian beauty, as Mr. Thigsby used to call it, the dirty-lace look of Spanish moss hanging from live oaks in Vonda Freeman's chain-linked yard. Vonda was right about one thing: I don't tell people in Smyrna what I'm thinking. I can't picture myself at a demonstration. I can't imagine.

After the Charleston shootings, Facebook pop-pop-pops with the Rebel flag. Every few days, a new firefight breaks out and the ghost of Mr. Thigsby weeps. I find myself staring into another void. I open Vonda Freeman's faculty page and gaze again into her light eyes. Vonda gazes back, zapped by the miracle of quantum-something-or-other into my condo. I could reach out and touch her face.

I do reach out. I stretch a hand toward the wavering screen. We're in the holy rollers' church. All around us, rollers sway and moan while we sit silent, side by side. The air's charged, as if a hurricane's about to swoop in, and outside the birds chatter, sly prophets planning where to meet after the waters rise. I feel Vonda's body warm against mine. It takes me a while to see that the preacher standing in front of us is Marcus, grown portly. They both know something I don't know. When Marcus summons me to rise, I realize I can translate that one line he keeps chanting.

Right on, I whisper, but no sound comes out. Marcus doesn't hear me. He doesn't see me, either.

I'm not there.

I'm not anywhere, and Vonda has marched off into the night without me. I hear birds chattering still, though the dark stretches deep. The screen pulses on, looking assiduously for its absent Facebook queen.

Nominated by Melanie Rae Thon

ACT

fiction by STEPHEN HESS

from NOON

Last spring, I declared to several of my friends that I intended to videotape myself performing a variety of basic, yet highly artificial acts. At the time, I had settled on three specific scenarios: reading the entirety of Thomas Bernhard's novel *Yes* aloud, attempting to erase every spot of snow cover on a stretch of sidewalk with my footprints after a winter storm, and walking through city streets to the point of injury, yet continuing on until the pain became unbearable. And although I never executed any of these schemes with a camera present, I practiced for the reading and also the snow erasure on several occasions. At the time, I was feeling melodramatic and depressed, and was also filled with such intense anxiety that I could not speak or write clearly, so I felt that recording myself would allow me to articulate a statement that would have otherwise escaped me, and for reasons I cannot explain, I felt the need to document the moment. It seems to me that this documentary urge is something most writers and artists, both amateur and professional, must confront at one time or another. I would not want to be so incendiary as to say that everyone has a common goal in "telling stories" or "making confessions," but I would say that the more basic notion of documenting, or recording something, is relevant to most, whether theirs is a story and or an antistory, a chronos or a kairos, and so on. The point is that I wanted to document something but I didn't, but I did the things I proposed to do anyway, so I can't say whether I lost or gained something, or merely gained a little when I stood to gain more or lost just a little or more than could have been imagined from the outset.

I will not hesitate to admit that, because I decided to continue expressing myself during a time when I could not properly rationalize my expressions, I incurred losses that could easily have been avoided. I not only lost my ability to make sense to myself, but also to those around me, which meant that I eventually lost friends. I was so excited to discuss what I then referred to as "the glut of violence in both everyday life and the news media," that I was constantly introducing and alluding to the subject in our conversations. Even on the occasion when it seemed that one of my friends had instigated a conversation on such and such a topic having to do with "the everyday violence of life" or "the phantasmagoria of horrific images" in such and such media, it was merely a continuance of one of the earlier and numerous discussions I had already initiated on the subject. At the end of my visit in their city, my friends told me that I had poisoned them with my words on this particular subject, and I agreed with them. I had poisoned them, but what I failed to admit at the time was that the concoction was not my own but had been repeated from the news, books, and articles I had been reading during my stay. Every time I heard these friends of mine who are no longer my friends say "everyday violence" or "phantasmagoria" I cringed, knowing that I had promoted the slogans and anthems of thinkers who I hadn't even bothered to take the time to understand. In conversation, I often find myself quoting philosophers and thinkers as if their works are pop songs, and although it gets me into trouble, I can't stop myself from doing it.

The point, however, is that I wanted to document something and I didn't. And while I have explained that my urge to document myself has something to do with expressing that which I cannot in language, such an explanation does not address more significant and conspicuous questions such as "Why do I not do what I repeatedly say I will do?" and "What are the adverse effects of this sort of behavior?" and "Would I actually enjoy hastening to do what I claim I want to be doing?" I'm not sociopathic or a liar or even a pipe dreamer, but I display symptoms and qualities shared by all of them.

The behaviors I wish to document are among the most automatic and obsessive that I practice. And while I'd never say that I want to be a performance artist, I have been known to say that I would like "to take up acting again, as I had done when I was a schoolboy" or "to fully dedicate myself to music," as I had also done periodically in the past. Who doesn't wish to expand their physical "boundaries" when they have begun to experience the full onslaught of aging? The second we recognize that our bodies are wretched and decaying on the surface, we wish to make them sacred and holy. Physically and mentally, sexually and aerobically, we abuse ourselves throughout middle age, especially during the years of its onset. Every time I see a jogger or a glass-walled room filled with middle-aged people exercising, I do not think of health or longevity, but rather, "This person or these people must be caught up in some vicious cycle of self-abuse," and I begin to imagine the potential symptoms and scenarios of their specific sicknesses. Right now, I'm abusing myself in a variety of ways, too, although I don't happen to frequent the local gym or track, but my body and my image and my sexuality, of course, are all fully involved and integrated into my idiosyncratic obsessions, as they are with all the joggers and exercisers and athletes out there. We're all juicing ourselves for something and, moreover, desperately seeking a vessel in which to capture and exhibit the product of our efforts.

Videotaping athletes has always made sense. It is natural to exploit their gracefulness and strength, their victories and defeats, and the survivors and casualties of their competitions. And while it may not be wise for me to look to sports for help with my own unrecognized projects, I am nonetheless compelled by the simplicity with which the omnipresent risk of injury in sports accelerates and condenses the risks of everyday life. It's obvious to say this, that all people face more or less the same risks at different molarities and frequencies, but the concept is made more palpable through images of athletes and skilled competitors. If, for example, I were to execute the video of myself walking to injury as I mentioned before, I would document the process of an everyday, low-impact activity causing injury, but, like the time I badly sprained my ankle when walking too much, it would take hours to execute, and, to the viewer, the risk and danger in a light-footed step would not be made available by a short excerpt or a still image from the video but only by viewing its entire duration. And if the viewer were only to see me walking with a limp, without any idea of the cause, he or she would immediately assume that the cause of my injury must be somewhere else, and of a greater force than a single step. Would it be enough to walk down the sidewalk alongside a shadowy figure, or with a police officer watching over me as if I'm performing a daylong sobriety test, or a nurse trailing behind me with a stretcher or an IV cart, or a cardboard cutout of myself threatening suicide with a pistol?

The other night I made a satirical list of some of the projects I've failed to complete over the past few years:

ARTIST DIRECTIONS (remember to credit me as the author when realized)

Raise the Stakes on the Dunking Booth: Place all your photos in a box and permit gallery visitor to run them through a paper shredder in your presence.

Childhood Image or *Discovery of the Name*: This performance features an adult writing his or her name repeatedly on a blackboard until he or she experiences a loss of fine motor control.

Ground Cover or *Accounting for the Total* or *A Life's Work*: Videotape yourself walking up and down a stretch of sidewalk that has been freshly covered with snow, attempting to erase every spot of snow cover with your footprints.

Planets of Desire or *The Endocrine Life*: Fearlessly approach strangers whom you are attracted to.

Nostalgia for a Future World Populated by Me: Make a list of everything you think is frivolous.

On the Mythic Potential of Appliances: A functional toilet (w/o seat) is placed in the center of the gallery, and a sign invites individuals to flush whatever they like. A plunger is provided to aid in the event of overflow.

The Visionary or *Future Time Seen*: BAROMETER HEAD MAN hangs lifeless from a noose. The barometer, however, is still functional. Is he dead?

And then, when I finished the list, I wrote a letter to myself:

Dear Me,

Why should I feel anxious about conceiving of projects and performances and videos I know I'll never complete, and even ones I don't want to complete? I have suspicions that I don't know whom I'm talking to when I'm talking on the phone, and sometimes it seems like names and details are unimportant so long as we can talk to each other without effort. Why should I care to be so exacting with names and faces, and why do important people always expect to be remembered? It only causes a great commotion when the name of such and such person of importance is misspelled. Most others would never care. If this weren't the case—wakes, for example—would be much more disturbing than they actually are. I know everyone thinks I'm a nihilist when I talk like this, but I'm not.

Sometimes, when I think about things like incomplete projects, or the fact that I've been living off the memory of who I was or else imagined myself to be two years ago, or that wakes are a whole lot less disturbing than they ought to be, I feel a tingle in my lips or, at other times, I sense a "halo" or a "crown" of numbness wrapping around my head.

Nominated by Noon, Elizabeth Ellen

THE BOATMAN

by CAROLYN FORCHÉ

from POETRY

We were thirty-one souls all, he said, on the gray-sick of sea
in a cold rubber boat, rising and falling in our filth.
By morning this didn't matter, no land was in sight,
all were soaked to the bone, living and dead.
We could still float, we said, from war to war.
What lay behind us but ruins of stone piled on ruins of stone?
City called "mother of the poor" surrounded by fields
of cotton and millet, city of jewelers and cloak-makers,
with the oldest church in Christendom and the Sword of Allah.
If anyone remains there now, he assures, they would be utterly
    alone.
There is a hotel named for it in Rome two hundred meters
from the Piazza di Spagna, where you can have breakfast under
the portraits of film stars. There the staff cannot do enough
    for you.
But I am talking nonsense again, as I have since that night
we fetched a child, not ours, from the sea, drifting face-
down in a life vest, its eyes taken by fish or the birds above us.
After that, Aleppo went up in smoke, and Raqqa came under a rain
of leaflets warning everyone to go. Leave, yes, but go where?
We lived through the Americans and Russians, through Americans
again, many nights of death from the clouds, mornings surprised
to be waking from the sleep of death, still unburied and alive
but with no safe place. Leave, yes, we obey the leaflets, but
    go where?

To the sea to be eaten, to the shores of Europe to be caged?
To *camp misery* and *camp remain* here. I ask you then, where?
You tell me you are a poet. If so, our destination is the same.
I find myself now the boatman, driving a taxi at the end
    of the world.
I will see that you arrive safely, my friend, I will get you there.

Nominated by Poetry, Jane Hirshfield
Alicia Ostriker, Carolyne Wright

STRANGER, THANK YOU

FOR GIVING ME THIS BODY

by TERESA DZIEGLEWICZ

from RHINO

> to break
> on Lakeshore Drive. For the eyes I turn
> to the radio as the lady
> in the red SUV slams
> on her brakes. Thank you for bringing me
> into this world,
> where my Pontiac crumples
> like crepe paper, where the airbag's white fist
> pummels my chest and burnt talcum erupts
> like confetti, stains my clothes
> with the scent of singed hair.

> Thank you for my skin against bug-blood stained glass
> as it shatters in the strobe of the headlights,
> for my legs that still stand, stumble
> to the cracked yellow line of my lane, as I mark
> its bandage of snow with my heels.
> I want to thank you

> for the college party
> that led to my conception, the cramped bedroom
> I can only imagine. How maybe your hands cold as comets
> curved against the bend of his back. How maybe your tongue
> moved in his mouth— in this moment that leads to
> your body

156

weaving velvet layers
of blood into my tongue, the cold bones of my hands.
Those small strands of DNA that swirl in your cells,
replicating to muscle, becoming the thing that moves
me. Stranger, I lie

in the ambulance, when asked
for my medical history.
I watch the wiper break geode of city,
the snowflakes reform
again and again, and I say
I know anything about my birth mother
but I mean, I've learned no name
for how we've never sat across a table,
fingers greasy with fries,
how it wasn't you who read to me each night,
taught me to make pizzelles and
Sunday gravy,
rushed to the emergency room.
But still, somehow, I know you

by the beautiful facts
of my fingers, my cracked sternum, the skin
of my chest
purpling with fireworks of blood.

Nominated by Rhino

ZOMBIES

by DANIEL HARRIS

from SALMAGUNDI

Historically, there are two entirely unrelated types of zombies, one dull and quiescent, the other rabid and infectious. There are, on the one hand, the somewhat soporific zombies who shuffle around such films as *White Zombie*, *Revolt of the Zombies*, and *I Walked with a Zombie*— macabre colonialist cautionary tales from the 1930s and 1940s often set in a tenebrous Caribbean where evil voodoo mesmerists resurrect dead slaves. On the other hand, there is George Romero's 1968 *Night of the Living Dead* in which, after a returning space probe from Venus explodes in the upper atmosphere, spreading either radioactive contamination or Venutian microbes, the dead arise to cannibalize the living. This one low-budget cult classic inspired a feeding frenzy that culminated in thousands of films, novels, video games, T.V. shows, apps, tshirts, action figures, board games, pet costumes, collectible dolls, mutant Mickey Mice, and cookie jars with lids made of slate grey ceramic brains—the spawn of a mercantile pandemic for which there is as yet no known cure.

While Romero's classic is as artful as a silent film, almost painterly in its stark shadows which slash across close-ups of anguished faces, it was dismissed by most critics when it appeared, with the notable exception of Pauline Kael, as the paradigmatic B horror film of the 1960s. Since its inception, the zombie film has lived up to its reputation as the opposite of the art film or, more specifically, of the historical costume drama whose audiences revel in dresses, props, and property as much as they do the actual story being told. Unlike the art film, the zombie film belongs to an actively distasteful genre, an impolite one, unfit for the BBC. Its sensibility is almost self-righteously puerile, as in the famous lawnmower scene in Peter Jackson's *Dead Alive* in which a character flips up his pull-cord Lawn-Boy and mulches a surging tide of zombies whose limbs and heads spin around the room like so many buckets of paint (80 gallons of fake blood were spilled in the course of three minutes of film); or in George Romero's 2010 *Survival of the Dead* in which a soldier ignites a zombie with a flare gun and then uses the ensuing bonfire to light his cigarette. In their exuberant carnage, zombie extravaganzas resemble such comedic gross-out films as *Animal House*, *Superbad*, and *American Pie*, movies in which characters smash beer cans on their foreheads, "pork" virginal coeds, masturbate in freshly cooked pies, and spit partially masticated cream cheese in their friends' faces during impersonations of popping pimples. Both the gross-out comedy and the zombie film appeal to the anarchistic temperaments of rude teenagers who delight in the odiousness of the body, wallowing in their repugnance for natural functions, making mud pies with urine and feces. That one film inspires horror, the other laughter, seems almost immaterial, for they are both splatterfests, ill-mannered saturnalias, orgies of crudeness and immaturity, the one giving us food fights in the cafeteria, the other onslaughts of ravenous hordes who toss kidneys and thigh bones if not donuts and dinner rolls.

In fact, the two are so similar in spirit that the zombie film often morphs into the gross-out comedy, as seen in the hugely productive industry of zombie parodies, *Shaun of the Dead*, in which an electronics salesman plays video games with a putrescent friend he keeps caged in the garden shed; *Cockneys and Zombies*, in which the retirees in a nursing home defend themselves, with amazing aplomb, with walkers and even egg whisks; and the suburban idyll *Fido*, in which zombies have been turned into domestic servants by means of protective collars that, at the expense of tantalizingly corpulent neighbors, too often malfunction. Zombie films bleed into comedy because they are already over-the-top, so desperate in their need to appall and repulse that they become parodies of themselves. There is no line to cross. The grotesque and the hilarious merge in a prepubescent frenzy of excretory slapstick.

Both the gross-out comedy and the zombie film involve a juvenile suspension of empathy in which other people are reduced to walking targets, no more than human bull's-eyes and tattered silhouettes at firing ranges, objects of adolescent aggression, devoid of thought and feeling and therefore destroyed with impunity. In Quentin Tarantino's *Planet Terror*, a character puts out his cigarette by casually grinding it in a zombie's eye, and in *Wyrmwood: Road of the Dead*, zombies, whose blood the living characters discover is combustible, are strapped to a truck like gas cans, stuck with an IV that runs directly into the empty tank, and exsanguinated for fuel. The misanthropic hero of *Zombie Hunter* kills the creature who ate the sole remaining Polaroid of his belated wife and child and then, in a fit of anger, disembowels it, rummaging through its intestines to recover the precious, if mucilaginous relic. Zombie films relax social edicts against dehumanizing others, who merely afford practice for aim, for guessing the trajectory of missiles and blows, for fixing the axes of a sniper's cross hairs on unpredictably clumsy creatures, whom the protagonist of J.L. Bourne's novel *Day by Day Armageddon* calls "stink ridden shit ball[s]," "seven-foot puss sack[s]," and "convulsing maggot pie[s]."

For this reason, zombies are the perfect non-characters of a gamer culture, providing a plethora of things to shoot at, hack, skewer, ax, chainsaw in half, thermo-detonate, ionize, and light-saber. Games like *Resident Evil* (which has inspired its own successful movie franchise, five films and counting) and *Call of Duty* (whose zombies have a second level of dehumanization in that they are not only dead but the ultimate pariah, Nazis) provide the perfect playthings for inactive misfits who prefer to hole up in their rooms staring at screens thumbing their Xbox 360 controllers, rather than running around outside throwing balls with their peers or racing on their bicycles. If less aerobic, video games allow adolescents to guide hypertrophied avatars bulging with muscles through deadly mazes while they themselves, gorging on Cheez-Its, never break a sweat. Zombie games provide surrogate exercise for surrogate bullies, offering a dark prequel to their future lives as over-weight, middle-aged Sunday quarterbacks watching football in their Naugahyde recliners.

The popularity of the contagious feeder lies partly in his status as an easy kill but also in the morbidity reports of the final decades of the twentieth century, perhaps the ultimate source of the genre's success. This period saw a number of disturbing and unprecedented biological outbreaks. In 1976, twenty-nine legionnaires died in Philadelphia, the same year the CDC diagnosed the first case of hemorrhagic fever or Ebola. Toxic shock syndrome debuted in 1980, and in 1981 five gay men in Los Angeles came down with a rare lung infection, Pneumocystis carinii pneumonia. Acquired Immune Deficiency entered the general vocabulary in 1982 but it wasn't until late 1983 that the CDC officially ruled out casual contact, food, water, air, or surfaces as sources of transmission. In the late 1990s, West Nile encephalitis appeared in New York

City, an instance of bioterrorism in the eyes of conspiracy theorists who felt that imams had been radicalizing, not just the mosques, but the mosquitoes and launched an entomological fatwa against the infidels living in the swamps of Staten Island and Queens.

As the international gene pool sloshed over sovereign borders and the public became increasingly disillusioned with the ability of modern medicine to fight off new threats, popular art met the challenge by ceaselessly reimagining a medical catastrophe that reifies pathogens as actual human beings, soulless shamblers who, not so much infect you, as devour you, with teeth and not replicating strands of DNA being the primary agents of infection. The process of transmission in zombie films is not a cough or a sneeze or a shake of the hand, as in the case of poor Gwyneth Paltrow whose gruesome scalping during her autopsy is one of the highlights of the medical thriller *Contagion*, but a bite, a juicy chomp with the crisp fracture of splintering bones and growls of gleeful gustation from the voracious huddle of the undead as they over-power their prey. In real life, the entry of a virus into the bloodstream is less cinematic. Transmission is silent, invisible, whereas Hollywood is loud and visually flamboyant, with cars exploding in fireballs and cities rattled by earthquakes collapsing into the chasms of gaping fault lines—spectacles inherently more dramatic than an organism's penetra-tion of a cell's glycoprotein membrane. Advertisers of antacids and toothpastes face the same problem as cinematographers of disease when they attempt to represent the action of their peptides on stomach gases or their sulfates on dental plaque—chemical reactions that they animate with firemen who turn their hoses on flaming intestines and cartoon superheroes who do battle with bacteria masked as bandits and bank robbers. When something eludes the senses, it is often anthropo-morphized, the complex rendered diagrammatically simplistic, the in-visible made manifest through flamboyant pictorial hyperboles.

The bite is the Hollywood director's answer to the invisibility of transmission. It is the equivalent of the bandit or bank robber in the toothpaste commercial, a metaphor for both the inaudible and the un-seen. The bite of the infected is no ordinary bite but an enhanced, PhotoShopped, audio-engineered bite, one heard from an unnaturally close point of view, often from within the sonic zone of the mouth itself, right next to the gnashing teeth, a bite that has been augmented by the aesthetic adjustments of special effects. Food advertisers often talk about the "perfect pour," a flawless, photogenic cascade of liquid as it spills in slow motion into a glass, and the directors of zombie movies are just as dedicated to the elusive goal of the perfect bite, a slimy display of rotten dentition with glistening strands of saliva and arterial spurts of the victim's blood, all to dramatize a moment too microscopic for the multiplex.

The zombie bite is also a dark, rebarbative fantasy of a culture obsessed with eating. Ingestion is an act of nourishment, but, in a society of bulimics and anorexics, it is also a terminal disease. The snapping jaws of the undead incarnate the new neuroses of eating, the dinner table having become a triage gurney on which the obese clog their arteries and the binge-and-purgers develop peptic ulcers and pancreatitis. In the face of such pathologies, popular art has created a satanic image of the glutton, not a zaftig roly-poly snoozing on his sofa, but a famished corpse who lives to ingest, who stuffs his maw with flesh, heedless of the civilities of table manners. The zombie is the new poster child of eating disorders which, as we see-saw up and down in the course of endless yo-yo diets, loom so large in our daily lives that they have acquired a sinister, supernatural dimension, one in which the dead rise from their graves to hoover up an ever-dwindling source of meals. Perhaps it is poetic justice for our intemperance that, after the apocalypse, we ourselves, once the feeders, become the food.

Like the bite, the zombie brain is subject to a host of rhetorical adjustments. Vampires die when stakes are thrust through their hearts, werewolves when shot by silver bullets, and zombies when their brains are destroyed. Brains are the occipital equivalent of their Achilles's heel. But the zombie's isn't a clean death. Its skull isn't simply pierced by a bullet or whacked with a hammer, hockey stick, golf club, drum majorette's baton, frying pan, cosh, cane; it explodes, it detonates, it shatters like a piñata. The zombie brain, it would seem, has far more volume than the skull that contains it, as if the grey masses within were under extreme pressure, vacuum-packed. Heads are not the real heads of living actors—however altered with blackened dentures and clouded cataract contact lenses–but complex incendiary devices designed by studio pyrotechnicians which detonate remotely, rupturing into sopping splatters of Karo syrup and food dye, the film industry's recipe of choice for a viscous form of hemoglobin that moves somewhat more lethargically than real blood and thus makes a more lurid impression.

Without such effects—bites as forceful as those of a T. Rex, heads that go off like grenades, blood that runs like molasses (indeed, that *is* molasses)—the zombie film as we know it today would not exist. It would be a Halloween parade of spastics garbed as ghouls and not the festival of ever more inventive forms of carnage that Hollywood cine-matographers have so brilliantly concocted. Once the province of in-spired amateurs like George Romero, who could cobble together an expressionistic masterpiece on a shoestring, zombie films now have the most bloated budgets in the business, like the Brad Pitt vehicle *World War Z* which, despite its mediocrity, cost nearly $200,000,000 to make, or the wildly popular television series *The Walking Dead*—another me-diocrity, atrociously acted and padded with lofty, philosophical filler—which costs nearly $3,000,000 per episode, or $60,000,000 per season. The latter employs no less than thirty full-time sculptors to achieve effects as gory as rotten heads being pushed like Play-Doh through hurricane fences and torsos so putrid they can be pulled in two like strips of taffy. A clean bill of public health in the last few decades would almost certainly have sapped the genre's momentum, but without major advancements in special effects and prosthetics—which, only fifty years ago, were limited to a shabby costume and some green paint but which now use robotic puppetry or "animatronics" and thick sheathes of vul-canized silicone–zombie films would long since have lapsed into obso-lescent period pieces. Instead, they are subject to a kind of special-effects arms race as the public becomes instantly inured to the ingenious de-signs of the animators and make-up artists. Ever escalating standards of realism have set for the zombie filmmaker an aesthetic trap, their costly effects whetting and never satisfying the audience's appetite for a perpetually unstable verisimilitude that constantly approaches but never achieves the Platonic ideal of naturalism, of being there in the flesh, a participant as well as a potential victim and not just a spectator.

The zombie plot is often childishly simple. We play the same game as toddlers: "chase." The dead chase the living—over and over and over again, no matter how big the budgets, how many extras are employed, or how many stars bite equally famous friends. Or, flipping the scenario, the living unwittingly chase the dead, entering the fateful room where dear old Uncle John, a little green at the gills, trapped in a closet or napping beneath a bed, lunges for his long-delayed dinner. One of Hol-lywood's oldest conventions is recycled with endless variation in one horror film after another: we follow a character (as well as a score, his often overbearing acoustical companion) down a hallway as he calls out someone's name, muffled by an echoing, portentous silence, until he opens a door and screams. The camera is always one step behind him so that the audience accompanies him down that hallway, looking over his shoulder. There is a one-second delay and the actor sees before we do the psycho-killer or the monster or the atrociously mutilated corpse sprawled on the carpet so that our reactions are mediated through his fear, through the rhetoric of the scream, which is often more terrifying than the spectacle itself. The killer in his ghost-face Edvard Munch mask is never allowed to simply present himself in all of his horribleness but must be glossed or annotated with the victim's facial expressions, a kind of physiognomic footnote that says "this is really shocking," an instruction, not a reaction, an aesthetic admonition or stage direction that manipulates us into a state of panic that we may not really feel.

The zombie genre, in short, is plagued by repetition and cliché. Aware of the audience's growing enervation, the author or director tries frantically to create novelty. He *could* prevent boredom by inventing new situations but this is a time-and-talent-intensive enterprise, and so, in the name of convenience, he resorts to costumes, much as Shakespeare is constantly updated in novel stagings that present Othello as a thug, Lear as the ailing dictator of a banana republic, and Macbeth as a chef in a restaurant in Glascow, as in an episode of the BBC's *ShakespeaRE-Told*. Similarly, there are Nazi zombies, coed zombies, stripper zombies, radioactive zombies, cybernetic zombies, Amish zombies, and even beaver zombies (hence the movie *Zombeavers*), zombies that have been superficially renovated, spiffed up, with exotic new wardrobes. The zombie genre is itself a zombie; it is dead, decadent, lifeless, but, with each new film, game, novel, is revivified by artists incapable of breaking free of its rigid formulae.

The vacuum at the center of this cinematic and literary tautology deforms the genre aesthetically. The zombie actor chews up, not only innocent survivors, but the scenery. Screen writers upholster and plump up the sagging conventions of zombie films with magniloquent disquisitions. This most immature of genres is prone to bombastic speeches. The writers of *The Walking Dead* fill the mouths of each season's characters with so much hard-won wisdom that they seem to be so many Hamlet epigones afflicted by the need to step toward the footlights and soliloquize the audience, to maunder on like victims of a high-brow Tourette's. In one of the main character's speeches from Season 5, a rambling elocution that brought tears to the eyes of the actor who plays him, Rick compares his experiences during the apocalypse to his grandfather's during World War II:

> Every day he woke up, he told himself, "rest in peace. Now get up and go to war." And then after a few years of pretending

he was dead, he made it out alive. And that's the trick of it, I
think. We do what we need to do, and then we get to live . . .
I know we'll be okay, because this is how we survive. We tell
ourselves that we are the walking dead.

Similarly, sagacious Hershel, a country vet who waxes profound, his
voice a quavering tremolo, virtually every time he walks on set:

You step outside, you risk your life. You take a drink of water,
you risk your life. And nowadays, you breathe and you risk
your life. Every moment now, you don't have a choice. The
only thing you can choose is what you are risking it for. Now
I can make these people feel better and hang on a little bit
longer. I can save lives. That's reason enough to risk mine.

When Shakespeare wrote *Hamlet* between 1599 and 1602, the re-
venge tragedy, the genre of which the play was a part, had already been
around for at least twenty years and was suffering from the audience's
fatigue with its conventions, an ennui that Shakespeare countered by
attempting to raise this most bloody of low-brow thrillers to a more
elevated, metaphysical level. Hamlet's great speeches can be seen as
part of an effort to remodel a dilapidated literary genre by endowing it
with a kind of gravitas it lacked through its early history. *The Walking
Dead* premiered in 2010, some 40 years after Romero invented the
genre, an expanse of time that has left the contemporary audience as
weary of the vitiated conventions of the zombie apocalypse as the Eliz-
abethan audience was of those of the revenge tragedy. Screen writers
of zombie films also attempt to break free of paralyzing and repetitive
topoi by trying to force the ultimate low-brow scary movie to fulfill a
function it is almost by definition unfit to serve, that of a sophisticated
and literary to-be-or-not-to-be meditation on life, death, and other great
quandaries of human existence.

The zombie genre is based on an incongruous form of pastoral, on
literary conventions as old as Hesiod's *Works and Days*, Theocritus's
Idylls, and Virgil's *Eclogues*. Like literature that evokes idealized bu-
colic settings, the zombie apocalypse is an anti-urban genre that plays
upon fears of over-population, of the lack of personal space in cities.
This sense of vulnerability on congested sidewalks and in traffic jams
generates nightmares about crowds of jostling pedestrians and road-
enraged drivers, which, after infection, become hordes, the moaning
swarms of the undead. It is only a small step from Manhattan's Sixth

Avenue, down which, during lunch hour, thousands of men and women crawl, their glazed eyes fixed on their cell phones, to the throngs of "walkers" that roam aimlessly through the streets of Atlanta in the first episodes of *The Walking Dead* or mill about the parking lot of the Midwestern mall in *Dawn of the Dead*, now a sea of thousands of spasmodic extras. The horde is just a lunch-hour crowd that bites.

It is because of the agoraphobic nature of the genre that, in the great international debate that rages on the Internet about slow and weak versus fast and strong zombies, filmmakers and novelists must come down squarely on the side of the former, lethargic laggards who don't attack but converge. Zombies are corporate revenants who are most dangerous in torpid packs, whereas, when traveling solo, they are fairly easily kept at bay, outpaced, shoved back, or just shut out by a slamming door, too feeble and cretinous to outwit the usually seasoned survivor. Those who make their zombies fast and strong, like the director of *World War Z*, in which the living dead sprint like athletes and "turn" within ten seconds of being bitten, or the director of the *28 Days Later* series, in which they have the superhuman strength of Marvell comic book characters, commit a grave aesthetic mistake: their hyperactive flesheaters move too swiftly to create the vast assemblies of extras in which hapless survivors are smothered and entrapped, sinking in the throng, the confluence of corpses that slowly congregates around them.

Overcrowding is what fuels our fear of zombies who are just surrogate components of the urban cattle crush. In the zombie pastoral, survivors living in cities flee to the sparsely populated countryside which, unhappily, turns out to be less Sir Philip Sydney's *Arcadia* than James Dickey's *Deliverance*, a macabre anti-pastoral where the rule of law has given way to rugged, selfish, and often autocratic individualism. Once they enter this impaired Eden, migrants from overrun cities revert to the lives of hunter gatherers scavenging through abandoned houses whose possessions aren't purchased so much as requisitioned, marked as one's inviolable territory, often in the face of others' more tenable claims. (The zombie plot almost always involves a house tour in which characters invade the inner sanctums of former occupants, the remnants of whose private lives they treat with careless disrespect, wolfing down their food and throwing themselves on their beds in muddy boots, much as pre-historic hunter gatherers were said to pollute the ecosystems in which they trespassed, stripping trees and bushes like locusts, hunting species to extinction, simply moving on when they had rendered one location uninhabitable.) It is in this Wild Wild West world of eat or be eaten that one encounters the deeply reactionary ideology of the zombie genre, which is in fact a Republican dystopia, a world of self-government in which the state has finally disappeared. This is life as the NRA imagines it, a libertarian paradise—or hell—one without law enforcement, without the National Guard, without (especially) circling black helicopters whose appearance in the sky signals to paranoid extremists the imminent takeover of the United States by the UN. Law devolves to the individual and his gun or, indeed, *arsenal,* a cache of semi-automatics, revolvers, and grenade launchers whose purchase no longer requires the permission of Diane Feinstein—no doubt already eaten—let alone background checks and permits issued by ATF agents, also long since some hungry housewife's snack.

The government invariably falls during the apocalypse and the military is thrown into ineffectual disarray. The public service announcements for shelters and escape routes broadcast on radio and television dwindle and then cease. One station after another goes off the air. The President "turns" and chases the Secretary of Health and Human Services around the White House. Indeed, in J.L. Bourne's *Day by Day Armageddon,* it is the widowed First Lady, now the Commander-in-Chief, who announces that she has ordered nuclear strikes on major U.S. cities to thin the ranks of the undead, which means that the seventeen people in the official line of presidential succession—from the Speaker of the House to the Secretary of Veterans Affairs—have succumbed to the epidemic. At the very moment big government is needed, it fails its citizens, betrays them, leaves them to their own devices, a despairing self-sufficiency that expresses profound disillusion with Washington, both its untimely intrusiveness and its perceived cynical withdrawal during crises. People who wait for the government to arrive and rescue them, for the Calvary, with a flourish of horns, to appear silhouetted on the horizon on horseback, are summarily eaten for their gullibility. Those in the Beltway have retreated to a few scattered bunkers where they are gnawing on each other's bones, leaving trigger-happy paramilitarists, living in Red States, the classic locale of the zombie plot, to protect their families to the best of their ability. Liberals in Blue States are simply grub, vittles for the undead, too namby-pamby and conscience-stricken to save themselves.

The crazed survivalist, often a disaffected member of the army or

167

police force, who has all of the training of the soldier and none of the camaraderie, frequently attracts disciples, giving rise to the second form of zombie government, that of charismatic tyranny, of cultish autocrats who capitalize on the fear and defenselessness of other survivors and exact slavish fealty to their whims, like the deranged "Governor" in *The Walking Dead* who creates his own fiefdom, a peaceful simulacrum of a small town complete with a Main Street of quaint shops even as he keeps his zombie daughter tethered to a chain in his office and collects severed heads still chomping for flesh. While celebrating right-wing militias and the hoarding mentality of Biblical eschatologists and "doomsday preppers," the zombie genre often makes an implausibly tendentious swerve to the left and warns of the potential Pol Pots, Idi Amins, and Kim Jong-Ils who arise during power vacuums when democracy is weakened or crippled.

The zombie genre is not only a cockeyed pastoral but a perverse Robinson Crusoe romance in which a culture that no longer knows how to survive, that cannot build its own shelters without the help of architects and contractors, that has abandoned food production to corporate giants like Mansanto, Dupont, and Dow, is forced to undergo an emergency tutorial on the essentials of subsistence. Feelings of helplessness in the face of the extreme division of labor, from plumbing and electricity to clothing and transportation, produce fantasies of remedial study in the basics of survival, pop culture reveries in which we recover lost standards of sufficiency. The zombie apocalypse, preeminently a right-wing rejection of the cozy embrace of big government for the self-rule of the lone gunman, also draws upon the appeal of back-to-the-garden ecological utopias, lefty pipe dreams about growing one's own food and living simpler lives on collective farms. The genre is riddled with ideological inconsistencies, with the delusions and manias of the doomsday-sayers, stocking their bomb shelters with MREs, residing cheek-by-jowl with the ideals of those advocating for the simpler lives of highly principled social drop-outs.

Why does a culture of plenty obsess over scarcity? Do we feel we are living in a fool's paradise, that plenitude is unsustainable, that we have pushed the planet beyond its limits? The comforts of civilization are fraught with anxieties about hardship and distress, fears that manifest themselves in popular culture, in novels and films that imagine a world depleted of its resources. Global warming, pandemics, nuclear war, terrorism, pollution all contribute to our sense of the precariousness of our affluence and privilege, apprehensions that lead us to create obsessive scenarios of decimation, annihilation, apocalypse. Zombies are the scolds of prosperity, loquacious lay preachers who remind us that the whole complex structure of civilization could collapse in an instant and we could find ourselves, between breakfast and lunch, scrounging for our next meal, even as they scrounge for theirs, us.

Nominated by Salmagundi

FREEDOM

fiction by RACHEL CUSK

from THE PARIS REVIEW

I asked Dale whether he could try to get rid of the gray.

It was growing dark outside, and the rain against the salon's big windows looked like ink running down a page. The traffic crawled along the blackened road beyond. The cars all had their lights on. Dale was standing behind me in the mirror, lifting long, dry fistfuls of hair and then letting them fall. His eyes were moving all over my image with a devouring expression. His face was portentous, and I watched it in the glass.

"There's nothing wrong with a few sparkles," he said reproachfully.

The other stylist, who was standing behind a customer at the next chair, half closed her long sleepy lids and smiled.

"I get mine done," she said. "A lot of people do."

"We're talking about a commitment," Dale said. "You have to keep coming back every six weeks. That's a life sentence," he added darkly, his eyes meeting mine in the mirror. "I'm just saying you need to be sure."

The other stylist looked at me sidelong with her sphinxlike smile.

"A lot of people don't find that a problem," she said. "Their lives are mostly commitments anyway. At least if it makes you feel good, that's something."

Dale asked whether my hair had ever been dyed before. The dye could accumulate, apparently, and the hair become synthetic looking and dull. It was the accumulation rather than the color itself that resulted in an unnatural appearance. People bought box after box of those home dyeing kits in search of a lifelike shade, and all they were doing was mak-

170

ing their hair look more and more like a matted wig. But that was apparently preferable to a natural touch of frost. In fact, where hair was concerned, Dale said, the fake generally seemed to be more real than the real: so long as what they saw in the mirror wasn't the product of nature, it didn't seem to matter to most people if their hair looked like a shop-front dummy's. Though he did have one client, an older lady, who wore her gray hair loose all the way to her waist. Like an elder's beard, her hair struck Dale as her wisdom: she carried herself like a queen, he said, streaming power in the form of this gray mane. He lifted my hair again in his hands, holding it aloft and then letting it drop, while we looked at each other in the mirror.

"We're talking about your natural authority," Dale said.

The woman in the next chair was reading *Glamour* magazine with an expressionless face, while the other stylist's fingers worked at her intricately tinseled head, painting each strand of hair and folding it into a neat foil parcel. The stylist was diligent and careful, though her client didn't once glance up to look.

The salon was a lofty, white, brilliantly lit room with white-painted floorboards and baroque, velvet-upholstered furniture. The tall mirrors had elaborately carved white-painted frames. The light came from three big branching chandeliers that hung from the ceiling and were duplicated in dazzling reflection all around the mirrored walls. It stood in a row of dingy shops and fast-food outlets and hardware stores. The big plate-glass shop front sometimes rattled when a heavy vehicle passed outside.

In the mirror, Dale's expression was unyielding. His own hair was a dark, artful mop of gray-streaked curls. He was somewhere in his mid-forties, tall and narrow, with the elegant, upright bearing of a dancer. He wore a dark, closely fitted jersey that showed the suggestion of a potbelly above his lean hips.

"It doesn't fool anyone, you know," he said. "It just makes it obvious that you've got something to hide."

I said that seemed preferable to having what you wished hidden on public display.

"Why?" Dale said. "What's so terrible about looking like what you are?"

I didn't know, I said, but it was obviously something a lot of people feared.

"You're telling me," Dale said glumly. "A lot of people," he went on, "say it's because what they see in the mirror doesn't feel like them. I say to them, Why doesn't it? I say, What you need isn't a color wash, it's a change of attitude. I think it's the pressure," Dale said. "What people are frightened of," he said, lifting the back of my hair to look underneath, "is being unwanted."

At the other end of the room, the big glass door jangled open and a boy of twelve or thirteen came in out of the darkness. He left the door standing ajar and the cold wet air and roaring noise of traffic came in great gusts into the warm, lit-up salon.

"Can you close the door, please?" Dale called in a peevish voice.

The boy stood, frozen, a panicked expression on his face. He wore no coat, only a gray school shirt and trousers. His shirt and hair were wet from the rain. A few seconds later, a woman came in after him through the open door and closed it carefully behind her. She was very tall and upright, with a large, angular face and mahogany-colored hair carefully cut in a bob that hung exactly at the square line of her jaw. Seeing her, the boy raised his hand to plaster his own hair sideways over his forehead. The woman stood for a moment, her large eyes moving around the room, and then she said to the boy:

"Go on then. Go and give them your name."

The boy looked at her with a pleading expression. His shirt was undone at the collar, and a patch of his pale, bony chest could be seen. His arms hung by his sides, the palms opened in protest.

"Go on," she said.

Dale asked whether I was ready to have my hair washed; he would go through the color charts while I was gone and see if he could find a match. Nothing too dark, he said; I'm thinking more browns and reds, something lighter. Even if it's not what you naturally are, he said, I think you'll look more real that way. He called across to the girl who was sweeping the floors that there was a customer ready to go down. She automatically stopped sweeping and leaned the broom against the wall.

"Don't leave it there," Dale said. "Someone might trip over it and hurt themselves."

Again automatically, she turned around and, retrieving the broom, stood there holding it.

"In the cupboard," Dale said wearily. "Just put it in the cupboard."

She went away and returned empty-handed, and then came to stand beside my chair. I rose and followed her down some steps to the warm, lightless alcove where the sinks were. She fastened a nylon cape around my shoulders, and then arranged a towel on the edge of the sink so that I could lean back.

"Is that all right?" she said.

The water came in a spray, with alternating passages of hot and cold. I closed my eyes, following the successions and returns, the displacement of one temperature by another and then its reinstatement: they were so different from one another, yet each was mildly uncomfortable to the same degree. The girl rubbed shampoo over my head with tentative fingers. Later she tugged a comb through the hair and I waited, as though waiting for someone to untangle a mathematical problem.

"There you are," she said finally, stepping back from the sink.

I thanked her and returned to the salon, where Dale was absorbedly mixing a paste with a small paintbrush in a pink plastic dish. The boy was now sitting in the chair next to mine, and the *Glamour*-reading woman had withdrawn, her hair still in its foil parcels, to the sofa by the window, where she continued to turn the pages expressionlessly one after another. Next to her sat the woman who had come in with the boy. She was tapping at the screen of her mobile phone; a book lay beside her on the seat. The other stylist was leaning with her elbow on the reception desk, a cup of coffee beside her, talking to the receptionist.

"Sammy," Dale called to her, "your client's waiting."

Sammy exchanged a few more remarks with the receptionist and then ambled back to the chair.

"So," she said, putting her hands on the boy's shoulders so that he involuntarily flinched. "What's it going to be, then?"

"Do you ever get the feeling," Dale said to me, "that if you weren't there to make things happen, it would all just go tits-up?"

I said it seemed to me that just as often the reverse was true: people could become more capable when the person they relied on to tell them what to do wasn't there.

"I must be doing something wrong then," Dale said. "This lot couldn't run a bath without my help."

He picked up one of a set of silver clips and fastened it to a section of my hair. The dye would need to stay in for at least half an hour, he said: he hoped I wasn't in a hurry. He took a second clip and isolated another section. I watched his face in the mirror as he worked. He took a third clip and held it between his lips while he separated one strand of hair from another.

"Actually I'm in no particular rush myself," he said presently. "My date for this evening just canceled. Luckily," he said, "as it turns out."

In the next-door chair, the boy sat staring interestedly at himself in the mirror.

"What do you fancy?" Sammy said. "Mohican? Buzz cut?"

He gave a sort of twitch of his shoulders and looked away. He had a soft, sallow face, with a long, rounded nose that gave him a ruminative expression. A strange, secretive smile was forever playing around his plump pink mouth. Finally he murmured something, so quietly that it was inaudible.

"What's that?" Sammy said.

She bent her head down toward him but he failed to repeat it.

"Strange as it might sound," Dale was saying, "I was quite relieved. And this is a person I really like." He paused while he fastened a section of hair with a clip. "I just keep getting this feeling more and more these days"—he paused again to fasten another—"that it's more trouble than it's worth."

What was, I asked him.

"Oh, I don't know," he said, "maybe it's just an age thing. I just feel like I can't be bothered."

There had been a time, he went on, when the prospect of spending an evening alone would have terrified him, would actually have seemed so weird and immense and empty that he would have gone anywhere and done anything just to avoid it. But now he found that he'd just as soon be on his own.

"And if other people have a problem with that," he said, "like I say, I can't be bothered with them."

I watched his dark figure in the glass, the fastidiousness of his quick fingers, the concentration on his long, narrow face. Behind him, the receptionist was approaching with a phone in her hand. She tapped his shoulder and held it out to him.

"For you," she said.

"Ask them to leave a message," Dale said. "I'm with a client."

The receptionist went away again and he rolled his eyes.

"I persist in the belief that this is a creative job," he said. "But sometimes you have to wonder."

He knew quite a lot of creative people, he went on after a while. It was just a type he happened to get on with. He had one friend in particular, a plumber, who made sculptures in his spare time. These sculptures were constructed entirely from materials he used in his plumbing job: lengths of pipe, valves and washers, drains, waste traps, you name it. He had a sort of blowtorch he used to heat the metal and bend it into different shapes.

174

"He makes them in his garage," Dale said. "They're actually quite good. The thing is, he can only do it when he's off his trolley."

He took a new section of hair and began to fix the clips around it.

"On what," I said.

"Crystal meth," Dale said. "The rest of the time he's quite a normal bloke. But like I say, in his spare time he gets himself tanked up on crystal meth and locks himself in his garage. He says that sometimes he'll wake up on his garage floor in the morning and there'll be this thing beside him that he's made and he's got no memory at all of making it. He can't remember a thing. It must be really strange," Dale said, inserting the last clip with pincer-like fingers. "Like seeing a part of yourself that's invisible."

He liked his friends—he thought he might have given me the wrong impression earlier—though he knew plenty of people who were still carrying on at forty the way they had been at twenty-five: he actually found it slightly depressing, the spectacle of grown men frenziedly partying, still shoving things up their noses and whirling like brides on packed dance floors; personally, he had better things to do.

He straightened up and examined his work in the mirror, his fingertips resting lightly on my shoulders.

"The thing is," he said, "that kind of life—the parties, the drugs, the staying up all night—is basically repetitive. It doesn't get you anywhere and it isn't meant to, because what it represents is freedom." He picked up the pink plastic dish and stirred its contents with the paintbrush. "And to stay free," he said, coating the brush with the thick brown paste, "you have to reject change."

I asked him what he meant by that, and he stood for a moment with his eyes fixed on mine in the mirror, the paintbrush suspended in mid-air. Then he looked away again, taking a strand of hair and applying the paste to it with careful strokes.

"Well it's true, isn't it," he said, somewhat petulantly.

I said I wasn't sure: when people freed themselves, they usually forced change on everyone else. But it didn't necessarily follow that to stay free was to stay the same. In fact, the first thing people sometimes did with their freedom was to find another version of the thing that had imprisoned them. Not changing, in other words, deprived them of what they'd gone to such trouble to attain.

"It's a bit like a revolving door," Dale said. "You're not inside and you're not outside. You can stay in it going round and round for as long as you like, and as long as you're doing that you can call yourself free." He laid aside the strand of painted hair and began to paint a new section. "All I'm saying," he said, "is that freedom is overrated."

Next door to us, Sammy was running her fingers through the boy's dark, unruly hair, feeling its texture and its length, while his eyes looked sideways in alarm. His hands gripped the chrome armrests of his chair. She swept the hair first to one side, then the other, looking closely at him in the mirror, then picked up her comb and made a neat parting down the middle. The boy looked immediately anxious and Sammy laughed.

"I'll leave it like that, shall I?" she said, "Don't panic, only joking. It's just so that I can get it the same length on both sides. You don't want to go around with your hair all different lengths, do you?"

The boy looked away again silently.

"What's it called," Dale said, "when you have one of those bloody great blinding flashes of insight that changes the way you look at things?"

I said I wasn't sure: a few different words sprang to mind.

Dale twitched his paintbrush irritably.

"It's something to do with a road," he said.

"Road to Damascus," I said.

"I had a road to Damascus moment," he said. "Last New Year's Eve, of all times. I bloody hate New Year's. That was part of it, realizing that I bloody hated New Year's Eve."

A group of them had been at his flat, he said. They were getting ready to go out, and he starting thinking about the fact that he hated it and thinking that everyone else probably hated it, too, but that no one was prepared to say so. When everyone had their coats on, he announced that he'd decided to stay at home.

"I just suddenly couldn't be bothered," he said.

"Why not," I said.

For a long time he didn't reply, painting the strands of hair one after another until I thought he either hadn't heard my question or was choosing to ignore it.

"I was sitting there on my sofa," he said, "and it just suddenly happened."

He stirred the paintbrush in the dish, coating each side again carefully with the brown paste.

"It was this bloke," he said. "I didn't really know him. He was sitting there doing lines that he'd laid out all neatly for himself on the coffee table. I suddenly just felt really sorry for him. I don't know what it was about him," Dale said. "He'd lost all his hair, poor bastard."

He unclipped a new section and began to paint it. I watched the way he distributed the paste all along the strand in even strokes. He started at the root but became more meticulous the further away from it he got, as though he had learned to resist the temptation to concentrate his labors there at the beginning.

"He had this funny, pudgy little face," Dale said, pausing with his paintbrush in the air. "It must have been the combination of the baldness and the funny face that did it. I thought, That bloke looks like a baby. What's a baby doing sitting on my sofa shoving coke up his nose? And once I'd started seeing it that way, I couldn't stop. Suddenly they all started looking like that. It was a bit like being on acid," he said, dipping his paintbrush again in the dish, "if I can cast my mind back that far."

Sammy had started gingerly snipping the boy's hair with a pair of scissors.

"What sort of things are you into, then?" she asked him.

He gave a little shrug, the secretive smile on his lips.

"Football?" she said. "Or the what's it called—the Xbox. All you boys are into those, aren't you? Do you play Xbox with your friends?"

The boy shrugged again.

Everyone obviously thought he was completely mad, Dale went on, for staying at home while all of them went off clubbing. He had had to pretend he was ill. Once upon a time it would have terrified him, the prospect of spending New Year's Eve alone, but on this occasion he couldn't get rid of them fast enough. He suddenly felt he'd seen through it, seen through them all. What he'd realized in his Damascene moment was that the people in his sitting room—himself included—weren't adults: they were children in overgrown bodies.

"And I don't mean," he said, "to sound patronizing when I say that."

"My little girl's about your age," Sammy was saying to the boy in the next chair. "You're what, eleven, twelve?"

The boy did not reply.

"You look about the same age as her," Sammy said. "With her and her friends it's all makeup and boys now. You'd think they're a bit young to be starting all that, wouldn't you? But you can't stop them. The problem with girls," she went on, "is they don't have as many hobbies as boys. They don't have as many things to do. They sit around talking while the boys are out playing football. You wouldn't believe," she said, "how complicated their relationships are already. It's all that talking: if they were outside running around they wouldn't have time for all the politics." She moved around the back of his chair, still snipping. "Girls can be quite nasty, can't they?"

The boy glanced over at the woman he had come in with. She had put down her phone and was now sitting reading her book.

"That your mum?" Sammy said.

The boy nodded.

"She must find you quiet," Sammy said. "My daughter never shuts up. Can you hold your head still, please?" she added, pausing the scissors in mid-air. "I can't cut it if you keep moving your head. No," she went on, "she never stops talking, my daughter. She's yakking all day from morning to night, on the phone to her friends."

While she spoke, the boy was moving his eyes up and down and from side to side while his head remained motionless, as if he were having an eye test.

"It's all about your friends at your age, isn't it?" Sammy said.

By now it was completely dark outside. Inside the salon, all the lights were on. There was music playing, and the droning sound of passing traffic could be faintly heard from the street. There was a great bank of glass shelves against one wall where hair products stood for sale in pristine rows, and when a lorry passed too close outside, it shuddered slightly and the jars and bottles rattled in their places. The room had become a chamber of reflecting surfaces while the world outside became opaque. Everywhere you looked, there was only the reflection of what was already there. Often I had walked past the salon in the dark and had glanced in through the windows. From the darkness of the street, it was almost like a theater, with the characters moving around in the bright light of the stage.

After that episode, Dale said, he had had a period in which every time he saw someone he knew or spoke to them—and increasingly with people he didn't know, with clients or strangers in the street—he was literally plagued by this sense of them as children in adults' bodies. He saw it in their gestures and mannerisms, in their competitiveness, their anxiety, their anger and joy, most of all in their needs, both physical and emotional: even the people he knew who were in stable partnerships—relationships he had once envied for their companionship and intimacy—now looked to him like no more than best friends in the playground. For weeks he went around in a sort of fog of pity for the human race, "like some bloke from the Middle Ages wandering about

178

in sackcloth ringing a bell." It was quite disabling, he said: some days he actually felt physically weak and could barely drag himself to the salon. People assumed he was depressed, "and maybe I was," Dale said, "but I knew I was doing something I had to do, I was going somewhere, and I wasn't going back if it bloody killed me." At the end of it, he felt empty, in the sense of minimalism, like he'd had a massive mental clear-out. Thinking back to that New Year's Eve, what he'd felt was that there had been something enormous in the room that everyone else was pretending wasn't there.

I asked him what it was.

He was squatting down behind me by now, painting the hair at the back, so I couldn't see his face. After a while he stood up, reappearing in the mirror with the plastic dish in one hand and the paintbrush in the other.

"Fear," he said. "And I thought, I'm not running away from it. I'm going to stay here until it's gone." He scrutinized the painted hair from all sides, like an artist examining a finished canvas. "It shouldn't be long now," he said. "We'll leave it to settle in for a bit."

He just had to go and make a quick call, if I would excuse him. He had his nephew staying with him at the moment; he ought to let him know that his plans for this evening had changed and that he'd be home after all.

"With any luck," Dale said, "he might even have found it in himself to cook something."

I asked where his nephew had come from, and he said Scotland.

"And not one of the trendy bits," he said. "For some reason my sister keeps herself in the arse-end of nowhere." He'd been there once or twice to visit her, and it was only forty-eight hours before he was seriously considering talking to the sheep.

The nephew was a funny fellow, Dale said: everyone had decided he was autistic or had Asperger's or whatever it is people call you these days when you're not like everyone else. He'd left school with no qualifications: when Dale went up to visit, he was unemployed and would sit throwing rocks down the hill into the quarry for amusement.

"He's changed a bit since then, fortunately. The other night he even asked me whether I'd used fresh herbs in the pasta sauce, or 'just' "—Dale made the inverted commas with his fingers—"the dried ones."

I asked how the boy had ended up coming to London, and Dale said it was after a conversation he'd had with his sister. She told him the boy had started saying things to her that were freaking her out, that he felt he was living in the wrong body or living in the wrong person or something like that.

"He doesn't say a word in months," Dale said, "and then he suddenly comes out with that. She didn't know what to make of it. She asked me what I thought it meant." He shrugged. "I'm a hairdresser," he said, "not a psychologist." He picked at a few stray strands on my head. "But obviously I had a hunch. I told him if he could pack a bag and get himself on a train, he could stay with me in London. I said to him, I'm not looking for company: I like my life just the way it is. I've got a nice flat and a nice business and I want to keep them that way. You'd have to do your share, I said, and I'm not putting someone up who doesn't work, because I'm not a bloody charity. But you'd have your freedom, I said, and London's a big place. If you can't find what you're looking for here, you won't find it anywhere. And a week later," Dale said, "the doorbell rings and there he is."

He hadn't been entirely surprised, he admitted: his sister had tipped him off a couple of days earlier, "just so I'd have time to hide anything she might not approve of." And for those two days, he did find himself having some second thoughts. He wandered around the rooms of his flat, noticing their cleanliness and order; he savored the peace of the place, his freedom to come and go as he liked, to return home after work and find it all just as he had left it. "The idea," he said, "of having someone always there, someone I had to talk to and clean up after, someone I would basically have responsibility for, because at sixteen you're really still a child and this one had never been outside a tiny Scottish village in his life: well, you get my drift," Dale said. "I thought, I must be insane, giving all this up."

I asked whether any of those fears had been realized, and he was silent for a moment. I watched him in the mirror, his arms crossed over his stomach, where the faint paunch stood out from his lean, wolflike frame.

Obviously at the beginning, he said, they'd had some moments. He had to teach his nephew to do things as he liked them done, and nobody learns in an instant: he of all people knew that, from training up novices at the salon. You need time, he said, time and consistency. But it had been two months now, and they rubbed along together quite well. The boy had found work as a trainee mechanic; he had a bit of a budding social life, and even came out clubbing with Dale on occasion.

"When I can be bothered to put away the pipe and slippers," Dale said, "and haul myself out the door. Shared life," he went on, "can never be the same as being on your own. You lose something," he said, "and I don't know if you ever get it back. One day he'll leave, and the thought has occurred to me that I'll probably miss him; that the place might feel empty, where before it felt complete. I might have given up more than I bargained for," he said. "But you can't stop people coming in," he said, "and you can't ask what's in it for you when they do."

He crossed to the reception desk to get his phone, and I looked at the boy in the chair beside me, whose wild dark hair was now cropped short. He was shooting frequent, imploring looks at his mother, who remained determinedly absorbed in her book.

"That's coming on nicely," Sammy said to me. "You going anywhere special tonight?"

I said that I wasn't, though I had to go somewhere the following evening.

"You're usually good for two or three days if he styles it properly," Sammy said. "You should be all right. Right then," she said to the boy, "let's have a look at you."

She put her hands on his shoulders and faced him in the mirror.

"What do you think?" she said.

There was no reply.

"Come on," she said, "what have you got to say for yourself?"

I saw the boy's mother glance up from her book.

"We've got a right one here," Sammy said. "A right man of mystery."

The boy's knuckles were white where they gripped the armrests of his chair. His sallow face was pale and clenched. Sammy released her hands and in an instant he had sprung to his feet and was tearing off the nylon gown that was fastened around his shoulders.

"Take it easy!" Sammy said, stepping back with her palms raised. "There's expensive equipment in here, you know."

With strange, lunging movements, the boy strode away from the chair toward the big glass door. His mother got to her feet, the book still in her hand, and watched as he yanked the door open and the black rainy street with its hissing traffic was revealed. He had pulled the handle so forcefully that the door continued to revolve all the way around on its hinges after he had let it go. It traveled farther and farther, until finally it collided heavily with the tiers of glass shelving where the hair-care products stood in their neat rows. The boy stood frozen in the open doorway, his pale face lit up, his hair as though standing on end, and

181

watched as the bank of shelves disgorged a landslide of bottles and jars which fell and rolled with a great thundering sound out across the salon floor, and then itself collapsed in a tremendous shrieking cascade of breaking glass.

There was a moment of silence in which everyone stood absolutely still, Dale with the phone in his hand, Sammy holding the boy's discarded cape, the mother with the book clasped in her fingers; even the *Glamour*-reading woman finally looked up from her magazine.

"Jesus fucking Christ," Sammy said.

The boy shot out through the doorway and disappeared into the wet, black street. For a few instants, his mother stayed where she was, in the glittering field of bottles and broken glass. She wore an expression of stony dignity. She stared at Sammy, her eyes unblinking. Then she picked up her bag, carefully put her book in it, and walked out after her son, leaving the door open behind her.

Nominated by The Paris Review,
Katherine Taylor

IT'S SOMETHING PEOPLE IN LOVE DO

by CHRISTOPHER CITRO

from SYCAMORE REVIEW

We were happy and wretched and cloudy
and setting fire to everything for warmth.
　　　　　Heather Christle, "Taxonomy of That November"

It's a late film, not one of their best, clogged
with a love interest that never really makes
your pants itch, but when the Marx Brothers
keep the train moving so the hero can make it
to town to record the deed and afford to marry
the girl of his dreams, they chop the whole
damn train up to feed the fire. Frightened
passengers in bustles and waistcoats watch
their seats axed from beneath them as women
cradle their children and men stand around
looking affronted. Then they hack up the walls
and the roofs, carrying armfuls of train forward
to turn into steam to keep things moving and
I'm not saying we should watch less old movies.
What I am saying is maybe everything's not
a metaphor for trying to pay the bills on time.
I love your credit score. It could pin my credit score
to the late summer soil and pee on its head.
My credit score would roll over and take it.
But what do you think of that chicken dinner
I made last night, how caramelized the thighs,
the bourbon from a plastic jug. How beautiful
that farmhouse looks passing by in the distance.

If we could get off this train we could go get it
and tear it to pieces with our teeth, tossing
hallways and lintels to the flames. Then we
could clean each other's face with our tongues.
It's called kissing. People in love do it

Nominated by Sycamore Review,
Tony Ardizzone, Lee Upton

ELEGY

fiction by **KEITH WOODRUFF**

from WIGLEAF

(R.W.W. June 4, 1998 – July 14, 1998)

Early morning. As he enters the chicken coop, the hens are quiet but for that low steady clucking. Calmly, the boy reaches into the first nest and gently takes the brown egg. He wants to get in and out without rousing the hens. Three eggs in his basket now. His chore each morning before school.

When he was younger, he thought the chickens beautiful. Noted their personalities. Named a few and even considered them pets. He feels nothing but contempt for them now, for the idiot flies that ping into his eyes and mouth, for the smell of chicken shit he carries onto the school bus. He reserves most of his hate for the rooster, though—just another tiny dictator too sure of his claim on the world. The rooster, who has entered the coop now and is watching the boy with its head lowered; the boy, who has one eye on the rooster and is now grabbing up the eggs more quickly as the hens cluck with growing alarm. Finally the rooster charges, a rush of red-orange feathers, and the boy kicks repeatedly at its head, feels the beak strike his shoe. *Fuck you*, the boy thinks, *I am taking your eggs you stupid fuck.* Like a boxer that won't stay down, the rooster comes at him again. This time, he kicks it so hard that feathers fly. It lies stunned in the straw for a moment before it's back, hopping up and down at the boy's feet and battering his legs with its wings.

Every morning they do this dance. The rooster is just doing his job. The boy gets that but feels they should have an understanding by now. That the rooster should back off and stop making his shit job of gathering eggs harder than it has to be.

He has gone for the eggs for so many mornings, he does it without thinking or seeing what he's doing. But this morning, he takes an egg that's still wet into his hand and it jars him, makes him pause and forget the rooster, though it will be years before as a father he remembers the moment, years before it truly breaks his heart.

Nominated by Wigleaf

TAUT RHYTHMIC SURFACES

by GEORGE SAUNDERS

from THE SOUTHAMPTON REVIEW

I didn't know James Salter well at all, personally. I only spent part of one day with him and Kay at the Hay Festival in Wales a few years ago. But I remember that day very fondly. It was such a thrill, really, to meet one of my writing heroes and find him everything that I had hoped he would be: sweet, funny, self- effacing, and generous.

But actually he had been a dear friend of mine for many years before that, and will continue to be a dear friend to me as long as I live through his prose. He did for me, and does for me, what any dear friend might do. He helps me sustain my sometimes faltering faith in an idea I base my life on: namely, that there is something sacred about working in prose; that purifying one's prose style is a form of spiritual dedication; that working with language is a beautiful and noble way to spend one's life. Every time I read his work I feel a kindred spirit there and am convinced all over again that the way we write a sentence can be every-thing: exploration, devotion, celebration. A person is never more him-self than when he's writing a sentence he'll later stand by. A mediocre stylist sounds like anyone else. The great stylist can be picked out in a few lines. Salter was one of those.

So what made his style so great? For me, the main quality of his style is its incredible surface tension. His paragraphs proceed so originally that they make the reader fear this originality will suddenly vanish. I remember once hearing a Fado singer in Lisbon whose voice and phrasing were so pure and so strange and she sang with such concentra-tion that you sort of feared for her. Could she keep that up? If not, what a letdown it was going to be. But she could keep it up and she did. And then she just stopped, leaving behind a stunned and transformed room. For me, Salter's prose is like that. It seems impossible that someone could be regarding the world with such an intense gaze, with such love-struck intelligence, making such a taut rhythmic surface, never uttering a single banal sentence, and you're a little afraid for him. Afraid that the prose will drop down into some more quotidian register or surrender something of its intensity because it sort of seems like it will have to. And then it doesn't. For whole books, it doesn't.

Although he's known as a realist, his sentences are often really strange. They appear at first to be straightforward, objective descriptions, but then they'll make some odd, Gogolian lunge you didn't expect, enacting some simultaneous world-expansion. For example, this, from his great story "Twenty Minutes:"

"Her father had lived in Ireland, where they rode into the dining room on Sunday morning and the host died, fallen on the bed in full attire."

At first, you're kind of like *what? Go back!* And then you're like, *Oh of course, that Ireland.* You hadn't known you knew about that Ireland and then suddenly from somewhere, you did. Later in the same story, he writes:

"Lights were appearing in parts of distant houses."

A simple sentence. A lesser writer's auto-seeking minimalism might have just said "lights were appearing in distant houses." But somehow, the addition of "parts of" makes it better. Better sonically, and also causes it to evoke better. Those distant houses, partly lighted, with lawns in front of them and people moving around inside appear in my mind more vividly than they would have if lights were appearing in distant houses. I don't know why. It's a tiny move, a small improvement, but that level of care enacted over the course of an entire work is, for me, the essence of James Salter's genius: the enacted certainty that such small improvements are not small at all, but are where the writer, in meaning more precisely, forces the story up to its own highest ground. The quality one feels reading his prose is that he was always choosing, that every breath of a story, every punctuation mark, every word, every juncture between sentences, had been carefully considered, reconsidered, reconsidered, and ultimately, grudgingly blessed. The goal of all this? To excise all banality. When banality is excised, what's left? Originality. Vitality. Curiosity. A feeling of real life on the page. Take this description of Dean's father from *A Sport and A Pastime*:

"He's wearing a blue batiste shirt that seems not to touch him anywhere, except at the neck and wrists which he is buttoning, a shirt that encircles him with an elegant slimness."

Now, there's no comma after "wrists," and for me somehow that causes the image to go cinematic and then beyond. Not only do I see that father, right in front of me in that beautiful shirt, but he is buttoning it, arrogantly buttoning it, that handsome, tan bastard, and I can smell his expensive cologne with which he is bullying me a little bit. I want to share one more bit with you and you should know that I wrote several hundred words explaining why this is so beautiful. But when I read my explanation after reading Salter's prose I felt like a terrible, inadequate pedant, so I'm just going to read it. A description of an outdoor meat market in Paris:

"Finally we emerge at the roaring iron galleries where meat is handled. It's like coming upon a factory in the darkness. The overhead lights are blazing. The smell of carnage is everywhere. The very metal reeks with an odor denser than flowers. On the sidewalk there are wheelbarrows of slaughtered heads. We stare down at the dumb victims. There are scores of them. The mouths are pink, the nostrils still moist. Warm knives with the edge of a razor have flensed them while their eyes were still fluttering, the huge, eloquent eyes of young calves. The bloody arms of the workers sketch quickly. Wherever they move, the skin magically parts, the warm insides pour out. Everything is swiftly divided."

There are certainly things to say about that. *Wow*, or *Holy shit*, *I quit*, or *Thank God that writer was among us*. But this is the lesson the true stylist teaches us: nothing we can say will improve our experience of that paragraph. Its beauties are many but they're irreducible. They have to do, yeah, with rhythm, with strategic omission, with the great sympathetic human heart being present behind the writing, all of that, yeah. But that's all post-game stuff. What makes that paragraph astonish is—about a million things, all happening at once. How did he do it? I have no idea. Great taste enacted with incredible discipline. A word-class ear refusing to be satisfied until it is truly satisfied. Or: extraordinary human being seeks magic, finds magic through tireless work.

My younger daughter has been reading David Foster Wallace recently and she reminded me the other day of a fundamental effect of reading a great stylist: his language takes over your head. Rereading James these last few weeks, the specific way he's taken over my head is this: I have grown vastly more fond of the things of the world. Doorways, food, sunlight, rivers, bodies, tablecloths, you name it. Accompanying this is a sense of how dangerous the beauty of the world is for us. How

189

our love for the world is what makes all this tragedy and comedy by calling up on us that fatal and essential thing: desire. Chekov said that art doesn't have to solve problems; it just has to formulate them correctly. The great problem that Salter formulated more correctly and beautifully than anyone is: given that the world is so gorgeous and we are dying within it, how should we live? We can't be in this world without having desire aroused. Once we start wanting and valuing and treasuring, the doom begins. Given the fact that, as the Stones said, we can't always get what we want, and if we do get it, we can't hold it. And even if we can hold it awhile, we can't hold it infinitely, and this is what the Buddhists call "samsari."

What James did so magnificently is make the case for desire, reminding us of how good it feels, how essential it is for us, how wonderful, how unavoidable, an inevitable and happy result of simply being alive— while at the same time reminding us that it's dangerous to desire. Or maybe, dangerous to simply desire, to believe that the satisfaction of desire is sufficient for a human being.

We can't live with desire and we can't live without it, we say.

Correct, says the Salter story.

This was a man, on the evidence of his prose, who found the world beautiful, believed that we make it more beautiful by interacting with it decisively, who believed that craft is more than just craft: it is a form of showing love for the world through attention and through care. It seemed he had a beautiful time here. I wish I could have known him better, but the essential Salter can still be known by all of us through those beautiful works of art that will continue to awe and instruct and inspire us for as long as people love the English language. His work will endure because it is full of a love for living that we crave to see modeled and be near.

From a speech at Old Souls Unitarian Church, New York City

Nominated by The Southampton Review

POEM IMPOSING ORDER

by KEITH RATZLAFF

from 1-70 REVIEW

The chestnut on the playground,
its pinkish flowers.
Three boys playing Hacky Sack.

And the fat guy with a basketball
imagines himself
lanky and light as a balloon—

which is a kind of perspective,
a way of being
able to dunk when you can't,

which is the oldest kind
of story,
the lie we tell ourselves.

So, today the game
is free throws
and the fat guy is hot.

What else could he be in this story?
Not a juggler
like the tree, not the boys

playing Hacky Sack who seem
equally miraculous.
And he shoots, imposing order

on the day. Each made shot
erases a scar,
some old humiliation—

which is a kind of forgiveness,
a way to tell
the story right the second time.

So draw the foul underneath,
shake it off,
square up, dribble twice,

say something for luck like
"Nijinsky."
Bend the knees—"Nijinsky"

because he likes the j as in
gigolo and juke,
the tough Slavic s-k-y.

Think rotation, think
follow through—
and his uncle's arm isn't mangled.

Follow through, think the ball
over the rim
and he's lost forty pounds—

no fifty—and he never insulted
the president's wife,
or betrayed his father,

then that day in Greece
never happened,
dogs pouring down the hillside,

then his brother isn't going blind,
then there's no shame
on his wife's face, no weeping.

Which is 10 in a row,
15, then 23,
then x which is his life,

the story when he gets home,
35 then 52,
and x is where has he been,

and so what if he's lying,
so what.
And x is shooting past dark,

until 75 and 85 and
95 in a row,
until the NBA scouts

disguised as two old men
pick up their hats
and go for a beer, until

x is the orange streetlights,
the multi-year contract,
the unfolding story where

I never go home,
And x means
there is no story,

no palimpsest,
just the world
retold, scraped clean.

Nominated by Andrea Hollander

BASIC TRAINING

fiction by MAHREEN SOHAIL

from A PUBLIC SPACE

Two months ago, our mother was admitted to the Noor Hospital for People Who Need Organs and New Teeth. My sister and I had just finished donating blood and were in the parking lot of the hospital, both of us sitting in our car with the doors open, taking great gulping breaths of fresh air to restore our energy. Around us, paramedics leaped out of screaming ambulances and tried stretching soldiers back to life. A young man in a blue kameez and a red sash leaned over a stretcher, his cheeks like small hard tumors in his face. He gently admonished the soldier, This is selfish, guy, pull yourself together, while his friend stood next to him taking quick, worried puffs from a joint.

A man walked up to us as we exhaled once and together, our heads between our knees. Sisters, he said, you look tired. We closed the doors against him and started to reverse out of there. When we were mid-way home we rolled down the windows and started talking about the special hatred we'd developed for little children. We agreed that they made us angrier than they'd ever made us before because now we saw them for what they really were (useless).

My sister and I determinedly refused to acknowledge the kids living on our street. They held balls, bats, dolls, chalk, twigs, badminton racquets, little clods of dirt, prams of younger siblings, the corners of their mothers' clothes, their own arms and legs (one or the other). They looked torn and used up, unspooling on the streets. Their parents orbited terraces above them, one eye on the children, the other on God knows what. Raheel Sb, next door, was a retired major and fancied himself a catcher of spies in these times of war. When he walked on his

194

terrace, he also kept his binoculars trained on the homeless uncle sitting cross-legged outside the general store. The store was famous for deep-frying its potato wedges and serving them up in oiled scraps of newspaper. When we drove back from the hospital that day, the sun was going down and the street we lived in smelled stale and salty, probably from the fries. Mosquitoes the size of our fists flew in the air and splattered themselves against our windshield. Raheel Sb pointed his binoculars at us once and then moved them away.

The man in the parking lot was back when we visited our mother in the hospital a week later. Our kameezes stuck to us because of the heat. I had just donated my hair; my sister had sacrificed a finger. There is a way for you to contribute to the war effort without giving of yourself quite so literally, he said, assuming that we were donating to the soldiers. Despite feeling out of sorts because of the sudden dearth of young men in the country, we ignored him. We recognized a line when we heard one. Driving home, we looked at how the women walking on the sides of the road clutched their clothes closer to their bodies in a way that was both extremely modest and very attractive to the boys growing up in the area (who had their pick now that their older brothers were dead or soon to be dead).

The third time we drove out to see our mother we could not stand it. We did not even go inside the hospital. Our hair lapped at our chins. While we were sitting there, the man came to our car window and asked us to come with him. The wind picked up and tunneled inside our car and tried getting into our eyes. The hospital's walls disappeared against our lashes. Perhaps two or four more people had died inside—hopefully and God Forbid though, not our mother. The man had a small moustache, so dark it almost looked blue, and small, bright brown eyes. He was wearing a white linen vest and a light black blazer. His name was Rafi and he needed us, he said. We are done being needed, we told him. It felt good to say it out loud. The hospital came back into focus. Not like that, he replied. You girls have egos!

We were so embarrassed by the immodesty of our thinking that we didn't say anything when he got into the back seat of our car. A man with such small hands cannot be harmful, we tried telling each other telepathically, with our backs straight against our seats and my sister's knuckles tight around the car's steering wheel. We were right; he didn't pull out guns and simply directed us around corners and down narrow alleys. Eventually we turned into a road far away from anywhere we had ever driven. One side of this road was lined by a high concrete wall that went on for quite a while. The other looked out into rows and rows of great oak trees. We parked before a small metallic gate which appeared to be the only entrance into the walled area. Rafi banged the inside of his palm flat against the metal and yelled, Oi!

We heard someone scratching behind the door. A head appeared over the top of the wall, a messy little boy, his face swollen and confused, as if he had just been beaten up, or asleep. He dropped out of sight again. We heard someone drawing back bolts.

The gate opened and we were led into a large field, grassy in patches. There were hundreds of little boys and girls inside. Large men wearing bright purple stood in the four corners of the walled area holding black rifles. The youngest of the children is three, Rafi told us proudly, the oldest is ten. Next to the gate was a raised wooden platform. Rafi also pointed out the large black speakers, one in each corner. Of course we had heard that they were picking up homeless children and training them for the cause in hideaways all over the country. But the children were not in Technicolor the way they had been in our heads. They were feral and dusty. The girls wore brown frocks that came down to their feet. The boys wore long brown robes.

Someone had taken a branch and gouged out lines in the grass so the field was divided into five identical looking squares. Each square holds forty children, Rafi said. In the distance, we saw a man in purple take aim and shoot a small girl who had been crying loudly. The air cracked and she fell to the ground like a mannequin. The children around her paused for a second and then backed away like performers in a circus, young and taut. They seemed full of rage as if directly feeding on the heat from the sun. One girl elbowed a gap-toothed little boy in the stomach. The toy grenade he had been playing with went flying. He lunged at her face with open hands until her lips started to bleed. My sister and I were only small-scale sinners. Like when the paramedics laid our mother out in the ambulance, and instead of feeling scared we were annoyed. When she screamed it was a long, shining sound that soared straight to the roof of our skulls.

Rafi climbed onto the wooden platform. The men in purple began to walk away. Rafi picked up a mega phone and spoke into it, his voice echoing around the field. He said, The ants are here—this directed at the children and accompanied by a short, flat wink at us. At first we thought we were the ants and glanced, insulted, down at our clothes as if we were late and poorly grown, but then we noticed that the roar of the children was directed at the re-entering men who were now holding big gray buckets as they walked back onto the field.

We start them off small, Rafi explained to us. Yesterday it was lady bugs followed by sedated squirrels. Today it's ants and kittens. We move on to the Human Enemy next week. The men grimaced as they pulled buckets in through the gate. The ants—fire ants, we noticed admirably—climbed over the handles of the buckets and bit their hands. The children ran to the men. They overturned the buckets and the ground crawled orange. It shook from so many small feet jumping in the air. Their stamping drummed into our heads like a song. We sweated with fear and heat. When all the ants were dead, the children continued scooping them into their hands. They tried to crush them into a fine red powder. It's protein, we heard one small boy woozily tell a girl who could only have been his sister. He had welts the size of boulders on his arms and legs.

We left for home when the children began to breathe normally again. We told Rafi we would be back tomorrow, perhaps in the evening. We are not ready yet, we said, implying, we later realized, that we would be ready soon.

At the hospital the next day our mother asked us about our lives and we told her about what we had seen. She laughed and called us her silly dolls. The secret made us feel happy and bloated, as if our insides finally matched our outsides. A nurse came in to help with the daily exercises. She lifted our mother's arms and legs carefully, one by one, as if she was a banana leaf and the hospital was inspecting her for holes.

Outside our mother's room, we noticed a little girl in the corridor. In our defense, she looked very bored. She must have been six. My sister bent down to her level and asked for her name and she told us it was Asya. We hadn't spoken to any children in months. We exchanged looks and asked Asya if she wanted to come with us for a ride while she waited, and she said yes, very shyly, her thumb and forefinger playing with a blue bead. In the parking lot, she squinted against the late evening sun and in the car she put her head out of the back window while we drove. Her hair fluttered against her face and she screamed into the wind to tell us that her brother had been sick forever. We felt very bad for her and almost turned back. But children are shaped by the shape of their country. In the long term, we consoled ourselves, we weren't really doing any harm.

Asya was frightened and unsmiling by the time we led her into the ground. Someone had turned the stadium lights on. Rafi's smile was too huge, his teeth like cracked white bones in his mouth. He held out his hand to the little girl, and she took it. We noticed she kept the hand with the beads clutched into a fist.

She began to cry when Rafi urged her—nicely, to his credit—to join the children in the center square. We begged him to wait for just a little while. He seemed resigned as he nodded. The sooner the better he warned, and we agreed in principle. We led Asya to the center block and sat with her on the grass, asked her to show us her beads, though she did not. The children were busy with a kitten activity. The men in the field kept re-entering through the metal gate holding pink, furless bodies that looked like rats. A four year old grabbed at one of the small animals a man set by her feet and held it up to her face. Its small paws wound in the air and it let out short, sharp cries. The girl scrunched up her face in concentration and tightened her grip around the kitten's neck. Rafi's moustache hair waving in apology. Some children found pieces of rope left over from previous exercises and fashioned nooses. One boy with a dark mole at the place where his eyebrow ended crushed a kitten with his foot so it lay splashed against the grass like a dark red clot. They continued like this until the sound of crying faded from the air.

We sat with Asya while all of this was happening until someone cut off the area's electricity and the field plunged into darkness. One of the men started a small fire in our square and some of the children wrapped themselves around its edges. A few children, who were farther away, edged closer to the fire. We saw a boy look both ways and cross the line that led from his block into ours before he was shot by a purple man.

Asya was the only one wearing a yellow dress, and the other children looked at her, ravenous. One little boy tried to rip it off so we punched him in his face. She began to cry again, and we got a little tired of her. Look, we said, trying to get her to smile. We hopped on one leg and then another, waved our hands around her face, stuck our fingers in our mouths and pulled them into wide grins. Some of the other children copied us. Mosquitoes hummed in the air and we heard planes approaching in the distance. The heat from the fire burned into our skin.

Panicking, we did the dance our mother had taught us when we were children. We spun as gracefully as we could. The children began to form lines behind us, straining their eyes to see, stumbling and laughing as they tried to keep up in the dark. Rafi watched from what seemed like far away, perhaps too tired to move closer, perhaps too slow to realize what was happening. Asya stopped crying and used her nails to dig out a small hole in the ground. She put her beads in it carefully before standing to join us. The night smelled like jasmine and grass. I should not have to string these scenes up in front of you like this to help you understand that the word *loss* has a weight that cannot be borne. We saw two children begin to kiss each other like adults by the fire and strained to ignore our hearts, finally beginning to beat, large and fearful, in our mouths.

Nominated by Asako Serizawa

GOOD HAIR

by SAFIYA SINCLAIR

from NEW ENGLAND REVIEW

> *Only God, my dear,*
> *Could love you for yourself alone*
> *And not your yellow hair.*
> > —W. B. Yeats, "For Anne Gregory"

Sister, there was nothing left for us.
Down here, this cast-off hour, we listened
but heard no voices in the shells. No beauty.

Our lives already tangled in the violence of our hair,
we learned to feel unwanted in the sea's blue gaze,
knowing even the blond lichen was considered lovely.

Not us, who combed and tamed ourselves at dawn,
cursing every brute animal in its windy mane—
God forbid all that good hair being grown to waste.

Barber, I can say a true thing or I can say nothing;
meet you in the canerows with my crooked English,
coins with strange faces stamped deep inside my palm,

ask to be remodeled with castaway hair, or dragged
by my scalp through your hot comb. The mirror takes
and the mirror takes. I've waded there and waited in vanity;

paid the toll to watch my wayward roots foam white,
drugstore formaldehyde burning through my skin.
For good hair I'd do anything. Pay the price of dignity,

send virgins in India to daily harvest; their miles
of glittering hair sold for thousands in the street.
Still we come to them yearly with our copper coins,

whole nights spent on our knees, our prayers whispered
ear to ear, hoping to wake with soft unfurling curls,
black waves parting strands of honey.

But how were we to know our poverty?
That our mother's good genes would only come to weeds,
that I would squander all her mulatta luck.

This nigger-hair my biggest malady.
So thick it holds a pencil up.

Nominated by New England Review,
Jaquira Díaz, Asako Serizawa, Shelley Wong

THE FUTURE CONSEQUENCES OF PRESENT ACTIONS

fiction by ALLEGRA HYDE

from THE GETTYSBURG REVIEW

When a boy wakes, he must not make a sound. He must kneel beside his bed in silent prayer, like the others in the room, and feel the weight of two minutes. He must feel joy too. And gratitude. If such sensations do not arise, a boy must report this to his Caretaker. A boy must strip his bed. He must fold his bedclothes lengthwise and lay them flat across two chairs, a pillow on each seat. A boy must dress in trousers, a frock, a vest. The frock must be fashioned from coarse cotton and must be blue or white, never an extravagant color, especially not red. A boy must comb his hair. Clean his teeth. A boy must not spit on the floor, however, as this is a vulgar act. All spitting should be directed toward the spit box. A boy must take his turn carrying the slops from the sleeping quarters out into a morning still dark and trembling with the groans of milk-heavy cows. A boy must not spill. If a spill occurs, a boy must not make vulgar pronouncements. Vulgar pronouncements include "hang it" and "plague on it." A boy must report all such phrases to his Caretaker. He must change into clean trousers, a clean frock and vest. The essentiality of cleanliness cannot be overstated. A boy must hurry to breakfast, for punctuality is likewise indispensable. At breakfast, he must kneel again in silence. Two minutes. A boy must eat with the other boys. His table must be one in a long row of tables, set with bone-white crockery, the dishes grouped by four to reduce the need for passing. A boy must first eat what appeals to him least—the thick porridge—and then proceed to tastier morsels—the apple slices—and he must completely clear his plate. A boy must remember the feeling of a stomach pitted hollow by hunger, fingers so cold they felt they would snap. A boy must sit still. He must not swivel his neck to search the faces of the others. He must not look for his father. If he finds himself doing so, he should report this to his Caretaker. A boy must be amenable. He must concede. He must not look for his father.

Charles Lane has always believed in the perfectibility of man. Always he has considered himself a voluntaryist, an abolitionist. He has abstained from meat, despite having butchers for brothers. An Englishman, aged a stately forty-six, he'd come to America because America—so hopeful and fertile and vast—seemed the place to start society anew.

This he tells the gray-eyed men in gray-blue shirts, the gray-eyed women in starched white dresses, who have gathered together to judge him.

"You are prepared," says a man rising gravely from his place on a bench in the assembly hall, "to sever all your worldly ties?"

Charles Lane believes himself prepared. Already, he feels at home among the Shakers, their well-pruned orchards, the pastures ringed by fence posts planted deep as spears. What restraint these people show! What prudent innovation! Just beyond the assembly hall stands a stone barn built in concentric circles for ventilating hay. Lodgings with windows installed at an angle to welcome in more light. Each room swept clean. Everywhere the smell of bread. Everyone well rested and solemn. These people do not proselytize, and yet their numbers swell even in the absence of progeniture. Merchants, midwives, students, sea captains, soldiers now among them. Methodists, Baptists, Presbyterians, Roman Catholics, Jews.

"You have no wife?"

Charles Lane sits pinned by the gaze of a gray-eyed woman, her face shadowed by a plain white bonnet. He clears his throat. He is not a man of the flesh, he tells her, though he uses many more words—words that wander back to England, Greavesian ideology, his staunch belief in abstinence—before returning to the present moment: the little son beside him, back erect against a wooden chair, feet dangling above the polished floor. William Lane. His father's greatest source of pride. His father's greatest source of shame.

"It is with the utmost conviction," says Charles Lane, addressing the whole assembly, "that I hold paternal love to have a deleterious effect on humanity's pursuit of spiritual ascension."

He trembles as he speaks. Two years already he has lived in America, years he squandered on a transcendental goose hunt, on a scrubby farm purchased with his assets, a communal catastrophe beset by freeloaders and halfwits, by a family—the Alcotts—who spoke of universal paradise yet could not see beyond themselves.

Fruitlands, they'd named the place. As if a ripe new Eden might have appeared in Massachusetts, born only of yearning.

"Beyond the narrow island of selfishness lies the continent of all-embracing love . . ."

Those were Bronson Alcott's words, in the commune's early days. The summer days when blackberries ornamented woodlands, and talk of Herodotus echoed through the gardens. The days when visitors came and spoke of staying. The days when such a geography still seemed reachable.

"But the winds are not always propitious, and steam is only a recent invention."

How quickly Bronson's homely wife, Abigail, had begun favoring her own children, giving them treats, little poems of encouragement. And all at the commune's expense. At his expense! Charles Lane would never act in such a manner; he would never undermine his son's chance to participate in ventures greater than himself.

"Brother?" says the gray-eyed woman.

It was the Alcotts' love for their own blood that spoiled the young utopia.

"Brother?" says the gray-eyed man.

Charles Lane gathers his thoughts, returns to the present moment: the assembly hall filled with unblinking faces, and beyond them—outside the polished windows—the lawns kept litterless even as maple trees shed their crimson autumn coats.

"I am prepared," says Charles Lane, "to take upon myself the cross."

The bonnets nod. The bearded give their chins a stroke.

"You have no debts?"

"Nay."

"You have no doubts?"

Charles Lane moves to sign the papers the gray-eyed men and women set before him. His eyes skim over "indentureship" and "William Lane" and "I will not take away the Said Children nor Control them." His mind has plunged ahead to a life unburdened by cupidity, the prejudices of family ties. A life restrained and orderly, conducted in the spirit of a Universal Family. His spine tingles with the final whisk

204

of the quill pen. He feels his past absolved: his future blooms. Thrumming with the buoyancy of the newly saved, he turns to clutch his son, kiss the boy's forehead, but little William is being led away.

When entering a house, a boy must uncover his head and hang his hat on a peg and wipe his boots on the foot scraper. He must shut the door gently behind him. If the door is slammed, a boy must step back outside, reenter, and close the door again. A boy must fear God. A boy must learn the teachings of Mother Ann, God rest her soul. He must learn that God is both a man and a woman and that Mother Ann, God rest her soul, was the second coming of Christ in female form. He must recognize the inherent equality of the sexes. That celibacy is the path to eternity. *Do all your work as if you had a thousand years to live.* Industriousness is revelatory. *And as if you knew you must die tomorrow.* A boy must welcome other boys: the boys, like him, from foreign shores, the colored boys and orphans, the broke farmhands. A boy must be willing to share in all things. He must have no private property. Private property includes a marred daguerreotype of one's mother, God rest her soul. *Private property puts the devil in you.*

"It would be wise, the construction of a preserve shop."

"Indeed, Brother, it would be wise."

"Such a bounty of apples this year."

"Such a bounty."

Elder Geary lets his body relax onto his cot. A clean white pillow welcomes his head, which is as bald and spotted as a farmyard egg. Around him, half a dozen Shaker Brethren have gathered to watch him die. The infirmary windows are open wide, despite the winter chill, to lesson his moribund stink. The Brethren are dry-eyed and thoughtful.

"I should like to see the children outfitted with new boots before winter," says Elder Geary.

"New boots before winter," echo the Brethren—except for one, who moves toward the window, pinching his nose.

For a moment, Elder Geary does not know the man: lean limbed, thin lipped, eyes as busy as mice. A stranger? An angel of death? Then he recalls the Englishman, joined some months ago, who had arrived with his single son.

"It would be wise . . ." Elder Geary falters on his words. He cannot help staring at the man—a Mr. Charles Lane, he now recalls—who had proven a satisfactory laborer, well behaved, but who had yet to bequeath the Shakers all his worldly goods.

He needed more time, Charles Lane had told them, to make arrangements.

A feeble excuse for a purported Believer.

"Brother?" The Brethren step a little closer, peer down into the old man's cot.

Charles Lane creeps closer as well, mouth breathing. "Such an exemplary soul," he says, his voice righteous and nasally. "He will be welcomed in the Kingdom of Heaven."

Elder Geary shudders. He feels the sweet drowsiness of death encroaching but cannot yet justify succumbing. What would Mother Ann think, witnessing her teachings so desecrated? Elder Geary had once followed the woman on her holy tour through Massachusetts—he'd heard her sing without words, heal without touch—and her principals of common property had galvanized his thumping heart. All Shakers, rich or poor, pooled their possessions so that all might aspire toward godliness. And yet this man, this Charles Lane—for all his voluble admiration of their Shaker customs—saw himself as an exception?

"Hear me!" Elder Geary sits bolt upright.

The attending Brethren step back from his cot in surprise.

"We have an unbeliever among us." Elder Geary lifts a shaking hand to point at Charles Lane.

The Englishman pales, but he offers the Brethren a creaky smile. "Elder Geary is delirious," he says. "The deathbed muddle, I fear. For I am as pious as—"

"We have a task before us." Elder Geary's voice rings far louder than it has in years, loud enough to escape the open window and to infuse the lightly falling snow. Throughout the village, fellow Shakers pause their daily chores. Drop brooms and wash buckets. Look toward the sky. "Our sacred order, our blessed order, must create two classes," says Elder Geary. He thinks again of Mother Ann, that blue-eyed woman so small in stature, yet limitless in spirit. "We have a task before us: we must separate the true believers from those who live their lives in sin."

With those words, Elder Geary falls back upon his cot, too weary to rise again. The room begins to darken. His senses fade. Yet even as Elder Geary drifts away, he hears the echo of his words:

". . . from those who live their lives in sin."

206

* * *

A boy must remember it is a privilege to be brought up among people of God, that beyond these grounds are the beggarly elements. The ravages of Babylon. To secure salvation, a boy must put his hands to work. His heart to God. He must learn to fashion brooms from bales of straw, and sieves from beechwood planks, and large oak casks to store molasses. He must learn to plant seeds. Pick apples. Dry sweet corn for winter. He must learn to drive a team of oxen, but he must not give an ox a human name, as this leads to wickedness. If a boy does give an ox a human name—Louisa perhaps—and kisses its snout and addresses it like a confidante, despite all instructions otherwise, he must discover that he will not be struck by rod or cane. He must discover, only, the disappointment of his fellow Shakers. Their heart-wrung sighs. Eyes cast to heaven, their prayers for his soul. He must remember his father's bidding. He must remember that this is what his father chose.

"You are in need of assistance?" The voice belongs to a woman, a schoolteacher, a Miss Sophia Foord. She bids her driver slow his horses, pause beside a man flagging them from the bank of a waterlogged road. Not far beyond she sees his coach in muddy disarray: axle splintered, reins tangled where the horses bolted free.

"My sincerest thank you," says the man—wide-eyed and effusive—as if rescued from the bowels of a beasty wilderness and not merely poor luck on an otherwise fine spring day. A reaction made even odder, thinks Miss Foord, by the looming bulk of a Shaker stone barn about a mile to the west. Walking distance, no doubt.

Normally, Miss Foord would avoid such stops, but the day is crisp and bright and vernal, sky-blue puddles jeweling the road, and she feels plucky, venturesome, and wild.

"Sincerely grateful," says the man again, even bowing slightly. "My coachman ran off." He points toward a ridge, nut-brown and raw from winter, the horse and human tracks braiding up its side. "I suspect—"

"Why, sir," interrupts Miss Foord, leaning from her coach window to study his face, "are you not an associate of that good man Bronson Alcott?"

Charles Lane sheds his grateful pretense. He looks at the sky, mutters, "I suppose you could say that."

Miss Foord is too excited to notice. "How propitious!" She claps her hands. Her driver coughs, loudly, but Miss Foord ignores him. "I heard your lecture in Boston—such wonderful ideas—the commune, what was it called? Berryfield? Fruitfarm? Fruitlands! I very nearly joined the whole endeavor!"

Charles Lane's scowl begins to melt. He stands a little straighter "Ah yes," he says, "Bronson and I were on our Penniless Pilgrimage. We—"

"But where are you headed?" She nods at the broken coach, its cabin shuttered by curtains. "The Alcotts have set up a lovely little cottage. I'm on my way to teach his daughters. You must come as well—with your son of course."

At "son," Charles Lane stiffens.

"Well that's settled then. You and your son will ride with me. There's plenty of room." Miss Foord says this brightly. If she has learned one thing as a woman, it is that sanguineness—when adequately applied— can prove a formidable force. She smiles at Charles Lane standing tense as a sapling beside the muddy road. Men and their pride, she thinks. She is not one to flirt, but today she feels a touch mischievous. Lowering her voice, so that the driver cannot hear, she says, "If there exists bad blood between you and the Shaker people, we will all understand. They are such dreary company."

Charles Lane rubs a hand through his thin hair. "It's not—"

"And if you're worried about your son's education, fear not!" Miss Foord blushes with excitement: her role in reuniting two distinguished men. "I'll be instructing the Alcott daughters in manifold subjects. Such savvy creatures—Louisa especially—and your son can join. Remind me, what is his name?"

Charles Lane stares at her blankly.

Miss Foord feels her excitement grow a little heavy. She looks again at the broken coach, then cocks her head. "Sir?"

"My son's name is William," says Charles Lane, avoiding her eyes.

Miss Foord nods. Her driver coughs again, rustles the horses' reins. "Well, go fetch him," she says. "And we'll be off."

If a boy leaves the house to attend school, or meals, or meetings, he must go with a Brother, and they must walk two abreast and synchronized, always starting with their right feet first. Neither may speak. They must move across the grounds like a cloud. A boy must not visit a Sister's quarters, except for errands—and then only for fifteen minutes. When speaking with Sisters, a boy must say "agreeable things about nothing." He must not, under any circumstances, bring up the

208

idea of departure. He must not bring up reasons why others have departed—others including his father—whom he must not consider his father but rather a man beset by sin. If a boy remains uncertain what to say, silence is best. During his allotted free time, a boy may roll trucks in the courtyard, but then he must only whisper.

Louisa May curls in the softness of a threadbare settee, a book held before her face like a parlor lady's fan. *Pilgrim's Progress.* Usually an engrossing read, but today Louisa May finds herself distracted by Mr. Lane—her parents' newest guest—ever pacing, pacing, back and forth across their cottage. Floorboards creak and squall. Around him: a flurry of bodies, speculation. The cottage, these past few days, has been especially cacophonous. Mr. Lane, Mr. Emerson, Mr. Thoreau, Miss Foord. They gather and talk. Come and go. Dust, stirred into the air like writhing apparitions, resettles on bookshelves already raucous with desiccated butterflies, wilting daisies, cobwebs, bits of ribbon. It's this clutter that often makes Mr. Lane scowl, and Miss Foord laugh, and allows the stealthy Mr. Emerson to "mislay" money for her ever-needy family.

"My son," says Mr. Lane, pausing his pacing to voice a coherent thought. "The Shakers won't return him. They won't even let me see him."

To Louisa May, this news is disappointing. She does not care for Mr. Lane. He is nothing like her much-adored Mr. Thoreau: almost a child himself, appreciative of the daisies she's started leaving on his doorstep. Mr. Lane has no interest in daisies. When they lived together at Fruitlands—his family and hers—she'd come to hate his chore charts and lessons on essential virtues (Obedience, Self-denial, Industry, Silence). But, at Fruitlands, Mr. Lane's son—William—had been her playmate.

Not that there had been much time for playing.

"I asked and asked to see my boy. I demanded." Mr. Lane half sits, half trips on a seesawing rocking chair. He steadies himself, rubs his hands across his cheeks, his skin as coarse as granite. Eyes cold as coal. "But those people, they just hold up the contract. Point to my signature. 'He's indentured,' they say."

Louisa May's mother offers Mr. Lane a lumpy pear.

Louisa May's father offers up recollections of old times: the summer nights spent philosophizing and singing and sharing at Fruitlands—leaving out the lesser bits: the calloused hands and arguments, the infirmities and empty bellies. The exodus.

"What else can I do?"

Mr. Lane chokes on his words, and Louisa May feels the heat of impending surrender: this man who once scorned her family for its bonds, now aching for his only son. From behind her book, she hears a sob escape his throat like the scraping grind of a millstone.

She waits for a sense of victory, but all she feels is sympathy.

She's never had a gift for grudges.

"Remind me," says Louisa May's mother in a manner that suggests she already knows, "why you couldn't stay among them, the Shakers. In your letters you made their way of life sound wonderful."

Mr. Lane throws up his hands. "They aren't serious enough," he says, though Louisa May has guessed, as her mother has guessed, that Mr. Lane—for all his talk of the comradeship and selflessness—could not fully commit his worldly goods to a collective cause.

Was it not the same at Fruitlands?

"You know," says Charles Lane, nearly squealing with disbelief, "the Shakers claim to be spiritually informed, and yet more than half will dine on meat!"

Louisa May wonders what has really left Mr. Lane so unsettled. His unreachable indentured son? Or that he could not enact his espoused ideals of a universal family?

"And their schooling, just outrageous—"

She is studying the man so closely that she fails to notice her mother come to stand beside her. A hand brushes Louisa May's hair, pats her shoulder.

"Perhaps," says Mrs. Alcott, "you could make the love argument." She glances at her husband, who has remained uncharacteristically quiet. Louisa May feels the grip on her shoulder tighten, the bruising press of her mother's unwavering affection. "As I see it, you can either leave William and return to England or you can go before the Shakers and declare the preeminence of paternal affection. That blood trumps all other bonds."

Charles Lane says nothing.

"You have tried that, haven't you? Expressing your love for your son?"

A boy must remember his lessons: That impartiality is more important than prosperity. Good manners eclipse intelligence. That a speck of dust might seem of little weight within the wider cosmos, just as a drop of water might be lost in the sea, but a barrel of dust, like a barrel of droplets, amounts to something more. The earth is composed of dust and droplets. Indeed, every atom of our universe adds up to something greater, just as every gesture a man makes amounts to his character. From *The Future Consequences of Present Actions*, the Shaker school-house guide: "A second is a short space of time, but without it there are no centuries."

Aboard the *Shenandoah*, a packet ship bound for Liverpool, the chief mate makes his evening rounds. The air is whip sharp. The sea, purple-dark and fidgeting. Most passengers have retired below for their evening meals, though a solitary figure persists on the upper deck, staring west. A man as immobile as a foremast.

"Cold aren't ye?" says the chief mate, approaching. He chuckles, eyeing the man's thin linen shirt, wet with sea spray and nearly translucent. "Wouldn't want to catch yer death, would ye, before we make our landing?"

The man, though visibly shivering, whirls around and sneers at the astonished sailor. "Weather," he says, with pious authority, "cannot assault the human soul."

Then he turns again to the horizon, as straight and thin as a pair of pursed lips.

A boy must think of the good times: the summer picnics, the nutting and the berrying, the swimming and the skating, the barn raisings and chopping frolics, the corn roasts. A boy must think of now and no other time. He must lie straight in his bed and strive to sleep in a manner that is unbroken and without dreams. If a boy has dreams, he must report them to his Caretaker. When entering the room to speak to his Care-taker, a boy must bow three times, kneel, then confess his every crooked step. Each wayward thought. He must then proceed to the meeting-house for worship, taking care not to gaze out upon surrounding fields, grasses feathery in the dusk, or the sky, stacked with clouds like the surf of a purpling sea. He must not wonder. He must not yearn. A boy must enter the meetinghouse and form two lines with the other children. His hands must be folded with the thumb and forefinger of the right hand covering the left. He must not laugh. He must not glare. He must sing low. When the time comes to dance, a boy must not scuff his feet. He must step with the right foot first, and he must step carefully so as to avoid the shoes of those in front of him. He must not rub against the wall or drift out of line. He must feel ecstatic but not too ecstatic. He must stop when the song stops and file out into night without speaking. A boy must have his evening chores complete before dark. He must never make a fire in a stove without supervision. There must be no wood piled near the stove nor the spit box set beneath the stove. The stove must always be shut tight before all leave the room. A boy must return to his sleeping quarters by nine. If a door is locked, a boy must not go on rattling and knocking. It is not meant to be opened.

Nominated by Melissa Pritchard

WHEN I THINK OF TAMIR RICE WHILE DRIVING

by REGINALD DWAYNE BETTS

from POETRY

in the backseat of my car are my own sons,
still not yet Tamir's age, already having heard
me warn them against playing with toy pistols,
though my rhetoric is always about what I don't
like, not what I fear, because sometimes
I think of Tamir Rice & shed tears, the weeping
all another insignificance, all another way to avoid
saying what should be said: the Second Amendment
is a ruthless one, the pomp & constitutional circumstance
that says my arms should be heavy with the weight
of a pistol when forced to confront death like
this: a child, a hidden toy gun, an officer that fires
before his heart beats twice. My two young sons play
in the backseat while the video of Tamir dying
plays in my head, & for everything I do know, the thing
I don't say is that this should not be the brick and mortar
of poetry, the moment when a black father drives
his black sons to school & the thing in the air is the death
of a black boy that the father cannot mention,
because to mention the death is to invite discussion
of taboo: if you touch my sons the crimson
that touches the concrete must belong, at some point,
to you, the police officer who justifies the echo
of the fired pistol; taboo: the thing that says that justice
is a killer's body mangled and disrupted by bullets

213

because his mind would not accept the narrative
of your child's dignity, of his right to life, of his humanity,
and the crystalline brilliance you saw when your
　　boys first breathed;
the narrative must invite more than the children bleeding
on crisp fall days; & this is why I hate it all, the people around me,
the black people who march, the white people who cheer,
the other brown people, Latinos & Asians & all the colors
　　of humanity
that we erase in this American dance around death, as we
are not permitted to articulate the reasons we might yearn
to see a man die; there is so much that has to disappear
for my mind not to abandon sanity: Tamir for instance, everything
about him, even as his face, really and truly reminds me
of my own, in the last photo I took before heading off
to a cell, disappears, and all I have stomach for is blood,
and there is a part of me that wishes that it would go away,
the memories, & that I could abandon all talk of making it right
& justice. But my mind is no sieve & sanity is no elixir &
　　I am bound
to be haunted by the strength that lets Tamir's father,
mother, kinfolk resist the temptation to turn everything
they see into a grave & make home the series of cells
that so many of my brothers already call their tomb.

Nominated by Poetry, Maxine Scates, Carolyne Wright

THE DREAMS OF KINGS

fiction by SUJATA SHEKAR

from EPOCH

Our morning begins like every other, with the shrill of the clock, the hiss of the pressure cooker in the kitchen, the rattle of pipes signaling the release of water for the regulation hour. We brush, bathe, comb our hair, tie our shoelaces, all with an economy of motion born from the need to maneuver in single-roomed homes, to step over our children still sleeping on the floor. We fume incense before our deities of choice and remember to take our lunchboxes from our wives before leaving.

Some of us walk to the train station. Others take a bus or auto-rickshaw, or a share-cab if we can afford it. We sniff the muggy air, which by late June in Mumbai feels like snorting jelly. Our collars go limp. Sweat coronas our armpits in quick semi-circles. We ignore our watches, let our phones vibrate, feel our cigarette packs grow heavy in our pockets. We stride, pause, turn, climb, our steps programmed to the arrival of the train at our respective stations on the Central Line.

The Kalyan—CST 7:14 A.M. Fast is our common ride. Those of us boarding at the starting point scramble for seats as the coach winds in, squeezing five to a bench that is meant to fit three. We gulp tea direct from thermoses and scarf down buns stuffed with potato fritters in the six minutes until the next stop, Dombivli. For here our number multiplies, already eighty or so in a coach that can hold two hundred but will soon stuff in close to twice that. We sidle between knees and pile onto laps, men on men, why not, for only the most gutter-minded commuter would mistake it for anything other than a desire to rest our feet for the hour or so of journey remaining. Radios turn on, a high-pitched voice analyzing prospects for the Twenty20 cricket match scheduled for that evening. A phone trills a Bollywood song, a bass-heavy number featuring the latest Eastern European wench in minimal clothes and agile hips, whose video clip has been looping on the local television channels through the past week. Not that we can see her, only hear her lip-synced breathlessness, but we shift in our seats, or laps, and hastily hit mute. A game of cards is suggested, rummy with two packs; the accountant among us keeps score.

Eleven minutes, and the platform of Thane station curves into view. The crowd hangs off the concrete edge, leaning in instead of back, arms outstretched to swing onto the train before it slows. Our bodies compress, our limbs smash against our trunks, our noses plunge deep into the napes, the shoulders, the middle of our neighbors' backs, breathe slow, breathe shallow, breathe not at all. The game of cards dies, the swivel of elbow, of lifting and dealing and showing, takes too much room. We chant a hymn, a paean to Krishna, yodeling inches from unbelievers' ears. Some of us nap standing, our bodies limp but aware, improvised meditation. We peruse ads, long memorized, stuck to the walls of the coach—tutorials for engineering entrance exams, call girl Dolly's telephone numbers, guru-led lessons for tantric poses, Stay-On Heavy-Duty condoms in raspberry and peach.

Thane to Mulund, the next station, takes three minutes on an average day. It is around now that time slows, and we, the daily commuters of the 7:14 A.M. Fast, ascend to a contemplative state. We retreat from our bodies, dim the feedback of our senses. We question our animal existence. We measure our inhalations as they grow short and observe from our new, elevated perspective how this messes with our brains and squeezes us formless, waiting. It is a vulnerable moment. And when the weather is like it is today, when the city itself outside the grilled and barred windows of the train seems to gasp with the heat, then the timing, as every B-grade flick and pirated novel and even the great mythological epics will have it, is ripe.

It matters little who catches the pickpocket first. Fingers the fingersmith, as it were. That adept practitioner of a classical art, the nail on his thumb shaved long and sharp to allow for a better grip, the half razor blade tucked up his cuff, the folded newspaper obscuring his face, and beneath that a set of nondescript features, just like ours. But we feel the difference between flesh on flesh and a lighter brush, stasis versus movement, forbearance versus purpose, and we pounce down

216

upon our own sides, our pockets, the front pockets, because the back holds nothing of consequence unless we are complete patsies and deserve to be stripped clean.

We grab the invading fingers, which twist as if on robotic wrists and slip from our grasp. Too late, too late, but wait, quick, here they are again, caught for good this time, definitely the same. How do we know? That thumbnail! We wrench. A cry of pain, louder than the wrench warrants. We move our grip from wrist to forearm to skinny collarbone, give vent to our own outrage. Where is it? The wallet, the cash bound with sacred thread, the blank check, the wedding ring, the sachet of stones on its way to being cut into garnets? We search his pockets, hands from every direction, too easy, too stupid. Too empty to be trusted. Rip the seams of his shirt, his fraying trousers, his faded vest, even his sagging underpants. Shred the soles of his sandals. Empty, empty, *empty*.

Mulund station arrives and leaves after the requisite one minute pause, fresh hordes of us clinging to the open sides of the coach with our fingertips, our weight held in place through some cosmic force of which we are unaware and therefore ungrateful, like creatures of a spinning earth. The next stop, Ghatkopar, is eleven minutes away. We recommence searching. We crank the pickpocket's jaws wide, thrust our index fingers between cheek and lower gum. Find another blade tucked in that abominable crevice at the cost of a bleeding finger, proof if we needed any, that we had the right man. But the cash is gone. It is not in the folds of his ears, or the crack of his ass, or the part of his hair, or in the web between his pungent toes.

An accomplice, naturally. There must have been. Maybe more than one, the loot slipped from hand to hand to hand in seconds, well before our initial pounce. Perhaps that compatriot was even now strolling down the footbridge of Mulund station, beyond our reach. The moment we realize this, we know it to be true. Acid leaps to our throats. Our eyes blush. Our palms itch and flex and curl. The train rocks as it gathers speed, as it always does on this midway stretch. We brace ourselves as if there were room to fall. Then we land the first blow.

Close quarters, there is less satisfaction. Hard enough impact, the whump of knuckles against tender cheek, but the spring-loaded action of swinging from the shoulder is quite another high. The force of the body resides in the wraparound muscle of the core. Ask any boxer. Ask us. We take a small, impossible step back. Create a ring of room, an amphitheater of justice. Unbutton our cuffs, roll them past our elbows, sling

217

our ties over our shoulders, position our glasses well up our nose. Shove our briefcases and doubts onto the luggage rack, where they are safe from errant punches and offered an undeniable view.

We take turns like our parents once taught us at the playground, ranging our assaults over the pickpocket's torso, parceling it out into manageable pieces, here, you take the neck up, you the shoulders and back, you the ribs, the heaving belly, the quivering buttocks, the flopping thighs, the soles of the feet that thrum on the steel floor of the train in a hypnotic rhythm, distinct from the clatter of wheels on track, and the hiss of the brakes as the train pulls into Kurla station; when did Ghatkopar come and go?

He curls like a shrimp, shielding his eunuch parts. Not fair, we cry! Let us skin your scrotum, let us deseed your Adam's apple, let us aim our instep, Messi style, at your delectable shins. We improvise. We scrunch up on the handlebars and slam down with our heels. We pry open his fingers and bend them back one by one, until they snap like the tips of the freshest and most succulent okra. We tattoo violet welts on his arms and do our best to make them even, symmetrical. Our momentum builds. The handlebars and floor grow greasy with blood; the pickpocket's nose is broken.

His spirit is not, as he tells us what to do with our mothers and our virginal sisters. He draws illogical cause-effect chains: you went to college, now work in big-big offices, fear God Allah Guru Christ Chistiwhatyouplease, how do you not know the meaning of mercy? I beg you, he bleats, and rolls with our blows like a tai-chi master. For seconds at a time, he goes quiet and soft, as if waiting in some interminable line, his jellyfished lips pursed into a smile. We redouble our kicks; our arms are tiring. We are unused to such exertion, us keyboard tappers, mouse pushers, ass lickers, clerks. Our knees emit ominous clicks.

Dadar station is the first where the train spits out more of us than it swallows. The scrum at the door to the coach thins, and before we can pause and recalibrate, prime ourselves for the post-interval show, the pickpocket leaps to his slippery feet and flings himself onto the platform and down the opposite tracks and off into the tin and tarpaulin shanties lining the station's sides. We yelp, we roar, we curse, we throw a shoe, but we cannot follow, we cannot leave our pulsing womb, and as the train moves on and we realize our man has made his escape, we utter a reluctant cheer. That last glimpse of him running for his life, the flash of his nude brown limbs, the daubs of red, the flaps of unnatural pink, ah, we wish we could paint, or at least take a photograph, frame

218

it in our wallets forever. What a joke that would make, a raised middle finger with a sharpened nail, to any prospective thief.

Byculla approaches, the penultimate stop. We smooth our hair, suck the bruises on our knuckles, mourn our footwear that now needs urgent re-soling. We meet each other's eyes, allow for modest smiles, stand with our legs braced wider apart than necessary. As the 7:14 A.M. Fast rolls to its final stop, Mumbai Victoria Terminus, that queen to our hive, that muse to our pension plans, we take our time dismounting.

We will pull through the day with unaccustomed verve, contradict our bosses on a minor but suddenly crucial point, treat ourselves to a mango softie ice cream and dig our tongue into the bottom of the cone like a child. We will ride the usual evening trains, and whistle as we walk to our homes. After dinner, we will fuck our wives with a vigor that will leave them sore and waddling. And once we have set our clocks to wake us the following morning, and the morning after that, and the next, and the next, and the nextnextnext, as long as our destinies let us, we will slip into the dreams of kings.

Nominated by Epoch, Liz Ziemska

MENTOR

fiction by MARK JUDE POIRIER

from CRAZYHORSE

When you meet him in 1980, he's eleven years old with a dusting of freckles and a choppy haircut that looks as if his mother did it at the kitchen table. Ears too big for his head. Cute, though, with dimples and a shy smile. He has seven siblings, but he's the only one of them here at Bellerive Country Day. You know he's gay by the way he nervously averts his eyes whenever you look at him. His voice is slightly girlish, too, but you can hear him fighting it, clipping his syllables and straining to speak from his chest. He's smart. You've seen his entrance exam. You're the assistant headmaster, in charge of admissions at this tony little school in the corner of Baton Rouge. His father taught at MIT before he moved his family down here last spring. With all those kids, a few of them babies, they don't have time for him. How could they? And they're Catholics. What would they do with a gay son? Shame him to suicide, that's what.

At first, you're careful about singling him out. He's always with Andy and Tim, anyway. The sixth-grade alpha males. You could address all three of them now, ask how it's going as they walk across the rich, green lawns between classes, playfully shoving each other, roughhousing in a way that doesn't initially make sense given his soft manners, until you consider that he has four brothers. Instead, you sneak up behind them, hear their conversation—video game prowess, an ugly girl named Rachel— and grab the back of his neck. Harder than you should, but not so hard that it bruises. He's startled but he's deferential. He understands that he's on scholarship and he's lucky to be here. You can imagine his time at Capitol Elementary, the public school he attended when his family first arrived: grouchy teachers, unruly kids with thick accents, crowded classes. He had likely never seen grits or po'boys, and probably skipped lunch, spending the lonely hour in a large cement pipe—a sad excuse for playground equipment—hiding from the heavy sun and reading Judy Blume paperbacks.

He holds up his end of the financial aid bargain. He's elected to student council and makes A's in everything except Spanish, which is taught by a humorless Cuban-American woman, whom you hate. She assigns him a B+, and writes in his narrative evaluation that he "has problems con-jugating verbs in the imperfect tense." If she keeps this up, you will make sure her contract isn't renewed. You're serious.

You call him into your office to discuss his grades. He's nervous as you guide him, gripping his sweaty neck. He's wearing a ball cap with velour wings sewn on its sides. A popular history teacher wears one with devil horns, and he started a trend among the students. You find the hats absurd. You ask him to remove it. It's what one does when entering a building, and especially before a meeting. You try to put him at ease by congratulating him for making the high honor roll. Only three of the twelve sixth graders did so. Now he's embarrassed. He doesn't likely hear many compliments at home. He's wearing light-blue corduroy surfer shorts. His legs are brown from the sun, and newly sprouted hairs curl over his drooping tube socks. His canvas Nikes are grubby and there's a small hole in the toe of his right one. He catches you looking at them. You watch his face as he tries to summon some dignity. He fails. On his way out, you squeeze his neck and tell him to keep up the good work.

For the next two years, you witness his puberty. He grows eight inches but doesn't seem to gain any weight. He's in the study hall you monitor, so you're with him every seventh period. He has begun to be more label-conscious and wears Ralph Lauren and Lacoste shirts. The colors are off, though, like he bought them on sale. A purple Oxford. A long-sleeved polo the color of margarine. You're familiar with all five of his

221

shirts and you notice how he rotates them. His hair is too long and still smacks of a home-cut, but at least he has stopped sporting those ridiculous winged and horned caps.

He wears pleated tennis shorts one day. His legs look so thin that you ask, "Are you eating enough?" His face flushes red as he mutters, "Yes." He's jerking off on average twice per day, you guess. You envision him kneeled in front of the toilet, his brother's *Sports Illustrated* opened to a Jockey underwear ad. But you know the men in the photos he studies while he masturbates are nothing like you. Their muscles are defined. And they aren't teachers in boring, humid, rednecky Baton Rouge. They don't bother him. They don't seek him out. They never grab his neck. They are not faggots, who spend their Sundays sunbathing and cruising the fruit loop in Capitol Park. "You must be losing a lot of protein," you say. You smirk when you say it, even raise an insinuating eyebrow, and his face melts before he opens his copy of *A Separate Peace*. He knows what you've implied. This makes you hard, but you're safely seated behind the desk.

You imagine driving him in your Fiat to the barber downtown on 3rd Street, getting him a proper haircut, and then ushering him to Burkman's, where you buy him several shirts in decent colors and patterns. You might encourage him to lift weights in the gym and put some meat on his bones. You'd spot him on the bench press, enter the showers with him afterward, horse around a little, permit yourself to slap his ass.

The summer before his ninth grade, Sara Blankenship, his academic advisor and math teacher, leaves Country Day and moves to Colorado. This means he will need an advisor in September. You decide to make yourself his advisor. You can do that; you're the assistant headmaster. You ignore the disappointment and fear on his face when you tell him in the fall, and instead focus on the fact that he gained some weight over the summer, that he's filling out. There's a smudge of a moustache pushing through his upper lip. He'll have to shave soon. When you ask him what he did over the summer, he tells you he got a job at Baskin Robbins and complains about the brown polyester pants he has to wear. "That's right. You're a bit of a dandy," you say. He looks away. You've essentially accused him of being gay, which was your intention.

Now that he's a freshman, his grades count for college admissions. You know he speaks fondly of Massachusetts, so when you spot him reading in the shade of a tulip tree by the science building, you say, "Hey, young scholar, how about we get you into Harvard?" You see something in his eyes, a gleam of interest and hope. You can't help but imagine him in Cambridge at eighteen, meeting other gay boys, and falling in love. You muse that after he has a few experiences, he'll return to Baton Rouge at Christmas break and knock on your door late at night with a bottle of wine.

He's ambitious and he takes both Spanish and French. He's in Accelerated Algebra. Six academic courses. You keep track of his grades, and when you hear from Mr. Marsden that he scored a B- on a history quiz, you hurry over to the art room, where you find him glazing a pot, and you tell him you need to see him in your office. Now. His friends Carl and Fred laugh. They know you're overly fond of him. But they don't matter.

He wears L.L. Bean hunting boots, even though the rain stopped last night and it's in the seventies and sunny. His job scooping ice cream affords him nicer clothes and decent haircuts, and he affects a New England prep school look with some success. You tell him you like his clover green trousers, that you have very similar ones. He doesn't respond. You grab the back of his neck like you do normally, only this time, you squeeze a little harder. You tell him to loosen up, that he's not in trouble, but by the time you reach your office, he hasn't uttered more than a few words.

You show him glossy college pamphlets and point out the photos of shirtless young men playing Frisbee on lawns spread before Neo-Gothic buildings. He pretends not to be interested. He crosses his arms tightly. He shakes his leg. Sweat beads on his upper lip—which he finally shaved. You convince yourself that you're helping him, but you allow your erection to form as you watch him squirm. You tell him he can finally be himself when he goes away to college. He acts as if he doesn't understand. But he knows exactly what you're implying. You're not subtle.

In late April, the students may request new advisors when they fill out their course selection cards for next year. He chooses Bob Bender, his math teacher. When you see this, it's as if someone has kicked you in the stomach. You nearly vomit and you have to step outside and feel the intense sun, which calms you until you look once more at his bubbly, effeminate handwriting: *Because Mr. Bender is my teacher and Mr. Roth isn't.* How could he do this to you? You've been an excellent advisor—caring attentive, thoughtful. You're not flamboyant or silly; you're an educator and an administrator. You believe you're rather handsome.

223

Objectively, you're not fat. You look younger than your thirty-seven years. And you're a nice guy. You have a wonderful sense of humor. What's his problem? You should have been so lucky to have a mentor like you.

A few minutes later, through your window you see him walking and laughing with Marina Gaudette, a sophomore. The two of them write for the student newspaper. You'd like to march out there, tell Marina you need to speak with him privately, pin him to the giant Cow Oak's trunk, force him to explain why he no longer wants you to be his advisor. "Be specific!" you'd demand. "Say it!" But you don't have to step outside again; he's heading for the office.

You find him in the small Xeroxing room, duplicating articles for the newspaper. You watch him for a moment. His posture is horrible. If he'd just pull back his shoulders like you've told him a hundred times. When he looks up, you see the fear on his face. His eyes widen. "Hi," he says, turning away, pretending to focus on aligning the document with the edge of the copier glass. You begin to cry. You can't help it. He stiffens when he notices your tears. You say, "How could you?" He says, "What?" You glare at him. Tears course down your face and drip from your jaw. You sniff. "I've been the best advisor you've ever had and the best advisor you will ever have." That's it. That's all you can say with your cracking voice. You leave him cowering, the white light from the copier wiping across his face. You're the college counselor, and he knows he screwed up. To hell with him. He can go to LSU with the dregs from his class. He won't attend college anywhere near Harvard.

You hurry into your office and slam the door loudly enough so he can hear. He must feel terribly guilty. Your hands tremble as you close the blinds, and unlatch your belt. Minutes later, as you wipe up the Saltillo tiled floor with tissues, you cry again.

He is one of three sophomores who tested into Pre-Calc, and because he's taking two foreign languages, this means the only English courses that fit in his schedule are Composition and AP British Literature. You teach AP British Literature. It's normally a class for seniors. You pride yourself on it being tough. You justify putting him in it because there are already sixteen students in Composition, which is for dumb kids and stoners. He's in your course. He won't know 'til the first day of school. You're his teacher now.

His work is mediocre. While most of the others in the class are se-
niors bound for the nation's best colleges, and he's only a sophomore,
he should be doing better. His essays are weak, with unsubstantiated
and undeveloped claims. He rarely contributes to class discussions. You
often have to tell him to stop talking to Trish, who sits next to him. They
gab and giggle in a way that almost seems like genuine flirting. You can
sense that he hates your class. At home, you're certain, he curses you
as he slogs through *Beowulf* or Marlowe or Wordsworth, turning the
flimsy pages of *The Norton Anthology* you forced him to buy.

He earns a C+ that first semester. You hesitate before you type it into
his grade report. You know his parents will come down hard on him. But
his mother's on your side. She has been since you first offered the schol-
arship almost five years ago. Even if he does break down when she asks
him about the low grade, the lowest he's ever received, and tells her that
you like him too much, that you harass him and that you fixed it so he'd
be in your class, his mother tells him he's being silly. She'd caution him
that he could lose his financial aid. "Be nicer to him," she'd say. "Being
nicer never hurts." Maybe he'll finally understand that you care for him
and his parents don't, not really.

For the first in-class assignment the following semester, he writes
about turning over a log in the woods behind his former house in sub-
urban Massachusetts to discover a tribe of red efts. In your signature
brown ink, you jot encouragingly in the margins. His essay is rich with
detail, meaningful, and seemingly heartfelt. He's trying. That C+ must
have shaken him. When you return the essays, you notice he smiles
when he sees he earned an A-, which is better than what Trish earned,
and she's a National Merit Scholar who recently gained acceptance to
Berkeley. You keep him after class to reinforce the praise you wrote on
his essay. He thanks you. You tell him he ought to put that much effort
into all of his essays. He says he has a biology test next period and he
has to go over his notes on the Krebs Cycle. Too specific. He's lying. He
wants to get away from you.

School's over for the day and you're walking to your car when a junior
named Caren or Cara asks if you've heard what happened. "He was
playing football and he bumped his head and he couldn't remember
what day it was or anything." You learn that he was standing at his
locker a few minutes later, examining his paperback copy of *Macbeth*,

unsure of what the play was about. He began to panic, and fortunately someone realized he was seriously hurt. He has amnesia, and his friend Eric is rushing him to the ER right now.

You call his house that night to check on him. One of his sisters answers. She tells you that he's still at the hospital and he has a concussion. They're keeping him there overnight. "Is he okay?" you ask. "I think so," the girl says, "but he's probably not going to school tomorrow." Of course not, you stupid bitch. You forget to ask which hospital, and you shouldn't call back or you'll seem as desperate as you feel. Now you can't visit him. You won't see him 'til Monday. Four days.

The autumn of his junior year, you receive his SAT score report. He did well. Well enough. Better than all twenty-two of his classmates—though, his is a weak class. Most are on drugs. You see him talking with his friends by the Coke machine and you hurry over. The look of annoyance on his face doesn't stop you from forging ahead. "What's up, lads?" you say. His friends hurry off. He doesn't. You praise him for his scores, and ask where he wants to go to college, but before he answers, you mention that you could have gone to Duke like your father and grandfather, but you wanted something different. You chose Reed College in Portland, Oregon. No one else from your school in Houston went there, which made it even more appealing. "I had a boyfriend within a month," you mention. "A poet from New Mexico." The strategically cavalier reference to your boyfriend makes him anxious. He looks around. He doesn't respond to your question. So you suggest he consider colleges far away, where no other students from County Day matriculate. "I have a year to think about it," he says, and the sixth-period bell rings.

You stay after school to watch him play tennis. His stance is wrong. His chest is constantly parallel to the net. He barely bends his knees. It's sadly evident that he's never had proper lessons. He's scrappy, though, and he beats his opponent from St. George's 6-2, 6-3. After the match, you walk over to the court to congratulate him and you seize his neck. It's sweaty. "Why do you always grab my neck like that?" he says as he ducks away from your grip. "Just a show of masculine camaraderie," you say. He rolls his eyes, and jogs off, and it becomes clear that he thinks you're a pathetic pervert. You flick a tiny green lizard from its perch on the net.

*　*　*

In March, the students choose from a long list of educational trips, each overseen by a faculty member and a few parents. You're leading a trip to Springer Mountain in Georgia, where the Appalachian Trail begins. Your group will hike and camp and study the "The American Literature of Nature: Emerson, Thoreau, Whitman, and Dickinson." You tell him about the trip, hope that he'll sign up for it, but he doesn't. Of course not. Instead, he and his buddies head down to New Orleans to presumably learn about jazz with Gene Babineux, a notoriously lenient physics teacher who will probably allow them to drink.

He may not be on your trip, but Michael, a sophomore, is. Michael has few friends at school and none of them is here on the trail, breathing the deliciously earthy air. Michael's plainly not interested in the poetry or prose you've assigned, but he hikes with gusto. You barely keep pace with him, and you ask him about school, about girls, about baseball and soccer. Michael's friendly. Michael answers in complete sentences and asks about you, about the sports you played in high school, about why you like literature, about your neighborhood, Spanish Town. Michael doesn't seem disappointed to share a tent with you, and he doesn't pull away when later that cool, damp night, you spit in your palm and reach over.

Michael remains silent when you spoon scrambled eggs into his tin camping pan the next morning. You hope Michael won't tell anyone. Michael won't. You're certain he won't, but last night was stupid, really stupid. You don't know Michael well enough. You barely noticed Michael before this trip. Michael may be very close to his parents. Michael could tell them. Michael might. You're gone, if he does. Maybe even arrested.

You'd normally attend every home baseball game, chat up the parents, but you don't—not with Michael at second base. During assembly one rainy morning, you catch Michael glaring hatred at you. You look away. A fifteen-year-old holds absolute power over you. That afternoon, you call your friend at Cimarron Academy in Oklahoma City. It's a nice little school with decent college placement. You tell him you need to teach there in the fall. You don't have to explain why you'll be leaving Country Day. He understands. He fucked up six years ago at a school in Connecticut.

You don't make an announcement to the students at this year's final assembly. They'll learn that you're gone in the fall. You're confident he'll eventually miss you; you've been an excellent teacher and a good friend, and he knows this down deep. But then you realize he will feel tremendous relief. He will not have to spend his senior year avoiding you.

A few years later, you call his mother, and she proudly tells you that he's at Dartmouth. You say, "That's wonderful." You're concerned. This is 1988 and Dartmouth is not hospitable to gays. You've read about their appalling student newspaper, how students were outed to their parents. What if he chose Dartmouth because of its conservative atmosphere, figuring he wouldn't be tempted? It's not your fault. You would have advised him against it. You decide to send him a genial note. You drive over to a shop for homo knickknacks in the 39th District and find the perfect postcard: a nude muscular young man holds an exploding champagne bottle in front of his crotch. You write how happy you are that he was able to go away to college. You ask him if he likes it, what he's studying. You ask if he has any other news. You leave your address and tell him to drop you a line, but you know that when he sees your brown ink scrawl his stomach will drop. He'll tear it up and toss it without reading it. He'll feel like you're gripping his neck again. The press of your palm and the clamp of your fingers will return with a sickening visceral immediacy.

He doesn't respond to your note, which is rude.

You have to leave Cimarron for the same reason you had to leave Country Day. You call a friend at The Driggs School in California, and soon, after a few interviews with the board members, you're the new headmaster there. You have a relationship with a twenty-five year-old fey Mexican you met at a gay bar in a strip mall in Riverside, but after a few months, you tire of him, his neediness, his poverty, the smell of sex. There are boys at the Driggs School, but none over the next several years is worth anything to you.

You're retired. You sport a blond mustache and you've abandoned Brooks Brothers blazers and bowties for loose-fitting drawstring pants and V-neck T-shirts. You wear comfortable clogs. You've returned to Baton Rouge and live again in Spanish Town, where you lived years ago, a block away from your former house, in a bigger bungalow that you bought for a song. Built in 1932. Hardwood throughout, except the kitchen, whose floor is poured cement. You love the sun. You love the food. You love running into former Country Day students. For the local arts paper, you write thoughtful and intelligent film and book reviews—a bit more sophisticated than this city is accustomed to, you fancy.

You're given a book to review, a collection of short stories set in Baton Rouge that features a photo of a plastic alligator on its slick dust jacket. He wrote it. It's his first book. How did you not know this? You can't help but well up with pride. You knew he was a writer. That essay he wrote about turning over a log in the woods was excellent. You taught him to love writing. He pretended not to listen in your class, but he did. He's a handsome man in his author photo. His bio mentions he studied fiction writing at Johns Hopkins and won an NEA fellowship. It mentions that he grew up in Baton Rouge. The book is dedicated to two of his friends from Country Day. You flip to the acknowledgements page. You're not listed. You thought you would be. Ungrateful prick.

You read the book in one sitting and immediately begin to type the review. You mention you've known him since he was a sixth-grader, and that all through his youth, he spoke fondly of the Northeast, where he had spent the first eleven years of his life. You write that he couldn't wait to get out of Louisiana, and this anti-Louisiana sentiment pervades his stories of losers and drug addicts and inbred, raccoon-eating Cajuns. You hope his mother cuts the review from the paper and leaves it for him on the nightstand when he's in town for a reading as part of his book tour. Maybe you'll discuss it with him over a few beers. He'll thank you for your thoughtful frankness.

There's a crowd at the bookstore for the local boy. You stand towards the back. His arms are thicker with muscle. He obviously goes to the gym like all gay guys do. He reads a technically competent story about a little boy lost in Cortana Mall. The audience loves the local references and laughs when they should. He glances out into the crowd and spots you, and you see shock on his face. He stutters a word, but only one, and in a few seconds, he's reading confidently again, like you're not out there in the audience, like you didn't review his book for the *Gambit Weekly*. Still, you made him stammer. You made him squirm. You did. And this buoys you and carries you to the front of the line to talk with him when he finishes his story. "I knew you were a writer even when you resisted," you say. "Hi, Mr. Roth," he mutters. "I wrote a review of your book," you say. "I know," he says and he grimaces at you. An older woman who's dripping in turquois jewelry taps him on his shoulder, he turns around, stands, and hugs her. They speak quickly and eagerly, and leave you there with the other people waiting in line to have him sign books. And you thought he might want to grab dinner and few drinks afterwards. You're a fool.

Years later, you read in an interview that he finished his latest novel on his back, felled by excruciating sciatic pain in his right leg so intense that he passed out and bumped his head on the floor of the apartment he shares with his partner, an oncologist. The reporter, who refers to him as 'one of today's preeminent Southern writers,' mentions his limp, his red walking stick that he calls "baton rouge."

You had sciatic pain a few years ago, so you sympathize. It was so awful that you had to piss in a jug, and crawl to the door when you ordered food from Spanish Town Market. You consider contacting him to tell him about Dr. Sarno, whose controversial theory is that back pain is a diversion meant to support the burial of uncomfortable unconscious emotions. If sufferers determine what's disturbing their unconscious, their physical pain disappears. It worked for you. You journaled about your callous parents for a few days, and then you focused on him, how he hurt you, and by the time you filled the journal, you could walk without wincing.

You imagine him discussing the foundations of his deep grief with his therapist: his emotionally absent and judgmental parents, the Catholic fear of hell, the years of loneliness and shame. But then his manner changes and he begins to spout acrimoniously about you. You were the only openly gay person in his life, and you made him think that gay men were creepy. And you taunted him and relished his discomfort. You pestered him. You pursued him. You grabbed his neck, and you knew he hated it but you kept doing it, and now it's as though the pain traveled down his spine and manifested itself as a bulging disc at L5. As he pushes away any remaining empathy he might have felt towards you and trudges through all the sickening moments and interactions, clinging to the word 'trauma' that his therapist uses to describe what you put him through, he says he wants more than anything to feel unmitigated rage, to wallow in it and make you fade, alongside his sciatica, into nothing.

But he can't do it, you know he can't, and you see him late at night, swallowing three hydrocodone tablets, praying that the waves of searing pain in his leg will subside—even a little—so he can sleep.

Nominated by Crazyhorse

230

BELIEF

by JAMIE QUATRO

from TIN HOUSE

Some mornings I wake up a Christian. On such mornings, upon waking, I feel a precognitive tug of joy in my body, a sense of delight I experienced regularly in childhood—my mind a blank page upon which someone is poised to write a message of bliss. On such mornings I know the tug of joy is a nudge from God, to remind me I am His child, I came to Earth trailing clouds of glory. How blessed, to feel divine approbation in my biological systems, unbidden. Today, out of gratitude, I will strive to please God with my actions. I will be the hands and feet of Christ, spreading love to every soul that crosses my path. I will not do this perfectly—there will be mistakes—but God will forgive. Has already forgiven.

I get up and brush my teeth. My husband has left the toilet lid up. The cat has vomited on my daughter's comforter. I will have to strip the duvet and wash it and take the comforter to the dry cleaner; as it is made of down, this will be expensive. My neighbor is late for carpool, which means my son will be late to school for a fifth time this semester, which will mean a weekend detention, to which I will have to drive him. At the grocery store a woman I recognize from church says she has read my book and that she would like to sit down with me and talk about it, and about my personal faith, and my stance on Christianity in general. At dinner no one talks except the daughter, who mostly complains. My husband cannot help our son with his calculus homework—the son yells, my husband yells back, I yell at both of them to calm them down. After the children are in bed, I drink wine, too much of it, and Jimmy Fallon says that China has officially surpassed America in economic

231

power, but—good news—America still has the best reality television anywhere. Also rap music. I have always loved Jimmy Fallon but tonight I loathe him. My husband sits down beside me with his glass of wine and I loathe him, too, for finishing off the bottle when I had planned on another glass, for his inability to assist our son with his calculus, for his shortness of temper with the son, and for his persistence in leaving the lid up despite my taping a note above the toilet. I also loathe my son for still requiring help with homework his junior year in high school, and I loathe the cat for always selecting fabric/upholstery on which to vomit. I loathe the woman at the grocery store who thinks my personal faith has anything to do with my art. I especially loathe myself for all this loathing. For the fact that, despite my intention to spread love, I have not only failed to feel love, but I feel only its opposite.

Before getting into bed, I read an essay in a book of essays by a brilliant atheist critic. This critic is someone I have met. He is kind, generous, compassionate, intelligent. He moves among people who are also all of those things. Every person I can think of who is kind, generous, compassionate, and intelligent is atheist or agnostic. None of them have to think about pleasing a divine being, no one is asking them to be grateful for anything, they inhabit a meaningless universe and will cease to exist when they die. Therefore, if they persist in kind, generous, compassionate, and intelligent behaviors, it is heroic. They are free to love, they loathe no one. Glorious. I fall asleep determined that tomorrow I will wake up an atheist.

*　*　*

Some mornings I wake up an atheist. On such mornings, upon waking, I do not feel the little tug of joy I used to feel regularly, in childhood. I sense no impending message of happiness. I feel only vacuity, the cold certainty that God is dead and everything I've ever felt of Him is the biological result of hormones, or a bright trigger spot in my brain, or psychology/wishful thinking, or what my parents told me. If I love anyone today, it will be the heroic effort of one tiny pointless accidental creature. There is no one watching, no one to please or displease. No mistakes or the need for forgiveness.

A lightness of spirit enters my being. I have nothing to lose and everything to gain. My daughter cannot find a shoe, and when I locate it beneath the slipcovered couch and bring it to her—though she blames me for losing the shoe, and making her late to school—I sing "Reunited" while she puts the shoes on. This makes her laugh. The woman who drives carpool is late picking up my son but I notice she has her phone to her ear and she is crying. She is recently divorced, her husband left her with three children, but she still keeps up her end of the carpool. The poor woman, I think. To be alone, and lonely and also a cosmic accident, extinction waiting at the end of all the suffering. I feel a tremendous measure of compassion and gratitude for her. Also, compassion and gratitude for myself, extinction likewise waiting for me, yet here I am, singing, returning a gentle word. At the dry cleaner an elderly man I've seen smoking cigars outside the Mountain Cafe brings in his suits and tells the attendant to please take good care of them, his deceased wife picked them out in 1953 and they're the only suits he's ever owned. The woman in the grocery store asks her question and I want to embrace her, tell her she needn't be so afraid. After dinner I think my son is heroic for trying to do, night after night, what his school requires of him, and I admire my husband for continuing to try to help him, even though he never took calculus himself and has told me, more than once, that calculus in high school is a waste of a year. And here's Jimmy Fallon presiding, making us laugh at ourselves, poor foolish smiling Americans. Poor serious driven Chinese. Desperate mammals giving life our heartiest effort. How worthy of kindness and generosity and compassion.

Before going to bed, it occurs to me that this all-encompassing compassion for humanity is what Christ taught and embodied. Lost sheep, paralyzed by their fear of death, in need of a shepherd who will enter into, suffer alongside of, die in the stead of. Then rise and overcome the thing they're most afraid of. Give them a fighting chance, something to hope for. The evil things they do en masse are necessarily repugnant to me, a perfectly loving being. The evil things they do cannot help but create a vast divide. But they should not have to bear the blame. It is not their fault. They have simply forgotten who they are. And as I am perfect in justice—all debts must be paid—I am also perfect in mercy, and therefore will become one of them and pay the cost in full. Breach the divide. Treat them as they deserve to be treated: divine beings worthy of love and forgiveness. Glorious.

I get into bed beside my husband, who says he feels like a failure with our son, and that he had a troubling conversation with a client who isn't satisfied with the strategic plan he created and may not renew my husband's retainer. Also that he misses me, physically, as it's been a week since we made love. The loathing for him returns—for the way he uses sex as a panacea—but here is my chance to live out the all-encompassing compassion of Christ. To look not only to my own interests but also to the interests of others.

I pull his hand out from beneath my T-shirt.

I really want to read tonight, I say.

Morning will be better timing, I say.

My husband rolls over. I open my book of essays by the brilliant atheist critic and fall asleep determined that tomorrow, I will wake up a Christian.

Nominated by Melissa Pritchard

MY DEAR MASTER LISZT

fiction by BEN STROUD

from OXFORD AMERICAN

My Dear Master Liszt!

I have become a slave owner. Yes, like you I believe in the freedom of all men—your Hungarians, the Poles, the Rumanians!—and in the role we artists must play—light-bringers, revealers of passion, sympathizers with the oppressed! But I have become a slave owner. It is a stain, a mark of rot. How many stains have I come to bear in these last weeks? They are countless.

I beg you, my dear Master Liszt, read this letter.

Fifteen years have passed since I was your student. Do you remember me? At the beginning of September, 1845, I came to Baden-Baden. I had learned from a newspaper that you were there, resting after seasons of touring and the disastrous festival at Bonn, and I presented myself, a graduate of the new conservatory at Leipzig. I called Leipzig a stifling place, pleaded with you to teach me, you who had always been so generous with students. A shining Érard stood in your rooms, and you commanded me to play. When I finished you told me to visit you each afternoon, promptly at three. Overjoyed, I did. I played, and you encouraged me. I treasure those hours, my dear Master Liszt. After two weeks of visits, though, I arrived and you were not there. Belloni, sitting at his usual desk and tending to your letters, told me you were late returning from the baths. As I waited I saw, on the Érard, a book. Curiosity stole over me. I seized it, discovered inside a list of all your students. I raced through the pages, searched for my name, found it at the list's very end. What had I most wanted, when I came to you? A kiss, like that which Master Beethoven once placed upon your forehead. Genius welcoming genius. What did I find? These words, which ache still in the deepest chambers of my very being: "Languid and mediocre.

Fingers good enough. Posture at the piano good enough. Enough 'enoughs,' the grand total of which is not much."

You returned, found me, my eyes red from too many tears, the book open on my lap.

"I am a mediocrity," I said.

You hung your head, placed a consoling hand on my knee, said it was true. I was a kind young man, but, yes, I was a mediocrity.

One who is not an artist—such a one does not understand. But you and I, my dear Master Liszt, we understand. The pronouncement was death. That instant I became like those poor gamblers I'd seen haunting the steps of the Kurhaus, ruined by a single turn of the wheel. What had I lost? All that I'd dreamt of. I would give no concerts before emperors. I would receive no cheering crowds. I would taste no sweets made in my honor by a city's foremost bakers. Trifles all, perhaps, but the outward sign of my true damnation: Never from my fingers would come true grace.

At last I looked at you. "What am I to do?" I said.

You smiled. Join my father's wheat business, you said. Marry a sturdy woman with pink rolls of flesh. Mediocrity is a gift. I would be happy.

I said, "No."

"Go over the wide seas then," you said. "Perhaps there your mediocrity will be taken for genius."

Do you remember any of this?

Irritated by my importuning, my dear Master Liszt, you meant your words as a rebuke. But I returned to Leipzig, sold all that I owned save for my collection of music and the clothes I could fit in a bag. Then I hurried to Hamburg, leaped onto the first boat I found, and crossed the wide seas to Cuba.

There, for two months, I played on the pianos at opera houses, in the villas of grandees. It was no good. In Cuba, too, my mediocrity showed. I thought to attempt another island. But at the ship offices I learned of Texas. Open country, just admitted to the United States. I needed a remote place, my dear Master Liszt, this I knew. I sailed to Galveston, port city of Texas, a buggy island with beaches of mud, and there I bargained for passage with a man going up country, and there, too, I bought my piano. No Érard, but a battered Tomkison, the best I could find, the best I could afford. We crossed the bay to the city of Houston and traveled north, north, north through thick forests of pine. Our road was a dirt track, and as we bounced on its ruts my poor Tomkison jangled in the back of its wagon. I thought it might well fall apart before

236

our journey ended! But no. It and I reached Henderson, Texas, the town I settled in, newly risen in those remote wilds, and the town from which these pages come.

Only in a place such as this, you said, might I be accepted as a genius—an ambassador of light!—a bearer of art, stirring passions in every breast! And, indeed, my dear Master Liszt, for fifteen years, in this far spot, it has been so.

Henderson has an academy, and for these fifteen years I have been its music teacher. To my students I proclaim emotion and the spirit as guiding stars, and for all the town I am a wonder, with my long hair, my twenty bright cravats, and my white gloves that, like you, I pull from my fingers and toss whenever I play. My townsmen consult me on the revolutions of '48, the fashions of Europe, the duties of the heart. Once each month, the owner of the finest plantation in the county, Mr. Tatum, feeds me the bear he hunts. Imagine this speck of rare opulence in our wilderness, his slaves waving peacock fans while we drink French wines and chart the fates of each figure in his bound Shakespeare! And Tatum has been but one of my regular dining companions, my dear Master Liszt. Here I am sought. Here I am regarded!

Here, too, I have been a man of romance. I fall in love with every young lady student, even those with pitted faces and sunken chins. I write poems on their music, slip kisses onto their hands, and when they ask me to put my fingers onto theirs, to show them the keys, I always oblige.

Is this not genius? How we act and are perceived? It is not. Fifteen years, my dear Master Liszt. For fifteen years I have pretended to genius, only pretended. For this I have been punished. For this I have been made to pay.

Do you know of the current great debate in this country, my dear Master Liszt? The unrest since the nomination of Lincoln? All summer, abolitionists have been riding in secret through Texas, setting fires, distributing guns and blades, preparing the slaves to revolt. Such, at least, have been the rumors printed in our newspapers week by week. I myself ignored them. Whenever Tatum, treating me to bear, leaned to me and asked what I thought, I would shake my head and tsk. Perhaps it has been one of my failings, a rot of my person, but I never spoke on matters touching slavery. Slavery is a contract between men, I would say if pressed, let it be what it will be. It is outside me.

Well—and then our town burned, my dear Master Liszt.

It happened on a night at the beginning of this month. I woke to shouting, looked out my window, and thought it dawn. Fire, I soon realized. I dressed quickly and helped my fellow townsmen carry water. When the true dawn came, we had mastered the flames. My house was spared. Most houses were spared. It was the shops in the center of town that were lost.

I stayed to help two Jews comb through the ashes. Brothers from Erfurt, they owned a shop where once a week I visited them to talk German while their women fried me potato pancakes. Some of their metal goods survived. Our hands wrapped in cloth, the metal hot still from the flames, we picked free what we could find.

Meanwhile, behind us, men gathered in the square. Principal men of the town, planters in from the county, a host of common folk. We had ignored the abolitionist threat, they said. We hadn't set up a watch. Now the abolitionists had struck. They were here, they must be uncovered, and they must be stopped.

Tatum called to me. "You're needed," he said, and before I could answer, he enrolled me in the Vigilance Committee. Griffin, a lawyer whose pig-eyed daughter has been both my student and a recipient of my poems, put a rifle into my hands.

In these circumstances, with fears running of abolitionists, I could not refuse. If I had—me, Miszner, who speaks of beauty and freedom— my own life would have been risked. So I believed. So I still believe, though now I count that thing, my life, worthless.

Whatley, a planter near in stature to Tatum, and with whom I have also dined, began to speak (over choice hams, we discoursed on Goethe and the passions that reside in all men, my dear Master Liszt). A Northerner lived in our town, he said. Bert Scofield.

I knew of this Scofield, though I'd never met with him. He owned a dirty tavern, of the kind I did not visit.

Whatley said it was a known fact that Scofield bought goods from slaves, goods stolen from their masters. Perhaps it was he who set the fire. The Committee marched to Scofield's tavern. It too had burned, and Scofield had fled. His absence was taken for admission. He was a secret abolitionist, the Committee soon declared. He'd hoped to lead the slaves into revolt. Horses were found, and half the Committee mounted them, galloped off to search the roads. I have no horse, and I am no rider. I stood with the rest and we idled, uncertain, in the August sun.

Then Hodges, the town's post clerk, from whom I have collected my sheet music, and with whom I have sometimes drunk iced lemonades at the Brick Hotel, said that Scofield had a slave woman. Missy May, a cook in his tavern. She should be questioned, he said. Tatum agreed. On his orders we broke up and looked for her.

I found her, my dear Master Liszt, I and my searching partner, Vansickle, the Latin teacher at the academy. Missy May was in the Presbyterian preacher's garden shed, hiding among his rakes. We told her to come out, and she did. Her skin was black as coal, and she was big with child.

The Committee brought her to the square. Tatum and Griffin put questions to her. At last she confessed: she herself had set the fire, on Scofield's orders.

The riders returned. One dragged something behind him. Scofield. The Northerner made a noise, my dear Master Liszt, that I cannot describe. The horseman, young Birdwell, one of my former pupils, a steady student with a good understanding of Chopin, dragged Scofield around the square—through the ashes—over the burned wood. I don't know how Scofield lived. The rope bound his neck. But there was that noise, that indescribable noise.

Even so, Scofield was dead when they untied him. Young Bird well and a few others hung his body from the courthouse oak. The Committee shot at it. The body turned and danced with the bullets. At last I thought it done. But then all the Committee looked at me. For I had not fired.

I raised my rifle, my dear Master Liszt, and I shot. My bullet struck Scofield's bloody corpse and made it swing.

Now I thought it was done. But, no, it still was not done. There remained the matter of Missy May, Tatum said. He called for a vote. The Committee decided—death.

To this Dr. March objected. "Her baby," he said.

Dr. March is the town's chief physician, a man of true intellectual gifts. With him I have had a running debate over which is the true master, spirit or flesh. I had strong hope of merciful words. Dr. March told the Committee that Missy May would give birth within weeks, that we could not kill her.

The Committee was dumbfounded. They stared.

"Let the baby come," Dr. March said. "Then kill her."

It was a blow, my dear Master Liszt. Missy May was guilty, I believed it. But this was brutality.

The Committee approved Dr. March's recommendation. Missy May was put in the jail. It was now past noon and we had been awake all night and all morning. Tatum told us to go to our homes and sleep.

And did I sleep? I was distraught by what I had witnessed, by what

I had been made to do. Vile. Yes, vile. Already I felt these stains. But, too, I was exhausted.

Over the next days the town settled. People came in from the country to see the ruins. I gave lessons to my private students. One of my maiden aunts—I have a whole collection of maiden aunts—asked if it was true that I had shot Scofield's body, then blushed with desire when I admitted it. A few nights after the fire I returned again to Tatum's. As we dined he talked of slave revolts in Virginia and South Carolina, of how it was a mark of honor, of bravery, to say that we too had put one down.

In this time, I took turns guarding Missy May. A handful of us in the Committee shared the work. Nearly everyone else, including the jailer, Smith, had hired themselves out to rebuild, and yet others were seeing to their crops. My first turn I brought sheet music, some of the new Wagner I've seen you touting in your essays—for even here, my dear Master Liszt, I can get the leading European papers—a little Berlioz, your *Transcendental Études*. (So flowing, my dear Master Liszt! The way the notes glide from stately progressions to tumblings that surpass the most agile of acrobats!) I wanted only to pass the time. I skimmed the music, stopped at certain intriguing passages to sing notes. I pretended Missy May was not there. I did not want to look at her, to think of her, to think of what was to become of her.

I concentrated mostly on your *Études*, and my second time through "Harmonies of the Night" I heard Missy May hum the notes with me. I turned to her. She stopped.

"Please, no," I said, "continue if it brings you happiness."

My dear Master Liszt, she had confessed to burning the town. And yet she was a fellow being. More! A mother, the light of two souls in her. I did not know what else to say. So I sang, and she hummed.

A mistake, perhaps, for it was a binding. Our voices are but instruments of our spirits, and these we joined. Our music was crude and reedy—it's true. But it was ours, and as we made it I looked at Missy May and saw her beauty, the ripe beauty of motherhood, the mournful beauty of a wild creature condemned. By the end of your "Harmonies of the Night," I loved her.

I feel too deeply. I know it. But you yourself loved the doomed Marie Duplessis, loved her because she was doomed. My love for Missy May was much the same. And greater, I dare say. Your Duplessis died of consumption, while my Missy May was to hang, and I—yes, I own it—was among those sending her to the noose. Which love-agony is the more tragic I leave it to you to decide.

Of course I said nothing to her. On my second turn as guard I brought your *Études*. Again I sang, again she hummed. But on my third turn as guard, after we went through your *Études*, Missy May spoke.

"Let me out," she said. "Let me run."

I shut away the song sheets. Angry! Yes, angry! Had it been a trick, my dear Master Liszt, her gentle humming? Was the passion she put into me only a coin with which to pay her way out, a cheap bribe to her jailer? So, in that moment, I wondered. So, in that moment, I thought. I felt myself abused. I told her she had confessed her guilt.

She had done nothing, she said. She had been frightened. She had told the Committee lies. I was not like the others. I sang to her.

All this she said to me, and my soul raged. I put my forehead to that copy of your *Études*. The Committee had voted, I told her. I must abide by the Committee.

We made no more music.

On my fourth turn as guard, she again said, "Let me out, let me run."

I did not answer. The rest of the time we passed in silence.

And then my fifth turn came. My fifth turn, my dear Master Liszt. At the writing of each of these words my hand has trembled. Now it shakes—riots—tries vehemently to refuse! As I approached the jail I heard laughter. A jail is not a place of laughter. I entered, saw men. Young men from out in the county, six of them, boys truly, boys I did not know. They had gotten into Missy May's cell, had bound her mouth, had pulled her clothes from her.

Need I detail the outrage?

They invited me to join them. I ran out, a coward, and waited for them to finish.

In Baden-Baden, when you showed me my mediocrity, I feared there was no life after, that I had as much as died. But no. This is when I died, my dear Master Liszt. From here there is no life after.

I sat with Missy May once the boys were gone. I sang the notes of your "Mazeppa." She did not hum.

My soul stormed, then and through all the hours after. That night I plotted to free Missy May. I purchased a jug of whiskey, brought it to the jail. I would get the guard drunk. I would let her out. I too would flee. That simple.

This time, as I approached, I heard a cry of pain and I saw men. Not like those boys before—these stood outside the jail. Ten, twenty of them. One was the lawyer Griffin. He grinned at the sight of the whiskey, called me a good fellow, and took the jug and passed it around. The baby was coming, he said. Two of his own slave women were in the jail with Missy May. I stayed and listened. Past midnight the cries calmed and I heard the sharp protest of a being new to the world.

The jug made its final round. "Noon," Griffin said to us.

Noon, my dear Master Liszt.

At noon the next day, the Committee gathered before the courthouse oak. Tatum and Whatley walked Missy May from the jail. Young Birdwell and Wiley Tipps—another of my students, a sensitive player with the slenderest fingers and a proclivity for Bach (what a waste, you see, all my fifteen years, what a waste!)—put the rope around Missy May's neck and lifted her. She fought, my dear Master Liszt. She jerked. She twisted. Then she hung dead.

I returned to my home, sat at my Tomkison, attempted "Harmonies of the Night," that étude to which she first hummed. I thought to mourn Missy May. But the notes came in rattling bursts. At last I stopped. I tore the songsheet and wept.

How many stains does my soul bear? How many failings do I count? And this is not yet the end, my dear Master Liszt. Read on, I beg you.

Missy May's baby was a girl and she was to be auctioned off, the money earned to be put in a relief fund for those who had suffered losses in the fire. I decided I would buy her, raise her, and in this way earn a measure of forgiveness.

The auction was held under that same courthouse oak, just one day after Missy May was killed. The bidding started at twenty-five dollars, rose to fifty. A female infant commands a low price, my dear Master Liszt. This I had learned in my years among the practice of bondage. I shouted two hundred. All looked at me. My townsmen wanted an explanation. I had prepared for this. In my blue suit and brightest cravat, my long hair washed and combed, I stood among them as Miszner the artist—the genius! It was my experiment, I said, to mold a perfect servant from her first suckling days.

A few of my townsmen chuckled. The auctioneer waited for more bids. A formality. I was overpaying for the baby and no one would challenge me. The auctioneer called "sold." The baby was mine.

I named her Anna, my dear Master Liszt, that name my mother and your mother share. I rented a wet nurse from Tatum. At night we three sat together. The nurse put Anna to her breast, then I held Anna. The nurse said I was natural with her, though I do not know if this was true or simple flattery. What does it mean, to be natural with a fresh-born soul? Anna spat her milk on me. She grunted. She fell asleep in the crook of my arm.

When I left those men inside with Missy May, I myself died. It is true. And yet I look back on these days with Anna and count them among the sweetest I have ever lived.

By now, my dear Master Liszt, you have surely guessed. At the end of the week Anna sickened. I sent for Dr. March. He said Anna had a fever. It was this hot summer. "Maybe if her mother had lived," Dr. March said. "No substitute for a mother." At these words he showed not an ounce of compunction. He told me Anna had one day left.

Her death was awful, my dear Master Liszt. I will not pretend otherwise. She vomited black vomit. She sweated. She cried and would not be comforted. Her mouth dried. By the end, her lips were flaked white.

I held her. I spoke to her in German. I told her sweet stories. I said her mother was waiting for her, that she was lucky, that this was no world for her. And I did not lie, my dear Master Liszt. For what life could she have here? I am not foolish. She and I living in harmony, father and child, in this Texas, this Rusk County? I owned her, my dear Master Liszt, but I could not guard her from the cruelties of this world, from its lusts.

Anna made it through to the dawn, and then she cried her last.

I did not know where Missy May had been buried. Two members of the Committee had taken her body out of the town, disposed of it someplace unmarked. So I petitioned Tatum to let me bury Anna among his dead slaves. He agreed. I had a little coffin made, and I dug the grave myself. I paid fifty dollars for a white stone angel. It shines in that poor, grim yard.

Thus ended my brief tenure as a slave owner.

Now mere days have passed, my dear Master Liszt, and already no one speaks of Bert Scofield, of Missy May, of Anna. When I left your rooms in Baden-Baden fifteen years ago, I dreamed of transmuting my mediocrity into genius, of leading my fellow men as a noble artist, of living above the world like a heralding comet or star. Now I am stained with these guilts, these failings uncountable. Have you read on, my dear Master Liszt? I pray you have. It is why I write to you who taught me falsely, who sent me to this Texas. These stains, these guilts, these failings, they are mine. Yes, I own them. But you have a share, and my words—they have brought that share to you.

Nominated by Oxford American

UNDOCUMENTED ALIEN (VERY ROUGH FIRST DRAFT REPORT, PROJECT JRD)

fiction by JOYCE CAROL OATES

from CONJUNCTIONS

LOST IN TIME

Test subject #293199/Joseph Saidu Maada (undocumented alien, home country Nigeria, b. 1990, d. 2016).

Most immediate and long-lasting effect of the neurotransmitter micro-chip (NTM) inserted in the cerebral cortex of the human brain appears to be a radical destabilization of temporal and spatial functions of cognition. (See Graz, S. R., "Temporal and Parietal Functions of the Human Brain," *Journal of Neuroscience Studies* 14:2 for a detailed description of normal functions.)

In test subject #293199 temporal destabilization was immediate and (seemingly) permanent; spatial destabilization was sporadic and unpredictable.

For instance, upon several (videotaped) occasions in the PROJECT JRD laboratory (Institute for Independent Neurophysiological Research, Princeton, New Jersey), test subject #293199 J. S. Maada demonstrated confusion and panic when asked to list events in a chronological sequence. Even those events that were made to occur within a single hour in the institute laboratory, which he had observed, were virtually impossible for Maada to "list" (it was noted that the subject seemed to have lost comprehension of what the term "list" means). If subject was allowed to view a videotape of the hour, he could list events on a sheet of paper as he observed them occurring, though after the elapse of a half hour, he would not remember their sequence except by consulting the list. Also, Maada did not appear to recognize himself in the video, or would not acknowledge himself. (*Who is that black face* Maada would ask, sneering and anxious. *I see him. He does not see me.*)

In the last several months of Maada's life, partly as a consequence (it is believed) of deteriorating vision, hearing, and cognitive functions, subject's paranoia was heightened so that he became convinced that a team of *black spies* had been sent to abduct him and return him to Nigeria to be imprisoned and tortured in collusion with the CIA. (See Lehrman, M., "Learned Helplessness and Conditioned Paranoia in Thirty-Year-Old African American Male/" *Johns Hopkins Neurophysiological Journal* 22:17. Though this paper [attributed to Dr. Lehrman but in fact 90 percent of it the work of his postdoc staff at the institute] is based upon PROJECT JRD classified experiments, it does not contain information that reveals the identity of the test subject or the laboratory in which the cycle of experiments took place. Thus, the age of the subject has been altered as well as other details pertaining to the subject's ethnic identity and legal status in the US, in conformity with Department of Defense regulations stipulating classified scientific material revised for publication in nonclassified journals.) Simultaneously, and with no awareness of the contradictory nature of his assumptions, test subject Maada was made to believe that he was a "privileged alien agent" sent to Earth on a "secret stealth mission" from one of the orbiting moons of Jupiter and that the nature of this mission would be revealed to him at the proper time, and not before. *Am I a ticking bomb!* Maada would ask slyly. *Or am I just a ticking clock! A heart!*

Over a duration of several months, Maada so lost his ability to register the sequence of what we call "time" that he was continually expressing surprise at encountering members of the S_____ family (with whom he was living in Edison, New Jersey; their name is redacted, at least in this rough draft of our report, since the entire S_____ family is "undocumented"/"illegal") in their cramped quarters in a brownstone tenement on Ewing Street, Edison. When the older children returned from school, if Maada was in his room and heard their voices, he would rush at them, demanding to know why they weren't at school, for it seemed to him (evidently) that they had just left, or had not left at all; concepts of "earlier"—"previous"—"subsequent"—"consequent"— were no longer available to him. The several children in the S_____ household, ranging in age from three to eleven, were very fond of

245

"Saidu" (as they called Maada), because he was "kind" and "funny" with them, like an older brother, and "very smart," helping them with their homework; but over the course of PROJECT JRD, as Maada's personality was made to "plasticize"(i.e., alter in a "melting" way) and other features of the experiments were initiated, the children did not know what to expect from their "Saidu" and began to avoid him.

When the several adults in the S_____ household returned from their low-income jobs in the Edison area, Maada frequently expressed great anxiety for them, and occasional impatience, that they had failed to go to work at all, and were risking their jobs, thus their livelihood and ability to pay rent, which would lead to their arrest and deportation, and his own.

For the "undocumented alien"—"illegal alien"—it is arrest and deportation that is the prevailing fear, and not, as it is for others of us (who are US citizens) a more generalized fear of the impenetrability of the future: *Death*, we can assume; but not the *how of Death*, still less the (precise) *when of Death*.

As early as 6/11/15, within three weeks of the start of his participation in PROJECT JRD, #293199/J. S. Maada began to have difficulty listing the chronology of events in his previous life: his arrival in the US as an engineering student at Harrogate University, Jersey City, New Jersey, at which time a student visa was granted in his name by the United States Department of State (8/21/07); his withdrawal from Harrogate on "academic grounds," at which time his student visa was declared null and void and he was issued a summons from the Department of State ordering him to report immediately to the Newark Immigration Authority (2/2/08); his (unlawful, unreported) move to Edison, New Jersey, as an "undocumented alien" given temporary shelter in the small, fiercely protective Nigerian community; his sporadic (and un-documented) employment in the Edison/Newark area as a cafeteria worker, busboy, hospital and morgue custodian, sanitation worker, con-struction and lawn-service worker, etc.; his (first) arrest by law enforce-ment officers (Newark) on grounds of creating a public disturbance, refusing to obey police officers' commands, and resisting arrest (5/21/15); his release from police custody dependent upon agreeing to participate "freely and of his own volition" in the National Defense Security (Classified) PROJECT JRD (5/24/15); his (second) arrest, Montclair, New Jersey (6/19/16) on more serious charges of sexual as-

246

sault, aggravated assault, assault with a deadly weapon (teeth, shovel), assault with the intention of committing homicide, and assault against (Montclair) law enforcement officers.

Following the altercation with law enforcement officers in Montclair, test subject J. S. Maada did not return to participate in the PROJECT. Injuries sustained at the time resulted in (emergency) hospitalization at Robert Wood Johnson University Hospital, New Brunswick, New Jersey, with the (federally mandated) proviso that no medical information regarding the patient could be entered in any hospital computer, and that access to the subject's room was restricted. Following the subject's death (6/30/16), his room was declared a *quarantine area* accessible only to the PROJECT JRD medical team, which performed the autopsy establishing cause of death as "natural": hypothermia, brain hemorrhage, respiratory, cardiac, and liver failure. (7/2/16) Per the contract signed by the test subject at the start of his participation in PROJECT JRD, his "bodily remains" became the property of PROJECT JRD and are currently stored in the research morgue at the Institute for Independent Neurophysiological Research on Rt. 1, Princeton, New Jersey.

(Information concerning NTM inserts, stents, surgical and chemical alterations to J. S. Maada's brain and body is not indicated in the [official] autopsy that has been sent to the test subject's family in Nigeria but is to be found in the [classified] autopsy on file with NDS (National Defense Security).

Though hundreds of pages of data have been recorded in PROJECT JRD computer files, the participation of test subject #293199/Joseph Saidu Maada in the cycle of experiments at the time of his demise is considered incomplete and unsatisfactory.

NOTE: As indicated above, this report is a rough first draft, a compilation of lab notes with some expository and transitional material put together by a small team of postdocs assigned to Dr. M. Lehrman working late at night in the depressing and ill-smelling quarters of the institute. If you have read this far, please do not be offended by our plea (of a sort) that allowances might be made for our (relative) lack of data concerning test subject #293199/Joseph Saidu Maada, whose full name was not available to us until this morning when we arrived at the lab to learn to our surprise that 1) #293199 was not coming today, as he had been coming every Thursday for months, and 2) #293199 would not ever be coming again, for any scheduled Thursday.

Oh. Shit—one of us murmured.

Weird. We'd got to know the guy kind of well, and now—

It is common practice in laboratories under the auspices of PROJECT JRD to refer to test subjects by their (classified) ID numbers and not by their (actual) names; so too test subjects are not told the (actual) names of the research scientists and medical authorities who work with them over the course of the cycle of experiments. (So far as Joseph Saidu Maada could know, the names on our badges—*Dr. R. Keck, Dr. M. Lui, Dr. J. Mariotti*—indicated who we actually are, and in addition to this (quasi) information we encouraged the subject to call us by first names closely resembling our own, actual first names: "Rick" for "Rich," "Michelle" for "Milhcent," "Jonny" for "Jonathan"). In this way, a desired *atmosphere of trust* was established, a crucial goal for all PROJECT JRD labs.

Also, as postdoc assistants to Dr. M. Lehrman, director of our institute lab, and not director of PROJECT JRD itself, we could not access some essential files without arousing suspicion. Each rank at the institute, as at PROJECT JRD, as at the Department of Defense, carries with it a degree of "classified clearance," and postdocs are of the lowest rank. (Just above lab technicians—we are sensitive about being confused with lab technicians who do not have PhDs as we do.) Hence the haphazard nature of this report, which we intend to correct in subsequent drafts, before submitting it to Dr. Lehrman, who will slash through it with a red pencil, correcting our mistakes (as he sees them), revising and excising, and providing (restricted) information of his own (which we will never see), to the director of PROJECT JRD, whose very name is not known to us but whose office is in the Department of Defense, Washington, DC.

(Unfortunately, the final draft of this report is due on Monday morning. If only we were outfitted with the more potent neurotransmitter chips inserted into J. S. Maada's brain, or, at least, one or two of the amphetamine biochemical boosters that kept the hapless test subject awake at night!)

Radical temporal destabilization seems to have intensified the subject's confusion about his (classified) role as a "privileged alien agent" with special powers (invisibility, ability to read minds, to pass through solid walls, and to perceive the shimmering molecular interiors of all things; to "detonate"—"demolecularize"—when directed by his commandant) and his (actual, literal) life as a manual laborer in the not-always-reliable hire of Adolpho's Lawn Care &. Maintenance of Montclair, New Jersey.

From the perspective of institute research scientists it would have been preferable that the test subject had not worked at all, and that he was available for their purposes at all times, like a laboratory animal that is kept, for his own safety as well as for the convenience of experimental researchers, in a cage; but J. S. Maada's disappearance from the Nigerian enclave in Edison would have aroused suspicion, it was believed. And so, inevitably, J. S. Maada's real-life activities impacted upon his role as an experimental subject, and presented serious limitations, which resulted in the tragic events of 6/19/16.

Precipitating factors include extreme heat on the day of the "assault" (a high of ninety-six degrees Fahrenheit in Montclair, New Jersey, by noon), protracted labor (the lawn crew had begun work at 7:00 a.m. at the E_____s' large, three-acre property; the assault occurred at 11:00 a.m.), and an evident miscommunication between Mrs. E_____and J. S. Maada that ended in a "violent outburst" on the part of the test subject, bringing to an abrupt and unforeseen halt the subject's participation in PROJECT JRD.

Possibilities accounting for Maada's extreme reaction following an exchange with Mrs. E_____ are: the stent in the subject's cerebellum had begun to work loose and/or one or another of the inserted microchips may have been malfunctioning. Usually "docile, reticent, cooperative, and naively unquestioning," the test subject allegedly became "excitable, belligerent, and threatening." According to witnesses, Maada lifted his shovel as if to strike the terrified Mrs. E_____ but decided instead to attack the Floradora bush, rending it into pieces; he then threw down the shovel, seized Mrs. E_____by her shoulders, and shook her violently as one might shake a doll with the intention of breaking it. Further, according to Mrs. E_____, Maada bared his "wet, sharp" teeth and lunged as if to bite her in the (right) breast.

By this time two of Maada's coworkers came shouting to the rescue of Mrs. E_____. Inside the house, a housekeeper called 911 to report the attempted sexual assault/homicide.

When Montclair police officers arrived at the E_____ residence they discovered the agitated (black, Nigerian-born) laborer "cowering at the foot of the property, by a fence"—"foaming at the mouth like a mad dog"—"rushing at us with a shovel." After "repeated warnings," officers had "no choice" but to open fire, seriously wounding but not (immediately) killing subject #293199.

Transcript of testimony of Mrs. E_____, to the Essex County prosecutor. 6/28/16

I did not condescend to Mr. Maada. I did not provoke him.

You can ask any of Adolpho's men—I am always very friendly when I see them. I will admit, most of the time I can't remember their names—their names are so exotic!

We couldn't possibly—personally—know which of the workers are undocumented—illegal. I would never dream of questioning anyone who works for us, who is obviously working very hard to send money back home to a wife and seven children, or a mother and eleven siblings, in God knows what poverty-stricken African or Central American country, still less would I register suspicion of their legal status. I suppose that some are Mexicans, and some are Filipinos, and some are African, and some are—Pakistani? Well, I don't know. They are all *foreign*.

Mostly, they are excellent workers. Sometimes, in the house, I see them working out in the sun, and start to feel faint watching. . . . Of course, as Adolpho has said, they are not like us. They don't mind sun and heat, they have been born nearer the equator.

So in all innocence I approached "J. S. Maada"—this is the name I would afterward learn—I will never forget!—to whom I had spoken the week before, at least I think that I had (it's hard to keep them straight, they look so much alike especially hunched over in the rose garden), and I told him that the Floradora rose had not worked out well where he'd transplanted it, so he would have to move it again, back to where it had been originally, except now there was an azalea bush in its place that he'd planted, and that would have to be relocated . . . I was not speaking rudely. I am not a bossy person! I was speaking slowly and carefully as you would speak to a child or a retarded person. For the man did not seem to comprehend my words. I could see his mouth working—but no sounds came out. He was sort of hunched over in the rose bed like a dwarf, with a back like a dwarf's back, but he was not small like a dwarf, and was sweating terribly, and "smelling" (well, I know he could not help it, none of them can help it, which is why we don't allow them to use the bathroom in our house or to come into the house for any reason)—it was a strong smell—-and was making me feel sickish. . . . He was not looking at me, his eyes were averted from my face. He had a very dark skin that seemed to suck in all the light, like an eclipse in the sky. He was polite and stiff and he was trying to smile but his face was contorted like a mask and I could see that he had cut his arm on some of the rose thorns but he did not seem to be bleeding like a normal person. It was like some kind of mucus leaked out, with a strange, sharp smell. And now I could see his eyes were not matching colors. The iris of one eye was a strange bright russet red and it was larger than the other iris, which was mud brown. Though his face was very dark it seemed to have begun to splotch with something like mange, or melanomas. It was very frightening to see—the black, "Negroid" skin seemed to be peeling off, but what was beneath?—a kind of pinkish skin, like our own skin if the outermost layer is peeled off, an unnatural pink, like raw meat. And now, the man was furious—at *me*. I could not believe how he lifted the shovel to hit me—screaming at me in a strange, brute language like the grunting of an ape—and then he struck the rose bush with the shovel—like a crazy man—and then he took hold of me and shook, shook, shook me and bared his wet, sharp teeth to b-bite . . .

(So agitated did Mrs. E_____ become, the prosecutor excused her from further testimony.)

Consequential, sequential. Without temporality, i.e., the measured unfolding of time, the human is reduced to something lesser than human.

J. S. Maada's first arrest, one day to be conflated with his second arrest, and yet a *causal factor* in the second arrest, had been in New Brunswick (5/21/15). Subject was waiting for a bus at State Street and Second Ave. at approximately 9:20 p.m. when two New Brunswick PD squad cars braked to a stop and police officers swarmed upon several "black youths" on the sidewalk. Subject demonstrated "suspicious behavior" by running panicked from the scene; after a scuffle, during which subject was thrown to the sidewalk and handcuffed, subject was arrested and taken to precinct with other young men.

Jailed in the New Brunswick Men's Detention, subject was ignored for forty-eight hours despite requests for medical attention (broken ribs, lacerated face, possible concussion), then discovered to be an "undocumented alien" from Nigeria whose student visa had expired.

251

NOTE: "Undocumented aliens" have no immigration status in the United States and may be arrested at any time and "removal proceedings" initiated. Legal help may provide options but these are temporary. Until individual is issued a green card (providing permanent residence, but not citizenship) or a student visa, he can be deported at any time.

Marriage with a US citizen automatically confers immunity to deportation by the State Department but does not confer citizenship.

Distraught subject was visited in the New Brunswick Men's Detention by a PROJECT JRD officer, who explained to him that deportation for undocumented aliens was mandated by the US State Department with one exception: if subject volunteered for a federal medical research program that he successfully completed, he would be issued a new student visa with which to attend "any university of his choice" and he would be eligible for a green card—that is, permanent residence in the US.

Gratefully, then, Joseph Saidu Maada agreed to participate in the project, which was explained to him as funded by both the United States Department of Defense and the United States Department of State. Contracts pertaining to Maada's willingness to waive his rights were signed with a flourish, though (strictly speaking) the undocumented alien does not share "rights" with US citizens. The seal of the state of New Jersey lent to these documents an authentic air. Among the test subject's personal remains, after his death, these documents were found, and reclaimed by the PROJECT.

According to the S_____ family, who had taken in the young man in his hour of need, after his expulsion from Harrogate University, Maada seemed certain that his application for US citizenship was being processed by a "special, secret court," and that he would soon become a citizen, and when he did, he would help the entire S_____ family to apply as well. *Saidu was a very kind young man, very helpful and loving with the children, especially our three-year-old Riki. When he first came to live with us he was not so talkative, and suspicious of everyone at the door but then later he became nervous and excitable and loud-laughing when there was nothing so funny we could see. With a wink he would say how he would pay us back one hundred times over for he was a "special-mission agent," one day we would be surprised.*

Maada had enrolled in the engineering program—"One of the Finest Engineering Programs in the World!"—at Harrogate University but his background in mathematics was inadequate and his ability to read and

252

write English was substandard. He had difficulty with all of his first-year courses but particularly Introduction to Computer Engineering in which he was given a grade of D- by a (Pakistani American) teaching assistant, who, he claimed, had taken a "hate" of him and whose heavily accented English Maada could not comprehend. His tuition to Harrogate had been paid by an international nonprofit agency and would not be continued after his first year. *It was kind of pathetic, these African students they'd recruited from God knows where. They weren't the age of college freshmen. They could speak English—sort of. Their tongues were just too large for the vowels. They had the look of swimmers flailing and thrashing to drown. They sat together in the dining hall, trying to eat the tasteless food. Their laughter was loud and kind of scary. White girls were particularly frightened of them, for the way the Africans stared at them with "strange hungry" smiles, they could feel "intense sexual thoughts" directed toward them especially if they wore shorts and halter tops or tight jeans, which (they believed) they had every right to wear and were not going to be "intimidated."*

Along with several other universities, Harrogate has been charged with fraud in soliciting young persons from abroad with "enticing and misrepresentative" brochures, "unethical waivers of basic educational requirements," and "worthless scholarships"; presidents of these universities travel to Africa, India, Korea, and China to proselytize shamelessly for their schools, which attract only a small percentage of (white-skinned, above-average-income) Americans and are not accredited in the US. The university does not clearly state that tuition and costs are nonrefundable as soon as the term begins and that "undergraduate living fees" are considerable. Harrogate University in Jersey City, New Jersey, has been several times indicted as perpetrating fraud—yet, even as a half dozen lawsuits pend, it is still operating in New Jersey.

After being asked to leave Harrogate, Maada was deeply shamed and disconsolate. With several other ex-engineering African students he made his way to Edison, New Jersey, where he lived with the S_____ family, fellow Nigerians who took pity on him and made room for him in their small, cramped apartment on Ewing Street. In Edison, Maada looked for employment wherever he could find it. He was paid in cash, and took pride in paying the S_____s whenever he could; they did not know details of Maada's personal life but registered surprise that Maada had been released from men's detention so quickly after his arrest, with no charges against him. Not only was Maada spared a prison sentence but he was guaranteed payment from the US government each month, in cash, which, combined with the cash he received from his numerous jobs, allowed him to pay the S_____s usually on time, and even to send money back to his family in Nigeria.

By a 2012 mandate of the Department of Defense, payments received by all participants in (classified) research projects throughout the United States are to be "at least one and a half times" the wages earned by the participant in his primary civilian job; this has been emphasized, for PROJECT JRD has committed to "zero tolerance" of exploitation of any of its subjects domestic or foreign.

LOST IN SPACE

As stated at the outset of this report, the destabilization of spatial functions of cognition in test subject #293199/Joseph Saidu Maada as a consequence of neurotransmitter microchips inserted in his cerebral cortex did not appear to be so extreme as the subject's temporal destabilization, though it was frequently a contribution to his general " disorientation."

Essentially, subject did not know "where" he was in the basic ontological sense of the term. He had exhibited some natural curiosity before leaving his homeland to fly (to Newark Liberty International Airport) and then to take ground transportation (bus) to Jersey City, New Jersey, to the campus of Harrogate University; but, if examined, he could not have said where these destinations were in relationship to one another, let alone to his homeland or, indeed, to any other points on the map,* nor did Maada, like many, or most, foreign visitors, have anything like a clear vision of how vast the United States is and of how staggeringly long it would require (for instance) to drive across the continent. Maada had no idea of his proximate position in the universe—he had no idea of the universe. When it was revealed to him via the commandant (NTM) that he was a native of a distant moon (Ganymede, one of the moons of Jupiter) sent to Earth on a mission that involved amnesia (no memory of Ganymede) and "surrogate identity" (quasi memory of Nigeria), he was initially eager to be shown photographs of Ganymede and Jupiter but soon became discouraged by the distant and impersonal nature of the images provided him at the institute. For—where did the people *live?* Maada wondered. All you could see was strangely colored rock and blank, black space that was very beautiful but did not appear to be habitable.

Before this, Maada had had frequent difficulty with his physical/ spatial surroundings in his "adopted" country. He could not begin to comprehend the New Jersey Turnpike with its many lanes and exits that seemed to repeat endlessly and to no purpose; if he was obliged to ride in a vehicle on the turnpike, being driven by Adolpho to a work site, he shut his eyes and hunched his head between his shoulders and waited to be told that he had arrived. Even on the Harrogate campus he was easily confused. Not only did the blank, buff-colored factorylike buildings closely resemble one another but walkways and "quads" appeared to be identical. Many of the (multiethnic) individuals whom he encountered at the university appeared to be identical. Often he became lost looking for a classroom; by the time he arrived, the class had ended, or perhaps it had never existed. Tests were administered like slaps to the head—he could not grasp what was being demanded of him, and he did not like the way his professors and TAs ("teaching assistants"—a term new to him) smiled at him in scorn, derision, and pity. For amid so many dusky-skinned persons, Joseph Saidu Maada was decidedly *black*.

Somehow, then, it happened that he was barred from the dour asphalt dormitory to which he'd been assigned, to share a "suite" with several other first-year engineering students from scattered parts of the globe. He was served a warrant: a notice of expulsion signed by the chancellor of Harrogate University and affixed with the university's gold-gilt seal. African American security officers, taller than he by several inches, burly, uniformed, and armed with billy clubs, arrived to forcibly escort him off campus with a warning that if he dared return he would be arrested and deported. His student visa had been revoked, his scholarship had been terminated. This happened so quickly, Maada had difficulty comprehending that he was no longer a *student* with much promise enrolled in one of the great engineering programs in the world but an individual designated as *undocumented, illegal,* who was shortly to be *deported.*

In "New Jersey" there was nowhere to go *on foot.* You could not use *instinct.* Blows to the test subject's head caused by the booted feet of enraged New Brunswick police officers contributed to his diminished sense of place and direction. In an apartment of three cramped rooms Maada could become hopelessly lost; as in a hallucination he might encounter his own self emerging through a doorway. A dingy mirror or reflecting surface told him what he already dreaded to know—there was "another" on the farther side of a glass whose intentions could not be known.

255

Later, the commandment would quell such fears. *You are one of many; and you are many of one.*

Since Maada had no idea where the institute was, how many miles from the apartment he shared with the S_____s in Edison, there was a kind of comfort in not knowing and in the certitude of not being able to know where he was taken. No one could possibly expect Maada to draw a map of where he was taken—he had virtually no idea where he *was*, before he was *taken*. Each Thursday, according to schedule, and in fulfillment of his contract, Maada was picked up by an (unmarked) van, to bring him to the institute for approximately twelve hours of neurophysiological experiments; soon after the onset of the NTM insertions in the parietal lobe of his brain, Maada had but the vaguest sense of direction, like a child on a fun-house ride who is dazed and dazzled and frightened and yet strangely comforted that the ride was after all a *ride*, prescribed by adults whose wisdom far surpassed his own.

On a typical Thursday, the test subject was instructed to wait in the early morning at a designated place, usually in the parking lot of a fast-food restaurant on Route 1, though sometimes in the parking lot of a discount store on Route 27; there was a busy intersection near the campus of Edison Community College on Route 27 that was a convenient place for Maada to await the van, for here he could easily blend in with other young men like himself, drawn to the college with a hope of bettering their lives and being granted US citizenship as a reward. Maada had been warned never to speak of waiting to be picked up by any vehicle. So zealous to obey the commandant, he did not speak to anyone at all, gesturing at his throat and shaking his head bemusedly to indicate that (possibly) he had a sore throat, laryngitis, if anyone tried to initiate a conversation with him. It was a continual surprise to the subject to glance around and discover the (unmarked) van gliding to the curb beside him like a vehicle in a space film, and braking silently to a stop. The driver, only just distinguishable through a tinted windshield, wore dark glasses, and gave no sign to Maada that Maada should make his way with seeming casualness to the rear of the van, where the doors would be opened for him, quickly, and quickly shut behind him.

It was with a sense of excitement and exhilaration that Maada climbed so trustingly into the van, to be borne however many miles to the institute, in the company of mostly dark-skinned men of about his age, sometimes younger, rarely older; these were individuals dressed like himself, in nondescript dark hoodies provided by the PROJECT and good-quality running shoes; at a glance you saw that their wrists were not cuffed and their ankles not shackled, for they were here voluntarily, as J. S. Maada was here voluntarily. There was little need to warn these men (they were all men) to remain silent, and to keep to themselves, for each believed the others to be spies who would report them to the CIA. Also, each knew that a surveillance camera was trained on the interior of the van, for (they knew) all US citizens were under surveillance at all times. The van was windowless—of course. There was no way to *look out*. The driver took the silent, slightly apprehensive men who avoided eye contact with one another on an ever-shifting, improvised circuit that might have taken them twenty miles from their pickup site, or five hundred yards. Their destination was the Institute for Independent Neurophysiological Research on Route 1, Princeton, New Jersey—a windowless three-floor rectangle that looked as if it were covered in aluminum foil, blindingly reflecting the sun—but of course none of the men ever saw the exterior of the institute.

The van passed into an underground garage and came to a halt. The rear doors were unlocked by unseen, deft hands. As Maada and the others disembarked, always very polite with one another, and maintaining their discreet eye evasion, PROJECT assistants were waiting to check their IDs (eyes, fingerprints) and to take them to their assigned laboratories. They had not a moment to glance about, to "get their bearings"—indeed, in the dim-lighted interior of the garage, which smelled of nothing more ominous than motor oil, there were no bearings to *get*.

Inevitably, the test subjects had no way of exercising any residue of a natural sense of space and direction, for they had no more information about where they were than blindfolded children forced to turn in circles until they were dizzy and in danger of fainting might have.

Joseph Saidu Maada was usually eager to cooperate with researchers. He was boyish, even energetic. He laughed often, if nervously. At the institute it was said of him that he resembled the youthful Muhammad Ali—so tall, so handsome, and so good-natured!—but that was at the start of his participation in the PROJECT.

After disembarking from the van, the test subjects were quickly taken to individual examination rooms in the institute. Their blood was drawn, and lab tests run. Some, like J. S. Maada, often volunteered to give more blood, for which they were rewarded with cash bonuses; but this was not required.

(Of course, after several months, when our research team began to replace Maada's blood with an experimental chemical solution mimicking the molecular structure of the blood, it was not "blood" drawn from his arm but a surrogate material designated as *blood [patent pending] in the reports. See also *plasma, *bone marrow, *nerves, *ganglia.)

From the examination room the subject was brought to Dr. Lehrman's laboratory, where the staff awaited him. Assiduous lab notes were kept by all, to be subsequently conflated; each session was videotaped, and copies sent at once to PROJECT JRD headquarters.

One of the consequences of the initial brain (microchip) insertions was a flattening of vision, so that to the subject much of the world looked like "walls"—"wallpaper" A three-dimensional world is a visual habit that can be broken readily in the human brain, if one knows how. Maada was more perplexed by this phenomenon than disturbed, for there was, in line with the simplification of images, a cartoonlike simplification of "depth"—you could feel that "depth" was missing from your visual field but you could not comprehend that it was "depth" that was missing.

Soon, without understanding what was wrong, and that it was his perception that was amiss and not the actual world, Maada began to puzzle over the S_____children, who did not seem (to him) to be the "right sizes." Especially his favorite, Riki, a lively three-year-old, appeared to be "different sizes," depending upon his physical proximity to Maada. For Maada might sight Riki at a distance, without realizing that it was a distance, and so the child would appear to Maada much smaller than he was, like a doll; without three dimensions to suggest depth, all was flattened, cartoonlike. Such experiences bewildered Maada, who could not have explained them, even before the impairment to his cerebral cortex, in clinical or intellectual terms. The diminution of the children in size was particularly frightening to Maada, who soon became convinced that Riki, the smallest child, was in danger of *going out*—as a flame is blown out.

Conversely, adults who seemed, to Maada, of a comfortably small, contained size at a distance, loomed large up close, and could be terrifying. The overall shifting sizes of persons and objects was disorienting to Maada, and eventually exhausting, but he learned to shut one eye so that the expectation of three dimensions (whatever "three dimensions" had come to mean) was not an issue.

In all, there would be eleven surgeries performed on Maada's brain, each for a distinct purpose. One of the more successful was the instillation of selected amnesia, through "erasures" of certain clusters of neurons in the brain matter surrounding the hippocampus, with the result that the subject could not remember that he'd had surgery, along with much else. To account for his part-shaved head, the subject was told that he'd had an infestation of head lice—his hair had had to be cut off and his head shaved in the affected area. The surgery left wounds and scars that had to be disguised with a scalp covering, in this case a "wig" that was a patch of hair matching the subject's own hair, which he could not remove from his head, and would not try to remove, under the impression that it was a "scalp flap" that had been secured with stitches. In addition, Maada was told that the patch contained toxin to repel lice. All this he seemed to accept without question.

Another of the surgeries concentrated on the agency of *will, willfulness*. With neurons in these areas "hosed clean," these were subdued.

Eventually, the "scalp flap" was enlarged, and a more serious, systematic neurosurgery was performed on the subject. (Of course, the subject was kept in an anesthetized state for such surgeries, which could require as long as nine or ten hours.) Exposed as a clockwork mechanism, the brain was readily examined by a team of experimental neuroscientists involved in the NTM project. Could one communicate with a region of the subject's brain without involving the subject ("consciousness") at all? Could one give contrary signals to parts of the brain, and force upon the brain a quasi consciousness, born of desperation? Could "consciousness" be chased into a region of the brain, like a rat into a cage corner? Maada, in his state of suspended animation, barely breathing, bodily functions monitored minutely, was an ideal subject, for he was in excellent physical condition and, in recent months in particular, inclined to *passivity*.

In a sequence of surgeries, parts of the subject's brain were excised and replaced with artificial devices—chips, stents. Such experimentation is crucial, for one day, and that day not far in the future, neurophysiological enhancements will be necessary to provide longevity to humankind, at least to world leaders and members of the ruling classes. One of the most innovative experiments developed at the institute has been the gradual replacement of a subject's blood with a chemically identical *blood that was not red but near transparent, a more practical blood composition in which white cells are better equipped to combat bacterial and viral invasions than "natural" blood.

In another yet more radical experiment, through electrical charges directly into the memory center of the subject's brain, circumventing conscious channels, the subject was informed in a vividly "mystical" dream that he was not an ordinary, mortal human being but a native of Ganymede, one of four large, beautiful moons of the sixty-seven moons of Jupiter. Given the code name "Joseph," the subject had been sent on a stealth mission to the Earth, to the United States, in the guise of a youthful, male native of the African nation Nigeria; to throw off suspicion, the subject was outfitted with a very dark, purplish-black skin, hyperalert senses (visual, auditory, olfactory), and "radioactive" eye sensors. In this guise, as "Joseph," the subject could see through solid objects; he could hear not only what was being said at a distance but he could "hear" thoughts. He knew languages instinctively—without needing to think, he "translated" these languages into thought. In this superior being, the thin scrim between consciousness and unconsciousness had been penetrated.

Of course, there have been unanticipated side effects of such experimentation: in several test subjects these have included convulsions, psychosis, and death. (So far as we know, none of these have been subjects in Dr. Lehrman's lab.)

Here, there. How do we distinguish?

Despite J. S. Maada's spatial destabilization, or perhaps because of it, the subject exhibited no difficulty in understanding, or imagining that he understood, how his cramped living quarters in Edison, New Jersey, were at the same time the open, unbounded atmosphere of Ganymede; he was not baffled that he could be *here* and *there* simultaneously.

Partly, this extraordinary mental feat was made possible by the near-total modification of the subject's basic memory—that is, the neural region in which were stored memories of the subject's earliest childhood and adolescence, altered to include purposefully vague "memories" of Ganymede. In a bold experiment the subject was shown photographs taken in Nigeria, initially landscapes of surpassing beauty, villages, celebrations, smiling children; suddenly, war-torn villages, hellish ruins, fires, corpses; men, women, and children strewn in the street, some badly mutilated, headless. Such powerful stimuli had a minimal emotional effect upon the subject, for an inhibitory microchip governed the firing of neurons in his brain. Where neurons fail to fire there cannot be conscious "thought"; where there is not conscious thought, there cannot be the retrieval of "memory"; and where no memory, no "emotion." (See Lehrman, M., "Neurotransmitter Inhibitory Functions in the Subcortical Human Brain," *Neuroscience Quarterly*, 1:3. [Another paper of which 90 percent was written by Dr. Lehrman's postdocs, names grudgingly acknowledged in an obscure footnote.])

Yet more ingeniously, microchip neurotransmitters were activated at a distance in the subject's brain by (remote) electrical stimulation sending "voices" to the subject, with such auditory acuteness the subject could not but believe that they were in the room with him and were *actual*; amidst these, secondary "voices" could be sent to confirm, or contradict, or drown out the initial voices, leaving the hapless subject utterly baffled and catatonic. In one phase of the experiment the subject was made to hear voices in his original (Yoruba) language but with unusual inflections as if being uttered by computers, or foreign-born persons, which produced a particularly unnerving effect in the subject; in another phase, the subject was made to hear "Ganymede" speech—a computer-generated language with a scrambled syntax. At all times the voice of the commandant could interrupt and redirect the subject. (This too was a computergenerated voice but its baritone timbre was soothing and "paternal.")

More recently developed has been a means of using the subject as a recording device without the subject's awareness, in Maada's case exchanges among Maada and some members of the S_____ family, when Maada sat down to meals with them; these in pidgin English or, presumably, Yoruba. No effort was made to translate these desultory conversations as they could have zero scientific interest.

Other sounds sent to the subject at a distance were thunder, music, dreams, an eerie whispering "breath" of outer space meant to simulate the sound of winds on Ganymede; each drew a specific reaction from the subject, ranging from fear to sorrow to intense, infantile joy, and each was experienced without question.

Electrical stimulations in the subject's brain stirred appetite and nausea, sexual desire and sexual repugnance, simultaneously. Shown photographs of (presumably) sexually stimulating images, like naked, nubile women and girls, the subject did not react as he might have reacted normally, when neurotransmitters blocked his reflexive reactions; conversely, shown photographs of (presumably) asexual images, the subject was stimulated to react sexually. (Of experiments performed upon him without his awareness this was perhaps the most distressing to the subject as Maada could not comprehend why he was beginning to have "sex desire" for such bizarre and inappropriate objects as clouds, towels, doorknobs, infants, and toddlers. Even in his diminished state, the subject retained a residue of human shame and conscience, and came to feel agitated about losing control of his "soul.")

As "Joseph," the test subject was required to carry a ("virtual") explosive device strapped to his body to be detonated by remote control at the direction of the commandant. This act of *martyrdom* was a test of Maada's/"Joseph's" loyalty to his Ganymede mission. Though perceived to be "anxious" and "distracted" at the prospect of a suicide mission, or what he believed to be a suicide mission, Maada did not question its necessity; a crucial incision in his brain had reduced the impulse to "question."

Such detonations might take place, for instance, when Maada and the S_____ family were sitting together at a mealtime; when Maada was shopping in a 7-Eleven store, walking along a crowded street in Edison, or traveling with his fellow lawn-crew workers in the rear of his employer Adolpho's truck. Detonation would be accomplished at a vastly long distance: electrical forces would be released on Ganymede, to travel to Earth at the speed of light. *Why?* was not a question to be asked, nor even *How?*—for Maada need do nothing but submit, and he would be blameless.

Each time Maada was directed by the commandant to prepare for the explosion, he became highly agitated, but only inwardly; his heartbeat accelerated, and his sweat glands oozed sweat. (Eventually, in a later phase of the experiment, the subject's heart was adjoined to a fine-meshed mechanism that was immune to "accelerating.") That Maada cooperated unresistingly in what would be (theoretically) his own demise confirmed the success of the NTM inserts; he'd been programmed to elevate the commandant over any (merely) human beings. Obedience was linked to the subject's "Ganymede destiny" and "Ganymede pride" though J. S. Maada's notion of his mythical homeland was almost entirely abstract: a rugged rock terrain resembling the badlands of Montana, of pitiless sunshine and shadows so sharp they registered to the eye as crevices.

In another experimental mission the subject was directed to make his way into the Martin Luther King Building & US Courthouse at 50 Walnut Street, Newark, New Jersey. Here, in this clamorous foyer, he was to pass through security undetected—of course, the explosives he was carrying were "virtual" and not "actual"—and without calling attention to himself in any way; he was then to enter a specially designated courtroom on the first floor, and take a seat inconspicuously at the rear. A PROJECT observer stationed at the site noted that Maada did not behave suspiciously in this public setting but exuded the slightly nervous yet eager-to-please air of a foreign visitor to the United States who is hoping one day to become a citizen. Here too the subject was convinced that he was "Joseph"—a "stealth missile" and potential "martyr" to be detonated by a remote control from one of the moons of Jupiter.

In Judge D_____'s courtroom, which was beginning to fill with participants and spectators, the test subject waited.

Even at such a time of intense concentration and preparedness Maada retained some residue of awareness from his former life. He could not, he reasoned, be blamed for anything that "happened"—it would "happen" through him but not by his hand. He was as innocent as a young child of knowledge of who the enemy was, and why the enemy, and himself with them, was to be annihilated in a cataclysm of flames and rubble in this austere old government building. US Federal Justice D_____ was to be "executed"—but why? An enemy of—whom? Was the US government involved in a stealth program to assassinate certain of its citizens, like Judge D_____? So long as Maada was innocent of such knowledge and merely following the directives of the commandant, he was innocent of the acts he precipitated, and this was a solace to him.

Saidu, what are you doing? Why?

But he was innocent of such knowledge, merely following the directives of the commandant. He did not need to lift a finger—to employ a finger—to "detonate"—for that would be done for him, like magic.

And yet abruptly, after forty minutes, the commandant's voice calmly informed him that the mission had been "suspended" for the time being and he was free to leave.

What relief he felt! Or no, not relief, a sudden vast, insatiable hunger.

In front of a vending machine on the ground floor of the courthouse Maada stood trembling. So many choices!—soft drinks, candy bars, chips. He could not decide what to purchase first. His hands were shaking so badly, he could not remove his wallet from his pocket. In a trance of euphoria he wept hot acid tears that ran in rivulets down his cheeks.

＊　＊　＊

And then, in late spring 2016 Maada began to misinterpret NTM sig-nals. Willful neurons in the test subject firing *in ways contrary to direc-tives.*

That this was happening in test subject #293199 after months of subject's near-total cooperation was in itself a significant if unexpected development. For no experiment is without valuable revelations!

Of course, *willfulness* in the subject J. S. Maada was intermittent and inconsistent. Resisting programmed directives did not represent an al-tered pattern of behavior in #293199 for there was no (discernible) pattern to it.

In the heat of early summer working with Adolpho's Lawn Care crew, Maada was observed shivering violently while others complained of heat; subject perspired heavily, yet continued to shiver with (apparent) cold. When NTM activity was inoperative, subject began to "hear" voices of a new and inexplicable sort. Though he could not have known of the microscopic stents in his brain, still less the cluster of strategi-cally placed computer chips, or the artificial "scalp flap" beneath a patch of hair, he began to obsess that there were "things" in his brain—grains of sand, staple-sized bits of metal, lice that crawled and sucked his blood. He came to believe that his heart had been replaced by "a kind of clock that ticks." His blood was no longer red but of the hue and substance of mucus. His skin, which had always been so rich and dark, was lightening in splotches, like a kind of cancer—from working in the sun? Yet, Maada could not *not work* for he needed the money to repay the S_____ family for their generosity to him and also to send back to his family in Nigeria (though his family had become distant and blank to him like faded faces on a billboard, and several messages from "voices" had called into question his actual blood relationship to them). Maada diverted his most anxious thoughts by scratching and peeling his skin, which seemed to give him an intense, sensual pleasure; be-neath were patches of sickly pale skin, both repugnant and fascinating.

Even when no NTM activity was initiated from the institute, subject began to experience "zapping" sensations in his brain and throughout his body. These came from a long distance, subject believed, traveling at the speed of light. His genitals were particularly sensitive to such signals—though in fact there were no signals. "Sex desire" for inani-mate objects like discarded Styrofoam cups bearing a residue of coffee or cola, carelessly opened cereal boxes, unlaced work boots swept upon

264

him at unpredictable times. He could not bear to touch the genital region of his body for such touch was forbidden, yet his hands moved of their own greed and willfulness, and were shameful to him. In the S_____family there was little privacy, which was shameful to him. *You smell funny, Saidu,* one of the older children said, wrinkling her nose. It was terrifying to him; the S_____family would evict him from their apartment; a voice not precisely but resembling that of the commandant suggested that it might be wisest to slash the S_____s' throats in their beds some night when all were sleeping peacefully, and then to slash his own. Yet an instant later, Adolpho was shouting at him: *Asshole! Wake up.* So tired he was falling asleep in the truck—he was falling asleep on his (shaky) feet. Losing his ability to see himself in relationship to other (spatial) beings. For it is *space* that prevents us being crushed together—as *time* prevents everything happening at once—but what is *space?* Shut his eyes, *space* vanished. Much was becoming scrambled, dismembered, dissected. It was repulsive to him, to observe his own body dissected by (white) strangers with handsaws and bloodstained surgical instruments. And his jaw hanging slackly open, and his eyes but half closed. Those corrosive acid tears leaving rivulets on his cheeks, and elsewhere, on his body, splotches and peelings. So vividly he saw the strangers with their sharp instruments, their wrinkled noses at the smell of his sawn-open torso—*Jesus, what a stink!*

Had it already happened?—or not yet? As if compressed on the head of a pin, everything was prepared to detonate.

When Adolpho came for them on a street corner in Edison in the twilit hour at dawn Maada had to summon all his strength to climb into the truck with the others. Where once he'd been the youngest member of the lawn crew, now his youth had drained from him—he'd become the oldest. His back was stricken with pain. All of the nerves of his back had been strung to breaking. His brain was swollen with pustules. Lice scrambled through the hole in his head, and into his hair. His left eye was plastic. He had slipped back in "time" as clumsily as you'd slip in dog shit on the sidewalk—he had become his own ancestor, a slave. On the moon of Jupiter, slaves had revolted in open, deep crevice pits as their captors had flung livid torches down at them. It had been a slave uprising, which had propelled him to Earth, to save the others. He yearned to know more of his mysterious and forbidden origin but the words that would have brought him knowledge began to break and crumble like a column of ants when a booted foot descends upon them.

Riding the massive lawn mower. A coworker had been kind enough to adjust the ear protectors against his ears. Yet hearing a babble and crackle of voices and laughter. Seeing figures amid the trees, which (though lifelike) he knew were not really there, for they were transparent like jellyfish; you could see through them.

At the S_____ estate working stooped in the sun. How many hours stooped and digging in the sun. Woman with a pig face. That skin—"white." Snout nose. Pig-eyes lewd and laughing. Pig-eyes dared to descend to the gnarl of misery at his groin.

What issued from the pig-mouth was confusing to him for he had already obeyed the pig-mouth. He knew. He was sure. Yet he was not sure for perhaps it had not happened yet.

Yet, *it had happened.* The Floradora rose was to be dug up another time and another time replanted.

Dug up and brought to the other bed, which is/was the first bed. And the azalea dug up, and hauled away to be replanted. It seemed to Maada that he had just performed these actions. He had performed these actions several times. The pig-woman had given him orders, and he had obeyed. Yet it was possible that the several times he had obeyed the pig-woman were collapsed to a single time and that time like the head of a pin, too small to see. Was there just one rose bed, and one hole?—but more than one Floradora rose? And what of the azalea? Trying to understand such a puzzle was like trying to push inside his head an object too big to fit inside his skull as well as oddly angled. Subject began to experience rapid zaps in brain, groin, fingers. Began to scream, grunt, tear like a ravenous animal with his teeth.

Pig-woman screamed, screamed. His coworkers screamed at *him,* pulling him off her.

It was the end. All of Ganymede would rejoice; a new martyr would enter the firmament.

The night before, this had happened.

Riki, who'd loved to cuddle with Saidu, shrank from him now, seeing something in Saidu's face that was beginning to twitch, splotch, and peel like sunburn. The iris of one eye was inflamed, half again the size of the other iris. And the strange smell like something rotted.

Riki laughed uneasily, and sucked his thumb, and began to cry when Maada stooped to play with him.

Yet Maada had no clear idea when this was. Riki was running away from him before he'd run toward him.

No! Go away, I don't like you.

Reached for the child, who was screaming with laughter. Or, screaming. Reached for the child, and the child's legs thrashed wildly.

Far away, on a moon of the great planet Jupiter, a remote control was being pressed. The detonation would be instantaneous.

Nominated by Conjunctions

ANY COMMON DESOLATION

by ELLEN BASS

from POEM-A-DAY

can be enough to make you look up
at the yellowed leaves of the apple tree, the few
that survived the rains and frost, shot
with late afternoon sun. They glow a deep
orange-gold against a blue so sheer, a single bird
would rip it like silk. You may have to break
your heart, but it isn't nothing
to know even one moment alive. The sound
of an oar in an oarlock or a ruminant
animal tearing grass. The smell of grated ginger.
The ruby neon of the liquor store sign.
Warm socks. You remember your mother,
her precision a ceremony, as she gathered
the white cotton, slipped it over your toes,
drew up the heel, turned the cuff. A breath
can uncoil as you walk across your own muddy yard,
the big dipper pouring night down over you, and everything
you dread, all you can't bear, dissolves
and, like a needle slipped into your vein—
that sudden rush of the world.

Nominated by Frank X. Gaspar

FUNNY BIRD SEX

by JOHN R. NELSON

from THE ANTIOCH REVIEW

> *"Man is the only animal that blushes. Or needs to."*
> —*Mark Twain*

We humans like to think our species is unique. "Man is the only animal for whom his own existence is a problem that he has to solve." (Erich Fromm) "Man is the only animal whose desires increase as they are fed; the only animal that is never satisfied." (Henry George) "Man is the only animal that can remain on friendly terms with the victims he intends to eat until he eats them." (Samuel Butler) Fire, underwear, irony, iPhones, art appreciation, AK-47s, judgment in the afterlife, life after offspring—all these set us apart, or so we believe. We're the animal with a touchy self-pride, the animal that insists on locating itself in a separate, usually higher category. Man is the only animal that laughs at the sex lives of other animals.

Take birds, for instance. To breed successfully, a bird must manage a few seemingly straightforward prerequisites. Find other members of your species. Choose one of the desired gender. Make sure your partner is alive. Easy enough, one would think, but would-be mating birds may fail absurdly on all three counts: wrong species, wrong gender, not even animate. In the 1950s, when scientists first experimented with stuffed specimens of birds, ornithologist Ludlow Griscom proclaimed: "One of the most extraordinary things about birds is their apparent inability to discriminate between a live bird and a dead one." Males of sexually dimorphic species, like quail, proved especially vulnerable to the charms of terrycloth mates. "The sexual behavior of male quail can be triggered by the visual cues of a receptive female," concluded researcher Michael Domjan, "even if those visual cues are provided by a taxidermic model of a female." Even when the sexes look alike, as in wrens, some males can't resist replicas. One cadre of scientists set out to test the limits of male indiscriminateness. Using wooden models of female turkeys, they systematically removed the tails, feet, and wings until all that remained were heads on sticks. The male turkeys were still good to go. Turkeys' tendency to overgeneralize isn't limited to prospective mates, for they'll also attack territorial rivals ranging from fellow turkeys to Pontiacs.

To be fair, partner recognition can be tough. In some species, males and females look so nearly identical that scientists can know gender only by dissection—not an option if you're aiming to mate. Eighteenth-century naturalist Gilbert White, struggling to distinguish birds by gender in first plumage, compared the problem to uncertain identification in our own species. Before secondary sex characteristics make gender evident, he noted, "A beautiful youth shall be so like a beautiful girl that the difference shall not be discernible." In fact, the difficulty extends far beyond birds or humans. Males of many animal species are "dim in their sexual discernment," says Robert Wright in *The Moral Animal*, and will try to breed with almost anything. Sure, it's funny to us that a turkey will try to hump a stick with a fake head. But what about the millions of human males who masturbate to representations of women, including "women" who are literally cartoons? If, as anthropologist Helen Fisher claims, every human develops a refined "love map" in seeking an ideal partner, some of us need to check our neural GPSs for malfunctions.

In the field, birders almost invariably titter or crack wise if they come upon copulating birds. Usually it takes two to tango—that is, two birders watching, preferably of different genders, for our species' sexual self-consciousness to kick in and express itself through attempts at humor. At the least we feel obliged to point out that, indeed, these animals are having sex right in front of us. On the face of it, bird coition seems an unpromising source of comic material. For one thing, it's usually over almost before it starts. Dunnock pairs, with astonishing coordination, can do it in under a second. Manakin copulation is so quick that we need slow-motion video to witness it. But for humans, there's humor even in this wham-bam-thank-you-ma'am rapidity, like a premature ejaculator on fast-forward. We're the species that grasps the world through identification and analogy. Unless we've become deadened, we're animals who think, or feel: "How would I feel if I were that animal?" When we laugh at birds, we laugh at ourselves.

For the same reason we may chuckle lewdly when hearing that

American kestrels copulate up to fifteen times a day, and northern goshawks up to 600 times per clutch. Not that it would be so amusing, much less erotic, to actually watch 600 goshawk copulations. Some of the comedy in bird sex comes from its deadpan matter-of-factness, its defiance of romanticized human projections. The male mounts, the couple briefly vibrates, the male hops off. And things may not even get that far. William Vogt, editor of *Bird Lore* and a leader of Planned Parenthood, used to watch a willet couple he named Will and Kate: "A neo-pagan poet would have been shocked at the lack of impetuousness in their love-making. At the slightest sign of negation from Kate, Will would turn his attention to other matters (usually food)." John Hay described similarly lackluster terns: "Efforts at copulation don't always succeed. A male may mount a female and stand on her back for minutes at a time in an absent-minded, half-hearted way before he climbs off, with nothing accomplished." C'mon, guys, you want to shout at these birds, get with the program! You call that mating? You'll never pass along your genes that way! You can almost hear Sarah Vaughan singing "You're So Blasé" on the soundtrack.

Bird sex isn't all about quickies and slackers. As with humans, bird pairings are rarely merely funny. Bird lovers have long been touched by the attentiveness, tender caresses, and sweet chatter of mating birds such as white-breasted nuthatches and eastern bluebirds. Konrad Lorenz, who kept jackdaws as pets, claimed that, well before they're "wed" through "physical union," a jackdaw couple becomes "betrothed," feeding, grooming, and supporting each other in a "heartfelt mutual defense league" strengthened by affection during their lives together. Though he granted that few birds "maintain a lasting conjugal state," Lorenz indignantly denied he was anthropomorphizing his birds: "You think I humanize the animal?" Belief in jackdaw love, he argued, "does not invest the animal with human properties, but, on the contrary, shows us the still remaining animal instincts in man." Albatrosses prove that a loyal bird bond, though hardly the norm, is not merely sentimental human myth. They may have, says Noah Strycher, "the most intense love affairs of any animal on our planet," and their near-zero divorce rate is probably the lowest of any bird species. Despite long and frequent separations, with thousands of miles between them, the birds invariably come back to their mates, to feed their young and snuggle together in sleep, head to breast.

If there's tenderness in mating birds, there's also rapture, or the appearance of rapture. Many observers have been bewitched by the elab-

271

orate, intense ballets of courting tricolored herons. The herons, like most animals, make the most of what they've got—long legs; long, flexible necks; plumes that can stiffen or quiver—to come together, curtsey and bow, sway and sidestep, dazzle and suggest, fan their lacy aigrettes, twist their slender necks into lover's knots, and preen together. Swan pairs will join in a celebratory strut-and-gloat "triumph ceremony" after the chivalrous swan lord vanquishes a rival suitor unworthy of his lady's attention. Long-billed dowitchers wait until after copulation to celebrate, hovering enrapt over mates and launching into rousing song. The most famous description of bird ecstasy is Walt Whitman's poem "Dalliance of the Eagles," which makes airplane sex seem a poor substitute:

> The rushing amorous contact high in space together
> The clinching, interlocking claws, a living, fierce, gyrating wheel,
> Four beating wings, two beaks, a swirling mass tight grappling,
> In tumbling turning clustering loops, straight downward falling.

As Whitman demonstrates, the real show comes before the show, not in copulation but during "courtship," a prim term encompassing a wide range of dynamic behavior. Bird courtship can be wonderfully impassioned. But for human observers, if not the birds themselves, there's a thin line between passion and comedy. If you're a female who likes to see male pride deflated—and what woman doesn't?—you need look no further than the come-on of the squat, tubby, long-nosed American woodcock, a far cry from love-locked eagles. "As an enticement to idle hens," says Peter Matthiessen, "it parades like a tiny peacock, bowing and puffing and raising its bill towards the heavens as it forces its head back, the better to display its chest; whereupon, rendered blind by its own pomp, it may stumble ignominiously, or trip on sticks." As they prance and boom and swell, greater prairie chickens (whose Latin name, *Tympanuchus cupido*, roughly translates as "Cupid with a kettle drum") seem designed as parodies of human male self-importance. With other species the humor lies in the sheer unlikelihood of what these guys consider seductiveness. Among lekking birds, where male groups display competitively in arenas, like bodybuilders, excitable males can get so caught up in macho one-upmanship that they wind up chasing each other around, seven or eight at a time, says Colin Tudge, "pounding along in a mock race—like Greek athletes, hurtling in silhouette around a vase." The females, evaluating, look on.

In his preface to *Joseph Andrews*, Henry Fielding theorized that the "true Ridiculous" arises from one spring only, affectation, which in turn stems from two causes, vanity and hypocrisy. Birds lack both capability and cause to be hypocrites, and it's probably unfair to attribute vanity to creatures who usually ignore mirrors. Nonetheless, when birders, especially women, get good looks at gorgeous birds, such as Baltimore orioles, they often exclaim, "He knows how handsome he is!" Do orioles know they're good-looking? I doubt it, but even if they do, simply showing off one's beauty is not sufficient to achieve Ridiculousness. No, even with the flashiest, most manic birds, the bite in the comedy comes not from male display alone but from the mortifying contrast between males' desperate sexual pleadings and the apparent boredom of females. While lekking males leap, spin, and zigzag around them, females nonchalantly wander about, glancing now and again but seeming preoccupied, as if composing the day's shopping list. Sure, eventually they agree to copulate, with the vast majority often choosing the same mate, but the climax is so anticlimactic, and there are so many scoreless losers.

It would be foolish to claim that laughter at bird procreation is a universal human trait. Do hunter-gatherers in Papua New Guinea giggle knowingly when they come across copulating birds-of-paradise? I have no idea. But in the West, with our Puritan tradition, there've been plenty of watchers who didn't find bird sex the least bit funny. In the film *The African Queen*, Rose Sayer (Katherine Hepburn) says to Humphrey Bogart's character, "Nature, Mr. Allnutt, is what we are put on this earth to rise above"—an attitude that led centuries of witnesses to denounce bird lechery. Certain species were singled out for shameless fornications, including the partridge—slang for "whore" in eighteenth-century England—and the barnyard rooster, which inspired "cock-alley" as a slang term for pudendum. One sixteenth- century Lutheran minister condemned house sparrows to death for their "scandalous acts of unchastity committed during the service, to the hindrance of God's Word and of Christian Doctrine."

Outrage over bird lust peaked in 1925 when American birdwatcher Althea Sherman published her "Case of the People of North America versus the House Wren." While accusing wren "felons" of nefarious sexual misdeeds and "diabolical disposition," Sherman chastised fellow bird lovers for putting up wren boxes, thus enabling wren adultery. She also censured the female flicker, "a weak-minded, inconsistent, frivolous

273

creature that is called from duty by the notes of any stray male," and one thrice-mated red-winged blackbird she called Brigham, "a true polygamist of the Latter-day Saints stripe" that treated her in a "vindictive, insolent manner." It's a shame Sherman never met Billy, a pet cockatiel who's been known to masturbate up to ten times a day. Personally, I've never witnessed avian masturbation—or maybe I have without realizing it—but for all we know, self-pleasuring may be a common practice, at least in pets. "Literature on bird autoeroticism is scarce," says biologist Tom Price of the University of Liverpool, but Price and colleagues are busy "building a database on the masturbatory habits of wild and captive birds."

Some people have also been shocked by the brutality of bird copulations, such as the serial "rapes" committed by mallards, but sexual violence has provoked much less indignation than wantonness, especially female promiscuity. Again, the humor here lies not in the behavior of the birds but in our own denial or dismay when evidence undercuts our biases. It's hardly news that female birds are often faithless. A century ago, Edward Howe Forbush, citing a tree swallow that left her "husband" for a stranger, concluded that "inconstancy is a failing common to birds as well as men." And those ditch-and-switch house wrens that Sherman deplored were finding new partners somewhere. In fact, we now know that "extra-pair copulations" by one or both partners occur within every bird family. For some, cheating is occasional; for others, promiscuity is so rampant that females seem to be competing for the title of World's Biggest Bird Slut. Prime candidates include salt marsh sparrows, whose nests almost always contain eggs from multiple fathers, and dunnocks, who may copulate twenty-five times a day and eventually get around to every male in the neighborhood. The sexual escapades of some species get so complicated that ornithologists can barely keep track of the players. Flamingos are just hopeless. Every last one of them, female and male alike, subscribes to AshleyMadison.com.

Yet many people, including some scientists, long resisted the mounting evidence of female promiscuity, whether because they'd idealized birds as paragons of marital fidelity, or idealized females as the virtuous glue that holds families together, or they just couldn't believe that Mother Nature would encourage such freewheeling chaos. We also don't like the idea that if birds, or other primates, make sexual choices out of genetic self-interest, then maybe we do, too. One objection to modern sociobiology is the premise that animal sexuality is all about strategy—what is called "epigamic selection"—and that promiscuity, in birds or people, is simply one of many possible strategies that might maximize reproductive success. Some female birds are monogamous for the breeding season only, until their offspring can fend for themselves. Some mate with the best available male until a superior partner comes courting—a situation that may produce steady tension, the males constantly on guard for rivals, the females waiting for wariness to slacken. In some colonial species, couples seem to consent to mutually beneficial open marriages; males have more offspring, females, better offspring. Other females don't consent at all, but are forced into copulations by wandering males. Among sexual creatures throughout nature, Colin Tudge concludes, "Sometimes the interests of both sexes coincide; sometimes they do not." Male skuas—in what seems a stretch to call a "strategy"—may simply leave the field to the females, who sometimes kill each other in fights over desirable males.

One problem in interpreting bird sex as "strategic" is that the term implies calculation and conniving. It's not as if these birds are thinking, "If I'm a golddigger, I'll do better by my kids," or, "A guy doesn't warble like that unless he's got some good stuff in there." Actually, we don't know what birds think; we know only what they do. And often birds "choose" a "strategy" when there's little choice in the matter. Gannets return to mates year after year, while seemingly similar frigatebirds mate and move on. The difference lies not in any predilection for straying but in the species' different breeding locations and food availability. Hummingbird females, "deserted" by their partners, incubate eggs and feed their offspring and themselves without help, but single motherhood isn't a viable option for species whose offspring won't survive incubation and infancy without the care of two parents. In the nineteenth century, Thomas Higginson, a great believer in avian domestic harmony, just couldn't accept that male hummingbirds are only for-a-moment fathers, neither feeding nor protecting their young. A century later, Ludlow Griscom scoffed at such sentimentality and objected to the use of any term—desertion, faithfulness—that suggested birds were capable of "moral obliquity." It was time, Griscom insisted, to face the unromantic facts of life about bird sex. Certain species, he acknowledged, are "supposed to pair for life, but surely not because they subscribe to the principle of monogamy." It is what it is.

If we could view bird sex with Griscom's cold-eyed objectivity, we might find no humor there at all, but human sentimentality is not only natural but necessary for our own reproductive efforts. Try as we might, we can't help but project our feelings onto others, human or bird. We know that female birds aren't rationally selecting their behavior from a menu of sexual strategies, yet we still wish these girls would make smarter choices. The flamboyant performances by lekking bird—male beauty pageants—led Charles Darwin to his theory of sexual selection: "To suppose that the females do not appreciate the beauty of the males is to admit that their splendid decorations, all their pomp and display, are useless; and this is incredible." But his theory was immediately resisted by critics complaining that females, even bird females, couldn't be that shallow. As Adrian Forsyth states in *The Natural History of Sex*, the theory seemed to require "vanity in one sex and wantonness in the other."

Sociobiology offers an explanation, that courtship is a contest between male salesmanship and female sales resistance, but it leaves questions unanswered: why are these females such capricious shoppers, and why do they keep falling for the same sales pitch when they know that the salesman will skip town the moment the deal is closed? Granted, ruffs put on a good show—among the most fantastical mating displays in the animal kingdom—but why do reeves (the females of the species) perversely opt for the gaudiest guy over demonstrably stronger, tougher rivals? And golden-collared manakin females seem to think that the serious business of procreation is just an excuse to watch a dance contest. Performing tricky steps at breakneck speeds, male wooers compete to outdance one another, and one study found that females chose dynamos who finished their steps in fifty milliseconds over slowpokes who took eighty milliseconds. That's cutting it fine. Female bowerbirds, meanwhile, pin all their chances on art criticism. Males compete in building bowers (which don't function as nests), and each female judges the bowers for ingenuity and sturdiness of construction, aesthetic arrangement of objects within the bower, or whatever it is she fancies. Finally she chooses a builder, they copulate, and that's the last she sees of him, as he brings in the next judge. Why, we wonder, don't these females choose good family men instead of these let-me-show-you-my-etchings rakes? "Maybe I would, if I could find one," a bowergirl might respond. "Where's my alternative? Show me a stay-at-home bowerboy. Have you got a better way of finding good genes?" Males remain intransigent in shunning any nurturing duties. "That's the way we roll."

Most disturbing, to some observers, are females that won't stick to proper gender roles. In 1998, says Colin Tudge, male investigators were appalled by the plight of male wattled jacanas, who were routinely dominated, hounded into sex, and then abandoned—left to incubate eggs and raise offspring that often weren't even their own—by bigger, stronger, bossy, harem-ruling females. Polyandry, in which females move from partner to partner, assigning all parental care to males, is rare among birds, but its gender-bending quality nicely illustrates how judgments of birds' sexual behavior reflect the interests of human observers. Phalaropes are the best known polyandrists, and I've yet to meet the woman who doesn't feel a sisterhood with the table-turning, tit-for-tat phalarope females. Neltje Blanchan, writing in the early twentieth century, also saluted the males as admirable househusbands, unlike the "selfish, dandified drakes of some of our wild ducks" that "desert their mates as soon as the first egg is laid."

Men, on the other hand, may feel some ambivalence as they watch a female phalarope badger and thump a male until he agrees to sex or risks drowning. At most, like Elliott Coues, they might manage a wry acceptance of the situation: "The fair sex conducts the courtship, and several of them may be seen in spring pursuing a modest male, who undertakes the role of St. Anthony without success, and when captured, submits with what grace he may to incubating such eggs as his flourishing partner assures him are his own." Other men have doubted that phalarope females are female at all because, well, they don't act female. Some confusion is understandable, given that female phalaropes are atypically larger and more colorful than males, though they tend to give themselves away by laying eggs. Franz de Waal observed a similar posture of denial in male primatologists who, confronted by mutually masturbating male bonobos, labeled the behavior "sham" or "pseudo" sex to distinguish it from real, heterosexual sex. As Bill Clinton explained, it depends on what the meaning of the word *is* is.

If there's any lesson to be learned here, it's the silliness of looking to birds to model morality or wise judgment in making reproductive choices. We're kin to birds, sharing some of the same needs, but truly we must be a pathetic species if they have to teach us gender roles or devotion to our spouses. Whether we need romance—for survival or spiritual fulfillment—doesn't depend on whether birds do. (If you're reading this, honey, I love you.)

The most striking feature of bird reproduction—more funny weird than funny ha ha—isn't its amorality but its variety, the many ways in which birds attract, select, consummate, and proceed to raise offspring. Flamingos, like some gulls and hornbills, use cosmetics, applying oil to their plumes to enrich the color; the most intensely pink birds are the first to breed. Great bustard females inspect males' cloacas for parasites before copulation, while the males prepare for inspection by ingesting huge, toxic blister beetles (sometimes too toxic) to kill their parasites. Males of some species use "mating plugs" to keep rivals from inseminating females, but they've also evolved penises that can displace the plugs. In fact, if it's weirdness you fancy, the whole subject of bird penises won't disappoint. Actually, instead of penises, most males have little lumpy cloacas, but some have sort of in-between appendages, "pseudo-penises," as in the old punch line "it feels like a penis, only smaller," while ducks' spiraling, explosive penises may be, at full extension, almost as long as the ducks. The more we know about the natural world, the weirder it gets, orderly yet seemingly arbitrary, pragmatic yet whimsical, a strange brew of mutations, historical contingency and whatever-works adaptability.

Certain humans like to pride themselves on their sexual inventiveness, but, whatever innovations they've come up with, some bird probably got there before them. Some males dance for their sex lives, or fly, or dance while flying. Some proffer food for sex, gifting fish, fruit, or flies as evidence of provider skills to often fussy females. Some sing prettily, with melody and finesse, while others—avian equivalents of heavy metal bands—go for amped-up volume. Wattled bellbirds, masters of ear-splitting foreplay, sing so loud they can blow the girls right off their branches. The lords of their realms prove their superiority through fierceness in combat or pomp in the face of danger, while the apparent losers, the "sneakers," bide their time on the fringes of territories, dash in, copulate, dash off. If you're looking for birds to justify, or at least illustrate, some particular sexual practice—fetishism, dinner dates, pick-ups—there's a bird out there to accommodate you. Well, almost any practice. Sado-masochistic hermaphrodites would be better served by earthworms.

"When you observe an animal closely," Elias Canetti once said, "you feel as if a human being sitting inside were making fun of you." If birds could laugh at the sex lives of humans—and we can't say for certain they don't—what would they find laughable? Our oversized, cumbersome penises, or the fact that so many of us have penises? Our incessant voyeurism, from porn to Harlequin romance? "Recreational" sex? Menopause? If we can joke about avian quickies, high-metabolism birds might roll their eyes at the length of our consummations. When will this ever end? Or, as animals that go through long refractory periods, indifferent to any sexual stimuli, they might snicker at our 24/7/52 randiness. Don't these people ever give it a rest? And these fanatically

278

sexy animals are the same ones that make a virtue of abstinence? How confusing it must all seem. And what do birds make of the fact that, during our copulations, we might mimic *them*? Consider a partridge perusing the *Kama Sutra*: "As a major part of moaning, she may use, according to her imagination, the cries of the dove, cuckoo, green pigeon, parrot, bee, nightingale, goose, duck, and partridge. . . . As passion nears its end, he beats her extremely quickly, until the climax. At this, she begins to babble, fast, like a partridge or a goose. Those are the ways of groaning and slapping." I'll confess to at least one occasion on which I crowed like a rooster post-coitally.

Perhaps, as fellow hormone-driven creatures, onlooking birds might be sympathetically philosophical. "You know," a partridge might say to his brother, "they're not really so different from us. I mean, one day we're bowing, spinning, crooning, running around like chickens with our heads cut off. The next day we couldn't care less. What's that all about? Who's running this show anyway?"

The idea of people laughing at bird sex ultimately takes us beyond birds, beyond sex, and maybe beyond people. "It is seldom that I laugh at an animal," Lorenz observed, "and when I do, I usually find out afterwards that it was at myself, at the human being whom the animal has portrayed in a more or less pitiless caricature, that I have laughed." But what makes us laugh at ourselves? For that matter, why laugh at anything? How did our species evolve to find life comic as well as struggle-and-death tragic? How did we get from being Neolithic hunter-gatherers to sedentary oglers laughing at cats on YouTube? When did the world turn funny?

Darwin used to wonder at the human ability to produce and enjoy musical notes, and scholars still debate whether our species' musicality is adaptive—evolved through natural selection—or a superfluous, non-adaptive by-product of evolution. Darwin also puzzled over the function of laughter; late in life, his observations of his son Doddy prompted him to write a sketch on the first signs of humor appreciation in infants. Researchers in fields from biology to linguistics haven't agreed on any unified theory of comedy, but one current hypothesis is that all mammals have a sense of humor, from ticklish rats to gorillas that play on words in American Sign Language. Laughter may have originated in our great ape ancestors, who emitted laughter-like pants when they realized, or were trying to communicate, that they were playing together, in mock combat, not really fighting. Like the apes we laugh, in surprise and relief, when we know we're safe, at least for the moment.

It's a theory as plausible as any other. I prefer to believe that, like singing dowitchers, humans first laughed after sex, expressing their delighted surprise that a biological compulsion could feel so good. Long before our species grasped any connection between sex and reproduction, or realized that play grows out of a drive to survive, we burst out at our bodies' potential for shared pleasure. Sex isn't fun because it leads to procreation; it leads to procreation because it's fun, and it can be fun whether you're gay, solitary, infertile, or using contraception.

The same idea applies to dancing. As with birds, human dance may have evolved as sexual display, but whatever the function, it feels good to dance—as couples, alone, or with fellow toddlers or fellow septuagenerians. Birds, too, I believe, find joy in the unnecessary, though for fear of being charged with anthropomorphism, scientists have been reluctant to credit bird fun. Some cranes dance throughout the year, compulsively or spontaneously, whether they're mating or not. In courtship, as in hunting, peregrine falcons will stoop at tremendous speeds, abruptly shift directions, and inscribe figure-eights in the air, but they'll also plunge and somersault, relishing their powers in flight, when there's no partner to witness, no prey in sight. We go on living so we can keep on loving, dancing, and laughing. Or flying.

If birds can't laugh now, they may still evolve the capability if they can endure the hard times we've brought them. Eventually they might progress to irony. Is irony adaptive? Does irony somehow help to enable human survival, or toleration of survival? I wish I knew the answer. It would be strange if it did, strange if it didn't. "The world," said biologist J. B. S. Haldane, "is not only queerer than we imagine; it's queerer than we can imagine."

Nominated by The Antioch Review

BULLY

by AMIT MAJMUDAR

from THE HOPKINS REVIEW

First day fake friend
With the knuckle-
Crusher handshake
Making new kids

Buckle pleading
By the bus stop:
Art Class vandal,
Safety scissors

Leaving jackknife-
Streaks on Andy's
Weekslong Van Gogh
(Oddly savvy,

Though, when sneering
*Just be glad I
Didn't slash your
Ear off for you):*

Rubber cement
Booger-flicker,

Aiming always
At our terror

Eyes: Touch-football
Blindside tackler
On the recess
Blacktop, cackling

At my swiftly
Swelling ankle...
By some just as
Human impulse,

Paul "the Mauler"
Miller pulled me
Up and crutched me
On his shoulder

To the nurse's
Office; next day,
Called me *shitskin*
Like before; the

Next night, one night
Short of summer,
Hunkered in a
Crawl space while his

Former jarhead
Father rounded
On his family
With a legal

Handgun, starting
At the upstairs
Crib and ending
In the basement,

Sparing only
Two beloved
Dobermans out
Back on chokechains.

Nominated by The Hoplins Review

FAMOUS ACTOR

fiction by JESS WALTER

from TIN HOUSE

The Famous Actor was rubbing my tit with his elbow.

He'd swept into the party not five minutes earlier, in old jeans and a plain gray T-shirt, and plopped down on the couch next to me, facing the other way. He was having a chat with a guy leaning on the arm of the couch. I heard him say, "Twelve pounds of muscle," and I heard him say. "Dude sandbagged that route," and I heard him say, "No, man, the Ducati Mach 1 came out in limited release in '64. I know 'cause I have one"—all while rubbing my left boob.

I looked around the party: forty or so people clustered in threes and fours, pretending not to look at the Famous Actor (even here in Bend, we know not to go goony around celebrities), but no one went more than four or five seconds without stealing a glance at him. Nobody but me seemed to notice what his right elbow was up to.

After a few minutes, he stopped elbow-fucking me and turned so that we were face-to-face. It was weird staring into those pale blues, eyes I'd known for years, eyes I'd seen in, what, fifteen or sixteen movies, in a couple of seasons of TV, staring out from magazine covers. He muttered something I couldn't quite hear.

I leaned in. "I'm sorry—what?"

"I *said* . . ." he bent in closer, so that his mouth was inches from my left ear ". . . the universe is an endless span of darkness occasionally broken by moments of unspeakable celestial violence."

I was pretty sure that wasn't what he'd said.

He laughed as if he recognized what an insane thing that was for someone to say. "You ever think shit like that at parties?"

I tend to think about crying at parties, or if someone might be trying to kill me. But I didn't say that. I don't very often say what I think.

"Hey," he said, "this is going to sound like a line, but . . . do you maybe want to get out of here?"

He was right. It did sound like a line.

And I did want to get out of there

"Okay," I said.

I disliked him from the moment I decided to sleep with him.

In one of his first movies, *Fire in the Hole,* he plays a scared young soldier. I can't even remember which war but it's not Vietnam. It's maybe one of the gulf wars, or Afghanistan, or something. It's a truly awful movie, but somehow too earnest to *really* hate. Still, you know you've made a bad war movie when they don't even show it on TNT. At the time he was cast, the Famous Actor was still known as the kid from the Disney Channel. I think the role in that war movie was supposed to launch him as an adult actor. But you got the sense that people watched the movie thinking, *Wait, what's the kid from* The Terrific Todd Chronicles! *doing carrying a rifle, for Christ's sake.* Still, I guess it did turn him into a real adult actor because he started doing more movies after that.

We made our way through the party. He didn't ask how it was that I didn't need to tell anyone that I was leaving. I was glad I didn't have to explain that I wasn't actually invited to the party.

There were a few people I knew outside and I wondered what they would say about him leaving with me. The Famous Actor climbed in the passenger seat of my Subaru. He sat on my makeup bag, held it up, then tossed it into the back seat. He had a small hiker's backpack with him, which he sat at his feet. "Must be weird to go to a party in Bend, Oregon, and end up leaving with me," he said

I shrugged. "There's always a party at that house. Everybody knows about it."

"No, I didn't mean the party. I just meant this probably wasn't how you figured your Friday night would go."

"This is my Wednesday," I said. I explained that I had Mondays and Tuesdays off from the coffee shop, so I always thought of Fridays as my Wednesdays. He looked at me as if he couldn't tell if I was crazy or if I was fucking with him. It's hard to explain, but I can make myself distant, make my face as blank as possible.

"Huh, funny," he said. He stared out the window as I drove. He hadn't buckled his seat belt and my car bonged at him.

"You know that thing I said at the party—about the universe being an endless span of darkness? It was really a comment on how it gets old, everyone looking at you like you're going to say something profound. Sometimes I play off that expectation by saying something totally crazy." He laughed at himself. "You know?" My car bonged at him again.

When he dies in *Fire in the Hole*, you can tell it's meant to be the emotional peak of the movie. The soldiers are walking through this destroyed city and a sniper's bullet zips into the spot where his neck meets his chest, just above his body armor. He slaps at the wound like he's been stung by a wasp, and only then does he seem to realize what's happening to him. That he's dying. It should be a profound moment. Those tuna-blue eyes get all wide and he frantically reaches around his back to feel whether the bullet has gone all the way through. His line is something like, *Sarge! Did it go through? Did . . . it . . . go through?* And then he just falls over. It's hard to say what's wrong with it, but it became one of those unintentional laugh lines. Like: *Sure, war is hell, but it's nothing compared to Terrific Todd's acting*.

He pulled a cigarette pack from his pocket. "You mind?" Natural Spirits. Naturally. I can't remember the last time I dated a guy who didn't smoke Natural Spirits. Every guy in Bend smokes them. He blew the smoke to the roof of the car, which answered by bonging at him again about his seat belt.

The Famous Actor explained that he'd been making a movie nearby— I knew this, of course; everyone knew they were filming a postapocalyptic movie called *The Beats* in the high desert, and we all knew the cast. Someone had told the Famous Actor that Bend was known for its rock-climbing, so he'd called a climbing guide and they'd gone bouldering that day. Then the guide invited him to the party.

I knew the dick-guide he'd called. Wayne Bolls. Wayne's website is covered with pictures of celebrities he's climbed with, like he's some old New York dry cleaner. *Starfucker Tours*, we call it in Bend. *We put the climber in climbing*.

"It's so great to get away from the bullshit," he said. I guess the bullshit was Hollywood, and wealth and fame—pretty much everything that everyone else in the world completely craves. He took a long drag of that cigarette. "But hey, Bend's a cool town, huh?"

I nodded. That's the worst thing about Bend. Its coolness. That and its size, how everyone thinks they know you.

He picked a piece of tobacco off his tongue. "For me it's just a treat to be around normal people."

I made a noise that must've sounded like a laugh.

"What's so funny?" He took another drag of his cigarette. "I'm serious." He seemed genuinely hurt. "I don't see why people have so much trouble believing that famous people just want to be normal."

In his last movie, *New Year's Love Song,* he is one of like a hundred celebrities paired off in parallel love stories. He was cast as the manager of a rock band that is doing a concert on New Year's Day in New York. The band is supposed to be a modern-day Fleetwood Mac, I guess—two young guys and two young girls—but without the hard drugs or anything else that made Fleetwood Mac interesting. The cute singer is married to the drummer and, as the band's tongue-tied manager, the Famous Actor needs to keep the press from finding out that they're divorcing until after the concert—although they never really make it clear why that would matter. The singer is played by the girl from that Nickelodeon show *You Can't Fool Tara!*—it was billed as a kind of Disney meets Nickelodeon thing; this was right after her whole sex-tape scandal, so the movie was meant to redeem her image or something. The movie ends with the Famous Actor's band manager character stumbling out on stage in Rockefeller Plaza and telling the singer that he's always loved her in front of, like, a jillion people. But here's what I don't get: Why do we find that romantic? Are men such liars that it's a turn-on to have so many witnesses? It's one of those movies that make you sad to be female, that make you want to stab yourself in the ovaries. It's truly a hateful movie, but I was still teary at the end, in a completely involuntary way, the way crying babies are supposed to make women lactate. "I want to start every year from now on with you in my arms," the Famous Actor says to the singer on the stage, in front of everyone in the world. There should be a German word for wanting to gouge out your own teary eyes.

"I like your apartment," the Famous Actor said. He walked around like someone sizing up a hotel room. He ran his hand along the spines of the books on my shelf and crouched in front of my albums. "Vinyl," he said. "Cool." When he got to a band he approved of, he would say the name. "Love this old Beck. Ooh, Talking Heads. Nice. The New Pornographers. Yes."

I put my keys on the kitchen table and looked through my mail.

287

There was a late notice for credit card bill, a late notice for a water bill, a solicitation for a fake college, and a postcard from my ex. The postcard showed some old 1960s tourist trap in Idaho called the Snake Pit. On the back he'd written, "Expected to see you here." It's this thing my ex and I have: we send each other old postcards with slights on them. I sent him one from Crater Lake on which I wrote: "The second biggest a-hole in Oregon." We never really broke up; he just moved to Portland with his band. Not that we had this great relationship. He always said I needed help. I always said he was a pig who fucked any girl who would have him. But I'll say this for him: he was *not* a liar. He told me all about it every time he strayed. He'd get back from some gig in Ashland or Eureka and say, "Dude, I got something to tell you." After a while I'd get anxious even seeing his name on my phone because I thought he was going to tell me about some new girl he'd junked. But I couldn't seem to break up with him. When he finally left for Portland I wasn't sad, just more deadened, the way I get. Sometimes I think our real problem wasn't his infidelity; it was his honesty.

I think we sent old postcards to say—*Hey. Still here.* I wondered if he'd be jealous if he saw who was in my apartment.

The Famous Actor plopped down on my couch. "It's so great to just be in, like, a fucking *apartment*! Right? You know? A *real place*? With just, like . . . walls . . . and furniture and books and a TV and real posters and . . ." I wondered if he was going to name everything in my apartment, room by room: dresser, nightstand, alarm clock . . . toothbrush, antibacterial soap, Tampax . . .

I opened my fridge. "You want a drink?"

"I'm in recovery," he said. "But you go ahead." He held up his pack of Natural Spirits again. "This okay?" When I said it was, he lit up, took a deep pull of smoke, and let it go in the air. "No, this is really nice," he said again. "Just what I needed." He pulled a piece of tobacco off his tongue again. Or, actually, I suspect that he pretended to pull a piece of tobacco off his tongue. He leaned his head back onto the couch. "I just get so fucking tired of . . ."

But he couldn't seem to think of what it was that made him so fucking tired.

In *Amsterdam Deadly* he plays a UN investigator who goes to The Hague to testify in the trial of a vicious African warlord. As soon as you see the cast you know he's going to fall in love with the beautiful blond

South African lawyer defending the warlord. The actress is that girl from *My One True*, and because she's as American as Velveeta she got knocked pretty bad for her South African accent, which sounded like an Irish girl crossed with a Jamaican auctioneer. Still, she and the Famous Actor really do have chemistry. Watching that movie is like watching the two best-looking single people at a wedding reception; not a lot of drama about who's going to fuck whom later. But if the romance in that movie is okay, the politics make no sense. The dialogue is like someone reading stories out of the *New York Times*. The Famous Actor has a speech near the end where he yells, "If the Security Council won't pass this joint resolution then *I* will get these refugees across the border to the safe zone!" Not exactly *Henry V*. I think sometimes movies, like people, just try too hard.

We had straight missionary paint-by-numbers sex: some foreplay, exactly enough oral to get us both going, then he pulled a condom out of that backpack he carried and rolled it over his dick. It was ribbed, which I could see he believed was thoughtful of him. There was nothing weird or obsessive or porny about the sex. Or particularly memorable. First sex is always kind of awkward, though; you don't yet know what the other person likes. Everything's basically in the right place, but it doesn't feel right, or it takes a minute to find.

First sex is like being in a stranger's kitchen, trying all the drawers, looking for a spoon. There was one point where he was over me, his eyes closed, head back, weight on his arms like he was doing a pushup, and it was kind of weird—like, *Oh, hey, look, Terrific Todd is boning someone. Oh wait, it's me.* But I shouldn't make it sound like the sex was bad. It was fine. Really, the only disappointing thing was how much stomach fat the Famous Actor had—I mean, really, when you have that much money, how hard is it to do a few sit-ups? Of course that might have been intentional, too, part of his normalcy campaign.

Afterward, we were lying on my bed naked and he was smoking another Natural Spirit. He smoked so many I wanted to buy stock in it. "That was great," he said. "And thanks for not taking a selfie or anything weird like that."

I must've made a face like, *Christ, are you kidding me?*

He sat up. "Oh, you'd be surprised how often that happens. I know actors who have, like, a contract they have women sign before they'll have sex." He named two actors of his generation, both of whom had been in movies with him. "I mean, can you imagine?" he asked. "Making a woman sign a contract before you fuck?"

He offered me his cigarette. I took a small drag. Those organic cigarettes tasted a little like dog shit.

"That's the part I really don't think people get." He picked another fake tobacco bit off his tongue. "You know? About fame? How dispiriting it is, how dehumanizing? It's like you're this . . . product. Right? I mean: I'm not some product. I'm a fuckin' person." He slapped his little intentional belly fat. "Right? Why can't people understand I'm just a regular guy?"

"I think people understand that," I said.

In *Big Bro,* he plays a guy in a fraternity whose older brother is a Wall Street trader who shows up after his divorce to act out some *Animal House* fantasies, only to find that frats now are full of serious students. The actor who plays the Wall Street brother had recently left *Saturday Night Live* and you can really tell the difference between someone used to making live audiences laugh and someone who falls into a giant birthday cake and reads lines like, "Oh boy! Here we go again!" to a Disney laugh track. Still, *Big Bro* was the Famous Actor's breakout. It must've made $200 million and it's watchable in part because the Famous Actor seems so easygoing and likeable in it (in other words, exactly like *no* fraternity guy *ever,* in the history of the world). People saw him differently after that. I think when an actor exudes such charm we assume the character must be close to his real self. But there's no reason to think that: he could just as easily be the selfish loser who raids his senile dad's retirement account in *Forty Reasons for Dying,* for instance. We really want to like people, even famous people.

It's not really possible to sleep next to someone the first time you've had sex together. That's something I'd like to take up with Hollywood if I ever get the chance: how they always cut from the kissing couple to them lying peacefully in bed postsex, snoozing with smiles on their faces. I'd like to grab some screenwriter by his ears: "Hey, *you* fuck a stranger and then try sleeping afterward!"

We were lying there on our backs, staring at the ceiling. He was smoking another cigarette. Our legs were touching.

"If you want me to go, I can call for a ride," he said.

"Only if you want to," I said.

"Cool," he said. "Yeah, cool. I'll stay. I like it here. It's chill."

I didn't say anything.

He sniffed. "I think people would be surprised at how hard it is for someone like me to find a place where I can just . . . you know—*be?* Where there's not some PA constantly buzzing around asking if I want a Sprite."

"You want a Sprite?"

He laughed a little, took a pull of smoke, and when he started to reach for his mouth, I watched him closely. He looked like he was picking something off the end of his tongue again, but I'll be damned if I saw any tobacco bits there. He looked right at me with those Pepsi-blue eyes.

"Sometimes I daydream about hiding out someplace like this. Just saying 'Fuck you' to the fake industry stuff and just dropping the fuck out. Not tell anyone either, just chill in Bend, Oregon, for a month, go out to breakfast, rock-climb, maybe get a bike, read poetry in the park, go to parties like last night, hang out with someone cool like you? Know what I mean?"

"Yes," I said. I didn't say the rest of what I was thinking, which was: Who *doesn't* daydream of that, of not having a job or any worries, playing around all day, riding a bike and reading poetry and having sex? The difference is that most of us would fucking starve to death in a week.

I started to imagine the Famous Actor hanging around my apartment for the next month like some unwanted houseguest. A month becoming two, and three, him smoking forty cartons of organic cigarettes and never finishing that book of poetry he was supposedly reading, me coming home every day to Terrific Todd marveling still at all the normal shit in my normal apartment—dish soap, spatula, salt pig, can opener!— that band of fat around his middle getting bigger and realer all the time.

He leaned over, got his tennis shoe off the ground, put his cigarette out on its sole, and put the butt in the pocket of his jeans. Then he propped himself up on one elbow—the one that I had gotten to know so well earlier. "Hey, can I ask you a personal question?"

Look, I don't mean to go all double-standard feminist—I mean, I wasn't some victim; *I'd* fucked *him,* too—but that seemed like such a guy thing to say right then. *Hey, remember a few minutes ago my dick was inside you? Well, now I was wondering if we could talk.*

"Sure," I said.

"It's just . . . I can't get a read on you."

I didn't say anything.

I get that a lot from guys.

291

Also, it wasn't technically a question.

"I just keep feeling like . . . I don't know . . . like you think I'm . . . kind of a douchebag or something."

Also not a question.

Toward the end of *Big Bro*, after this huge party where Snoop Dogg inexplicably shows up with a bunch of hookers, the rest of the frat pulls the Famous Actor's character aside and tells him that his big brother has to go. He's nearly gotten them all expelled and they're all flunking classes and in danger of losing their fraternity charter. It's probably the most moving scene in the movie, the Famous Actor telling his brother he's got to leave. "Hey, Charlie, *these* are my brothers now," the Famous Actor says, "but they'll never be . . . *my brother*." Chastened for his boorish behavior, the older brother slinks away sadly. Of course, he doesn't really go away, but shows up three minutes later with Mark Cuban and Donald Trump to save the day at his brother's oral presentation in his business class.

"I don't think you're a douchebag," I said to the Famous Actor.

"No, I think you do." He sat up higher.

"It's not that," I said. "It's just . . . " What are you supposed to say—after years of therapy to untangle your difficulty in forming relationships, your self-destructive behavior, the depressive periods and suicidal thoughts? And some narcissist expects you to pillow-talk it out?

"Seriously," he said, "I need you to tell me what you think of me."

What I thought of *him*? That his insecurity was infinite? Instead, after a minute, I said, "You'll always be my brother."

You have to wonder how a movie like *Big Bro 2* even gets made. In it, the younger brother has graduated from college and been hired by the older brother's company, which has somehow morphed from a Wall Street firm in the first movie to a tech company in the second. They're about to unveil this new kind of biocomputer, but an evil tech company called Gorgle wants to take over the brothers' company, so the old *SNL* comedian has to gather all the old frat guys together to use their special skills to defeat—Ugh, you know, it actually hurts my head to even think of the plot of that movie. It's like having to recount all the sexual positions your parents might have used in conceiving you. The best thing I can say about the second *Big Bro* is that the Famous Actor is barely in it, and only because he's clearly fulfilling some line in a contract that required his presence in a sequel. The *SNL* guy's career had stalled, and most of those frat guys would've starred in animal porn just to work again, but the Famous Actor had gone on to become the Famous Actor by then. He seems truly apologetic in the six or seven scenes he's in— like, I'm sorry America. I really am sorry.

He had that same sorry look on his face as he sat on the edge of the bed and looked back over his shoulder at me. "You know, I think you're not being very generous."

"Sorry," I said.

"I mean, maybe *you're* the asshole. Did that ever occur to you?"

"Yes," I said.

He turned away. "You can't know how weird this fame shit is. It's like you're see-through. Everyone assumes they know everything about you, but you know what? Nobody knows a fucking thing about me!" He stood and rubbed his forehead. "Always trying to be what people want—after a while, it's like you don't even know how to trust yourself anymore. You're always second-guessing, like, *Wait, how do I talk again? Is this how I react to things or how I want people to see me react?* And when no one's watching, you feel totally fucked—like, *Am I even here?* You don't know how hard that is—to not know yourself!"

He really seemed to think famous people were the only ones who didn't know themselves.

"Then I meet someone like you, someone I might genuinely like, someone I don't want to think that I'm a celebrity dickhead . . . and what do I do?" He laughed. "Act like a dickhead."

He walked across my tiny bedroom to my dresser. Behind a pile of clothes there was a picture of me with my sister, the last picture of us before she disappeared. He picked up the picture and stared at it. In the picture I'm eleven and Megan's thirteen and we're standing in front of the hammer ride at the county fair. We both have huge grins on our face and Megan's giving the thumbs-up because we're so proud of riding that scary ride together. Three months later she would run away from home. We never found out what happened to her, if her body is somewhere or if she's working as a hooker in Alaska or whatever. She could be in the Taliban, or she could be in the circus, or she could be rotting in a field in Utah. That was the hardest thing for my parents— just never knowing. Our house was a tomb after that; my parents never the same. The Famous Actor stared at the picture a moment and then put it down. He turned and faced me.

"So if I've been a little self-absorbed, I apologize."

"It's fine," I said.

"No," he said. "It's not fine." He was getting worked up again. "You can't just say, *It's fuckin' fine* and then keep acting like some zombie! You can't fuckin' do that! You have to give something back! You can't just sit there in judgment thinking that I'm an asshole and not give me the chance to show you I'm not! I mean, am I asking too much? For a little human interaction!"

"What's my name?" I said.

He stared at me for a few seconds. "Aw fuck," he said.

If I was trapped on an island or something and I could only have one movie to watch, but it had to be one of *his* movies, I'd choose *Been There, Done That*. It's telling that my favorite of his movies is one where he's just a supporting actor. I think it's hard for even good actors to carry a whole movie. He's great as the gay brother of the heroine, who has come back to her family's home in 1980s Louisiana with her black boyfriend. He has several opportunities to go too broad with the gay brother, or go all AIDS-victim-TV-movie-of-the-week or something, but he's really restrained. And when the gay brother ends up being the most racist person in the family, the Famous Actor turns in a really nuanced and smart performance. It's even a little bit brave. I suspect it's what happens when you work with a great director. But I also think there's something deeper that he managed to find in himself in that movie.

He snapped his fingers and pointed at me. "Katherine!"

I shook my head.

"But it's something with a *K* sound, though, right? Caroline or Cassidy or . . ."

"Sorry."

He had his eyes closed, concentrating. "You work at a bar."

"Coffee shop."

"Well *fuck me*," he said. "Fuck me fuck me fuck me." He opened his eyes, as if suddenly finding out someone he'd known for years was not who he thought they were.

"You had a lot on your mind," I said. "And your elbow."

He shook his head—like, *Can you believe me?*

"Don't worry about it," I said. "I suspect it's harder to not be a douchebag than people think."

He gave a little laugh, but I think, of all the things I said, that might've hurt the most. The condescension and truth of it. I felt okay then, in control of things.

"Well, thanks for understanding, Katherine," he said, "or whatever your name is."

I just smiled.

He reached into his backpack for his phone. "I should probably—" He turned on his phone and it buzzed and buzzed. He began reading messages. "Oh shit."

"Girlfriend?"

"What?" He scowled. "No. No. I have an earlier call tomorrow than I thought. I'm gonna have someone come get me."

"Sure."

He pressed a number and put his iPhone to his ear. "Hey. It's me. I'm at this girl's house. Yeah, in Bend. I know. I know. Hey, is there any way . . ."

He didn't have to finish the sentence. I guessed there were a lot of sentences he didn't have to finish. "Yeah. Cool. Just a sec." He looked up at me. "Hey, what's the address here?"

In *Been There, Done That,* he has a great scene where he has a beer with the black boyfriend, who, it turns out, is super religious and has a problem with gay people. It ends with the two of them laughing together, two otherwise decent men confronting their old biases. As Hollywood pat as it sounds, the scene comes off as entirely genuine.

I have to say, right before he left, it felt that way in my apartment, too. Genuine. Like we'd come through something. He took a quick shower, and came out dressed in the same jeans and gray T-shirt.

He bowed. "Well, nameless queen of Bend, it was a pleasure to meet you tonight. Thank you."

I'd put a T-shirt on.

"Can I kiss you goodbye?"

I said he could.

It would be hard being with an actor. Figuring out what's real. That goodbye kiss he gave me—honestly, I don't know if I've ever been kissed like that: one hand behind my neck, the other on my waist. It was a great, generous kiss and I felt myself opening up to him, more than I had in bed. In fact, the kiss was so good I started to think about that laughter in *Been There, Done That.* I mean, clearly, they weren't *really* laughing like that, but in a way they sort of *were.* I guess in acting, you become the very thing you're portraying. In sex scenes, if you act turned on, you get turned on. Act like something is hilarious, it becomes hilarious. And that's how that kiss was—

My God, if that kiss wasn't real, I don't even care. I'll take fake over real any day. I've seen real.

Maybe it's that way with our lives, too. Normal people. I mean, we're all acting all of the time anyway, putting on our not-crazy faces for people, acting like making someone a cappuccino is the greatest thrill in the world, pretending to care about things you don't, pretending *not* to care about things you do care about, pretending your name isn't Katherine when it is, acting like you have your shit together when, the truth is, well—

I didn't want to look out the window as he left—it seemed like such a stupid movie-cliché thing to do—but I couldn't help myself. I looked out. He gave a small glance over his shoulder to my window, but I think the light was wrong and he couldn't see my face. Then he flicked at his hair and jumped into the passenger seat of a blue Audi, which zipped away. I imagined his Big Bro driving the car. I imagined the Famous Actor lighting up a Natural Spirit while the car bonged at him to put on his seat belt. He hated seat belts. It was three in the morning. I wasn't tired.

I looked around my apartment.

The Famous Actor was in a serial killer movie, too. It's called *Over Tumbled Graves* and he plays this young cop, the love interest of the girl detective hunting a serial killer. It might be the only movie of his that I've never seen—because of Megan, I guess. If you suffer night terrors and insomnia you sort of learn to avoid serial killer movies. Not that I begrudge him being in it. We all make choices. And he generally makes good ones. I just read that he is getting a franchise superhero in one of those reboots. And that he's engaged to the girl who is going to play Blue Aura in the same movie.

I'm really glad for him. He's been through a lot the last year. It wasn't even two weeks after the postapocalyptic movie finished production in Bend that I read that the Famous Actor was going back into rehab. Of course, I might have been the least surprised person in the world.

The morning he left, I rubbed lotion on my arms so that I wouldn't start scratching. I cried for a while, then I cried for crying. I went back to bed but I couldn't fall back to sleep. I had to be at the coffee shop at six. I repeated the steps: Get out of bed. Keep moving. Take care of yourself. I got up to take a shower. That's when I noticed my medicine cabinet door was slightly ajar. I opened it all the way. He had cleaned it out. The Zoloft I take for depression. The Ativan I take for anxiety. The Ambien I sometimes have to take to sleep. But not just that. He took the Benadryl and the Advil and the Gas-X. He even took the Lysteda I sometimes take when I get these ungodly heavy periods. I can't imagine what he thought he was going to do with that one. Two days later I got a visit from a nice young woman from the production company. I signed the nondisclosure documents without negotiating. She gave me a check for six thousand dollars. All I had to do was promise never to mention his name. But what's a name anyway?

That morning, as I stood there, staring at that empty medicine cabinet, I felt the strangest sense of pride in him. Warmth. Love, even. Well, look at you, I thought, you are normal—as normal as the most fucked-up barista in Bend, Oregon. Relax, Terrific Todd, wherever you are, you're one of us.

Nominated by Kim Barnes, Don Waters

DESIRED APPRECIATION

by SOLMAZ SHARIF

from THE KENYON REVIEW AND *LOOK* (GRAYWOLF PRESS)

Until now, now that I've reached my thirties:
All my Muse's poetry has been harmless:
American and diplomatic: a learned helplessness
Is what psychologists call it: my docile, desired state.
I've been largely well-behaved and gracious.
I've learned the doctors learned of learned helplessness
By shocking dogs. Eventually we things give up.
Am I grateful to be here? Someone eventually asks
If I love this country. In between the helplessness,
The agents, the nation must administer
A bit of hope: must meet basic dietary needs:
Ensure by tube, by nose, by throat, by other
Orifice. Must fistbump a janitor. Must muss up
Some kid's hair and let him loose
Around the Oval Office. *click click* could be cameras
Or the teeth of handcuffs closing to fix
The arms overhead. There must be a doctor on hand
To ensure the shoulders do not dislocate
And there must be Prince's "Raspberry Beret."
click click could be Morse code tapped out
Against a coffin wall to the neighboring coffin.
Outside my window, the snow lights cobalt
For a bit at dusk and I'm surprised
Every second of it. I had never seen the country
Like this. Somehow I can't say yes. *This is a beautiful country.*

298

I have not cast my eyes over it before, that is,
In this direction, is how John Brown put it
When he was put on the scaffold.
I feel like I must muzzle myself,
I told my psychologist.
"So you feel dangerous?" she said.
Yes.
"So you feel like a threat?"
Yes.
Why was I so surprised to hear it?

Nominated by The Kenyon Review, David Baker

MIRACLE FRUIT

fiction by ETHAN CHATAGNIER

from NEW ENGLAND REVIEW

At seven pm, three quarters of the recessed lights in the main office space are programmed to turn off. What's left is deemed bright enough for the custodial staff to do their work, but what I love, looking out at it through the interior window of my office, is that the glow of all the screensavers creates a faint aurora over the top of all the cubicle walls almost like that of a town at night hidden just beyond a ridge. I know it's just a silly image, but it gives me the sort of comfort I imagine God would feel looking at a snow- dusted Swiss village and allowing himself to forget the rest of the troubled world for a while. I stay late like this because it's the easiest time to handle the real, unbureaucratic work of thinking, planning, analyzing data, and so on. I also use the time to care for my *synsepalum dulcificum*, misting it, trimming it, adding a little peat or some acidifying fertilizer, and for whatever reason these diversions provide me with the greatest clarity of thought I have all day. But I also like to stay late because, unlike at home, where my mother salts the air with her misery, the solitude here feels purposeful.

Tonight, I'm just finishing up a request for access to our latest acquisition. All the other project leads had theirs in last week, but I've been trying to get my wording, my logic, just right, in the hopes that a strong argument will matter more than who was first to the starting line. But I know how it will go. Corn and soy will get the first crack at it. My wheat is beating yield estimates and making the company lots of money too—which I'm certain is why I haven't been talked to despite all the surveillance footage of me staying late to mommy a potted plant—but

I know a lot of people are starting to see me as some sort of deluded prophet for continuing to believe that wheat has a place in the future.

I finish up my request and e-mail it to Meadows anyway. In an office environment, logic can only do so much.

Before I go, I plug in the humidifying contraption I've put together. *Synsepalum dulcificum* is from the jungles of west Africa, and the store-bought warm-water humidifier I bought just wasn't enough, so I've connected a space heater to a litter box full of water, and wired in a little fan to circulate the humid air. Security has surely sent someone to investigate the strange contraption I've set up in my office, just to check, but there's little point. Anyone with a keycard for this facility has the knowhow to make a bomb, even the technicians. Maybe even the custodians. It doesn't take an engineering degree to see this setup is climate control for my shrub. It's been a lot perkier since I switched to this method. In the first half of the year it didn't bloom, but now it has eleven green buds on it, and all of them are starting to blush.

I like walking out to the deserted parking lot as well, no claustrophobia of cars, nobody yammering into a cell phone or blasting bad music, but tonight there is another car, a Camry with Avis stickers, and it's parked right next to mine. Leaning against it is a slender, copper-haired woman wearing a fitted trench coat and kitten heels who is definitely not from Nebraska.

"Can I ask you about Aeon, Dr. Schuyler?" she asks.

"Mother Jones?"

"New York Times."

Surprising. To someone like me, our Aeon acquisition is front page news, but most people would rather see pictures of a beheading or read a new brownie recipe. It's good that someone is paying attention, I think. But it's bad news when a *New York Times* reporter ambushes you in the dark of an empty parking lot rather than contacting the corporate media office. It means this is just the slight visible outgrowth of a story already being tracked, of documents already being compiled and pieces put together. It means you are not just the person who picked up the phone. You were chosen. And why was I chosen? Because I am unmarried, because I have no children, because I own a small home outright and scrupulously save 60 percent of my income? All information readily available on a tax return form. A few days of observation would reveal me to be the type to arrive first and leave last from work, the type to care for an elderly parent whose one remaining joy is complaining, and the type to carefully tend a backyard garden that I'm rarely home to enjoy. She is betting that I am the right combination of idealistic, lonely, and with little enough to lose that I might throw myself on the sword. She suspects that if confronted with a beautiful woman I will want to speak to her, to please.

How close is she to right?

I tell her I can't help her. She hands me her business card anyway. Sharon Saxon—what a newspaper name. She counsels me not to bring the card back to this place.

❀   ❀   ❀

When I get home, my mother tells me that all those dials on the washing machine do nothing. As with a baby toy, they are simply knobs that click. Cold and hot are the only true settings. The rest are illusions. This is just the latest of her modern horrors. They're all she has these days. The chunky spaghetti sauce is the same as the non-chunky spaghetti sauce. The chunks in chunky peanut butter are microplastics. There are little bugs that look like dust. They look just like dust, but they are bugs. How can you tell, Mom? You can't. Last month she said her earwax smelled savory, like mushrooms with rosemary, like duck fat. No matter how good it smells, I told her, don't eat it.

"Hot and cold is all I need," I say, regarding the washing machine.

"Garage doors cause cancer. You should put yours on manual."

She's reached an age where there's no listening going on. She's all output. She prefers afghans now, though I offer her good quilts. Any chair she sits in instantly takes on the aura of a rocking chair, even the sofa. She's unhappier now than her own mother was at this age. She broke the world record. I bring her a bowl of SpaghettiOs.

"I fed you kids vegetables."

"Ketchup and canned beans."

If I bring her zucchini she'll say, "You know how I feel about zucchini." The same if I bring her kale or celery or butternut squash. She'll accept SpaghettiOs, mac and cheese, pork and beans—Depression food, pun intended—but she always offers that disclaimer: I fed you kids vegetables. The O's are made with rice flour now. Pretty much all pasta is, besides the luxury stuff. The sauce is sweetened with corn syrup. It's soybeans in pork and beans. The sauce is sweetened with corn syrup. The cheese powder is synthetically produced flavor crystallites. The milk you make it with is soy milk. The butter you mix in is hydrogenated corn oil with synthetically produced flavor crystallites.

"Why don't you go out to the garden?"

She does, though she's eaten only half of her bowl. She leaves it on the end table and heads out back. Even though she fails to finish her meals, her midsection is growing, though it seems to be airy and insubstantial, like a loaf of rising bread dough. Is it a tumor, or a gland issue, or just following the dada rules of the aging body after sixty? I don't know. Her health is a house of cards I don't want to blow on.

She's on the bench in the garden, making it seem like a rocking chair. Around her there's amaranth, leeks, chard, varicolored carrots, rare potatoes, the shoots of onion and garlic bulbs. There's a big bush of rosemary and a bit of thyme. Of the trees, the fuyu persimmon, ponderosa lemon, and alma fig are bearing fruit. I pluck a fuyu and take a bite. Its flesh is crisp but the flavor, with traces of cinnamon, butter, and apple, is almost too delicate to exist.

"Why don't you have a fig for dessert?" I ask.

"You know how I feel about figs."

❀   ❀   ❀

The Aeon seed bank was the last major seed bank in the world. It was in Annecy, France, not far across the border from the Geneva office of the United Nations, which, along with a dozen other foundations and entities, had subsidized its existence. But it was still a French property, still under the aegis of the French government, and with the spiral toward bankruptcy looming, they were vulnerable to Manticore making an offer they could hardly believe, let alone refuse. The papers and magazines that made a stink about the purchase comforted their readers with editorials arguing that transporting one and a half billion seeds in cold storage from eastern France to Nebraska was a logistical problem that would take at least five years to solve. What they didn't know was that Manticore had been working on the problem for eight years. Only a few conspiracy nuts were right about that part, though they destroyed any credibility with claims that Manticore had manufactured the French fiscal crisis to begin with.

On the first day of delivery, a line of semi trucks stretches out of the campus and six miles down the highway. Exhaust hangs above the string of them like a heat mirage. Each carries a specially equipped refrigeration trailer, and at four ports the semis back in and robotic overhead cranes hook the trailers and carry them on a track system to a pre-programmed spot in the main refrigeration chamber, where they automatically hook into the facility's power system. No manual labor is required.

303

The protesters who come to lie in front of the trucks are late, show-
ing up at seven-thirty AM like me. The first trucks had queued up at five.
The procession is so slow, though, that they have no trouble lying down
in front of an arbitrary truck and halting the line there. But a crowd of
state police has been on the scene since eight and the company has a
cart full of coffee urns set out for them, and they haul the tree-bearded
activists out of the street pretty much as soon as their backs touch the
ground. They leave unmolested the protesters standing on the shoulder
with picket signs that read BIODIVERSITY IS PUBLIC PROPERTY
or show poorly painted images of a globe locked in a jail cell. I'm a
little embarrassed to agree with them. But then, they are looking at the
issue from only one angle. Our population is growing at an exponential
rate, and crop yields at a linear rate. Already we have 9 billion people
on a planet that can only feed 8 billion. Despite all the seeming logisti-
cal impossibilities, ten-year projections have the population at 10 bil-
lion and food production at enough for 8.1 billion. And what happens
when the food wars migrate to countries with nuclear arsenals?

There are two weeks of days like this, trucks creeping patiently along
the highway, dejected protesters using one hand to hold picket signs
and the other to check their phones. There are a lot of plant species in
the world. Some of the seeds in this collection are from plants no longer
extant, plants waiting to be revived, though mostly they wait in vain.

At the end of the second week of transit, Meadows calls me into his
office and tells me I can have access to anything not earmarked by corn
or soy, carte blanche, for one year. No need to file project memos and
wait for approval, so long as I track what I use in the master database.
It's an unprecedented level of access, an unprecedented cutting of red
tape.

"Mind your deadlines, and don't take on too much."

"I've got a few big ideas."

"It all expires after a year."

"What happens in a year?"

I look at him. He looks at me. He's mastered the expression that says:
I'm a scientist; I wish these weren't the realities we lived with; I care.
He's even better at it than I am.

"Pete," he says, as I'm leaving. I stop in his doorframe. "You're doing
important work."

"Everyone is, right?"

Our part of the campus is utilitarian, but the Carthy Building, which
faces the road, is designed to welcome corporate affiliates, board mem-

bers, diplomats, and congressional representatives. It houses a tropical courtyard with one of the top-ranked koi ponds in the world. I don't know who ranks these things, but it is marvelous. Unreasonably calming. I spend the rest of the day there. I'm thinking about my most ambitious projects, narrowing them by those I can get off the ground within a year and by those with a reasonable chance of success. But mostly I'm thinking about nothing. Mostly I'm trying not to think about what happens in a year.

Sharon Saxon has been waiting for me in the parking lot every Tuesday night. She must be seeing signs that I'll crack, though I'm not sure what they are. I haven't stopped combing my hair. I'm still brushing my teeth. The Tuesday after my meeting with Meadows, I snap a berry off the *synsepalum dulcificum*, perfectly red now, the shape of a grape tomato but a few shades darker. She's out there, all right. Her attire has mutated from what you'd wear to a client meeting to what you'd wear on a date. I imagine it's like a lockpick testing out a lock. A skirt now, respectable but shiny. Higher heels. A blouse coincidentally the same shade as my berry. Though how trustworthy is any coincidence when you're dealing with an investigative reporter? One of those silly jackets women wear that only go down as far as the ribs.

"Your father would tell you to wear a coat," I say.

"A gentleman would offer me his own."

I look down at the sleeves of my thin sweater.

"Sorry. I'm from Vermont."

"I know." She manages the aura of a smoker without having a cigarette, a real miracle of science.

"I don't really want to know how much you know about me."

"Yes, you do. Just not all at once."

What I like is not her in her professional garb or her date clothes, not an inch more or an inch less of leg, not a certain amount of décolletage or the right heels. I like the process of it all, despite the constructions, despite the obvious ends fueling all these different means. What can I say? Who doesn't want to feel like a lock being picked?

"Any news?"

"No news," I say, as usual. But this time I hold out my closed fist, and she puts her hand under it, open. I place the red berry in the bowl of her palm.

"Eat this," I say. "Then eat a lemon."

On the way home I stop at the hardware store and buy ten feet of four-inch PVC and a few plastic totes.

Sharon Saxon is sitting in my garden early Wednesday morning when I head out with my watering can and trowel. She's holed up in the corner of my park bench, wearing the kind of sweats that fancy people jog in, and she lights up when she sees me. She's waiting for a "good morning" or something, but I've decided to play it coy. Coy is as close to charming as a plant geneticist can get.

"It took me about three hours to convince myself you weren't trying to poison me."

"You're here, aren't you?"

"And I kept thinking it was some kind of code. But what is this berry, what's the lemon supposed to mean? "

"Did you try it?"

"Yeah, I finally went out and bought a bag of fucking lemons. This is incredible, Pete. Did you make it?"

I laugh. "The climate of west Africa made it, and a thousand individual pressures. Though it's anyone's guess as to why it's a selected-for trait. Nothing too useful, or it would be more common. *Synsepalum dulcificum*. They call it the miracle fruit."

"Have you thought of selling this to New York chefs? They'd pay a fortune for something like this."

"Don't tell me you're not familiar with the pleasure of keeping a secret."

My mother shuffles out the back door with a bowl of Frosted Flakes, leaving the screen open behind her. She's up two hours earlier than usual. Either Sharon woke her hopping the fence, or she sensed my happiness and has emerged to destroy it. She sits down in the other corner of the bench while I go on watering.

"There's a great beauty in the amazing diversity of plant life. Not just in the jungles, but in a place like this. It was never just grass, despite what the movies show. And the plainsmen who grazed it to death were not immune to its beauty. They just had families to feed."

"I sense a point emerging."

"So, one way of looking at it is that I have an overly generous definition of family."

All the while, we can hear my mother crunching her cereal. She watches Sharon Saxon with as much of a twinkle in her eyes as I do.

"Would you like a persimmon, Mom?"

"That sounds delightful," she says.

I feel it too, Mother. I didn't know you could.

"Sharon?"

"Any more magic fruits?"

"Miracle. And only at the office."

"Then sure, a persimmon."

We all take bites and soak up the flavor slowly. I wait for my mother to say something like "toothpaste is made of recycled taxidermy," but apparently she doesn't want to offer her insights to the larger world.

"So what is the other way of looking at it?" Sharon asks.

"Just don't paint me as some kind of Mengele, okay?"

"What do you have?"

Nothing, I say, but a scent on the wind.

But I suggest that maybe she should keep her hotel reservation open.

❆ ❆ ❆

Fall gives way to winter, though the work we do makes the shift increasingly less relevant.

Meanwhile, I snoop around the work intranet. I lack the skill to avoid leaving digital footprints, but I buy myself some time by wearing Meadows's shoes. The oscillating cameras in his corridor are surprisingly easy to time. He doesn't lock his office and he doesn't log out of his computer and he doesn't delete his e-mail. And how much did the company pay that video production company for its cybersecurity training? I want to write it on a Post-it and leave it on his monitor.

The memo isn't hard to find. I knew the gist from that patented look-between-scientists he offered when he gave me my deadline. But since I have an idea what the *New York Times* would tell me to do with my gist, I need something more detailed. And there it is: a memo that says that the security risks of holding on to the bank outweigh its value as an asset; that says it would be more detrimental *to the company* [emphasis mine] if the bounty of these seeds escaped containment than if the smallpox virus did; that recommends incineration. Attached was a suggested schedule for the incinerations: Flowers, vines, and other non-fruiting plants first. Then non-orchard trees. Then fruit and nut trees. Then bulbs and vegetables. Last, grasses and grains.

First they came for the Socialists, et cetera, et cetera.

Meanwhile, I'm bringing home a bucket of ammonium nitrate fertilizer from work every day and carting it down to my workshop in the basement. They track how much of this stuff people buy at hardware stores and nurseries. Not at the company.

Meanwhile, my mother has kept asking about Sharon Saxon and, what can I say, I've created a lie that keeps the two of us happy. Sharon thinks she might extend her stay even after she finishes her story. She's been taking me out to dinners to conduct interviews, but we often get lost in discussions irrelevant to Manticore, conversations about nature and history and the unforgiving beauty of selection both natural and artificial. My mother still tells me that television technology has always been flatscreen, that they built a big empty space inside the old blocky TVs because they weren't sure how people would react, but she tells me over a plate of wild rice and home-cooked vegetables.

In truth, Sharon has been waiting for me Tuesdays, as always, and I've given her little bits of information, but mostly seeds. Every Tuesday, a new batch. *Albuca spiralis. Randia Ruizana. Musa acuminata.* I don't know that she'll plant them. I don't know that she can keep them alive if she does. I just know that they're out. Two seeds in my hand become two seeds in her hand.

* * *

Imagine a kid lighting off his first firecracker, surprised that the sound of its blast is less impressive than the pop of a shaken soda can. The word *blast* becomes instantly ridiculous. There you have the blast that failed to shake the world or even the little old cornhusker state when the news broke that Manticore Incorporated planned to destroy the world's greatest store of biodiversity. The *New York Times*: page four. Another round of beardy protesters lying down in front of basic delivery trucks and some op-eds aimed at the already converted. Still, I go into work prepared to be served with papers or taken into custody or led by security down some ill-lit hallway, never to return. Dust Meadows's keyboard for fingerprints and they've got me. Ask around among the custodians and they've probably got me. Instead, Meadows is gone and there's a meeting in which they caution us to neither initiate nor accept contact with him pursuant to the settling of a legal action. In fact, they say, if anyone sees him, walk straight out of the room, crawl beneath the windows, and call security from the first phone you see.

Sorry, bro. You never should have gone into administration.

The suit brought against Manticore is dropped after initial hearings. No one has standing to sue, the judge says. No individual can claim harm. In his twelve-page decision, the judge writes that he is not happy with having to make this decision. He sympathizes with the people who wrote to him saying the incineration would be a crime against humanity.

No, he wrote, it was a crime against something else. A crime, probably, against something worse, but something unfortunately not protected by the law. It seems logical. He's doing his job. I'm not really doing mine anymore. Wheat and rice are being planted over by the hectare anyway. Once they're gone, corn and soy can duke it out for who has better numbers. There can be only one.

Sorry, wheat. You should have been more calorific.

❁ ❁ ❁

Snow in the parking lot, and Sharon standing tall in it like a candle asking if I can find any documents relating to Manticore's involvement in the French recession. She knows that would be out of my division even if it were more than a rumor. Even asking shows her desperation. She looks harried now, like a wife. It's much more beautiful, hair frizzed, eyes bagged, like a person who exists in the world.

I tell her I'll find what I can. I know what that will be.

Security has clamped down since the leak. Cameras have been added to cover blind spots. IT has been given the authority to publicly yell at people with stupid passwords. The only way for me to search around is with my own login information, and that only gets me into a space with very well-defined fences. I'm likely to get only one shot at testing those boundaries, and I'm not ready to take it yet. What does it matter? I keep wondering. The memo I gave Sharon *was* the smoking gun. Unless Manticore is planning to toss some babies into the incinerator with the seeds, no one is going to care. Given the quandaries of overpopulation, some might not even balk at that. Crop yields—we all bow to that god now.

But I've told her I am waiting for my opportunity. Still doing what? Working up the nerve; working in my basement; cultivating fantasies; ferrying plants across the Styx, borne back ceaselessly against time.

Brugmansia arborea. Rafflesia arnoldii. Strongylodon macrobotrys.
Sharon. Harper. Saxon.

Seeds passing from my hand to hers, little things, dried and hard and unassuming, displaying no pomp at all the information they contain. *Phoenix dactylifera.* The Judean date palm, extinct for six hundred years, was resurrected from a two-thousand-year-old seed lost in a jar. This is no more than the pit of a date, the thing you spit out when you eat one.

I tell Sharon she'll have to come to my house to get what I've found. I tell her she doesn't have to Batman into the garden, but she does anyway. It's warm again, and she's there on a morning in April during which there's a whole different crop of fruit and vegetables. Only the ponderosa lemons are the same. Oh, tired but hopeful eyes. Is there a more heartbreaking sight?

I smile a smile I've been saving up for her. I unclasp my fist in front of her, my big reveal: two red berries just longer than olives. We chew the pulp away from the pits and swirl it around in our mouths to coat as much of the surface as we can. It tastes like almost nothing. The secret, I tell her, is its glycoprotein, uncreatively named miraculin, which binds to the taste buds and blocks bitter and sour compounds. The properties, of course, were known long before the mechanism.

By the time I've finished my pedantry, it's taken effect. We set upon the lemon tree. We bite into them without peeling them. The insides taste like lemonade. The white pith tastes like meringue. We eat whole lemons this way, not bothering to spit out the seeds. I yank other things out of the garden: arugula, which now tastes like some kind of crazy herb sorbet; rhubarb like raspberry jam; radishes like sweetened ice. But we go back to the lemon tree. It seems to be what this was made for—ambrosia, jellied light bulbs. The miracle doesn't keep our bellies from feeling full, from growing hot with acid, but we keep going.

The miraculin lasts about thirty minutes. We start to pucker as the lemons turn back into lemons. We look at each other and laugh, but it's hard to keep up as we feel our teeth ache, our throats burn, our stomachs roil, and the truth that we've just gorged on raw lemons becomes once again unavoidable. I tell her I want a favor before I give her the document I've found. I tell her my mother's grown fond of her, that she doesn't get out much. I ask her to drive my mother around town for half an hour, showing her whatever she wants to see. When I go inside, my mother is already up making coffee and sparing me her theory that it was all ground at the same time in one great coffee bean holocaust. I let her know about Sharon taking her out for a spin.

"Oh," she says, brightening. "Then I should put on something more presentable."

She comes out of her room wearing slightly moth—holed but still bright pastels from a friendlier decade. I tell her she looks nice.

Once they've gone, I head down to the basement. It's a simple enough calculation, scaling the reactants down and filling the empty space in the pipe with chalk. I'd made it big enough to destroy half of the re-frigeration chamber at the seed bank. I thought of putting it in an in-termodal container and driving a big rig up to the loading docks, letting the routing system deliver it. But of course there's no way to get it through security, and there's no point. What good is a bomb for saving something from destruction? We scientists with our strange meditative acts. Too fancy for yoga or Sudoku. But this one doesn't have to go to waste. I think I've got the right amount to just destroy my own base-ment. The living room and kitchen, if my decimal points are off. The blast will certainly be small enough to spare the garden, though I have little hope that anyone will tend it.

I write out the document on a piece of stationery and place it like a bookmark in chapter six of Genesis in my mother's Bible. I've never been religious, but I do believe in parables. I leave the book on the park bench out back. It is not the document she's hoping for. It simply says *Sorry. There is nothing to be done.* I leave it next to a little brown bag containing the eight remaining miracle berries. I consider writing out the rest of what follows, but decide not to be one of those men who needs to inflict his pain upon the world.

But here is what I would write if I were. The problem all along has been with trying to see myself as the savior in this parable, or at least a Good Samaritan. But my role is much smaller than that, much plainer. I've realized I'm here simply to update an old verse for a modern age:

God saw evil in the hearts of men. He repented of having made them. God planned to flood the earth, but he had some reservations. He had Noah build an ark. Noah built according to God's specifications, includ-ing the coating of pitch, and he ushered into it all the animals of the world—birds, cows, walkers, creepers, and so on—and he secured them in their cells. Then the great flood came and drowned the Earth, but the ark was buoyed safely up. It floated on the water awhile, above the drowned world. Long enough for Noah to take some comfort in the work he'd done. Then after a while, whether because God willed it, or because he didn't care enough to stop it—and let the angels debate over whether it's a meaningful difference—the ark caught fire. The ark sank.

Nominated by New England Review

DIXON

fiction by BRET ANTHONY JOHNSTON

from VIRGINIA QUARTERLY REVIEW

A star-smeared night, the usual briny and humid haze of the brush country in August, and Dixon was hauling twenty cases of stolen toys up from the Rio Grande valley. They were in the bed of his truck under a blue tarp. He took care to drive the speed limit and flash his blinker. If the border patrol at the Sarita checkpoint asked, he'd claim a delivery mix-up. If the guards were white, he'd blame it on Mexicans.

The toys had been slated for Dairy Queen kids' meals, a promotion for a book series called *Pegaterrestrials* in which the characters were half alien and half winged horse, but that morning the office phone rang and a collectibles dealer had offered three grand for the lot. Dixon was forty-two and he'd managed the franchise outside Harlingen for four years. He knew he'd be fired, maybe arrested, too, but he also knew better than to give himself time to reconsider. He loaded the cases into his truck between customers. When the afternoon crew arrived, he went to the filling station to top off the tank. He checked his tire pressure and brake lights. Then he drove home and had supper with his wife, hamburger meat fried with peppers and onions. Afterward, they ate Blizzards he'd brought for dessert and he told her not to wait up.

Dixon pressed his swollen knuckles to the cold paper cup and felt a soothing. Trish saw it, looked away. She said, "You're doing all this for someone named Cornbread?"

"I'm doing it for the money. Three grand gets us closer to the twenty-eight days."

"Three grand from a man named after bread you cook in a skillet," she said.

"Sounded more teenager than man."

"Where does a teenager get that kind of cash?"

"Where does anyone?"

Trish licked her red plastic spoon. She said, "Did you put the pistol back in the truck?"

"I'm doing it for Casey," he said. Their daughter was fifteen. She'd been asleep in her bed since Dixon had carried her there the night before.

"A man got arrested this morning," Trish said. "He was driving a hearse and had dope in the cadaver, an old woman stuffed full of pot."

"He didn't think the creek would rise."

"I never understand what you mean by that."

"My father used to say it," Dixon said. He wanted to get going. The deal was to meet Cornbread at a Kingsville taxidermy shop by ten. He said, "It means we'll be all right."

"If your knuckles aren't broken, they're getting close. I can put some ice in the cooler for your drive."

"After I get home," he said.

"Part of me wishes you hadn't gone so easy on those boys."

"I doubt that's the word they'd use."

"You know my meaning, Dixie," she said.

"I need to scoot," he said.

"The man with the hearse probably figured the cadaver would confuse the dogs," Trish said. She was rinsing the plastic spoon. Their drawers were full of Dairy Queen flatware.

"What time do they start admitting patients at Bayview?"

"The story was on the news," she said. "It happened at Sarita. That's all I'm saying. It happened where you're fixin' to go."

His headlamps washed out on the pavement. The air pushing through the vents smelled of creosote and trapped heat. Dixon wished the truck's radio still worked. He hadn't missed it for years, but tonight he wanted distraction. The drive was too flat, too dim and quiet. Occasionally, a sharp and radiating pain singed his knuckles; he should've accepted that cooler with ice. He alternated hands on the wheel. Outside Raymondville, plastic grocery bags were snagged on barbed wire fences. They looked like jellyfish.

How long since he'd come up this way? They used to go to Corpus for Casey's school clothes because the valley stores weren't up to snuff.

There had been trips to see the replica Columbus ships dry-docked by the museum and the air shows at the Army depot. Mostly, they'd drive up to go bird hunting near the King Ranch. For Casey's twelfth birthday, they'd given her a .20 gauge. Dixon taught her to press her cheek to the shotgun as she's patterning the dove, to keep her eyes on a shot bird as it falls, to track them where they like to eat—wheat fields and sunflower crops and gravel roads. He didn't know what other fathers did with their daughters; the greatest luck of his life was having the only girl he'd know how to raise.

An hour into the drive, his cell lit up. Felipe, his assistant manager, had an irate customer.

"She's got three kids here," Felipe said. "They want the new toys."

"That promotion doesn't start until tomorrow. We aren't allowed to pop the cases earlier," Dixon said.

"I know, but the kids are losing their shit and we're trying to close. I thought I'd just slip her a couple, but I can't find them."

"Give her free Blizzards," Dixon said.

"We already shut down the machine. Before her, we hadn't had a customer for an hour. Did we move the cases?"

"Give them extras of the old ones."

"What about tomorrow? I'm scheduled to open and if the toys aren't here, I can't—"

"They didn't grow goddamn legs," Dixon interrupted. "Hell, Felipe, they didn't just walk out the goddamn door."

Before Shawn Milford, Casey's interest in boys had not extended beyond hunting experience—how old they'd been when they got their first guns, what kind of shells they loaded, how many birds they'd brought down in a day. She was in competition with them, not love. At fourteen, she still played cards and went bowling with her parents, made honor roll, washed dishes without being asked. So when the cop called Dixon last year, he figured it for a prank. Panhandling? The word itself seemed vaudevillian. And yet it was no joke. Others were on the hook as well, a crew of friends whose names neither Dixon nor Trish recognized. But the cops knew Milford—he was nineteen, a burnout. No question that he concocted the scam where the kids had spread out through the mall, claimed to have been separated from their church group, and begged for bus fare. Security footage showed they'd been running the con for weeks. Casey spent the day at the police station but

314

got off with a warning. She cried and shook and apologized when Dixon picked her up, but he knew he'd been given a gift. She'd be too scared to court more trouble in the future.

But then came truancy notices and calls from Ivan at the pawnshop: Casey was hocking her mother's tennis bracelet, Dixon's circular saw, the .20 gauge she'd gotten for her birthday. Then came so many nights of her sneaking out her window that Dixon drilled it shut; he counter-sunk six screws from outside so she couldn't work on them from her bed. Dixon talked to her by himself, so did Trish, and they talked to her together. She saw a counselor at school and started reading books to old folks at the retirement home. Then she got suspended for fighting Alma Santos in the cafeteria. Casey said Alma had been the instigator, but only Dixon believed her. Trish accused him of cutting Casey too much slack, of seeing good where there was only shit. A month ago, Casey came home in a police cruiser with pupils the size of quarters. The cops had been called on a noise complaint and when they arrived at the apartment Milford shared with his brother, they found a bowl party.

"A what?" Dixon had asked the officer. Casey was still in the cruiser, her cheek pressed to the window.

"Kids dump a bunch of their parents' pills in a bowl, then spend the night munching on them like popcorn. No one ever knows what they're taking."

"Where's Milford?"

"County," the cop said. "His brother, too."

"How long?"

"Up to the judge. With all those pills, they might be in for a stretch."

"Too bad," Dixon said.

Then he crossed the yard and gathered his daughter from the squad car. She was dead weight in his arms, like her bones had turned to gruel.

The next time his phone buzzed, the night was full dark and the call lit the cab. Trish said, "Why are you the one on the road?"

"Do what?"

"If Mr. Cornbread wants his toys so bad, why didn't he make the drive down?"

"DQ has security cameras," he said.

"They're working again?"

315

"Safety first," Dixon said.

"This doesn't add up," Trish said. "We didn't think it out."

In truth, Dixon had suggested delivering the toys tonight because Cornbread said he wouldn't have access to a truck until next week. Waiting that long seemed careless, cowardly.

"I guess she hasn't emerged yet," he said.

"I checked on her. She kicked the covers off."

"She'll sweat some of it out. That's all to the good."

"She still smells like that glue," she said.

"It's in her hair," Dixon said.

"Like those resistoleros," she said. There'd been articles in the paper about homeless kids addicted to huffing Resistol across the border. The cobbler's glue was cheap and legal in Mexico. It suppressed hunger. Dealers sold it in baby food jars.

"She'll hate us more if they have to cut her hair to get it out," Trish said.

"Bayview will have better shampoo," he said. "She doesn't hate us."

"They start admitting at eight. I didn't answer you earlier."

"We'll be the first in line," he said.

"I made some tuna in case she wakes up wanting real food. I thought you might want some when you got home, too."

"Nothing would taste better," he said.

"Felipe called," Trish said. "I let the machine get it."

"We talked. He needed help closing out the register."

"How far to Sarita?" she said.

"Coming up," he said. "I can see the lights."

"I told you about the woman stuffed with pot, right?"

"Yes ma'am," he said.

"Cornflake should've come here. You shouldn't be driving all that way. Your poor hands."

"I didn't want him to know where we live," he said.

"Maybe he was thinking along the same lines."

"We're all right," he said.

"That's what you keep saying," she said.

The Sarita checkpoint was bleached in artificial light. Dixon had to lower his visor as he idled behind a tractor-trailer being searched by two guards. One was white, the other was Mexican. Flashlights, clipboards, handcuffs, and side arms. The Mexican guard led a German shepherd around the truck on a leash. He opened the trailer and waved his light inside: wooden crates of grapefruit. Dixon rolled down his window and the night swamped in, heavy as wet wool. He fidgeted with the vents. He could feel his pulse racing under his jaw. His knuckles were throbbing too and he concentrated on the pain as a way of calming himself. After a sedan pulled up behind him, he realized he'd been considering reversing out and hooking a U-turn back to Harlingen.

The rig heaved into gear and rumbled out of the checkpoint. Dixon pulled forward. The white guard stepped in front of the truck, waving him closer then motioning for him to kill the engine. Dixon considered asking if he could keep it running, explaining that the starter was on its last legs, but he turned the key instead. The guard flipped a switch in his booth and a strip of spikes hinged up from asphalt. The other guard set to circling the truck with the dog.

"Where you off to?" the guard asked.

"Kingsville," he said.

"Carrying any firearms or illegal drugs?"

"I've got a .38 under my seat," Dixon said, hoping such honesty would pay off later. He added, "Permit's at home."

The guard scratched a note on his clipboard just as the tailgate dropped down and rocked the whole truck. It was like jumping a curb. The guard with the dog whistled and his partner went to see what he'd found.

When the guard returned, he said, "What's with the boxes?"

"Toys for kids' meals. I manage the Harlingen DQ. We got the Corpus shipment."

"You said Kingsville."

"I'm meeting another manager there. He's hauling them the rest of the way."

The guard surveyed the truck's cab: paper trash on the floorboards, sun-split dashboard, cell phone on the passenger seat. He glanced to the rear. In the mirror, the other guard shrugged. Dixon put both hands on the wheel, a mistake.

"What happened to your knuckles?" the guard asked.

"Punched the wall when I saw we got the wrong shipment."

"With both hands?"

"Not my finest hour," Dixon said. His shirt was soggy against the seat. If he floored the gas, he'd make it no farther than fifty feet past the spikes. Then, a memory: Casey used to love the sound of balloons popping. When she had chicken pox, Dixon had blown up a bag's worth of balloons and burst them with his pocket- knife to make her laugh.

The guard had been talking. "Sir," he repeated, "I need to see your license."

Dixon fished out his billfold. The guard checked the ID picture against his face. He wrote something else down, then passed it back.

"Can I get hold of the Corpus manager?" the guard asked.

"He's on the road. I don't know his cell, but his name's Milford. If he ever passes through, your time wouldn't be wasted searching his car.

"If he's got something to hide, we'll find it," he said.

"I heard about the hearse," Dixon said. "It's bad in the valley too—heroin, glue, pill parties."

"Is your firearm loaded?"

"Unloaded. It's just a paperweight."

"And if I make a call, I won't have trouble finding it registered in your name?"

"None at all," Dixon lied.

The guard held his gaze. He wasn't gauging whether Dixon was lying—Dixon suspected he knew the truth—but whether the infractions were worth his effort, whether whatever danger Dixon posed was tolerable. Without warning, the tailgate slammed shut. The guard moved to the booth and flipped the switch. The spikes flattened. The guards walked to the sedan behind him. Dixon had to crank the ignition three times before it turned over.

Excepting his pistol and Casey's .20 gauge, Dixon had sold all of their guns. They'd gone one by one to the pawnshop—when he was short on rent, when the starter on the truck first gave out, when Trish's hours got cut at the deli counter. He kept the pistol because he'd never lived without one; the .38 had belonged to his father and had traveled from one house to the next with Dixon. He kept Casey's shotgun because it had once meant so much to her and he hoped it would again. After she tried pawning it on her own, he'd locked it in the gun cabinet in his and Trish's bedroom. The key was taped under his nightstand drawer.

For the last hour of the drive, he'd been thinking of Casey as someone suffering temporary amnesia. She was in a fugue state. Getting her out of this sludge could be as simple as reminding her of the life before.

All he needed to do was jar her memory. He could manage it. They'd play cards and go bowling. They could even start hunting again, maybe head up to the Hill Country for pheasant. If the taxidermy shop where he was meeting Cornbread did solid work, he'd have one of her birds mounted. Hang it above the television or in her room. When he'd laid her in her bed last night, Dixon was struck by how unfamiliar the room had become. Her plush toys and bright posters had been replaced by a wheelless skateboard, a lava lamp, and barren walls. Maybe they'd hang a bird on all of her walls, he thought now. Give her more to brag about, build her confidence. Trish would call his thinking naïve, but Dixon knew it would work. He could hardly wait.

The taxidermist's gravel lot was empty. A lamppost swayed over the squat building, but the casing and bulb were busted. What little light there was spread from the Party Barn across the road. A line of cars ten deep waited at the drive-through liquor store; one was an ice cream van. Before he stepped from the truck, Dixon slipped the pistol into the back of his waistband.

He thought about walking to the Party Barn to get a bag of ice for his knuckles, but didn't want to risk missing Cornbread. He checked his phone and peered through the shop window. Cupping his hands around his eyes, he could make out mounted heads of deer, javelina, a caribou. He squinted but couldn't discern the quality of the work. A rattlesnake arrested in midstrike, fangs bared. An armadillo on its back guzzling a Lone Star bottle. A lynx in a fierce pose, a marlin arching on the far wall, an owl spreading its wings. All of the animals' dull glass eyes seemed fixed on Dixon.

When he turned from the window, a young man stood in the street: Cornbread. He was pacing in the turning lane, trying to time his crossing. Cars barreled by in both directions and Dixon feared he'd be hit. After a minute without an opening, Cornbread tried darting out and forced a 4x4 pickup to swerve. The driver laid into his horn and kept on it for a hundred yards. Cornbread waved an exaggerated wave; it looked like he was trying to flag down a helicopter. Dixon wondered if he was on something. When traffic finally eased, Cornbread bolted across. He ran in a flailing, childish way. One of his shoes flew off and he had to kneel to retie it on a parking block.

"You're early," Cornbread said, bent at the waist, breathing heavy.

He looked about Casey's age, but smaller. He said, "We're in line at the Party Barn. I didn't want you to think I flaked. I almost got run over by a truck."

"You brought the money?"

Cornbread dug in his pocket and came up with a roll of cash. Before handing it over, he doffed an imaginary cap. Dixon fanned out the bills—twenties, fifties, a few hundreds. He counted them twice, then again, arranging them to face forward. Cornbread had closed his eyes. His head bobbed to music only he heard.

Dixon said, "Help me get these boxes out of the truck."

Cornbread clapped his hands and cut a jig in the gravel.

They unhooked the tarp, lowered the tailgate, and began unloading. Cornbread worked as though he was still hearing the music, as though he could barely restrain himself from dancing. He looked not like a kid buying stolen goods, but like he'd randomly happened upon something he'd coveted for years. Once enough of the cases were on the ground, Cornbread swung himself into the truck bed and passed what remained to Dixon.

His phone vibrated. Trish's name appeared on the screen and he sent it to voicemail.

"We have a flea market booth," Cornbread said after they'd gotten all the boxes out of the truck. "We sell collectible toys. Each of these cases has one ultra-rare figure. Collectors pay out the ass for Pegater-restrials."

"How old are you?" Dixon asked.

"Eighteen. I'm little for my age," he said.

"I thought you had to be twenty-one to buy anything at Party Barn."

"My friend's older," he said. "He's the ice cream man."

Dixon was trying to fold the tarp, awkwardly trapping a corner with his chin and getting nowhere, but when Cornbread noticed him struggling, he came to help. They folded it like a sheet, finished in no time.

Cornbread said, "We called about ten Dairy Queens before yours. I didn't think you'd show up."

An idea had been forming without Dixon's knowledge. It whorled outward as imperceptibly as a growing shell, recognizable only after taking its full and inevitable shape. Dixon said, "What about the extras?"

"Do what?"

"You said you sell the rare toys. What happens to the leftovers?"

"They're worthless. We'll blow them up with firecrackers."

"Sell them to me," Dixon said.

Cornbread looked toward Party Barn. The ice cream van was next in line.

"We'll pick out the ones you need, then I'll take the rest back to Harlingen," Dixon said. He felt awake and alive, sure of himself, the future. He said, "Five hundred for the lot?"

"Can we still have a few of the regulars to explode?"

"You bet," Dixon said. "Now show me how to spot the special ones."

Cornbread opened the first box, ferreting through the common figures until he found one. The toy was bright chrome—eagle wings, the muscled body of a thoroughbred, an alien's smooth head and teardrop eyes. Cornbread studied it like a jeweler, handled it as delicately as he would a newborn chick. What drew children to such outlandish creatures? Dixon wondered. Had Casey read any *Pegaterrestrial* books? That he didn't know galled him. She'd always loved animals, declaring once that she wanted to be a zebra when she grew up, and in a way Dixon couldn't explain, he equated her hunting with an affection for the birds, an abiding desire to be closer with them. He'd ask her about such things when they drove to the Hill Country. Across the street, the ice cream van was entering Party Barn. Cornbread was still regarding the special figure with no small amount of awe. Dixon opened another box and located the chrome creature easily. Then he moved onto the next one, then the next and the next. He opened case after case and his knuckles hardly hurt at all.

The day before yesterday, Casey hadn't come home from school. They called her phone, left messages, waited. They paced the floor, stopping occasionally to part the blinds and watch the street, willing her to appear in the distance. Trish kept supper warm, then after a couple of hours they conceded to pick at their food in fraught silence. Every little noise sounded like the door opening. Finally, Dixon wiped his mouth with a DQ napkin and said, "I'll rustle her up."

He took the .38 from the gun cabinet and went to the Milford brothers' apartment. No surprise that they were gone, too. He lingered in the parking lot, but then set out. Trish was at home redialing Casey's phone. She called the hospitals and border patrol. She called the police, who said nothing could be filed until Casey had been missing for twenty-four hours. She called Bayview Hospital, the rehab facility in Corpus, and scribbled rates on the back of an overdue electric bill: *28 days =* *3600.00*. She called the morgue. The man who answered recognized their last name and said her husband had just left, said they'd get in touch if someone matching Casey's description arrived, said not to call back. She called Dixon to tell him whom she'd called and to ask where else he'd gone.

He'd gone to the mall and pawnshop and her friends' houses. He stopped for gas and left the truck running for fear of it not starting again. He drove out to the citrus groves, her school, the retirement home where she read her books. He checked the underpasses where users camped. Nothing. Everywhere, nothing. His prevailing sense was of having always just missed her. No evidence supported it, but the notion of lagging one step behind weighed more heavily every hour. Phantom visions of her appeared in storefronts and on street corners. "Where are you, little girl?" he caught himself saying out loud. He'd emptied a tank of gas. The night was leaden, clouds scudded by and disappeared. *Think*, he thought. *Think*.

What he thought was this: *The world is too goddamn big*. If she'd headed out after the first school bell rang, she could've been in San Antonio by lunch, in Houston by midafternoon, in Dallas by supper. Or she could be within minutes of where Dixon was now. She could be unconscious or terrified or crying out for her father. He was near a motor court that rented by the hour when dizzying nausea took hold. He pulled to the curb and tried to vomit but nothing came. He stepped into the empty street and pivoted in a circle, as if scouting a spot to crouch in a field and wait for a flock of quail. The memory of her safety, of a life where he could trust the day to deliver her home, had withered and scattered. There were new rules now. Or the rules were unchanged and he'd failed to understand them until this moment.

He went to St. Pius, where Casey had been christened. He prayed and lit a candle. He doubled back the way he'd come.

Dixon and Cornbread had culled the special figures from the cases by the time the ice cream van jostled into the parking lot. Headlights slashed across them, briefly whiting out the taxidermy shop's windows. The driver made a wide and fast arc that sent gravel pinging around, then reversed toward them. He braked and doused everything in a red glow.

The driver walked with a cane. He was shirtless, roped with skinny muscle, Dixon's age. His cigarette was near down to the filter. He extended his hand to Dixon and said, "Call me Moose."

"Moose and Cornbread," Dixon said.

"Sounds like an old-time meal," Cornbread said.

Moose smiled without conviction. Smoke ribboned into his eyes, but he seemed not to notice. He said, "Why are my cases open?"

"He wants to buy back the commons," Cornbread said. "We pulled the specials."

The tip of Moose's cigarette flared and smoke went through his nose. He caned his way over to the cases. He said, "What price are you offering?"

"I was thinking five hundred would do it. Cornbread says they're worthless."

"Worthless to us," Moose said, nudging a box with the tip of his cane, "but I'd wager they're worth a job to you."

"I could throw in another hundred."

"The price is a thousand."

"For something you're going to burn up with firecrackers?"

Moose squinted toward Cornbread, then Dixon. He said, "Then how about that pistol of yours? Would that square us?"

Dixon saw where this was going. He said, "We'll leave things be. Everyone can leave happy."

"I wish we could, bubba."

"Do what?"

"You decreased the value when you cracked the seals on the cases. They're not worth what I paid anymore. I'll need to collect a refund."

"My understanding was that you were only interested in the special figures."

"My understanding was that I was paying for unopened cases," Moose said.

"That's my bad, Moose," Cornbread said. "I just figured since the specials were what—"

"How about the three thousand," Moose cut him off, "your Saturday Night Special, your piece of shit truck, and we keep all the toys?"

"Our deal was for the cases and I delivered them," Dixon said and started for the truck. A line of traffic charged by and sounded like a long, heavy wave plowing the shore.

"Hey, bubba," Moose said, laughing. "I'm just jerking you. Of course you can have these no-nothing toys. How about six hundred and we call it a night?"

"Six hundred and we're done?" Dixon said. "Six hundred and we'll hallelujah the county."

Dixon peeled off the cash. Moose grinned with the cigarette still clenched in his teeth—a show of shared enterprise—and limped over to take the money.

323

"How come you brought that pistol?" Moose said as Dixon loaded a case into the truck. "Didn't pick Cornbread for a friendly?"

"It's been a rough few days."

"Your knuckles tell that story just fine," Moose said.

Dixon expected Cornbread to help with the cases, but he stayed by the ice cream van. He was nothing but downcast eyes and stillness. No one spoke. For a while the only sound was gravel crunching beneath Dixon's boots.

Then Moose flicked his cigarette into the parking lot and said, "Thing is, bubba, I've had a rough few days too, and the more I think about you toting a gun here, the more it chafes me."

"Selling those toys will cure that," Dixon said, stowing another case.

"It just makes me think you have untoward plans for me and my little buddy over there."

Dixon's back was to him. He closed his eyes and tried to figure the best move, tried to find some combination of words that would get him on the road.

"So, bubba," Moose said, "here's what's going to happen."

Dixon's eyes were still closed when he heard the air slicing behind him. The blow coursed through the hollows of his bones like quicksilver until there was too much weight to bear and Dixon felt the ground go out from under him. His chin cracked the tailgate as he fell. His mind pulled away from him, a reverse spiral as he hit the gravel. He thought of shot birds dropping from ice-blue skies. He thought of Casey in the back of the squad car with her eyes like coins, thought of her draped in a Texas flag, thought of limp and lifeless bodies filled with cold water and jellyfish, and then his thinking ceased and there was nothing except a soundless and enveloping blackness. Then, increasingly, not even that.

The night before, when he'd passed once more by the Milford apartment, the windows were leaking light. He drove onto the patchy grass and bounded up the concrete stairs two at a time. The door was slightly open. He pushed it the rest of the way with the barrel of the pistol.

A bucket of cobbler's glue sat on a wicker table, the air in the apartment thick with a viscous odor—the glue, yes, but also dank sweat and mildew, aerosol and rotting food, the ripe and chemical smell of semen. A Texas flag hung on the wall over a plaid couch pocked with cigarette burns. All of the lights were on. A calico cat, likely a stray that had just come through the open door, was licking a grease-scabbed skillet on the stove. The cat paid him no mind. In the bathroom, the toilet seat was up and the water was dark with days of urine. Empty cans and bottles spilled from the tub. He took care where he stepped on his way to the bedroom. The door was shut, but he didn't want to hit a creaking floorboard; he tested each step before putting his full weight on it, as if worried the floor would collapse. What a time to think of how he and Trish used to tiptoe through the house after Casey got to sleep as an infant. Now, as then, he put his ear to the door. He heard a window unit working hard. He turned the knob slowly, bracing for when it clicked and he could peek inside.

Casey. Asleep on a bare mattress on the floor. No box spring. She wore an oversized T-shirt and nothing else. Even with only the slice of light from the hall, he could see that the soles of her feet were black with filth. The Milford brothers were naked beside her.

One of them lay curled in a ball and the other on his stomach. The room was freezing, sixty degrees at most. No pillows, no blankets. Another bucket of glue beside the bed. Used condoms on the carpet. He slipped into the room without lowering the pistol. His arm trembled. Sweat in his eyes, bile in his throat, the sense of standing on a threshold that divided before and after. Then came a harsh clattering racket from the kitchen, a sharp and ringing noise that quickly wobbled into silence—the cat had knocked the skillet to the floor. Dixon expected the noise to rouse one or all of them, but no one stirred.

Then Casey rubbed her face with the heels of her hands. She yawned. She smiled, and it seemed a lifetime since he'd witnessed such beauty. He hid the gun behind his back.

"Daddy," she said, groggy, "did you bring me a Blizzard?"

Before he could answer, her eyes lidded and she was back asleep. He lifted her from the bed and backed out of the room and carried her to the couch. The cat was cleaning itself on the wicker table. Dixon shooed it away. He snatched the flag from the wall and draped it over Casey. She snuggled into it, tucking the fabric under her chin. He kissed her cheek and whispered, "I'll be right back, Caybird." He hadn't called her that in years, had entirely forgotten about the nickname, and yet, now, there it was. He took up the bucket of glue.

The brothers hadn't moved. The room was loud with the struggling air conditioner. He left the lights off, locked the door behind him, and beat the brothers until he lost feeling in his hands. Before he left, they were whimpering and pleading, slumped in different corners of the room, too disoriented to even stand. Dixon flipped on the light. The brothers pressed their bloodied faces to the walls. Whether out of fear or a reaction to the sudden brightness, Dixon didn't know. Nor did he know if they'd remember or understand what had happened once they sobered up. To make sure, he emptied the bucket of cobbler's glue over each of their heads.

He woke in the taxidermist's parking lot with gravel notching into his cheek. He worked a pebble out of his mouth with his tongue. Coughing sent an electric pain down his spine. He tried raising himself but couldn't. His ears rang. He tasted copper and minerals and his own mealy blood. He tasted hamburger fried with onions and peppers.

He made it to his knees and stayed there. Saliva hung from his mouth to the gravel. The swelling on the back of his head felt like a bone spur, a cranial anomaly that had grown so fast it tore through the skin. There wasn't enough of him anymore. A breeze dragged itself over the parking lot, and when the air hit the gash, Dixon understood it was deep enough for his flesh to fold open. He thought he could feel grit in it. He reached to the top of his truck's tire and levered himself up. His eyes wouldn't focus. Then they did. The parking lot was abandoned. Party Barn had closed. His watch and phone were gone. His pistol, too, and the money.

But his keys were in his pocket, and when he turned to lean against the truck and rest a little, he saw that most of the toy cases were still there, too. He couldn't gauge if this was good or bad news. He tried to figure the odds of Moose returning, but his thoughts kept petering out. Too many angles to consider. They made his head throb. He loaded the cases as fast as he could, but all of the bending over gave him vertigo. His vision kept twisting, shifting everything to the left. Each step was like trying to balance on a raft being pitched by waves. He draped the boxes with the tarp again, though not as thoroughly. He doubted it would hold to Harlingen.

He worried they'd taken his battery or cut the fuel line, worried the engine had given out again on its own, but the ignition turned. After several miles, he remembered to click on his headlights. The truck listed across the highway's double yellow lines, and when Dixon jerked back into his lane, the cases slid across the bed. He drowsed. He lowered his windows to fill the cab with wind and noise that would keep him awake. The speedometer needle tipped toward eighty, eighty-five. The truck rattled. Trish would say he should've known better.

Not that all was lost. He was making decent time. The drive was halfway done and the tarp was holding. There was no checkpoint heading south, and when Sarita passed on the other side and he saw his two guards doing their work, a particular relief washed over him: He didn't have to worry about them again. His head had eased up some. He felt one step removed from the current moment, which likely meant he had a concussion, but with that distance came clarity. The future seemed as certain as the past. He'd return the toys to Dairy Queen before going home and he'd keep his job. Trish would clean him up enough to get Casey admitted to Bayview, then they'd go to the minor emergency clinic. He'd scrounge the money for Casey's treatment before she was discharged from the hospital. He had almost a month. There were ways. Sell the truck. Visit Ivan at the pawnshop. Go to other Dairy Queens where he knew the managers, pluck the special figures from the cases, open up his own goddamned flea market booth.

When he pulled into the driveway, Trish was on the porch. She held her phone with both hands, which made her look like a woman praying. What Dixon believed was that their air conditioner had crapped out again, and he hated that his wife and daughter had been suffering through the soupy heat. He wondered if there was enough room on his credit card for a motel. Even just a few hours of comfortable sleep would do them all a world of good.

"You look chewed up and stepped on," Trish said. "You look like you've been hit with a bag of nickels."

"Things could've gone smoother out there, I'll tell you that."

"I thought you were dead. You never called me back."

Dixon walked to the porch and she rose to inspect his wound. The blood on his shirt embarrassed him; he should've washed up at Dairy Queen after returning the toys. Trish had him bend into the floodlight. She said, "You need stitches."

"It'll keep till after Bayview," he said.

She cocked her head, confused, like he was a stranger who'd called her name on the street. He wondered if he'd slurred his speech, if the blow to his head was compromising him in ways he couldn't parse.

"I called the police," Trish was saying. "They came and took my statement."

Now Dixon was confused. Now she was the stranger calling his name. He said, "Police?" Trish said, "You didn't listen to my messages?"

"Cornbread brought reinforcements," he said. "They took my phone. The money and pistol, too, but we can still get her into—"

"Oh, Dixie," she interrupted. "Oh, honey."

"You were right. I didn't think it out. I should've had him drive up here and—"

"She's gone, baby. The cops are out hunting for her."

"Gone? What does gone' mean right now?"

"Her window," she said.

"I had her window drilled shut."

"Someone undid it," she said. "They even left the screws on her windowsill."

Dixon couldn't get his bearings. His eyes lit on his patchy yard, the dark neighborhood, the stars in the sky like buckshot, and his wife talking under it. He felt connected to none of it, completely untethered.

"The last time I saw her was around eleven," Trish said. "She ate some tuna on the couch then went back to her room. I called to tell you."

"What time is it now?"

"Almost four."

"She could be halfway to Cancún," he said. "We had a nice talk," Trish said. "She asked if you were mad and when you'd be back. Maybe she was distracting me while they undid her window, but she seemed sincere. I brushed some glue from her hair and she hugged my neck before going back to bed."

"I'm not mad at her," he said.

"I told her that," she said.

"Good," he said.

"I'm furious, though. I'm just seeing red, but I knew you'd be more forgiving."

She meant *too* forgiving. There was no disdain in her tone, but Dixon still heard the accusation: He'd been too timid, too relentless in his optimism, too faint of heart. Had he handled things differently, they'd be in a better spot now. He couldn't say she was fully wrong.

The morning was glomming, every surface beaded with condensation. First light was an hour away, but cars were already moving into the streets. People were heading to work or coming off overnight shifts. Dixon wondered how he and Trish would appear to someone driving by. Like a couple whose air conditioner had died? Like they'd been up all night fighting? Or would the scene, in the shallow glow of the floodlight, look happier? Dixon could easily recall mornings like this when he was busy packing the truck to take Casey hunting. Trish had always

328

woken up to see them off and they'd always let their daughter sleep until it was time to leave.

"Is there any tuna left?" Dixon asked.

"Plenty," Trish said. "She just had a few bites."

"I should eat something, then get cleaned up. She doesn't need to see me like this when she gets home."

"I'll run you a bath," she said. "It'll feel good to soak and I'll get a better look at your head that way."

Trish went into the house. Dixon waited until he saw light come through the bathroom window then climbed the porch and made his way to their bedroom. The key for the gun cabinet was still taped under his nightstand drawer. Only now did he realize he'd been expecting otherwise. He listened for Trish coming down the hall as he took out the .20 gauge, but she was in the kitchen slicing a tomato for his sandwich. The smell of coconut bubble bath wafted; the tub was filling and Dixon hoped Trish would check the water before it flooded. He slipped out the front door quietly, concealing the gun with his leg. The morning was already brighter, a long seam of color on the horizon. His knuckles were aching again. His head thrummed and his vision undulated, as if he were watching the world through a fast-moving stream. But his thoughts were sharp, concerted. When he saw Trish pass from the kitchen and disappear down the hall, he dropped the truck into neutral and let it roll backwards from the driveway. Of course, he worried the engine wouldn't crank, but it came to life without trouble. A promising sign, Dixon thought, a signal of good things to come.

Nominated by Virginia Quarterly Review, Don Lee

SAD SONG

by CHASE TWICHELL

from SALMAGUNDI

It's ridiculous, at my age,
to have to pull the car onto the shoulder
because Bob Dylan and Johnny Cash
are singing "Girl From the North Country,"
taking turns remembering not one girl,
but each of their girls, one and then the other,
a duet that forces tears from my eyes
so that I have to pull off the road and weep.
Ridiculous! My sadness is fifty years old!
It travels into sorrow and gets lost there.
Not because it calls up first love, though it does,
or first loss of love, though both
are shawls it wears to hide its wound,
a wound to the girl of which
all men sing, the girl split open,
the sluice through which all of childhood pours,
carrying her out of one country
into another, in which she grows up
wearing a necklace of stones,
one for each girl not her,
though they all live together here
in the North Country, where the winds
hit heavy on the borderline.

Nominated by Salmagundi

I WILL LOVE YOU IN THE SUMMERTIME

by CHRISTIAN WIMAN

from THE AMERICAN SCHOLAR

Twenty years ago, while watching some television report about depression and religion—I forget the relationship but apparently there was one—a friend who was entirely secular asked me with genuine curiosity and concern, "Why do they believe in something that doesn't make them happy?" I was an ambivalent atheist at that point, beset with an inchoate loneliness and endless anxieties, contemptuous of Christianity but addicted to its aspirations and art. I was also chained fast to the rock of poetry, having my liver pecked out by the bird of a harrowing and apparently absurd ambition—and thus had some sense of what to say. One doesn't follow God in hope of happiness but because one senses—miserable flimsy little word for that beak in your bowels—a truth that renders ordinary contentment irrelevant. There are some hungers that only an endless commitment to emptiness can feed, and the only true antidote to the plague of modern despair is an absolute, and perhaps even annihilating, awe. "I asked for wonders instead of happiness, Lord," writes the Jewish theologian Abraham Joshua Heschel. "And you gave them to me."

I thought of this moment not long ago when one of my four-year-old twin daughters walked wide-eyed and trembly into my room at night. My wife was traveling. The girls are accustomed to my being gone and have learned to allay their anxieties with the prospect of airport presents, but they are less sanguine about the absence of their mother. There had been a vociferous territorial dispute at the kiddie pool and then a principled aesthetic disagreement (over the length of my hair in a chalk drawing) that was decided by a bite. Still, I thought we were managing pretty well. Dinner was lively, the ice-cream bribery effective, and after story time, poem time, I-love-you time, I slipped out of their room without a fuss. About an hour later, though, I looked up to find my blond-haired blue-eyed scarily intelligent sprite of a child Eliza standing in the doorway.

"Daddy" she said, "I can't sleep. Every time I close my eyes, I'm seeing terrible things." I am a lifelong insomniac. I used to freak my own parents out when I was a small child by creeping quietly into their room and opening up their eyelids with my fingers in an effort—so the story goes—to see what they were dreaming. And in fact I began this very essay between two and four one morning when "[m]y thoughts were all a case of knives," to quote the 17th-century poet and priest George Herbert. So I was sympathetic to my daughter's plight.

I suggested she pray to God. This was either a moment of tremendous grace or brazen hypocrisy (not that the two can't coincide), since I am not a great pray-er myself and tend to be either undermined by irony or overwhelmed by my own chaotic consciousness. Nevertheless, I suggested that my little girl get down on her knees and bow her head and ask God to give her good thoughts—about the old family house in Tennessee that we'd gone to just a couple of weeks earlier, for example, and the huge green yard with its warlock willows and mystery thickets, the river with its Pleistocene snapping turtles and water-bearded cattle, the buckets of just-picked blueberries and the fried Krispy Kremes and the fireflies smearing their strange radiance through the humid Tennessee twilight. I told her to hold that image in her head and ask God to preserve it for her. I suggested she let the force of her longing and the fact of God's love coalesce into a form as intact and atomic as matter itself, to attend to memory with the painstaking attentiveness of the poet, the abraded patience of the saint, the visionary innocence of the child whose unwilled wonder erases any distinction between her days and her dreams. I said all this—underneath my actual words, as it were—and waited while all that blond-haired, blue-eyed intelligence took it in.

"Oh, I don't think so, Daddy." She looked me right in the eyes.

"What do you mean, Eliza? Why not?"

"Because in Tennessee I asked God to turn me into a unicorn and"—she spread her arms wide in a disconcertingly adult and ironic shrug—"look how that's worked out."

What exactly does that mean: *to pray?* And is it something one ought to be teaching a child to do? And if we assume for a moment that it is indeed an essential thing to "learn," then what exactly ought one to pray for? A parking space? To be cured of some dread disease? For the emotional and spiritual well-being of a beloved child? To be a unicorn? For one night of untroubled sleep?

The Polish poet Anna Kamienska died in 1986, at the age of 66. She had converted to Christianity in her late 40s, after the unexpected death of her beloved husband, the poet Jan Spiewak. People who have been away from God tend to come back by one of two ways: destitution or abundance, an overmastering sorrow or a strangely disabling joy. Either the world is not enough for the hole that has opened in you, or it is too much. The two impulses are intimately related, and it may be that the most authentic spiritual existence inheres in being able to perceive one state when you are squarely in the midst of the other. The mortal sorrow that shadows even the most intense joy. The immortal joy that can give even the darkest sorrow a fugitive gleam.

Anna Kamienska, then. A devoted and tormented Catholic, whose faith brought her great comfort and great anguish, often at the same time. No doubt this is precisely the quality that attracted me to her when I first came across a couple of passages from her diaries, high in the air above downtown Chicago in Northwestern Memorial Hospital, blood in my tubes and blades in my veins. I had—have—cancer. I have been living with it—dying with it—for so long now that it bores me, or baffles me, or drives me into the furthest crannies of literature and theology in search of something that will both speak and spare my own pain. Were it not for my daughters, I think by this point I would be at peace with any outcome, which is, I have come to believe, one reason why they are here.

Not long before her death, Anna Kamienska wrote what I think is her best poem (available in English, at any rate), a stark, haunting, and insidiously hopeful little gem called "A Prayer That Will Be Answered." The title is worth some stress, in both senses of that word: "A Prayer That *Will Be Answered.*"

> Lord let me suffer much
> and then die

Let me walk through silence
and leave nothing behind not even fear

Make the world continue
let the ocean kiss the sand just as before

Let the grass stay green
so that the frogs can hide in it

so that someone can bury his face in it
and sob out his love

Make the day rise brightly as if there
were no more pain

And let my poem stand clear as a windowpane
bumped by a bumblebee's head

  —tr. by Clare Cavanagh and Stanislaw Baranczak

This is an uncanny poem, giving God all power (the continuance of the world) and no power (it was going to continue anyway). The poem is implicitly apophatic, you might say. That is, it erases what it asserts: it is a prayer to be reconciled to a world in which prayer *does not work*. "Ah my dear God! . . . Let me not love thee, if I love thee not," writes George Herbert at the end of one of his own greatest poems ("Affliction I"). "We pray God to be free of God," says the 13th-century mystic Meister Eckhart. Behind Kamienska's poem, infusing it with an ancient and awful power, is the most wonderful and terrible prayer one can pray: "Not my will, Lord, but yours." That's Jesus in the Garden of Gethsemane before the Roman soldiers come to take him to his death, just after he has sweated blood, begged God to let the cup of suffering pass him by, and wept to leave this world that he has come to love so completely and, it seems, helplessly. And then: Not my will, Lord, but yours. It's difficult enough to pray a prayer like this when you're thinking of making some big life decision. It's damn near impossible when your actual life is on the line, or the life of someone you love, when all you want to pray is *help, help, help*.

Not my will, Lord, but yours.

Kamienska's poem is uncanny in another way too—and triumphant.

"If you want me again," writes Walt Whitman near the end of "Song of Myself," "look for me under your bootsoles," and this poem has a similar ghosting effect, gives its author a kind of posthumous presence. "And let my poem stand clear as a windowpane / bumped by a bumblebee's head." This, it turns out, has happened. The poem is indeed as clear as a windowpane, and we the readers, all these decades after Kamienska's death, are bumping our heads upon it. The prayer has been answered, and to feel the full effect of this poem is to feel a little ripple of spirit going right through the stark indifferent reality to which the poet sought to be reconciled.

*　*　*

For a long time I tried to write a poem that had as its first line "Are you only my childhood?" By *childhood* I meant not only the encompassing bubble of Baptist religiosity in which I was raised, but also that universally animate energy, that primal permeability of mind and matter that children both intuit and inhabit ("The park lives outside," as one of my little girls said to the other when they were going to sleep), that clear and endlessly creative existence that a word like "faith" can only stain. By you I meant You. I took dozens of different tacks for the poem, but it was all will, and thus all wasted. Years passed. Then recently, in a half-dreaming state in the middle of the night, I heard myself ask the question again: "Are you only my childhood?" And from deep within the dream, a voice—it was me, but the voice was not mine—said, with what seemed to be genuine interest and puzzlement: "Why do you say *only?*"

*　*　*

> Ah, my dear angry Lord,
> Since thou dost love yet strike,
> Cast down, yet help afford,
> Sure I will do the like.
>
> I will complain, yet praise.
> I will bewail, approve.
> And all my sour-sweet days
> I will lament and love.

George Herbert again. It's likely he wrote the poem—"Bitter-Sweet," it's called—between the ages of 37 and 40, when he had just swerved from a disappointing political career into parish ministry, was newly and

335

very happily married, and obviously dying of tuberculosis. "And all my sour-sweet days / I will lament and love." Destitution and abundance. Submission to God and aggression against God. What might it mean to pray an honest prayer? Well, maybe it means, like Meister Eckhart, praying to be free of the need for prayer. Maybe it means praying to be fit for, worthy of, capable of living up to the only reality that we know, which is this physical world around us, the severest of whose terms is death. Maybe it means resisting this constriction with the little ripple of spirit that cries otherwise, as all art, even the most apparently despairing, ultimately does. And maybe, just maybe, it even means praying for a parking spot in the faith that there is no permutation of reality too minute or trivial for God to be altogether absent from it. If Jesus' first miracle can be a kind of pointless party trick—he turns water into wine! voilà!—maybe the lesson that believers are meant to learn from this is that we have to turn *everything* over to God, including those niggling feelings and hesitations we have that the whole rigmarole of sifting scripture like bird's entrails, and bowing one's suddenly brainless head, and "believing" in something more than matter—this is all just a little ridiculous, isn't it? An embarrassment even. The province, perhaps, of little children.

* * *

I can't tell a story of one daughter without including the other. Fiona, then. The olive-skinned and night-eyed child, the lithe and little trickster sister: Fiona.

When our girls were just two years old, we spent a summer in Seattle, where I had lived for a while many years earlier. It was the first break I had managed to take from my editing job in a decade, and it was only eight months after I had undergone a bone marrow transplant. Time had a texture that summer, an hourly reality that we could taste and see. The girls went to a wonderful little daycare in the mornings so that my wife and I could write, and then we all came together in the afternoons to do something fun in the city. We had the same nightly ritual that we do now. I'd read to the girls and tuck them in before my wife took over, and the last thing I'd say every night was "I love you," and they would always reply promptly, "I love you too, Daddy." But one night after my declaration, Fiona was silent. She just kept staring at the ceiling.

"Do you love me too, Fiona?" I asked, foolishly.

A long moment passed.

"No, Daddy, I don't."

"Oh, Fiona sweetie, I bet you do," I said.

Nothing.

"Well," I said finally, "I love you, Finn, and I'll see you in the morning."

And then as I started to get up, I felt her small hand on my arm and she said dreamily, without looking at me, like a little Lauren Bacall, "I will love you in the summertime, Daddy. I will love you . . . in the summertime."

I have told this to a couple of people who thought it was heartbreaking, but I was so proud, I thought my heart would burst. I will love you in the summertime. What a piercing poetic thing to say—at two years old. And for weeks I thought about it. A year later, just after that dream I related above, I even wrote a poem about it. I will love you in the summertime. Which is to say, given the charmed life we were living there in Seattle and all the grace and grief that my wife and I felt ourselves moving through at every second: I will love you in the time where there is time for everything, which is now and always. I will love you in the time when time is no more.

Now, do I think that's what my Athena-eyed and mysteriously interior two-year-old daughter meant by that expression? No, I do not. But do I think that sometimes life and language break each other open to change, that a rupture in one can be a rapture in the other, that sometimes there are, as it were, words underneath the words—even the very Word underneath the words? Yes, I do.

❊   ❊   ❊

When Jesus says that you must become as little children in order to enter the Kingdom of Heaven, he is not suggesting that you must shuck all knowledge and revert to an innocence—or, worse, a state of helpless dependence—that you have lost or outgrown. The operative word in the injunction is *become*. (The Greek word is *strepho*, which is probably more accurately translated as "convert," a word that suggests an element of will and maturation.) Spiritual innocence is not beyond knowledge but inclusive of it, just as it is of joy and love, despair and doubt. For the hardiest souls, even outright atheism may be an essential element. ("There are two atheisms of which one is a purification of the notion of God," says Simone Weil.) There is some way of ensuring that one's primary intuitions survive one's secondary self; or, to phrase it differently, ensuring that one's soul survives one's self; or, to phrase it differently, to ensure that one's self and one's soul are not terminally separate entities. To *ripen* into childhood, as Bruno Schulz puts it.

So perhaps one doesn't teach children about God so much as help them grow into what they already know, and perhaps "know" is precisely the wrong verb. "Trying to solve the problem of God is like trying to see your own eyeballs," writes Thomas Merton. It has been my experience that most adults will either smile wryly at this and immediately agree, or roll their eyes and lament the existence of this benighted superstition that pretzels intelligence into these pointless knots, this zombie zeal that will not die. It has also been my experience that there are on this earth two little children who, if told this koan by a father inclined to linguistic experiments, will separately walk over to the mirror and declare that in fact, Daddy, they *can* see their own eyeballs.

"I want only with my whole self to reach the heart of obvious truths." Thus Anna Kamienska near the end of the fractured, intense, diamond-like diaries that circle around and around the same obsessive concern: God. I know just what she means. The trouble, though, as her own life and mind illustrate, is that, just as there are simple and elegant equations that emerge only at the end of what seems like a maze of complicated mathematics, so there are truths that depend upon the very contortions they untangle. Every person has to earn the clarity of common sense, and every path to that one clearing is difficult, circuitous, and utterly, painfully individual.

Here's an obvious truth: I am somewhat ambivalent about religion—and not simply the institutional manifestations, which even a saint could hate, but sometimes, too many times, all of it, the very meat of it, the whole goddamned shebang. Here's another: I believe that the question of faith—which is ultimately separable from the question of "religion"—is the single most important question that any person asks in and of her life, and that every life is an answer to this question, whether she has addressed it consciously or not.

As for myself, I have found faith not to be a comfort but a provocation to a life I never seem to live up to, an eruption of joy that evaporates the instant I recognize it as such, an agony of absence that assaults me like a psychic wound. As for my children, I would like them to be free of whatever particular kink there is in me that turns every spiritual impulse into anguish. Failing that, I would like them to be free to make of their anguish a means of peace, for themselves or others (or both), with art or action (or both). Failing that—and I suppose, ultimately, here in the ceaseless machinery of implacable matter, there is only failure—I would like them to be able to pray, keeping in mind the fact that, as St. Anthony of the Desert said, a true prayer is one that you do not understand.

Witness

Typically cryptic, God said three weasels
slipping electric over the rocks
one current conducting them up the tree
by the river in the woods of the country
into which I walked
away and away and away;
and a moon-blued, cloud-strewn night sky
like an x-ray
with here a mass and there a mass
and everywhere a mass;
and to the tune of a two-year-old
storm of atoms
elliptically, electrically alive—
I will love you in the summertime, Daddy.
I will love you . . . in the summertime.

Once in the west I lay down dying
to see something other than the dying stars
so singularly clear, so unassailably there,
they made me reach for something other.
I said I will not bow down again
to the numinous ruins.
I said I will not violate my silence with prayer.
I said *Lord, Lord*
in the speechless way of things
that bear years, and hard weather, and witness.

Nominated by The American Scholar

ELEGY WITH GROWN FOLKS' MUSIC

by SAEED JONES

from TIN HOUSE

"I Wanna Be Your Lover" comes on the kitchen radio
and briefly, your mother isn't your mother—
just like, if the falsetto is just right, a black man in black
lace panties isn't a faggot, but a prince,
a prodigy—and the woman with your hometown
between her legs shimmies past the eviction notice
burning on the counter and her body moves like she never
even birthed you. The voice on the radio pleas,
"I wanna be the only one that makes you come
running." Some songs take women places men cannot
follow. Spinning, she looks at but doesn't see you,
spinning, she sings lyrics too fast for you to pursue,
spinning, she don't have time for questions like:
What is this nasty song and where did she learn
to dance like *that* and *why*, and who is this high-pitched
bitch of a man who can sing like a woman and turn
your mother not into your mother but a woman,
not even a woman, but a box-braided black girl, a fast
girl, a chick, a Vanity 6, and how far away she is from you
right here in the same living room, dancing
with the song's hook in her throat. And you hate
the voice coming through the radio because another
sissy has snatched your dreams and run off with them
and because you're young and don't know the difference
between abandoned and alone just like your mother's

340

heart won't know the difference between beat
and attack. She will be dead in a decade and maybe
you already know what you're losing without knowing
how, but you're just a boy for now and your mother
is just a woman, just a girl, body swaying, fingers
snapping and snakes in her blood.

Nominated by D. A. Powell

NATURAL HISTORY

by CAMILLE T. DUNGY

from BOSTON REVIEW

The Rufous hummingbird builds her nest
of moss and spider webs and lichen.
I held one once—smaller than my palm,
but sturdy. I would have told Mrs. Jeffers,
from Court Street, if in those days of constant flights
between Virginia and the West I'd happened
on that particular museum. Any chance
I could, I'd leave my rented house in Lynchburg.
I hated the feeling of stuckness that old city's humidity
implied. *You need to stop running away so much,*
Mrs. Jeffers would say when my visits were over
and I leaned down to hug her. Why her words
come to me, the woman dead for the better part
of this new century, while I think of that
nest of web and lichen, I cannot rightly say.
She had once known my mother's parents.
The whole lot of them, even then, in their twenties,
must already have been as old as God. They were
black—the kind name for them in those days
would have been Negroes—and the daily elections
called for between their safety and their sanity
must have torn even the strongest of them down.
Mr. Jeffers had been a laborer. The sort, I regret,
I don't remember. He sat on their front porch
all day, near his oxygen tank, waving occasionally

to passing Buicks and Fords, praising the black
walnut that shaded their yard. She would leave
the porch sometimes to prepare their meals.
I still have her yeast roll recipe. The best
I've ever tried. Mostly, though, the same Virginian
breeze that encouraged Thomas Jefferson's
tomatoes passed warmly through their porch eaves
while we listened to the swing chains, and no one
talked or moved too much at all. Little had changed
in that house since 1952. I guess it's no surprise
they'd come to mind when I think of that cup
of spider webs and moss, made softer by the feathers
of some long-gone bird. She used to say, *I like it
right here where I am. In my little house. Here,
with him.* I thought her small-minded. In the winter,
I didn't visit very often. Their house was closed up
and overheated. Everything smelled of chemical
mothballs. She had plastic wrappers on the sofas
and chairs. Everyone must have once
held someone as old and small and precious as this.

Nominated by Jane Hirshfield, D. A. Powell, Maxine Scates, Philip White

COUNSELOR
OF MY HEART

fiction by LYDIA CONKLIN

from THE SOUTHERN REVIEW

After crossing Memorial Drive onto the bank of the Charles, Molly let her quasi girlfriend's dog off leash. Chowder bounded next to her, limbs flapping against the snow—so puppyish she wanted to push him over. But nothing could annoy her now, not even the stupid dog. She had a day off from the hot dog stand. The air smelled like fire.

She was just wishing the dog away when she became half-aware of the squirrel skittering over the frozen river, making the sound of a rake dragged over plastic. Later she'd wonder why she didn't turn and face the squirrel, seriously question his purpose on the ice. Did he think he'd buried a nut out there? *Had* he, actually? Was it floating, swollen, an inch above the river bottom?

Chowder took his time noticing. He was a foolish dog, though German shepherds are supposed to be bright. Perhaps the white ones, rabbity and smiling, had the smarts bleached out. Beth, whom Molly was dating, had owned Chowder for ten years. Ten frustrating years, Molly imagined, though she'd only met Beth last year. She could picture the rodent-like puppy the dog must have made, the cakes he must have flattened, the urine he must have sprinkled on carpets like holy water.

When Chowder saw the squirrel, he didn't stop to point or stare, judge distance or his probability of success. He tore off across the frosty grass and rinds of stale snow and slipped onto the river. He turned wild for a second, properly vicious. His hackles went up and his tail flagged, his teeth golden against his white coat. Even when his paws slipped, they slipped together, all four at once, so he sailed farther and faster across the ice.

Just as Chowder was about to seize the squirrel, she heard thunder and the ice gave way.

For a heartbeat his tail stuck out, the bottlebrush whiter than the ice or the overcast sky. Molly wondered if anyone was watching from the Weeks Footbridge or the Leverett Towers or the mysterious factory across the river. But then Chowder was gone and the squirrel was gone and Molly was still standing on the bank. She hadn't even taken a step.

There was a hole in the river now. A gray-blue shadow that didn't look big enough to swallow a Chihuahua, much less a shepherd and a squirrel. Molly watched the hole for longer than any mammal could hold its breath, then realized she should've run to the edge, at least tried the ice, before letting the dog go.

Walking back through Harvard Square, dusk hazing the air, Molly felt the weight of the leather leash around her neck. She was balling it up to stick in her bag when a kid in a "Veritas = Beer" shirt said, "All you need is a dog!"

A shot of acid hit Molly's throat. She wanted to spank the kid but instead she asked, "Are you volunteering?"

She returned to Hurlbut Hall, more commonly known as Pukeass Hall, to the first floor suite where Beth was a tutor. Molly was staying with Chowder while Beth presented a paper in Delaware. Harvard tutors were allowed to have pets on the first floor. Beth said that was because the dogs could exit quickly without sloughing dandruff on the stairs and halls. Some of the students on the upper floors had sensitivities.

"You mean allergies?" Molly asked. That was reasonable. Molly was surprised they let a dog in the dorms at all.

"No," said Beth. "If there were allergies I wouldn't be in Hurlbut. But some of the students are sensitive."

That was an understatement. The Harvard kids were at Beth's door from dawn until dawn again. There was never a moment you could crawl between the sheets without some wiener tapping that tight knock that said, *While I acknowledge in theory that I'm being a pain, I nevertheless require your immediate response.*

The freshmen wanted advice about applying to medical school or to report G-Chat alerts that were turned up too loud and poop residue on the toilet seat and gum plastered over showerhead holes. The gum was intended to increase water pressure but just ended up steaming people in mint. Beth indulged the students like precious, dear children, nodding deeply at their monologues, sometimes even tapping their shoulders and rolling her eyes at their pain.

Molly entered the suite. There were armchairs in the front room, everything layered with overlapping rugs and Southwestern blankets. There were too many patterns but that was what you needed to make a dorm cozy when you were in your late twenties and no longer willing to surrender to bluish industrial white.

When she sat down she felt, for an instant, the smiling muzzle of Chowder in her lap. This was the first time she'd sat on the chair without him burrowing in, as though out of sweetness, and then taking a drag of her crotch. Beth wasn't coming back until later tonight, but Molly should call and tell her what had happened. Beth loved Chowder more than she loved Molly, or her family, or herself. Only God knew why.

Molly listened to the ocean on the receiver for a while before dialing out of the Harvard system. Beth was in session or in the hotel revising. Her presentation was in an hour, and her phone would be off. Molly would leave a message using her ghastliest voice. Delivering the news would be easier when Beth called back expecting something dire.

But then, suddenly, Beth was on the line.

"I have to get dressed in two minutes," she said, as if they were already midconversation. "Judith Butler is here. I can't believe no one told me. I have to raise the barn. I have to."

Beth always mixed up aphorisms, which Molly found endearing, considering Beth was in her fourth year of a comp lit PhD program. She'd finished her course work but couldn't begin her dissertation until she accumulated three first-author publications. She was presenting a paper today at a conference called "Bodies that Matter."

"Then raise the barn," Molly said. Usually she hated talking about Beth's stress, which washed over Molly like secondhand smoke, reminding her of all the careers she wasn't pursuing, all the progress she wasn't making. But right now she'd take any topic over Chowder.

"How am I supposed to raise the barn if I've been writing this paper for three months and I've already raised the goddamn barn a thousand times, like practically out of the atmosphere, and now I can't raise it any higher or everything's going to topple like some kind of, I don't know, tower of napkins? Whatever that's called?"

Molly pictured a soft, wobbling skyscraper. Beth's versions were always better.

"My talk's in an hour, Molly. You never call. Why now?"

The leash was coiled on the floor, spring-loaded like it might strike. If Molly dumped the news on Beth now, her presentation would be ruined. "I guess I'll talk to you when you get home."

"OK. Kiss the beast."

Molly tried to hang up before that last part. A pang ripped her shoulder. She should've told Beth. But she shouldn't have let Chowder off the leash in the first place. As long as she was wishing.

She leaned back in the armchair. She'd wait until the panel started, and then she'd leave a message. She tried to relax into the stiff upholstery, taking in these last few hours of calm, but she couldn't hold still. She kept noticing Chowder's accessories and thinking about how they would never be squeezed or squished, thrown or caught, eaten or slurped up again. So she gathered everything dog-related and stuffed the whole mess under the sink. She stacked his bag of kibble on the last inch of drooly water in his bowl. She piled the squeaky T-bone steak on the pack of Snausages and added a clump of fur that had floated around the room for weeks, like a fuzzy flying saucer. It felt good to snatch the soft disk out of the air and confine it.

But she still couldn't rest; she needed something to get the relaxing started. Ever since she was fifteen, she'd leaned on substances at times like this. Just thinking about her adventures was enough to make her grin. She'd mixed NyQuil with root beer, huffed computer keyboard cleaner, and never said no to cocaine, even if it had that grainy yellow look and was mostly lactose or baking soda. Even now that she was living the domestic life, she needed a boost sometimes, though she tried to hide the worst from Beth. A couple glasses of wine usually did the trick, but alcohol wasn't allowed in freshman dorms. Fortunately, Molly had a sandwich bag of pot for emergencies.

Sometimes Beth let her smoke in the bathroom, the last room in the railroad suite, with her head out the window, at night, when no one was on Prescott. This seemed more incriminating than smoking inside and lighting a cranberry-scented candle afterward, but Beth was more afraid of the little Harvard shits than the campus police or even the real police. Right now, though, it didn't matter. Molly had killed Beth's dog. She smoked right there in the armchair.

Molly's own apartment was in Allston, across the river, where there were no rules or snotty students. But life in Allston wasn't paradise. She had cockroaches and rats. Not mice, but rats. She'd had mice at first, had wished away the one-ounce fluffs only to meet bulge-backed, two-pound goblins that dragged themselves across the floor without bother-

347

ing to scamper. If you yelled or stomped they just planted their hips and stared, as though saying, *You're sixty times my body weight and that's the best you can do?* Even so, she preferred her place to this womb of eighteen-year-olds. She felt caught with Beth, too domestic. She was afraid of how much she liked just hanging out and having sex, watching TV, reading for the first time in years. Wasn't she too young to be this boring?

Ever since Molly graduated from Northeastern four years ago, she'd been working at the vegan hot dog stand and playing as many shows as she could get at T.T.'s and the Lizard Lounge and sometimes, if she was lucky, Club Passim. She had a couple good songs, one about a boy riding the Hi-Line through Montana, one about coming out in fourth grade. She had some bad songs, too—she knew they were bad—but she had to play them for filler.

She first saw Beth at a gig, from her perch atop her rickety industrial stool. She noticed Beth because she was older, heavier, and more fastidiously dressed than her normal fan base. Large-bosomed and prim, Beth was a virgin at twenty-seven. She reminded Molly of a counselor at a summer camp she'd never attended, who was critical of the children but stood naked before them. Who taught them how to pull the udder of a cow with slipping, lubricated fingers and didn't realize how sexual it was. Molly referred to Beth among her coworkers as Counselor of My Heart. After five friend dates she cornered Beth before a screening of *Happy Together* at the Brattle and kissed her. To Molly's surprise, the involvement actually went forward from there. Beth had come close to saying she loved Molly the other day, at least Molly thought she did. Her eyes were glassy with nervousness, and she said she had to tell Molly something. Molly changed the subject fast. Maybe she didn't believe Beth could love her, being so much smarter, so much more put together. Not dependent on substances. Not a failed musician.

Molly got viciously high. But no matter how high she got she couldn't stop thinking about Chowder. She saw that pale wolf's tail sticking out of the ice, pictured paws pedaling in water thick with cold. She needed a distraction, so she found her travel guitar, three-quarters size and a gift from Beth, which frankly was higher quality than her official guitar. She warmed up on scales and picked out a new tune. Just A-D-A-D-A-D-G, plain as can be. She tried to make it funny. Tried to cheer herself up so she could forget for a minute. "Counselor of my heart," she sang. "Counselor of my heart, don't come home too soon. Counselor of my heart, I hope your flight's delayed."

Just as she wound down the first verse, there was a tight rap at the door. Molly put out the joint and kept playing. "Will you forgive me, counselor of my heart? Will you still sleep with me like you do so well?"

The rapping continued. The Harvard kids were so urgent. They even brushed their teeth urgently, specks of blood flinging onto the mirrors. They washed their faces until they shone like peeled beets. On their eyelids were fierce marks where they bore down too hard with eyeliner pencils.

Molly composed one more verse, "Counselor of my heart, will you survive today? Will you get a new dog, a smart dog, a graceful dog? Golden dogs, gorgeous dogs, sexy dogs, Harvard dogs?" before she had to admit the kid wasn't leaving. She flicked the smoke away and pulled the door open an inch.

A boy stood in the fluorescent-lit hall. He had unfashionable glasses and sandy hair and wore flannel pants and a T-shirt that read "Give Bone Marrow" above a rubbery, grinning femur.

"Excuse me, ma'am," he said with odd formality, considering his outfit. "Has Beth Barrett yet returned?"

"No." Molly tried to limit her interactions with the students. If anyone said "Hi" to her in the hall, it was always that hi-I-have-a-question voice. *Hi, I have ulterior motives. Hi, I want to take advantage of you really fast.* Molly started to close the door.

"Wait," the boy said. "Who's on duty? The third-floor guy? There's a problem."

"There's no problem," Molly said. "Why don't you run along?"

"But it smells like marijuana. I think it's from six-A."

"That's no concern of yours."

Molly couldn't read the boy's expression because the lenses of his glasses were so dense and uneven. As he shifted, his eyes broke up.

"Where's the dog?" he asked. "Beth said someone was staying with the dog."

Molly didn't like that "someone." It sounded too much like "anyone," even though she didn't call Beth her girlfriend yet, wasn't ready to have a real girlfriend. Just like she wasn't ready to have a real job or a real musical career, as if she had the option for either.

"I don't hear him. Chowder. Chowder."

Molly cracked the door wider. The kids pushed and pushed but they didn't know themselves what for. "Come in." She didn't want him shouting about drugs and the dog so the RA on the third floor could hear. That kid was only a junior himself and not much more mature than the freshmen. Even he sometimes whined to Beth, bleating his dull troubles.

The kid entered the room. "Beth said I could walk Chowder anytime. I want to walk him."

Molly slouched against the wall, as if claiming her territory by osmosing into it. There was a quality in this kid that made her want to thoroughly disappoint him. "This isn't a good time."

Molly had come over to find students weeping in the armchair, the shepherd huffing their crotches. From the intensity of their wails you'd have guessed they were failing or brokenhearted, but they were usually upset about a cavity or a B-. Beth left the door open to guard against lawsuits, but Molly closed it now.

"Sit down." The boy was skinny, a slice shaved off some other boy. He picked up the leash, held it distastefully, like a snakeskin.

Molly remembered him now. She'd seen him with Beth in the hall, cuddling the shepherd's big head, his fleece matted with fur. He was probably one of those kids with a dog back home who couldn't stand a life free of gamy smells and feces handling.

"Sit down, please." Molly took the leash. "And stop grabbing things that don't belong to you." The Harvard kids, for all their intensity, just wanted to be treated like children. They relaxed when following orders.

Molly closed the door to Beth's bedroom, creating the possibility that Chowder was somewhere in the suite, even though the softest rap sent him rocketing to the door, woofing with his tongue out, ecstatic to meet whomever might emerge from beyond the wooden frame. Rapists and serial killers, he welcomed them all.

The boy sat down.

"Who are you?" he asked. "I've seen you."

"I'm Beth's, you know, person." Saying that out loud felt weird. Molly didn't know if she'd ever before admitted to an official relationship with Beth, or anyone for that matter. The fumbling sentence was out before she considered that perhaps Beth did not want students knowing she was gay. Perhaps that was why "someone" was watching the dog. Of course, Molly was wearing a man's flannel and had shaggy, short hair. She was always around, and there was only one bed.

The boy's eyes inflated. "Beth's, like, a gay lesbian?"

"Yup." In fact, Beth's sexuality wasn't official. She hadn't come out to her family or friends. She didn't even know the term "come out," but said "come forth," as in, "Do you think Larry Summers will ever come forth from the closet?" (Her gaydar was also abysmal.) But she sure

350

acted gay enough. Molly had long thought the information should be public. And she'd always known she'd have to follow through while high. She relit the joint, watching the fleshy machine of the boy's brain kick into gear.

"You're smoking marijuana."

Molly wagged her eyebrows. "Sure about that, kid?"

"James," he said. Then, defiantly, he reached out his knobby hand for the joint. She let him have it because, why not? Everything was going to shit today, and she was too high to care. James took a drag, his eyes filling with water.

"You don't have to hold it in for an hour."

He let the smoke leak out his nostrils, trying not to snort at the burn. It was nice to share with someone for once in her life, even a rookie. Beth never caved to a drag, even on her most anxious nights. "Pot makes me paranoid," she said. Or, "Pot makes me stupid." It wasn't until she said, "Pot makes me gassy" that Molly realized pot didn't make Beth anything because she'd never tried it.

After they'd been smoking for a while, James's eyes went pink and he slumped into the armchair, painting his pajamas with a full coat of dead dog hair. Why was he in pajamas at six o'clock in the evening? Because the Harvard students wore their pajamas all day, all over town: their genitals bouncing in sweat pants, their stomachs expanding against the forgiving pressure of elastic waists.

"So," James said. "Tell me. Where's the dog?"

At first Molly thought she wouldn't say. Why would she, when he could use it against her later? Plus he was just an entitled kid; he wouldn't understand her position. But one of the symptoms of Molly's high was babbling. And once she started talking she couldn't help telling the whole story.

She described Chowder going down the bank, how she could've grabbed his brush of tail while he was still on land, if she'd only reacted quickly enough. She told him each nuance of how she felt during the entire episode: How at first she wanted to laugh at the tail disappearing, how funny it was, like a cartoon where the world could break open. How her next thought was relief. She actually considered that Chowder hadn't pooped yet, and now she wouldn't have to touch it. But then she thought of Beth, and a fist squeezed her heart.

"I didn't even go on the ice," Molly said.

"That would've been stupid," James said. "If he fell through, you obviously would have."

He said it like he was answering an exam question, without consideration for the feelings involved. "I should've tested the edge. At least so I had."

James fingered his eyes so hard that Molly couldn't tell if the resultant tears were from grief or physical pain. "Chowder, Jesus. What a dog."

"I know," said Molly, and now that he was dead, she sort of meant it. There was something of value in all that dumb affection, probably.

"You must really love her," James said.

Molly didn't want to walk into a trap, but she was curious. "Why do you say that?"

"You're crying over a dog."

"You're crying, too." He was, though his tears didn't dilute his rational tone of voice.

"They're just dogs. He was sort of old, right? Dogs die. They just die. You know, at our farm? Dogs were always dying. We threw the extra litters into Canada."

"I thought you were from Greenwich." Everyone here was from either New York City or Greenwich, Connecticut, or other less popular rich towns.

"What? No. Minnesota." James struggled up in the chair, trying to achieve a more dignified posture. He threw out a hand in a loose gesture. "The point is, they're animals. They do the best they can. Like people come here more for Chowder than Beth. He did his job, and now he's gone."

"Not naturally, though." Molly squeezed her eyes shut, trying not to picture Chowder's claws scraping the river bottom, his eyes popping blood vessels.

"Still."

Molly was beyond high, out of her mind. She was deep in the sky above Prescott Street, watching the plain square roof of Hurlbut Hall. She was seeing how Beth loved her with a consuming energy. Beth was the smartest person Molly had ever known, the most patient with Molly's flimsy musical career, her fake job. Who cared about her prudishness, her stress? Those features hardly mattered when you looked at their life together. "Yes, I do. Very much."

"Do what?" asked James.

Molly shook the hot idea from her head. "Never mind."

Molly and James rallied to make a cake. They stirred together quantities of flour, sugar, Swiss Miss, maple syrup, minimarshmallows, frozen blueberries, and rice milk. They left the mixture lumpy because James insisted it would be tenderer that way.

They put the cake in the oven with the heat all the way up so it would be ready faster. They smoked again. Then they fell asleep in the armchairs.

When Molly woke, the door was open and the smoke alarm was screeching high, even wails. She could've slept through all that if it weren't for Beth crying, "Are you OK? Molly?" Hearing her name spoken by Beth, even loudly and sharply, always got to her. Molly sat up, stood up, stumbled, and fought for the kitchen through the smoke. Somehow she managed to turn off the oven and remove the battery in the alarm and open all the windows in the front room and hallway before she even realized she was moving. Smoke alarms were not uncommon rivals for her.

The air thinned, and Molly squinted. James was still asleep in his chair, and Beth was standing in the doorway in a dress shirt with her breasts pushing gaps between the buttons. She held a leather duffel.

"Molly?" she said. "What's going on?" She didn't seem sure which way her voice should tip.

"We forgot the cake," Molly said. "I'm sorry."

"Why is James Masterson here?" Beth looked at James as if he was a ferret who'd crawled in out of nowhere. She was cold, furious. A smell came off her, the wrong kind of hormone.

"I'll get rid of him."

Molly couldn't believe how badly she'd messed up. Why was it always her instinct to bury a mess with another mess? Once at a party she'd hid a wine stain with a turned-over plate of deviled eggs.

As soon as she could make her feet move again she shook James awake, his mouth spilling drool down his bone marrow shirt.

"Hi, girls," he said.

Beth stared at Molly like she didn't know who Molly was. Molly hoped it wasn't a relationship-ending stare. She suspected it was.

"Come on, James," Molly said. "Let's go to bed." She grabbed his arm, but it was limp.

"Oh, my murderer," he said. The words were hollow and chilling. Molly flinched. She had to get him out of here.

"He's high," Molly said. "I'm going to walk him home." She got James to stand, but he couldn't stabilize. She had to pass Beth with the boy held out in front of her like a floppy shield. Beth peered into James's fogged-up eyes and said, "James?"

"Thank you for all you do. On behalf of all students. Sincerely." He saluted her and relaxed against Molly's support, deflating.

In the hall, Molly propped him against the wall.

"Are you really that high?" Usually White Kush didn't have a late-onset effect, but you never knew, especially with kids. He could have "sensitivities."

"Didn't I do a good job?" He looked like a puppy now, his sandy hair flipped up. "I thought if I acted that bad I could pretend tomorrow I don't remember. That would be good, right? That would get you out of trouble?"

She guessed that made sense. If James had been coherent there would have been a whole different scene. Beth would've insisted on questioning him, and no one could stand up to Beth's questions, not even Molly. "Why'd you call me a murderer, though?"

"Come on," he said. "You killed her dog. We can't hide that from her."

Molly wanted to hit him. He was an entitled brat just like she'd always suspected, meddling in her affairs without a blip of remorse. But she made herself breathe. And then she realized he was right. She did have to tell Beth about Chowder. Of course she did. That would be the first question when she reentered the suite. And now there was an opening. *Why did James Masterson call you a murderer? Oh, that? Because I am one.* She could've slapped herself for forgetting to leave a voice mail while Beth was on her panel. At least James didn't tell Beth that Molly had outed her. And she was glad to have talked to James about her relationship, actually. She knew now, for certain, that she loved Beth. But she might be too late.

When she entered the suite, the cake was on the burners and Beth was fanning smoke out of the window with a rag. "What are you doing? Why was James here? Why is a cake burning in the oven? Why is the dog food under the sink? And where is Chowder?"

The questions rushed at Molly, pricking her skin. Beth would find out any second what had happened. There were only a few more moments left in her life where Beth wouldn't know. Molly covered her face against the assault. "I'm high."

"Great. I'll add that to the list of delightful events that occur when I leave for two days. You corrupt my students; you give them drugs. Jesus. I could lose my job." She held her hand to her mouth.

"I'm sorry." Saying the words felt like eating an insubstantial snack, just reminding you how hungry you were.

"Oh, great. That makes it all OK. Everything's solved now, because you're sorry."

That was it. Beth had unplugged something deep in Molly's core. She thought of poor, idiotic Chowder at the bottom of the river. She thought of James Masterson's innocence, gone. She thought of her relationship with Beth, ending tonight, just when Molly had decided it was what she wanted. And there was nothing she could do to change any of these things. She leaned against the cold tiles and cried. She cried so hard she had to run to the bedroom and lie on the quilt and just keep crying, the bed a mossy landscape beneath her, pulling her in.

Beth loomed in the doorway. "Are you for real?"

Molly nodded into the quilt. Then she shook her head. She wanted to stop crying, but holding it in just made the sobs bounce out more erratically.

"Relax," Beth said. "They're not that innocent."

"But your job," Molly said. "And the dog."

Beth paused. Molly could tell she knew something was seriously wrong and wasn't sure if she was ready to find out what. Maybe Beth was thinking of what James had said, wondering who the murderer was. There were only so many people it could be. Maybe, hopefully, Beth thought something worse had happened than actually had. But nothing could be worse, not for Beth.

"Where's the dog?"

It wasn't fair to tell her this way, really, courting her pity first. Even though she didn't like the dog taking up half the bed, didn't like that Beth hugged and fondled him when she could've hugged and fondled Molly, didn't like the white hair on her mostly black wardrobe or cupping shit—a thin skin of plastic the only protection against that sick warmth—she was thinking now about Beth alone. What if Beth ended up not really being gay, or what if the relationship got too serious for Molly and she left? She didn't like thinking about Beth stuck in Hurlbut with all these kids, no Molly, not even Chowder.

"He's dead," Molly said. She'd blown her load earlier, describing the incident to James with nuance and remorse. Now the plain truth was out, ugly and unwieldy. She sponged her tears with the corner of her flannel. Then she described what had happened. Beth shook her head. She put her fingers on her forehead and closed her eyes. When Molly was done, they went minutes without talking, Beth raising a finger whenever Molly tried to start saying something. After a long time, Beth said, "Show me."

"What do you mean?" Molly flashed on pulling the soggy body out of the river.

Beth put on her boots, and Molly had no choice but to do so, too. Free of the cake smoke, Prescott was like the top of a mountain, the air so thin you had to breathe fast to get enough. They took Bow Street to Memorial Drive and crossed to the river.

There were just a couple of pinpricks of light in the sky. They were probably airplanes and satellites but maybe they were planets, and for now, at least, Beth wouldn't leave her side. Even though it was dark, the ice on the river was lit white as though illuminated from below.

Beth tried to walk down onto the ice but Molly stopped her. "It's dangerous."

That's all Beth needed to hear, logical Beth. When her cheeks caught the glow of the river, Molly saw they were wet. Molly tried to hold her but Beth shoved her away. Beth didn't have to say anything—Molly could see the hate in her face, her lip tangled under her teeth, her eyes hooded and fierce.

They looked at the river for a long time. Molly switched her weight from one foot to the other. She was dying to know what would become of the two of them, but she had to wait. Now that things were on the edge of over, Molly couldn't stand it. She couldn't give up the intellectual discussions with Beth as they walked along the Charles, going to old movies on big screens, traveling to the city to try new teas. So it was a boring life, who cared? No one could be wild forever. Would she really rather snort cut cocaine in the bathroom of a naked party in Jamaica Plain?

The hole was gray in the white ice and didn't look like it went all the way through to the water. Maybe a shell had formed since that afternoon, so now Chowder had a roof over his head, a warped view of the winter sky.

Beth walked back to Hurlbut. Molly didn't know if she should follow or take the footbridge to Allston. But there was the cake and the mess in the suite. At least she could clean up. Then, if Beth wanted, she'd leave.

Beth got ready for bed as though Molly weren't there. Molly's hands shook as she pushed the disintegrating sponge over the burners. She was about to wash the cake out of the pan when she found it was white inside, that only the edges were black. The middle was fluffy and wet with blue explosions where the berries broke under heat. The high temperature must have flash cooked the interior; it made an uncommon, silky texture. Molly dug cake out of the black pocket and heaped it on a plate. The cake looked like rice or porridge, but was soft and, when Molly tried it, sweet. She was so hungry that she wanted to eat all of it. But instead, she brought it to Beth. Maybe if there were another element in the room, Beth would forget how angry she was.

"What is this?" Beth asked when Molly held out the plate with arms stretched long and trembling, trying to keep herself as distant as possible.

"Blueberry vanilla hot chocolate cake." That sounded better than it was.

Beth took a bite. She made a face but kept eating. Molly watched her chew, waiting to be told to leave. Beth hated sweets, and made slow progress. Molly hoped she was eating as a grudging sign of forgiveness. Or maybe, at least, she was delaying.

Beth turned off the light and put the plate on the floor. For a moment, Molly stood there in the dark. But then, since she hadn't been told not to, she got undressed. She laid herself down stiffly, facing the ceiling. She felt like if she moved at all it would be over.

"I know he's just a dog," Beth said, her voice shaky, her breath smelling like stress and travel.

Molly couldn't believe Beth was saying that. Beth, whose dog had been her main concern for years, her golden boy, her heir. Molly didn't know what to say. So she said, "Animals have a purpose. Then they leave." James's words sounded lame in her strained voice.

"You shouldn't have let him off the leash. You don't have enough control." Beth shifted onto her back, a quarter roll toward Molly. "I'll have to pay off James Masterson. Jesus."

"I'm sorry." Molly felt like she was getting used to saying this. Like she could go on apologizing forever, knocking chips off the block of what she'd done.

She reached through the sheets and found Beth's wrist. She squeezed it, like they used to do in Girl Scouts, in a circle while singing. The gesture was stupid, but it was all she had. Beth turned in the blue light and looked at Molly as if she was from a different world.

"I fucked up. But I have to tell you something."

"What?" Beth sounded skeptical, as if maybe Molly had killed another of her animals, or corrupted poor James Masterson in even more twisted ways.

Molly took a breath. She thought of that dead dog, once full of joy. "I'm in love with you." It came out like bad acting. She wanted to stuff the words back down her throat.

Beth's eyes worked over each piece of Molly's face. "That's crazy." She shook her head. "That's rat-shit crazy."

Beth would yell at Molly for an hour in the morning. She'd cry every night before bed for days, sleep with the leash tight around her forearm like tefillin. The leather would go soft from how hard she gripped it, would lose its ability to harness a cat. She wouldn't say she loved Molly for months. Sometimes she'd barely even look at her. Molly would suffer. Maybe more than she deserved.

But for now, Molly tried not to think about the future. She rolled on top of Beth, their bodies gluing with thick warmth. She focused on the love that was between them now, however hard it could be to find.

Nominated by The Southern Review, Emma Duffy-Comparone,
Sarah Frisch, Meghan O'Gieblyn, Barrett Swanson

BEACH CITY

by JAQUIRA DÍAZ

from BREVITY

We talked about Miami Beach like it belonged to us, convinced that the tourists who came down to swim in our ocean and dance in our nightclubs were fucking up our city. We were seventeen, eighteen, nineteen-year-old hoodlums, our hair in cornrows, too-tight ponytails, too much hairspray, dark brown lip liner, noses and belly buttons pierced, door-knocker earrings, jailhouse ankle tattoos. We didn't have time for boys from Hollywood or North Miami, busters who drove their hoopties with the windows down because they didn't have A/C, calling out to us trying to get phone numbers as we crossed Washington Avenue or Lincoln Road, our chancletas slapping the sidewalk.

What did they know about surfing during hurricane winds, fucking on lifeguard stands, breathing under water? What did they know about millions of stray cats pissing in the sand dunes, entire flocks of rogue seagulls dropping shit torpedoes, about refugees and kilos of cocaine and bodies washing up on our shores?

We were the ones who knew what it meant to belong here, to be made whole during full moon drum circles, dancing, drinking, smoking it up with our homeboys. We knew what it meant to bloody our knuckles here, to break teeth here, to live and breathe these streets day in, day out, the glow of the neon hotel signs on the waterfront, the salt and sweat of this beach city.

One night we parked Brown's Mustang behind the skating rink on Collins, hoofed it to the beach. We took our bottles of Olde English

359

and Mad Dog 20/20, the six of us passing a blunt and listening to 2Pac's "Hit Em Up" blaring from somebody's radio, and every time they sang, "Grab your Glocks when you see 2Pac," the boys grabbed their dicks, and we all laughed our asses off. Brown danced, stripping off his clothes while we cheered him on, me and A. J. keeling over, slapping our knees. Flaca, China, and Cisco climbed to the top of the lifeguard stand, singing, "Go Brown! Go Brown!" When he was down to just boxers, Brown gave up, and we booed him, threw our balled-up socks and sneakers at him.

Me and A.J. were out behind the lifeguard stand, sand between our toes, feeling for each other in the dark. We ran around laughing and laughing, and I took his hand, danced circles around him in slow motion.

I don't remember when A.J. first told me he loved me, or even if he told me, but I knew. I felt it every time he came around, every time our thighs touched while sitting together on China's couch, or when the six of us had to squeeze into Brown's Mustang and I sat sideways on his lap, my lip brushing against his ear, his arms around my waist. Or when we stayed up all night talking even though he had to get up early for school the next morning—something I didn't have to worry about since I was a high school dropout. Or on nights when the liquor and the weed made my head spin, the heat and the high coming down on me all at once, and only A J. around to keep me from falling.

Down by the shore, Brown was so fucked up he dropped to his knees, then lay down sideways on the sand. Later, we would all carry him back to his car. Flaca would drive us to her place a few blocks away. We would all stagger up the stairs to her little studio, put Brown to sleep in the bathtub, and smoke Newports on the balcony. He would wake up with the munchies an hour later. "You got any cheese?" he'd call out from the bathroom. Cisco would grab an entire pack of Kraft Singles from Flaca's fridge, and the two of us would toss them into the tub, slice by slice, while Brown tried to catch them in his mouth.

But before all that, the six of us dancing and running around on the beach, China chugging down Mad Dog, Flaca and Cisco kissing on the steps of the lifeguard stand, and A.J. looking at me under the moonlight, a cloud of smoke all around us, I wrapped my arms around him and said, "Don't let me go."

We were laughing, hitting the blunt.

We were the faraway waves breaking, the music and the ocean and the heat rising rising rising, like a fever.

We were bodies made of smoke and water.

Nominated by Brevity

ABOUT THE TONGUE

by CHRISTOPHER TODD ANDERSON

from TIPTON POETRY JOURNAL

My tongue is a prodigy. If it had arms
and legs, it would be on talk shows.
It is a genius, it is buff and agile. Eyeless,
it tells sweet from sour, bitter from salt.
It could be the world's best carnie
or con man. It can wrestle its lover
all night in the dirtiest hotel in Joplin,
then spend the next morning singing
Verdi and feasting on satsuma oranges.

Sometimes words line up at its tip
like third graders on a diving board,
then plunge into the clean blue air.
Though it can pronounce *diphtheria*
and *Quetzalcoatl*, it can spit and slather,
dangle and curse like any workworn lubber.
Lock it in its toothy cage and, like Houdini,
it twists itself free. You will never net it
nor pull it ashore. Watch as, slick as an eel,
it swims upstream through a river of gin.

Nominated by Tipton Poetry Journal

ABSOLUTE RYTHM

by DAVID WOJAHN

from BLACKBIRD

> *I believe in an absolute rhythm, a rhythm . . . in poetry that corresponds exactly with the emotion or shade of emotion to be expressed.*
>
> —*Pound*

Siri, show us a picture of an iamb.
& the pixels gathered on the phone screen,

Half-moon married to slash, scythe
Beside spear-shaft. Crescent or chalice,

Then a wheat-stalk bending to autumn zephyrs.
& yes, the hearts'-blood coursing:

Drumtap, birdcall, ringtone. Resplendent
Atavistic pictograph. Sympathetic magic,

Impious to demean it to *concept*, to *symbol*,
To *sign*. The tattooist took your phone,

Turned it & its pictures in his hand. Ponytail,
Harley T-shirt, lots of bling. *Shouldn't be too hard to do,*

He said. & the instrument began its hum
& sable infusion—your right wrist,

The left clutching Kent's calm hand.
Now you're showing it off to the six of us

Crowding the restaurant table, your hair nearly back
From the latest chemo. Head half bent,

You pick at your salad. At your desk,
You tell us, under the drafts of poems

You thumbtack to your wall—pin them
The way the rest of us would slap up Post-Its—

You pause sometimes beneath the desk-lamp halo
& contemplate the fresh dark ink above

The indigo rivulet of vein.
You have three months. Later, the first-year

Med students in the MCV basement
Will pause to examine it—absolute rhythm,

Arranging their tools beneath the vapor-
Light glare. Lancets poised, they ready themselves

To receive your gift, yet another
Of your legacies. Dear friend, your faith

Lay always in unsealing, in the gnosis we carry,
Luminous & mortal within. But also outliving us,

Outliving us in word & act. You'd say this better
& more plainly, in some anecdote

From one-stoplight Chatham,
Seasoned with some lines from Dickinson, Welty,

Or Kitty Wells. Toward the end your poems
Issued forth daily, fiercer & more knowing

Than any of us deserved. Absolute rhythm,
Where *sorrow is ecstatic*. Grant us

The skill to learn their august cadences.
The waitress brings to-go bags. By stealth,

You've picked up the tab again. The rain has
Almost stopped & the parking lot shimmers in a pewter

Intractable light. Now the hugs & handshakes.
Turning, I glimpse the raven-black

Inscripting ink once more, glinting with raindrops,
Pulsing & quickened along your wrist.

Nominated by Rosellen Brown, James Harms,
David Hernandez, William Olsen

MILK

fiction by YE CHUN

from THE THREEPENNY REVIEW

The boy follows the man, eyes on his pants, and mumbles, "Sir, please buy a rose, buy a rose for your girlfriend." The man's legs move faster; the boy grabs one of them, wraps his skinny arms and legs around it and presses his small buttocks on the man's leather shoe, and says the words again to the leg.

The spring afternoon has gone sultry, the air the texture of rotten fruit. The man is on his way to a sales meeting. He didn't meet his sales quota and before the child approached him had been rehearsing his explanations in his head. He tries to shake his leg free, but the child tightens his grip. People circle past them: a few giggle, a few gape back to see how he reacts. His face flushes red. He bends down and snatches the child's wrists and tosses him away from his leg. The child looks up at his face for the first time, stunned, as though he's just realized that he was not merely dealing with a leg, but an unpredictable man several times his size. And he must also have sensed what's coming: the man kicks him, the shoe landing on his small rib cage. The child flips over on the pavement, groans, curls into a ball, and cries, "Mama, mama—"

A woman runs toward them on the pavement, yelling in some rural dialect the man can't quite understand. But judging by her tone, he's sure she's calling him names or cursing him in the worst possible way. She kneels down by the child, picks him up, and clasps him to her chest. The child's cry turns into wail; he looks as heartbroken as any other wailing child, though the pathetic rose is still clutched in his hand. The woman rocks him, strokes his ribs. Sallow-faced, ill-dressed, she must have been lurking somewhere by the roadside, blending right in with other urban poor whom the man has stopped paying attention to.

People gather around them, gawking like their eyes have finally found a free feast. The man's head buzzes, face hotter. "Are you his mother?" he shouts down at the woman. "What kind of mother lets her child pester people on the street?"

Then he turns, quickly, not wanting to hear one single word from the woman. He walks away as fast and steady as his body can manage, controlling the impulse to run, and slows down only after he's sure the woman's gaze no longer reaches him. Then he breathes and it feels like the first real breath he's taken since he bent down to grab the child—those wrists thin and pulsing like a chicken's neck. The man has never felt comfortable watching vendors wring chicken necks in the market. He'll grimace and avert his eyes. *I'm not a bad person*, he imagines saying to the woman whose face still seems to hover right in front of him, its misery and rage so sharp-toned that it reduces the dusty street, dusty plastic-looking palm trees, dusty pedestrians with their idiotic stares to nothing but a stage setting. *I'm not a bad person.* He imagines the woman's face soften and himself taking a ten-yuan bill from his wallet and stuffing it in the child's little grimy hand. Then, like an uncle, he'll hold the child up and make faces at him until he laughs.

But he knows that's not what he'll do. He'll keep walking and rehearse his explanations for the failure to meet the sales quota and pray he keeps his job. That's all he can do and will do. He takes another breath. As the humid air fused with dust and exhaust fills his lungs, the city distorts—its skyscrapers, shops, multi-lane streets, vehicles lose their edges and density, fattening with moisture, grease, and the incessant despairs and high hopes steaming out of people's heads. All around him the city is swelling and his feet are hardly touching the ground. He has become a stick figure, a splinter the city is about to push out of its inflated flesh.

The woman carries the crying child to the side of the pavement, under a palm tree. The child murmurs, "Mimi, mimi." The woman sighs, lifts her blouse, and the child presses his mouth to her breast. People gawk and shake their heads. She lowers her eyes and sees their shoes—tennis shoes, leather shoes, canvas shoes, high-heels, sandals, flats—nice shoes that know where their feet are taking them. She shields the child's face with a hand: it's better he doesn't see any of these shoes, better still he forgets where they are. The blind fortune-teller told her this was a hard time for them, but things would get better in three years. "Luck star will then shine above your son's head." He raised his opaque, scarred eyes. She paid him five yuan and that was all she got—a promise of a turn of fortune in three years. Can she keep her milk flow that long? She felt foolish. She needed the five yuan for food, not a fortune that wouldn't turn until three years from now. But still, three years is better than five or ten, or no luck at all.

She came to the city to look for her husband, whom she hasn't heard a word from since he left after the Spring Festival. She called the construction company he worked for; they said they hadn't seen him since he'd left for home before the festival. She went to the village fortune-teller, giving him her husband's year, month, day, and hour of birth and, as payment, a bucket of frogs her son helped her catch. The old man flipped the brittle pages of his yellow book, wrote down four columns of words with ink and brush, squinted his eyes at a brittle page again, and shook his head: "His longevity star is clouded this year. I see possible falling, a tall building, and serious or fatal injury." She held her breath. "A building in the south," he added, "in the city where he builds them tall buildings."

The woman took her son to the city. She found the construction company; they told her the same thing they'd said on the phone. She told them what the fortune-teller had told her. They asked her to go talk to other construction companies—there are tons of them in the city, they told her, and her husband could be working for any of them now. She and her son wander around the city, looking up at scaffoldings to see whether he is there. It's hard to tell: they all look alike from down here—a helmet, a little torso, a pair of doll arms and legs. She waits with her son on the roadside for them to come down. She asks them about her husband; they shake their heads or mention another company or building under construction for her to check. At night, she and her son sleep behind park bushes or under viaducts. She doesn't want to go back to her village until she finds her husband and warns him of his ill fortune ahead. She'll make sure he goes home with them, where there're no tall buildings and the inevitability of falling.

She has no money left so she begs. She tries to tell people her story, but they walk away. "They think we're fake," an old beggar woman from the same province told her. "They don't care about us, but some still pity children. Have your son sell flowers. That may still work." So she picked a less bruised rose from a flower shop's trashcan and had her son sell it like other children on the street—except that people don't pity children either.

She's kept her milk flow for a time like this. She always knew there would be a time like this. The child's small shoulders stop shuddering. His fingers loosen around the rose that lies by his feet like congealed blood. She looks up at the scaffolding across the street and the small figures of construction workers printed on the sky. Any of them could be her husband or could have been her husband. One dizzying misstep could be a step into the nothing down below and when that happens, you won't even see his body.

She wants to curse those people sparing no pity for her son, but she's tired. She needs to save the rest of her energy for her body to continue to produce milk. She doesn't have much milk left and their fortune will not turn until three years from now. She wishes she had a place to go, a private place where she could lie down with her son, close her eyes, enjoy this little pleasure of giving and taking, this little numbing sensation that's slowly spreading over her body. Any time now she's going to close her eyes. The shoes, legs, and wheels around them will disappear. She and her son will turn into some gossamer matter, hide somewhere in the air, until things get better for them.

A man is walking in this direction. He sees the mother and son on the side of the pavement under a palm tree. He takes out his smartphone from his messenger bag, pauses in front of them for a second, and snaps a shot. The woman doesn't even notice, her eyes drooped, her half-exposed breast coarse-skinned and sallow-colored like her complexion. The boy is obviously too big for this: he looks like he's tried his best to curl himself in her arms, but most of his legs still spill onto the pavement. Only the utter unselfconsciousness of his close-eyed suckling resembles that of a baby's.

The man goes back to his apartment and makes instant noodles and sits down in front of his computer. He has recently started a blog called "Critical Eye," a title he's having second thoughts about and considering changing into something less explicit. He posts social commentaries, often in the form of snapshots he takes with his smartphone on the street. Though his blog hasn't got much traffic, he has noticed a quickening of his senses as he goes about his daily life. He's no longer a passive passerby, his life no longer an unanchored fuzziness with perfunctory routines and a job that organizes his hours into rest, work, wants, and small gratifications.

Now he freezes moments he finds provocative, forms opinions, and makes them visible to anyone surfing his way. Sometimes, sitting in his cubicle or walking home from work, he feels he's simultaneously inhabiting the city and roaming a space ungoverned by gravity, where he's just about as free as one can be.

But when he posts his blog entries, his photos and words gone public, he can't help but feel an unease, a weak-hearted uncertainty that his posts will be scrutinized or attacked, vulnerable like insects left for dissection.

After he uploads the photo, he comments: "We are a decade into the 21st century and our country is becoming one of the strongest economic powers in the world, yet, here in our city that we claim to be a world-class metropolis, a woman is nursing a five- or six-year-old on the street as though they were in a remote 19th-century village. Why is this happening?"

He clicks "Post" and slurps his noodles. He reads his post; it reads sound. He was going to simply write, "This doesn't look good—nursing such a big child in public," but thought it would be too simplistic. He checks some of the blogs and websites he frequents and then checks back to see whether he's got any comments. There are none. He surfs more and checks back again. Still none. No response is almost worse than a negative response. He thought this post would provoke: the photo alone should catch attention and his commentary should generate a public debate.

But there's no response and he feels as though he has been sucked into a black hole where other surfers and bloggers swirl around just as involuntarily, propelled by a force none can control. They are trapped but they think they are free. They think they're living a different life from their daytime personas that perform duties and nod to their supervisors and get a paycheck. They think they are living a fuller, more connected life here in the virtual space, but they are actually engulfed in a black hole where no one cares about anyone else, just as in the reality life. He puts his computer into the sleep mode and goes to bed.

He dreams of a woman lying so close to him he can feel the buzzing heat and electricity radiating from her body. It's his ex-girlfriend, who by now must have become someone else's wife and maybe even a mother. But somehow she came back to him. Has she kept a key to his apartment? Did she sneak in, tiptoe to his bed, and lie down by him?

Gently, she palms his head with one hand and with the other cups her breast to his mouth. His penis swells up and as her hand slides down his torso and wraps around it, he sucks on her nipple and milk flows out. The liquid only surprises his tongue for a second before it calls back an ancient euphoria—he feels as if he were soaring into a galaxy of burning stars and becoming part of its radiance and order, fervor and harmony. As he comes, he wakes up. His ex-girlfriend is not with him. He's alone in his small, stuffy room. His computer sits on the desk like a large toad. His dirty clothes litter the floor. The air smells of semen, sweat, and greasy hair. In his mouth he tastes nothing but fetid breath.

But still he remembers the smooth, luscious milk on his tongue and the wondrous feeling of soaring and peace. He closes his eyes and tries to will the true-to-life sensation back into being—his ex-girlfriend's flesh blended with his, her breast throbbing in front of his face. He opens his mouth, closes his lips around the nipple where the elixir will flow onto his parched tongue.

A woman surfing the internet stumbles upon the photo on the man's blog. She once lived in that city; now she's living abroad. Since she became a mother she has wished she were there instead of here—if nothing else, she would at least have someone to talk to in her native tongue, another mother raising a child. The boy being nursed in the photo is much bigger than her son, who has finally fallen asleep on her lap. She's weaning him. She has nursed him for eighteen months, has suffered cracked nipples, plugged ducts, and bouts of mastitis. But her son's demand for her breasts has not dwindled. He wants to nurse before sleep, before nap, after sleep, after nap, during the middle of sleep and nap and during other activities. He grabs her breasts as if they were his. She wants her body back. She craves spicy food and caffeinated tea, wants to wear dresses, not nursing bras and breast pads. She wants her body to be touched and fondled by her husband, and when that happens, she doesn't want her breasts to leak milk.

Her husband is not at home again. Got some work to finish, he said on the phone. When he does come home, he sleeps on the couch in the living room, says he needs his sleep so he can get up and work and support the family. It suited her well at the beginning, when she loved to snuggle with her son alone on the big bed, her body willingly letting its white ribbon of milk flow into his mouth, as though his intake was also her intake, her giving so complete it merged into taking. They were locked in the cycle of give and take, forming a circle with no beginning or end to allow another's entrance. When her husband touched her, she recoiled from the intrusion. When he held the baby, the baby screamed for her. He spends less and less time with them.

When she asks him to change the baby's diaper, or give him a bath, or take him out for a walk, "because he's your son too," he looks grudging. He fumbles the diaper on the baby loosely and poop leaks out and she has to wash him again. The walks he takes with the baby tend to be short, "because he was screaming the entire time and people thought I kidnapped him." Once she caught him holding the baby upside down, dangling in front of his legs, bigheaded like a frog, with blood pooling in his puffy face, too startled or strained to make a sound. She'd just finished her weekly shower and instinctively knew she needed to be gentle. She crouched down to take hold of the child's head and eased him into her arms, putting his wronged face to her wet breast. "That's enough," she then said to her husband, still suppressing a scream in her throat. "Just leave!"

Maybe it's all her fault—she pushed him away. And it's all her fault, too, that the baby is addicted to her milk. Didn't she give him her breast when she wanted him to go back to sleep so she could sleep longer, give it when she wanted him to take a nap so she could rest, give it again when he was fussy so she could have some peace? She's been weaning him for weeks, slowly cutting down the sessions, first daytime, then night. Now they've come to the last and most trying session—the one he has been depending on to fall asleep at night. Earlier, he battled with her, reaching for her breast, and when pushed away, reaching again. He bawled and whimpered. She stuffed cotton balls in her ears. She rocked and sang and yelled and patted him, till he finally drifted off in exhaustion.

She's surfing the internet because there's nothing else she can do right now. There're a lot to do—dishes need to be cleaned, toys need to be picked up, soiled clothes need to be washed, but she's afraid if she moves, the child will wake up and want to nurse again. The whole battle will repeat and she'll be too tired for that. And she knows her breasts will be filling up soon. She'll need to go to the bathroom sink and squirt the milk out instead of giving it to her son, who wants it so much and can't understand why his mother is denying him the very thing that she used to offer him so abundantly.

She sees the photo of the countrywoman nursing her big son on the street in the city she used to live in and begins to cry. Heat leaps up her eye sockets and tears burn out before she knows it. She looks at her baby: his lips open to a zero; his blue-veined eyelids tremble as though there was a storm below. She holds him to her face, crying as silently as she can. The child wakes up, gazes at her, alarmed. He reaches his little fingers to her cheek, as if to find out through touch what she's actually doing. It must be an expression he hasn't seen much before, even though he's made it thousands of times in his one-and-a-half years of life. He stares at her. He's about to cry himself, his little face already folding into those familiar creases. She tries to stop herself, wiping her eyes. "I'm okay," she says to him. "I'm okay." But she continues to shudder. Her milk is filling up. The child smells it and lifts his mouth to the breast close to it, but he hesitates, examines her face, afraid she'll push him away again. Her crying must have something to do with that. He's making the connection. But it's all too much for him. His sorrowful face lifts to her breast. "Mimi, mimi," he pleads.

Nominated by The Threepenny Review, Jessica Roeder

HOW WE BUILT OUR HOUSE

by THOMAS R. MOORE

from SAVING NAILS (MOON PIE PRESS)

We built our house of wind and salt,
of seeing and touching. Our shovels

bit in, our wooden-handled hammers
beat rhythms. We learned berm,

window spacing, roof pitch. We
chainsawed joists to length, then

spiked with a kind of awe at our
dexterity. We felt the mystery of plumb,

and when rains blew in we smelled
the pine. The rafters became our heart

and we nailed high the green bough.
Now grace shines off the gray metal

roof and together we listen to the barred
owl's call, watch the blossoming peach.

Nominated by Moon Pie Press

CONDITION

by ERICA DAWSON

from BENNINGTON REVIEW

If it don't mean a thing without the swing
of a gavel, if a trace of doubt can trump
a circumstance, oh beautiful for skies
too small.

      Today, the paper boasted this—
Five local policemen tied to the KKK—
italicized as if to shout, I'm new

here. When I went outside, thinking I knew
something of Frost's birches, that endless swing
of left to right, the afternoon did trump
up stillness. Today, I am reading the sky's
pastoral. Cumuli passing for this
creature or that one, stallions, maybe K-
9 dogs, maybe the alphabet with K
then O, maybe this sentence: *That kid knew
he had no business here.*

         I find the swing,
far off, of scales. The winning suit and trump
card in a game of spades.

        Today, the skies
are angled sides in the A-frame of this

big house we built and then forgot. And this
one cracking rafter, rotting, looks ok
for now. But, later, it's old wood all new
and gnarled. Later, knots are knees. There's the swing
of a young girl's legs.

        I'm telling Donald Trump,
today, the story of a woman. How the skies
came out of her wherever. Spacious skies.
Dark skies. Grown woman skies. Coalsack at this
time of the month is deep. That kind-of K
you see in Crux, that's her. The bloody new
moon, her. Mister, you're going to have to swing
a huge dick if you're going to hit it.

     Trump
came out of *triumph*. Trump: to play a trump
on; win a trick.

       Tonight, I'm running skies
through my sewing machine, connecting this
evening to morning, ironing on K
for force. I hang it on my windows, new
and needing blackout shades.

        Tonight, the swing
of things. Tonight,

      if any world was new
ever. If Trump. Ok. If even this.
If swinging skies were spume preserved in amber.

Nominated by Bennington Review

BURN SCARS

by PHILIP CONNORS

from N+1

> *Like any Romantic, I had always been vaguely certain that sometime during my life I should come into a magic place which in disclosing its secrets would give me wisdom and ecstasy—perhaps even death.*
>
> —Paul Bowles

> *Infrared waves just below twenty hertz associated with approaching thunder seem to have strange effects on the temporal lobe in some part of the population, to wit producing feelings of baseless awe and ecstasy.*
>
> —Norman Rush

I thought I heard a shout from far below. Snug in the cocoon of my sleeping bag, face averted from the honey-colored sunrise pouring through the windows, I could not at first remember where I was and why. For a moment I experienced the tingly, dissociative terror one feels on waking from a bad dream—only to realize I was waking into one.

The shout came twice more before I recognized the voice and hollered back. It belonged to Teresa, fiancée of my friend John, whom we had both been mourning for three weeks. She had started up the mountain on foot before daybreak, a steep two and a half miles from the trailhead. Sleep eluded her past about three in the morning, so she found ways to make use of the dawn hours, fueled by plenty of coffee. For me the trouble was the night, but I stumbled through with the time-tested crutch of whiskey, neat.

During a dozen summers of lookout duty I had mostly spent my nights in a cabin at ground level, in another mountain range entirely, but there was no cabin on John's peak, only the tower—a spacious live-in model. I invited Teresa up the stairs, feeling almost embarrassed at having to proffer an invitation. She had spent far more time there than I had, hanging out with John; I was merely an emergency fill-in, on loan from a different ranger district twenty miles east. A fire there the previous summer had left my home tower surrounded by a 214-square-mile burn scar: a bird's nest marooned in a charscape. There wasn't a whole lot left to catch fire in that country, so my boss figured he could spare me for a few weeks while I covered John's shifts on Signal Peak, and my relief lookout worked extra to cover mine.

I slipped into my pants and donned a hat while Teresa's hiking boots rang on the tower's metal steps. Given her intimate understanding of the profession, she refused to climb an occupied lookout without permission from its resident caretaker, a recognition that fire towers serve not merely as scenic overlooks for tourists but as actual work spaces for lookouts, some of whom consider pants optional.

Rare is the pleasure hiker whose appreciation of the wild is capacious enough to include a surprise confrontation with a hairy human ass. Nonetheless, an unsettling number of visitors disregarded the sign at the base of the tower informing the curious that the structure had an official purpose, and that permission was required to climb it during its annual period of occupancy, roughly April through August. People being people, a few began their thoughtless trudge up the stairs without even a hollered warning. Maybe this impertinence had something to do with the implausibility, in our day and age, of someone still getting paid to stare out the window at mountains all day; maybe certain humans could no longer be bothered to read from a surface other than a screen. In any case, when John had ruled the roost he would tweak trespassers by meeting them partway in their ascent and telling them he was in the middle of some very important paperwork, and if they would wait at the base of the tower for ten or fifteen minutes—twenty tops—he would have the *I*s dotted and the *T*s crossed and be glad to share the view. Then he would return to his glass-walled perch on stilts and laugh to himself. The fact that there was no paperwork was part of what we loved about the job.

I joined Teresa on the catwalk. We stood against the railing looking north toward the big mountains, where tinsel tufts of cloud hovered over the creases in the land, the canyons and the river valleys. It was one of those mornings of fresh-scrubbed serenity that made the forest look like a world at the dawn of time—a view so magnanimous with earthly beauty it made me want to live forever, even as I was more aware than usual that I would not.

Although her days as a freak on a peak were behind her, Teresa still surpassed me by almost two decades of experience in the lookout's game, having worked thirty seasons in total, most of them on two mountains—Black Mountain, Bearwallow—in our shared home forest, the Gila of southern New Mexico. She last occupied Bearwallow the year before I showed up on the Gila; my first season coincided with her venturing north to work towers in Oregon and Idaho, so I had missed out on the pleasure of hearing her voice on the two-way radio. Hearing it now, in person, I felt sadness and gratitude at once; the sadness would have been there either way, with or without her presence, but I was grateful I wouldn't feel compelled to hide it from her, as I would have from the average day hiker—that on the contrary I could share it with her, and share in hers. Perhaps in this way we could soften it for each other just a little.

In the distance we could see the Gila Wilderness, the original American experiment in protecting wild country from incursion by industrial machines. In 1924, as an idealistic young forester, Aldo Leopold had convinced his superiors in the Forest Service to draw a jagged boundary line around the only mountains left in the American Southwest not carved up by roads and keep them that way. His plan made the Gila the world's first Wilderness with a capital W, meaning no automobiles, no tourist developments of any kind, all travel demanding the exertions of animate flesh, either one's own or that of a horse: the model for what would become, forty years later, the Wilderness Act. True to Leopold's vision, this exercise in willed restraint had preserved, for ninety years and running, a big enough stretch of country to allow for packing with mules on a trip lasting two weeks during which the pack string never once crossed its own tracks. Even if he weren't venerated as the high priest of American ecology, having forever changed the way we think about the natural world thanks to his visionary land ethic, Leopold would be remembered for changing our relationship with some pretty big chunks of it—none more resonant with symbolism than the Gila. For some of us it remained not only the first Wilderness but the best: more than half a million acres of grassland, mountain, and mesa, the major sky-island bridge between the southern Rockies and the northern Sierra Madre.

Teresa had seen more of that place than anyone I knew, and I never tired of hearing her stories of riding the trails with old-time mule packers, or floating the river's forks at flood stage in a battered boat. These were uncommon pursuits, to put it mildly. Packing with mules had always been so, and those who boated in that country ran the Gila River's main stem, not the smaller and gnarlier headwaters forks. Those forks were too small, offered too many challenges, involved too much boat-dragging and bushwhacking. I had never heard of anyone else attempting to float them. For Teresa, that was part of the allure: the difficulty, the novelty. That, and the occasion for solitude. Hers was an undomesticated sensibility of an especially intense kind, fueled by a passion for wild creatures and native flora, making for a life lived around ranchers and firefighters and others who worked outdoors, fuel-wood cutters and horse breeders and their ilk. She had more than held her own in that world. She was what was called an "old Gila hand"—*hand* being the most respectful moniker bestowed on humans in wild country, and *old* not an epithet but an honorific.

Her adventures had hardly been limited to the Gila. She had once run the Green River solo, from northern Utah to Lake Powell, 430 miles in six weeks. Back in the 1980s, she had gone horseback from the Mexican border to Canada, a six-month journey on the second day of which she was thrown from her mount, suffering a broken arm on impact. For most people, that mishap would have derailed the trip, or at least postponed it. Teresa was not most people. As fortune would have it, she found her way to a nearby ranch owned by a semiprofessional rodeo cowboy who happened to have some casting material handy; he typically used it on the calves he practiced roping, whenever the rope broke one of their legs. Calf-roping tended to result in a lot of broken legs, which healed relatively quickly when properly set. His expertise made for an impeccable cast on her arm, and he sent her on her way with some extra plaster, in case she needed to repeat the job herself.

But that was long ago, in what sometimes seemed to her another life entirely. During one of her last seasons as a lookout she had been poisoned by too much time spent in a tower infected with hidden mold. A subsequent tick bite bequeathed her a blood-borne pathogen and set her on an excruciating medical odyssey that lasted several years and only really ended after she spent long sessions in a hyperbaric chamber. At age 63, having lived hand-to-mouth for decades to feed her jones for adventure and avoid what she viewed as the suffocating expectations of the culture, namely marriage and motherhood, she had surprised herself by having a change of heart about marriage. In her capacity for solitude and all-around hardihood she made the perfect partner for John, but they had been granted only eleven months together. Now she was walking around with his ashes in a plastic bag and looking a little lost.

It felt like the right sort of day for spreading some of those ashes. The breeze was barely a whisper in the tops of the pines below us; their needle clusters glinted like pom-poms in the slanted sunlight. As the ribbons of ground fog began to lift and dissolve, we could see mountains way beyond the forest boundary, over in Arizona and down on the Mexican border. We both understood the gravity of what we were about to do and so we held off a while longer, not wanting to rush toward a reckoning. Instead we stood on the catwalk and watched the forest come to life, sometimes speaking quietly, sometimes pointing to something on the landscape, sometimes silently attentive as the hummingbirds buzzed around the feeder and the shadows shortened and the air began to warm. After a while I left Teresa alone with the view and went inside the tower to make myself some oatmeal with nuts and dried fruit, and a cup of coffee, extra-strong, with a generous pour of cream.

As I did so, the other lookouts began to call in service over the radio—first Jean on Black Mountain, then Hedge at Lookout Mountain, and on around the horn, one by one, Eagle Peak, Mogollon Baldy, Mangas Mountain, Fox Mountain, Saddle Mountain, Bearwallow, Hillsboro Peak—until all of us had been accounted for but me. Some days I liked to go first and others I preferred to go last, and often the ritual round of morning voices called to mind the first few lines of Gary Snyder's poem "The Lookouts":

> Perched on their bare and windy peaks
> They twitter like birds across the fractured hills
> Equipped by science with the keenest tool—
> A complex two-way radio, full of tubes.
>
> The most alone, and highest in the land,
> We trust their scrupulous vision to a man:

Or woman, I always added, adjusting the cadence to make the poem more inclusive, not to mention more accurate. The lookouts I admired most were women, so this zeal for accuracy was more than academic. Four of them—Teresa, Jean, Sara, and Rázik—counted a hundred fire seasons worth of experience altogether, a deep reservoir of knowledge about the country that, one had to believe, would never again be duplicated. Jean worked the loneliest of all the towers, seeing fewer visitors than any of the rest of us by far, sometimes only six or eight in a summer. Sara and Ráz split time equally at Baldy, since the hike in was so long—twelve miles—it didn't make sense for one of them to work the relief schedule of four days on and ten days off and spend half the time coming and going. Sara had spent more summers on her mountain—

thirty-three straight—than John and I combined on ours; Ráz liked to joke that Sara knew the country so well she could tell you precisely which tree had started the fire. At twenty-four seasons of service herself, Ráz was no slouch when it came to understanding the lay of the land. She was 72 years old and as spry as most people half her age. I doubted I would be alive at 72, much less fit enough to hike twelve miles each way to work.

I joined the 9 AM chorus by pressing the transmit button on my Bendix-King VHF radio full of tubes and carefully enunciating, "Silver City dispatch, Signal Peak, in service." It felt peculiar to say words John had uttered on more than a thousand mornings. The name Signal Peak didn't feel right in my mouth, but that's where I was, so that's who I was, for the moment.

My spasm of discomfort passed as I moved into the daily routine of measuring the morning weather, a set of gestures identical for each of the ten lookouts on the forest: note the location and intensity of lightning in the previous twenty-four hours, eyeball the sky for its percentage of cloud cover, check the rain gauge for any precip since 9 the day before. Hold an anemometer into the wind, noting direction and range of speeds and maximum gust. Dip a sling psychrometer in distilled water, dampening the cotton sleeve that hugged its wet bulb; twirl the psychrometer's twin thermometers in the shade of the catwalk, producing readings from both the dry bulb (conventional air temperature) and wet bulb (cooler temperature created by evaporation from the dampened cotton). Discern the relative humidity from the difference between the two with the help of a handy chart. Write all this in the logbook in preparation for calling it in to the dispatcher.

"Silver City dispatch, Signal Peak, morning report," I announced, those two little words in the middle again sounding off—not just to me but to everyone listening.

Once I finished on the radio, Teresa suggested a morning stroll. We descended the tower and walked down the trail until we came to an opening in the trees, on a ridge overlooking the rounded peaks of the Twin Sisters to the south. John had come there often with his wife, Miquette, back when they first staffed the tower, back when Miquette was still alive. In 1999, she had been hired as the primary lookout, he as her relief, and they both liked the view from a natural stone bench just below the top of the ridge: thick ponderosa pine rolling down the slopes of the Pinos Altos Range, giving way eventually to piñon-juniper country, and beyond it the cougar-colored grasslands. John spread some of Miquette's ashes in the clearing after her death, back in 2003.

Now it was his turn to join her.

In their last months together, John played caretaker while Miquette succumbed to cancer. This happened not long after my first summer as a lookout ended, so I didn't know him at the time, other than as one of many voices on my two-way radio. He later said it was the most difficult thing he had ever done, and in some ways the most meaningful.

Having been informed the disease was incurable, they embarked on a journey John called "hospice in a motor home." Thanks in part to an unexpected bequest from Miquette's godmother, the two of them had lived on the road for years, dropping anchor in different campgrounds for a week or a month at a time, moving across the mountains and deserts from New Mexico to Idaho; they didn't want their journey to end in some godforsaken institutional room. Ignoring the doctors' appalled warnings to the contrary, they packed up her crutches and oxygen tanks, her gauze patches and pill bottles, and set off toward a secret valley in California where they had stayed many times before. "It was as romantic, in its own intimate way, as a honeymoon," John later wrote of that week, in an essay he shared with friends.

They continued west to a campground on the Pacific coast, where the host, apprised of their situation, waived the two-week stay limit. As was their way, they continued to make connections until the very end. Folks stopped by to see whether they needed help, fellow RVers brought tapioca pudding to share with Miquette—part death watch, part social hour. When the end drew near they bowed to necessity and joined her family in Santa Cruz. "On New Year's Eve, with a sigh, Miquette slipped gently away," John wrote. "Outside the bedroom window, fireworks sparkled in the midnight sky."

Feeling an urge to bend his grief to some good purpose, John signed up to become an air angel, flying sick patients in need of emergency medical care to distant hospitals free of charge in his own private plane. He constantly reminded himself that, although the end had come too soon for her—she had died at 56—Miquette had lived out her dreams. As a little girl she loved horses so much she wanted to be one; she also fantasized about living in a tree house. After she met John they lived in the shadow of 14,000-foot peaks in Colorado, tucked amid a grove of aspens on the edge of a meadow, where they cared for a large herd of horses. Later they took up seasonal residence on Signal Peak, in a sort of deluxe tree house above the Gila. The timing and manner of her death had not undone the fact that hers had been, in many ways, a charmed life.

So had John's, mostly. As with all of us, there were areas of his personal history shadowed in varying degrees of darkness, but on the day of his death, age 62, he was happier than he had been in some time, excited to be planning a new honeymoon on which he would fly his Cessna Cardinal around the American West with Teresa, golfing at a different course in a different state each day—a major concession on her part, golf being far afield from her own interests, but what the hell, the things we do for love. Instead the plane was orphaned in a hangar at the Grant County Airport, and there would be no teeing off in Arizona one day and Utah the next, not to mention no more air-angel flights with him at the helm.

On the stone bench, Teresa and I shared a few tears, a few laughs. John's laughter still echoed in our memories, and sometimes we merely felt like displaced conduits for it. Never parsimonious with his emotions, he would have appreciated the sight of us crying one minute and giggling the next—and sometimes both at once—as we sifted through what we remembered most vividly about him.

I sometimes thought of him as the blue-eyed gringo incarnation of a Mudhead Kachina, the drumming, dancing clown in Hopi ceremonies: partial to mischief and merriment, and the most gregarious lover of solitude I had ever known. His laughter, his most winning characteristic, tumbled forth in staccato waves, his belly shaking, his torso rocking back and forth from the hinge of his waist like a seesaw. He had a kind of bebop laugh that reminded me of Dizzy Gillespie's solo on "Salt Peanuts"—supple and exuberant, the individual notes crowding one another as if in a hurry to be free. When children visited his lookout tower, he delighted in showing them how he could make a flower of his lips by painting them with lipstick, drawing in hummingbirds for a drink of sugar water straight out of his mouth. I found the tube of cherry-colored Wet 'n Wild in the drawer where he kept his weather instruments; its gauche branding first made me laugh and then ruined me for half an hour with all it evoked of him.

The sight of that lipstick was nothing compared with my initial glimpse of his handwriting in the logbook, which detailed the major events of his last hours:

Noonish	Past lookout Bart Mortenson family arrives. Bart was a lookout here in the 70s. He honeymooned here
12:32	Smoke report: Azimuth 247° 30', Township 16S, Range 14W, Section 32—small white column—BART FIRE
12:39	Smoke more dense, still white color
12:57	Engine 672 on scene
13:00	Mortenson family spreads Bart's ashes north of tower. Nice singing of hymns drifting inside
13:05	BART FIRE getting a broader base. Lat/Long 33° 55' 32.1" x 108° 12' 46.8"
19:00	Out of service

Shortly after writing the words "Out of service" on the evening of June 7, 2014, he saddled his horse, Sundance, and set off on a ride along the Continental Divide Trail, passing by the spot where he had spread Miquette's ashes eleven years earlier. When he didn't call in service the next morning, two friends—his relief lookout, Mark Johnson, and his supervisor, Keith Mathes—set out ahead of a search-and-rescue team to hunt for him. The hunt did not last long. Both John and the horse were found where they fell; Sundance's massive bulk had crushed the torso of his rider. Neither betrayed signs of having struggled. Those of us who loved John kept telling ourselves that whatever the reason for the fall—a horse heart attack, the evidence suggested, although we would never know for sure—he had gone quickly, doing something he enjoyed, in a place he loved.

At least he died with his boots on, I told Teresa, inanely, when we met in the hours after his body was found.

"Not quite," she said. "Classic John: the bastard was wearing his tennis shoes. If he'd had his cowboy boots on, who knows, he might've been able to get out of the stirrups in time."

Those of us with long experience sitting watch over the Gila sometimes joked that we were not so much fire lookouts anymore as morbid priests or pyromaniacal monks—officiants at an ongoing funeral for the forests as we had found them when we first assumed our posts. All of us had come seeking solitude, adventure, the romance of wild mountains, and a taste of the sublime; we got everything we had hoped for and more, including pyrotechnics on a landscape scale. The job never lasted long enough—six months maximum, more like four or five in a typical season—but it beat working down in the neon plastic valleys.

Nationwide, our numbers dwindled by the year, our sort of work a casualty of "development" and the schemes of the techno-titillated, who looked forward to the day when the last of us would be put out to pasture by satellites, drones, and high-definition infrared cameras linked with pattern-recognition software. We had been reduced from several thousand to a few hundred in the span of half a century, and the trend showed no sign of reversing; quite the contrary. The only question was how long we would last. Squinting in just the right light, after just the right number of drinks, I found it possible to envision an alternate reality in which I toiled alongside the rest of the creative class in the panopticon of the social-media surveillance economy, another insufferable white guy curating my personal brand—a tiny celebrity on a miniature stage—and art-directing amateur photo shoots of what I ate for lunch. That might still be my future. But not just yet. Not quite.

In the sunset days of a doomed vocation, I had lucked into a lineage of mountain mystics and lone rangers. We were paid in US dollars to read the meaning in clouds and discern the difference between positive and negative lightning. It seemed almost an oversight on the culture's part that the job still existed at all. Those of us who kept with it across the decades became walking repositories of bird-migration and weather patterns, fire history and trail conditions. For days and sometimes weeks on end we studied maps, performed seasonal maintenance on our facilities, and luxuriated in silence and solitude; some of us even learned to kiss hummingbirds. Then a storm moved over and the fires busted out, one or two or a dozen in an afternoon, and we earned our keep triangulating smokes, alerting crews to sudden changes in wind and fire behavior, guiding smokejumpers toward good trails on which to hike out after demob. It was hard to imagine jumpers on loan from Alaska or Montana, dropped from the sky into a remote place they had never seen before, getting that sort of intelligence from a high-def camera—*angle toward the ridge northwest of you above the scree field for about two-thirds of a mile, then look for the rock cairn at the base of a big Doug fir, and follow the trail east from there until it drops down to the creek bottom*—but the gadget fetishists never bothered to imagine that we offered more than merely a pair of eyes, that the evolving palimpsest of knowledge we accrued about the country might have some real and practical value beyond that of an adorable curio from an age before the world went virtual.

Those of us who worked on the Gila had the good fortune to watch over the forest that, for the sake of the health of the land, was allowed to burn more aggressively than any other in the Lower 48. We had witnessed the triumphs of progressive fire management, even played a small role in them, participants in a new pyromancy that no longer saw wildfire as a despised disruption of the natural order, a menace, a scourge. After most of a century of total suppression, the fire managers of the Gila National Forest had sculpted that new attitude into a strategy—let a few fires burn, when and where conditions were favorable, generally in the middle elevations of the wilderness areas, away from the settled edges of the forest—that helped preserve one of the healthiest ponderosa-pine stands in the Southwest.

The country outside the forest boundary was essentially a sacrifice zone to cattle grazing, denuded so thoroughly it was a study in desertification. The forest's fringes had been transformed as well, also badly overgrazed for more than a century, crisscrossed by roads and off-road-vehicle trails, and overgrown with unburned brush. In certain areas, woodcutting—for cooking, heating homes, making lumber, and smelting copper ore—had altered the forest structure, and throughout the region top predators, notably Mexican gray wolves and grizzly bears, had been the object of a relentless effort at zoöcide. Against all odds the wolves were making a comeback, but the grizzlies were likely gone forever.

The heart of the country nonetheless remained a land without roads, one of the wildest we had left, licked frequently by flame since at least the end of the Pleistocene and all the more beautiful and resilient for it. At McKenna Park, the place in the state of New Mexico farthest from pavement, you'd have to be lobotomized or a filthy aesthete not to sense something magical about the country: the scent of earth unbroken by human tools, a pine-oak savannah that called up a primeval feeling in the blood. The whole interwoven pattern of life there flourished amid frequent low-intensity burns; it had been and remained a fire-adapted ecosystem. The ponderosas dropped their lowest limbs to prevent fire climbing into their crowns, giving the forest a distinctive, open look. Nearly every living tree was blackened at its base—evidence of wildfire as handmaiden to evolution.

For close to four decades, the mantra on the Gila had been that fire was good, fire was necessary—the land had burned for millennia, after all, with no paramilitary force to stamp out smokes until the first years of the 20th century—but the size and character of the burns were changing. All across the planet, forests were undergoing an alarming die-off due to drought, disease, and beetle infestation, not to mention logging and slash-and-burn agriculture on an industrial scale—an apoc- alyptic acceleration of tree murder. Even in the world's first Wilderness, theoretically protected from destructive human activity, the effects of global warming were evident in the form of unstoppable megafires. They reinforced the fact that no place on earth was safely sealed off from the effects of human activity.

"One of the penalties of an ecological education is to live alone in a world of wounds," Aldo Leopold wrote seven decades ago. An ecological education is easier to come by in the 21st century than in Leopold's time; the penalty now is not to live alone with the burden of the knowledge— there is plenty enough company—but to feel helpless to stanch the losses foreordained by our pollution of the atmosphere with heat-trapping gases: losses of forests and ice, losses of habitat and species. We are in the midst of an irreversible ecocide. To fully grasp what our appetites have done to the nonhuman life of this planet would be to combust in guilt and grief.

In the two fire seasons preceding the summer of John's death, the forest saw the two biggest burns in its known history. First came the Whitewater-Baldy Fire in May 2012, which set a state record when two fires merged and burned five hundred square miles of the Mogollon Range, forcing Ráz and Sara off their mountain for most of the summer. It was followed eleven months later by the Silver Fire, a burn that chased me from my peak in a helicopter as half of the Black Range succumbed to flames. Taken together, the two fires roamed across nearly half a million acres. There wasn't much to do about them but marvel at the heat and smoke and what they wrought, which included, at their hottest, the incineration of the normally moist, dense woods of the high country: Douglas and corkbark fir, blue and Engelmann spruce.

The drier, warmer land below, on the flanks of the mountains and along the high mesas, was meant to burn frequently and had—the his- torical record suggested a couple times a decade was about average. But the big fires had taken the kind of old, big trees—living near 10,000 feet and above, and along the cool north-facing slopes slightly lower— that, according to tree-ring analysis, typically saw consuming fire just once every century or three, and then only in small patches. Now they were going away in massive stand-replacement events, and it felt silly to hope for their eventual return in a warming world. They were gone, and they weren't coming back.

On John's last day as a lookout, the open-ended memorial enlarged to include not just big old trees but one of our predecessors. It unnerved me to learn that John had saddled his horse and ridden to his death within hours of witnessing, out his tower window, those rituals honoring the memory of Bart Mortenson. The resonance of all the little details made for a paradoxical feeling, a retroactive sense of foreboding: the loved ones of a fellow lookout bearing the man's ashes to the mountain; the mention of that now poignant word, *honeymoon;* John's honoring the memory of the man by bestowing his name on a fire—*BART FIRE*—a mere seven hours before the fire in his own eyes went out.

The first thing you noticed about John were those lively, almost effervescent blue eyes. As lustrous as polished turquoise, they gave him an expression that appeared never to say no to the world, although that hadn't always been the case. "It took me some time to animate my face," he had once written, in a notebook discovered by Teresa after his death.

I thought I knew what he meant. When I learned he was a fellow Minnesotan, I tried once and only once to engage him on the subject, but he pivoted away so abruptly, with a look of such dread in those normally avid eyes, that I felt I had poked my finger in a wound. Only later would I learn that he had been present when his best friend accidentally killed himself while fooling around with a gun in the woods during the winter of their senior year of high school. The mere mention of the state where this had occurred was enough to make him recall the scene as if it had happened yesterday, although forty years had passed. He remembered just as vividly his parents' reaction to the tragedy, his father picking him up at the police station afterward, not saying a word as they drove home in terrible silence, and his mother turning away in disgust when he walked through the door, as if he had committed a murder.

It was not the sort of story one dropped as an icebreaker at parties. He trusted me with it, I suspect, because I first shared with him the fact that my brother had ended his life with a bullet from a semi-automatic assault rifle. Sometimes you just have a feeling about people, and from the beginning of our acquaintance I judged him to be the kind of man who was capable of absorbing such knowledge with sensitivity and grace. From the very beginning, in fact: I shared my brother's story with him the first time I saw him face-to-face, at an end-of-season gathering of lookouts in summer 2003.

Come to think of it, I suppose you could say I dropped it as an icebreaker at a party. Mark Hedge, the resident sage on Lookout Mountain, had invited four of us to his place at Elephant Butte for beer around the backyard fire pit; for some in attendance, including me and John, it would be our first chance to connect faces with familiar voices on the radio. That was the day John spread Miquette's ashes near the tower where they had lived four summers together. He knew he was going to spend time with other lookouts that evening, and although he hadn't met us all in person yet, the thought of our company gave him the courage to do a thing he had been putting off for months. Within an hour of having shaken hands, we were both in tears over the loss of people we had loved. We began in mutual candor; it would have felt phony to proceed any other way thereafter.

Shared some months later, his story of having paid witness to a friend's death by gunshot revealed that we were blood brothers of a sort. Each of us, in the wake of a bullet's destruction, had checked into the guilt suite at the Hotel Sorrow and re-upped for a few hundred weeks, he at 17, I at 23.

"I reviewed my life and it was also a river," Herman Hesse wrote, in the voice of Siddhartha, a sentence that stayed with me through the years. Whenever I recalled it I felt an impulse to revise it for my own purposes and replace the word *river* with the word *fire: I reviewed my life and it was also a fire.* My life was more like a series of fires, each of which moved through similar phases, from a thunderous moment of ignition—the lightning strike of a brother's suicide, the incendiary dissolution of a marriage—to the full flaring heat of grief, followed by a long, slow cooling, a landscape of ashen remains, and, finally, purgation and rebirth. It occurred to me more than once to share my plagiarized sentiment with John, including him in it—*I reviewed our lives and they were also fires*—but I never had, and now I never would. I had erred in assuming that tomorrow remained a perpetual possibility for that combination of elements forged in friendship and known as *us.* For me, tomorrow might still come. Probably would, in fact. For him, and for us, there would be no such thing.

Shortly after the fatal gunshot, John left the exurbs of Minneapolis and began a life of travel and adventure that took him across the country and around the world, including a yearlong trip through Mexico and South America and a stint of expatriate living in Spain. His work life included an exotic mélange of duties: bartender, gentleman rancher, private investigator, PR man for a race-car team, claims adjuster for Lloyd's of London. At the time of his death, he was president and part owner of an airplane-repair shop. The job about which he liked to reminisce most involved his misadventures as a deputy marshal in Telluride, Colorado, where he and his boss, committed to gentler forms of justice than the code books called for, adopted the motto *Better us than the real guys.*

He possessed a colorful and mysterious backstory and lots of fancy toys even as he cultivated a reputation as a midwestern penny-pincher, partial to torn blue jeans and thrift-store sweatshirts, liable to haggle over the cost of just about anything. He surrounded himself with all the trappings of old-school machismo, the whole suite of midlife-crisis totems—airplane, Jeep, motorcycle, Pantera sports car, GT40 race car—while conducting his emotional life in the most open and vulnerable way possible. He liked to fly high and drive fast; he liked sitting in one place for months, watching mountains. He lived simply in a house of four hundred square feet; he owned a forty-foot mobile home he liked to call his "land yacht."

The last time I saw him alive it was with our mutual pal Mark Johnson, John's relief lookout on Signal Peak. My girlfriend and I joined John and Mark for dinner and a beer, and when we were through Mark was the first to leave. Before he did so, John opened his arms as if welcoming a good-bye hug; Mark leaned in, and John gave him a kiss full on the lips. All this, appropriately enough, at a bar called Wrangler's, which catered to the clientele one would expect from a place by that name. It struck me as the first time in my entire life I had witnessed two straight dudes kiss each other on the lips with real affection and no self-consciousness in a public place. The surprise of bearing witness to it was surpassed only by the surprise of realizing I was a little bit jealous.

On the other hand, when I mentioned John's death to the first friend I encountered after hearing the news, my friend said: "You know, that guy was a real asshole." Stuart said that John had come into his metal-fabrication shop one day, seeking a quote on a minor welding project. When Stuart gave him one, John blanched and began—cheapskate that he was—to bargain for a lower price. Stuart countered that he had given him a fair price: take it or leave it. John grumbled in a way that left Stuart feeling abused and insulted. John left and never returned.

More even than haggling for better deals, the man loved needling bureaucratic authority. Even as a lowly agency employee (pay grade GS-4) with no health insurance, no retirement benefits, and a merely seasonal appointment (forestry technician—lookout), he wrote long, deeply researched letters of complaint to the chief of the US Forest Service about the waste of running reconnaissance flights over a forest already covered by the eyes of ten lookouts. "Dear Chief Tidwell," one such missive began, "I am a fellow Forest Service employee. I work as a fire lookout . . . rest assured my office is nicer than yours." After this cheeky opening, he spent nine pages and several thousand words attacking the agency's rationale for using expensive, accident-prone aircraft to detect fires and guide slurry planes in a place such as the Gila. His objections encompassed both the practical—wasteful spending of tax dollars, leaded-gas emissions over the wilderness—and the philosophical, the latter grounded in the knowledge that the landscape we loved and claimed as part owners along with the rest of the American public was stolen from the Apache in a genocidal war. With the red man subdued and removed, red flames had been cast as a savage force that could be tamed only by efforts on a military model. Seen in that light, firefighting—with helicopters, slurry bombers, and paratrooper smoke-jumpers—was simply a way of perpetuating the endless war on the land. Despite a reputation as the most forward-thinking forest in the country when it came to fire, the Gila still suppressed more than 90 percent of new wildfire starts. Some old habits die hard, none more so than those involving the tools of warfare, funded by unlimited sums of emergency money.

A part of John hoped, vainly as it turned out, that he would be called on to answer for his litany of heresies by the "chain of command." Meanwhile he remained on a friendly, first-name basis with the aviation officers of the Gila, who always said hello via the air-to-ground frequency when they flew over his mountain on their redundant recon missions. He thought their work bogus and profligate, not to mention needlessly risky with human life, but that didn't prevent him from liking the people who did it, or they him. He loved to fly circles over beautiful country—and had to admit it was quite the caper for the flyboys and flygirls to have found a way to get paid for doing precisely that.

About ten days into my hitch as his stand-in, I hiked down to the scene of his death to pay homage. For reasons I couldn't fully explain, probably having to do with both my fear of death and the allure of it—the big dark, the long sleep—I wanted to spend some time in the place where he had breathed his last breath.

Over the years, I had become, quite in contrast to anything I had ever dreamed—who would imagine such a thing ahead of time?—a connoisseur of burn scars. My first such forays involved backpack trips to the interior of the Gila's wilderness areas, but more recently the burns appeared inclined to come to me.

The earth where John fell to his death had burned in the Signal Fire a little more than a month earlier. His last big wildfire as a lookout, it had left another new burn scar calling out for exploration. The smoke started on Mother's Day afternoon, when target shooters threw their spent shells in a hollow stump just off the Signal Peak Road. The heat from the cluster of shells set the stump to smoldering, and it smoldered long enough to ignite the grass and pine needles surrounding it. (The shooters slipped away and were never identified.) Aided by steady winds at thirty miles per hour and up, the grass fire quickly swept into the timber; once in the treetops it became a running crown fire, with flame lengths of fifty feet and more. These sorts of fires—started accidentally by humans—were often the hottest kind, because they tended to happen not, as with lightning, in conjunction with rain, but rather on dry, windy days, early in the season, before the summer monsoon greened the grass and brought the fuel moistures back up. On windless days the goofuses who were careless with fire tended to catch their own mistakes before the fires spread. On windy days they turned tail and ran, leaving the fight to the Forest Service.

The Signal Fire ran up the flank of the mountain in a hurry, wind-driven all the way. Only the arrival of a backdoor cold front that first night stopped it from growing ten times larger than its final tally of 5,484 acres. Overnight, the humidity rose and temperatures dropped into the twenties; more crucially, the prevailing west wind changed to a light east one, turning the fire back on itself—but not before John and Teresa were forced to flee down the mountain on foot. After their departure, the fire crested the ridge at the base of the tower, and the heat half-melted the flamingos John had arranged in wry imitation of a sub-urban lawn. The fire essentially died there, leaving one side of the mountain green, the other black, with malformed pink plastic birds marking the boundary.

Two weeks later, the fire was cold when three students from a local charter school flew over the burn scar in a private plane, assessing the changes to a forest transect they had laid out for a class project in eco-monitoring. It was the last thing they would do with their promising young lives. "On May 23, 2014, at 1553 mountain daylight time, a Ray-theon G36 airplane, N536G, impacted terrain near Silver City, New Mexico," the National Transportation Safety Board report stated. "The private pilot and three passengers were fatally injured. The airplane was destroyed."

> The airplane was returning from a local flight and the pilot flew a tight downwind leg for landing on runway 35, possibly due to a direct crosswind in excess of 20 knots. During the base turn, the airplane overshot the final course, and the pilot used at least 60 degrees of bank to correct the airplane back on course and over the runway. The airplane then bounced and touched down at least 20 knots above the manufacturer's published approach speed with about 1,810 ft remaining on the runway. The airplane's airspeed began to rapidly decrease, but then several seconds later, the airplane's airspeed increased as the pilot rejected the landing. The airplane did not gain significant altitude or airspeed then began a slight right turn. The airplane's roll rate then sharply increased, and the airplane quickly descended, consistent with a stall, before colliding with a transmission wire and terrain. Examination of the airframe and engine did not reveal any pre-impact anomalies that would have precluded normal operation. Strong, variable, gusty wind, with an environment conducive to the formation of dry microbursts, was present at the airport at the time of the accident. Several lightning strikes were recorded in the vicinity of the accident site around the time of the accident. It is unknown if the presence of lightning or wind impacted the pilot's in flight decision-making in the pattern, on approach, or during the attempted go-around. The circumstances of the accident are consistent with an in-flight encounter with a

strong tailwind and/or windshear during climbout after the rejected landing.

John had reported the presence of the small fixed-wing near his tower that afternoon, in keeping with lookout protocol; he later reported the smoke plume from the crash, aware from the moment he saw it what it meant. The deaths of those kids, coming so soon after they had circled his tower, shook him badly. Two were 16 years old, the other 14. All were members of the Aldo Leopold High School science team, which had won the Envirothon state championship six weeks earlier. A thousand people turned out for their memorial.

The young man among them, Michael Mahl, had been a gifted guitarist who also played drums, ukulele, and mandolin; he performed most Sundays at a church in Silver City led by his pastor grandfather. The two young women, Ella Jaz Kirk and Ella Myers, had participated in a writing workshop I conducted at the school not long before their death. Ella Myers wrote a novel at the age of 12 and had been accepted at an elite film school in Chicago; Ella Kirk, the youngest, played violin and piano, wrote her own songs, and collected more than 6,400 signatures on her self-authored petition to protect the Gila River from a billion-dollar dam project cooked up by scheming bureaucrats in Santa Fe. She testified about the issue before a state legislative committee with a poise I doubt I could have matched. Those kids' lives, seemingly limitless in their potential, were, in a way, casualties of the fire as surely as the mixed conifer on the north slope of the mountain. That John died inside the burn scar shortly after the crash only compounded the fire's eerie aftereffects: loss layered on loss.

From the mountain one could see almost the entire burn, the pattern it had chewed across the land quite obvious: west to east, with an uphill push to the top of the divide along the southern perimeter. It was far from the most spectacular fire I had witnessed, but it had more personal resonance than most. It was to be the last smoke on which I collaborated with John; I gave him an azimuth on it from my vantage, so he could pinpoint how far north of his tower it was before he bailed off the mountain. Now, staring at the burn scar day after day up close, I felt as if I would be shirking a duty if I didn't venture into it. One evening, after signing off the radio, I decided it was time for a walk through the ash.

It didn't take long to discover the scene of John's death; the smell tipped me off from fifty yards away. The body of Sundance still lay where it fell, and his bay-colored hide stood out in a landscape that was now monochrome, the bare earth and fire-scarred trees streaked and daubed with white vulture droppings, like a halfway-finished Pollock painting. John's body had been retrieved by Forest Service friends and colleagues, but rules and regs did not call for the removal of a half-ton of horseflesh from national forestland, and the birds had made a feast of it. In the afternoons, I sometimes watched them circling the ridge southeast of the tower, as many as two dozen at a time riding thermals over the crest of the divide, spinning in languid gyres, dark against the light-blue sky—lazy-looking but never not vigilant. Sort of like lookouts.

The trail ran along a steep slope on the southern edge of the burn. Sundance had fallen hard to the downhill side, his neck bent around a charred tree trunk. In the two weeks since, his carcass had shrunk until the hide draped over the bones like a tattered blanket. Beneath that blanket, inside the rib cage, something scratched and scrabbled— something alive. I stood and listened for a while, touched in some very old way, even sort of honored to eavesdrop on the process of flesh re-entering the food chain by the traditional method. The sound said all you needed to know about the pickins being slim: a dry scraping, sig- nifying that the carcass had been worked over pretty well already. I tossed a small rock at it, then another, half-fearing the appearance of a tiny bear cub, which would imply the presence of its mother nearby.

Instead a vulture poked its head from inside the horse's body cavity. It crawled out into the light, glanced over its shoulder at me, beat its heavy wings, and took flight through the bare branches of the ghost forest: meal interrupted.

The turkey vulture, a study in paradox: from a distance so graceful, gliding on invisible currents, air riffling its fingerlike wing tips; at close range so hideous, with its raw red head, greasy brown feathers, and contemptuous yellow eyes. Misfortune its sustenance, death what's for dinner. "Your ass is somebody's else's meal," Gary Snyder wrote, in his essay "The Etiquette of Freedom," and more than once I had imagined my corpse—after an accidental fall from my fire tower—picked clean by *Cathartes aura*, ensuring my remains would soar one last time over mountains before falling back to earth as scavenger's excrement. What can I say? The days are long in a lookout tower. But not until that mo- ment, as I stood over the bag of bones called Sundance, had I known by name a creature who'd passed through a vulture's digestive system.

It occurred to me to wonder whether John might have chosen the same fate, had he been given the option. It would have been like him to skip the expense of cremation.

A peculiar thing happens once you've been a lookout for many seasons. Radio protocol demands that you forgo your given name and identify yourself by the name of your peak. For several months each year you are not Sara Irving or Rázik MaJean, Teresa Beall or Mark Hedge, Jean Stelzer or John Kavchar; you are the name of a mountain. Mogollon Baldy. Bearwallow. Lookout Mountain. Black Mountain. Signal Peak. The longer you keep the job, the more intimately your identity becomes entwined with that mountain.

At the same time, in our shared vigilance, scattered across the sky-island ridge tops, we come to feel ourselves a part of more than just a mountain, a part of something grand and dignified, a club of splendid misfits, delightfully at odds with the drift of the culture. Eventually the voices of our fellow freaks on peaks become aural talismans, sources of comfort and connection amid a sometimes enigmatic solitude.

It's not merely the radio that provokes this transformation. By living and working where we do we become intimate with the moods of a wild and moody place, its flora and fauna, its susceptibility to extreme weather; we discover which of the north-face snowbanks melts last, where water collects in the rainy season, which trees lure convergent lady beetles by the thousands until their bark turns a writhing orange. We learn the songs of birds and the names of flowers, the spooky thrill of monsoon-season mornings waking up inside the clouds. We discover where to find food in the time of ripeness—wild raspberries, prickly gooseberries—and where other creatures find theirs.

Our terse radio commo ratifies an evolving external reality. The work has made of the mountains a gift to us, and we honor this gift by assuming and intoning their names. John had been Signal Peak; Signal Peak had been John, for every summer of the new millennium, just as Mogollon Baldy had been Sara and Ráz, and Lookout Mountain Hedge, and Black Mountain Jean. No matter how many times I repeated those two little words, I couldn't make them comfortable in my own voice, calling in service each morning, calling in my smoke and weather reports. I was not Signal Peak and never would be. Only John could eyeball the sky and with whimsical precision call in a morning report of 17.5 percent cloud cover. Only John could get away with naming a harmless end-of-season smoke the Jell-O Fire. To have tried such a trick would have marked me as a pretender.

His presence permeated the two hundred square feet of penthouse real estate where I cooked and slept and kept watch that June, and sometimes I had to leave the tower and wander the mountain for twenty minutes just to get away from him. He was there in the vase of plastic flowers set on the windowsill; he was there in the bag of Smokey Bear lapel pins kept handy as swag for visitors with kids. Even something as simple as a can of refried beans in the pantry reminded me of our routine for Continental Divide Trail thru-hikers, those creatures of seemingly limitless fortitude whose route brought them first to my mountain, then his, on their journey from Mexico to Canada. By the time they reached me they had traveled 100 miles through the desert—the bare beginning of their 3,000-mile journey along the spine of the Rockies. If they arrived at my tower after quitting time, I would offer a swig of tequila as we looked upon the country they had traveled to get there and the route that lay ahead. Once they returned to the trail, whether that same evening or the next morning, I would radio John and let him know visitors were on their way, ETA twenty-four hours, give or take, and he would do the prep work on a batch of nachos. We had never met a thru-hiker who wasn't tickled by the gift economy of the Gila's high peaks: aperitif at my tower, appetizer at John's. All they had heard of the place were rumors of its rough beauty and its capacity for inflicting bodily punishment, and here they were, being treated like visiting dignitaries.

The moment had arrived for John to become one with the mountain. Teresa opened the plastic bag. We dipped our hands in his ashes, extracted pinches between our fingertips, let them float off below us, toward a cluster of surviving century plants. His ashes mingled there with the ashes of the Signal Fire, his final form mingling with his final major burn; within weeks, perhaps even days, a good rain would flush some of the ash and loose soil down drainage, a nutrient recharge for the banks of the creek bottoms and, for a bit of his remains, one last ride through a piece of country he had known better than nearly anyone alive.

I was surprised to find myself reminded of the Catholic masses of my childhood, when the priest, arms uplifted, would intone over the Eucharist the words of the doomed savior at his last supper: *Take this, all of you, and eat, for this is my body. . . . Do this in memory of me.* John had been intimate with those same rituals, and we had talked about how one is never quite a former Catholic, only a recovering Catholic, the liturgy having been absorbed on an almost molecular level by our spongy young minds. For us, the metaphors had been more enduring than the faith, none more so than those of Ash Wednesday, when our foreheads had been traced by the priest's thumb, the cross-shaped smudge a reminder of mortality and mourning, a harbinger of what lay in store for us all:

For you are dust, and to dust you shall return . . .

Simultaneously—unprompted by word or gesture—Teresa and I each licked our fingers, wanting to take a bit of him into ourselves. I suppose some might view this as macabre, perhaps even some kind of health hazard, but we had both inhaled the smoke of huge burns, as had John during his fifteen years on the mountain. The taste of ash on the tongue was becoming more familiar all the time, as historic fires devoured the mixed conifer of the Southwestern high country. The forests would evolve and become something else—spruce and fir succeeded by aspen, pine replaced by locust and oak. What they had been for millennia was now, like John, a memento etched in flame.

As the day's heat increased, a few proto-cumulus began to form. Teresa and I tossed another pinch of John into the air, watched the motes drift and swirl downslope on the breeze. We shared a bitter laugh at the irony of her having finally found a man she cared to stand by for the long run—only to have him maroon her at the altar in the most theatrical fashion possible.

She gestured at the sky: "Looks like you're about to be in business." We hugged and said good-bye, and she set off down the trail, back toward home, where she would spend the next year and a half in a longer and more complicated relationship with John's possessions than she had with the man himself.

Her departure left me alone to the spectacle in the sky. And what a spectacle: the ancient drama of monsoon moisture streaming north off the Gulf of Mexico, meeting the furnace of the desert and rising over the mountains, the resulting cumulus clusters expanding like popcorn kernels, their bottoms slowly darkening and tendrils of virga beginning to fall, and finally the first hot flash of a ground strike in the middle distance. By midafternoon, dry lightning jabbed the mesas to the north every few seconds, and new smokes were popping up. I called in three in the span of an hour. Still unfamiliar with the terrain from John's vantage point, I misplaced one of them by two miles. The crew sent to suppress it found it anyway, in plenty of time.

That evening, off the clock and out of service, I took a couple of pulls from the tequila bottle John had left behind. I uncapped his tube of lipstick and made myself up in the reflection of his handheld signal mirror. Lips puckered, a sad clown waiting for a hummingbird's kiss, I couldn't help thinking that the man I would have liked to ask about the contours of the country, the man who could have alleviated my ignorance, was forever unavailable. No longer up above the country keeping watch, he was now a part of it—and a part of me.

Nominated by n+1, Dominica Phetteplace

LANGUAGE LESSON FOR ONE

by PUI YING WONG

from CONSTELLATIONS

If I knew French
I would speak its music,
its melancholy.

If I knew French
I would ask questions
like how much, where is,

be comfortable with words
like money, lost.

I'll rescue this French verb book,
4000 of them pressed together

between navy-blue covers
for traveling artists.

This afternoon,
no one needs it more than I.

I'll learn a few words,
words that have no equivalent
in English or Chinese.

Like the word for loneliness,
not the one that means
without friends or love,

but the kind you find
between horizon and the sea,

or homesickness,
the kind you feel when you are home.

Nominated by Constellations

WEEKEND TRIP

fiction by ANNE RAY

from THE GETTYSBURG REVIEW

On our way to the yearly party Yahlie's friends throw, we encounter a woman and her baby. The drive is one day from Santa Fe to Amarillo, one to Austin. Maybe Yahlie and I will do it in less, with our feet up on the dash and Styrofoam cups of soda in the cup holders. She and I felt the need to get out of town. In our house, the stereo is broken, and we can't find the cable to hook up the VCR we found. Texas feels like a step down from where we've come from, devilish and mean. Her friend Kirsten, who Yahlie says is belligerent and doesn't listen, said we could stay for a while, which we might. We have $220 between us.

We're out in the open. It's hot in the car, Yahlie's shrunken white car. It has a whole assortment of stuff in the back. A basketball, an enormous foam hand that fits over one's own hand, guitar strings, pennies. She's driving. It's her turn. We have the windows down, and the air is coming in, filching our oxygen. Out here it's more yellow than gold, and nothing at all is green, and everywhere unidentifiable objects are supplanting the landscape. A roly-poly silver mechanism, mounted on a flatbed trailer, the size of a jet engine. A silo with a roof too big for its shaft. Where we have come from, one state over, is softer, redder. Out here seems unkind. But I love the road. I love it like a lost pet. The plan is to find better work when we get back, better than two banquet jobs. We'd been doing this thing where we'd try to get scheduled for the same shifts, and one of us would sneak out after a while and work waitressing at the Cowgirl, shifts we bilked from our friend who had a boyfriend she got free rent from. I'd say, "Yahlie's in the back slicing lemons." "Kate's out back having a cigarette," Yahlie'd say. It was get-

103

ting three paychecks for two jobs. In honor of this, we'd sometimes order three plates of huevos for the two of us.

"I hear Ambrose Bierce is buried somewhere out here," she says.

"That must be true," I say. I stare through the windshield and its pockmarks, about to nod out.

"Where Kirsten lives is nothing like this," she says. "They have trees and lots of friends."

She gets this wistful look on her face. She and I have been sharing a tiny casita that we moved into after we met in a weird rooming house that was formerly a school for the deaf. We'd discovered we both dropped out of college at the same time, on opposite coasts. When we met she had seemed very scared, and I had felt somewhat assured. Since then, that had ebbed and flowed so many times that I was sometimes confused by who we were. The year before, she'd been in Israel on a farm. The year before, I'd been at a prestigious East Coast architecture school, faking it. I'd left only a few credits shy of finishing. Sometimes she talked on the pay phone at the Cowgirl in Hebrew to her sisters, who were in Michigan.

A ways outside Austin we stop and get sandwiches in a town with a carved wooden Indian at nearly every doorway and four shops selling the same things. The restaurant has a checkered tablecloth and no lights on, only the sunlight through the window. As we eat, mayonnaise expands in my mouth, the lettuce bruises as I touch it. We drink two glasses of soda so cold it leaves a ringing in my ears. We hear the air conditioning, like a combine running. Yahlie eats in enormous bites, steals fries off my plate with her slim hands. The waitresses sit at the table near the window, staring out.

"You eat so slowly. When I eat with you it takes all day," she says.

"It does not. And what else have you got to do, anyway, besides eat with me?"

When we get inside air conditioning, our conversations return to our usual, a little like Franz Liszt playing the piano, a little like prison inmates. She waits for me to finish the BLT.

We pay the woman and thank her. Outside, the heat is a force field. One cloud has appeared from somewhere to cover the sun. Sky's a hollowed-out bone.

Yahlie says, "Why does one have to go so far from the city, even a small city, to find a place where the values of mass production have not infiltrated the food? Why do we still eat everything out of a can? Instead of those delicious sandwiches?"

"Because we're broke," I say. "And you don't know how to cook."

She laughs her snorting laugh. "My belly hurts," she says. "I need to walk around."

I can tell she's writing an economic white paper in her head as we walk off the food, belching. She twists one piece of hair between two fingers.

"We either have too much food or not enough," she says.

Except I could have eaten three more of those sandwiches. It wasn't too much. In our house we eat instant soup and apples that I cut open on my desk, shuffling my papers out of the way, because the kitchen has no room for a table, or pintos and cheese from Felipe's, loaded up with the free parsley and green chile, dented cans of beer from the squalid bar in town, or the assortment of leftovers from the caterer. Twenty cold shrimp rolls. Half a tray of cut fruit, all the strawberries gone. A sleeve of melba toast.

We walk across the wooden walkways they've built around the town square—the kind that if we wore cowboy boots, we'd thump across ominously, spurs jangling—a dry fountain with a couple trees in the center. A guy in a gleaming red pickup screams past. I can hear the metal thrumming from his stereo through the closed windows. Then we pass one little store, a vintage store. I can see someone behind the counter.

"Let's go in here," Yahlie says.

Inside it's cold, dusty, with painted floorboards, a welcome mat. For sale is a Formica table, a carpeted couch, a velvet Elvis, a twelve-string guitar mounted in a frame, a restored Radio Flyer, stuff rich New Yorkers might dispatch staff to Texas to acquire. Country-swing records, high-waisted Jordache jeans with gold stitching, Walter Mondale campaign buttons in a teacup on the counter. Gem of a store. The kind of place Yahlie and I could kill two hours in.

A woman stands behind the glass counter, a sack of price tags emptied out in front of her. She has a look on her face like she'd been dreaming something sweet, or randy. Perched on a stool next to her is a bassinet holding a gurgly baby. I smell stinking diaper.

"I wonder if all this stuff has been here since the forties," Yahlie says, "and they just put up a sign that says Vintage." She finds an entire rack of plaid shirts in absurd color schemes, each with three buttons on the cuffs, arrows stitched on the breast pockets.

"Oh yeah," she says and picks one in khaki and AstroTurf green, tries it on behind a curtain in the back. She comes out, and it's not quite too small. "You look like Patsy Cline," I say.

"All I need," she says, "are some white patent-leather cowboy boots and a blond wig and I'd be Dolly Parton. I'm buying it."

While she's changing I wander back, pull back a brocade curtain hiding another room lit by a plastic chandelier, the walls wooden panels painted white, the ceiling shining tin. Every surface holding an object. Tea cups, old suitcases, a yellowing needlepoint in a frame. I can barely move, feel I might knock something over and ruin it. Like being inside a Christmas tree. I find a wooden chair. It's the green of a nickel at the bottom of a fountain, all chipped and crackling. Several others sit nearby, part of a set. But this one, it's more rough than all the others. I look at it and hear some far-off jukebox reverb, see the sun go down over a bluff, dancers shuffling, a woman singing into a microphone in a hall lit by strings of lights. This was the one its owner sat in. Every night, till it had to be given up. The tag says $60.

"You ready?" Yahlie says. She looks at the chair. "Whoa, sixty bucks."

We go to the counter to pay, and the woman has the baby against her shoulder, a white towel on its skull like a nun, and she holds it as she rings Yahlie up, one-handed. She has on one of the plaid shirts also, two yellows. She kneels slowly under the counter and retrieves a plastic bag, struggles to open the crinkly cellophane with the tips of her fingers. She shakes it with her one free hand. She can't be more than ten years older than we are. But still she seems young to have a baby. Yahlie asks, "How old is your baby?"

"Oh, she's seven months."

"She's adorable," Yahlie says. "What's her name?"

"Her name's Pearl," the woman says and smiles like she has a secret or that same randy, sweet dream still on her mind.

It's a name I've only imagined people having, women who waved to ships with handkerchiefs.

"That's a great name," Yahlie says.

The woman finally has the shirt in the bag and slides it across the counter.

"Thanks," she says. "And look."

With her free hand she untucks the yellow plaid shirt, and on her stomach is a tattoo, the word *Pearl* in a script I've never seen, a sweet, buttery flower of a thing.

Yahlie makes a little gasping noise. "That's amazing!" she says.

"She's the person I always wished I was," the woman says as she smooths down her shirt. "She's the chance I never had, so I gave her the name I always wished I had. We couldn't get any store space in

Austin so we're out here, just us and our antiques. All the shops in Austin are picked over, nothing good left. I think I got all the Bakelite jewelry in Texas right here. You can buy these shirts in Austin shops, but they're all from the eighties, John Travolta era. These are the real deal. You can tell from the tight weave, the heavy fabric, and the extra button on the cuff. You all should go out dancing."

She strokes the baby's back, taking the towel down, finally done talking. Her hair lies in a sandy-colored curl around her face, spilling down around the baby's head, which is smattered with fuzz in the same color. She rocks from heel to heel, and Pearl burbles.

"What did she say?" Yahlie says. "Cue ball? Did she say cue ball?"

"She says all kinds of things," the woman says. "Sometimes in her little talking, I hear the weirdest words. I can't wait till she starts talking real; she'll say the most amazing things."

Right then she lifts up one hand and waves out the front window. We turn and see a man in a baseball cap waving back, ambling past.

I stand there waiting, and Yahlie coos over the baby some more. I've never heard her do this in all the time we've been kicking around like two birds in the same cage. Who are you, talking in a voice with this lilting, whiny swirl? You can light four cigarettes with one match, and you drink six cups of coffee a day, and you fall asleep with the door to our house unlocked.

"We have dancing here in the veterans' hall, and every Sunday there's barbecue. Stop by, I'll take you if you're back by. My name's Beverly. Bev."

"That's a nice name too," Yahlie says.

The woman shrugs. "I don't know, it doesn't mean anything. It sounds made up."

Something about the way Yahlie is standing with her shoulder to me makes me go to the back room and pick up that chair and bring it to the counter.

"Think I'll buy this too."

I take out my wallet. There are seventy-four dollars in there.

"Great!" Bev says, ringing it up. "This is such a nice piece."

Yahlie is looking at me with that squinched, judgmental stare.

"What?" I say.

"You don't want the other ones too? Whole set back there," Bev says.

"I'll take just the one."

She rings me up, taking my cash. I'm ready to leave and edge toward the door with the chair. "It was so nice to meet you, Pearl!" Yahlie says, giving a little wave. Then Bev says, "You all got a car running out there?"

407

I can't tell if she means a car with the key in the ignition or a car that is not a complete piece of shit.

"Yeah," Yahlie says. "We're driving my car."

"Hate to impose if you got somewhere to be, but I thought I'd ask if you might give me a ride someplace. Somebody owes me money, and I think I can get it today if I could just get over there."

Yahlie and I look at each other.

"That is, I mean the two of us," Bev says.

Somewhere in the store is a ticking clock. The baby makes a noise. Yahlie's eyes are open wider than usual. Bev seems impossibly big and curvy standing behind the counter. I feel small and scrawny. The sun looks unreasonably bright through the shaded windows. Bev has squinted eyes, a deep, bloodless laugh line. Yahlie and I are staring each other down. Sometimes, I'll think I know what thing she wants to do and instead she does another. I think she wants to leave, and she keeps us sitting at the bar talking to two yahoos from Colorado Springs.

Before I have a chance to say anything, she decides for us.

"Sure!" she says, like we've been invited to the moon.

"Well, thanks. Sure appreciate it," Bev says, wandering off to some back room. "Just lemme get Pearl's stuff," she calls.

Now Yahlie's smiling. "What about the party?" I say, mumbling so Bev can't hear.

"We'll get there," she says. "This is exactly what we need."

"Why?" I say. "Why is this what we need?"

"Why'd you buy that?" she says. "Why do you need that chair?"

"You don't like it?"

"I do like it; I do like it."

Bev comes back with a lumpy bag over one shoulder and a wad of keys in one hand, and with the other she scoops up Pearl in her bassinet.

"Still your turn to drive," I say to Yahlie.

"All right!" she says.

Bev locks the store, and we walk outside on the wooden planks, back around to where the car is parked.

"Can't thank y'all enough for this," Bev says, standing at my elbow.

"Sure," I mumble.

Yahlie opens the car doors, an oven inside. "Wait," I say. "This chair won't fit in here with all of us."

"Oh, that's okay," Bev says. "We can come back for it." Then she puts the bassinet on the roof of the car, takes the chair, Pearl baking, and scurries to the store, unlocks it, and sort of bumps the chair through the door.

"Okay," I say. We get in the car, Bev in the back with the bassinet beside her. The diaper smell swirls, like something wafting up from a sewer, with fried funnel cake, and for a second I think I might barf. Yahlie's face is twisted, her nose crumpled into a sneer. She pushes the buttons in her arm rest, and the automatic windows roll slowly down.

"She need a seat or something?" I say.

"No," Bev says. "Y'all remember how to get on Route 1?"

"Where we headed?" Yahlie asks.

"Past Roundtop. We're not going far. I'll tell you when to turn off."

Except I forget what "far" means out here, and we drive twenty miles on Route 1 to another town altogether, where street signs appear on the sides of the road with names like sons and daughters, Gretchen and Randolph and MacKenzie, and the asphalt is fossilized. In the back, Bev talks.

"I got a couple of cousins out this way, and they tell me there's a great place to get some pie around here. Can't thank y'all enough. I just got my car back from the shop last week and didn't drive it but two days before whatever they said they fixed wasn't fixed and left me stuck at my store all night. Fuckin' assholes, I'm going to give them hell till they give me all my money back. Plus I got this ex, he owes me money. Y'all know anything about computers? Somebody gave us one, and I'm still trying to figure out how to turn it on."

Yahlie puts on the tape we were listening to, two guys singing over some reggae. The street signs roll past, and the names change to German, Hauptstrasse and Augsburg. Bev bites one fingernail.

Bev and I speak at the same time.

"So who owes you money again?" I say.

"Where you two got to go after this?" she says.

I turn around, and we wait for each other to talk. Yahlie answers before either of us. "We're going to Austin," she says. "See some friends."

Pearl starts to moan, but not really a moan, more like a hum, a hum with a skip.

"What's wrong, sweet pea?" Bev says.

After another couple of short hills, Bev says, "That's it," and Yahlie has to hit the brakes. The tires burr. We turn past a mailbox propped on a crooked piece of rebar jutting out of the ground. At the end of a driveway lined with a few cratered trees and pieces of things—a stained mattress, a tricycle, a pile of skinny PVC pipes, cinder blocks—is a dented trailer. We're in a haze of dust. Yahlie stops the car.

"Actually it's right back there," Bev says, pointing, her finger between the front seats.

Yahlie inches the car forward on the road past the trailer until I see there is another house, adobe like our casita, cracked and sinking into the ground. "That's it," Bev says. On the walls of the house, on the outside, is a faded poster with cars and someone's face. A screen door with a hole in it. Yahlie stops; Bev climbs out.

"Could you hold her?" Bev says to me. She's holding Pearl out at me like she might shove her through the window, and I smell the smell again.

"Could I what?"

"Just hold her for one second while I run up there?"

She has a rolled-up piece of paper in one hand, like it materialized from nothing, tucked under her thumb as she holds Pearl, and if I don't take her, she'll just drop her there in the dirt and split, so I open the door, and next thing, Pearl is in my hands. Bev gives me a punch on the shoulder with two fingers, like she's my crazy aunt, and says, "Thanks, doll," and walks fast through the dirt toward the house. I have my hands under Pearl's armpits, and she's making the same noise, hum, hum. She's heavy, like a full gallon jug.

Or a dictionary. The dictionary my parents owned and I flipped through, looking at all the tiny illustrations. If the dictionary were her and had a beating heart.

"What the hell is this lady doing?" I say.

"Dunno," Yahlie says. She giggles a little and shuts off the car.

Bev pounds on the casita door. She lifts a fist and beats, her arm like a mace, and yells. Between strokes she stands there, arms loose at her sides. She yells when she pounds so we can't hear what she's saying. She grabs the doorknob with both hands and pushes with her foot.

"What kind of a scam do you suppose *this* is?" Yahlie says, laughing, thumping the gas pedal with her foot.

"I think this is what's known as the breaking-and-entering scam," I say. "I tried to ask her, but you didn't let me. Goddamn, the baby needs a diaper change."

"Okay, okay," she says. "We'll go right after this. You're not comfortable with other people's discourses."

I never know what to say when she says stuff like that. Why use such a word? I feel like a flock of birds has flown into the cage.

410

After a minute Pearl mumbles again. Yahlie says, "One of her eyes is smaller than the other."

So it is. One an almond, one a skipping stone. Pearl twists her head back and forth, from my face to the house. I sit there with the door open, one foot in the dirt.

"And she's fatter than you are," Yahlie says.

She *is* fatter than me. She's like I imagine an elf would be. I am a skeleton compared to her.

Bev is still whacking at the door.

"Why isn't she crying?" I ask. "You'd think she would be crying, since her diaper's all shitty."

"Dunno," Yahlie says. "Poor baby with a shitty diaper."

"I think she must be used to this."

"Used to what? Being all poopy?" Yahlie laughs her sniveling laugh, the one she has when she knows I'm not going to laugh at her joke.

"No, being left with strangers. This lady's leaving her with *us*? She's not thinking straight. And I don't think that door's going to open."

Pearl squirms. I have her held away from me. I should hold her to my chest, but I can't. She seems to weigh more now. Pearl looks right at me, and I can see the way she'll be when she's older and looks at someone and says what she wants most in the world, and I think, I've got a person's whole body in my hands. A wedge of fear rises up into my ribcage. I can see myself in the rearview mirror, the back of Pearl's head below my chin. The two of us reflected together. Under my eyes are gray half-moons, like bruises.

Yahlie says, "You want me to hold her?"

"No," I say. And it has that edge that happens without my meaning to; I am shutting the door on her, that blister that rises up between us. "I can do it," I say.

"Okay," she says. "*Fine*."

Bev is at the house looking through the window, her hands around her eyes. I get a twinge in my chest, and my arms are tired. Yahlie is sulking, leaning on the windowsill. I get the feeling like something is coming, and I want to get the hell out of here. And if there's one thing I can't stand, it's Yahlie sulking.

"Okay," I say. "You hold her."

I give Pearl to Yahlie. She says, "That's right, sweet pea." I get out. Bev turns away from the house and takes a couple steps, like she's about to give up, then she sees me and stops. The scabbed yard between me and her seems like a long way. I should just let her give up. The place is a trap about to close. I walk across the dust, and as I get closer, I see her eyes, creases circling them, a wrinkle in her skin that isn't going anywhere.

"I can't get the door open," she says.

"I can see that," I say.

"You got an idea about how to do it?"

"You sure you don't want to come back later? Maybe whoever it is will be back then. Somebody could see us."

"Nobody's going to see us."

"How do you know?"

"Because I did it once before," she says.

She leans on the post holding up the awning built out over the roof. I put a foot up on the crusty patch of adobe that is serving as a porch. Bev isn't a bit scared, like it's all the same to her, breaking and entering, bobbling the baby on her knee. I want her to see that I am scared, but I realize, then, that I am not. The collar of her shirt is rumpled.

"How'd you do it that time?"

"It was open," she says. "I thought the door would be open."

I go to the door, rattle the doorknob. It gives a little, and I'm thinking there must not be any deadbolt. A weak lock.

I'll admit to one thing about this happening: Up until right then, I had only watched this sort of thing on television, and I didn't believe that I was strong enough to do it. But I know about doors, about roofs, and windows, chimneys. Soffit, fascia, rake, slope. From my father, who could build everything. From my failure at architecture. Yahlie doesn't know this about me, that I know anything besides where to buy tacos and how to pump my own gas.

I knew where to kick.

"You have to be fast, though," I say.

I stand back and kick the door with the heel of my boot. The sound is hollow. It doesn't open. I kick again, then it cracks open and hits something inside. I have to stop myself from saying, Yes! The door doesn't swing; I was expecting it to swing. The doorjamb is barely broken.

The foyer is dark, and it smells of a thousand burned breakfasts and vinegary coffee and fertilizer, and daylight comes in from somewhere in the back. Bev stomps past me and tramples a pair of work boots on the floor. To the right is a dining room with a table full of papers and jars, a tarnished chandelier hanging. I can hear Bev thumping around, opening drawers. I squint outside past the drapes and can barely see the car, can't see Yahlie. The papers are all faded newspapers; the jars are all half-filled with liquid, something stewed and putrid. The smell knocks me away.

To one side is a dim bedroom, and to the other, through a cramped arch, is the kitchen. Dishes sit scattered everywhere, the counters lined with soda cans. All Mountain Dew. Some are bottles, all dusty. Another arch has an enormous chunk knocked out of it so it seems to droop. It leads to a room carpeted in brown shag, dark except for a flickering TV, set to the news with the sound down. Bev is against a wall lined with dressers, ruffling her hands through some drawers.

I say, "So what the hell are you looking for? Wanna find it quicker?"

"My ex owes me money," she says. She slams a drawer and walks toward where the daylight is coming from, what I suppose is another bedroom. She stops and stares, her arms hanging.

The light streams through a sliding glass door, and in the bedroom is a man in a wheelchair.

"You didn't hear me knocking?" she says in some twangy accent that wasn't there before.

His chair takes up almost the entire room. Another TV sits against one wall, a neatly made bed on the other. He is staring at us, frozen, frowning. Between his eyes—a green that seems to be almost yellow—between two dark eyebrows is a line that looks as though it were drawn with charcoal. A plastic tube snakes downward from somewhere behind his neck. One hand is on the wheelchair's joystick, about to push it. He has a mustache and two-day stubble. Mountain Dew cans in here too. His other hand rests on a tiny tray attached to the chair's arm. Tied to the chair's other arm is a piece of black cloth with some design on it I can't see, maybe a flag. He looks strong. A shakiness begins around my knees, and I want out of there. Any second, a guy in a truck will roll up and see the busted door. Yahlie is out in the car.

"Arman been here today?" Bev asks. I can't understand what name she says. Armand? Herman? The man doesn't answer. His lips seem to be moving, closed, churning underneath the mustache.

"Arman taking real good care of you as usual, right?" she says in a voice all sarcasm.

"Look," I say, "we've got to go."

She ignores me. She seems to be awaiting an explanation of some kind. On the wood-paneled wall, I see a shelf with a stereo and a lamp, some magazines, another Mountain Dew bottle. Outside are two squares of concrete. He has an okay view—the land slopes slightly away from the house, must catch the sunset.

413

"Bev, let's go," I say, hoping he won't hear me.

"Just a sec," she says, a horse's bite to her voice. To him she says, "You can tell him I was here, that I came looking for what he owes me. He can figure it out for himself whether I found it or not."

The line between the man's eyes seems to stiffen, and he is not looking at Bev but at me, and I can see that he will tell anybody whatever the hell he wants.

Then she stalks off, like she's made her point and that's that. I try not to look at the man as I follow her, but I do anyway, and his eyes are shifted as far in their sockets as possible, watching me. I don't say one thing to him. The shallowest thought pops into my head—can he move his neck.

Bev goes to the kitchen, starts opening cabinets, yanking on drawers.

"Okay," I say to her. "Now we really have to go. You didn't say anyone was here."

"I didn't know he was here."

"The dude's in a wheelchair," I say. "How could he not be here?"

"You don't know anything," she says. "Quit getting in the way so I can find it, okay?" She looks up at me, her iceberg of a jaw jutting away from her face.

She yanks on one more drawer. Inside is mismatched silverware—she pushes it around, finds an envelope. She flips it open, and inside is a wad of what looks like tens and ones. She lets out a long sigh.

"See?" she says. "All done." She walks out the open door, crossing the long distance to the car. I could fix it, fix the door just like it was. There are no cars out front but Yahlie's. She's in the front seat with the baby. I leave the door, follow Bev out. She jumps in the backseat.

"Oh," she says. "Sorry." She laughs nervously. She stands up, twitters around to the front, and lifts Pearl out of Yahlie's hands.

"Were you a good girl?" she says.

"Yes, she's a good girl," Yahlie says.

"Can we go?" I say, and Yahlie gives me a mean look.

Yahlie turns the car around in its wind-up-toy way. As we go back on the main road, Yahlie driving cautiously, a rickety pickup blows past in the other direction, breaking the sound barrier, someone with his bare arm hanging out the window. In the rearview I see Bev whip her head around.

"What color was that?" she says. "What color? Blue? Blue?"

"Keep driving," I say.

"I *am*," Yahlie says.

"I know you are. I didn't mean it like that. Jesus."

The road spools back the way it came. A string of unimportant questions forms in my head: Can he talk? Does he watch TV? How does he take a shit? I try to push the feeling away. Yahlie doesn't turn the tape on. The two of them in the back seem to creep over my shoulder, and I have to look out the window at the road's white line.

Bev sits in the back and starts singing to Pearl, sounding like June Carter as she holds Pearl's hands, teaching her to clap, singing, "The wheels on the bus go round and round, round and round." But then in the middle, she seems to forget that Pearl is on her lap, and she looks out the window, starting another song.

"I do believe, in all the things you see."

The return drive seems to take seconds, a drive Bev might do every day. Maybe this is what she does every time she runs out of cash, and this is like going to the supermarket. We leave her at the shop. As she gets out, setting the bassinet on the ground to put Pearl inside, Yahlie asks, "Got a ride home?"

"Oh, sure. My friend picks me up when she gets done at the restaurant. But y'all did me a special favor, taking me out that way."

"What about the chair?" I say.

"Oh, right," she says, and we all get out of the car. She walks bumping the bassinet against her hip, sets it down again. She unlocks the store. She doesn't let me in. She skitters the chair out on the concrete, its legs screeching.

"Y'all enjoy."

The chair sits like a throne, ruined. The store is dark and she's gone and it's all over. Yahlie sucks air in and blows it out.

"Good thing you bought *that*," she says.

She is a cruel person sometimes. I think of just leaving it there. But it's mine, I bought it. I look at it, and I can't leave it. Separated from all the others. I pick it up and wrench it into the backseat.

"Dipshit," I say. "It was your idea to drive out there to begin with, and you're going to give me a bunch of shit for buying a chair? What are we doing? It's like what, three thirty? And we're how far from the interstate? You're the one who wants to go to Kirsten's party."

"You are so impossible to be around," she says.

Both of us stand on the wooden sidewalk waiting for the other.

"You drive," Yahlie says.

The car whirs, and we can't go without keeping the windows down. The sky, now a preposterous blue.

415

We drive for a while, and I contemplate how to suggest that we skip the party, but it seems impossible, now that we've driven all this way. We stop at a casino gas station once it gets dark. Yahlie goes inside, frowning, counting how much money she has left. I stay behind.

Another time, we were at a rodeo with some guys. She hated it, the ropes, the shrieking; she thought the horses were frightened. I thought of it right then, sitting on the back of the car in the waning heat. She had sat hunched on the wooden bench and kept saying, "It's just so awful." I said, "You want to leave?" And she was so upset that she couldn't even shake her head no. I wasn't thinking about the horses, or her. I was enjoying the feeling of tapping someone's back in comfort. I wasn't being true. She sat there, her tan face turning the color of cantaloupe. My tapping her back seemed to do nothing. So I stopped, and I watched the calf roping. I had to leave her sitting there. Why did I do that? Why did I leave her there like that, staring at her feet while I watched calves being lassoed and tied?

I sit on the back of the car, clammy, with the lights flashing and the sense that a wasp is hovering nearby and must be shooed away.

When she returns, she says, "I'll drive," even though it's still my turn.

When we get to Kirsten's ranch house, paper lanterns rise up, lighting the whole house. There are fifteen or so people under the carport with lawn chairs. Through the windows I see a lamp turned on.

We park, and as we get out, somebody shouts, "What took you so long?" like they've known us forever and have thrown this party just for us.

A girl with black hair and skin like a china saucer comes up and says, "Hey!" As we walk up the dying lawn, something returns to Yahlie, that lightness of hers.

"We thought you were Todd coming back with the beer," the woman says. She hugs Yahlie.

"This is Kirsten," Yahlie says to me.

"You guys," Kirsten says, "later you should check out the installation in the carport. So glad you guys could participate."

I don't know what the hell she's talking about. Kirsten shows us inside. Two brocade couches and a plastic shelf full of books, two desks, one with two computers on it.

"Kirsten is writing her dissertation," Yahlie says.

"Yep," Kirsten says. "Write my dissertation, then get fucked up. That is my plan."

"Good plan," Yahlie says.

I knock my foot on an amp and pass a guy, a weedy stallion of a guy, with a petulant lip, a Grand Canyon dimple, an entire sleeve of tattoos, all tinted green.

"Cheers," he says.

I nod at the guy.

"Hi," says Yahlie.

"How are you, dollface?" says Kirsten and kisses him on the cheek. Whatever languid game exists between women, with men as the spoils, she will be the winner. I look at Yahlie, since this is usually the type of thing we agree on exactly without having to say a word, but I can't catch her eye.

Yahlie goes off with Kirsten, and I try to handle the chatter. I stand in the kitchen for a while, find a beer, and drink under the light of the stove. The guy with the tattoos comes up and stands near me, his arm on their funk-brown refrigerator.

He says to me, "So what's your story?"

I run through some possible answers.

"We're from New Mexico. Except I'm not originally. I'm from the suburbs."

"Cool," he says. He nods, a marionette head.

"What's your story?" I ask.

"I'm getting my doctorate in Latin American studies."

"Oh. I'm an architect. Except not right now, I mean. Or I will be. Maybe."

He nods his head, scratches a green tattoo. I open my mouth to say one other thing, but only air comes out. He looks at me from the corner of his eye.

"You have a nice laugh," he says. "Just the right amount of nervous. I like it."

Someone gets his attention. "Danny," they say, and he wanders off.

I stand there for a moment in the swirl of people in the kitchen, empties lining the countertops, and the smell of that man's house returns, and I feel I want to run away.

I go to the bathroom and pull down my jeans. I look at my stomach, flat as a crushed tumbleweed. In the crotch of my underwear is a smear of blood. In the front of my stomach, I feel a roiling. I piss and it feels cold. I try to think about what my laugh sounds like. I think of that man

417

looking out the sliding glass door at the same wicked sun, rising every day.

In the chattering room I can't see Yahlie. I search for another beer and go outside to the carport. The art consists of ancient science movies on 16 mm projected onto the wall. No one around. I sit on a lawn chair. The film is of black string, twitching. It reaches a picture of a mountain, then returns to the string. The same thing over and over, it must be broken. String, mountain. The audio still runs, stuff about moving glaciers, the extraction of oil from the earth.

After a while Yahlie comes out. "These people aren't anything like I remember," she says. She sips her beer. The light from the projector hits underneath her chin. She says, "I loved that lady's tattoo. She's alone in the desert with that baby, and she was so happy."

"She didn't seem so happy," I say.

"You didn't ask me about the baby."

I try to think how to explain what was in that house.

"I'm sorry I called you a dipshit," I say. "I'm sorry I didn't ask. How was the baby?"

"It's okay," she says. "You were talking about yourself when you said that."

She pauses and looks out into the driveway.

"The baby didn't make a sound," she says, "just stared at the door the whole time."

"Jesus," I say.

"I wanted to take the baby with us," she says. "Either of us would be better than that lady."

I look at her. "Not sure about me," I say. "But you would. You would be."

I catch her eye and it says, Thank you.

"Listen " I say. "I might be hungover tomorrow."

"That's right," she says. "Shit faced again!"

"Great," I say. "Then you can drive."

She turns, and the light disappears from her chin. "I want you to drive," she says.

"Why?" I say.

"Because I drove all day. So," she says, lifting her hand in a lilting way, as though presenting me with some small object, "you should quit drinking now so you'll be sober when I'm drunk."

"Okay," I say. "Done. Herewith, my last evening beer."

She says, "Look, I can fix this." She gets up and fiddles with the projector. "Was the house creepy?"

"Yeah. It was. There were soda cans everywhere. It was creepy. It was."

She twists a knob, and the projector starts winding. "Look at that," she says. "I got it."

She looks at the projector like it's a statue she just carved. The tape winds neatly, and once that mountain appears, the picture continues, a pan across valleys, a distant forest. The light from the party makes her cheeks yellow. I stand up and stick my hand in a crevice in the projector, its light shining on my fingers.

"You want to go back inside?" she says.

"I'm thinking about it," I say.

The audio tape beeps and now says stuff about molecules. The paper lanterns above us swing. A breeze has appeared from nowhere. I feel like for a second it might be winter. I walk behind the carport, look up at the roof of the house and the clean, golden line it makes in the sky, wander back. I feel the urge to go for a long walk in the dark and look for lights in the windows of other people's houses.

I sit back down and she is still there.

"You know what?" I say.

"What?" she says.

"You know what?"

"What?!" she says, and begins to laugh. That laugh.

I am tempted to tell her all of it from the beginning. Or the end. The man in his wheelchair. How he looked at me with that look that said, Everything is wrong.

"It's just that—"

"It's just *what*?" she says. "Stop fucking around."

"It's just that I wonder if I'll ever be pregnant again."

She has been twisting her hair and stops.

"That's all," I say.

She sits very still, and I can see that it has ebbed again so that now I am the one who's afraid.

"Why do you say that?" she says.

I couldn't talk for a second. I had to wipe my face because I was crying. I was thinking about my laugh, and how it sounds compared to hers. But that wasn't what I was thinking about. Also, his look said, Things will be right. Then one of the lanterns sways in the breeze again and begins gently hitting the carport wall, ticking. A cicada clicks in the trees behind the house.

"It just might not be in the cards for me," I say.

419

What I don't say is, Because if I ever sat still I might die. Because I don't believe I'll ever be lucky, because I think I'm a slum. Because right here, it's enough.

"Yes, it is," she says, softly, her eyes ringed in gold.

The certainty of it! It felt like a gift. I wondered if this was the moment when a door might open, when this feeling would become something I could just pass through the window, or sell to someone for a high price, or just abandon on a wooden sidewalk.

Nominated by Robert Long Foreman

A SMALL SACRIFICE FOR AN ENORMOUS HAPPINESS

fiction by JAI CHAKRABARTI

from A PUBLIC SPACE

From his balcony, Nikhil waited and watched the street as hyacinth braiders tied floral knots, rum sellers hauled bags of ice, and the row of elderly typists, who'd seemed elderly to him since he'd been a boy, struck the last notes of their daily work. Beside him on the balcony, his servant, Kanu, plucked at the hair that grew from his ears.

"Keep a lookout for babu," Nikhil shouted to Kanu. "I'll check on the tea."

Kanu was so old he could neither see nor hear well, but he still accepted each responsibility with enthusiasm.

The tea was ready, as were the sweets, the whole conical pile of them—the base layer of pistachio mounds, the center almond bars that Nikhil had rolled by hand himself, and on the top three lychees from the garden, so precariously balanced, a single misstep would have upset their delectable geometry.

When he returned to the balcony he saw Sharma walking up the cobbled lane, his oiled hair shining in the late afternoon light. The typists greeted him with a verse from a Bollywood number—Sharma's boxer's jaw and darling eyes reminded the typists of an emerging movie star—and Sharma shook his head and laughed.

Kanu limped downstairs to let Sharma in, and Nikhil waited in the living room while the two of them made their way up.

"And what is the special occasion?" Sharma said, eyeing the pile of confections with a boyish grin.

Nikhil refused to say. He allowed Sharma to have his fill, watching with satisfaction as his fingers became honey-glazed from the offering.

Afterward, when they lay on the great divan—hand-carved and older than his grandmother's ghost—Nikhil breathed deeply to calm his heart. He feared the words would be eaten in his chest, but he'd been planning to tell Sharma for days, and there was no going back now. As evening settled, the air between them became heavy with the sweetness of secrecy, but secrecy had a short wick.

"My dearest, fairest boy," he said. "I want our love to increase."

Sharma raised his eyebrows, those lines thickly drawn, nearly fused. Who better than Sharma to know Nikhil's heart? Who but Sharma to take it all in stride?

"I desire to have a child with you," Nikhil said.

Nikhil had trouble reading Sharma's expression in the waning light, so he repeated himself. His fingers were shaking, but he took Sharma's hand anyway, gave it a squeeze.

"I heard you the first time," Sharma said.

A rare cool wind had prompted Nikhil to turn off the ceiling fan, and now he could hear the rum sellers on the street enunciating prices in singsong Urdu.

He touched Sharma's face, traced the line of his jaw, unsure still of how his lover had received his news. Likely, Sharma was still mulling—he formed his opinions, Nikhil believed, at the pace the street cows strolled.

Nikhil waited out the silence as long as he could. "Listen," he finally said. "The country is changing."

"A child diapered by two men," said Sharma. "Your country is changing faster than my country is changing. What about the boys from Kerala?"

They had learned about a schoolteacher and a postal clerk who'd secretly made a life together. Unfashionably attired and chubby cheeked, they seemed too dull for the news. A few months ago, locals threw acid on their faces. Even in the black and white of the photographs, their scars, along the jaw, the nose, the better half of a cheek. Ten years since man had landed on the moon, and still.

"We are not boys from Kerala. We are protected."

No ruse better than a woman in the home, Nikhil had argued over a year ago, and eventually Sharma had agreed to a marriage of convenience. Kang, who had loved Nikhil through his childhood and even through his years of chasing prostitutes, had arranged for a village woman who knew about the two men's relationship but would never tell.

Nikhil rummaged through his almirah and returned with a gift in his hands. "You close your eyes now."

"Oh, Nikhil." But Sharma closed his eyes, accustomed now perhaps to receiving precious things.

Around Sharma's neck, Nikhil tied his dead mother's necklace. It had been dipped in twenty-four carats of gold by master artisans of Agra. Miniature busts of Queen Victoria decorated its circumference. A piece for the museums, a jeweler had once explained, but Nikhil wanted Sharma to have it. That morning, when he'd visited the family vault to retrieve it, he'd startled himself with the enormity of what he was giving away, but what better time than now, as they were about to begin a family?

"Promise you'll dream about a child with me."

"It is beautiful, and I will wear it every day, even though people will wonder what is that under my shirt."

"Let them wonder."

"You are entirely mad. Mad is what you are."

Nikhil was pulled back to the divan. Sharma, lifting Nikhil's shirt, placed a molasses square on his belly, teasing a trail of sweetness with his tongue.

Nikhil closed his eyes and allowed himself to be enjoyed. Down below, the rum sellers negotiated, the prices of bottles fluctuating wildly.

Afterward, they retired to the roof. Their chadors cut off the cold, but Nikhil still shivered. When Sharma asked what the matter was, Nikhil kissed the spot where his eyebrows met. There was another old roof across the street, where grandmothers were known to gossip and eavesdrop, but he did not care. Let them hear, he thought, let them feel this wind of enormous change.

The next morning, while Sharma washed, Nikhil said, "I want you to toss the idea to your wife. Get Tripti used to the matter."

Sharma dried himself so quickly he left behind footprints on the bathroom's marble floor. "Toss the idea to my wife. Get her used to the matter," Sharma said, before he changed into his working clothes, leaving Nikhil to brood alone.

Tripti would have few issues with the arrangement of a child, Nikhil believed. After all, at the time of her marriage to Sharma, her family was mired in bankruptcy, her father had left them nothing but a reputation for drink and dishonesty, and she herself—insofar as he recalled

423

from his sole meeting with her, at the wedding—was a dour, spiritless creature who deserved little of the bounty that had been provided her. What little else he knew was from Kanu's reports. Extremely pliable, Kanu had first said. Then, closer to the wedding: A little stubborn about the choice of sweets. She wants village kind. On that note, Nikhil had wilted—let her have her desserts, he'd said, the wedding paid for, and the matter removed from mind.

The next few days, when Sharma was away at the village and at the foundry, Nikhil paced around the house, overcome by the idea of a child. He'd always dreamed of becoming a father but had never believed it would be his due until this year's monsoon, when, in the middle of a deluge, his forty-two-year-old sister had given birth to a girl. The rain had been so fierce no ambulance could ferry them to the hospital, so the elderly women of the family assumed the duties of midwifery and delivered the child themselves. The first moment he saw his niece he nearly believed in God and, strangely, in his own ability— his *right*—to produce so perfect a thing.

He couldn't bring Sharma to his sister's house to meet his new niece, so the next week he'd spent their Thursday together sharing photos; if Sharma experienced the same lightness of being, he didn't let it show. All Sharma said was, "Quite a healthy baby she is."

It was true. She'd been born nine pounds two ounces. The family had purchased a cow so that fresh milk would always be available.

Nikhil convinced himself that Sharma had opened his heart to the idea of fathering, but the exuberance of this conclusion led to certain practical questions. Sharma's wife would be the carrier of the child, but where would the child live? In Sharma's house in the village, or in Nikhil's house here in the city? If she lived in the village, which Nikhil admitted was the safer option, how would Nikhil father her, how would she receive a proper education?

These questions consumed the hours. When he went to check on his tenants, he was distracted and unable to focus on their concerns. A leaky toilet, a broken window, the group of vagrants who'd squatted outside one of his properties—all these matters seemed trivial compared to his imagined child's needs.

The next week, the afternoon before he would see Sharma again, he stepped into a clothing store on Rashbehari Avenue to calm his mind. It was a shop he'd frequented to purchase silk kurtas for Sharma or paisley shirts for himself. He told the attendants he needed an exceptional outfit for his niece. They combed the shelves and found a white dress with a lacy pink bow. He imagined his daughter wearing it. From his dreaming he was certain a girl would come out of their love—Shristi was what he'd named her—Shristi enunciating like a princess, Shristi riding her bicycle up and down Kakulia Lane.

Early on, they'd agreed Nikhil would avoid the foundry, but he was feeling so full of promise for Shristi that he did not deter himself from continuing down Rashbehari Avenue toward Tollygunge Phari, nor did he prevent himself from walking to the entrance of Mahesh Steel and asking for his *friend.*

Sharma emerged from the uneven music of metalworking with a cigarette between his lips. His Apollonian features were smeared with grease. His hands constricted by thick welding gloves, which excluded the possibility of even an accidental touch. When he saw Nikhil, Sharma scowled. "Sir," he said, "you'll have the parts tomorrow."

Though he knew Sharma was treating him as a customer for good reason, the tone still stung. Nikhil whispered, "See what I have brought." He produced the perfect baby girl dress.

"You have lost your soup," Sharma whispered back. Then, so everyone could hear, "Babu, you'll have the parts tomorrow. Latest, tomorrow."

Nikhil tried again, "Do you see the collar, the sweet lace?"

"You should go to your home now," Sharma said. "Tomorrow, I'll see you."

But that Thursday Sharma failed to visit. Nikhil and Kanu waited until half past nine and then ate their meal together by lamplight.

Thursdays because it was on a Thursday that they had met three years ago, that time of year when the city is at its most bearable, when the smell of wild hyacinth cannot be outdone by the stench of the gutters, because it is after the city's short winter, which manages, despite its brevity, to birth more funerals than any other time of year. In the city's spring, two men walking the long road from Santiniketan back to Kolkata—because the bus has broken and no one is interested in its repair—are not entirely oblivious to the smells abounding in the wildflower fields, not oblivious at all to their own smells.

He supposed he had fetishized Sharma's smell from the beginning, that scent of a day's honest work. The smell of steel, of the cheapest soap. The smell of a shirt that had been laundered beyond its time. The smell of his night-bound stubble. He allowed his hand to linger on Sharma's wrist, pretending he was trying to see the hour. An hour before sunset. An hour after. He did not remember exactly when they parted. What did it matter.

What mattered were the coincidences of love. The day he saw Sharma for the second time he counted among the small miracles of his life.

Sharma was drinking tea at the tea stall on Kakulia Lane. He was leaning the weight of his body on the rotting wood of the counter, listening to the chai wallah recount stories. Later, he would learn that Sharma had landed a job at a nearby foundry and that this tea stall was simply the closest one, but in that moment he did not think of foundries or work or any other encumbrance, he thought instead of the way Sharma cradled his earthen teacup, as if it were the Koh-i-noor.

Oh, he had said, did you and I . . . that broken bus . . . What an evening, yes?

A question that led to Thursdays. Two years of Thursdays haunted by fear of discovery, which led to a wedding, because a married man who arrived regularly at Kakulia Lane could not be doing anything but playing backgammon with his happenstance friend. What followed was a year of bliss. He considered this time their honeymoon. They were as seriously committed as any partners who'd ever shared a covenant, and shouldn't that show?

Sharma did visit the following Thursday, though the matter of his absence the week before was not raised. Instead of their usual feast at home, they ate chili noodles doused with sugary tomato sauce at Jimmy's Chinese Kitchen, along with stale pastries for dessert. Sharma was wearing Nikhil's family necklace under his shirt, with just an edge of the queen's image peeking out from the collar. Seeing his gift on his lover's body released Nikhil from his brood, and for the first time that night, he met Sharma's gaze.

"You're cross with me," Sharma offered.

It wasn't an apology, but Nikhil was warming to the idea of a reconciliation.

"Anyway, Tripti and I have been discussing the issue of the baby."

Tripti and I. He so rarely heard the name Tripti from Sharma's lips, but that she could be in league with him, discussing an *issue*? Unjust was what it was.

"It's in part the physical act. We eat our meals together. We take walks to the bazaar or to the pond. But that, no, we do not do that."

"Don't worry," Nikhil said. "I shall do the deed. I shall be the child's father." While it was unpleasant to imagine the act of copulation itself, he'd studied the intricacies of the reproductive process and believed his chances were excellent for a single, well-timed session to yield its fruit.

"But you can barely stand the smell of a woman."

What passed over Sharma's face may have been described as amusement, but Nikhil refused to believe his lover wasn't taking him seriously—not now that he'd opened his heart like a salvaged piano. "Sharma," Nikhil said. "It shall be a small sacrifice for an enormous happiness."

"Oh Nikhil, do you not see that we are already happy? Anything more might upset what we have. We should not tempt the gods."

Nikhil ground away at the pastry in his mouth until the memory of sweetness dispersed. The things Sharma said. As if there were a cap on happiness in this world. It was Sharma's village religion talking again, but there was something more. He sensed in the way Sharma held his hands in his lap, the way he kept to the far side of the bed when they retired for the night, that Tripti had wormed something rotten into him. He was vulnerable that way, Sharma was.

When Nikhil awoke the next morning, Sharma had already departed, but in the bathroom, which he'd lovingly reconstructed from Parisian prints, with a claw-foot tub and a nearly functioning bidet, he found Sharma's stubble littering the marble sink. Sharma had always been fastidious in the house, taking care to wipe away evidence of his coming and going, and the patches of facial hair offended Nikhil. He studied their formations, searching for patterns. When nothing could be discerned, he called for Kanu to clean the mess.

Only one train went to Bilaspur, a commuter local. For two hours, Nikhil was stuck next to the village yeoman, who'd gone to the city to peddle his chickens and was clutching the feet of the aging pair he'd been unable to sell, and the bleary-eyed dairyman, who smelled of curd and urine. The only distraction was the girl with the henna-tinged hair who'd boarded between stops to plead for money, whose face looked entirely too much like the child he envisioned fathering.

When he reached the Bilaspur terminus, he was relieved to see the rows of wildflowers on either side of the tracks, to smell the bloom of begonias planted by the stationmaster's post.

It wasn't difficult finding Sharma's home. With money from the foundry and regular gifts of cash from Nikhil, Sharma had purchased several hectares of hilltop land and built a concrete slab of a house, garrisoned with a garden of squash, cucumber, and eggplant, and with large windows marking the combined living and dining area. Nikhil found the structure too modern, but that was Sharma's way—he had never swooned over the old colonials of Kakulia Lane.

From inside the house, Nikhil could hear the BBC broadcast, which was strange given Tripti didn't understand English. Nikhil tiptoed toward the open living room window, and from there he spied. Sharma's wife was holding a book on her lap, mouthing back the words of the BBC announcer.

"BER-LIN WALL," she said. "DOWNING STREET."

She had a proud bookish nose—adequately sized for the resting of eyeglasses—a forehead that jutted too far forward, reminding Nikhil of a depiction of Neanderthal gatherers, and the slightest of chins, which gave to her appearance a quality of perpetual meekness. Her sari was stained with years of cooking. Her only adornments were the bright red bindi on her forehead and the brass bangles that made music whenever she turned a page.

There were certain topics Nikhil and Sharma had left to the wind, foremost the matter of Sharma's marriage. In the beginning, Nikhil experienced a shooting pain in his abdomen whenever he thought about Sharma and Tripti coexisting in domestic harmony, though over the past few months that pain had numbed; the less he'd thought of Tripti, the less she existed, but here she was now—the would-be mother of his child. He rapped on the grill of her window.

"Just leave it there," Tripti said without looking up from her book.

It was the first time she'd ever spoken to him. Her voice, which was composed of rich baritones, seemed rather forceful, and her demeanor, that of the lady of a proper house, left him feeling uncertain about his next move. At last, he said in a Bengali so refined it could have passed for the old tongue of Sanskrit, "Perhaps you've mistaken me for the bringer of milk. I am not he. Madam, you know me but you do not know me."

The words had sounded elegant in his head, but when spoken aloud he flushed at their foolishness.

She looked up to study his face, then his outfit, even his shoes now rimmed with the village's mud. "I know who you are," she finally said. "Why don't you come inside?"

He had not planned beyond this moment. He had allowed his feet to step onto the train at Howrah, imagined a brief meeting, a quick exchange at the doorstep, ending with a mutually desirable pact.

"I can't stay long," he said. Sharma would be home in another hour, and Nikhil had no wish to see Sharma in the same vicinity as his wife.

While he settled into the living room, Tripti puttered around the kitchen. The house was decorated with wood carvings and paintings of gods and goddesses. Parvati, the wife of Shiva, smiled beatifically from a gilded frame, and her son the remover of obstacles was frozen inside a copper statuette. From the plans Sharma had gloated over, he knew a hallway connected the three bedrooms of the house—one for Tripti, one for Sharma, and the last a prayer room—and he wondered now who slept where, how their mornings were arranged, what politics were discussed, what arguments were had, where the laundry was piled.

Tripti brought two cups of tea and a plate of sweets. "Homemade," she said. He'd been raised to fear milk sweets from unfamiliar places, but out of politeness, he took the first bite—a little lumpy, only mildly flavorful.

"Sharma is always praising your cooking," he said, but it was a lie. They never bothered to discuss Tripti's cooking; in fact, Nikhil had teased that they were lovers because of his talents in the kitchen. Still, it felt appropriate to compliment this woman, and he continued in this fashion, standing to admire the Parvati painting, which he described as "terribly and modernly artful."

"Nikhil Babu," she interrupted. "Are you here to discuss the matter of the child?"

He sighed with relief. Until that moment, he'd been unsure about how to broach the subject.

"You know," she said. "We discuss our days. We may not be lovers, but we are fair friends."

He experienced what felt like an arthritic pain in his shoulder, but it was only the collar of his jealousy. At least they were not *best* friends.

She pointed to the book on her coffee table, an English language primer. "Unfortunately, it's just not on our horizon. You see, I'm going to university. I shall be a teacher."

"University," he said. "But you did not even finish eighth grade."

"That is true, but at Bilaspur College, the principal is willing to accept students who display enormous curiosities."

He found it improbable that she would be able to absorb the principles of higher learning, but he had no particular wish to impede her efforts. Education was a challenge he understood. "You want to improve yourself? Wonderful. If you are with child, I will have tutors come to you. Not professors from Bilaspur College. Real academics from the city."

But it was as if she had not heard him at all. She submerged a biscuit in her tea and stared out into the garden.

"Whose happiness are you after, Nikhil Babu?" she said. "Yours and yours only?"

He found himself grinding his teeth. The great bane of modernity. Though the country had opened itself to the pleasures of the other world—cream-filled pastries, the films of Godard, a penchant for pristine white-sand beaches—he did not care for the consequences, the dissolution of ordering traditions, with whose loss came poor speech, thoughtless conduct. A village woman addressing him without the slightest deference.

"Perhaps you should enroll in a school for proper manners," he said.

Tripti eased her teacup down. He followed the geometry of her sloping wrist, but there was no break of anger in her face.

"Listen," he said. But how could he explain that his want for a child had become rooted in his body, in the bones of his hands and the ridge of his knee, where just that afternoon the girl on the train who'd emerged from the rice fields to beg in the vestibules, whose outstretched palm he would normally loathe—there was no way to lift the country by satisfying beggars—had touched him. Had he not smiled back and touched her hair?

"If you're planning to catch the last train back," she said, "it's best you go now."

He chewed another of Tripti's lumpy sweets. When properly masticated, it would have the consistency to be spat and to land right between Tripti's eyes. But Tripti had turned away from him and resumed her studies. Soon he was all chewed out; he had to show himself out of the house.

By the time he reached the train station, the six o'clock was arriving at the platform. He squatted behind the begonias by the stationmaster's post and waited to see if Sharma was aboard. With the afternoon's disappointment, he felt he deserved to see Sharma's face, even if only

430

covertly. See but remain unseen. In that moment, he could not have explained why he did not peek his head out of the tangle of flowers, though a glimmer of an idea came, something to do with the freedom of others—how, in this village of Sharma's birth, unknown and burdened, Nikhil could never be himself. Sweat pooled where his hairline had receded. How old the skin of his forehead felt to the touch.

As passengers began to disembark, those who were headed for the city clamored aboard. He looked at the faces passing by but did not see Sharma. The first warning bell sounded, then the second, and the stationmaster announced that the train was nearly city bound.

He saw Sharma as the crowd was thinning out. He was walking with someone dressed in the atrocious nylon pants that were the fashion, and perhaps they were telling jokes, because Sharma was doubled over laughing. In all their evenings together, he couldn't recall seeing Sharma laugh with so little inhibition as now, so little concern about who would hear that joyous voice—who would think, What are those two doing? He watched Sharma walk along the dirt road toward his house, but it was an entirely different progress; he was stopping to inspect the rows of wildflowers on the path, to chat up the farmer who'd bellowed his name.

He kept watching Sharma's retreating form until he could see nothing but the faint shape of a man crossing the road. It was then he realized that the city-bound train, the last of the day, had left without him; he sprinted into the stationmaster's booth and phoned his house. It took several rings for Kanu to answer. "Yello?"

"Oh, Kanu," he said. "You must send a car. You must get me. I am at Bilaspur."

The connection was poor, but he could hear Kanu saying, "Babu? What is happening? What is wrong?"

There was no way to express how wounded the afternoon had left him, and he knew the odds of securing a car at this hour, so he yelled back into the phone, "Don't wait for me, Kanu. Make dinner, go to bed!"

He asked the stationmaster if there were any hotels in the village. A room just till the morning, he said. The stationmaster shrugged and pointed vaguely in the direction of the dirt road.

There were no hotels, he soon discovered. Either he would sleep underneath the stars or he would announce himself at Sharma's house to spend the night. He was certain he couldn't do the latter—what a loss of face that would be—but the former with its cold and its unknown night animals, seemed nearly as terrifying.

He paced the town's only road until he grew hungry. Then he headed in the direction of Sharma's house, following a field where fireflies alighted on piles of ash. He had no wish to be discovered, but in the waning daylight that would soon turn into uninterrupted darkness, he felt as anonymous as any of the mosquitoes making dinner of his feet.

When he reached the entrance to Sharma's house, he could smell the evening's meal: lentil soup, rice softened with clarified butter. He could see the two of them together in the kitchen. Sharma was slicing cucumbers and Tripti was stirring a pot. The way Sharma's knife passed over the counter seemed like an act of magic. Such grace and precision. Soon, he knew the lentils and rice would be combined, a pair of onions diced, ginger infused into the stew, the table set, the meal consumed. He watched, waiting for the first word to be spoken, but they were silent partners, unified by the rhythm of their hands.

They moved into the dining room with their meal, and he crawled to the open kitchen window. Sharma had left his mother's necklace on the kitchen counter, next to the cheap china atop the stains of all meals past. What he was seeing couldn't be dismissed: Sharma had treated his greatest gift as if it were nothing more than a kitchen ornament. Nikhil's hand snaked through the window to recover the heirloom, and he knocked over a steel pan in the process.

Sharma rushed to the kitchen and began to yell "Thief, stop" as if it were a mantra. Nikhil scurried down the hill, the necklace secure in his grip, and when he paused at the mouth of the town's only road and turned back, he thought he saw Sharma's hands in the window, making signs that reminded him of their first meeting, when in the darkness those dark fingers had beckoned. Nikhil almost called back, but too much distance lay between them. Whatever he said now wouldn't be heard.

Nominated by Steve Adams

ABRACADABRA

by KATHLEEN LYNCH

from TULE REVIEW

When our mother yelled *Stop that or I'll box
your ears!* I thought she meant chop them off
and put them in a Roi Tan cigar box.

A few years later, a local State Fair side-
show magician sawed a pretty older girl right
through the middle. We screamed, yet she

danced back to us, all smiles and sequins, her
breasts bouncing the way I hoped mine would
someday—a transformation I prayed for daily.

When mom wrung her hands over her many
& various worries, whispering *I'm simply beside myself,*
I tried to picture that diaphanous other version

of our mother—not a ghost, but not all there like
a real body—a mystery vapor-vision that mimicked
her hand-wringing, pacing—always beside her.

Years later, when I knew something more
about metaphor, she told me *You've lost your head*
when I married him and brought him home.

Fast forward to a woman, me, in my bed decades
later, now master of my own arts of appearance
and disappearance, and my cold acquaintance

with how close one can come to death and not die.
He sleeps, never sees my subterfuge when I grab my
head by its sturdy helmet skull, give it a good

crank to the right, lift it and set it on the nightstand.
"Head" is my night watchwoman, observant crone.
She stays alert, enjoys the way moonlight limns

our bodies—his, forty-two years later, still lean, sinewy
bent to my shape; mine, slumped, rounded, in the pose
of a person asleep but, really, quite beside herself.

Nominated by Tule Review

DISPATCH FROM FLYOVER COUNTRY

by MEGHAN O'GIEBLYN

from THE THREEPENNY REVIEW

The August before last, my husband and I moved to Muskegon, a town on the scenic and economically depressed west coast of Michigan. I grew up in the state, but most of my friends have left it, or else are too beleaguered by children to answer their phones. We live in a trailer in the woods, one paneled with oakgrained laminate and beneath which a family of raccoons have made their home. There is a small screened-in porch and a large deck that extends over the side of a sand dune. We work there in the mornings beneath the ceiling of broadleaves, teaching our online classes and completing whatever freelance projects we've managed to scrape together that week. Occasionally, I'll try to amuse him by pitching my latest idea for a screenplay. "An out-of-work stuntman leaves Hollywood and becomes an Uber driver," I'll say. "It's about second chances in the sharing economy." We write the kinds of things that return few material rewards; there is no harm in fantasizing. After dinner, we take the trail that runs from the back of the trailer through an aisle of high pines, down the side of the dune to Lake Michigan.

Evenings have been strange this year: hazy, surreal. Ordinarily, Michigan sunsets are like a preview of the apocalypse, a celestial fury of reds and tangerines. But since we moved here, each day expires in white gauze. The evening air grows thick with fog, and as the sun descends toward the water, it grows perfectly round and blood-colored, lingering on the horizon like an evil planet. If a paddle-boarder happens to cross the lake, the vista looks exactly like one of those old oil paintings of Hanoi. For a long time, we assumed the haze was smog wafting in from

Chicago, or perhaps Milwaukee. But one night, as we walked along the beach, we bumped into a friend of my mother's who told us it was from the California wildfires. She'd heard all about it on the news: smoke from the hills of the Sierra Nevada had apparently been carried on an eastern jet stream thousands of miles across the country, all the way to our beach.

"That seems impossible," I said.

"It does seem impossible," she agreed, and the three of us stood there on the shore, staring at the horizon as though if we looked hard enough, we might glimpse whatever was burning on the far side of the country.

The Midwest is a somewhat slippery notion. It is a region whose existence—whose very name—has always been contingent upon the more fixed and concrete notion of the West. Historically, these interior states were less a destination than a corridor, a gateway that funneled travelers from the east into the vast expanse of the frontier. The great industrial cities of this region—Chicago, Detroit, and St. Louis—were built as "hubs," places where the rivers and the railroads met, where all the goods of the prairie accumulated before being shipped to the exterior states. Today, coastal residents stop here only to change planes, a fact that has solidified our identity as a place to be passed over. To be fair, people who live here seem to prefer it this way. Gift shops along the shores of the Great Lakes sell T-shirts bearing the logo *Flyover Living*. For a long time, the unofficial nickname for the state of Indiana was "Crossroads of America." Each time my family passed the state line, my sisters and I would mock its odd, anti-touristic logic ("Nothing to see here, folks!").

When I was young, my family moved across the borders of these interior states—from Illinois to Michigan to Wisconsin. My father sold industrial lubricant, an occupation that took us to the kinds of cities that had been built for manufacturing and by the end of the century lay mostly abandoned, covered, like Pompeii, in layers of ash. We lived on the outskirts of these cities, in midcentury bedroom communities, or else beyond them, in subdivisions built atop decimated cornfields. On winter evenings, when the last flush of daylight stretched across the prairie, the only sight for miles was the green and white lights of airport runways blinking in the distance like lodestars. We were never far from a freeway, and at night the whistle of trains passing through was as much a part of the soundscape as the wind or the rain. It is like this anywhere you go in the Midwest. It is the sound of transit, of things passing through. People who grew up here tend to tune it out, but if you stop and actually listen, it can be disarming. On some nights, it's easy to imagine that it is the sound of a more profound shifting, as though the entire landscape of this region—the north woods, the tall-grass prairies, the sand dunes, and the glacial moraines—is itself fluid and impermanent.

It's difficult to live here without developing an existential dizziness, a sense that the rest of the world is moving while you remain still. I spent most of my twenties in south Chicago, in an apartment across from a hellscape of coal-burning plants that ran on grandfather clauses and churned out smoke blacker than the night sky. To live there during the digital revolution was like existing in an anachronism. When I opened my windows in summer, soot blew in with the breeze; I swept piles of it off my floor, which left my hands blackened like a scullery maid's. I often thought that Dickens's descriptions of industrial England might have aptly described twenty-first century Chicago. "It was a town of machinery and tall chimneys, out of which interminable serpents of smoke trailed themselves for ever and ever, and never got uncoiled." Far from the blat of the city, there was another world, one depicted on television and in the pages of magazines—a nirvana of sprawling green parks and the distant silence of wind turbines. Billboards glowed above the streets like portals into another world, one where everything was reduced to clean and essential lines. *You Are Beautiful*, said one of them, its product unmentioned or unclear. Another featured a blue sky marked with cumulus clouds and the words: *Imagine Peace.*

I still believed during those years that I would end up in New York, or perhaps in California. I never had any plans for how to get there. I truly believed I would "end up" there, swept by that force of nature that funneled each harvest to the exterior states and carried young people off along with it. Instead, I found work as a cocktail waitress at a bar downtown, across from the state prison. The regulars were graying men who sat impassively at the bar each night, reading the *Tribune* in silence. The nature of my job, according to my boss, was to be an envoy of feminine cheer in that dark place, and so I occasionally wandered over to offer some chipper comment on the headlines—"Looks like the stimulus package is going to pass"—a task that was invariably met with a cascade of fatalism.

437

"You think any of that money's going to make it to Chicago?"

"They should make Wall Street pay for it," someone quipped.

"Nah, that would be too much like right."

Any news of emerging technology was roundly dismissed as unlikely. If I mentioned self-driving cars, or 3-D printers, one of the men would hold up his cell phone and say, "They can't even figure out how to get us service south of Van Buren."

For a long time, I mistook this for cynicism. In reality, it is something more like stoicism, a resistance to excitement that is native to this region. The longer I live here, the more I detect it in myself. It is less disposition than habit, one that comes from tuning out the fashions and revelations of the coastal cities, which have nothing to do with you, just as you learned as a child to ignore those local boosters who proclaimed, year after year, that your wasted rustbelt town was on the cusp of revival. Some years ago, the Detroit Museum of Modern Art installed on its western exterior a neon sign that read EVERYTHING IS GOING TO BE ALRIGHT. For several months, this message brightened the surrounding blight and everyone spoke of it as a symbol of hope. Then the installation was changed to read: NOTHING IS GOING TO BE ALRIGHT. They couldn't help themselves, I guess. To live here is to develop a wariness toward all forms of unqualified optimism; it is to know that progress comes in fits and starts, that whatever promise the future holds, its fruits may very well pass on by, on their way to somewhere else.

My husband and I live just up the hill from the grounds of a Bible camp where I spent the summers of my childhood, a place called Maranatha. People in town assume the name is Native American, but it is in fact an Aramaic word that means "Come, Lord," and which appears in the closing sentences of the New Testament. The apostolic fathers once spoke the word as a prayer, and it was repeated by people of faith throughout the centuries, a mantra to fill God's millennia-long silence. When the camp was built in the early years of the last century, a more ominous English formulation—"The Lord is Coming"—was carved into the cedar walls of the Tabernacle. Everyone is still waiting.

From Memorial Day to Labor Day, the grounds are overrun with evangelical families who come from all over the Midwest to spend their summer vacations on the beach. They stay for weeks at a time in the main lodge, and some stay for the whole summer in cottages built on stilts atop what is the largest collection of freshwater dunes in the world. My parents own one of these cottages; so do my grandparents. Each year, a representative from the DNR comes out to warn them that the dunes are eroding and the houses will one day slide into the lake— prophecies that go unheeded. Everyone plants more dune grass and prays for a few more years. I once pointed out to my mother that there is, in fact, a Biblical parable about the foolish man who builds his house on sand, but she chided me for my pedantic literalism. "That parable," she said, "is about having a foundational faith."

We moved here because we love this part of Michigan and because I have family here. Also, because it's cheap to live here and we're poor. We've lost track of the true reason. Or rather, the foremost reasons and the incidental ones are easy to confuse. Before, we were in Madison, Wisconsin, where we were teaching college writing and juggling other part-time jobs. As more of this work migrated online, location became negotiable. We have the kind of career people like to call "flexible," meaning we buy our own health insurance, work in our underwear, and are taxed like a small business. Sometimes we fool ourselves into believing that we've outsmarted the system, that we've harnessed the plucky spirit of those DIY blogs that applaud young couples for turning a tool-shed or a teardrop camper into a studio apartment, as though economic instability were the great crucible of American creativity.

On Saturday nights, the camp hosts a concert, and my husband and I occasionally walk down to the Tabernacle to listen to whatever band has been bused in from Nashville. Neither of us is a believer, but we enjoy the music. The bands favor gospel standards, a blend of highlands ballads and Gaither-style revivalism. The older generation here includes a contingent of retired missionaries. Many of them are widows, women who spent their youth carrying the gospel to the Philippines or the interior of Ecuador, and after the service they smile faintly at me as they pass by our pew, perhaps sensing a family resemblance. Occasionally, one of them will grip my forearm and say, "Tell me who you are." The response to this question is "I'm Colleen's daughter." Or, if that fails to register: "I'm Paul and Marilyn's granddaughter." It is unnerving to identify oneself in this way. My husband once noted that it harkens back to the origins of surnames, to the clans of feudal times who identified villagers by patronymic epithets. John's son became Johnson, etcetera. To do so now is to see all the things that constitute a modern identity—all your quirks and accomplishments—rendered obsolete.

This is among the many reasons why young people leave these states. When you live in close proximity to your parents and aging relatives, it's impossible to forget that you too will grow old and die. It's the same reason, I suspect, that people are made uncomfortable by the specter of open landscapes, why the cornfields and empty highways of the heartland inspire so much angst. There was a time when people spoke of such vistas as metaphors for opportunity—"expand your horizons"— a convention, I suppose, that goes back to the days of the frontier. Today, opportunity is the province of cities, and the view here signals not possibility but visible constraints. To look out at the expanse of earth, scraped clean of novelty and distraction, is to remember in a very real sense what lies at the end of your own horizon.

Many of our friends who grew up here now live in Brooklyn, where they are at work on "book-length narratives." Another contingent has moved to the Bay Area and made a fortune there. Every year or so, these west-coasters travel back to Michigan and call us up for dinner or drinks, occasions they use to educate us on the inner workings of the tech industry. They refer to the companies they work for in the first person plural, a habit I have yet to acculturate to. Occasionally they lapse into the utopian, speaking of robotics ordinances and brain-computer interfaces and the mystical, labyrinthine channels of capital, conveying it all with the fervency of pioneers on a civilizing mission. Being lectured quickly becomes dull, and so my husband and I, to amuse ourselves, will sometimes play the rube. "So what, exactly, is a venture capitalist?" we'll say. Or: "Gosh, it sounds like science fiction." I suppose we could tell them the truth—that nothing they're proclaiming is news; that the boom and bustle of the coastal cities, like the smoke from those California wildfires, liberally wafts over the rest of the country. But that seems a bit rude. We are, after all, Midwesterners.

Here, work is work and money is money, and nobody speaks of these things as though they were spiritual movements or expressions of one's identity. In college, I waitressed at a chain restaurant, the kind of place that played Smashmouth on satellite and cycled through twenty gallons of ranch dressing a week. One day, it was announced that all employees, from management to dish crew, would hereafter be referred to as "partners." It was a diktat from corporate. Everyone found this so absurd that all of us, including the assistant managers, refused to say the word without a cartoonish, cowboy twang ("Howdy, pard'ner"), robbing it of its intended purpose, which was, of course, to erase the appearance of

440

hierarchy. This has always struck me as indicative of a local political disposition, one that cannot be hoodwinked into euphemism. When you live at the center of the American machine, it's impossible to avoid speaking of mechanics.

Winters here are dark and brutal. On weekends, my husband and I will drive into town, where there are five or six restaurants that have different names but identical menus. Each serves fried perch and whitefish sandwiches, plus a salad section that boasts an EPCOT-like *tour du monde:* Chinese salad, Taco salad, Thai chicken salad, Southwest salad. In Michigan, they still—thankfully—believe in iceberg lettuce, or, as one menu has it, "crisp, cold iceberg lettuce." At the more high-end Muskegon restaurants, you can order something called a Wedge Salad, which is a quarter-head of iceberg covered in tomatoes, bacon bits, and what appears to be—but is not, actually—a profane amount of blue cheese *and* French dressings. "Oh shit," my husband said the first time I ordered one in his presence. "They forgot your dressing." Of course, anyone familiar with iceberg heads knows that they are baroquely layered and dense; you truly do need all that dressing. People in Michigan understand these things.

But even here, in Muskegon, there are headwinds of change. At the farmers' market, there is now one stand that sells organic whole-bean coffee and makes pour-overs—the only place in town—while you wait. The owner, Dave, wears white Oakley's and speaks as though he learned about the artisanal revolution at a corporate convention. "The best places are those that have five things on the menu," he tells us. "Don't make it complicated, man. Just make it good." Across the street from the market is a farm-to-table restaurant where you can order sous-vide octopus and duck tortellini. A sister restaurant recently opened next door, Whistlepunk Pizza, a sparse stone-oven joint whose ingredients list, scrawled on brown paper, includes maque choux and swiss chard sourced from local farms. A "Whistlepunk," reads the restaurant's website, "is an affectionate term given to the newest member of a logging camp."

Muskegon is, in fact, an old logging hub, a mill town once known as the "Lumber Queen of the World." It's tempting to see in such gestures evidence of the hinterland becoming conscious, an entire region rising up to lay claim to its roots. It would be easier to believe this if the coveted look in *Brooklyn Magazine*, about ten years ago, were not called "the lumberjack."

There are places in the Midwest that are considered oases—cities that lie within the coordinates of the region but do not technically belong there. The model in this mode is Madison, Wisconsin, the so-called Berkeley of the Midwest. The comparison stems from the 1960s, when students stormed the campus to protest the Vietnam war. The campus mall is still guarded by foreboding Brutalist structures that were built during that era as an intimidation tactic. I taught in one of these buildings when I was in graduate school. The other TAs complained about them, claiming they got headaches from the lack of sunlight and the maze of asymmetrical halls. I found them beautiful, despite their politics. During my first day of class, I would walk my students outside to show them the exterior. I noted how the walls canted away from the street, evoking a fortress. I pointed out the narrow windows, impossible to smash with rocks. "Buildings," I told them, "can be arguments. Everything you see is an argument." The students were first-semester freshmen, bright and bashful farm kids who had come to this great metropolis—this Athens of the prairie—with the wholesome desire to learn.

Those buildings, like all the old buildings in town, were constantly under threat of demolition. Many of the heavy masonry structures had already been torn down to make way for condo high rises, built to house the young employees of Epic—a healthcare software company that bills itself as the "Google of the Midwest." The corporate headquarters, located just outside town, was a legendary place that boasted all the hallmarks of Menlo Park excess: a gourmet cafeteria with chefs poached from five-star restaurants, an entire wing decorated to resemble Hogwarts. During the years I lived in Madison, the city was flush with new money. A rash of artisanal shops and restaurants broke out across town, each of them channeling the spirit of the prairie and its hardworking, industrial ethos. The old warehouses were refurbished into posh restaurants whose names evoked the surrounding countryside (Graze, Harvest). They were the kinds of places where ryes were served on bars made of reclaimed barn wood, and veal was cooked by chefs whose forearms were tattooed with Holsteins. Most of the factories in town had been turned into breweries, or the kind of coffee shops that resembled an eighteenth-century workshop—all the baristas in butcher aprons and engaged in what appeared to be chemistry experiments with espresso.

Meanwhile, the actual industry, unhidden in the middle of the downtown, looked as though it had never been used. There were gleaming aluminum silos and emissionless brick chimneys. In the prairie stockyards near my apartment, blue railroad cars were lined up like children's toys. Beyond the fences, giant coils of yellow industrial hose glimmered in the early morning light, as beautiful as Monet's haystacks. I doubt that any visitor would see in such artifacts the signs of progress, but when you live for any period in the Midwest, you become sensitive to the subtle process by which industry gives way to commerce, and utility to aesthetics.

Each spring arrived with the effulgent bloom of the farmer's market. The sidewalks around the capitol became flush with white flowers, heirloom eggs, and little pots of honey, and all the city came out in linen and distressed denim. There were food carts parked on the sidewalk, and a string quartet playing "Don't Stop Believing," and my husband and I, newly in love, smoking on the steps of the capitol. We kept our distance from the crowds, preferring to watch from afar. He pointed out that the Amish men selling cherry pies were indistinguishable from the students busking in straw hats and suspenders. It was strange, all these paeans to the pastoral. In the coastal cities, throwbacks of this sort are regarded as a romantic reaction against the sterile exigencies of urban life. But Madison was smack in the middle of the heartland. You could, in theory, drive five miles out of town and find yourself in the great oblivion of corn.

In the early days of our relationship, we were always driving out to those parts, spurred by some vague desire to see the limits of the land— or perhaps to distinguish the simulacrum from the real. We would download albums from our teen years—*Night on the Sun, Either/Or*— and drive east on the expressway until the sprawl of subdivisions gave way to open land. If there was a storm in the forecast, we'd head out to the farmland of Black Earth, flying through the cropfields with all the windows down, the backseat fluttering with unread newspapers as lightning forked across the horizon.

Madison was utopia for a certain kind of Midwesterner: the Baptist boy who grew up reading Wittgenstein, the farm lass who secretly dreamed about the girl next door. It should have been such a place for me as well. Instead, I came to find the live bluegrass outside the co-op insufferable. I developed a physical allergy to NPR. Sitting in a bakery one morning, I heard the opening theme of *Morning Edition* drift in from the kitchen and started scratching my arms as though contracting a rash. My husband tried to get me to articulate what it was that bothered me, but I could never come up with the right adjective. Self-satisfied? Self-congratulatory? I could never get past aesthetics. On the way home from teaching my night class, I would unwind by listening to a fundamentalist preacher who delivered exegeses on the Pentateuch and occasionally lapsed into fire and brimstone. The drive was long, and I would slip into something like a trance state, failing to register the import of the message but calmed nonetheless by the familiar rhythm of conviction.

Over time, I came to dread the parties and potlucks. Most of the people we knew had spent time on the coasts, or had come from there, or were frequently traveling from one to the other, and the conversation was always about what was happening elsewhere: what people were listening to in Williamsburg, or what everyone was wearing at Coachella. A sizeable portion of the evening was devoted to the plots of premium TV dramas. Occasionally there were long arguments about actual ideas, but they always crumbled into semantics. What do you mean by *duty*? someone would say. Or: It all depends on your definition of *morality*. At the end of these nights, I would get into the car with the first throb of a migraine, saying that we didn't have any business discussing anything until we could, all of us, articulate a coherent ideology. It seemed to me then that we suffered from the fundamental delusion that we had elevated ourselves above the rubble of hinterland ignorance—that fair-trade coffee and *Orange You Glad It's Vegan?* cake had somehow redeemed us of our sins. All of us had, like the man in the parable, built our houses on sand.

A couple weeks ago, there was a mass baptism in Lake Michigan. There is one at the end of each summer, though I haven't attended one in years. It was a warm night, and so my husband and I walked down to watch, along with my mother and my sister and her two-year-old daughter. The haze was thick that evening, and it wasn't until we were nearly upon the crowd that we could see it in its entirety: hundreds of people standing along the shore, barefoot like refugees in the sand. Out in the water, a pastor stood waist-deep with a line of congregants waiting their turn in the shallows. Farther down, there was another pastor standing in the lake with another line of congregants, and even farther down, near the rocks of the channel, a third stood with yet another line of people. The water was so gray and still, the evening air so windless, that you could hear the pastors' voices as they recited the sacramental formula: "Buried with Christ in baptism, raised to walk in the fullness of life." Whenever someone emerged from the water, everyone on the beach cheered and clapped as the congregant waded back through the mist like a ghost, his clothes suddenly thin and weighed down with water.

My mother saw someone she knew in the crowd and walked over to say hello. A small drone flew over the water, hovering over each of the pastors, and then darted along the shoreline. My sister pointed it out. "It must be filming," we decided. The beach was clean from a recent storm, empty except for some stray pieces of driftwood, bleached white and hewn smooth as whale bones. The seagulls were circling in frantic patterns, as though trying to warn us. Usually they glide over the beach in elegant arabesques, but there was no wind on this night, and they flapped like bats, trying to stay afloat.

The whole scene seemed to me like a Bruegel painting, a sweeping portrait of community life already distilled by time. I imagined scholars examining it many years in the future, trying to decipher its rituals and iconography. There was something beautiful in how the pastor laid his hands over each congregant's face, covering her hand with his own, something beautiful in the bewildered look on the congregant's face when she emerged from the water. Although I no longer espouse this faith, it's hard to deny the mark it has left on me. It is a conviction that lies beneath the doctrine and theology, a kind of bone-marrow knowledge that the Lord is coming; that he has always been coming, which is the same as saying that he will never come; that each of us must find a way to live with this absence and our own, earthly limitations.

The crowd erupted again in cheers. I was watching my niece run through the surf, watching my sister pretend to chase her. Each time the crowd cheered, she threw her hands above her head, as though it were for her. The drone made its way toward us, descended and hovered there, just above the water.

"That's unsettling," I said. The machine was idling above the water, appearing to stare us down. It was close enough that I could see the lens of its camera, a red light going on and off, as though winking at us.

"It knows we're not believers," my husband whispered.

"Let's go," I said. We made our way into the crowd, hoping to disappear within it. Everyone was dressed in brightly colored shirts and smelled of damp cotton. We passed my mother, who was laughing. The voices of the pastors carried irregularly across the water, and once we were deep in the crowd, their incantations seemed to overlap, as though

445

it were one voice, rippling in a series of echoes. "Buried with Christ . . . Raised to walk in the fullness . . ." Things were ending and beginning again, just as everything is always ending and always beginning, and standing there amidst the sea of people, I was reminded that it might not go on like this forever. We made our way to the shore, where the crowd thinned out and the sand was firm with water, and beyond the fog there appeared, on the horizon, the faintest trace of a sunset.

Nominated by The Threepenny Review,
Lydia Conklin, Barrett Swanson

ON GAY PARENTING

by ANDREW SOLOMON

from THE THREEPENNY REVIEW

People often ask me when I came out, generalizing from the experience of many young people who announce themselves to the world on a particular afternoon. But I did not divorce my reticence in a single sharp break. Rather, I seeped out like a spreading wine stain. I told someone; I told a few more people; I denied what I'd said; I said it again, to someone else; I wished it away; I told my family; I denied it to the people I was sleeping with; I admitted it to those people; I denied it to my family; and so on. I had been completely closeted for two decades and I took another decade to declare myself even to myself. I apologize now to the pretty women I couldn't love enough and to the handsome men to whom I couldn't commit, to the tolerant friends who met them all with equal faith and to the blinkered parents who did not.

Since then, coming out has been an almost daily exercise. I am forever weighing whether I have the wherewithal to mention my husband, John, to an elderly someone on a train, or a brusque someone in a shop, or a fundamentalist someone to my left at dinner. It crosses my mind; it is often relevant; I can choose not to mention it, but then I have to live with the feeling that I am perhaps hating myself, or deferring to other people's tedious disapprobation. Then I have to wonder whether I am merely imagining such disapprobation. Would I have needed to mention a wife at this moment if I had one? Am I the one who is being aggressive when I deploy the word "husband" in a conversation with someone I think will be unnerved by it?

When I began writing about my experience of clinical depression, friends asked whether I wasn't distressed by taking so public a stance

447

about mental illness, and I had to explain repeatedly that I had done the closet once and wasn't going to do it again. Overcompensating, I made an ostentation of my candor. I had become allergic to secrets, so much so that I sometimes forgot that you can have privacy even when you don't disguise your identity. I often supposed the choice was between circumlocution and broadcast. The problem is that even as you reveal the mysteries in your past, you are accumulating them in the present: complete honesty is the stuff of post-mortem, not autobiography. I found it easier to be honest about external events than about internal ones; I made my own life sound more lyrical than it was and expressed enthusiasm about identity challenges I mostly regretted—those entangled with my being American, Jewish, gay, depressed, unathletic, half a stone heavier than I'd have liked, not a morning person. I aspired to dignity but not pity and I found both. Children had laughed at me when I was a child and people were laughing at me again. I was lonely.

Oddly, I am nostalgic for that loneliness. A few months ago, I had to go through all of my photo albums, starting from early childhood, in conjunction with a film project with which I am involved. The photos taken before I turned eighteen felt as though they were of someone I knew only vaguely; images of other people in those albums conjured more emotion than those of me. The photos taken between the time I left for university and the time I met John filled me with paralyzing nostalgia for the exhilarating, difficult times in which I became myself. The ones from the past fifteen years, since John and I found each other, felt so recent that it was hard to credit them with being documents of the past at all.

Though my meeting John was the beginning of an authentic claim on happiness, our early years together found me still only an intermittent champion of gay pride. Then we had children. Children confiscate your mask, leaving you far more exposed than lovers can. You can manipulate the valences of your own concealment, but once you have children, you have to bear in mind how your point of view becomes theirs and you are morally obligated to become an exemplar of self-esteem. No one much wants to be belittled, but we tolerate slurs surprisingly often for ourselves; for our lionized children, we demand freedom from insult. I'd had a facile answer when people asked me whether I had a wife but had to summon a more vigorous one when they now asked whether my son had a mother, because while the first question sometimes seemed patronizing, the second often seemed accusatory.

Gay parents are habitually made to feel that we must somehow love our children twice as much as anyone else to prove we have the right to be parents at all. We are expected to be thankful for having obtained rights that most people have enjoyed since time immemorial. I am grateful for the husband and children I couldn't have had before those rights were conferred, and indebted to the people who have made lives such as mine possible. For the rights themselves, however, I prefer not to be any more appreciative than I am for having a fire department, snow removal on public roads, Internet access, freedom of religion, or any of the other benefits that accrue to the population at large.

In February, I spoke at a literary festival in Cartagena, Colombia, and at the end of one of my talks there, an elegantly dressed Colombian woman stood up to ask a question. She mentioned research indicating that children brought up in gay families were on average better adjusted, said she had wondered why that might be so, and offered her own theory: men and women argue a lot. I was rather charmed by the notion that gay spouses would be strangers to quarrelling, that same-sex parents might see the world so similarly as to banish discord. Alas, I must offer in the interests of full disclosure that my husband and I occasionally have different points of view.

I was, however, taken with her proposition. For many years, the only model of family consisted of a mother, a father, and a few biological children. That definition has gradually expanded to include step-parents, gay and lesbian families, open adoptions, increased foster care, single parents by choice, and single parents by happenstance. Yet we still expect these evolving structures to replicate the old archetype, assume they have nothing better to give than imitation.

People still ask my husband and me which of us is the mom—which, as one lesbian friend pointed out to me, is like asking which chopstick is the fork. This pressure on us to embody normative traditions can be paralyzing.

Our son doesn't have a mother and a father. He has two fathers. A single mother I know is always attracting sympathy for how hard it must be to be "both Mom and Dad." But she is not Mom and Dad; she is a single mother, which is its own rich phenomenon.

So, there you have the further misperception from which we must emerge. All men are created equal but not identical. New family structures are different from mainstream ones. We are not lesser but we are not the same, and to deny the nuance of that asymmetry is to keep us almost as ensnared as we were when our marriages and families were impossible. Acquiescence to historical standards is still commonly recognized as the essence of good parenting, but I would emphasize the equal power of imaginative breaks with tradition. Modern families are different from Victorian ones; rich lives are different from poor ones; old parents are different from young parents; Asian mothers are different from British ones. The ways my family and I love one another are as radical as they are profound.

Nominated by The Threepenny Review,
Joan Murray

THE MÉNAGE

fiction by LOUISA ERMELINO

from MALAFEMMENA (SARABANDE BOOKS)

I didn't know Rosie then, when she lived on the beach in Calangute with her old man and the English couple. I could see her from my house when she would come out in the mornings to sweep. They were all four of them tall and beautiful, I remember, both the English girl and Rosie with wild red hair. They kept to themselves and I wasn't interested in new friends. I was too busy licking my wounds.

There were whispers about them, about what was going on in that house, but for me, it was all a scandal. You could find me on the beach in a dress, a black dress, if you can believe it, among the naked and the loinclothed. It takes time to take off your clothes when you were raised by Irish nuns in a country founded by Puritans.

One morning I saw Rosie's old man leave. I could tell he was leaving because he was wearing clothes. He had a rucksack over one shoulder and he was walking toward the road, sinking to his ankles in the soft sand with every step. And then there were three. The Englishman and his redheads in that house on the beach.

❖   ❖   ❖

Calangute was the first beach you hit in Goa when you came in from Panjim. You thought you were in paradise at first: white sand and swaying palms, everyone young and tanned and undressed, whitewashed houses with an ocean view for a few rupiahs, chillums firing on every porch, sunset parties with *Abbey Road* playing over and over on a tape deck until the batteries ran out. The local priest delivered *ganga* on his bicycle and the coconuts fell off the trees.

451

But rumors were rife. Was it the French chef from Grenoble who stole cameras from the Swedes to buy a goat to roast on a spit for his birthday? Had the Dutch girl really sold her baby to Father Damien who brought it to the nuns in Cochin? Was it true that religious pilgrims had bitten off several toes from the body of St. Francis Xavier in the Basilica of Bom Jesus in Old Goa?

The stories traveled on air, they appeared in mangoes, they wrapped themselves in sarongs and I took them in, swaying in my hammock on my porch overlooking the sea, but mostly I obsessed about Rosie and the English couple, watching Rosie bend over in front of her house with a broom of twigs and then step into the darkness of the open doorway.

I stayed around for a while, until neighbors stole my clothes and men got tiresome. Claus was indifferent and Achilles gave me a sexually transmitted disease. I was done with the East.

The day I left, the ménage were sitting cross-legged in a circle eating lychees. It was the season. I had never seen them all three together in one place and I stood a long while watching as they pulled the fruit from the branches and peeled off the rough pink-brown rind. The Englishman fed the redheads the slippery white flesh with his fingers; Rosie fed the English girl and the English girl fed Rosie. The English girl stood and the Englishman reached up and held her arm but she pulled away and disappeared into the grove of palm trees behind the house. Rosie and the Englishman got up and went inside, one following the other.

It was none of my business what was going on but I did think about walking over and looking in through the slot of the window, squinting into the cool dark of that white stucco house, but I didn't. Instead I took what hadn't been stolen and caught a *becak* to the bus station.

So there I was in Australia, in Sydney, working in a pub that recreated the Tyrolean Alps. I wore an appropriately humiliating costume and pink suede clogs and one Friday night came home to find Rosie holding court in the living room of the house I shared with three expat Pommies and a local actress.

More stunning than I remembered, an Indonesian batik sarong tight on her hips, Rosie told stories. She nodded to me when I came into the room and ignored me when I walked out.

She found me later and we hit it off, Rosie and I, and we left together for Bali on Garuda Airlines. It wasn't until weeks later that I told her I had been in Goa.

"Really?" she said. "When?"

We were lying side by side on rope beds in a shack on Kuta Beach.

"Not sure exactly. A year ago? Two?"

"Ah, yeah," she said, and rolled on her side and started picking at the mold that was growing on the leather bag she had carried from Sydney.

"Nice, that, Goa," she said. "Christ, it's good to be out of Aussie."

"You were living in a house on the beach . . . in Calangute."

"Right. Then it got fucked. All those junkies. Everyone started moving to Anjuna." She turned back to face me. "What were you doing there, darling?" she said.

"Nursing a broken heart."

"Oh, that." She laughed.

"You don't remember me at all?"

"Not likely. Not much in common. This heart of mine doesn't break."

I suspected as much, which is why I had left Sydney with her. I thought I could learn something.

"Goa," she said. "Ian and Cynthia.' Her voice was low and sultry. "That was a story."

"Tell me," I said, and when she started to talk I lay back and closed my eyes.

They had met on the beach, Cynthia and Ian and Rosie and John. They had all just arrived when Father Damien stopped his bicycle and asked if they were looking to rent a house. Ian said yes straightaway and they followed the priest as he walked his bicycle along the sand. They were ill-matched couples in many ways but they had a common language and the joke that both Rosie and Cynthia had that wild red hair.

"John wasn't so happy with the set-up," Rosie was saying. "He thought Ian was a bit of a bully, and you know, he was. He was big, threatening even, and he just took over."

"So John wanted to leave?"

"He did, after a while. At first we swapped partners, then we really got into it and John started getting bummed because it always ended up all about Ian. John would walk in with a newspaper cone of mandarins and find me and Cynthia and Ian all tangled up and Ian would say, 'C'mon, mate, join the party,' and in the beginning John tried but it wasn't his thing. Complicated, foursomes are. Me, I was just having a good time. I liked John well enough but John was straight. He'd been to university. He was taking some time off to see the world, but me and Cynthia and Ian, we had nothing else going on."

I could have told her then that I had watched John leave, that I had seen Ian feeding his redheads lychees from his fingers. I could have told her that I was in the John camp. I didn't know the Ians and Rosies and Cynthias of the world, with their fearlessness, their disregard for consequences. They both attracted and repelled me.

There were a lot of them moving around in those days, shoulder to shoulder with the seekers and the students taking a break. There was opportunity for stealing and fleecing and most of all, smuggling, to feed a dream of easy money, to finance a life on the bum. There was duplicity and desperation and stupidity.

"And John left, just like that?" I said. Rosie took a long, deep toke on the joint she had rolled.

"Not that easy. He got me alone and said something like: 'What in fuck's name are you doing? Let's get out of here, away from this freak.'"

"But I told him to fuck off. That Goa was a blast. The beach, the dope . . . it was one big blast. He came at me, pushed me down, started kissing me, talking in my ear, and then Ian comes in and moves right in between us. 'Groovy,' Ian says, taking my hand, putting it against his hard-on, moving his body against John. The next thing I know, the two of them are rolling around on the floor. John took the worst of it. Ian punched him bloody. John got up, packed his gear, and didn't even look back at me when he walked out."

"What happened to him?" I said. Rosie made a face.

"Fuck if I know," she said.

"So it was the two of you and Cynthia?" I said, taking the joint from her, rolling onto my back. It was so hot I could barely move. We were waiting for the rains.

"Right. Ian said it was all about me but Cynthia was having a hard time of it and I would hear him telling her how he loved her best but he loved me, too, and she had to love me, that we were family. The Trinity, he called us. The Trinity, and guess who sat at the top of the fucking triangle?"

"So what happened?"

"What always happens. We ran out of money. If John were there, he could have wired his mum and dad, but any of us? Forget it. Ian hadn't spoken to his in years, didn't even know if they were alive. Cynthia's had cut her off when she left England, and mine? They might have sent some but fucked if I was going to ask."

I watched a gecko stalk a horrifyingly large spider near the ceiling. Rosie was drifting off, stoned, but I wanted to hear the rest so I poked her awake with a toe and she laughed. "Ian started freaking out," she said. "His drugs were getting expensive. We had to pay the rent on the house. Then one night Ian said something about Cynthia and I maybe getting paid for what we gave away for free. 'I'd be right there,' he told us. 'Make sure nothing happened to you. Only businessmen . . . we could hit one of the really flash hotels up in Bombay.' Cynthia clocked him right under his eye with a teacup, the kind you broke when you finished drinking the tea. 'Bugger off, you disgusting arsehole,' she said. She might have spit in his face. She followed me outside and we put our arms around each other and realized it was us against him."

Rosie was sitting up now, enjoying her own story. "But we couldn't let him go," she said. "Ian was like that. Bluebeard, we called him. The three of us got back together that night; Ian even squeezed out a few tears, begging us to forgive, telling us how much he loved us, how we were his family, how he'd figure something out. We fell asleep in a huddle and he never brought it up again."

Rosie nodded off and, this time, there was no waking her.

If it wasn't sex, Rosie explained, it was going to have to be drugs. When Ian came up with an elaborate scheme to bring hashish into England, pure Pakistani from Chitral with the gold stamp in the corner of the brick to prove it, the redheads didn't think twice. Ian had a van that he and Cynthia had driven out East. They would drive it back the way they had come, this time with dope hidden inside, crossing some of the toughest borders in the world: Pakistan, Afghanistan, Iran, Turkey, Greece, countries where drug smugglers were locked up for life, executed, disappeared.

The redheads put their faith in their old man. He wasn't like some others, who sent their birds alone, convincing them that their gender would save them. They were all together in this.

The ménage was high on the future. Bad news didn't travel. It was only the triumphant who returned flashing wads of hard currency and new clothes that told the tale.

"We made it all the way to Rome," Rosie said. "They took that van apart at every border. We thought we were buggered once or twice. We sat at the Iranian border for three days. They banged, they dismembered, they shook. They knew we had it but they couldn't find it. We knew we had an advantage. Cynthia and I were distractions. They dug Ian because he had two wives and maybe our red hair drove them around the bend. Two of us, and Cynthia with skin white like milk glass, but they still wanted to find the dope. And they had all the time in the world. But so did we."

"Where was the dope?"

"Ha! Bloody brilliant, Ian was. You had to give him that. He suspended it in glass containers inside the gas tank. Everyone stashes it in doors and panels and floorboards but they always find it when it's in the body of the car. Remember when every stall in the market was flogging false-bottom suitcases and hollow Buddhas?" Rosie shook her head. "Stupid, that was,"

I didn't remember but I did want the rest of the story. I could see Rosie losing interest. She found a bag of cashews and said something about going for a swim. "And then?" I prodded. She poured cashews into my hand. They were spiced and salted and I licked my fingers and asked her again. She stretched her long freckled arms above her head,

"So we got to Rome, all the way to effing Rome and we were dead broke. Ian got out some dope to sell, just enough to get us to London. We made it all the way to Rome and ended up busted for a couple of joints."

"Jesus," I said.

"Jesus is right. We went to jail. Ian in the men's part, Cynthia and I in the women's. It was a trip, Italian jail. Nuns ran it and with a bit of lire, you could have anything you wanted. Cynthia and I plastered the walls of our cell with pages ripped out of fashion magazines. We had a standing order for chocolate and fags, English ones, Rothman's, Dunhill. We played with the babies when we got really bored. Didya know? In Italy, you keep your baby with you in jail. The women were in for smuggling cigarettes and murdering their cheating men. But the food! Spaghetti twice a day. *Nudo,* they called it, naked spaghetti. Nothing on it, not even salt. And every meal those Italian birds would smack their lips. 'Mmmm,' they'd say. 'Pasta!' Sometimes Cynthia and I would just have lollies and chips, we couldn't look at another limp string of wet noodle."

Rosie turned over on her stomach, folded her hands under her chin. "My mum and dad came up with the money for a lawyer. Poor luvs."

"You got off?"

"Cynthia and I did three months. Then, free as birds." She laughed at the pun. "Two innocent young girls drawn into crime by, what else? The sweet talk of a bad man."

"You gave Ian up?"

"You could say that."

"What happened to him?"

"In prison, for a very long time, I'm afraid, He was pissed he took the rap. Selling dope was one thing but worse was the morals charge. The judge said he corrupted us, Cynthia and I, *le innocente*. You should have seen us in court. We looked like schoolgirls. My mum sent us the sweetest flowered dresses." Rosie faced me when she said this.

"And Cynthia?"

"We kissed for the last time at the Rome airport."

"Didn't you feel bad for Ian?"

"Oh, darling, have you not learned anything?"

I should have by now, I thought. I wanted to tell Rosie I was trying, which was why I was here with her. I wasn't wearing dresses on the beach anymore.

The rains began and shook the tin roof. Water leaked along the openings near the ceiling. The gecko had caught the spider and was feasting in a corner. We would have to wait if we wanted to go for a swim.

Rosie said she had a better idea. We should find ourselves some rich blokes, she said. We shouldn't have to buy our own dope or pay for a room. Enough, she said, with these long-haired freaks. Tomorrow we should go over to that new resort, the Inna Grand. We would book a suite and lay out by the pool.

"How can we afford that?" I said.

She leaned over and kissed me on the mouth. She traced an eyebrow with a delicate finger. "Honestly, luv," she said. "What do you think happened to all that dope in the van?" Then she took me in her arms and together we listened to the rain.

Nominated by Sarabande Books

I TOLD THE WATER

by TARFIA FAIZULLAH

from MICHIGAN QUARTERLY REVIEW

I told the water   You're right
   the poor are
         broken sidewalks
   we try to avoid
Told it   the map of you folds into corners small enough
   to swallow   I told the water
You only exist because of thirst
   But beside your sour membrane   we lie
       facedown in dirt
The first time   my father threw me into you
   I became hieroglyph   a wet braid
      caught   in your throat
I knew then   how war was possible
   the urge
to defy gravity   to disarm another
     I knew then we'd, kill
to be your mirror   You   black-eyed barnacle
        You graveyard
of windows   I told the water
Last night I walked out onto your ice
         wearing only my skin
   Because you couldn't tell me   not to

Nominated by Michigan Quarterly Review,
Christine Gelineau, Richard Kostelanetz, Maxine Scates

PORTRAIT OF THE ALCOHOLIC WITH RELAPSE FANTASY

by KAVEH AKBAR

from ZYZZYVA

You're in a car and crying and amazed
at how bad it feels to do bad things. Then

you're in a hotel bathroom with blood
on your undershirt and the smell of a too-

chlorinated pool outside. You know
one hundred ways to pray to the gods

rippling beneath that water. Confess, tangle,
pass through. Once your room is dark

they come inside, dripping wet. When you show
them the burnt place on your arm,

they show you the bands of flesh cut
from their thighs. You suck their tongues,

trace the blisters under their wings. It's so lucky,
this living forever all at once. When you turn

on the lights, you're inconsolably
glad. You could stop this whenever, but why?

Nominated by ZYZZYVA, James Kimbrell, David Kirby,
Jessica Roeder, Rachel Rose, Jessica Wilbanks

GUNPOWDER

by REBECCA HAZELTON

from SOUTHERN INDIANA REVIEW

What if I did request that incendiary
                    touch, the slow-burn
        of too much, the bleaching kiss of a man
who twisted my mouth
        into the words he wanted to hear?
                            If it's written, it's written,
                but what's read differs.
What looks alchemical
            shakes out chemical, hundreds of years later,
rigor is revealed as metaphor,
            a story about
            a mixture of grains, ground in alcohol,
dried and packed—how I wanted
                    to be more than process,
        to be the bright impurity wronging the ratio.
                        Did I love him for his acrid smell?
            For the way he threatened to ignite
just by shuffling in, all three parts of him uneasy?
                        In friction, we see what rubs
                    and what breaks off, and in the fiction
        we tell others, there is an explanation
                        for fire and its hungers.
    I said *love,* and that is a match.
        I said *believe me,* and that was powder.

Nominated by Southern Indiana Review,
Alan Michael Parker

LATCHKEY

by NICK NORWOOD

from THE GREENSBORO REVIEW

Remember that first time
you let yourself in—
stunned by the sheer
silence of it all,

the sunlight blooming
on mute, blank-faced
walls. And how you
stormed, then,

from room to room
blistering furniture
and framed photos with your
hollering, commanding

the sunlight to go away
go away go away
because you wanted
to be alone.

Remember how you
yelled yourself
dizzy—exhilarated
and scared.

And how you
eventually dropped
into a chair
and watched

the sunlight
creep silently across
floors, up walls,
and let itself out.

Nominated by Melissa Pritchard

HOW TO SHOOT AT SOMEONE WHO OUTDREW YOU

by DAVID MEISCHEN

from THE GETTYSBURG REVIEW

The morning I learned of Hank Locklin's death, I disappeared right out of my life, jolted elsewhere by a single fragment of the deluge spilling from my web browser. March 9, 2009, was an ordinary Monday morning. A breeze drifted through my central Austin neighborhood. I was sixty years old. I'd long since quit listening to stations that call themselves country—that wasteland of loud pop ballads cowboyed up with twang, with steel guitar and fiddle. A name, then, a simple Internet death notice. A voice, singular as the whorl tipping my ring finger. Opening words to a song. And five decades dropped away beneath me.

> Please help me I'm falling . . . in love with you.
> Close the door to temptation, don't let me walk through.

I found myself in the bare dirt yard of the Meischen homestead some two hundred miles south—any Saturday afternoon of my youth—my father's leatherbound transistor radio, big as a school lunch box, standing on a cement block beneath the windmill, heartache pouring out of it while my brothers and I chamoised the car. Simultaneously, I could feel my feet moving over dance-waxed hardwood at the Rifle Club Hall of Orange Grove, Adolph Hofner and the Pearl Wranglers on the little, raised stage, a cousin circling the floor in my arms, my parents, my aunt and uncle somewhere among the dancers, all of us humming along, entranced by Locklin's moving little tale of a good man falling and knowing he oughtn't and falling anyway. Because the song, the fall, the narrative drive is quite simply irresistible. The song is the story and the story is the dance, the knowledge that the song immersed in us—that a fall is coming, that even if, like my parents, you have the luck of marrying the person you fall for, of not falling for another, a final fall is coming anyway. One of you will die before the other, as did my mother after forty-nine years of marriage, her loss the heartbreak of my father's life.

I remember them so young, Valerie and Elwood Meischen. When we were infants, they carried us into the Rifle Club and put us on a pallet against a wall near their table. After we found the use of our legs, they let us roam. A group of us ages three to five would gather in front of the bandstand, holding hands in a rotating circle, a dance-hall version of "Ring Around the Rosie." We learned the art of couple dancing from patient mothers, more often just by imitation. I loved the whirl of the dance floor during a polka. One Saturday night, my cousin Lana and I decided it was time to join the spinning couples. I took the stance I'd learned for the two-step—right hand at the small of Lana's back, left hand raised to take her right—and we took off onto the floor in a kind of sideways run, moving and turning until we collided with a couple who knew what they were doing. Then we'd take our dancers' stance and propel ourselves counterclockwise around the floor again. It was a clumsy business, but it worked. By the time I was fifteen and Lana thirteen, we'd transformed our polka into performance art, turning circles that would have dizzied more cautious souls, interrupting our breathless turns by letting go at the raised hand, slipping back until my right grasped her left, and then doing overhand and underhand moves adapted from other steps we'd learned along the way. Sometimes other couples stopped and gaped at us—admiringly, we thought, though likely they just wanted to get out of the way, stepping aside while the crazed show-offs spun by in a blur—Lana and I moving, moving as if the fire burning in us would never burn low.

While it burned, we learned the jitterbug, again by imitation. In 1965, twenty years after the war, every band that played the Rifle Club still had "In the Mood" on the playlist, saxophone sometimes missing from the opening riff, though it was the song's irrepressible beat we were after. Country ensembles played it by request, a break from covers of Ernest Tubb, Marty Robbins, Patsy Cline, Ray Price, George Jones, Tammy Wynette. Czech and German groups too—we called them old-timey bands. And none was better than Adolph Hofner, the Czech-

German bandleader who played Texas dance halls for decades. Affable, curly-haired, always a sparkle in the eye, Hofner had roots in Western swing and a recording contract with Bluebird Records in 1938, two years before Glenn Miller's tune propelled jitterbug aficionados onto the floor.

By the sixties, in my part of South Texas, a modest proportion of any dance crowd still knew the jitterbug—generally couples who'd learned it in their dating years or younger folks chasing the energy high it offered. There was more room on the floor then, more space between couples, more room to admire the other dancers, to learn from them. My parents were deft at this dance from the war years, but no one could jitterbug like Lana's parents, Wilton and Madeline Meischen. They made it look effortless. They made it look cool, and I use the word *cool* here in both senses. As Aunt Madeline and Uncle Wilton skimmed the floor to "In the Mood," they looked like the couple to be. And even in August—the Rifle Club was not air-conditioned—they danced as if perspiring were beneath them, their movements so smooth neither appeared to be leading, so fluid Wilton and Madeline were no longer themselves. They had become the dance.

All I knew then was that I loved the jitterbug, loved the challenge, the tempo, the rapidly changing moves, the chance to impress. What occurred to me later is something that lay beneath the level of conscious knowledge, that I only felt during the years the jitterbug had its way with me: the real magic lay in dancing a step our parents had been dancing since they were our age—doing the dance they were doing and sharing the dance floor with them while they were doing the dance we were doing. Our parents moved in us; they moved through us, the movements of the moment connecting us to a ritual that had been going on long before our parents learned to jitterbug and would continue long past our own ephemeral efforts. Dancing truly entered— dancing when you disappear into the dance—is both of the moment and timeless. The jitterbug I so loved has nothing in common with the haiku I came to admire decades later, except one feature: measured moments that are both now and always.

My brothers learned to dance, but for them the draw was girls— dancing as courtship, as mating ritual. I was a girlie boy, though, a queen's flamboyance knocking frenetically inside me. No one spoke the words for who I was; I had no words myself. But at the Rifle Club, I was free; the dance floor welcomed all my unarticulated energy. Like my brothers, I wanted a girlfriend, marriage, children. The coupled life was the only life I knew—husband and wife, aunts and uncles, grand-parents. Family. Still, dancing didn't fluster or distract me. I didn't have to worry—or hope—that some kind of fire would kindle in me when the tempo changed and I paired up with a girl I had a crush on, the song moody and slow now, something about straying and redemption:

I was wrong the day I left you—I let the world lead me astray.
If you'll say that you forgive me, you'll make the world go away.

Don't get me wrong. The girl was not merely incidental, a prop to help me get where the dance was going. I loved female company, loved dancing with my cousins, my mother, my aunts, eventually my high-school girlfriend. But with lyrics by the great Hank Cochran—the voice of a prodigal yearning for unearned grace—it was the story, the age-old refrain of love, loss, betrayal, the shimmering hope of forgiveness that moved me through a slow tune. First, last, always, it was the music itself—the mesmeric movement of the dance—that drew me in.

During the late fifties, Rod and the Westernaires played a number of Saturday night gigs in Orange Grove. They disappeared, mirage-like, as quickly as they'd arrived. My father was in charge of scheduling bands for the Rifle Club. I might have asked him what happened to them, though I didn't. Twice in recent years, I've gone to Google, searching for a glimpse, a trail of crumbs, a fragment. Nothing. Given how distant the memory, how perfectly encapsulated, perhaps Rod and his Westernaires were a daydream I embedded in personal history, though I doubt it. Memory insists.

Here's the part that has not let go.

I am eight. I am standing at the foot of three unimposing steps lead-ing up to the bandstand. I hear steel guitar and fiddle. I hear honky-tonk piano. They enter at the eardrum and find their way to my right foot, poised on the first step in front of me, tapping out the beat. At the mike, there is Rod; to either side and behind, the Westernaires. They wear flashy attire—a cross between Rex Allen in full rodeo preen and a Western-themed marching band prancing down the gridiron—smart satin cowboy shirts with fancy stitching at the yoke and silky fringe at the cuffs, fancy cowboy slacks with a pleat above the ankle so that when they tap their feet to a lively two-step, the hems of their pants dance like a baton twirler's skirt. I am in love without knowing it, and not just with the dandy outfits. Rod, you see, is gorgeous—cheeks, chin, and jawline straight out of a Gillette commercial. Sideburns. Hair dark and shiny as raven feathers. He's at the mike—*singing* to the mike—lips almost touching the mike.

I look and look—fingered strings and keyboard moving in me, snare drum pulsing in my tapping foot—too young to know that I am in love with more than the music, too young to know what it means, this endless moment watching a man sing. And years from the impulse that will move me from looking at a man to reaching for him, years from understanding that, free as I feel dancing, there is no place for me in the music, the dance hall, the story spun out by the words I am learning by heart.

My father was a happy man on dancing nights, sidestepping the moody, brooding impulse I often mistook for the man. There was darkness in him and perhaps good reason for it. Youngest son of a farmer who killed himself in 1941, Elwood Meischen stepped in where his father had left off, wrestling a hundred acres of cleared brush, thin soil over hardtop caliche, unirrigated fields in country hospitable to prickly pear, agarita, and mesquite. In 1950, as I approached two and my sister sailed past three, Daddy drove to town and asked the bank president for a job. My grandmother lived on the farm with us. Grandma owned the place; she could work like the stubborn, second-generation German farmer she was. Still, Lillie Meischen made a fifth stomach to fill, besides which her resident daughter-in-law was Catholic. I'm sure Daddy anticipated further arrivals. Larell Meischen joined the family in 1951, Vance following in '52. For all the years of my raising and a couple of decades beyond, Elwood Meischen worked full time at Farmer's State Bank of Orange Grove and managed the arduous labor that went into a modest farm of modest means.

Automation came late to small farmers in South Texas. We had a puny tractor, and that was about it. Until the mid-sixties, our cotton was picked by hand, my brothers and I dragging sacks down the rows beside migrant crews who eked a living from this backbreaking work. July 4 was Daddy's one summer holiday from the bank. While friends, neighbors, cousins took to a picnic table or a set of water skis, my father and his sons regularly hauled baled hay out of the fields and stacked it for winter feeding. There was no point complaining. We were raised by parents who didn't expect their lives to be easy or their children to mouth off about it. Bellyaching might get you in a worse fix than hard work in hot weather. Tears were even riskier. "I'll give you something to cry about," Daddy would say, following through if need be. No idle threats in our house.

The farm dictated the terms of our daily lives. It shaped my father, molding him into an often intractable man, precipitating what I have come to think of as the most difficult relationship of my life. The road to town was only ten miles, but when we drove from a week of work to a night of dancing, we might as well have teleported to another planet. Along the way, invisible but happy body snatchers got hold of Daddy, so that when we walked into the Rifle Club, he no longer even looked like the stern paternal figure who loomed over my days. The abduction I speak of here was true of others too, with much the same explanation. Which is that something about dancing transformed all of us.

During high school, I worked for Uncle Wilton, running the cash register at what we used to call an icehouse, sorting soft-drink bottles, and running the ice crusher in a vault set well below freezing. As a nephew, I was often included in lunches with my uncle and his family. After a summer of such, I began to think of Wilton and Madeline Meischen's relationship as "stormy." I had only one marriage to compare, and talker that I am, I was regularly stunned mute by the things my aunt and uncle said to each other over an absolutely delicious meal. But the body snatchers grabbed them too on the way to the Rifle Club. Aunt Madeline had perhaps the most infectious laugh I knew growing up—and the shortest tether on her patience. Uncle Wilton had a heart too kind by miles—paired with a temper so mercurial you could get whiplash just watching when he got his dander up. Her impatience, his short fuse—these were shed easily as an unnecessary summer jacket when they got out of the family car and walked into the Rifle Club. Aunt Madeline laughed; Uncle Wilton grinned as if his teeth were made for gleaming. He put his right hand at the small of her back. She raised her right lightly to his left. They danced.

And this miracle of my life growing up: at the Rifle Club Hall, my father and I were happy at the same time and in the same place. We didn't seek each other out. Daddy went his way and I went mine. I danced with Mother, with Aunt Madeline, with wives they knew, brushing past Daddy when I approached their table to ask for a dance. Whatever discomfort we felt otherwise—the father who worried too much, well versed in judging his offspring; the son too young to understand worry, well versed in feeling judged—at the Rifle Club I could dance past Daddy and smile, watching him be happy. He could dance past me and toss off one of the wacky wisecracks that otherwise seemed reserved for others.

I am my father's son. I didn't see it at the time. I'm not sure he did either. Picture him: Daddy was a hefty man when I was coming up. He was farm-work strong, with thickly muscled arms. Deep voice, heavy gait, firm handshake. And his firstborn son—my middle name his first—was a slip of a kid, impossibly skinny, hands flailing about like spooked birds caught indoors. "Light in the loafers" would have been the perfect way to describe me on my feet, waving at folks on Main Street, saying "Hi!" and again "Hi!" in a voice that danced right up the scale.

And yet. My father was a talker—storyteller, jokester, clown. He loved entertaining people, loved all eyes on him, all ears. I'm told I started talking at eighteen months. I can attest I haven't stopped since. I've been turning my life into stories for as long as I can remember. I can play the clown with the best of them.

A confession: When I was thirteen, fourteen, fifteen, I saw my father as impossibly moody, impossibly judgmental, his moods and judgments tinged by anger. I promised myself—*promised*—that I would not be a moody, angry father. Thirty years went by, and then one day in my early forties, I woke to a stunning fact. I was a moody, angry father.

Flip sides of a coin. I share both sides with the man who fathered me.

The antic energy running like an undercurrent at the Rifle Club reached its apex with the Paul Jones, an orchestrated group dance that had much in common with highly rule-bound childhood games passed down through generations. Hard to say who loved it more—Daddy or his eldest son. Here's how the South Texas version worked.

The bandleader would announce a Paul Jones, upon which the band launched into a polka. I don't remember if one particular tune was reserved for this dance. It doesn't matter. Folks paired up and entered the counterclockwise motion. To someone watching, the moving floor of dancers looked like a slow-motion, oversize carousel, a time-lapse kaleidoscope, as colorful skirts merged and swirled in ever-changing patterns. Until the bandleader blew his whistle, the signal for couples to disengage. The women moved into a circle at the center of the hall, the men into a slightly larger circle around them. Men circled to the left, women to the right, moving their feet in a shuffle that marked the polka beat. This interlude was a chance to catch your breath, to greet or wink at dancers you knew as they spun by in the other circle, to wonder who the dance would pair you with next. Because when the whistle blew, you paired up—man and woman, woman and man—with the person opposite you in the other circle. And launched into the polka again. Until the whistle blew: back into man and woman circles. And when the whistle blew again: a new polka partner. With an eager crowd the Paul Jones could go on and on, circles circling, dancers dancing out of themselves.

At such moments, our bodies are instruments of something else entirely, some other force. We might call that force God, timelessness, cosmic energy. You choose. And if for you dancing goes beyond mating ritual, if the dance itself is what you love—you know what can happen. You know that on a good night, with the right partner, the right surge of energy, you can dance out of the body that otherwise binds you and into something rare, inspired, exhilarating. At the risk of overstepping myself, I might even call it sacred.

Running can be like this. Those who run for the sheer love of running know this to be true, that running takes you out of yourself. And there's a scientific explanation—what we know about endorphins and their role in brain chemistry. But that kind of thinking can be reductive, can make us think that running and dancing are just cheaply purchased avenues to a purely physiological rush. I say it's more than that. I say endorphins are a vehicle too. They can take us elsewhere.

Sex can too—sex and love—even sex coupled with opposing emotions, as when the body says *I want* and a voice in the head says *no*, pleasure grappling with judgment.

In the fall of 1965, several weeks before my seventeenth birthday, I found myself on a country road after sunset, high beams carving a tunnel in starless dark. The man beside me at the wheel had crossed a significant boundary. I was an adolescent; he was not, though the gap meant little to me. This man was in the same age bracket as older boys I'd known riding the bus to school when I was nine or ten years old. They were several years past high school by now, but I saw them as eternal seniors—old enough to purchase alcohol but decades behind my father, his brothers and friends. Which is to say that nothing about my companion on the night in question even remotely suggested *adult*, let alone authority figure.

Were it not for a bit of foolishness two summers before, nothing might have happened on that night-drenched road. In the weeks before I started high school, though, another boy and I, having found ourselves alone in the dark behind closed doors, had let ourselves handle each other. We had nothing in common except that mutual masturbation electrified us.

Two years later, on what was to be an ordinary drive between Orange Grove and the family farm, my left hand fell into the driver's right. And I insist on the verb. I know what Freud would say: there are no accidents. Experience tells me otherwise, tells me intentions didn't figure at the outset, even in the reflexive movement of fingers and thumb by which the driver and I were holding hands. Dancers do this without thinking. And so we rode along, passenger and driver, this simple touch between us, rode on through a stretch of stillness, the loveliest calm of my life, enclosed together in the November night. Until memory fired, crucial signals leaping across synaptic gaps, and I wanted what hands can do with a man in the dark when no one is looking.

I marvel, looking back, at the shameless expertise with which I orchestrated what came next, relaxing my neck so that my head lolled to the side as if I'd fallen asleep, my torso leaning, leaning, as happens when someone nods off in a car. My right hand found its way to his hand holding mine and lit there briefly. No sign from him. I put my hand on his thigh—again like a movement in sleep—and let my fingers rest there. But that wasn't what I was after. My fingers slipped upward, upward, and touched the tongue of fabric at his fly. A beat. Another. A ridge of hardness throbbed beneath my fingertips, and the current surged in me. The driver shifted, scooting forward on the car seat ever so slightly, flexing his hips beneath my hand. I reached beneath his fly, fingered the zipper there, warm as blood, grasped the zipper tab between thumb and forefinger, tugged gently. The zipper gave. I slipped inside, fingered another opening, slipped inside again. Felt flesh as warm as fever. A pulse.

The driver took his right hand from my left, grasped my right wrist firmly, and removed my hand from his pants. "I know you're awake, David. Sit up, now. We can't do this." There was something raw in his voice, a kind of pain I had not heard spoken before. A kind of longing.

I sat up, slid back to my side of the car, and slipped out of myself, nothing left of me but cold awareness of this boy who has unzipped a man's pants and reached inside, touched eager, happy, touch-me flesh. Tethered here, riding out the silence, wide awake in the night, I can see. This boy has no place here, has no place else to go. He has stopped doing what he started. He knows without knowing that he will not stop wanting what he wants.

Family members, schoolmates, my high-school sweetheart—anyone who knew me then could make a game of guessing the driver's identity, but the obvious choices would be wrong, wrong, and wrong again. The locals who wanted what I wanted had learned to hide their hunger behind a shit-kicker slouch, a twangy sneer, smooth moves with a woman on the dance floor.

When I was twenty-six, at a popular South Texas eatery, with lots of drinking and joking and noise, a man my father's age, someone I'd known all my life, leaned over where I was sitting, as if to say something beneath the voices, and put his tongue in my ear. He was a father several times over, married for decades, with children my age. I had danced with his wife at the Rifle Club when he danced by with one of the other wives, winking in our direction. This intimate thing he did to me, a deeply private gesture in a wildly public space—it might have been a joke, the drunken hetero aping taboo behavior. But I recognized the current passing from him to me, a surge of wanting never spoken, aching to become a whisper in the ear he touched with his tongue. *Know me. Please.*

I knew. I'd been down the road with my anonymous driver. The law would have called him a man, but I passed that age soon enough myself. Hindsight revealed him for what he was—a boy fumbling his way into manhood and failing and trying again. Several friends I've told about this chapter in my sexual history—a therapist too, whom I saw in my early forties—have looked at the age gap and suggested a victim-abuser relationship. To this simplistic assessment, all I can say is that I was seventeen and then eighteen, that I'd been driving a tractor unsupervised since the age of ten or eleven, driving to and from town on my own since the age of fourteen, assuming adult responsibilities in a world that expected such. I knew exactly what I was doing the night I put my hands on this man and each time thereafter when I devised a way to be with him where others wouldn't see. I made adult if con-

472

flicted decisions about my first serious sexual relationship; any anguish I suffered as a result was adult anguish. I was no one's victim. From the beginning, then, I knew what we were doing was not child's play. What drew me was primal; it was dangerous. I faltered in my will to resist, faltered before church authority too. I knew just how powerful was the impulse moving in me when the parish priest, recognizing my voice in confession, threatened to expose me. Still, I didn't stop.

I suppose I might have chosen to end what we were doing, might have summoned the will, though I don't see how. And stopping would have changed nothing, which is to say that every fiber of me wanted him. And not in the way of the moody Top 40 songs I poured my heart into, Bobby Hatfield's astonishing rendition of "Unchained Melody," for example. The lyrics, the voice, are fueled by pure, unconflicted desire:

> I've hungered for your touch . . . a long, lonely time.
> Time goes by so slowly. And time can do so much.
> Are you still mine?

Desire without guilt—the loneliness that comes of wanting a *woman* who might not want you back—*this* is what I wanted. Listening to the Righteous Brothers, to the power in Hatfield's voice, I was able to believe in the possibility, though that kind of sexual love was always in future tense, always enclosed in the parentheses of marriage. But the man I was actually having sex with—I did not want him to be mine, did not want him to love me. He tried to tell me that he did—once, maybe more—as our hands went hungrily to work. I stopped him, appalled. I didn't want love. I wanted to crush myself against him, tear him out of his clothes, feel the heat in him, the heart beating beneath his skin. The moments when I knew I would go to him, the moments after—these were agony—wanting the one thing I didn't want, loving what I hated, hating *him* because he made me want him, because he was ready to say words I loathed.

Fifty years later I listen to Jeff Buckley singing "Hallelujah," and I remember what I felt with a man I first touched on a road in the dark, seventeen years old, absolutely unprepared for the wreckage that was coming. Buckley's nimble fingering pulls me in—a light, almost imperceptible waltz tempo running beneath the melody so tenderly, it puts me in mind of Wordsworth, though what I hear when Buckley's voice comes in, Leonard Cohen's lyrics raw in him, is suffering recalled in something like tranquillity. Fingers on the strings move in me like the ghost of myself on a dance floor long empty of anything except memory, right hand at the lower back, left hand raised to take the hand of a man I never danced with.

The words, the voice, the notes of the guitar: *this* is the kind of love I didn't want, the kind of love that didn't care what I wanted, that strapped me to a kitchen chair and broke me open:

> Maybe there's a God above,
> But all I ever learned from love
> Was how to shoot at someone who outdrew you.
> And it's not a cry you can hear at night—
> It's not somebody who's seen the light.
> It's a cold and it's a broken Hallelujah.

Praise and anguish in each and every breath, a kind of despairing gratitude distilled into a single word—*Hallelujah*—repeated, repeated: a litany, a rehearsal that doesn't heal the wound inflicted by this kind of love.

During the long, long months as I passed seventeen and then eighteen, I lived two lives. Really three. Expert at compartmentalizing, I spent most days happily immersed in the humdrum of school and farm life— chores in the morning; bus ride to school, classes with friends and girl-friend; farm work in the afternoons; homework and television evenings before bed. Dancing had always taken me out of this life and onto another plane. It was a special godsend during those years. At the Rifle Club I could still narrate a man-and-woman story of my own, the life that was supposed to be mine someday. Intermittent sessions with the man no one knew about took up fewer circles on the clock than Saturday night dances, likely less than a dozen hours total in the year and a half we regularly unbuckled each other. But he was the defining experience of my crossing into adulthood, a harbinger of the life to come, though much denied, much resisted, much delayed.

For too long I carried inside me the dance I learned from the Meischens who came before—Valerie and Elwood, Wilton and Madeline—

gone now, all four of them. Theirs was not to be my story, though I made it so for years, finally without regret. Because unexpected blessings came out of my futile persistence, my hesitation, my indirection—out of the intricate web of deceptions that snared both me and those I loved. I call three such blessings by name. Karl Meischen, my son, born September 8, 1980. Jack Meischen, also my son, born October 16, 1982. And Scott Wiggerman—love of my life—companion and lover since February 28, 1997, husband and lover since October 23, 2013.

If, like my father, I can lay claim to a difficult life, I know it was circumstances that made the years hard for Daddy—his own father's suicide, the harsh demands of the farming life, the need to feed and clothe his family through meager seasons. The challenge, even, of learning to love a son who didn't fit the mold. As for me, the central hardship of my life I can trace directly to myself. I am Elwood and Valerie Meischen's eldest son, born to love another man. For half a life I wanted another story, my parents' story, to be mine—a story of husband and wife.

I remember a morning years ago when Daddy woke to one of his moods and couldn't shake it. I was twelve, thereabout, and for some reason on the morning in question, I rode to town with him instead of walking to the school bus. Grandma Meischen lived in town by then; she'd left the farm when I was five. Daddy dropped me at her house before work at the bank. His mother noticed the state he was in—it would have been hard not to—and on that particular morning, she was out of patience.

"You ought to get down on your knees," she told Daddy, "and thank the good Lord." Her forefinger jabbing the air in front of his nose, Grandma delivered a rant, the drift of which was that her son was to shake off his sullen mood, pray thanks to his savior, count the blessings that were his. She said that several times. "Count your blessings."

Watching this little woman tailor my towering father to the boy he would always be to her—being there at this moment among so many others—was a saving grace of my childhood. Seeing that someone could speak to my father the way he often spoke to me. And get away with it. Every time his mother stopped to take a breath, Daddy slumped a little lower and said simply, "Aw, Momma."

His mother was an indisputable blessing of my father's life, and he knew it.

I say much the same here. I am blessed in the man who fathered me, in the woman I called Mother, in the story I learned going dancing with them, though eventually I had to make it my own. I learned that from them too—pure German hardheadedness—the will to make the story mine.

Nominated by The Gettysburg Review

AUBADE FOR NON-CITIZENS

by LO KWA MEI-EN

from THE BEES MAKE MONEY IN THE LION

(CLEVELAND STATE UNIVERSITY POETRY CENTER)

and NEW ORLEANS REVIEW

Alien status, a blue bourgeois dress, the hustle of Rome. A
    waltz—
zoom out—the citizen ingenue's cool, cool crinoline and
    persona
buckling her silhouette into the ahistorical hourglass. *I have*
    no story,
your shout into this century's solar wind, a yellow ribbon on a
    bomb
compromised by compromise, a citizen's birthright, a little box
xeroxed white, the alien body folded like a french flap in the
    epic
determination to predetermine the alien body in the here /
    now.
War is a feed. To be angry is to be fed up; citizens eat blood,
education aside. I should explore, not go off. The future,
    the TV
vectoring the colonists' self-portrait, thumbs up for this
    handmade
family, zoom in—Citizen 2 karaokes in low gravity (*Zou Bisou*
    Bisou),
unlikable kiss shot back to Earth. The camera winking, stiff
grafts in the ship's greenhouse not trembling at the speed
    of light,
turmeric tumescing quietly, and the brilliant soldier of a pear
    sapling.

Here on Earth, the rapist pledges, fear femmes my waist,
   it wastes

sure as the sun is wasting. Zoom out—the atomic story is
   smooth

in places if no one is protagonist but particle in motion or
   minor

residue of emotion's creation myth. I don't know why I love
   us, I

just do. Zoom in. Citizen 4 weeps, eats a webcam, *eff-you-s*
   HQ,

quarantines herself to the brink with paper porn. Citizen 1
   goes by PJ.

Kick kick, my grief is underfoot, empty bucket and an enemy
   on top

promised a drink of water for love, the landing we couldn't
   stick,

last zoom—every alien has a face. My face, a flipbook, a free
   pass to

outré worlds. Reassignment of number, denial of trial. A glass
   wall.

Might-be-colonists put the finger to the screen to zoom out
   or in,

napping on—baby, wake up, the foreign body just fell in the
   dream—

Nominated by Cleveland State University Poetry Center, Shelley Wong

WHEN YOU DIED

by JANE WONG

from FOUNDRY

Five years of fireflies in oil; five years of ants gnawing
through red flags; five years of pockmarked suns, your face:
each ray, each sweltering August; five years of unraveling,
hair loosening from your crown like a rotten tooth;
five years of how easy it is to split a frog in two; five
years of pollen in your mouth, that bitter buzzing;
one year of leeches along the spine, fattening; two years:
are rats good to eat? Another year: sun-licked pots;
your birth year: the cold bones of a stranger's hand;
the quiet year: no one wants to look at a gaping
fish, swallowing water endlessly; the sixth year:
to place these flowers on or in the graves?

Nominated by Foundry, Molly Bendall

REIGN OF EMBERS

by CECILIA WOLOCH

from THE AMERICAN JOURNAL OF POETRY

"In the dark time will there also be singing?"
"Yes, there will be singing about the dark time."—*Bertolt Brecht*

•

I. (Aftermath: Paris)

Can you make a song of the love of death?
(*And how does it go?* the poet asks.)

Some had been singing before they died.
Some had been bringing the food to their lips.
Some had been kissing. Some had been drunk.
Some had been screaming, *God is good*,
as they fired into the crowd.

Can you make a prayer from the love of death,
from the fingerprint of the finger
blown off the assassin's hand?

Can I love my enemy as myself?

Bless the almighty, the powerless.
Bless the boy who was circumcised
at thirteen. Bless the imam's knife.
Bless the girls who are being raped,
who are strapping on suicide vests.
Bless them remotely, as they detonate.
Bless whoever made the bomb.

How do you fight the love of death?
I ask my friend, who says, *You can't.*
It only takes eighteen years to grow
a suicide bomber from a child
and they have this figured out.

But who are *they*? I ask.

On the small screen, flickering, I watch
a young man unfolding, refolding a shirt —
the shirt he wore that night, he says.
Whose blood? He doesn't know.
Can I put it away now? he asks.
I don't know what to do with it.

Can I make a prayer of this?

Some died with the food still in their mouths.
Some died with the music playing, still.
Some died in one another's arms.
Some were dragged away to live —

hands trembling, lighting a cigarette,
It's monstrous, the young man says,
when I saw what a bullet could do.

A flower of flame.
A blossom of blood.
A shower of gold-hot sparks.
A blast.

Can you make a song from death?
I ask my friend. He says,
Go to sleep.

•

II. (MacBeth)

The murderer says, *I am one, my liege,*
whom the vile blows and buffets of the world

481

have so incensed that I am reckless
what I do to spite the world.

Some died having dreamt of this —

to cleanse the world of infidels,
to plant a black flag in the sand
where there is no law, no love
but the love of death.

Whose god? Whose flag?

●

III. (Ratline)

One source says the source is everywhere.
One source says the source is our enemy.
One source says the source is us,
with our blundering, with our greed.

Big, shining vehicles crossing the desert.
Shining machines in clouds of sand.
Black flags visible for miles.

Some died having dreamt of this.

One man says, *It's the Russians again.*
One man says, *It's a pipeline, moving oil.*
One man says, *No, a pipeline moving gas.*
One man says, *It began as a shadow movement*
of the U.S. government.

One source says children are being taught
to fire weapons, to throw grenades.
The face of their teacher obscured in the film.
The faces of mothers everywhere.

One source says they are not blunders
but part of a plan to divide the world.

A little truth, a little honor —
is that such a hard thing to wish?

Blood on the pavements of Paris, Beirut,
covered with wreaths and candles now.
One girl from Los Angeles dead,
dark-haired and young, with a name like a flower.

•

IV. (Chateau Marmont, West Hollywood)

He says it's going to take a hundred years to clean up the mess
we've made. By *us* he means Britain, France, the U.S. His
country, and mine. Our complicity. Bombs going off over
children's heads, a rain of dust and broken concrete and, in
the piles of rubble, limbs, torn flesh. He's sitting back in his
chair in the elegant suite in the elegant hotel.

I've got one leg tucked under my hip, one pump kicked off,
something sweet in my mouth. I'm trying to shut up for once
in my life, and just listen. He knows more than I know, I guess,
about what's going on in the Middle East. Who these *holy
warriors* are, who's putting the money into their hands for
more guns and more bombs, who's selling them weapons,
who's buying their oil, who, in the first place, put them in
place, thinking they'd be their best instruments. "It's a very
sophisticated operation," he says, and stutters a bit. *Sophis-
ticated. Sophistica-ted. Sophisticated P.R.* "It's like Hollywood,"
he says, about the videos I'm afraid to watch, the beautiful
propaganda—flashes of fire, flags waving, raised fists—because
I'm afraid I'd get sucked in. "And these kids," he says, "these
kids, they have nothing else. And they're stupid, really *stupid*."
He almost spits the word in disgust. Across the room, our
friend has dozed off sitting up in her chair in their elegant
suite—she's tired, or she's had too much wine. Later, she'll
wake and smile at us, stand up and stretch and go to bed. He'll
walk me back through the private garden, past the pool where
someone yells *fuck—fuck this* or *fuck that*, or *fuck you—*
though I can't see who, through the leafy dark, just the bright
blue eye of the swimmerless pool. And we'll stand for a while

in a crowd of the wealthy young on the sidewalk along Sunset
Boulevard, the valets parking expensive cars for the guests of
the elegant hotel. And I'll wonder, *where does their money
come from, how did they get so much?* Some young women
hobbling on heels so high they look like tilted dolls; some with
faces so famous, so faultless, they don't look human anymore.

•

V. (Dawn Raid in St. Denis: Abdelhamid Abbaoud)

And if you're so in love with death
why are you hiding now?
Why have you barricaded yourself
with your guns against their guns?
Who are you, and who are *they* —
masked as you mask yourself, blacking out
your only human face.

And who was the girl, falling in flames,
and what was the flower of her name?

Were you there, when the shots rang out
and some lay down and some crawled away
and some were hunted, still, like rats
in the basement rooms of the concert hall?

We ran through a maze,
one woman says, *We found a nook
and tried to make ourselves
as small as we could get.*

In St. Denis, still, the bullets flare
where they've flared since dawn, *like fireworks.*
And you are barricaded, still, and still
love every death but your own.

(*They seemed afraid,* one young man said
of the men who took hostages, in the end;
in the end, they hadn't wanted to die.)

484

How to make a song from the love of death?
How to make a black mask of the dawn,
of your own once-human face?

No children will go to school in St. Denis today.
There would be no books in the world you'd make
but the book you call *holy*
and have drenched in the blood
of the only world there is.

•

VI. (News)

One source says it's a *rat line* moving weapons
from Libya through Turkey to Syria.
One source says it's the Turkish president's son
getting rich transporting the terrorists' oil.

One source says the oil is put onto tankers,
then shipped to Malta, to Israel.

One man says, from his prison cell,
"You need to think like a woman,
for men only fight for power."

•

VII. (The Sixth Day: St. Denis/Alfortville)

The detonations went on for hours.
That's how *enormous* the arsenal was.
Almost incalculable, they say,
the weapons stockpiled
in those rooms, the rounds
of ammunition fired.

And those dead inside so dead,
at last, they could not be identified.

A floor collapsing, a ceiling collapsing,
one young woman's body
exploding in flames.

Are you safe? I type, *Keep safe*,
to my friend in another Paris suburb
where a *safehouse* has been found:
two rooms, abandoned, strewn with trash —
pizza boxes and chocolate wrappers,
rubber tubing and used syringes —

here the camera swerves, and stops.

Are the children safe? I type
to my old love whose daughter is named
for one white flower, in Arabic,
whose son is, almost, already, the age
of the young men who attacked,
who were not much more than boys.

One father bows his head and says
he'd prayed that his son was already dead —
the son who had kidnapped his younger brother,
thirteen, and taken the boy to Syria.
One father opens his arms and says,
This country gave us everything.
One young man's father comes to the door.
Did you know, did you know?
the reporters ask.
Did I know? he says. *Did I know?*
If I had known,
I'd have killed him myself

How to make a prayer from the love of death?

They'd been drug dealers, petty thieves,
they'd been in prison, they were young,
then they put on the black masks of warriors
and called this *holy war, jihad*
and call, in death, for the end of the world.

Let this not be the end of the world.

But who put the weapons into their hands?
On whose hands, now, the blood
of the young turned to flowers, turned to flame?

Have we chosen the wrong men to lead us?
Have we made the wrong people rich?
Have we put power into the hands
of those who love power as much as death?

How will I know my enemy, in the end,
if the air is full of poison gas?

A man kneels in the street
where wreaths have been lain
and tells his small son, *Yes,
the flowers protect us.*
The child believes.

The young woman whose body fell in flames
had only begun to wear the veil.
She didn't know what it meant, they say,
she was smitten with her cousin,
she was in love with him, she screamed,
He's not my boyfriend! as she fell.
The detonations went on for hours.
The dead in the rooms behind the barricade
could not be identified.

They had been drug dealers, prisoners, thieves.
They had been *welcomed with open arms.*
They had been boys, once, given to suck,
— as all boys are, in these times —
on the pornography of violence
in which a woman becomes a bomb,
in which the flower of her sex becomes
a passageway to death.

Can they be forgiven?
Can we?
Can the god in the girl still rise up, sing?

•

VIII. (Veering)

And let he who is without sin
cast the first stone.
And let she who is without blame
fall blamelessly, in flames.
And let our rocket launchers not fall
into the hands of our enemies.

But who are our enemies now?

A *rat line*, some say,
transporting weapons
from Libya to Syria.
A *shadow government*, some say,
transporting the terrorists' oil
across Turkey to the sea.

Two million children fleeing
into the arms of what country now?

A *medieval moment*, says my friend,
the child of the children of children of slaves.
Some people who have everything
don't want anyone else to have anything.

A man in prison in Kirkuk, Iraq,
from a family of seventeen,
who'd worked building car bombs
to feed his family —
What other work could he get? he asks.
What other choice did he have?
When the Americans came in,
they got rid of Saddam and gave us this.

488

Under Saddam, we were starving,
but at least we were alive.

And the god of the men
who paid for the bombs
is not his god, he says.
Their god is not my god.

And the boys in Europe who flocked to Syria
wanted adventure, wanted blood.
Wanted the Hollywood
Hollywood promised them.
Wanted a god who loved them best.

Death to the infidels.
Death to Nohemi Gonzalez,
who sat in a Paris cafe with her friends.
Death to Abdelhamid Abaaoud,
who planned the attacks in which how many died?
Death to the man in prison in Kirkuk
sentenced to death. More death.
How many deaths to feed whose god,
to empty the world of infidels?

A boy with a stone in his hand rears back.
The sky fills with falling stars.

Have we veered off-course?
Have we tilted the world
toward rat line, poison gas?
Have we made of our weapons a god
who will not answer when we call?

•

IX. (Lauren: Los Angeles)

Or have we loved wrongly all along?

A young woman comes to my door in Los Angeles,

years since I saw her last,
and with something pleading in her eyes,
something harmed. (*I would not have you harmed*.)

I invite her to sit, I pour wine.
She asks for a cigarette, a light.
She wasn't much more than a girl when we met,
she was my student, a favorite, then.

Now she's tasting the smoke, which is bitter.
Now she's drinking the wine, which is sweet.
Now she's asking if I'm afraid.

We talk, we agree on the shadows between us:
everywhere, blame, lines blurring, crossed.
The shadow governments, shadow wars,
the shadow weapons in shadow arms.
And the man who'd lived for two years in her house,
who'd slept in her bed and shared her food,
called her from prison last week for help,
having beaten another woman badly enough
to have finally broken the law.
A felony, she says, *I was just lucky it wasn't me.*

I tell her that I was *just lucky,* too.
That we're all lucky to be alive.
Because some women die for love.
Some women die in the name of love.
Some women died unnamed, unloved.

The young woman in St. Denis
whose name is on no one's tongue,
calling out from the midst of the explosions,
Help me, help me, please.
Calling out, *He's not my boyfriend* —
the last words to ever leave her mouth.
Then the detonation, the bomb,
her body turning to flame in the air,
her head and her spine, two separate pieces,

cinder and bone on the pavement below.
Who ever loved that girl? I wonder,
who loved to party, to drink and smoke,
who her own friends called *clueless*
— and these were her friends?

Whose mother and father had given her up,
as a child, into foster care,
who had lived nowhere and everywhere,
who had only begun to wear the veil,
who *didn't understand what it meant*,
who stood flaming in the sky a moment
then, burning, fell through the air.

Stupid, I think, *stupid kids*
who thought they loved death
until death came for them.

And my young friend, ash in her palm,
trembling a little, agrees.

And Paul, on the road to Damascus,
hearing the voice of Christ in the wind
asking, *Why do you persecute me?*
turned, in terror, to love, called love
the fulfillment of the law.
Love is the fulfillment of the law.

But where is the law when you need the law?

A young man had tried to flee the concert hall
in the midst of the chaos and bullets and blood;
he'd climbed out a window and clung
to a bare wall three stories above the street;
just below him, a woman, also clinging,
but slipping, *I'm slipping*, she sobbed,
I'm pregnant, I can't hold on.
So the young man pulled himself back inside
— what could he do?—and ran down the stairs

and pulled her to safety—was she safe?
And so he was caught, himself, held hostage
by the terrorists barricaded below —
because, in the end, they'd been terrified.
In the end, they'd not wanted to die.
Because the body wants to live.
They sat with their backs against a wall,
young men like him, but with guns in their arms.
And one threw a wad of cash at his feet
and, *Do you love money?* he asked.
And when the young man told him, *No,*
the young man with the gun said, *Burn it, then.*

Later, his body so pulverized
he could not be identified
except by the prints of one fingertip, spit.

And how did the other young man survive?

And the young cops in the street stood trembling
among the body parts, broken glass,
the dog they'd loved blown apart in the barrage,
the pavement blood-stained
when dawn finally came.

And where is the law when you need the law?
Where is love, as she falls in flames?
My young friend smoking a cigarette.
The dark machines screaming through the sky
over Damascus as we speak.

•

X. (Elizabeth: Los Angeles)
They had a power for death we wanted. —W.S. Merwin

And are these, then, the holy wars?
Is this *jihad, martyrdom*
for a heaven so filled with virgins
the seams of heaven explode?

Now a mass grave has been found,
filled with the corpses of women too old
to have been the warriors' wives, or their slaves.

But who put the weapons into their hands,
who took their money, drank their oil?

We're riding downtown in a car-for-hire,
my friend beside me, whose sight is failing,
her hand resting lightly in my hand;
the sleek car gliding through the gleam
of *the City of Angels*, Los Angeles,
our dark-skinned driver glancing back
in the rear-view mirror, smiling at us.

Guess where it is, he asks,
my favorite country in Africa?

Because my friend likes to talk to strangers,
she likes to ask them where they've been
and she's asked, and he wants us to ask him
where his favorite country is,
he wants to tell us,
So tell us, she says.

Rwanda, he answers, his smile
lighting up in the rear-view mirror,
because, after the genocide there,
so few men were left alive,
it's a country of women and children, now,
a new country of the young.
And the women who've taken the law
and the government into their hands
hold everyone accountable, he says.

Because all the warriors are dead.
Because they killed one another so well.

Allahu Akbar, God is great,
or maybe just *good*, and good is enough.
My friend, who is losing her sight,
for whom light is failing, thanking him.

Nominated by The American Journal of Poetry

MAYBE MERMAIDS AND ROBOTS ARE LONELY

fiction by MATTHEW FOGARTY

from STILLHOUSE PRESS

1

And just because his skin is steel doesn't mean he feels nothing. Maybe they're at a beach and she's in with the tide. Or maybe they're at the tops of skyscrapers, a city between them and all they can see is each other: her with the curls that fall in a tangle over her shoulders and the dress that drapes her fins, him with the earnestness of a logic board. Wherever it is they find each other, he has to believe in the possibility because if this isn't possible, what is?

Maybe they have coffee or a drink. She's intelligent, passionate about the sea. He's funny. She touches his arm and there's a spark. Later, they're at his factory, afterhours. In the breakroom, he finds salt and a jug of water. They lay under his favorite socket. He's barrel-chested, cylinder limbs heated drunk with her coursing energy. She's an electrical drug; her lips tap his circuit veins. He says, "I'd rust for you." She says, "You leave me breathless." Her grip is firm. His alloys green her clamshell breasts.

2

Maybe it's morning then and they're still at the factory when the first shift comes in.

Or maybe they woke early. They're already at the shore among schools of surfers. There's sand in his hinges; he feels unplugged. She says she has to go back. She says, "I wish you would come."

And maybe that's it. He lets her leave. Maybe his heart is a heat sink, a dull organ that shields his mainframe from her glow.

Or maybe it's clockwork, his heart, and maybe there's a screw that's twisted, a gear that slows. His LED eyes fade. There's an electric tear. He says, "I wish I could go."

A wave flows in. She ebbs out with it.

3

At the factory, he ratchets parts on the line, his hard drive looping that last image—her arms extended, hair trailing behind, the flip of a fin as she dives under, her wake shimmying the surface. Maybe that's when his memory loads an image of a surfer shedding a wetsuit.

In the closet, there are sheets of silicone rubber, bottles of glue and sealant, spools of thread. He lays them over a worktable, looms it all into the shape of him, his metal hands mechanical, methodical. If he could sweat, he'd wipe his brow. The moon sets in the high factory window.

4

At the beach, his pincers clamp at the sleeves, fit the wetsuit over his tin-can body. He goes awkwardly into the water, his feet softly sinking into the wet sand and the wet sand sucking thick against his step, against the pull and fall of his metal limbs. The water rises to his articulated joints and rises further. A broken wave washes against his mechanical chest, splashes the gloved whole of him and recedes to the warm of the air and then splashes again, higher, and recedes, the cool of it fogging the plastic mask he's sewn in to see. He loses his axis. The sea bottom descends. The sea floor gives way to water. He's surrounded by it. He's in it. His metal body buoys, and for a moment he floats, free—feels the surface as archived memory—before realizing it's a feeling he was never meant to have felt. He flails for it and from his flailing he floats down and he flails more and he goes deeper, floats further underwater, airless, deep and dumb.

He wonders whether robots can drown. He wonders whether she's forgotten him. Or whether maybe he's in the wrong ocean, or it's all just a cruel glitch. She's a failure of programming; she doesn't exist. Maybe this is what happens in the night when the factory is closed and it's dark: idle robots dream of mermaids.

Or maybe that's when she catches him, thrashing for life, fishhooks her arms under his. He says, "I'm sorry. I'm not programmed to swim." And she smiles, takes his hand, says, "Then don't let go."

Nominated by Stillhouse Press

TELEMACHUS

fiction by JIM SHEPARD

from ZOETROPE: ALL STORY AND GRAYWOLF PRESS

To commemorate Easter Sunday, the captain has spread word of a ship-wide contest for the best news of 1942, the winner to receive a double tot of rum each evening for a week. The contestants have their work cut out for them. Singapore has fallen. The *Prince of Wales* and the *Repulse* have been sunk. The Dutch East Indies have fallen. Burma is in a state of collapse. Darwin has been so severely bombed it had to be abandoned as a naval base. The only combatants in the entire Indian Ocean standing between the Japanese Navy and a linkup with the Germans, who are currently having their way in Russia and North Africa, seem to be us. And one Dutch gunboat we came across a week ago with a spirited crew and a crippled rudder.

We are the *Telemachus*, as our first lieutenant reminds us each morning on the voice-pipe: a T-class submarine—not so grand as a U, but not so dismal as an S. Most of us have served on S's and are grateful for the difference, even as we register the inferiority of our own boat to every other nation's. The Royal Navy leads the world in battleships and cruisers, we like to say, and trails even the Belgians in submarine design.

In the chaos following Singapore's surrender we've been provided no useful intelligence or patrol orders. A run through the Sunda Strait between Java and Sumatra ended in a hail of enemy fire on the approaches to Batavia. At our last dry dock the Ceylonese further undermined our morale by invariably gazing out their harborside windows at first light to see if the Japanese had arrived. We have no idea whether we will find any more ports available to us now that we've shipped back out to sea. We have no idea whether we will find more torpedoes once we've expended our store. "Heads up there, boys," our captain joked to those of us within earshot of his map table last night. "Is there anything more exhilarating than carrying on alone out on the edge of a doomed world?"

"Sounds like Fisher's childhood, sir," Mills responded, and everyone looked at me and laughed.

They view me as a sorry figure even by the standards of their meager histories. As a boy I was a horrid disappointment, pigeon-chested and gap-toothed, and as grandiose as I was untalented. The only activity for which I was any use at all was running, so I ran continually, though naturally not in competitions or road races but just all about the countryside, in fair weather and foul. It brought me not a trace of schoolboy glory, though it did at times alleviate my fury at being so awful at everything else.

The characterization my parents favored for me was *out of hand,* as in, *What does one do when a boy gets out of hand?* My stepfather inclined toward the strap; my mother, the reproachful look. Her only brother had been killed in the first war, and her first husband had come to a bad end, as well; and my stepfather never tired of pointing out that a disapproving countenance was her solution to most of life's challenges. He said about me that by the time I was out of short pants and he was forced to introduce me at pubs or on the street, friends sympathized.

My father had been presumed lost at sea on a bulk cargo ship that had gone missing between Indonesia and New South Wales. When I asked if he had loved me, my mother always replied that it hurt too much to recall such happiness in any detail. When I pressed for particulars nonetheless, she said only that he had been quick to laugh and that no man had possessed a greater capacity to forgive. When I asked my aunts they said they'd barely known the man, and when I asked if he'd been pleased with me, they said they were sure that had been the case, though they also remembered him not much liking children.

My stepfather viewed my running as a method of avoiding achievement or honest labor and marveled at my capacity for sloth. He pressed upon me *Engineering Principles for Boys* and *Elementary Statistics* and all sorts of other impressive-looking volumes I refrained from opening. He asked if I was really so incurious about the world of men, and I reassured him that I was very curious about the world of men, and he responded that in such case I must bear in mind that the world of men was the sphere of industry, and I clarified that I meant the *adventurous* world of men, that arena of tropic seas and volcanic cataclysms and cannibal feasts and polar exploits. He said that if I wanted to grow up a fool I might as well join the navy, which was precisely what I had already resolved to do.

Mills told everyone when he arrived aboard that he'd been one of those posh boys who'd gone to boarding school where at great expense he'd been provided rotten food and insufficient air and exercise, and so submarine duty oddly suited him. His father had been great with speculation and then it had all gone smash and he had hung himself. Mills remembered his mother sitting in the drawing room during the months that followed with all the bills that she didn't dare to open, since there was no money to pay them, and he remembered thinking that it would be a good thing for her if she had one less mouth to feed. He'd been a chauffeur, a silk-stocking salesman, a shipyard hand, and the second mate of a sailing ship before signing on with His Majesty's Navy.

As gunner's mates we bunk in the torpedo stowage compartment, between the tubes. He calls me "the Monk" because even in our tiny living space I never bother with pictures or photographs. I carry what I want to see in my head. Everything else feels like clutter.

"Our mate here doesn't know how to take things easy," he says by way of explanation to our fellow torpedomen. He seems to think he panders to my whimsies with a resigned good humor.

Mills was assigned to us at Harwich as a replacement for a mate we'd lost to carbon monoxide poisoning when a torpedo's engine had started prematurely in the tube. He asked me confidentially what sort of boat he was joining, and I recounted our most recent patrol, which I described as three weeks of misery that we'd endured without sighting a single enemy ship. We'd run aground and been unsuccessfully bombed by our own air force. We'd damaged our bow in a collision with the dock upon our return. He said that on *his* most recent patrol they'd surfaced between two startled German destroyers, each so near abeam that their bow wakes had spattered onto the submarine's deck. He and his captain on their bridge had just gaped up at the Germans above them, since they'd been beneath the elevation of the German guns, and too close to ram without the destroyers ramming one another. He said they'd pitched back down the conning tower ladder with the Germans still shrieking and cursing them. He said they'd mostly worked the arctic reaches out of Murmansk, sinking so much German tonnage that the Russians had presented them with a reindeer.

He said he was pining for a nurse he'd met in the Red Cross who, last he'd heard, had been sent to London and now no doubt was pouring lemonade over the wounded in the East End. Her father upon first meeting him had cordially asked, "And who or what are *you*?" and her mother, upon his reply, had remarked only that people had been doing dreadful things at sea for as long as she could remember. He said that every time he'd managed to arrange some privacy with the nurse and attempt a liberty with her she'd begged him instead to "do something useful," though he'd been encouraged by her remark about her father that no man had ever behaved so badly with the ladies and gotten away with it.

Occasionally when he was particularly displeased with the lack of vivacity in my responses he'd say that he didn't suppose I had any of my own experiences to relate, and I'd assure him I had very few, though I had in fact before I left home conceived an intense and inappropriate fondness for a cousin on my mother's side. This cousin's own mother in her house displayed a photograph of herself and my lost father alone under an arbor, peering at one another and smiling, but when I asked about it, the woman appeared faintly stricken and was no more informative than my mother. When I was fourteen and my cousin twelve I lured her into a neighbor's garden and in my overheated state crowded my face in close to hers, alarming her. Bees drowsed above a flower she'd been examining. She turned to fix her eyes upon my mouth, and when I moved still closer she backed farther away. She was chary around me during our visits afterward but also took my hand under tables in dining rooms and once, having run into me unexpectedly in a hallway, put a finger to my lips. In my fantasies I still imagine an unlikely world in which I would be allowed to marry her and she would want to marry me. In the packet of correspondence I received upon arrival in the Pacific my mother noted that my cousin Margery had let on that I was writing *her*, at least, and my cousin in her response to my letters asked apropos of nothing if I remembered a day years earlier during which I had acted very odd in the garden beside my home. When off duty I lie in my berth between tubes five and six and wonder what others would make of someone who can conceive of tenderness for only one other being, and a tenderness improper at that.

That hallway encounter occurred the month following my eighteenth birthday, soon after which I served my first sea duty on the HMS *Resolution,* an elderly battleship that had been hurriedly refitted, and still dreaming of my cousin I stumbled around its great decks on those tasks I was able to execute, grateful for the small mercy of remaining unnoticed. We sailed around the Orkneys in seas so tumultuous that during one gale our captain threw up on my feet. The other excitement about which I was able to write my cousin transpired one calm morning when we all turned out on the quarterdeck to witness the spectacle of the second pilot ever launched from a seaplane catapult. The first had broken his neck from the colossal acceleration. The second had been provided a chock at the back of his head for support.

I detailed for her my impressions of my first submarine, the *Seahorse*, and the way I'd almost fallen overboard when hurrying across the narrow plank onto its saddle tanks while the chief petty officer watched from the bridge, expressing his displeasure at my insufficient pace. How intimidating I'd found its insides, its lower half packed with trimming tanks, fuel tanks, oil tanks, electric batteries, and so on, and its upper all valves and switches and wiring and cables and pressure gauges and junction boxes, and how I'd had to learn from painful experience which valve was likely to crack me on the head over which station, and the revelation that above the cramped wooden bunks were cupboards and curtains. I described how the conning tower became a wind tunnel when we surfaced and the diesels were sucking in air, and how the diesels themselves were a pandemonium of noise in such confined space. I described a rare look through the periscope, as I glimpsed far more clearly than I'd expected a flurry of tumbling green sea that blurred the eyepiece like heavy rain on a windscreen and then swept past.

There was much I chose to spare her. On our first sea trial the piston rings wore away and exhaust flooded the engine room and everyone had to work gas-masked at their stations, sweating and panting and ready to faint. On our second one of our own destroyers tried to ram us and then, after we'd identified ourselves, reported that it had pursued without success two German U-boats. On our practice emergency dives everyone threw themselves down the conning tower ladder, trampling each other's fingers, and not even shouted orders could be heard above the awful Klaxon. On training maneuvers we lost the torpedo-loading competition, the navigation competition, the crash-dive competition, and the Lewis gun competition. On our second practice torpedo attack everything went according to plan, and when I reported accordingly to our torpedo officer he said, "Are you hoping for a prize?"

With nowhere to go we are headed vaguely toward the Andaman Sea off the west coast of Indochina, diving by day and gasping in relief in the cooler surface air at night. Every few days the captain announces our itinerary. He long ago resolved whenever possible to keep the crew informed, since it is his belief that we have a right to know what we are doing and why, and as security is hardly an issue aboard a submarine.

It is impossible to verify whether the wireless silence has to do more with our forces' standing orders not to give away our positions to the enemy's direction-finders, or with the total unraveling of our efforts in the region. The captain finally patched through to HQ Eastern Fleet and was told to stand by and then nothing more. A week later a Dutch merchant ship we raised on the horizon reported its understanding that the Eastern Fleet had abandoned even Ceylon, and fallen all the way back to Kenya. That, the captain announced, for the time being left the decision to us whether to quit the field or to strike a blow with what we had. He was choosing the latter.

The crew is divided about his verdict. On the one hand, as our torpedo officer advised us, at such a dark time perhaps even an isolated victory could do something to buoy morale. It took only one U-boat to sink the *Royal Oak* in Scapa Flow. On the other hand, alone and unsupported, if we were to attack a fleet of any size at all our chances of escape would be infinitesimal. Run into the right ship, he said, and we could find ourselves in all the papers. Run into the wrong one, Mills replied, and we could find ourselves with seaweed growing out of our ears.

The captain has elected to ignore the few enemy merchant vessels we spy, in order to hoard our likely irreplaceable torpedoes for capital ships. When we're surfaced and the circumstances seem safe he has the wireless operators continue to request information. Upon crossing the tenth parallel he announced over the voice-pipe that as far as he knew the entirety of the Royal Navy's fighting strength had now fled the Indian Ocean for the Bay of Bengal.

Despite the limitation of shifts to four hours, with everyone so cramped and hot and miserable it's an ongoing effort of will to recall what we are supposed to be doing or monitoring every waking second of such a long patrol. Even in the head a lapse in focus can have calamitous results, as any mucking up of the sequence of valve operations to empty the lavatory pan will cause its contents to be pressure- sprayed into the inattentive crewman's face.

Because of the chaos in Ceylon we were revictualed with one type of tinned food only: a peculiar soap-like mutton that's been breakfast, lunch, and dinner for the past three weeks. Those who complain are reminded that it all tastes of diesel oil, anyway. We have weevils in our biscuits, as if we're serving under Nelson at Trafalgar.

A bearing seized in one of the engines and the engineers spent three days disconnecting and slinging the piston; the resulting vibration was so severe our conning tower lookouts couldn't see through their binoculars. Now with that addressed we wait for a ship large enough to engage, and those who complain about the uncanny solitude are reminded what the alternative will mean.

In our berths Mills suggests it's a miracle we've made it this far. He came aboard sufficiently early in our Norway patrols to wish that he hadn't, and he often compares the two theaters for their relative miseries: off Norway we couldn't cook on the surface because it was too rough, whereas here it's impossible when submerged due to the heat. He claims we were even more fatuous then. When the French surrendered we were all upset since it meant the end of shore leave for the rest of the summer, and we spent those months living quietly, fed by wireless rumors, and one day intercepted a plain-language signal pleading for rope and small boats from anyone in the vicinity of Dunkirk. As we were many miles north, all we did by way of response was to wonder at the reason for the break in radio discipline, while we sailed about like imbeciles, puzzled at such empty seas.

After Dunkirk the expectation was that the Germans would invade from either Normandy or Norway, and the RAF had to concentrate on France, so that left our submarine fleet to provide adequate advance warning of any flotilla from the north. The Royal Navy had a total of twelve submarines to dedicate to that work, including ours. Together we were responsible for 1,300 kilometers of Norwegian coastline, although the good news was that military intelligence had decided we could focus on those few ports from which a sizable offensive force could be mounted. Our orders upon sighting such a formation were to report and then to attack. To report would require us to surface within view of the enemy, which would render the attack part of the directive irrelevant unless their gunners were blind, and the real question would be whether we'd even finish the broadcast. Each submarine had been provided with a padlocked chest of English pounds and Swedish kronor so that those of us bypassed by the invasion could in the event it was successful refuel in Göteborg or some other neutral port and then cross the Atlantic to carry on the fight from the New World.

To evade Luftwaffe patrols, particularly given the onset of white nights, by June we were submerged nineteen hours daily, and gambling that we could recharge our batteries and refresh our oxygen supply between enemy air sweeps. Those who lost that bet were devastated on the surface. At the end of nineteen hours our atmosphere was so thin that matches wouldn't light and even at rest we heaved like mountain-climbers. American and German submarines "were equipped with tele-scopic breathing tubes that could breach the water like periscopes, but when we proposed the same for our submarines we were told there was no tactical requirement for such a fitting. Our Treasury feared spending a million pounds to save a hundred million, our captain said bitterly, and its ranks were filled with rows of mincing clerks cutting corners.

As our periods submerged lengthened, our medical officer lectured us in small groups about the danger signs of carbon dioxide poisoning. Night after night just as breathing became all but impossible we were saved by a little low cloud providing just enough cover to surface. With the hatches opened, the boat revived from the control room aft to the engine room, though that didn't do much for the torpedo room, so Mills and I and our mates were allowed to come to the bridge two at a time for fifteen minutes of fresh air.

But we weren't safe even below. In calm weather the Norway Deep is clear as crystal, and we could be seen down to ninety feet, which we learned on our first day off the coast when six dive-bombers took their turns with us before heading home.

Around the solstice some nights never did get fully dark, and in the horrible half-light one after another of our boats was destroyed when it was finally forced to surface: the *Spearfish*, the *Salmon*, the *Sturgeon*, the *Trusty*, the *Truant*, the *Thames*. By July losses totaled 75 percent of those ships engaged. During one of our agonizing waits on the sur-face two Me-109s dropped out of the clouds and we could hear the *pom pom* of their cannon fire over the watch's screaming as he plummeted down the ladder, and while we submerged a gunner's mate snapped in his distress and beat himself senseless by pounding his forehead against his torpedo tube. He had doubled his jersey up over the steel first, to muffle the sound.

The invasion failed to materialize but we remained on station never-theless, weathering the autumn and winter storms. During the worst of them we alternated at the watch, poking our faces and flooded binoculars into the wind's teeth, riding up wall after wall of steep and chaotic waves, and maintaining a twenty-four-hour vigilance in case the impossible happened and an enemy funnel materialized, the captain struggling to keep the sextant dry long enough to snatch a star sight and gain a clue as to our whereabouts. In the heaviest gales the breaking waves poured in over the conning tower and filled the control room below, sparking the switchboards and washing through the entire ship. The hatches had to stand open because when the diesels could no longer draw air they stalled, so a stoker with a great suction hose would squeeze atop the tower beside the watch, absorbing the battering as he pumped the water back out.

One moonless night soon after surfacing I was on watch with the captain and two others, and all around in the darkness ship after ship appeared out of the mist, the hulls of transports rising above us like slabs of cliffs. We had run head-on into a full convoy, ascending inside the ring of their escorts, whose attentions were all trained out to sea. There was no time to dive and attack from periscope depth, nor to estimate the correct angles.

"What's the old rough rule?" the captain whispered, extending his hand toward the first transport. "If the enemy is slow, give him nine degrees of lead, or the width of a human hand at arm's length." With his fist as a gunsight over the bow, he set the firing interval through the voice-pipe, then shouted, "Fire!" At the launch of each torpedo we could feel the ship lurch slightly backward, and before leaving the bridge we watched a huge column of water erupt from one of our targets, followed by a thump. He shouted, "Dive!" and plunged down the ladder, and underwater we heard two more huge, far-off bangs at the correct running ranges, and the entire crew cheered. We went deep for hours, hanging silently, those of us off duty forbidden even to move since the clink of a dropped key could expose us, while we listened to the concussions of the sub hunters' depth charges glowing closer, then farther, then closer, until finally the German Navy seemed to run out of explosives.

On my last leave at home after the Norway patrols my cousin Margery insisted on bringing me round to her favorite pub and there a whole series of men with whom she seemed utterly at ease insisted on buying me drinks. "I didn't know you had a favorite pub," I told her, and she said, "Why would you?" She added that I should see her friends, and that her background had not prepared her for the amount some girls could drink. I asked if she had a favorite friend and she cited a girl named Jeanette who had an up-to-date mother who allowed them to smoke in the house. I continually had to repeat myself over the din of the place and when she finally asked with some exasperation why I couldn't speak up, I told her that almost everyone in the crew had what the doctors called fatigue-laryngitis from having reduced our voices to whispers for months in our attempts to outwit the enemy's hydrophones. She apologized, and when I told her it was nothing she took my hand.

One of her friends from a table nearby after a harangue with his mates asked me to settle the matter of whether the English had in fact invented the submarine. "Not hardly," I answered, and he said but hadn't the English always led in naval innovations? Who'd invented the broadside? Who'd converted the world from sail to steam? From coal to oil? And what about turret guns? "What about them," I asked. And Margery chided him that I wasn't allowed to talk shop, and that we needed some privacy to discuss family, thank you.

Once we were left alone she asked how my family *was* getting on, and I told her that my mother had reported she was enduring both my absence and the nightly bombing raids with a puzzling calm. When I asked after her family, Margery reminded me that they all remained greatly concerned about her older brother Jimmy, who was with the RAF and had already lost many friends. She said that now when he returned home on his leaves her mother and sister wore hypnotized looks and their conversations never strayed from speculations about the weather. And that Jimmy had in confidence told her some horrible stories. I suggested that perhaps he shouldn't have, and she responded that she'd known her entire life that the world beyond her home was stunning and heartless, and that all she'd ever heard from her mother about the protection afforded by an adherence to the rules was wrong. While she was speaking she seemed to scan the room first and then to focus on the nearer details of my face.

On our way home in the darkness of the blackout she said that she'd always been fond of me, and I said that she couldn't imagine how fond I'd been of her, and she pulled me into an alley and kissed me, and my chest felt like it did when I was running as a boy, and as her kiss continued her mouth flooded mine with pleasure. When I got hold of my senses I gripped her head and kissed her back. Finally she pulled away and said that we had to get home. While we walked she remarked that *there* was some rule-breaking for you: first cousins, kissing.

We stopped on her front step. She was lit for a moment when some-one waiting up for her peeked through a blackout curtain. She said I should take care of myself. I grasped her hands, still dumbstruck and happy. She asked if she could tell me something, and then waited for my assent. She said that during some of the family gatherings we spent seated beside one another at dining tables it had been for her as if the stillness we made together were like a third person who was neither of us and both, and that when she'd felt the most sad and alone it had helped to imagine herself creeping into that third person who was half hers and half mine.

Did I have a sense of what she meant? she asked after a moment. I told her I did, though some part of it had confused me, and I worried that even in the darkness she could hear that. Well, she said, maybe it would come to me, and she said good night, and kissed my cheek, and the next morning I was off to the Pacific.

We sailed for Singapore through Gibraltar with a merchant convoy bound for Alexandria, and left the convoy to stop over in Beirut, which provided our first sight of a camel outside of a zoo, and where we painted our gray ship dark green for its Far Eastern tour, and from there proceeded to Haifa and Port Said and the Red Sea and on to Aden and the Pacific War. The entire time I castigated myself for the inadequacy of my response to my cousin's overtures. Before we'd left Harwich the captain had addressed the crew, announcing that we could all settle back and prepare ourselves for a long journey filled with in-describable discomforts. We'd taken him to be joking.

Our initial view of Singapore was a towering column of black smoke on the horizon. When we docked at the naval base the captain went ashore in his whites to inquire as to where to lodge his men. He found everyone in headquarters burning records, and was told that our allot-ted accommodation had been destroyed by bombs that afternoon.

While he searched for an alternative we remained aboard. The bombing resumed, and with the harbor too shallow to dive, the hatches had to be kept shut or the splashes from the impacts would swamp us. A few of the torpedomen beside me who I thought were dozing turned out to have fainted from the heat. Everyone else just waited. We were all losing so much sweat the decks were slick underfoot. After an hour of the concussions one of the stokers went wild and tore down all the wardroom pinup girls before his mates restrained him.

Around sundown the captain returned, with the news that he'd finally located the rear admiral for Malaya inspecting the chit-book in the rubble of the officers' club, and he'd offered us his house in the hills. A commandeered truck transferred those off duty, and the rest of us had to make do in the boiling confines of the boat.

The next morning black clouds hung over the entire waterfront from the burning oil and rubber dumps and we refitted and loaded any supplies that we could in the chaos. The last provisions aboard were crates of Horlicks malted milk and Australian cough drops. When we cast off, one old woman with a spade was digging herself a private air-raid trench in the garden of the Raffles Hotel. To the east the sky was filled with high-altitude bombers, and once clear of the harbor we submerged, and as we rounded the channel buoy the captain at the periscope reported a convoy of our own troop transports arriving. He could make out the standards of the Argyll and Sutherland Highlanders. The whole ship went silent at the thought of what they were disembarking into.

We chugged three thousand miles west. We started leaking oil. One night I worked my way back to the wardroom, where the chief and the captain were sitting and talking quietly so as not to disturb the sleepers. They invited me to join them, and as they chatted about where they might be this time the following year, and the perversities of women, and the favorite pubs they had known, I fell asleep with my head on the wardroom table, and for days afterward they joked about how much they apparently had bored me. A gunlayer on his watch at last spotted a swallow, and the next afternoon a stoker sighted an old boot, and in the end we made Colombo Harbor in Ceylon. For two weeks no one had spoken except to give or to acknowledge orders.

The captain suggested we use our week in port to become human beings again. Mills responded that he would commence his rehabilitation with a nice, invigorating fuck. Our chief was carried ashore with dengue fever and instructions to rest up and then to report with a clean bill of health and no nonsense. Despite the direness of our situation those of us on liberty took real showers and shaved our beards on the harbor tender and then escaped to the four corners of the city. I found myself at the Colombo Club, which given the circumstances had been opened to enlisted men. I passed the time strolling about the lawns and staring at the women. I listened to their husbands' leisurely comments about sporting events. The captain commandeered a deck chair in the mornings, and after a few drinks took to playing something he called bicycle polo, which always left him limping. A lone Hurricane trailing smoke flew over, circled back, and belly-landed on the club green, after which the pilot climbed out and proceeded directly to the bar. Upon drawing any attention I disappeared. Nights I dreamt incessantly and awoke so soaked with sweat I could smell my room from the hall.

I returned to my running, ascending the steep steps to the top of the cable-tram, where I'd arrive bathed in sweat and then come right back down while the natives along the way looked on, amazed. They seemed to think Englishmen were prone to this sort of thing.

I went out drinking by myself. One night I happened upon Mills and our stoker petty officer, and the petty officer slipped on some stairs and rolled all the way to the bottom and then vomited. Mills said, "You know what they say: 'If that's the navy, all *must* be well with England.'" After I woke in the gutter of a bazaar without my billfold, Mills insisted I go out drinking with them.

We bought rounds for crewmembers of the *Snapper* celebrating a sunk Jap submarine. The Japs had attacked a Dutch merchant ship and then machine-gunned the survivors in the water, so after the *Snapper* sank the sub, the crew beat to death with spanners the two Japs they'd fished out. They said that off the west Australian coast they'd been laboring into harbor in heavy seas when an American submarine had surfaced and ripped right by them like they were standing still. They said that in Australia girls welcomed sailors at the gangways with crates of fresh apples and bottles of milk.

We met Mills's cousin, who'd been left behind in hospital when his ship had fled the port. He'd served as a messcook aboard a destroyer in Manila and loved the Philippines because he'd had multiple girlfriends and Scotch had been seventy-five American cents per bottle. For little more he'd maintained a love shack in the bush, a one-room hut up on stilts. The toilet and shower had emptied below without benefit of pipes and the only running water had been from heaven. All the palm trunks nearby were encircled with steel mesh to keep the rats from stealing the coconuts. In the bar he stripped his shirt to show us his tattoos, including a smiling baby's face over one side of his chest that was labeled *Sweet* and another on the other side that was labeled *Sour* and *Twin screws, Keep clear* on the small of his back.

He loved the story of the *Snapper* crew rescuing the Japs to beat them to death. He'd befriended a sampan man in Manila who'd rowed British officers around the harbor to visit the town or to shoot snipe, and for years the man had told anyone who'd listen that soon the Japanese would invade, and he'd been more accurate than any prognosticator in London. And when the Japanese did arrive they'd crucified him on his boat for ferrying the enemy. Mills's cousin had spied his body as the destroyer fought its way out of the port.

Three more went down with dengue fever before we departed Ceylon: our messcook, which allowed Mills's cousin to come aboard as his replacement; the junior engine-room rating; and a torpedoman. Mills and I showed the new torpedoman his station, and while he peered with dismay at the hideous and antiquated confusion of corroded pipes and valves and levers, Mills advised him that another way of looking at the situation was that hardly any other crew had been granted our abundance of experience and survived.

A merchantman that staggered into harbor turned out to be carrying a mail packet that included letters for both Mills and myself. Mills had heard from his Red Cross nurse, who'd also sent a photograph. He teared up when he showed me. When he noted my response he protested that just because he was no celibate that didn't mean he'd forgotten her.

I received three letters posted over a span of eleven months from my stepfather and the prelate's daughter and my cousin. My stepfather had attached to his note a newspaper clipping of the bomb damage on our street. He wrote that my mother had discovered the neighbors' cat dead in the rubble of the back garden gate, that she had been keenly hurt by my refusal to write, and that she dispatched her regards nonetheless, along with the news of an old classmate of mine also in the navy whose wife had just given birth. He added that when it came to me he often wondered if I would ever reach the top of fool hill.

The prelate's daughter had sent a photograph of herself, too, and confided that she'd shared with her father what we now meant to one another and that he'd asked her to leave his house. She wanted to know what she should now do. She was referring to a night I'd been on leave from the *Resolution* and had encountered her outside a tearoom in Harwich. It had transpired that she was bereft from another sailor failing to meet her as promised, and I had offered to walk her to the navy yard in consolation. She'd dried her eyes and put an arm around my waist and cheered herself with my stories of my own haplessness. We necked next to others in the darkness under the Halfpenny Pier and she opened her skirt to my hands. She whispered how much we liked one another, and it sounded so piteous that I stopped, and she seemed to think we'd gone

511

far enough in any event. She'd saved her chewing gum in her palm and she signaled we were finished by returning it to her mouth. Before we separated on King's Head Street she'd written down my name and posting and her address, and handed me the latter.

Margery wrote that she hoped I was well, and that she now at her family's insistence languished in a remote place where nothing momentous was likely to happen. She wrote that previously her nights in London had been long periods of enforced inactivity in her building's shelter, waiting for the all-clear, and that after one bombing she'd emerged to find a woman's body covered in soot and dust and had stooped to uncover its face. She wrote that in the middle of a memorial service for one of her mother's best friends she'd retired to a dressing room and wept at her own cowardice. She said her family often inquired if she had any word of how I was getting on, and that her little niece had asked her if I sank all of the bad people could I then swim home. She said she recognized our relationship had been at times an unconventional one but she hoped that I wouldn't hold this against her, and that with whomever I chose to share my life I would be happy. She also enclosed a photograph of herself, in a sundress, almost lost in the dappled light and shadow of a willow tree. I began any number of responses to her letter, all of which I rejected as insufficient.

When rumors started circulating about our impending patrol I spent mornings looking for myself in the mirror, as if I'd fallen down a well. In the days before our departure a senior medical officer gave us each the once-over. "Here's an interesting phenomenon," he remarked. "Let's have a look at your fingernails." I held out my hand and he indicated the concentric ridges. "Each ridge is a patrol," he said. "The gaps between correspond to the lengths of your leaves ashore." I looked at him. "Purely psychological," he said.

On our last night in Ceylon all the offshore watch returned in various states of intoxication, and the captain sentenced them, somewhat wryly, to ninety days on our own ship in the loathsome heat and overcrowding. "Very good, sir," one of the drunken mates said in reply, and the captain answered that the mate could now make it one hundred and twenty days.

After two weeks in the Bay of Bengal everyone is feeling lethargic and suffering from headaches. Some of the crew haven't shaved during the entire patrol and resemble figures from another century. Running on the surface at night we slip past sleepy whales bobbing like waterlogged hulks. Our medical officer taps out on a tiny typewriter a new edition of his *Health in the Tropics* newsletter, which he titles "Good Morning." This week's tip is: "If you have been sweating a lot, wash it off, or at least wipe it off with a hand towel, since the salt that your sweat has pushed out of your pores will irritate the skin." The only ship traffic we've encountered has been trawlers and junks, and the captain has decided that in such cases we'll just lie doggo and watch them move past. We find our new torpedoman all over the ship, his eyes around our feet, looking for dog-ends. When we're off duty Mills can instantly sleep and I lie awake. Sometimes when I can no longer stand my own company I go to the wardroom. There I find the captain or the chief alone at the table with binoculars slung round his neck and his head on his arms.

Mostly we're immersed in a haze of inactivity. We dove to evade a flying boat sighted by our starboard lookout. A heavy bomber swept directly overhead on a northerly course but did not appear to have noticed us. The 0400 watch reported that three small vessels he couldn't identify had altered course toward our location, then turned in a complete circle for no apparent reason before continuing on their transit.

We are perpetually in one another's way, tormented by septic heat sores, bodies that stink, and endless small breakdowns on the ship. The only clean-off available is a little torpedo alcohol applied to the rankest spots. Wet clothes never dry. Condensation is everywhere. Shoes are furred with mold and our woolens smell worse than the head. The batteries have begun to fume and refuse to charge. The periscope gland leaks. In the night we passed one of our own bombed-out merchant ships, listing miserably. The tinned mutton when opened is now often slimed over, and even the roaches won't touch it. Mills claims he can't imagine this going on much longer, but his cousin says that if this has to be done it's better that we should do it, since we know what we're about, and newcomers would likely cost their friends their lives.

I'm jolted from my bunk by a tremendous blast, and then a second and a third, and when I reach the wardroom everyone is celebrating and I'm told that our target was an ammunition ship. The captain is permitting the crew to go up to the bridge three at a time to enjoy the spectacle, and upon my turn explosions are still sending flame and debris high into the sky. All who've been bellyaching for days and begrudging each other a civil word are suddenly thick as thieves and best of friends, since with one solitary success all the clouds are dispelled. But soon after that come the sub hunters, and we hang still for twelve hours at one hundred and eighty feet while they thresh around above us like terriers at a rabbit hole. Off-duty crew lie in their bunks trying to read thrillers or magazines. Those working sit right on the deck at their stations to ensure they make as little noise as possible. The chief pores over a technical journal. The captain draws the green curtains round his berth. With the first depth charge a few lights are put out and a roach falls stunned to my chest. The second cracks a glass gauge before me and the welding on a starboard casing. The third knocks me to the floor and the remaining lights go dark and water spritzes from a joint. Pocket torches flash before the emergency lamps come on. More detonations reverberate, farther away and closer, farther away and closer.

The hunters persist until the humidity coalesces into an actual mist and the thinning air plagues everyone with crushing headaches and nausea, and then our hydrophone operators finally report our pursuers moving away.

When we're running on the surface again I find Mills contemplating his photo of the Red Cross nurse, his chin on his filthy mattress. I ask her name and he responds only that one of the last things she requested was that he take the time to consider what she might want, and what she might like, but that instead he gave her the sailor's lament, that he'd soon be shipping out and that they'd perhaps never see one another again, and so she allowed him the kiss and some of the other liberties he'd been desiring. Before his train departed she told him through the carriage window that he was the sort of man who was always at the last second catching his ride in triumph or missing it and not caring. "I think she meant I was selfish," he finally adds, and then turns to me to discover I have nothing to contribute. "What do you think of selfishness, eh, Fisher?" he asks, and some of the torpedomen laugh. "So here we are," he concludes. "Sweating and grease-covered and alone and miserable and sorry for ourselves." And a memory I banished from my time with Margery surfaces: We stood on her front step after our kisses, and she waited for me to respond to what she had confided about the stillness we made together. While she waited she explained that she was trying to ascertain where she could place her trust, and where more supervision would be needed. And when she received no response to

514

that either, she said that if I wanted to swan around the world pretending I didn't understand things, that was my affair, but that I should know that it did cause other people pain.

Another long stretch of empty ocean, which the captain announces as an opportunity for resuming the paper war, and everywhere those of us off duty get busy with pencils writing our patrol reports or toting up stores expended and remaining. Our boat continues to break down. Each day something or other gets jiggered up and someone puts it right. The chief initiates a tournament of Sea Battle, a game he plays on graph paper in which each contestant arranges his hidden fleet, consisting of a battleship, two cruisers, three destroyers, and four submarines and occupying respectively four, three, two, and one square each, while his opponent attempts to destroy them by guesswork, each correct guess on the grid counting as a hit. I'm drawn to the competitions but decline to participate. "That's the way he is on leave, as well," Mills tells everyone. "The Monk likes to watch."

Off Little Andaman Island we pass a jungle of chattering monkeys that cascades right down to the shore. For safety we stay close to the coast in the darkness, and the oily-looking water is filled with sea snakes and jellyfish so that when we surface at nightfall horrid things get stuck in our conning tower gratings and crunch and slide underfoot. The captain takes a bearing on the black hills in the starlight and those of us on watch can hear nothing but the water lapping against our hull and the fans quietly expelling the battery gases. Every so often a rock becomes visible. A little vacant jetty. In the morning we dive in rain like sheets flapping in the wind.

The mattresses grew so foul the captain had them rolled and hauled up through the conning tower and thrown over the side. The coarse pads left on our bunks rub open blisters and sores and our medical officer recommends cornmeal and baking soda to dry the mess. Our new torpedoman had the fingernails and top joints of his first three fingers crushed in a bulkhead door in a crash dive. I helped the medical officer with the bandaging and afterward was surprised at his annoyance. "You could have answered a few of the boy's questions," he complained. "He's new on the ship and looking for a friend."

Mills has begun agitating quietly with other members of the crew to petition the captain to head home, wherever "home" now remains, before it's too late. He explains that his philosophy is to be neither reckless nor overly gun-shy, but to evaluate the situation in light of whether we have any chance at all to make a successful attack and survive to report it. He claims that while the miracle of encountering a lone ammunition ship is all well and good, it's only a matter of time before we confront an entire convoy. He asks for my help to rally support for his position and I agree, and he says we can start with the torpedo officer since his shifts and mine align for the next few days. Each night when I return from duty Mills asks if I've talked to the TO yet and I tell him I haven't.

The next night the watch reports a debris field and the captain goes up to have a look. When he descends to the wardroom the wireless operator says, "It seems that we've finally given them a dose of what they've been giving us, eh, sir?" and the captain answers that it's British wreckage we're sailing through.

At breakfast there are complaints about the mutton, and to provide perspective Mills's cousin tells of having eaten in a mess so rancid they'd had to inspect each mouthful on the fork to ensure there was nothing crawling in it.

Twelve bleary hours later I'm seven minutes late for the dawn watch. The captain is on the conning tower, too, and the enraged mate I'm relieving shoulders past me and heads below. The fresh air smells of seaweed and shellfish. In the heat the sea is so calm it looks like metal. Mist moves across our bow in the early sun. I apologize and the captain remarks that as a midshipman he was flogged for "wasting three minutes of a thousand men's time" by piping a battle cruiser's crew tardy to its first shift. I tell him that when I'm sleepless for long periods I sometimes don't properly attend to things, and after a silence he answers that he had a great uncle who always claimed about himself that he didn't attend to things, and that this great uncle went off to the Crimean War, where as Lord Raglan's aide-de-camp he was more or less responsible for the Charge of the Light Brigade.

He stays on the bridge with me, evidently enjoying the air. "Did you know that *Telemachus* in Greek means 'far from battle'?" he asks. I tell him I didn't.

In the face of the blank sky and still water I return to the problem of how to respond to my cousin's letter. I imagine describing for her all these dawns I've collected on watch: gold over the Norway Deep, scarlet off Singapore, silvery pink in the China Sea. I imagine recounting the morning the sun was behind us and a spray from the bow was arching across the deck so that we carried with us our own rainbow. In my last attempt I wrote that there wasn't much I could say about my position, but that things were presently quiet and I was in excellent health and she shouldn't worry, and then I stopped, since every other man in the crew had the same fatuous and unfinished letter in his locker, as well. I imagine telling her how vividly I could see her face as we left Harwich, the dockyard walls slipping past us like sliding doors, opening up vistas of the harbor, our stern coming round as docile as an old horse. I imagine telling her how some part of me anticipated the Pacific as if a way to discover my father's fate. The sadness of my final glimpse of our escort vessel as it signaled its good-bye and dropped back to its station on our port beam.

Later that day a commotion pulls me from my bunk. The watch spotted something far off in the haze and the captain has taken us to periscope depth. When I get to the wardroom he's climbing into his berth and telling the chief that he'll resume observation in ten minutes and that it's going to be a long approach. In the meantime the chief is to redirect our course to a firing bearing, instruct the torpedo room to stand by, and order the ship's safe opened and the confidential materials packed into a canvas bag and the bag weighed down with wrenches.

The torpedomen are excited, since most believe that Thursdays and Saturdays are our lucky days. Mills is not hiding his dismay. He suggests to the TO that the captain use the wireless to inquire if the Admiralty thinks this action worth the risk, but the TO reminds him that such communications would reveal our position. Mills informs the TO that much of the crew shares his unease and the TO looks around at each of us until finally Mills tells me that if I'm not on duty I'm in the way. As I turn to go he asks when I stuck the photograph over my bunk but doesn't ask who it is.

Back in the wardroom the captain is out of his berth and at the periscope. When the sweat dripping over his eyebrows steams the lens, he wipes it clear with tissue paper the chief hands him. He finally murmurs that the convoy looks to be five miles out and that he estimates it will pass about a quarter mile in front of us. He reports that we've chanced across an escort carrier. He reports that the convoy's rear is lost to the distance, but in its vanguard alone he can make out two destroyers and three sub hunters.

517

"In this calm and in this channel, once they see our torpedoes' wakes there will be nowhere for us to hide," the chief tells him, as though reciting the solution to an arithmetic problem, and the captain keeps his face to the eyepiece.

"Perhaps the wise course is to live to fight another day, sir?" our navigator asks. No one answers him. In the silence it's as if my stomach and legs are urging me on to something.

The chief questions whether we should put on a little speed to close the gap still further, and the captain replies that in this calm any telltale swirl or turbulence would give us away even at this range, and that instead we'll just settle in and get our trim perfect and let them come to us.

We can hear our own breathing. The captain orders the forward torpedo tubes flooded and their doors opened. Our hydrophone operator indicates multiple HEs bearing Green 175 and closing rapidly. "Are we really going to do this?" our navigator asks again, barely audible. The captain senses the oddity of my presence and glances over before returning his attention to the eyepiece. "Our shipboard wraith," he jokes quietly, and the chief smiles, and I feel a child's pride at the separateness that I've always cultivated.

Then the captain clears his throat and re-grips the handles and calls out a final bearing, and issues the command to fire numbers one through six, and the entire ship jolts with each release. Mills reports in a strangled voice that all tubes have fired electrically, and soon thereafter our hydrophone operator reports that all torpedoes are running hot and straight.

And the image of what I wish I could have put into a letter for my cousin at once appears to me, from the only other time I was allowed at the periscope, along with the rest of the crew, when on a rough day near a reef in a breaking sea we found the spectacle of porpoises on our track above us, leaping through the avalanches of foam and froth six or seven at a time, maneuvering within our field of vision and then surging clean out of the water and reentering smoothly with trailing plumes of white bubbles, all of them flowing together, each a celebration of what the others could be, until finally it seemed as if hundreds had passed us, and in their kinship and coordination had then vanished into the impenetrable green beyond our reach.

Nominated by Zoetrope, Sandra Leong

EVERYTHING YOU WANT RIGHT HERE

fiction by DELANEY NOLAN

from ELECTRIC LITERATURE'S RECOMMENDED READING

Natalie was pulling the slot machine lever, dropping in coins from a little yellow purse she held in her lap. I was drinking my fourth daiquiri, which was also yellow.

"This honestly tastes like real bananas," I said.

Natalie said, "I think you must be bad luck today." She held the lever until I took two big steps back. Then I took a third step back. Then she finally let go of the knob and the slots display spun its crazy numbers. You'd think that would've shown on her face, but we were all in the same romantic forever twilight of the casino, and in the reflection on the plastic she looked bored, like an angel. Her hair was big, full of that funky-smelling hairspray: shiny, flammable, rough to touch.

We were standing near the one window in Game Room Twelve, which was tinted dark but still showed the red desert going on outside, the same for miles, thousands of miles, I guess. Jermy, who works janitorial on our floor, told me once that the desert led to a massive sinkhole, that magnificent quantities of sand were pouring into the sinkhole day after day, and that eventually we would pour in, too, all of us, the casino and the games and the residents and everything. But that is ridiculous. There might be one sinkhole. But we can't be surrounded by sinkholes, not in every direction. Statistically, we're going to turn out fine, in the long run.

Then there was a bright *ding!* and Natalie whooped because she'd won: out of its mouth the machine spilled a waterfall of shiny tokens, each one small enough to fit in her palm. She said, "I've never played this game before," and applauded a bit, folding her one free hand over and clapping her own fingers, before adding, "not in this room, anyway—not this machine, at least."

"Do you want some breakfast?"

"I'm not really hungry."

I peeked over her head toward the lobby. "Did you see the fountain of cane sugar today? It's really going." I put my hand flat against her shoulder. "It's got to be this high."

Natalie kissed the tips of my fingers and looked at my face and put another coin in. "This is the one," she said, rubbing her hands. And she was right: suddenly all the lights started blinking at once, and the machine started singing a kind of psycho song. People from the next stool over and the next stool over after that stood up and came to see what was going on. "Twenty bucks says she just won the grand prize," said a man in golf shorts.

"You're on," said a woman next to him. She whipped out her wallet and then started juggling it back and forth.

"I got four cherries," Natalie sang, and a single, big, fat, golden coin rolled into the dispensing tray. She picked it up with both her hands and kissed it and then asked, "What did I win?"

Which is how we got the tomato plant.

Natalie had called all our neighbors, our friends, and the front desk receptionist by the time we got to the cash-in counter. We were still examining the coin when a man in a white suit walked over, slapped me on the back and said, "Sir, you star, you MVP, you've struck gold, you champ; congratulations, sir!" Behind him was another man with a curl of earpiece wire running along his neck, and sunglasses, which struck me as funny—I couldn't remember the last time I saw sunglasses.

I told him I hadn't done anything. I pointed to Natalie. The man in the suit introduced himself as the floor manager and spoke into a walkie-talkie; after a few minutes some lugs with a cart wheeled over the tomato plant.

It was just a thin stalk with a few scraggly leaves moving shyly upwards, dwarfed by the cart itself. There was a real crowd by then. Natalie moved toward the plant, but the floor manager got to it first, picked it up and handed it to her while everyone clapped. One girl started to cry, in a hiccupping, cheerful way, fanning herself with a scorecard.

"There's nothing that makes me happier," the guy in the suit said, "than seeing our residents win."

Afterward, he escorted us upstairs, chatting happily about how we deserved everything we got. At the door to our home he had his assistant take pictures of the three of us, everybody giving each other firm, friendly handshakes. He wished us luck, and left us alone.

Every day for the next two weeks, friends and strangers would show up, knock on our door, and ask to see the tomato plant. Natalie was keeping it wrapped up in a blanket between two of the candy jars on the counter of the kitchenette, where it would get lots of sun. We all would stand in front of it, eating marshmallows, crammed in the tiny kitchen watching it, popping the marshmallows into our mouths one by one, like at any moment it might wake up and talk to us.

"I can't remember the last time I saw a plant," Natalie said quietly on the first afternoon. "A real plant, I mean, in real life."

"Me neither."

"When that pipe broke last year," said our neighbor Beth, "I spent two hours outside."

"I would chop off all of my fingers," added her husband thoughtfully, "just to eat a peach." He sounded sad.

The tomato plant had come wrapped in these glitzy pink beads, and Natalie wouldn't take them off, even though they spelled out the name of the casino in big tacky script letters: "Les Sables Chanceux", it read. It meant "The Lucky Sands", but I thought it sounded like a snobby ranch.

We'd been living in the southern section, where all the roulette tables were, for about four years by then. Like a lot of people, we'd stopped in thinking it was temporary, and then stayed for a little longer, and then just stayed. I don't even remember where we'd been headed before we stopped. I want to say Utah, maybe—I think Natalie had found a postcard with a picture of Utah on it, and in the picture there was a gigantic lake. But I guess the both of us knew that Utah wasn't going to be better than anywhere else. No lake, only the same sand, shaping itself into the wind. We'd made it to Les Sables, which I think is somewhere in Kansas, and decided we needed a nice long break.

Natalie and I used to fight a lot, before. Regular marriage fights—I pretend to laugh too often; she criticizes me too much. I wouldn't say we had issues, but we'd gotten married in our twenties, and after two decades together even our thinnest problems had had time to accumulate into thicker, heavier ones, like stacks of plastic transparencies that eventually stop being transparent. But when the sand started to come up and cover everything and everybody, the fighting sort of died off. We just didn't have the energy for it anymore. And now, here, in the casino, we're too busy to think about it: there's sixty-two floors, live music every night, a mile-long tunnel lit by epileptic laser shows, and twice a year, on the Fourth of July and Christmas, they fill the empty swimming pool up with marshmallow Fluff and we all put on our bathing suits and go wild. The next day everyone goes around real embarrassed.

The last fight I can remember happening at all was in our first casino year: a man had been running from suite to suite, screaming that he'd just reserved the whole floor, that we had to get out. Natalie had stood in the doorway while he threatened her with eviction, and she'd broken his cheekbone with a lamp. Everyone got to stay where they were.

On a banner in the buffet hall, big bubble letters declare Les Sables to be the biggest building in the tri-county area. But I think this seems kind of unfair, because everybody knows it's the only building in the tri-county area. You don't really appreciate the place's size most of the time, but I remember once getting a tour that included the basement, and it was just incredible: the stockpile of dry goods, canned frosting, dehydrated potato, huge sacks of rice, going on and on in every direction without a break, like it was going to keep right on to the edge of the earth.

"When's it going to make a tomato?" Natalie asked one morning after the visitors had left. She raised her hand to touch it but then let her hand just hover there.

"I've got no idea."

"Maybe it's a dud."

"Maybe we're doing this all wrong."

Natalie picked up the phone and pushed zero. "Front desk?" she said. "Yes, hello, could you tell me how long it takes a tomato plant to make a tomato?" She listened for a minute, making quiet hums of agreement. Then she hung up, saying, "He didn't know. But he did say that he's pretty sure we're supposed to tie the plant to a stick, so that it can get tall without falling over. He also might come up later to look at it, if that's okay."

"A stick?" I said. I looked at the plant. It was just a few inches tall, green with leaves, skinny all over, trembling if we so much as breathed on it. "Where are we supposed to find a stick?"

Every other Sunday, Natalie and I have date night. Date night is when we go to watch a movie in the cinema and we get a SugarShake with two straws. We like seats near the front. We've seen most of the movies a few times by now. Natalie's favorite is a Chinese film— something romantic with long, slow zooms of men beginning to cry.

There aren't any English subtitles but she says she likes the challenge and understands it a little more each time. Certainly, each time she watches it she cries a little harder.

My favorite is when the projectionist blows off his shift and instead they just show the loading screen, which is a looped video of sleepy, distant clouds, floating weightlessly across a warm blue sky. Sometimes Natalie and I stay for the whole two hours, watching the clouds.

A few days after Natalie won the plant, I was getting ready for date night, rinsing off my shaving razor when I noticed that Natalie was still in her pajamas. We did, sometimes, stay in our pajamas all day, but usually not on date night. She was leaning over the counter and talking to the plant in a low voice I couldn't make out.

"Nat?"

"Shh."

I stepped into the kitchen. "What are you doing?"

Natalie pressed her lips together and straightened up. She pinched the loose skin at her neck. "I thought it would like the sound of my voice," still quietly. I felt a twist in my stomach: I could see that she was lonely and that she wouldn't tell me about her loneliness. This is a terrible thing to know about your wife.

I came and wrapped my arms around her so that I was looking over her head and she was looking into my shoulder. "We'll be back in a few hours. It'll be good to get a change of scenery."

She was completely limp. She felt like a bag of unhappy laundry.

"Try getting dressed," I suggested. "It always helps me, when I start to feel—to feel claustrophobic. Get dressed like you're going out somewhere, like anything could happen." I pushed her gently toward the closet.

That night, it was the clouds again. They moved across the screen with nowhere to get to. It looked like the sky over our old house in Morgantown. Summer, hot, cicadas, moles in the tulip bed. But it isn't fair to compare the present, movie-screen sky with the old, real sky: the past gets to stay the same, frozen, shining, while the present is always shifting, and maybe getting worse.

I first met Natalie at the Waterfront Place Hotel in Morgantown. I was there on business, marketing medical devices in doctors' offices. She was there for a convention for people who ran convention centers.

Natalie was at the reception desk, giving a family directions to Ruby Memorial. I'd liked that right away—trying to help people, even though she didn't have to. She was kind about it, not bossy. She held the door as they left and I noticed that, too. I took out the case which held the equipment I was going to be presenting later that day. When the last people left, waving their thank yous, it was just us in the lobby. She'd wandered over to see what I was putting together.

"It's medical equipment." I held it up as I twisted a microphone into place. "A handheld device for people who've lost their voice box."

She picked it carefully from my hands and placed it under her jaw line.

"Electrolarynx," she said, and her voice was twinned by the machine. I could hear the sound of her smiling.

The plant got taller. In the second week, Natalie said it looked hungry, and she poured some soda pop on it. It lost a leaf or two, but it didn't die. We went back to spritzing it with tap water. And then one morning, three and a half weeks after Natalie brought it home, we saw it: a tiny green hint of a fruit, the size of a thumbnail.

Natalie rushed out to grab someone's attention and I stayed, breathing on the plant, seeing its leaves shiver. Go on, I whispered to the plant. *You're doing a really good job*. I was thinking about how I was inhaling pure, clean oxygen, like how I'd seen pictures in old textbooks: the cycle of molecules, moving around inside the plant body.

Then Natalie called me from the corridor—she wanted me to come with her to the kitchen of the lobby restaurant, she said, because she wanted to bring up a chef and show him how a real tomato ought to look. "Green," she shook her head, all the way down in the elevator, "I must have forgot that it ought to look green—and all this time they've been feeding us these shit red knock-off tomatoes from tins."

I followed her down and then through the lobby to the buffet hall.

"The chef," Natalie said to the hostess, who was standing at the podium by the door, painting her nails. "I need to see the head chef."

The hostess waved over a server. "She wants to see Allen," she said. The server disappeared, and a minute later came back with a large bearded man in a splattered apron holding a can opener. He looked warm; physically, I mean—he looked pink.

"I need to show you—"

His face lit up. "You're the tomato lady," he interrupted. He had thick fingers, which he dug under his apron strings.

Natalie straightened.

"I been wanting to let you in a project," said Allen. "A project I been working on for a time now."

"Great," I said quickly, before Natalie could answer, because I wanted to see the kitchen, had always been curious, and I took her hand and followed him.

Allen led us past the buffet table, past the gummy animal salad bar, past the donut brisket and the starch soup tureens and soda pools. He pushed through the swinging doors into a room that led to a series of rooms, with a wide conveyor belt on the side. As we entered, it was trundling out a huge tin labeled POTATO with a picture of a potato on it. With a practiced grace, Allen sprung open the tin and in one smooth movement emptied the gel inside into a nearby pot of steaming water. He moved as though he were unaware that we were still behind him, performing his duties swift and correct. Then he continued, hardly breaking his stride, gesturing for us to follow.

We passed ladles and sacks and piles of brown square parchment packages labeled MOLASSES. In the fifth narrow room, he looked around as though someone may have followed him. Then he moved his hand over a trapdoor in the zinc counter and, in some way we couldn't see, swung up the latch. He fished in with one meaty paw, biting his tongue, and then pulled out a small plastic jar.

Inside were three brown, dry-looking sticks, curling in on themselves.

"You all know what this is?" He spoke very low. Before waiting for an answer, he unscrewed the top and tilted it towards our noses.

We breathed in. It was cinnamon. The smell came up and with it came Christmas, grandmothers, hot buttered rum, jack-o-lanterns, wassail, Indian summer, yellow leaves, porcelain mugs, knit sweaters, wood fires, pastries steaming on a pan held with an apron wrapped around your hand. We breathed in and breathed in but you can only smell a thing so long, continuously, before it disappears even with you watching, like a good dream you try sleepily to catch.

"Where?" said Natalie breathlessly.

Allen screwed the cap back on, a little jealously, it seemed to me. "Years ago—I won, too. Not a jackpot like you. A smaller thing. The slots: three apples in a row. I used to have more. I saved it for special occasions. But even with my saving, I started to see it would run out. Now I haven't used one in a good while." He opened the trapdoor, again in a way I couldn't see, and put it back inside. "I thought maybe— whenever you get ready with that tomato—I got a recipe." He said recipe like it was a curse word.

"What sort of recipe?" Natalie's eyes shone.

"Candied tomatoes," Allen said proudly, and clapped his hands together.

Natalie took my arm. The conveyor belt buzzed and started up again with a chunking sound.

"You'll let me know when they're ready—right?" said the chef.

"We should go check on the plant now," I said, backing towards the other rooms. A white plastic tub moved smoothly past us on the belt.

In our suite, I lay on the kitchen floor while Natalie walked on my back. We'd spent a couple hours at the roulette table before coming back up, and sometimes hunching over the wheel like that made me sore. It seemed like bad luck to go back to the same slot machine as before, so we went to the poker table instead. I was having a lousy few rounds, so I mostly sat and watched Natalie, the other players, the dealer, the window. The dealer's hands dropped the playing cards and crisply gathered them up again. His nails were bitten back, showing the beds, red and raw.

If you squint real hard, so much that your eyes are closed, the lit-up ceiling of the casino could be sky, and the dark green carpet could be actual ground. But then you always see the window burning—the hot white sky and the dunes that just get bigger and bigger, and whatever they hold, the bones of cattle, skeleton of cacti, probably rusted-out cars, and plus all around you are the beeps and jingles and hot laughter of the people and machines, so it's hard to pretend, really.

A lady came by with a tray of blue-pink lollipops and I grabbed one, crunched it down, put the white paper stick in my breast pocket. The thing is, in the casino you tend to get into a routine, and it makes time go weird—you're walking past a bank of video poker screens when you realize a week's gone by without you really noticing. So at some point around last year I started holding on to leftover bits from meals, just to remind myself: time is passing, time is passing. This is your life. It really is.

Natalie folded. She'd broken even, like she usually did.

We didn't bring up Allen's plans about the tomato until we got into the elevator.

"I don't want it to be candied," Natalie had said.

"Me neither."

That was all. The question had hung around the stale air on the way up, fogging up the fluorescent light, bouncing back at us from the mirrored walls: what do you do with a thing you have to ruin to enjoy?

When the doors opened on our floor, the maid was standing by her trolley in front of our room, lifting the keycard from the lanyard around her neck.

"We don't need service!" Natalie shouted abruptly, startling us all. The maid blinked while we hurried over.

"Privacy, please," I said quickly, and we'd slammed the door in the maid's round face.

Now Natalie stepped off my back and sat against the cupboards next to me. I turned my head and felt crumbs sticking to my cheek.

"We have to protect it," she said.

"Yes."

"People will come."

I sat up and sat so that my legs crossed beneath her bent knees. I squeezed her calves, soft and white. Natalie used to be beautiful, tan; she is still beautiful, but a different kind, and pale as the rest of us. It used to strike me as strange to be pale when outside there was always sun, sun, sun, but now that desert out the window is just like the mural of a tropical island painted next to a motel swimming pool: you won't ever get there, and you have to just use it to enjoy the dingy place you're really at.

Natalie and I had a trick. We'd been doing it since our first week at Les Sables. We'd walk next to one another down the laser tunnel like totally normal people. Then, as we passed someone, splitting slightly so that we were walking on either side of them, we'd suddenly throw up our hands and scream like goblins and then sprint, fast as we could, to the opposite end of the tunnel. We never actually saw the person's reaction, but nearly every time we did this, one of us would have to stop before reaching the end of the tunnel, out of breath from hysterical laughing.

It was her idea, and the morning after we met the chef she suggested we give it a go. We'd been strange and distracted all day. She said it'd help us work out nervous energy.

I got dressed and washed, and I put the tomato plant in the hiding place we'd chosen for whenever we went out: in the musty cabinet under the sink. Its leaves brushed the plastic pipes down there. I always felt guilty for leaving it in the dark. We were about to leave when there was a knock on our door. I looked through the peephole. The floor manager, in his white suit, was smiling in the hallway, his face ballooned and alien from the glass's warp.

"It's him," I hissed.

"The chef?"

"The guy in the suit. The one who gave us the plant."

We both stood there. We didn't know what to do—here was the man who had given us our favorite thing. We couldn't just lock out the man who had given us our favorite thing.

I opened the door just as he was lifting his fist to knock. His smile got bigger.

"Our star players! Our MVPs!" He walked in and slapped me on the shoulder, air-kissed Nat. "Our favored guests. Our lucky ducks."

"Is something wrong?" Nat asked.

His smile went down a notch. Then it was just a regular smile. "Why would anything be wrong?"

Neither of us could come up with an answer to that.

"I was hoping you two could do me a favor." He sat on the arm of the couch.

"We'd love to help if we can," said Natalie.

"We have an event this week—an award ceremony—just a little thing we're putting on. We hoped you would join us, present one of the awards." He delicately picked one of Nat's long hairs off the couch arm. "'Best Janitor,' 'Happiest Waiter.' That sort of thing."

"Do we have to give a speech?"

"I don't like speeches," I added. "I don't like giving them."

"No speech." He threw his hands away from him like he was holding garbage. "Just presenting. You two—I don't know if you know this— you're something of a celebrity couple, now that you're growing those tomatoes. We thought it'd be fun to include you."

I didn't want to. And she didn't want to. But in front of us stood the man who had given us our prize. We agreed. The next day, a bellhop showed up outside our door with a new jacket and slacks for me, a dress for Natalie in sugary pastels. A card, event details written inside in careful black script; all of this nested in blue tissue paper, paper we kept, because Natalie said it was too pretty to throw out. She had this drawer where she kept beautiful things. She wouldn't let anyone into it, not even me. She put the tissue inside and closed the drawer.

The ceremony was held in the lounge. Natalie and I and everyone else who was on the giving-end of the award stuff were overdressed: I wore the fine dress jacket, and the janitor wore the janitorial uniform; the waitresses wore jeans. The floor manager in his white suit stood on stage saying Thank you in about a million different ways: We appreciate etc., we couldn't do it without etc., we are indebted etc., etc. There were bonbons on Styrofoam plates. I ordered daiquiris and then changed it to martinis and then to regular beer. I was embarrassed, didn't know where to put my hands. Kept them in my lap. I didn't like being the one with the shiny gold statue in my hands to dole out to winners.

I was picking cotton candy apart on my plate. A slim, balding guy who worked one of the craps tables was seated next to me.

"Who'd you vote for?" I asked him.

A blank look. "We don't vote."

"Right. I was only joking." Some chords of music started up as someone new took the stage. Natalie, on my other side, was whispering and laughing with a maid. She was always better than me at it—at being a person with people. "Are you in the running?"

"I don't know. I guess." He looked down at his plate. His fingernails, I noticed, were bitten down—way down, red and raw and painful looking. As I watched, he reached up to his scalp and plucked one of his own short hairs; then another, then another. He was doing it absently, a kind of nervous habit that I wondered if I should warn him off.

"Least there's free food, huh?"

He nodded.

"Got any tips for me for my next go at the craps table?" I tried.

He looked at me and gave a weak smile. "Luck of the draw."

"How long you been here?"

The dealer shrugged. As I watched, he plucked the cotton candy from his plate, set it aside, and then folded the paper cone carefully and tucked it away in his pocket.

Someone came and tapped us on our shoulders, signaling that we'd take the stage soon. We followed them, weaving around tables, up to the wings of the stage.

"Now, to present the award for 'Straightest Teeth,' our celebrity couple—the Tomato Growers!" Mild applause stirred around the room as we stepped on.

The lights were hot and white and made me squint. They were too bright; I couldn't see the face of the man as he waved us toward the podium. We stepped up and held the plastic gold statue. It looked like a squat hump, an anthill, a buttock—I realized much later that it was supposed to be a sand dune.

"The award goes to—" I opened the card and Natalie read the name.

"Jeffrey Krugman."

The man I'd been talking to stood up and came to the stage. People clapped; I shook his hand; he took the statue and turned around and left the stage. We left the stage. The man's voice boomed on cheerfully. Nat leaned against me; I put my arm around her and pulled hair back from her face. It was time to go home, or where we lived. We left the dinner, left the beers. The pneumatic door clicked the man's voice away from us into silence as we walked out. Our steps were quiet in the carpeted hallway. Fluorescent lights showed me the flaws in her makeup. I wanted to kiss her, to apologize for being in this place, unable to leave or taste anything real. I wanted to tell her that I knew the world wasn't very good, but she was a good thing in it. When we opened the door to our suite, all the lights were shining, the closets open, clothes on the floor. Sand ticked at the window over the sink. Natalie flung open the cabinet doors under the sink. The tomato plant was gone.

We checked the other cabinets, we checked the garbage disposal. Natalie called the front desk, sobbing, and four employees rushed up to help us look. We all spread out in the little hotel suite, scouring it for the plant, for footprints, for a trail of potted soil, something to help us learn who had taken it.

The headwaiter tucked his tie carefully into his shirt and moved around on his hands and knees. The busboy started tipping furniture, in case the tomato plant was hidden under the couch.

"Is this it?" asked the headwaiter. He held up a piece of fake straw that'd fallen from somebody's hat.

"No," I said.

"It's already dead," Natalie cried. I tried to put my arm around her again, but she shook me off, too upset to be touched. "The chef's taken it," she went on. "We all know that he did!"

The waiters looked at each other, and I looked at Natalie. Her nice eye makeup was making dark shapes in the shadows under her eyes where exhaustion usually shows.

"Wasn't he at the ceremony?"

"I didn't see him! He was up here!"

She was already moving out the door. She took my hand and pulled me behind her, and all six of us rushed out, crammed back into the mirrored elevator. In the lobby we marched toward the kitchen, past the roulette wheels, past the baccarat table, past the bar with its free shots of corn syrup.

"Can I help—" began the hostess as we entered, but Nat stormed past her, slamming through the swinging door into the kitchen. The hostess and the rest of the group followed, crying out that we weren't allowed.

"Wait," yelled the hostess, but we slammed into the second room.

The chef was there, on the floor. He was hitting his head with the flats of his hands. He said it was gone, it was gone.

Natalie took a knife from the block on the counter. She pointed it at him, jabbing it in the air on every other word: "What did you do? Where's our tomato gone?"

"Not the tomato, no, no; the cinnamon—the three sticks of cinnamon—the man in the suit took them. He came here. He took them away."

The chef led us to the floor manager's office, and Natalie was trying to kick down the door. A crowd had gathered by then. They weren't cheering, exactly, but people were worried that something bad was going to happen, and then under that worry, excited that something bad might happen. I wasn't sure whether to help, but finally I joined Natalie and threw my own weight against the door at the same time she did. On our third try, the lock buckled, and the door swung open, banging against the wall.

It took a second to make sense of what I saw, but Natalie was already screaming. The floor manager had an old camping stove, the kind you might take with you on a road trip, and above the roaring flame of the burner was a shallow metal pot. What it held was hardly a sauce—the few small tomatoes were crushed into pulp in the pan, a watery mash of seeds and skin, barely staining the cinnamon sticks. There couldn't be more than a couple of spoonfuls. It amounted to practically nothing. It smelled incredible.

I slammed the door shut behind me and quickly dragged a filing cabinet in front of it, afraid others would charge in and snatch it away. In the corner of the room, the tomato plant was already decimated. The manager was holding a plastic spoon in the pot, his hand stilled where it had been stirring. I slowly understood that he must have been watching us, all this time, to find the lost spices so he could have the last of every good thing for himself.

"It's too late," I heard Natalie say. The knife drooped from her hand and pointed at the floor.

"No, no," the manager breathed, looking frightened, holding up a hand to keep us back. Someone was pounding their fist on the door, asking if we were okay. "Look—you can have some. We can each have just, just a taste."

Natalie didn't say anything. She went over to the plant, which lay on its side, dirt spilling onto the floor. She sat on her heels near the manager and cradled the stem, then looked up, past me, past the casino, out into the net drawing tight around the rest of our lives.

531

While she crouched there, the manager suddenly snatched up the pot, held it to his lips, and started, ridiculously, to gulp it all, the tiny bit there was, some stray thin juice running a red line from the corner of his mouth. But it was too hot, of course. He choked and yelped, sputtering and dropping the pot which landed on the desk, slopping over and spilling half on the camping stove's burner so that the flames went out and we could hear the sharp hissing of the gas. The filing cabinet that I'd propped against the door shook as people pounded to be let in.

"Wait!" I yelled, and at the same time, Natalie struck out wildly from the floor with her right arm, slashing at the manager's legs. She caught him behind the knee and he buckled, went down with a cry. He lay there, clutching his leg and howling like a child.

She stood up over him, heaving, and as I moved toward her, reaching for her shoulder to calm her down, to bring her back to me, the door slammed open, banging the file cabinet into the wall. The two men with sunglasses and radio wires burst in and went straight for Natalie, went for my wife who was crying in anger.

"You can't," I said, stumbling as they shoved past me. "That's ours," was all I managed.

"I *gave* it to you," came the manager's wobbly voice from the floor beyond the desk. "It belongs to me."

The security men grabbed Natalie's arms, pulling them behind her back. She looked, finally, at me, and I can imagine now how I must've looked: my hands up, pathetic, tired, knowing already that we were defeated. She closed her eyes and tossed the knife hopelessly toward the camping stove, where it clattered. There was only the tiniest spark.

The gasoline that had been leaking from the stove for a couple minutes caught in a quick roar that made us all jump back, Natalie and the guards hitting the wall just behind them. One of them held onto her arm even as he stumbled and fell, bringing her down suddenly. From where I crouched on the ground, I could see the moment when the back of her neck connected with the jutting metal windowsill. Her head bent back, much too far back, her lovely skull cracking hard on the tempered glass, before she fell to the floor. It only took a second.

Someone was yelling on the other side of the office door. It was very warm. I crawled to where she was. Her eyes were open. I held my hand over her face. I was about to touch her, but when I did, what would I discover? Behind me, papers or files burned on the desk. The manager was moaning, holding his leg. I was about to touch her face. There she was below me on the floor, her eyes open. I was making words but all the sound had drained out of them, and I went to touch her face, and there was ash floating down onto her ears, into her open eyes, and I was about to touch her face but the guard pulled on her arm and her whole body moved bonelessly, a terrible thing to see, her arm flapping whitely against the carpeted floor, like she wasn't Natalie anymore at all, as the moment resolved cleanly in front of me and revealed that our story would end this way, that my hero finally wound up with nothing.

After Natalie died, I couldn't play anymore. I couldn't really move or want things. At some point, I rode the handsome glass elevator up to our suite alone. I finally opened and went through her drawer of beautiful stuff: The tissue paper. A glass ashtray. A poker chip that someone had broken a piece off of, so that it looked a little like Pacman. She'd kept the picture of Utah, like she'd still thought we'd make it there. She'd had all these tiny hopes that she kept bundled in secret, protecting them from everyone, including me. The manager said he wouldn't press charges. I went back to the electric laser tunnel, but it was just me, walking down a hallway. They were just colored lights. They were just people, going about their business.

In the apartment, I watched out the window. There's nothing at all out there, so you forget to look: the wind turns up thin tornados of sand, and at night, the glow of casino lights stretch off into the dark, pooling into the valleys, crowding out whatever stars or galaxies might be left up above. The night of the accident, the on-site doctor, once he got there from the baccarat tables, told me her neck had fractured so that she'd been paralyzed, but had been alive—alive for a few minutes— until she suffocated there on the floor. He should not have told me. I have to work hard at unknowing. On the floors below me, electric music from the machines sang and tumbled on.

After a couple of days, I went to the exit door. It's in the lobby, behind some luggage and empty vending machines. I stopped at the front desk and left my wallet behind; said *thanks* to no one in particular. The metal pushbar of the exit door was all dusty. There's a sign above it that says "Emergency Only, Alarm Will Sound," but no alarm sounds—no one tries to stop you or anything, you just leave.

Nominated by Electric Literature

SPECIAL MENTION

(The editors also wish to mention the following important works published by small presses last year. Listings are in no particular order.)

POETRY

Tony Hoagland — New Strategy (The Sun)

Lisa Badner—This is Not an Obituary (New Ohio Review)

Lisa Bellamy — Black-Eyed Susan (New Ohio Review)

Gabrielle Calvocoressi — Most Days I Want to Live (Southern Indiana Review)

Brandi Martin — For Then the Eyes of the Blind Shall Be Opened to Todd (Willow Springs)

Tom Montag — The Old House (The Lake)

Travis Mossotti — Black-Hole Camaro Enters the Mojave (Tar River Poetry)

Morgan Parker — Hottentot Venus (The Paris Review)

David Thacker — When Everything's Your Body (Colorado Review)

Lindsay Wilson — Blood Sausage (Raleigh Review)

Afaa Michael Weaver — East Baltimore, Fried Chicken (Prairie Schooner)

Rajiu Mohabir — Myotis Lucifugus (Verse Daily)

Adrian Matejka — After the Stars (Southern Indiana Review)

Naomi Shihab Nye — Hummingbird (Mizna)

Yona Harvey — On Literacy (Prairie Schooner)

Paisley Rekdal — The Wolves (Poetry)

Sharon Olds — Donner Party Mother Ode (Threepenny Review)

Wayne Miller — On Progress (New England Review)

Kevin Young — Homage to Phillis Wheatley (Kenyon Review)

Bob Hicok — Standing Up (Southern Review)

Jaswinder Bolina — Pornograph, With Americana (Omni Verse)

James Cummins — Ode to A Mockingbird (Agni)

William Wright — Understudy (Kenyon Review)

Emari DiGiorgio — The Grand Opera of Boko Haram (Heart)

J. Allyn Rosser — My Mother Addresses Everyone in the World (Ploughshares)

Betsy Sholl — To A Bat Fallen in the Street (Upstreet)

Katie Condon — Praying Naked (Narrative)

Leila Chatti — Hometown Nocturne (Narrative)

Dorothy Chan — Composition (Blackbird)

Lynne Thompson — Red Background (North American Review)

David Kirby — Look, Slav (Shenandoah)

Al Maginnes — Guardian (Grub Street)

Richard Cecil — Unsent E-mail to Kurt Brown (River Styx)

NON-FICTION

Ellen Collett — Undue Familiarity (The Sun)

Andre Dubus III — Carver and Dubus, New York City, 1988 (Five Points)

Phillip Lopate — My Red Relations (Mount Hope)

Gabriel Heller — Every Moment Is An Act Of Faith (The Sun)

Fazilhaq Hashimi — "How Can They Write About Anything But Pain?" (Electric Literature)

Florina Rodov — The Homemade Abortion: a Caged Bird, a Quinceaneara, and the American Dream (Electric Literature)

Sophie Beck — Pinterest for the Apocalypse (Missouri Review)

Edward Hoagland — The Miner's Lamp (New Letters)

Peter Selgin — The Strange Case of Arthur Silz (The Gettysburg Review)

Marilyn Abildskov — Goodness (Witness)

Barrett Swanson — Calling Audibles (Missouri Review)

Katharine Haake — War Protest (Santa Monica Review)

T. Kira Madden — The Feels of Love (Guernica)

Matthew Neill — Wanting to Die (Guernica)

Elissa Washuta — Apocalypse Logic (The Offing)

Jenny Shank — L'Homme De Ma Vie (Barrelhouse)

Jaclyn Moyer — On Wheat (The Normal School)

Peter Selgin — Swimming with Oliver (Colorado Review)

John Landretti — Nameless Season (Orion)

Eliese Colette Goldbach — White Horse (Alaska Quarterly Review)

Francisco Cantú — Crossing the Rio Grande (Orion)

Lia Purpura — All the Fierce Tethers (New England Review)

Saskia Vogel — Sluts (The Offing)

Kristin Ginger — How to Bury an Elephant (Slice)

Elissa Schappell — On Writing & Resistance & Miami Sound Machine (The Hopkins Review)

Jacob M. Appel — Why Get There from Here? (Fourth Genre)

Alison Hawthorne Deming — Coming Home to Earth: What Purse Seines, Pumpjacks, and a Twitter Feed from Space Taught One Worried Citizen about the Beauty of Climate Change in 2016 (Georgia Review)

Naira Kuzmich — On Grief (Massachusetts Review)

Kristin Allio — Buddhism for Western Children (The Southern Review)

Aisha Sabatini Sloan — D is for the Dance of the Hours (Ecotone)

Elena Passarello — Twinkle, Twinkle, Vogel Staar (Virginia Quarterly Review)

Carol Mersch — A Trial By Fire (The Big Roundtable)

Judith Barrington — The Walk Home (Creative Nonfiction)

Elliott D. Woods — The Fight for Chinko (Virginia Quarterly Review)

Sophie Beck — Returning the Gaze (The Point)

Victoria Blanco — Desert Race (Fourth Genre)

Brian Broome — The Red Caboose (Creative Nonfiction)

Susannah B. Mintz — White Matter (Epiphany)

Kaitlyn Teer — Drawing a Breath (Prairie Schooner)

Ben Jeffrey — After the Flood (The Point)

Thomas Mira y Lopez — Overburden (The Georgia Review)

Scott Latta — Spring, Miss Nelson's Class (The Southampton Review)

Shuchi Saraswat — The Journey Home (Ecotone)

Steven Kurutz — Fruitland (True Story)

Jonathan Burgess — Chai Party (War, Literature and The Arts)

Molly McCully Brown — Bent Body, Lamb (Image)

Deborah Thompson — Canine Cardiology (Bellevue Literary Review)

Dubravka Ugrešić — The Scold's Bridle (World Literature Today)

Sarah Bryan — Life and Death of the Father of Modern Miniature Golf (Southern Review)\

Maurice Carlos Ruffin — Fine Dining (Virginia Quarterly Review)

Peter LaSalle — Driving in São Paulo at Night with a Good Friend Who Has Died (Southern Review)

Barbara Hurd — Glimpses (Orion)

Joe Wilkins — A Place of First Permission (Orion)

Genese Grill — Re-Materialization, Remoteness, and Reverence: A Critique of De-Materialization in Art (The Georgia Review)

Joshua Wheeler — The Light of God: America's Pastime in the Age of Drone Warfare (The Iowa Review)

FICTION

Julian Zabalbeascoa — No One Here is Going to Save You (The Gettysburg Review)

David Stuart MacLean — Golden Friendship Club (Bennington Review)

Ann Patchett — Switzerland (One Story)

Erika Krouse — When in Bangkok (Kenyon Review)

Lygia Fagundes Telles — Seminar on the Extermination of Rats (Glossolalia)

Teresa Burns Gunther — Wild Places (Alaska Quarterly Review)

Ishrat Husain — Tales From The Toofaan Express (Fiction International)

Josie Sigler — The Flying Sampietrini (Provincetown Arts)

Sara Houghteling — The Thomas Cantor (Narrative)

Selena Anderson — Wig Violence (The Georgia Review)

Rebecca Schiff — Sports Night (Catapult)

Ariel Dorfman — Outliving Kafka (The Iowa Review)

Tamas Dobozy — Four by Kline Caro (Agni)

Jack Driscoll — Calcheck and Priest (Michigan Quarterly Review)

Eric Boehling Lewis — Newlyweds (Oxford American)

Melissa Pritchard — Hotel Majestic (Ploughshares)

Victor Lodato — The Tenant (Granta)

Christine Schutt — The Dot Sisters (Noon)

R.O. Kwon — Angels (Noon)

Farah Ali — Bulletproof Bus (J Journal)

Steven Gillis — Daddy (Michigan Quarterly Review)

Austin Smith — The Herd (The Threepenny Review)

Rick DeMarinis — Sparrow's Tale (The Antioch Review)

Jill McCorkle — The Last Station (The Southern Review)

Ye Chun — A Drawer (Gulf Coast)
Alice Mattison — Vegetables (Fifth Wednesday Journal)
Richard Burgin — Olympia (Per Contra)
Ann Beattie — Panthers (Paris Review)
Sarah Braunstein — Authority (Harvard Review)
Ramona Ausubel — Club Zeus (Tin House)
Onyinye Ihezukwu — Real Papa (The American Scholar)
Viet Thanh Nguyen — The Committed (Ploughshares)
Eireene Nealand — Gagarin's Shoelaces (Chicago Quarterly Review)
Stephen Dixon — Just What Is (Boulevard)
Jenniey Tallman — We Are Persistence Runners (Electric Literature)
Eric Thompson — The King of India (Glimmer Train Stories)
Maggie Shen King — A House of Her Own (Ecotone)
Leslie Pietrzyk — Give the Lady What She Wants (The Gettysburg Review)
Iris Smyles — Dating Tips for the Unemployed (East)
Julia Elliott — Clouds (Conjunctions)
David Brainard — In the Desert (New England Review)
Ben Eisman — Right-Hearted (New England Review)
Aamina Ahmad — The Discarded (Ecotone)
Brad Felver — Queen Elizabeth (One Story)
Polly Duff Kertis — Chicken Skin (The Literary Review)
Aaron Steven Miller — The One Arm (American Short Fiction)
Gwen E. Kirby — We Handle It (New Ohio Review)
Arinze Ifeakandu — God's Children Are Little Broken Things (A Public Space)
Adam Klinker — St. Lucy's Day (Chautauqua)
Amber Caron — The Handler (Southwest Review)
Emma Duffy-Comparone — The Sacrifice (Agni)
Jensen Beach — Migration (*Swallowed by The Cold*, Graywolf)
Melanie Rae Thon — The Bodies of Birds (Image)
Alice Denham — What Rich Is (Confrontation)
Poe Ballantine — Torpedoes D'Amour (The Sun)
Ariel Dorfman — Amboise (Zyzzyva)
Fatima Bhutto — Kabul (Zyzzyva)
E J. Levy — I, Spy (The Missouri Review)
Timothy Dumas — The Colonel's Boy (The Hudson Review)
Cary Mandel — Tuesdays with Moira (Witness)
Christine Sneed — Older Sister (New England Review)
Bradley Bazzle — Trash Mountain (Third Coast)

Kerry Neville — Remember to Forget Me (Arts & Letters)
Laurie Baker — Love Them All, Trust No One (Arts & Letters)
Adam O'Fallon Price — Tough Crowd (Epoch)
Richard Newman — The Winners (The Spectacle)
Nick Fuller Googins — Honeymoon Bandits (Willow Springs)
Matthew Lansburgh — Driving North (Michigan Quarterly Review)
Sylvie Bertrand — One of Them (Epiphany)
Manuel Martinez — Miami Don't Know (African American Review)
Clare Thompson-Ostrander — The Manual for Waitresses Everywhere
   (Glimmer Train Stories)
Ellen Prentiss Campbell — Sea Change (Broadkill River Press)
Tanaz Bhathena — The Final Examination (Upstreet)
Hunter Choate — The Amazing Uros (Pleiades)
Sofia Samatar — His Hollow (Obsidian)
A.A. Weiss — Challenger (Moon City)
Chase Burke — Some Memories of Brett Favre (Yemassee)
Zino Asalor — Fugar (New Madrid)
Bryan Washington — Lot (Transition)
Ben Fowlkes — Knuckles (failbetter)
Robin MacArthur — Creek Dippers (Edges)
Cecca Austin Ochoa — Still Life (Kweli Journal)
Brian Doyle — A Sprawl of Brothers (Harvard Review)
Joan Murray — Collectors (Ploughshares)
Alia Ahmed — The Comfort Weaver (The Hudson Review)
Joshua Cohen — The Last Last Summer (n +1)
Dionne Irving — Treading Water (The Missouri Review)
Phil Sultz — From Lake Effect Diner (The Hopkins Review)
Stephen O'Connor — The End of the End of the World (Conjunctions)
Maurice Carlos Ruffin — The Children of New Orleans (Agni)
Kent Nelson — Learning About Now (The Gettysburg Review)
Gunnhild Øyehaug — Eye Blister (Ploughsares)
Rachel Heng — Vegetarian (Prairie Schooner)
Constance Lindgreen — A Case in Point (Gascony Writers Anthology)
Lara Prescott — Aedinosaur (Crazyhorse)
Callan Wink — Upside Down (The Idaho Review)

PRESSES FEATURED IN THE PUSHCART PRIZE EDITIONS SINCE 1976

A-Minor
The Account
Adroit Journal
Agni
Ahsahta Press
Ailanthus Press
Alaska Quarterly Review
Alcheringa/Ethnopoetics
Alice James Books
Ambergris
Amelia
American Circus
American Journal of Poetry
American Letters and Commentary
American Literature
American PEN
American Poetry Review
American Scholar
American Short Fiction
The American Voice
Amicus Journal
Amnesty International
Anaesthesia Review
Anhinga Press
Another Chicago Magazine
Antaeus
Antietam Review

Antioch Review
Apalachee Quarterly
Aphra
Aralia Press
The Ark
Art and Understanding
Arts and Letters
Artword Quarterly
Ascensius Press
Ascent
Aspen Leaves
Aspen Poetry Anthology
Assaracus
Assembling
Atlanta Review
Autonomedia
Avocet Press
The Awl
The Baffler
Bakunin
Bamboo Ridge
Barlenmir House
Barnwood Press
Barrow Street
Bellevue Literary Review
The Bellingham Review
Bellowing Ark

Beloit Poetry Journal

Bennington Review

Bilingual Review

Black American Literature Forum

Blackbird

Black Renaissance Noire

Black Rooster

Black Scholar

Black Sparrow

Black Warrior Review

Blackwells Press

The Believer

Bloom

Bloomsbury Review

Blue Cloud Quarterly

Blueline

Blue Unicorn

Blue Wind Press

Bluefish

BOA Editions

Bomb

Bookslinger Editions

Boston Review

Boulevard

Boxspring

Briar Cliff Review

Brick

Bridge

Bridges

Brown Journal of Arts

Burning Deck Press

Butcher's Dog

Cafe Review

Caliban

California Quarterly

Callaloo

Calliope

Calliopea Press

Calyx

The Canary

Canto

Capra Press

Carcanet Editions

Caribbean Writer

Carolina Quarterly

Cave Wall

Cedar Rock

Center

Chariton Review

Charnel House

Chattahoochee Review

Chautauqua Literary Journal

Chelsea

Chicago Quarterly Review

Chouteau Review

Chowder Review

Cimarron Review

Cincinnati Review

Cincinnati Poetry Review

City Lights Books

Cleveland State Univ. Poetry Ctr.

Clown War

Codex Journal

CoEvolution Quarterly

Cold Mountain Press

The Collagist

Colorado Review

Columbia: A Magazine of Poetry and Prose

Conduit

Confluence Press

Confrontation

Conjunctions

Connecticut Review

Constellations

Copper Canyon Press

Copper Nickel

Cosmic Information Agency

Countermeasures

Counterpoint

Court Green

Crab Orchard Review

Crawl Out Your Window

Crazyhorse

Creative Nonfiction

Crescent Review

Cross Cultural Communications

Cross Currents

Crosstown Books

Crowd

Cue

Cumberland Poetry Review

Curbstone Press

Cutbank

Cypher Books

Dacotah Territory

Daedalus

Dalkey Archive Press

Decatur House

December

Denver Quarterly

Desperation Press

Dogwood

Domestic Crude

Doubletake

Dragon Gate Inc.

Dreamworks

Dryad Press

Duck Down Press

Dunes Review

Durak

East River Anthology

Eastern Washington University Press

Ecotone

El Malpensante

Electric Literature

Eleven Eleven

Ellis Press

Empty Bowl

Ep;phany

Epoch

Ergo!

Evansville Review

Exquisite Corpse

Faultline

Fence

Fiction

Fiction Collective

Fiction International

Field

Fifth Wednesday Journal

Fine Madness

Firebrand Books

Firelands Art Review

First Intensity

5 A.M.

Five Fingers Review

Five Points Press

Florida Review

Forklift

The Formalist

Foundry

Four Way Books

Fourth Genre

Fourth River

Frontiers: A Journal of Women Studies

Fugue

Gallimaufry

Genre

The Georgia Review

Gettysburg Review

Ghost Dance

Gibbs-Smith

Glimmer Train

Goddard Journal

David Godine, Publisher

Graham House Press

Grand Street

Granta

Graywolf Press

Great River Review

Green Mountains Review

Greenfield Review

Greensboro Review

Guardian Press

Gulf Coast

Hanging Loose

Harbour Publishing

Hard Pressed

Harvard Review

Hawaii Pacific Review

Hayden's Ferry Review

Hermitage Press

Heyday

Hills

Hollyridge Press

Holmgangers Press

Holy Cow!
Home Planet News
Hopkins Review
Hudson Review
Hunger Mountain
Hungry Mind Review
Ibbetson Street Press
Icarus
Icon
Idaho Review
Iguana Press
Image
In Character
Indiana Review
Indiana Writes
Intermedia
Intro
Invisible City
Inwood Press
Iowa Review
Ironwood
I-70 Review
Jam To-day
J Journal
The Journal
Jubilat
The Kanchenjunga Press
Kansas Quarterly
Kayak
Kelsey Street Press
Kenyon Review
Kestrel
Lake Effect
Lana Turner
Latitudes Press
Laughing Waters Press
Laurel Poetry Collective
Laurel Review
L'Epervier Press
Liberation
Linquis
Literal Latté
Literary Imagination
The Literary Review

The Little Magazine
Little Patuxent Review
Little Star
Living Hand Press
Living Poets Press
Logbridge-Rhodes
Louisville Review
Lowlands Review
LSU Press
Lucille
Lynx House Press
Lyric
The MacGuffin
Magic Circle Press
Malahat Review
Manoa
Manroot
Many Mountains Moving
Marlboro Review
Massachusetts Review
McSweeney's
Meridian
Mho & Mho Works
Micah Publications
Michigan Quarterly
Mid-American Review
Milkweed Editions
Milkweed Quarterly
The Minnesota Review
Mississippi Review
Mississippi Valley Review
Missouri Review
Montana Gothic
Montana Review
Montemora
Moon Pie Press
Moon Pony Press
Mount Voices
Mr. Cogito Press
MSS
Mudfish
Mulch Press
Muzzle Magazine
n + 1

Nada Press
Narrative
National Poetry Review
Nebraska Poets Calendar
Nebraska Review
Nepantla
Nerve Cowboy
New America
New American Review
New American Writing
The New Criterion
New Delta Review
New Directions
New England Review
New England Review and Bread Loaf
    Quarterly
New Issues
New Letters
New Madrid
New Ohio Review
New Orleans Review
New South Books
New Verse News
New Virginia Review
New York Quarterly
New York University Press
Nimrod
9X9 Industries
Ninth Letter
Noon
North American Review
North Atlantic Books
North Dakota Quarterly
North Point Press
Northeastern University Press
Northern Lights
Northwest Review
Notre Dame Review
O. ARS
O. Bl k
Obsidian
Obsidian II
Ocho
Oconee Review

October
Ohio Review
Old Crow Review
Ontario Review
Open City
Open Places
Orca Press
Orchises Press
Oregon Humanities
Orion
Other Voices
Oxford American
Oxford Press
Oyez Press
Oyster Boy Review
Painted Bride Quarterly
Painted Hills Review
Palo Alto Review
Paris Press
Paris Review
Parkett
Parnassus: Poetry in Review
Partisan Review
Passages North
Paterson Literary Review
Pebble Lake Review
Penca Books
Pentagram
Penumbra Press
Pequod
Persea: An International Review
Perugia Press
Per Contra
Pilot Light
The Pinch
Pipedream Press
Pitcairn Press
Pitt Magazine
Pleasure Boat Studio
Pleiades
Ploughshares
Poem-A-Day
Poems & Plays
Poet and Critic

Poet Lore

Poetry

Poetry Atlanta Press

Poetry East

Poetry International

Poetry Ireland Review

Poetry Northwest

Poetry Now

The Point

Post Road

Prairie Schooner

Prelude

Prescott Street Press

Press

Prism

Promise of Learnings

Provincetown Arts

A Public Space

Puerto Del Sol

Purple Passion Press

Quaderni Di Yip

Quarry West

The Quarterly

Quarterly West

Quiddity

Radio Silence

Rainbow Press

Raritan: A Quarterly Review

Rattle

Red Cedar Review

Red Clay Books

Red Dust Press

Red Earth Press

Red Hen Press

Release Press

Republic of Letters

Review of Contemporary Fiction

Revista Chicano-Riqueña

Rhetoric Review

Rhino

Rivendell

River Styx

River Teeth

Rowan Tree Press

Ruminate

Runes

Russian *Samizdat*

Salamander

Salmagundi

San Marcos Press

Santa Monica Review

Sarabande Books

Sea Pen Press and Paper Mill

Seal Press

Seamark Press

Seattle Review

Second Coming Press

Semiotext(e)

Seneca Review

Seven Days

The Seventies Press

Sewanee Review

Shankpainter

Shantih

Shearsman

Sheep Meadow Press

Shenandoah

A Shout In the Street

Sibyl-Child Press

Side Show

Sixth Finch

Small Moon

Smartish Pace

The Smith

Snake Nation Review

Solo

Solo 2

Some

The Sonora Review

Southern Indiana Review

Southern Poetry Review

Southern Review

Southampton Review

Southwest Review

Speakeasy

Spectrum

Spillway

Spork

The Spirit That Moves Us

St. Andrews Press

Stillhouse Press

Storm Cellar

Story

Story Quarterly

Streetfare Journal

Stuart Wright, Publisher

Subtropics

Sugar House Review

Sulfur

Summerset Review

The Sun

Sun & Moon Press

Sun Press

Sunstone

Sweet

Sycamore Review

Tab

Tamagawa

Tar River Poetry

Teal Press

Telephone Books

Telescope

Temblor

The Temple

Tendril

Texas Slough

Think

Third Coast

13th Moon

THIS

Thorp Springs Press

Three Rivers Press

Threepenny Review

Thrush

Thunder City Press

Thunder's Mouth Press

Tia Chucha Press

Tiger Bark Press

Tikkun

Tin House

Tipton Review

Tombouctou Books

Toothpaste Press

Transatlantic Review

Treelight

Triplopia

TriQuarterly

Truck Press

Tule Review

Tupelo Review

Turnrow

Tusculum Review

Undine

Unicorn Press

University of Chicago Press

University of Georgia Press

University of Illinois Press

University of Iowa Press

University of Massachusetts Press

University of North Texas Press

University of Pittsburgh Press

University of Wisconsin Press

University Press of New England

Unmuzzled Ox

Unspeakable Visions of the Individual

Vagabond

Vallum

Verse

Verse Wisconsin

Vignette

Virginia Quarterly Review

Volt

The Volta

Wampeter Press

War, Literature & The Arts

Washington Writer's Workshop

Water-Stone

Water Table

Wave Books

West Branch

Western Humanities Review

Westigan Review

White Pine Press
Wickwire Press
Wigleaf
Willow Springs
Wilmore City
Witness
Word Beat Press
Wordsmith
World Literature Today
Wormwood Review
Writers' Forum

Xanadu
Yale Review
Yardbird Reader
Yarrow
Y-Bird
Yes Yes Books
Zeitgeist Press
Zoetrope: All-Story
Zone 3
ZYZZYVA

THE PUSHCART PRIZE
FELLOWSHIPS

The Pushcart Prize Fellowships Inc., a 501 (c) (3) nonprofit corporation, is the endowment for The Pushcart Prize. "Members" donated up to $249 each. "Sponsors" gave between $250 and $999. "Benefactors" donated from $1000 to $4,999. "Patrons" donated $5,000 and more. We are very grateful for these donations. Gifts of any amount are welcome. For information write to the Fellowships at PO Box 380, Wainscott, NY 11975.

SUSTAINING MEMBERS

Margaret A. Ahnert
Dick Allen
Susan Antolin
Hilaria & Alec Baldwin
Jim Barnes
Ellen Bass
Ann Beattie
John Blondel
Rosellen Brown
David Caldwell
Bonnie Jo Campbell
Mary Casey
Lucinda Clark
Suzanne Cleary
Martha Collins
Linda Coleman
Stephen Corey
Lisa Couturier
Ed David
Josephine David
Michael Denison
Dan Dolgin & Loraine Gardner
Jack Driscoll
Wendy Druce
Penny Dunning
Elizabeth Ellen
Alice Friman
Carol & Laurene Frith
Ben & Sharon Fountain
Robert Giron
Myrna Goodman
Jeffrey Harrison
Michele Helm
Alex Henderson
Lee Hinton
Jane Hirsfield
Helen Houghton
Mark Irwin
Diane Johnson
Don Kaplan
Peter Krass
Edmund Keeley
Wally & Christine Lamb

Linda Lancione
Sydney Lea
Stephen O. Lesser
William Lychack
Maria Matthiessen
Alice Mattison
Robert McBrearty
Rebecca McClanahan
Rick Moody
John Mullen
Joan Murray
Neltje
Joyce Carol Oates
Osiris
Daniel Orozco
Pamela Painter
Barbara & Warren Phillips
Horatio Potter
C.E. Poverman
Elizabeth R. Rea
Stacey Richter
Valerie Sayers
Schaffner Family Fdn.
Alice Schell
Dennis Schmitz
Cindy Sherman
Grace Schulman
Lydia Ship
Jody Stewart
Sun Publishing
Summerset Review
Elaine Terranova
Susan Terris
Upstreet
Glyn Vincent
Rosanna Warren
Michael Waters
BJ Ward
Diane Williams
Kirby E. Williams
Henny Wenkart
Eleanor Wilner
Sandra Wisenberg

SPONSORS

Altman / Kazickas Fdn.
Jacob Appel
Jean M. Auel
Jim Barnes
Charles Baxter
Joe David Bellamy
Laura & Pinckney Benedict

Laure-Anne Bosselaar
Kate Braverman
Barbara Bristol
Kurt Brown
Richard Burgin
Alan Catlin
Mary Casey

Siv Cedering
Dan Chaon
James Charlton
Andrei Codrescu
Linda Coleman
Stephen Corey
Tracy Crow
Dana Literary Society
Carol de Gramont
Nelson DeMille
E. L. Doctorow
Karl Elder
Donald Finkel
Ben and Sharon Fountain
Alan and Karen Furst
John Gill
Robert Giron
Beth Gutcheon
Doris Grumbach & Sybil Pike
Gwen Head
The Healing Muse
Robin Hemley
Bob Hicok
Jane Hirshfield
Helen & Frank Houghton
Joseph Hurka
Diane Johnson

Janklow & Nesbit Asso.
Edmund Keeley
Thomas E. Kennedy
Sydney Lea
Stephen Lesser
Gerald Locklin
Thomas Lux
Markowitz, Fenelon and Bank
Elizabeth McKenzie
McSweeney's
John Mullen
Joan Murray
Barbara and Warren Phillips
Hilda Raz
Stacey Richter
Schaffner Family Foundation
Cindy Sherman
Joyce Carol Smith
May Carlton Swope
Glyn Vincent
Julia Wendell
Philip White
Kirby E. Williams
Eleanor Wilner
David Wittman
Richard Wyatt & Irene Eilers

MEMBERS

Anonymous (3)
Stephen Adams
Betty Adcock
Agni
Carolyn Alessio
Dick Allen
Henry H. Allen
John Allman
Lisa Alvarez
Jan Lee Ande
Dr. Russell Anderson
Ralph Angel
Antietam Review
Susan Antolin
Ruth Appelhof
Philip and Marjorie Appleman
Linda Aschbrenner
Renee Ashley
Ausable Press
David Baker
Catherine Barnett
Dorothy Barresi
Barlow Street Press
Jill Bart
Ellen Bass

Judith Baumel
Ann Beattie
Madison Smartt Bell
Beloit Poetry Journal
Pinckney Benedict
Karen Bender
Andre Bernard
Christopher Bernard
Wendell Berry
Linda Bierds
Stacy Bierlein
Big Fiction
Bitter Oleander Press
Mark Blaeuer
John Blondel
Blue Light Press
Carol Bly
BOA Editions
Deborah Bogen
Bomb
Susan Bono
Brain Child
Anthony Brandt
James Breeden
Rosellen Brown

Jane Brox
Andrea Hollander Budy
E. S. Bumas
Richard Burgin
Skylar H. Burris
David Caligiuri
Kathy Callaway
Bonnie Jo Campbell
Janine Canan
Henry Carlile
Carrick Publishing
Fran Castan
Mary Casey
Chelsea Associates
Marianne Cherry
Phillis M. Choyke
Lucinda Clark
Suzanne Cleary
Linda Coleman
Martha Collins
Ted Conklin
Joan Connor
J. Cooper
John Copenhaver
Dan Corrie
Pam Cotney
Lisa Couturier
Tricia Currans-Sheehan
Jim Daniels
Daniel & Daniel
Jerry Danielson
Ed David
Josephine David
Thadious Davis
Michael Denison
Maija Devine
Sharon Dilworth
Edward DiMaio
Kent Dixon
A.C. Dorset
Jack Driscoll
Wendy Druce
Penny Dunning
John Duncklee
Elaine Edelman
Renee Edison & Don Kaplan
Nancy Edwards
Ekphrasis Press
M.D. Elevitch
Elizabeth Ellen
Entrekin Foundation
Failbetter.com
Irvin Faust
Elliot Figman
Tom Filer
Carol and Lauerne Firth

Finishing Line Press
Susan Firer
Nick Flynn
Starkey Flythe Jr.
Peter Fogo
Linda Foster
Fourth Genre
John Fulton
Fugue
Alice Fulton
Alan Furst
Eugene Garber
Frank X. Gaspar
A Gathering of the Tribes
Reginald Gibbons
Emily Fox Gordon
Philip Graham
Eamon Grennan
Myrna Goodman
Ginko Tree Press
Jessica Graustain
Lee Meitzen Grue
Habit of Rainy Nights
Rachel Hadas
Susan Hahn
Meredith Hall
Harp Strings
Jeffrey Harrison
Clarinda Harriss
Lois Marie Harrod
Healing Muse
Tim Hedges
Michele Helm
Alex Henderson
Lily Henderson
Daniel Henry
Neva Herington
Lou Hertz
Stephen Herz
William Heyen
Bob Hicok
R. C. Hildebrandt
Kathleen Hill
Lee Hinton
Jane Hirshfield
Edward Hoagland
Daniel Hoffman
Doug Holder
Richard Holinger
Rochelle L. Holt
Richard M. Huber
Brigid Hughes
Lynne Hugo
Karla Huston
Illya's Honey
Susan Indigo

Mark Irwin
Beverly A. Jackson
Richard Jackson
Christian Jara
David Jauss
Marilyn Johnston
Alice Jones
Journal of New Jersey Poets
Robert Kalich
Sophia Kartsonis
Julia Kasdorf
Miriam Polli Katsikis
Meg Kearney
Celine Keating
Brigit Kelly
John Kistner
Judith Kitchen
Stephen Kopel
Peter Krass
David Kresh
Maxine Kumin
Valerie Laken
Babs Lakey
Linda Lancione
Maxine Landis
Lane Larson
Dorianne Laux & Joseph Millar
Sydney Lea
Donald Lev
Dana Levin
Gerald Locklin
Rachel Loden
Radomir Luza, Jr.
William Lychack
Annette Lynch
Elzabeth MacKiernan
Elizabeth Macklin
Leah Maines
Mark Manalang
Norma Marder
Jack Marshall
Michael Martone
Tara L. Masih
Dan Masterson
Peter Matthiessen
Maria Matthiessen
Alice Mattison
Tracy Mayor
Robert McBrearty
Jane McCafferty
Rebecca McClanahan
Bob McCrane
Jo McDougall
Sandy McIntosh
James McKean
Roberta Mendel

Didi Menendez
Barbara Milton
Alexander Mindt
Mississippi Review
Martin Mitchell
Roger Mitchell
Jewell Mogan
Patricia Monaghan
Jim Moore
James Morse
William Mulvihill
Nami Mun
Joan Murray
Carol Muske-Dukes
Edward Mycue
Deirdre Neilen
W. Dale Nelson
New Michigan Press
Jean Nordhaus
Celeste Ng
Christiana Norcross
Ontario Review Foundation
Daniel Orozco
Other Voices
Pamela Painter
Paris Review
Alan Michael Parker
Ellen Parker
Veronica Patterson
David Pearce, M.D.
Robert Phillips
Donald Platt
Plain View Press
Valerie Polichar
Pool
Horatio Potter
Jeffrey & Priscilla Potter
C.E. Poverman
Marcia Preston
Eric Puchner
Osiris
Tony Quagliano
Quill & Parchment
Barbara Quinn
Randy Rader
Juliana Rew
Belle Randall
Martha Rhodes
Nancy Richard
Stacey Richter
James Reiss
Katrina Roberts
Judith R. Robinson
Jessica Roeder
Martin Rosner
Kay Ryan

554

ADVISORY COUNCIL

Rick Bass
Charles Baxter
Madison Smartt Bell
Marvin Bell
Sven Birkerts
T. C. Boyle
Ron Carlson
Andrei Codrescu
Billy Collins
Stephen Dunn
Daniel Halpern
Edward Hoagland

John Irving
Ha Jin
Mary Karr
Joan Murray
Wally Lamb
Rick Moody
Joyce Carol Oates
Sherod Santos
Grace Schulman
Charles Simic
Gerald Stern
Charles Wright

CONTRIBUTING SMALL PRESSES FOR PUSHCART PRIZE XLII

(These presses made or received nominations for this edition.)

A

A&U: 25 Monroe St., #205, Albany, NY 12210

A Public Space, 323 Dean St., Brooklyn, NY 11217

Aaduna, 144 Genesee St., Ste. 102-259, Auburn, NY 13021

Able Muse Review, 467 Saratoga Ave., #602, San Jose, CA 95129

About Place, 4520 Blue Mounds Trail, Black Earth, WI 53515

The Account, 2501 W. Zia Rd., #8204, Santa Fe, NM 87505

The Adroit Journal, 3805 Locust Walk, Philadelphia, PA 19104

Aerogram, PO Box 591164, San Francisco, CA 94159

Agni, Boston Univ., 236 Bay State Rd., Boston, MA 02215

Airlie Press, P.O. Box 82653, Portland, OR 97282

Akashic Books, 232 3rd St., Ste. A115, Brooklyn, NY 11215-2708

Alaska Quarterly Review, ESH 208, 3211 Providence Dr., Anchorage, AK 99508- 4614

Alfie Dog Limited, Schilde Lodge, Black Lane, Tholthorpe, North Yorkshire Y061 1SN, UK

Algonquin Books of Chapel Hill, 225 Varick St., New York, NY 10014

Alice James Books, 114 Prescott St., Farmington, ME 04938

Alternating Current Press, PO Box 270921, Louisville, CO 80027

American Journal of Poetry, 14969 Chateau Village Dr., Chesterfield, MO 63017

American Literary Review, 1155 Union Circle, #311307, Denton, TX 76203

The American Scholar, 1606 New Hampshire Ave. NW, Washington, DC 20009

American Short Fiction, 109 West Johanna St., Austin ,TX 78704

Amethyst Arsenic, ELJ Pub., PO Box 904, Washingtonville, NY 10992

Amphorae Publishing Group, 4168 Hartford St., St. Louis, MO 63116

Anaphora Literary Press, 1898 Athens St., Brownsville, TX 78520

Anchor & Plume, PO Box 80142, Baton Rouge, LA 70898

Animal, 264 Fallen Palm Dr., Casselberry, FL 32707

Anomalous Press, 853 29th Ave., San Francisco, CA 94121

The Antioch Review, PO Box 148, Yellow Springs, OH 45387-0148

Antrim House Books, 21 Goodrich Rd., Simsbury, CT 06070

Apogee Journal, 418 Suydam St., Apt. 1L, Brooklyn, NY 11237

Appalachian Heritage, Berea College, CPO 2166, Berea, KY 40404

Apple Valley Review, 88 South 3rd St., #336, San José, CA 95113

Apt, 81 Lexington St., #1, Boston, MA 02128

Aquarius Press, P.O. Box 23096, Detroit, MI 48223

Aquila Polonica, 10850 Wilshire Blvd., #300, Los Angeles, CA 90024

Arcadia Magazine, PO Box 2905, Oklahoma City, OK 73101

Archaeopteryx, Newman Univ., 3100 McCormick, Wichita, KS 67213

Arcturus Magazine, 1 W. Superior St., #2610, Chicago, IL 60654

The Ardent Writer Press, 1014 Stone Dr., Brownsboro, AL 35741

Arizona Authors, 6939 E Chaparral Rd., Paradise Valley, AZ 85253

Arkana, Univ. of Central Arkansas, 201 Donaghey Ave., Conway, AR 72035

Arroyo Literary Review, C.S.U. English, MB2579, 25800 Carlos Bee Blvd., Hayward, CA 94542

Arsenic Lobster, 1830 W. 18th St., Chicago, IL 60608

Arts & Letters Journal, Campus Box 89, Georgia College & State University, Milledgeville, GA 31061

Ashland Creek Press, 2305 Ashland St., #C417, Ashland, OR 97520

Askew, P.O. Box 559, Ventura, CA 93002

Aster(ix), Univ. of Pittsburgh, 5200 Cathedral of Learning, Pittsburgh, PA 15260

Asymptote, #84 Zhongshan North Rd., Section 1, #13-7. Taipei, 10444, Taiwan

At Length, 716 W. Cornwallis Rd., Durham, NC 27707

Atlanta Review, c/o Georgia Tech, Atlanta, GA 30332-0165

Atticus Review, 22 Hickory Rd., West Orange, NJ 07052

Aunt Lute Books, PO Box 410687, San Francisco, CA 94141

Autumn House Press, 87 ½ Westwood St., Pittsburgh, PA 15211

Autumn Sky Poetry Daily, 5263 Arctic Circle, Emmaus, PA 18049

Awst, P.O. box 49163, Austin, TX 78765-9163

Azure, PO Box 21322, Brooklyn, NY 11202

B

Bad Knee Press, 528 N. Mansfield Ave., Los Angeles, CA 90036

Bacopa Literary Review, 4000 NW 51st St., G-121, Gainesville, FL 32606

The Baltimore Review, 6514 Maplewood Rd., Baltimore, MD 21212

Bamboo Ridge Press, PO Box 61781, Honolulu, HI 96839-1781

Banshee, 18 Pacelli Rd., Naas. Co. Kildare, Ireland

Barrelhouse, 793 Westerly Parkway, State College, PA 16801

Barrow Street Journal, 4 Bayview St., Highlands, NJ 07732

Bartleby Snopes, 2219 Grimm Rd., Chaska, MN 55318

Bat City Review, 1 University Station, B 5000, Austin, TX 78712

Bayou Magazine, U.N.O., 2000 Lake Shore Dr., New Orleans, LA 70148

Beecher's, Wescoc Hall, Room 3001, 1445 Jayhawk Blvd., Lawrence, KS 66045

Belletrist Magazine, 3000 Landerholm Circle SE, Bellevue, WA 98007

Bellevue Literary Review, NYU Medicine, 550 First Ave, OBV-A612, New York, NY 10016

Bellingham Review, MS-9053, WWU, 516 High St., Bellingham, WA 98225

Beloit Fiction Journal, 700 College St., Box 11, Beloit, WI 53511

Beloit Poetry Journal, PO Box 1450, Windham, ME 04062

Beltway Poetry Quarterly, 626 Quebec Pl., NW, Washington, DC 20010

Bennington Review, 1 College Dr., Bennington, VT 05201

Big Roundtable, Columbia Univ., MC3800, 2950 Broadway, New York, NY 10027

Big Table, 383 Langley Rd., #2, Newton Centre, MA 02459

Big Yes Press, PO Box 4344, San Luis Obispo, CA 93403

The Binnacle, 19 Kimball Hall, Univ. of Maine, 116 O'Brien Ave., Machias, ME 04654

bioStories, 175 Mission View Dr., Lakeside, MT 59922

bird's thumb, 701 S. Wells St., #2903, Chicago, IL 60607

Birmingham Poetry Review, English Dept., UAB, Birmingham, AL 35294-1260

BkMk Press, UMKC, 5100 Rockhill Rd., Kansas City, MO 64110-2446

Blackbird, PO Box 843082, Richmond, VA 23284

Black Mountain Institute, 4505 S. Maryland Prky, Las Vegas, NV 89154

Black Pear Press, 3 Station Rd., Hartlebury, Kidderminster, Worcestershire, DY11 7YJ, UK

Black Warrior, Univ. of Alabama, Box 870170, Tuscaloosa, AL 35487

Blink Ink, P.O. Box 5, North Branford, CT 06471

Blood Orange Review, WSU, Avery Hall 202, Pullman, WA 99164-5020

Blue Fifth Review, 267 Lark Meadow Circle, Bluff City, TN 37618

Blue Heron, N66W38350 Deer Creek Ct., Oconomowoc, WI 53066

Blue Light Press, 1563 45th Ave., San Francisco, CA 94122

Blue River, 3878 California St., Omaha, NE 68131

Blueshift Journal, 29 Ivana Dr., Andover, MA 01810

Bluestem, English Dept., Eastern Illinois University, Charleston, IL 61920-3011

BOA Editions, 250 North Goodman St., Ste. 306, Rochester, NY 14607

Bodega Magazine, 451 Court St., #3R, Brooklyn, NY 11231

The Boiler, 119 Peach St., Denton, TX 76201

Book Ex Machina, P.O. Box 23595, Nicosia 1685, Cyprus

Books and Boos Press, PO Box 772, Hebron, CT 06248

Booth, Butler Univ., English, 4600 Sunset Ave., Indianapolis, IN 46208

Bop Dead City, 212 Wildoak Dr., Birmingham, AL 35210

Border Crossing, 650 W. Easterday Ave., Sault Ste. Marie, MI 49783

Boston Review, PO Box 425786, Cambridge, MA 02142

Bosque Press, 508 Chamiso Lane, NW, Los Ranchos, NM 87107

Bottom Dog Press, Firelands College, P.O. Box 425, Huron, OH 44839

Boulevard, 6614 Clayton Rd., PMB 325, Richmond Heights, MO 63117

Box Turtle Press, 184 Franklin St., New York, NY 10013

Boxcar Poetry Review, 3508 NE 158th Ave., Vancouver, WA 98682

Brain, Child, 341 Newtown Turnpike, Wilton, CT 06897

Brain Mill Press, 1051 Kellogg St., Green Bay, WI 54303

Brain, Teen, 341 Newtown Turnpike, Wilton, CT 06897

Breakwater Review, 12 Thorpe St., #1, Somerville, MA 02143

Brevity, 265 E. State, Athens, OH 45701

The Briar Cliff Review, 3303 Rebecca St., Sioux City, IA 51104-2100

Brick, P.O. Box 609, Stn. P, Toronto, Ontario, M5S 2Y4, Canada

Brilliant Flash Fiction, 1 Saint Patrick's Square, Laytown, County Meath, Ireland

British Columbia History, PO Box 21187, Maple Ridge, BC V2X 1P7, Canada

Broad River, PO Box 7224, Gardner-Webb, Boiling Springs, NC 28017

Broad Street, English, VCU, PO Box 842005, Richmond, VA 23284

Broadstone Books, 418 Ann St., Frankfort, KY 40601-1929

The Broken Shore, 15 Sandspring Dr., Eatontown, NJ 07724

Buffalo Almanack, 418 W. Maynard Ave., Durham, NC 27704

Burnt Pine Magazine, 1723 Palo Verde Dr., Rapid City, SD 57701-4463

Burrow Press, P.O. Box 533709, Orlando, FL 32853

Butcher's Dog, 17 January Courtyard, Gateshead, NE8 2GL, UK

C

C & R Press, 1869 Meadowbrooke Dr., Winston-Salem, NC 27104

Café Irreal, PO Box 87031, Tucson, AZ 85745

Caliente Media, 320 Araneo Dr., West Orange, NJ 07052

California Quarterly, 23 Edgecroft Rd., Kensington, CA 94707

Caribbean Reads, PO Box 7321, Fairfax Station, VA 22039

The Caribbean Writer, UVI, RR 1, Box 10,000, Kingshill, St. Croix, USVI 00850

Carve Magazine, PO Box 701510, Dallas, TX 75370

Catamaran, 1050 River St., #118, Santa Cruz, CA 95060

Catapult, 1140 Broadway, Ste. 704, New York, NY 10001

Catherine Pratt, Publisher, 75 Front St., Noank, CT 06340

Cave Wall Press, PO Box 29546, Greensboro, NC 27429-9546

Cease, Cows, 133 Chaucer Manor Lane, #C, Kernersville, NC 27284

Cervena Barva Press, PO Box 440357, W. Sommerville, MA 02144

Chaffey Review, 5885 Haven Ave., Rancho Cucamonga, CA 91737-3002

Chattahoochee Review, 555 North Indian Creek Dr., Clarkston, GA 30021

Chatter House, 7915 S. Emerson Ave., Ste. B303, Indianapolis, IN 46237

Chautauqua, Creative Writing Dept., 601 South College Rd., Wilmington, NC 28401

Cheap Pop, 6021 Mission Trail, #3, Granger, IN 46530

Chicago Literati, 611 Stevens St., Geneva, IL 60134

Chicago Quarterly Review, 517 Sherman Ave., Evanston, IL 60202

Chiron Review, 522 E. South Ave., St. John, KS 67576-2212

Chrome Baby, 445 S. Western Ave., #303, Los Angeles, CA 90020

Cider Press Review, P.O. Box 33384, San Diego, CA 92163

Cincinnati Review, Univ. of Cincinnati, PO Box 210069, Cincinnati, OH 45221-0069

Citron Review, 291 Walnut Village Lane, Henderson, NV 89002

Cleaver Magazine, 8250 Shawnee St., Philadelphia, PA 19118

Clementine Unbound, 855 York Rd., Carlisle, PA 17015

Cleveland State University Poetry Center, 2121 Euclid Ave., RT 1841, Cleveland, OH 44115

Cloudbank, PO Box 610, Corvallis, OR 97339-0610

Clover, 203 West Holly St., Ste. 306, Bellingham, WA 98225

Coal City, English Dept., University of Kansas, Lawrence, KS 66045

Coda Review, P.O. Box 257, Thetford Center, VT 05075

Codorus Press, 1301 15th St. NW, #802, Washington, DC 20005

The Collagist, G. Blackwell, 2905 E. Jackson St., Pensacola, FL 32503

Colorado Review, Colorado State Univ., Fort Collins, CO 80523-9105

Columbia Poetry Review, 600 So. Michigan Ave., Chicago, IL 60605

Comment, 185 Young St., Hamilton, ON L8N 1V9, Canada

Compose, 544 Fishermens' Point Rd., Shuniah, ON, P7A 0J4, Canada

Concho River Review, ASU Station #10894, San Angelo, TX 76909-0894

Confrontation, English Dept., LIU/Post, Brookville, NY 11548-1300

Conjunctions, Bard College, Annandale-on-Hudson, NY 12504-5000

Connecticut River Review, PO Box 516, Cheshire, CT 06410

Consequence Magazine, P.O. Box 323, Cohasset, MA 02025

Constellations, 127 Lake View Ave., Cambridge, MA 02138

Contrary, S. Beers, PO Box 100, Pendleton, OR 97801-1000

Copper Nickel, Univ. of Colorado, Campus Box 175, Denver, CO 80217

Cossack Review, 422 Yorkshire Dr., Cameron, NC 28326

Counterpoint, Soft Skull Press, 2560 9th St., #318, Berkeley, CA 94710

The Courtship of Winds, 55 Cortland Lane, Boxborough, MA 01719

Cowboy Jamboree, 10695 Old Hwy 51 N, Cobden, IL 62920

Crab Creek, P.O. Box 1682, Kingston, WA 98346

Crannóg Magazine, 6 San Antonio Park, Salthill, Galway, Ireland

Crazyhorse, College of Charleston, 66 George St., Charleston, SC 29424

Creative Nonfiction, 5119 Coral St., Pittsburgh, PA 15224

Creative Talents Unleashed, PO Box 605, Helendale, CA 92342

Cultural Weekly, 215 W. 6th St., #801, Los Angeles, CA 90014

Cumberland River Review, English Dept., Trevecca Nazarene Univ., Nashville, TN 37210

Cutthroat, A Journal of the Arts, PO Box 2414, Durango, CO 81302

D

Damaged Goods Press, 5485 Woodgate Dr., Columbus, GA 31907

Dash, Cal State Fullerton, English, PO Box 6848, Fullerton, CA 92834

Dead Housekeeping, 914 S. 10th St., Mount Vernon, WA 98274

december, P.O. Box 16130, St. Louis, MO 63105

decomP, 726 Carriage Hill Dr., Athens, OH 45701

defenestrationism.net, 13 Oxford St., Chevy Chase, MD 20815

Delmarva Review, PO Box 547, Secretary, MD 21664

Denver Quarterly, English Dept., 2000 E. Ashbury, Denver, CO 80208

Diode Editions, 18221 150th Ave, DOH 3129, Springfield Gardens, NY 11413-4010

Dime Show Review, PO Box 760, Folsom, CA 95630-0760

District Lit, 2016 N. Adams St., #312, Arlington, VA 22201

The DMQ Review, 16393 Bonnie Lane, Los Gatos, CA 95032

Dos Gatos Press, 6452 Kola Court NW, Albuquerque, NM 87120-4285

Douglas & McIntyre, PO Box 219, Madeira Park, BC V0N 2H0, Canada

Dragonfly Press, P.O. Box 746, Columbia, CA 95310

Dreams and Nightmares, 1300 Kicker Rd., Tuscaloosa, AL 35404

Driftwood Press, 8804 Tallwood Dr., #24, Austin, TX 78759

Duende Journal, Goddard College, 123 Pitkin Rd., Plainfield, VT 05667

E

ELJ Publications, P.O. Box 904, Washingtonville, NY 10992

East Bay Review, 1720 Laguna St., #E, Concord, CA 94520

EAST Magazine, 153 Main St., PO Box 5002, East Hampton, NY 11937

Eclectia, 6030 N. Sheridan Rd., #805, Chicago, IL 60660

Ecotone, UNCW, 601 S. College Rd., Wilmington, NC 28403-3201

805 Lit + Art, 1301 Barcarrota Blvd W, Brandenton, FL 34205

Ekphrasis/Frith Press, PO Box 161236, Sacramento, CA 95816-1236

Electric Literature, 1140 Broadway, Ste. 704, New York, NY 10001

Eleven Eleven Journal, 1111 Eighth St., S.F., CA 94107

Elm, 300 College Ave., Eureka, IL 61530

Empty Sink, 2330 Boxer Palm, San Antonio, TX 78213

The Emrys Foundation, PO Box 8813, Greenville, SC 29604

Encircle Publications, P.O. Box 187, Farmington, ME 04938

Enizagam, Oak. School for the Arts, 530 18th St., Oakland, CA 94612

Epigram Books, 1008 Toa Payon North, #03-08, 318996 Singapore

Epiphany Literary Journal, 71 Bedford St., New York, NY 10014

Epoch, 251 Goldwin Smith Hall, Cornell University, Ithaca NY 14853

Event, PO Box 2503, New Westminster, BC, V3L 5B2, Canada

Exit 7, WKCTC, 4810 Alben Barkley Dr., Paducah, KY 42001

Exit 13, 22 Oakwood Ct., Fanwood, NJ 07023

Exposition Review, 915 Ocean Ave., #203, Santa Monica, CA 90403

Expound, 5822 N. Campbell Ave., #1, Chicago, IL 60659

Eye to the Telescope, SFPA, 117 McCann Rd., Newark, DE 19711

F

Fabula Press, 752 A/2, Block P, New Alipore, Kolkata, West Bengal, India 700053

Fairy Tale Review, English Dept., Univ. of Arizona, Tucson, AZ 85721

Fantasy and Science Fiction, PO Box 8420, Surprise, AZ 85374

Faultline, English Dept., UC Irvine, Irvine, CA 92697-2650

Fawkes Press, 6209 Timberwolfe Lane, Forth Worth, TX 76135

Femspec, 1610 Rydalmount Rd., Cleveland Heights, OH 44118

Fiction International, English Dept., SDSU, San Diego, CA 92182-6020

Fiction Week Literary Review, 887 So. Rice Rd., Ojai, CA 93023

Fiddlehead, Box 4400, Univ. New Brunswick, NB E3B 5A3, Canada

Field, 50 North Professor St., Oberlin, OH 44074-1091

Fifth Wednesday, P.O. Box 4033, Lisle, IL 60532-9033

Finishing Line Press, P.O. Box 1626, Georgetown, KY 40324

The First Line, PO Box 250382, Plano, TX 75025-0382

Fithian Press, PO Box 2790, McKinleyville, CA 95519

Five Oaks Press, 6 Five Oaks Dr., Newburgh, NY 12550

Five On the Fifth, 120 W. Lytle Ave., State College, PA 16801

Five Points, Georgia State University, Box 3999, Atlanta, GA 30302

Flapperhouse, 31 Ocean Parkway, #5J, Brooklyn, NY 11218

Flash, Univ. of Chester, English, Parkgate Rd., Chester, CH1 4BJ, UK

Flash Frontier, 267 Lark Meadow Cr., Bluff City, TN 37618

Fledging Rag, 1716 Swarr Run Rd., J-108, Lancaster, PA 17601

The Flexible Persona, 1070-1 Tunnel Rd., #10-244, Asheville, NC 28805

Flock, 6525 Greenway Dr., C28, Roanoke, VA 24019

Florida Review, PO Box 161346, Orlando, FL 32816-1346

Flying Island, 214 S. Third Ave., Beech Grove, IN 46107

Flying South 2016, 546 Birch Creek Rd., McLeansville, NC 27301

Flyway, English Dept., 206 Ross Hall, Iowa State Univ., Ames, IA 50011

Foglifter, 267 Divisadero St., San Francisco, CA 94117

Folded Word, 79 Tracy Way, Meredith, NH 03253-5409

Foliate Oak, Univ. of Arkansas, 562 University Dr., Monticello, AR 71656

Fomite, 58 Peru St., Burlington, VT 05401-8606

Foothill, 165 E. 10th St., Claremont, CA 91711-6186

Forage Poetry Journal, 1803 Windcrest Dr., Lilburn, GA 30047

Fordham University Press, 2546 Belmont Ave., University Box L, Bronx, NY 10458

Forge, 4018 Bayview Ave., San Mateo, CA 94403-4310

48th Street Press, 6 Bodnarik Rd., Edison, NJ 08837

45th Parallel, 4700 SW Research Way, Corvallis, OR 97333

Foundry, 10 Halley St., Yonkers, NY 10704

Four Way Review, 2581 N. Stowell Ave., #D, Milwaukee, WI 53211

Fourteen Hills, Creative Writing, SFSU, 1600 Holloway Ave., San Francisco, CA 94137

Fourth Genre, 434 Farm Lane, Rm 235, MSU, East Lansing, MI 48824

The Fourth River, Chatham Univ., 1 Woodland Rd., Pittsburgh, PA 15232

Freedom Fiction, Nirli Villa, #7, Village Rd., Bhandup West, Mumbai - 400078, India

Front Porch Journal, Texas State Univ., 601 University Dr., San Marcos, TX 78666

Fugue, University of Idaho, 200 Brink Hall, Moscow, ID 83844-1102

Full Grown People, 106 Tripper Ct., Charlottesville, VA 22903

G

Gargoyle Magazine, 3819 13th St. N., Arlington, VA 22201-4922

Gemini Magazine, PO Box 1485, Onset, MA 02558

The Georgia Review, University of Georgia, Athens, GA 30602-9009

The Gettysburg Review, Gettysburg College, Box 2446, Gettysburg, PA 17325

GFT Press, 14260 W. Newberry Rd., #174, Newberry, FL 32669

Ghost Ocean Magazine, 136 Pearl St., Fort Collins, CO 80521

Gigantic Sequins, 209 Avon St., Breaux Bridge, LA 70517

Gingerbread House, 378 Howell Ave., Cincinnati, OH 45220

Gingko Tree Review, Drury University, 900 N. Benton Ave., Springfield, MO 65802

Gival Press, PO Box 3812, Arlington, VA 22203

Glass Lyre Press, PO Box 2693, Glenview, IL 60025

Glass Poetry Press, 1667 Crestwood, Toledo, OH 43612

Glassworks, Rowan Univ., 201 Mullica Hill Rd., Glassboro, NJ 08028

Glimmer Train Press, P.O. Box 80430, Portland, OR 97280-1430

Glint, Fayetteville State U., 1200 Murchison Rd., Fayetteville, NC 28301

Gnarled Oak, 9412 Billingham Trail, Austin, TX 78717

Gold Line Press, USC, 3501 Trousdale Blvd., THH431, Los Angeles, CA 90089-0354

Gold Man Review, 22218 Elkhorn Pl., Cottonwood, CA 96022

Golden Foothills Press, 1443 E. Washington Blvd., #232, Pasadena, CA 91104

Good Men Project, 252 Marcia Way, Bridgewater, NJ 08807

Gorilla Press, PO Box 651, Blackduck, MN 56630

Granta, 12 Addison Ave., Holland Park, London W11 4QR, UK

Gravel, Univ. of Arkansas, Box 562, Monticello, AR 71656

Graywolf Press, 250 Third Ave. N., Ste. 600, Minneapolis, MN 55401

The Gravity of the Thing, 17028 SE Rhone St., Portland, OR 97236

great weather for MEDIA, 515 Broadway, #2B, New York, NY 10012

Green Hills Literary Lantern, Truman State Univ., English, Kirksville, MO 63501

Green Mountains Review, Johnson State, 337 College Hill, Johnson, VT 05656

Green Writers Press, 34 Miller Rd., West Brattleboro, VT 05301

Greensboro Review, UNC, Greensboro, NC 27402

The Greensilk Journal, 228 N. Main St., Woodstock, VA 22664

Griffith Review, PO Box 3370, South Brisbane, QLD 4101, Australia

Grist, 301 McClung Tower, Univ. of Tennessee, Knoxville, TN 37996

Grub Street, Towson Univ., English, 8000 York Rd., Towson, MD 21252

Guernica Editions, 1569 Heritage Way, Oakville, ON L6M 2Z7, Canada

Guidelights Productions, PO Box 233, San Luis Rey, CA 92068

Gulf Coast, University of Houston, Houston, TX 77204-3013

Gulf Stream, 3000 NE 151st St., ACI-335, North Miami, FL 33181

Gyroscope Review, 1891 Merrill St., Roseville, MN 55113

H

H. O. Tangager Press, 1412 W. Washington St., Boise, ID 83702

Haight Ashbury Literary Journal, 558 Joost Ave., San Francisco, CA 94127

Hamilton Arts & Letters, 92 Stanley Ave., Hamilton ON, L8P 2L3, Canada

Hamilton Stone Review, P.O. Box 457, Jay, NY 12941

Hand Type Press, P.O. Box 3941, Minneapolis, MN 55403-0941

Harbor Electronic Publishing, 84 Mt. Misery Dr., Sag Harbor, NY 11963

Harbour Publishing Co., P.O. Box 219, Madeira Park, BC V0N 2H0 Canada

Harvard Review, Lamont Library, Harvard Univ., Cambridge, MA 02138

Harvard Square Editions, 2152 Beachwood Terrace, Hollywood, CA 90068

Hayden's Ferry Review, P.O. Box 870302, Tempe, AZ 85287-0302

Headmistress Press, P.O. Box 275, Eagle Rock, MO 65641

The Healing Muse, 618 Irving Ave., Syracuse, NY 13210

Hedgehog Review, Univ. of Virginia, P.O. Box 400816, Charlottesville, VA 22904

Hedgerow Review, 71 South Pleasant St., Amherst, MA 01002

Helicon West, 3200 Old Main Hill, Logan UT 84322-3200

Hermeneutic Chaos Press, 109, DDA SFS Flats, Madipur, New Delhi - 110063, India

Heyday, P.O. Box 9145, Berkeley, CA 94709

HiConcept Magazine, 46 Ocean Ave., Bayport, NY 11705-1819

Hidden Charm Press, 246 South Huntington Ave., #9, Jamaica Plain, MA 02130

High Country News, P.O. Box 1090, Paonia, CO 81428

Hip Pocket Press, 5 Del Mar Court, Orinda, CA 94563

Hippocampus Magazine, 222 E. Walnut St., #2, Lancaster, PA 17602

Hobart, PO Box 1658, Ann Arbor, MI 48106

The Hollins Critic, P.O. Box 9538, Roanoke, VA 24020-1538

The Hopkins Review, Johns Hopkins Univ., 3400 N. Charles St., Baltimore, MD 21218

Hub City, 186 West Main St, Spartanburg, SC 29306

The Hudson Review, 33 West 67th St., New York, NY 10023

Hunger Mountain, Vermont College, 36 College St., Montpelier, VT 05602

Hypertrophic Press, P.O. Box 423, New Market, AL 35761

I

I-70 Review, 5021 S. Tierncy Dr., Independence, MO 64055

Ibbetson Street Press, 25 School Street, Somerville, MA 02143

Ice Cube Press, 205 N. Front St., North Liberty, IA 52317

The Idaho Review, Boise State, 1910 University Dr., Boise, ID 83725

Illuminations, College of Charleston, 66 George St., Charleston, SC 29424-0001

Illya's Honey, PO Box 700865, Dallas, TX 75370

Image, 3307 Third Avenue West, Seattle, WA 98119

Indiana Review, 1020 E. Kirkwood Ave., Bloomington, IN 47405-7103

Indiana University Press, 1320 East 10th St., Bloomington, IN 47405

Indiana Voice Journal, 3038 E. Clem Rd., Anderson, IN 46017

Indianola Review, 1616 West Salem Ave., Indianola, IA 50125

Ink & Letters, 1120 N. Louisa Ave., Shawnee, OK 74801

Inkerman & Blunt, PO Box 310, Carlton South, Victoria 3053, Australia

Inklette, Opp. Rangmahal, New Market, Bhopal-462003, Madhya Pradesh, India

Insomnia & Obsession, 7 Mayfield Ave., Akron, OH 44313

Intellect Publishing, 6581 Country Rd. 32, #1744, Point Clear, AL 36564

Interviewing the Caribbean, PO Box 6133, Christiansted, VI, 00823

Into the Void, 13 Weston Crt., Weston Park, Lucan, County Dublin, Ireland
The Iowa Review, 308 EPB, University of Iowa, Iowa City, IA 52242
Isthmus, PO Box 16742, Seattle, WA 98116

J

J Journal, 524 West 59th St., 7th fl, New York, NY 10019
Jabberwock Review, MSU., P.O. Box E, Mississippi State, MS 39762
Jacar Press, 6617 Deerview Trail, Durham, NC 27712
Jacaranda Books, #304 Metal Box Factory, 30 Great Guildford St., London
    SE1 0HS, UK
Jalada Africa, PO Box 45140, Nairobi 00100, Kenya
Jelly Bucket, 521 Lancaster Ave., Mattox 101, Richmond, KY 40475
Jellyfish Review, Medit. 1, D15KC, TJD, 11470 Jakarta Barat, Indonesia
Jersey Devil Press, 3722 Keagy Rd. SW, Roanoke, VA 24018
Jet Fuel Review, English, Lewis Univ., 1 University Pkwy, Romeoville, IL
    60446- 2200
Jewish Fiction, 378 Walmer Rd., Toronto, ON M5R 2Y4, Canada
Jokes Review, 3921 A Webster St., Oakland, CA 94609
The Journal, Ohio State Univ., 164 Annie & John Glenn Ave., Columbus, OH
    43210
Juked, 3941 Newdale Rd., #26, Chevy Chase, MD 20815
JuxtaProse, 339 West 2nd South, #204, Rexburg, ID 83440

K

Kadimah Press, PO Box 4563, Deerfield Beach, FL 33442
Kelsay Books, 24600 Mountain Avenue 35, Hemet, CA 92544
Kelsey Review, MCCC, 1200 Old Trenton Rd., West Windsor, NJ 08550
Kenyon Review, Finn House, 102 W. Wiggin St., Gambier, OH 43022
Kerf, College of Redwoods, 883 West Washington Blvd., Crescent City, CA
    95531
Kestrel, Fairmont State Univ., 1201 Locust Ave., Fairmont, WV 26554
Keystone College Press, 1 College Green, PO Box 50, La Plume, PA 18440
Kore Press, PO Box 42315, Tucson AZ 85733-2315
Kweli Journal, P.O. Box 693, New York, NY 10021
KY Story, 2111B Fayette Dr., Richmond, KY 40475
KYSO Flash, P.O. Box 1385, Marysville, WA 98270

L

The Lake, 11 Durbin Rd., Chessington, KT9 1BU, UK
Lake Effect, Humanities, 4951 College Drive, Erie, PA 16563-1501

Laurel Review, MWMSU, 800 University Dr., Marysville, MO 64468

Lavender Review, P.O. Box 275, Eagle Rock, MO 65641-0275

Leaf Press, Box 416, Lantzville, BC, V0R 2H0 Canada

Licorice Fish Books, Tanygrisiau, Blaenau Ffestiniog, Gwynedd, LL41 3SU, UK

Light, 1515 Highland Ave., Rochester, NY 14618

Lime Hawk, 10 Cross Highway, Redding, CT 06896

Lips, P.O. Box 616, Florham Park, NJ 07932

Lit.cat, 1640 Waterwood Circle, Anchorage, AK 99507

Literary House Press, Washington College, 300 Washington Ave., Chesterton, MD 21620-1197

Little Fiction/Big Truths, 24 Southport St., #353, Toronto, ON M6S 4Z1, Canada

Little Red Tree Publishing, 509 W. 3rd St., North Platte, NE 69101

Little Star, 107 Bank St., New York, NY 10014

The Lives You Touch, P.O. Box 276, Gwynedd Valley, PA 19437-0276

Locked Horn Press, 4638 Hawley Blvd., San Diego, CA 92116

Long Island Poetry Collective, 16 Francesca Dr., Oyster Bay, NY 11771

Longreads, 288 Wall St., #2, Kingston, NY 12401

Longridge Review, 524 Buttolph Dr., Middlebury, VT 05753

Longshot Press, 1455 Larkspur Ave., Eugene, OR 97401

Lost Tower Publications, 40 Southfield Way, Tiverton, Devon, EX16 5AJ, UK

Louisiana Literature, SLU 10792, Hammond, LA 70402

Louisville Review, Spalding U., 851 South 4th St., Louisville, KY 40203

Loving Healing Press, 5145 Pontiac Trail., Ann Arbor, MI 48105-9238

Lowestoft Chronicle Press, 1925 Massachusetts Ave., #8, Cambridge, MA 02140

Lummox Press, PO Box 5301, San Pedro, CA 90733

Luxembourg Review, 16 rue Nicolas Adames, L-illy, Luxembourg City, Luxembourg

M

The MacGuffin, 18600 Haggerty Rd., Livonia, MI 48152

Madcap Review, 245 Wallace Rd., Goffstown, NH 03045

The Magnolia Review, PO Box 731, Bowling Green, OH 43402

Malahat Review, University of Victoria, Box 1700, Stn CSC, Victoria BC V8W 2Y2, Canada

Manhattan Review, 440 Riverside Dr., #38, New York, NY 10027

Marin Poetry Center Anthology, 10 Crystal Creek Dr., Larkspur, CA 94939

Massachusetts Review, Photo Lab 309, 211 Hicks Way, Amherst, MA 01003

Masters Review, 1824 NW Couch St., Portland, OR 97209-2119

Matador Review, 1019 S. Oakley Blvd., #2, Chicago, IL 60612

Matchbook Stories, PO Box 23595, Nicosia 1685 Cyprus

Matter, 919 Pleasant St., New Orleans, LA 70115

The Meadow, VISTA B300, 7000 Dandini Blvd., Reno, NV 89512

Menacing Hedge, 424 SW Kenyon St., Seattle, WA 98106

Meridian, Univ. of Virginia, P.O. Box 400145, Charlottesville, VA 22904

Mercer University Press, 1400 Coleman Ave., Macon, GA 31207-0001

Metaphorosis Magazine, Box 851, Neskowin, OR 97149

Michigan Quarterly Review, 915 E. Washington St., Ann Arbor, MI 48109-1070

Michigan Writers, P.O. Box 2355, Traverse City, MI 49685

Mid-American Review, Bowling Green State Univ., Bowling Green, OH 43403

Midway Journal, 77 Liberty Ave., #10, Somerville, MA 02144

Midwest Review, UW-M, 21 N. Park St., #7101, Madison, WI53715

Midwestern Gothic, 957 E. Grant, Des Plaines, IL 60016

Milkweed, 1011 Washington Ave. So., Ste. 300, Minneapolis, MN 55415

The Minnesota Review, Virginia Tech, ASPECT, Blacksburg, VA 24061

Misfit Magazine, 143 Furman St., Schenectady, NY 12304

The Missing Slate, 1027 Cherokee Rd., Louisville, KY 40204

Mississippi Review, USM, 118 College Dr., #5144, Hattiesburg, MS 39406

Mizna, 2446 University Ave. West, #115, Saint Paul, MN 55114

Mobius, Journal of Social Change, 149 Talmadge, Madison, WI 53704

Modern Creative Life, 813 Eagle Run Dr., Centerville, OH 45458

Molotov Cocktail, 1218 NE 24th Ave., Portland, OR 97232

Mom Egg Review, PO Box 9037, Bardonia, NY 10954

The Mondegreen, 1162 7th St., Arcata, CA 95521

Monkeybicycle, 611-B Courtland St., Greensboro, NC 27401

Monster House Press, PO Box 1548, Bloomington, IN 47402

Moon City, English Dept., MSU, 901 South National Ave., Springfield, MO 65897

Moon Pie Press, 16 Walton St., Westbrook, ME 04092

Moonpath Press, P.O. Box 445, Tillamook, OR 97141-0445

Moonrise Press, PO Box 4288, Sunland, CA 91041-4288

Moss, 30 Columbia Pl., #AF, Brooklyn, NY 11201

Mothers Always Write, P.O. Box 282, East Greenwich, RI 02818

Motherwell Magazine, 23 Birchfield Dr., Glasgow, G14 9FG, Scotland

Mount Hope, Roger Williams U., One Old Ferry Rd., Bristol, RI 02809

MousePrints, 43200 Yale Ct., Lancaster, CA 93536-5375

Mouthfeel Press, PO Box 824, Huntsville, TX 77342-0824

Mud Season Review, 110 Main St., #3C, Burlington, VT 05401

Muddy River Poetry Review, 15 Eliot St., Chestnut Hill, MA 02467

Muse-Pie Press, 73 Pennington Ave., Passaic, NJ 07055

Muzzle, S. Edwards, 1800 Jason Dr., #328, Denton, TX 76205

n+1, 68 Jay St., #405, Brooklyn, NY 11201

Narrative, 2443 Fillmore St., #214, San Francisco, CA 94115

Narratively, 30 John St., Brooklyn, NY 11201

Nashville Review, 2301 Vanderbilt Pl., Nashville, TN 37235-1654

Nat. Brut, 5995 Summerside Dr., Unit 796032, Dallas, TX 75379

Nat'l Federation of State Poetry Societies, 499 Falcon Ridge Way, Boling-brook, IL 60440-2242

Natural Bridge, English Dept., UMSL, One University Blvd., St. Louis, MO 63121-4400

Naugatuck River Review, PO Box 368, Westfield, MA 01086

Nerve Cowboy, PO Box 4973, Austin, TX 78765

New Delta Review, LSU, Allen Hall 9, Baton Rouge, LA 70803

New Directions, 80 Eighth Ave., Floor 19, New York, NY 10011-7146

The New Engagement, 10730 No. Oracle Rd., #11201, Tucson, AZ 85737

New England Review, Middlebury College, Middlebury, VT 05753

New England Review of Books, PO Box 15274, Boston, MA 92215

New Lit Salon Press, 513 Vista on the Lake, Carmel, NY 10512

New Madrid, FH - 7C, Murray State University, Murray, KY 42071

New Millennium Writings, 4021 Garden Dr., Knoxville, TN 37918

New Ohio Review, Ohio University, 360 Ellis Hall, Athens, OH 45701

New Orleans Review, Loyola Univ., 6363 St. Charles Ave., New Orleans, LA 70118

New Pop Lit, 400 Bagley, #1953, Detroit, MI 48226

New Rivers Press, 1104 7th Ave. S., Moorhead, MN 56563

New South, Campus Box 1894, Georgia State Univ., Atlanta, GA 30303

New Southerner, 1450 Highgrove Rd., Coxs Creek, KY 40013

New Verse News, Les Belles Maisons H-11, Jl. Serpong Raya, Serpong Utara, Tangerang-Baten 15310, Indonesia

New York Literary Magazine, 8401 NW 90th St., Medley, FL 33166

Newfound Journal, 4505 Duval St., #156, Austin, TX 78751

Newtown Literary, 61-15 97th St., Rego Park, NY 11374

New York Quarterly, PO Box 2015, Old Chelsea Stn., N. Y., NY 10113

Nightjar Press, R. Baomann, 817 N. Forest Dr., Tallahassee, FL 32303

Nightwood Editions, Harbour Publishing, PO Box 219, 4437 Rondeview Rd., Madeira Park, BC V0N 2H0 Canada

Nimrod, Univ. of Tulsa, 800 South Tucker Dr., Tulsa, OK 74104

Ninth Letter, 608 S. Wright St., Urbana, IL 61801

No Tokens, 300 Mercer St., #26E, New York, NY 10003

Nodin Press, 5114 Cedar Lake Rd., Minneapolis, MN 55416

Nomadic Press, 2926 Foothill Blvd., #1, Oakland, CA 94601

Noon, 1324 Lexington Ave., PMB 298, New York, NY 10128

The Normal School, 5245 N. Backer Ave., M/S PB 98, CSU, Fresno, CA 93740-8001

North American Review, Univ. of Northern Iowa, Cedar Falls, IA 50614-0516

North Carolina Literary Review, ECU Mailstop 555, Greenville, NC 27858-4353

North Dakota Quarterly, 276 Centennial Drive, Grand Forks, ND 58202-7209

Northern Virginia Review, 2645 College Dr., Woodbridge, VA 22191

Nostrovial Press, 2041 Miramonte Ave., #37, San Leandro, CA 94578

Notre Dame Review, B009C McKenna Hall, UND, Notre Dame, IN 46556

O

O. C. 87, Inc., 1601 Market St., #2525, Philadelphia, PA 19103-2301

O-Dark-Thirty, 5812 Morland Drive No., Adamstown, MD 21710

Obsidian, Illinois State U., Campus Box 4241, Normal, IL 61790-4241

Ocean State Review, U.R.I., 60 Upper College Rd., Kingston, RI 02881

Ocean View Publishing, 595 Bay Isles Rd., #120H, Long Boat Key, FL 34228

Off the Coast, PO Box 14, Robbinston, ME 04671

Offing Magazine, PO Box 22730, Seattle, WA 98122

Ohio State Univ. Press, 1070 Carmack Rd., Columbus, OH 43210-1002

Ohio University Press, 31 S. Court St., Athens, OH 45701-2979

Old Cove Press, 445 Bristol Rd., Lexington, KY 40502-2436

Old Mountain Press, P.O. Box 66, Webster, NC 28788

Olive Press, Univ. of Mount Olive, 634 Henderson Dr., Mt. Olive, NC 28365

One Story, 232 3rd St., #A108, Brooklyn, NY 11215

One Teen Story, 232 3rd St., #A108, Brooklyn, NY 11215

Ooligan Press, Portland State Univ., PO Box 751, Portland, OR 97207

Open Country Press, 400 W. Broadway, Ste. 101, Missoula, MT 59802

Opiate Magazine, 1719 Gates Ave., #3C, Ridgewood, NJ 11385

Orchards Poetry Journal, 24600 Mountain Ave. 35, Hemet, CA 92544

Oregon Humanities, 921 SW Washington St., #150, Portland, OR 97205

Origami Poems Project, 1948 Shore View Dr., Indialantic, FL 32903

Orion Magazine, 187 Main St., Great Barrington, MA 01230

Osiris, 106 Meadow Lane, Greenfield, MA 01301

Outlook Springs, 43 Cushing St., Dover, NH 03820

Outrider Press, Inc., 2036 North Winds Drive, Dyer, IN 46311

Oxford American, P.O. Box 3235, Little Rock, AR 72203-3235

P

Pacific Literary Review, 2317 E. Lynn St., #2, Seattle, WA 98112

Pacific Standard, 801 Garden St., #101, Santa Barbara, CA 93101

Painted Bride Quarterly, Drexel Univ., English Dept., 3141 Chestnut St., Philadelphia, PA 19104-2875

Panorama, 68 Spruce Lane, Cambridge, VT 05445

Paper Darts, 750 SW 9th Ave., #710, Portland, OR 97205

The Paris Review, 544 West 27th St., New York, NY 10001

Parody, PO Box 6688, Portland, OR 97228

Passages North, English Dept., N.M.U., Marquette, MI 49855-5363

Paterson Literary Review, 1 College Blvd., Paterson, NJ 07505-1179

Peach, 7040 Bear Ridge Rd., N. Tonawanda, NY 14120

Peacock Journal, 12701 Eldrid PL, Silver Spring, MD 20904

Pembroke Magazine, P.O. Box 1510, Pembroke, NC 28372-1510

Pen America, 588 Broadway, #303, New York, NY 10012

Penny, 1825 Buccaneer Dr., Sarasota, FL 34231

Permafrost, Univ. of Alaska, P.O. Box 755720, Fairbanks, AK 99775

Perugia Press, PO Box 60364, Florence, MA 01062

Phantom Drift, P.O. Box 3235, La Grande, OR 97850

Philadelphia Stories, Sommers, 107 West Main St., Ephrata, PA 17522

Phoebe, George Mason Univ., MSN 2C5, 4400 University Place, Fairfax, VA 22030

Phoenicia Publishing, 207-5425 de Bordeaux, Montreal QC H2H 2P9, Canada

Phrygian Press, 58-09 205th St., Bayside, NY 11364

The Pinch, English Dept., 467 Patterson Hall, Memphis, TN 38152

Pine Mountain Sand & Gravel, 1266 Avon Dr., Cincinnati, OH 45229

Pinesong, 131 Bon Aire Rd., Elkin, NC 28621

Pinyon Publishing, 23847 V66 Trail, Montrose, CO 81403

Pithead Chapel, 1300 S. 23rd St., Apt. A, Lincoln, NE 68502

Pittsburgh Poetry Review, 1216 Middletown Rd., Greensburg, PA 15601

Pizza Pi Press, 24 Bower St., #2, Medford, MA 02155

Pleiades, Univ. of Central Missouri, English Dept., Warrensburg, MO 64093-5214

Ploughshares, Emerson College, 120 Boylston St., Boston, MA 02116

PMS, poemmemoirstory, University of Alabama, HB 217, 1530 3rd Avenue So, Birmingham, AL 35294-1260

PN&E Magazine, 876 East 225th St., Ste. 3A, Bronx, NY 10466

Poem-a-Day, 75 Maiden Ln., New York, NY 10038

Poet Lore, 4508 Walsh St., Bethesda, MD 20815

poeticdiversity, 6028 Comey Ave., Los Angeles, CA 90034

Poetry Box, 2228 NW 159th Pl., Beaverton, Or 97006

Poetry Breakfast, 5 Columbine Dr., Jackson, NJ 08527

Poetry Magazine, 61 West Superior St., Chicago, IL 60654

Poetry Northwest, 2000 Tower St., Everett, WA 98201-1390

Poetry Pacific, 1550 68th Ave. W., Vancouver, BC V6P 2V5 Canada

The Poetry Porch, 158 Hollett St., Scituate, MA 02066

Poetry South, Mississippi University for Women, 1100 College St., W-1634, Columbus, MS 39701

The Poet's Billow, 6135 Avon St., Portage, MI 49008

Poets and Artists, 604 Vale St., Bloomington, IL 61701-5620

Poets Wear Prada, 533 Bloomfield St., #2, Hoboken, NJ 07030-4960

The Point, 2 N. LaSalle St., Ste. 2300, Chicago, IL 60602

Pond Road Press, 221 Channing St. NE, Washington, DC 20002

Pool, 11500 San Vicente Blvd., #224, Los Angeles, CA 90049

Porkbelly Press, PO Box 11113, Cincinnati, OH 45211

Port Yonder Press, 6332 33rd Avenue Dr., Shellsburg, IA 52332

Post Road, 140 Commonwealth Ave., Chestnut Hill, MA 02487

Posit, 245 Sullivan St., #8A, New York, NY 10012

Post Road, Boston College, 140 Commonwealth Ave., Chestnut Hill, MA 02467

Potomac Review, 51 Manakee St., MT/212, Rockville, MD 20850

Pouch, 4186 Beryl Dr., Bellbrook, OH 45305

Prairie Journal Trust, 28 Crowfoot Terrace NW, PO Box 68073, Calgary, AB, T3G 3N8, Canada

Prairie Schooner, UNL, 123 Andrews Hall, Lincoln, NE 68588-0334

Prelude, 589 Flushing Ave., #3E, Brooklyn, NY 11206

Press 53, 560 No. Trade St., #103, Winston-Salem, NC 27101

Prime Number Magazine, 560 No. Trade St., #103, Winston-Salem, NC 27101

Prism International, UBC, Buch E462 - 1866 Main Mall, Vancouver BC V6T 1Z1, Canada

Prism Review, Univ. of La Verne, 1950 Third St., La Verne, CA 91750

Prodigal, 18082 Grassy Knoll Dr., Westfield, IN 46074

Progenitor, A.C.C., Campus Box 9002, 5900 S. Santa Fe Dr., Littleton, CO 80160

Prolific Press, PO Box 113, Harborton, VA 23389

Prospect Park Books, 2359 Lincoln Ave., Altadena, CA 91001

Provincetown Arts, 650 Commercial St., Provincetown, MA 02657

Provo Canyon Review, PO Box 971084, Orem, UT 84097

Prune Juice, 9564 Montgold, White Lake, MI 48386

Public Books, 20 Cooper Sq., #517, New York, NY 10003

Puerto del Sol, NMSU., PO Box 30001, Las Cruces, NM 88003-8001

Pulp Literature Press, 8336 Manson Ct., Burnaby, BC V5A 2C4, Canada

Puna Press, PO Box 7790, Ocean Beach, CA 92107

Pusteblume Journal of Translation, Room 119, 685 Commonwealth Ave., Boston, MA 02215

Q

Quarterly West, Univ. of Utah, English/LNCO 3500, 255 S. Central Campus Dr., Salt Lake City, UT 84112-9109

Queen Mab's Tea House, 2857 N. Troy St., 2nd floor, Chicago, IL 60618

Quiddity, PO Box 1046, Murphysboro, IL 82966

Quiet Lightning, 734 Balboa St., San Francisco, CA 94118

Quill and Parchment, 2357 Merrywood Dr., Los Angeles, CA 90046

R

r.kv.r.y literary journal, 72 Woodbury Dr., Lockport, NY 14094

Rabbit Catastrophe Press, 147 N. Limestone, Lexington, KY 40507

Radar Poetry, 19 Coniston Ct., Princeton, NJ 08540

Radius, 65 Paine St., #2, Worcester, MA 01605

Ragazine, 254 Outlook Ave., Youngstown, OH 44504

Raleigh Review, Box 6725, Raleigh, NC 27628

Raritan, Rutgers, 31 Mine St., New Brunswick, NJ 08901

Rattle, 12411 Ventura Blvd., Studio City, CA 91604

Raven Chronicles, 15528 12th Avenue NE, Shoreline, WA 98155

Red Fez, 10812 SE 166th St., Renton, WA 98055-5217

Red Hen Press, 1335 N. Lake Ave., #200, Pasadena, CA 91104

Red Mountain Press, PO Box 32205, Santa Fe, NM 87594

Red River Review, 4669 Mountain Oak St., Fort Worth, TX 76244-4397

Redactions, 604 N. 31st Ave., Apt. D-2, Hattiesburg, MS 39401

Reservoir Journal, 511 1st St. North, #302, Charlottesville, VA 22902

Rhino, The Poetry Forum, PO Box 591, Evanston, IL 60204

Ricky's Back Yard, 1882 Nicolet, Montreal, QC, H1W3K9, Canada

Rising Phoenix, 6 Ashley Court, Downingtown, PA 19335

River Styx, 3139A South Grand, Ste. 203, St. Louis, MO 63118-1021

River Teeth, Ashland University, 401 College Ave., Ashland, OH 44805

Rivet, 667 2nd Ave., San Francisco, CA 94118

RMFW Press, 303 S. Broadway #200-129, Denver, CO 80209

Roanoke Review, English Dept., 221 College Ln, Salem, VA 24153-3794

Rockhurst Review, 1100 Rockhurst Rd., Kansas City, MO 64110

Room Magazine, P.O. Box 46160 Stn. D, Vancouver, BC V6J 5G5, Canada

Rove, E. Barnett, 435 E.70th Terrace, Kansas City, MO 64131

Rum Punch Press, JCHS, 920 S. Jefferson St., Roanoke, VA 240131

Ruminate, 1041 N. Taft Hill Rd., Ft. Collins, CO 80521

The Rumpus, 419 Hawthorne Ave., Palo Alto, CA 94301

Rust + Moth, 2409 Eastridge Court, Fort Collins, CO 80524

The Rusty Toque, 2-680 Shaw St., Toronto, ON M6G 3L7, Canada

Sad Magazine, 3112 Windsor St., #1, Vancouver, BC V5T 4B1, Canada
Salamander, Suffolk Univ., English, 8 Ashburton Pl., Boston, MA 02108
Salmagundi, Skidmore College, 815 N. Broadway, Saratoga Springs, NY 12866
San Pedro River Review, P.O. Box 7000-760, Redondo Beach, CA 90277
Sand Journal, L. Pfister, Prinz-Georg-Str. 7, 10827 Berlin, Germany
Santa Monica Review, 29051 Hilltop Dr., Silverado, CA 92676
Sarabande Books, 2344 Dundee Rd., Ste. 200, Louisville, KY 40205
Saranac Review, SUNY, English, 101 Broad St., Plattsburgh, NY 12901
Saturnalia Books, 105 Woodside Rd., Ardmore, PA 19003
Scarlet Leaf Review, 26-1225 York Mills Rd., Toronto ON M3A 1Y4, Canada
Scarlet Tanager Books, PO Box 20906, Oakland, CA 94620
Scribendi, MSC06-3890, 1 University of New Mexico, Albuquerque, NM 87131
Scrutiny Journal, Meckes, 18 Lanark Rd., Chapel Hill, NC 27517
2nd and Church, PO Box 198156, Nashville, TN 37219
Seems, Lakeland Univ., W3718 South Drive, Plymouth, WI 53073-4878
SFA Press, P.O. Box 13007 - SFA Station, Nacogdoches, TX 75962-3007
The Shallow Ends, 2122 E. Carolina Lane, Tempe, AZ 85284
Sharkpack Poetry Review, PO Box 6288, Holliston, MA 01746
She Writes Press, 1563 Solano Ave., #546, Berkeley, CA 94707
shebooks, 490 Second St., 2nd floor, San Francisco, CA 94107
Sheep Meadow Press, PO Box 84, Rhinebeck, NY 12514
Sheila-Na-Gig, 203 Meadowlark Rd., Russell, KY 41160
Sibling Rivalry Press, P.O. Box 26147, Little Rock, AR 72221
Sick Lit Magazine, 7851 Brook Meadow Lane, Fort Worth, TX 76133
Sierra Nevada Review, SNR 2157, 999 Tahoe Blvd., Incline Village, NV 89451
Silver Birch Press, P.O. Box 29458, Los Angeles, CA 90029
Sinister Wisdom, P.O. Box 144, Riverdale, MD 20738
Six Hens, 274 Redwood Shores Pkwy, #318, Redwood City, CA 94065
Sixfold, 10 Concord Ridge Rd., Newtown, CT 06470
Sixteen Rivers Press, PO Box 640663, San Francisco, CA 94164-0663
Sky Blue Press, 4514 Spotted Oak Woods, San Antonio, TX 78249
Slag Glass City, English Dept., 2315 No. Kenmore Ave., Chicago, IL 60614-7485
Slapering Hol Press, 1755 York Ave., #33-E, New York, NY 10128
Sleet Magazine, 1846 Bohland Ave., St. Paul, MN 55116
Sleipnir, 3201 W. Pecan Blvd., McAllen, TX 78501
Slice Literary, 150 Oak Lane, Dayton, ME 04005
The Sligo Journal, Montgomery College, Takoma Park, MD 20912
Slippery Elm, University of Findlay, #9611,1000 N. Main, Findlay, OH 45840-3653
Slipstream, Box 2071, Niagara Falls, NY 14301

Slush Pile Magazine, 1749 W. Silver Lake Dr., Los Angeles, CA 90026

Smartish Pace, P.O. Box 22161, Baltimore, MD 21203

SmokeLong Quarterly, 2127 Kidd Rd., Nolensville, TN 37135

So Say We All Press, 3505 Texas St., San Diego, CA 92104

Solstice, 150 E. Robinson St., #1409, Orlando, FL 32801

Somondoco Press, 952 Frederick St., Hagerstown, MD 21740

The Song Is..., 523 N. Horners Ln, Rockville, MD 20850

Sonora Review, English Dept., University of Arizona, Tucson, AZ 85721

The Southampton Review, 239 Montauk Hwy., Southampton, NY 11968

The Southeast Review, English, Florida State U., Tallahassee, FL 32306

Southern Humanities Review, 9088 Haley Center, Auburn Univ., Auburn, AL 36849

Southern Indiana Review, USI, 8600 Univ. Blvd., Evansville, IN 47712

The Southern Review, L.S.U., 338 Johnston Hall, Baton Rouge, LA 70803

Southwest Review, PO Box 750374, Dallas, TX 75275-0374

The Sow's Ear Poetry Review, 1748 Cave Ridge Rd., Mount Jackson, VA 22842

Spark, 1704 Fountain Ridge Rd., Chapel, NC 27517

Spillway, 11 Jordan Ave., San Francisco, CA 94118

Spirit Fire Review, 3038 Clem Rd., Anderson, IN 46017

Split This Rock, 1301 Connecticut Ave. NW, Washington, DC 20036

(the) Squawk Back, 17-15 Greene Ave., #1R, Ridgewood, NY 11385

Star 82 Review, PO Box 8106, Berkeley, CA 94707

Star Line, W5679 State Road 60, Poynette, WI 53955-8564

Still, 89 W. Chestnut St., Williamsburg, KY 40769

Stillhouse Press, 4400 University Dr., #3E4, Fairfax, VA 22030

Stillwater Review, Poetry Center, Sussex County College, Newton, NJ 07860

Stoneboat Literary Journal, P.O. Box 1254, Sheboygan, WI 53082

Stonecoast Review, 40 Sidewinder St., Beaufort, SC 29906

Stoneslide Media, 4 Elm St., Guilford, CT 06437

Storm Cellar, 1901 St. Anthony Ave., St. Paul, MN 55104

Story Quarterly, English Dept., Rutgers, 311 N. Fifth St., Rm 424, Camden, NJ 08102

Strange Days Books, Chimaras 6, 74100, Rethymno, Crete, Greece

String Town Press, PO Box 1406, Medical Lake, WA 99022

subTerrain, P.O. Box 3008 MPO, Vancouver, BC V6B 3X5, Canada

Sugar House Review, PO Box 13, Cedar City, UT 84721

The Summerset Review, 25 Summerset Dr., Smithtown, NY 11787

The Sun, 107 North Roberson St., Chapel Hill, NC 27516

Sun Star Review, PO Box 14682, Portland, OR 97293

Sundog Lit, 429 Woodward Ave., Kalamazoo, MI 49007

Sybaritic, 12530 Culver Blvd., #3, Los Angeles, CA 90066

Sycamore Review, English Dept., Purdue University, 500 Oval Dr., West Lafayette, IN 47907

Synchronized Chaos, 636 Palouse St., #3, Walla Walla, WA 99362

TAB: The Journal of Poetry & Poetics, Chapman University, One University Drive, Orange, CA 92866

Tahoma Literary Review, 6516 112th Street Ct. NW, Gig Harbor, WA 98332-8697

Tammy, J. Novak, 2320 Scarff St., Los Angeles, CA 90007

Tangent Books, Unit 5.16, Paintworks, Bristol BS4 3EH, UK

|tap| Literary Magazine, 123 Kittleberger Park, #2, Webster, NY 14580

Tar River Poetry, East Carolina University, MS 159, Greenville, NC 27858-4353

Tayen Lane, 3475 rue de la Montagne, Montreal, Quebec H3G 2A4, Canada

Tell-Tale Chapbooks, 246 South Huntington Ave., #9, Jamaica Plain, MA 02130

Terrain.org, P.O. Box 19161, Tucson, AZ 85731-9161

Terrapin Books, 4 Midvale Ave., West Caldwell, NJ 07006

Tethered By Letters, 2217 S. Grant St., Denver, CO 80210

Texas Authors, 1712 E. Riverside Dr., #124, Austin, TX 78741

Texas Review Press, SHSU, Box 2146, Huntsville, TX 77341-2146

That Literary Review, Huntingdon College, 1500 East Fairview Ave., Montgomery, AL 36106-2418

Third Coast, Western Michigan University, Kalamazoo, MI 49008-5331

32 Poems, English Dept., Washington & Jefferson College, 60 South Lincoln St., Washington, PA 15301

Thomas-Jacob Publishing, P.O. Box 390524, Deltona, FL 32739

3: A Taos Press, P.O. Box 370627, Denver, CO 80237

3 Elements Review, 198 Valley View Rd., Manchester, CT 06040

Three Rooms Press, 561 Hudson St., #33, New York, NY 10014

Threepenny Review, PO Box 9131, Berkeley, CA 94709

Thrush Poetry Journal, 889 Lower Mountain Dr., Effort, PA 18330

Tiger Bark Press, 202 Mildorf St., Rochester, NY 14609

Timberline Review, 2108 Buck St., West Linn, OR 97068

Tinderbox, 6932 Kayser Mill Rd. NW, Albuquerque, NM 87114

Tin House, 2601 NW Thurman St, Portland, OR 97210

Tipton Poetry Journal, 642 Jackson St., Brownsburg, IN 46112

The Tishman Review, PO Box 605, Perry, MI 48872

Transition Magazine, 104 Mt. Auburn St., #3R, Cambridge, MA 02138

Transom Journal, 2543 Trevilian Way, Louisville, KY 40205

Tree Light Books, 136 Pearl St., Ft. Collins, CO 80521

Trestle Creek Review, North Idaho College, 1000 W. Garden Ave., Coeur d'Alene, ID 83814

Trinacria, 220 Ninth St., Brooklyn, NY 11215-3902

True Story, 5119 Coral St., Pittsburgh, PA 15224

Tule Review, Sacramento Poetry Center, 1719 25th St., Sacramento, CA 95816
Tupelo Press, P.O. Box 1767, North Adams, MA 01247
Turnip Truck(s), 305 Cleveland St., Lafayette, LA 70501
The Tusk, 1477 Bedford, #4, Brooklyn, NY 11216
2 Bridges Review, NY City College of Technology, 300 Jay St., Brooklyn, NY 11201
Two Cities Review, 1 Hanson Place, Apt. PHA, Brooklyn, NY 11243
Two Lines Press, 582 Market St., Ste. 700, San Francisco, CA 94104
Two of Cups Press, 4811 Hickory Woods Dr., Greensboro, NC 27410
Two Sylvias Press, PO Box 1524, Kinston, WA 98346
Two Thirds North, English Dept., Stockholm University, Stockholm, Sweden
Typehouse Magazine, PO Box 69721, Portland, OR 97268

U

U.S. 1 Poets' Cooperative, PO Box 127, Kingston, NJ 08528-0127
Ugly Duckling Presse, 232 Third St., #E-303, Brooklyn, NY 11215
Umbrella Factory, 2540 Sunset Dr., #125, Longmont, CO 80501
Under the Gum Tree, Studio J, 1812 J St., #21, Sacramento, CA 95811
Under the Sun, Tenn. Tech U., English, Box 5053, Cookeville, TN 38505
University of Arizona Press, PO Box 210055, Tucson, AZ 85721-0055
University of Evansville Press, 1800 Lincoln Ave., Evansville, IN 47722
University of Hell Press, 0524 SW Nebraska St., Portland, OR 97239
University of Iowa Press, 119 West Park Rd., 100 Kuhl House, Iowa City, IA 52242
University of North Texas Press, 1155 Union Circle #311336, Denton, TX 76203
University of South Carolina Press, 1600 Hampton St., Ste. 544, Columbia, SC 29208
University Press of Colorado, 5589 Arapahoe Ave., #206C, Boulder, CO 80303
Up the Staircase Quarterly, 716 4th St., SW, Apt. A, Minot, ND 58701
Upset Press, PO Box 301025, Brooklyn, NY 11230
upstreet, P.O. Box 105, Richmond, MA 01254-0105
Utne Reader, 1503 SW 42nd St., Topeka, KS 66609

V

Vallum, 5038 Sherbrooke West, PO Box 23077 CP Vendome, Montreal, QC H4A 1T0, Canada
Valley Voices, MVSU 7242, 14000 Highway 82 West, Itta Bena, MS 38941-1400
Vassar Review, 124 Raymond Ave., Box 464, Poughkeepsie, NY 12604
Veliz Books, PO Box 920243, El Paso, TX 79912
Vestal Review, 127 Kilsyth Rd., #3, Brighton, MA 02135
Vignette Review, 611 Stevens St., Geneva, IL 60134

Vinyl, 1614 NE Alberta St., Portland, OR 97211

Virginia Normal, Literature Dept., 1 Hayden Dr., Petersburg, VA 23806

The Virginia Quarterly Review, 5 Boar's Head Lane, P.O. Box 400223, Charlottesville, VA 22904-4223

Visitant, 183 31st St., Brooklyn, NY 11232

Voice Catcher Journal, PO Box 8814, Portland, OR 97207

The Volta, Univ. of Arizona, English Dept., ML445, Tucson, AZ 85721

vox poetica, 160 Summit St., Englewood, NJ, 07631

W

The War Horse, 609 Columbus Ave, 16-R, New York, NY 10024

War, Literature & the Arts, 2354 Fairchild Dr., Ste. 6D-149, USAF Academy, CO 80840-6242

Washington Square Review, 58 W. 10th St., New York, NY 10011

Water~Stone Review, MS A1730, 1536 Hewitt Ave., St. Paul, MN 55104

Watershed Review, CSU, Chico, 400 West First St., Chico, CA 95929

Waxwing Magazine, 3336 N. Schevene Blvd., Flagstaff, AZ 86004

Wayne State University Press, 4809 Woodward Ave., Detroit, MI 48201

Waywiser Press, PO Box 6205, Baltimore, MD 21206

West Branch, Stadler Center for Poetry, Bucknell Univ., Lewisburg, PA 17837

West End Press, PO Box 27334, Albuquerque, NM 87125

West Marin Review, P.O. Box 1302, Point Reyes Station, CA 94956

Westchester Review, Box 246H, Scarsdale, NY 10583

Whale Road Review, 3900 Lomaland Dr., San Diego, CA 92106

Whiskey Island, CSU, 2121 Euclid Ave., RT 1820, Cleveland, OH 44115

White Pine Press, 5783 Pinehurst Court, Lake View, NY 14085

Whitefish Review, 708 Lupfer Ave., Whitefish, MT 59937

Wild Fig Books, 726 N. Limestone, Lexington, KY 40508

Wild Horses, PO Box 904, Washingtonville, NY 10992

Wigleaf, 114 State Hall, Univ. of Missouri, Columbia, MO 65211

Willow Springs, 668 N. Riverpoint Blvd., #259, Spokane, WA 99202

Winter Tangerine, 3820 E. McCracken Way, #4, Bloomington, IN 47408

WMG Publishing, PO Box 269, Lincoln City, OR 97367

The Worcester Review, PO Box 804, Worcester, MA 01613

Words Without Borders, 2809 W. Logan, Chicago, IL 60647

Workers Write! P.O. Box 250382, Plano, TX 75025-0382

World Literature Today, 630 Parrington Oval, Ste. 110, Norman, OK 73019-4033

World Weaver Press, PO Box 21924, Albuquerque, NM 87154

Woven Tale Press, PO Box 2533, Setauket, NY 11733

Writing Disorder, P.O. Box 93613, L.A., CA 90093-0613

Writing Knights Press, PO Box 9364, Canton, OH 44711

Y

Yemassee Journal, English, USC, Columbia, SC 29208
Yarn, 86 Highview Ave., Melrose, MA 02176
Yes Yes Books, 1614 NE Alberta St., Portland, OR 97211
Your Impossible Voice, Biscopink, 30 Heyman Ave., S. F., CA 94110

Z

Zephyr Press, 400 Bason Dr., Las Cruces, NM 88005
Zoetic Press, PO Box 1354, Santa Cruz, CA 95061
Zone 3 Press, APSU, P.O. Box 4565, Clarksville, TN 37044
Zoetrope, 916 Kearny St., San Francisco, CA 94133
ZYZZYVA, 57 Post St., Ste. 604, San Francisco, CA 94104

CONTRIBUTORS' NOTES

KAVEH AKBAR's debut poetry collection, *Calling A Wolf A Wolf,* is just out from Alice James Books. He was born in Iran and now teaches at Purdue University.

CHRISTOPHER TODD ANDERSON teaches at Pittsburg State University in Kansas. His poems have appeared in *River Styx, Tar River Poetry* and *Crab Orchard Review.*

ELLEN BASS is the author of *Like A Beggar* from Copper Canyon Press, 2014. She teaches at Pacific University.

REGINOLD DWANE BETTS lives in New Haven, Connecticut and has appeared in two previous Pushcart Prizes.

TOM BISSELL's most recent book is *Apostle: Travels Among the Tombs of the Twelve* published in 2016. He is the author of nine books and last won a Pushcart Prize in 2005.

JAI CHAKRABARTI is A Public Space Emerging Writer Fellow. His work has appeared in *Barrow Street, Coffin Factory, Union Station* and elsewhere.

ETHAN CHATAGNIER won the Larry Levis Prize in poetry. His stories have appeared in *Five Point, Witness, Michigan Quarterly Review* and elsewhere. He lives in Fresno, California.

YE CHUN has published two books of poetry, a novel in Chinese and a collection of translations. She teaches at Providence College in Rhode Island.

CHRISTOPHER CITRO is the author of *The Maintenance of the Shimmy-Shammy* (Steel Toe Books). Recent poems have appeared in *Meridian, Crazyhorse* and the *Missouri Review.*

LYDIA CONKLIN's fiction has appeared in *The Gettysburg Review, Narrative* and elsewhere. She has received fellowships from MacDowell, Yadoo and Emory University. She lives in Princeton, New Jersey.

PHILIP CONNORS lives in El Paso, Texas. He recently completed his fifteenth season on fire watch duty in New Mexico's Gila National Forest, where he invites those who doubt the existence of global warming to visit and contemplate the megafires responsible for the loss of hundreds of square miles of once majestic spruce-fir and mixed conifers. He is the author of two previous books and his essay will be expanded into a book to be published in 2018 by Cinco Puntos Press.

FRANCISCO CONTÚ served as a Border Patrol agent in the deserts of Arizona, New Mexico and Texas. He is the winner of the 2017 Whiting Award and a Fulbright Fellow. His book *The Line Becomes A River* will be published in 2018.

RACHEL CUSK's story is re-printed from her book *Transit* (FSG). She lives in England.

ERICA DAWSON lives in Tampa, Florida and teaches at the University of Tampa.

JAQUIRA DÍAZ has published in *Rolling Stone, The Fader, The Guardian, The Sun* and *Best American Essays 2016*. She lives in Gambier, Ohio.

BRIAN DOYLE was editor of *Portland Magazine* and author of several novels. He won the John Burroughs Medal for distinguished nature writing. His essays appeared in *The Atlantic Monthly, Orion, The American Scholar* and elsewhere. He died in the spring of 2017.

CAMILLE DUNGY is the author of four poetry collections, most recently *Trophic Cascade*. Her poems have appeared in *Best American Poetry* and *100 Best African American Poems*.

THERESA DZIEGLEWICZ works at *Crab Orchard Review*. She has received honors from St. Louis Poetry Center and The Academy of American Poets.

LOUISA ERMELINO is the author of three novels: *Joey Dee Gets Wise, The Black Madonna,* and *The Sisters Malone*. She is the adult book director of *Publishers Weekly* and lives in New York City.

TARFIA FAIZULLAH's poems have appeared widely in both the United States and abroad and have been translated into Bengali, Spanish, Persian and Chinese. She was recently recognized by Harvard Law School as one of 50 Women Inspiring Change.

CAROLYN FORCHÉ is the author of four books of poetry, most recently *Blue Hour*. She is a recent recipient of the Windham-Campbell Prize and teaches at Georgetown University.

MATTHEW FORGARTY is the co-publisher at Jellyfish Highway Press. His fiction appeared in *Passages North, Fourteen Hills, Smokelong Quarterly* and elsewhere.

DANIEL HARRIS's most recent books are: *Celebrity* and *A Memoir of No One in Particular*.

REBECCA HAZELTON is the author of *Fair Copy* and *Vow*. Her poems have appeared in *Poetry, The New Yorker* and *Best American Poetry*.

STEPHEN HESS died in 2015. His past work has been included in *Noon, Sleepingfish, Unsaid,* and *New Orleans Review*.

BLAIR HURLEY lives Ontario, Canada. Her debut novel is forthcoming from W. W. Norton.

ALLEGRA HYDE is the author of the story collection *Of This New World*, which won the John Simmons Short Fiction Award. She lives in Huston, Texas.

BRET ANTHONY JOHNSON is the author of the novel *Remember Me Like This* which was a *New York Times* Notable Book of the Year. He is the author of the short story collection *Corpus Christi*. He teaches at Harvard University.

SAEED JONES's debut collection of poetry *Prelude to a Bruise* was named a 2014 finalist for the National Book Critics Circle Award. Jones is also executive editor for culture at BuzzFeed and appeared in *Pushcart Prize XXXVIII*.

LAURA KASISCHKE received the 2012 National Book Critics Circle Award for poetry. She has published nine novels, eight books of poetry and a short story collection.

CHRISTOPHER KEMPF is the author of *Late In the Empire of Men* which won the 2015 Levis Prize from Fourway Books. He received an NEA Fellowship and Stegner Fellowship from Stanford University.

RON KOERTGE is the author of a dozen novels and novels in verse. His latest books are: *Lies, Knives and Girls In Red Dresses* and *Coaltown Jesus*. His latest poetry collections are available from Red Hen Press.

ADA LIMÓN is the author of *Bright Dead Things*. She teaches at Queens University of Charlotte and lives in Lexington, Kentucky.

KATHLEEN LYNCH won the Black Zinnias Press poetry award for *Hinge*. She is the author of several chapbooks and lives in Sacramento, California.

AMIT MAJMUDAR is a nuclear radiologist who lives in Westerville, Ohio with his wife and three children. He is the author of three volumes of poetry, most recently *Dothead*. His forthcoming book is a verse translation from the Sanskrit of the *Bhagavad Gita*.

REGINALD MCKNIGHT is the Hamilton Holmes Professor of English at the University of Georgia. His books include: *White Boys, He Sleeps* and *I Get On the Bus*. He has won several prizes including an O'Henry award, a Drew Heinz prize, a Whiting award and a NEA Fellowship.

LO KWA MEI-EN's poem was originally published in the *New Orleans Review* in 2015 and then again in *The Bees Make Money In the Lion* (CSU Poetry Center 2016).

DAVID MEISCHEN, co-founder and managing editor of Dos Gatos Press, lives in Albuquerque, New Mexico with his husband. His essay is part of a memoir in progress.

THOMAS R. MOORE has published three books of poetry and his poems have appeared in over thirty literary journals. He currently serves as Poet Laureate of Belfast Maine,

BRIAN MORTON's novels include *Starting Out In the Evening* and *Florence Gordon*. He teaches at Sarah Lawrence College.

JOHN R. NELSON has contributed work to *The Missouri Review, Harvard Magazine* and birding journals in Great Britain and the United States. He lives in Gloucester, Massachusetts.

DELANEY NOLAN's work has appeared in *Ecotone, Guernica, The Indiana Review, Snap Judgment* and elsewhere. She lives in Winston-Salem, North Carolina.

NICK NORWOOD teaches at Columbus State University and is Director of the Carson McCullers Center for Writers and Musicians. His poems have appeared widely including on NPR's Writer's Almanac.

JOYCE CAROL OATES is the recipient of The National Medal of Humanities, the National Book Critics Circle Ivan Sandrof Lifetime Achievement Award and the National Book Award. Her most recent novel is *A Book of American Martyrs* (Ecco, 2017).

MEGHAN O'GIEBLYN's essays have appeared in *n+1, The Point, The Guardian, The New York Times* and *Best American Essays 2017*.

MARK JUDE POIRIER has written two novels, two story collections and a graphic novel. Film scripts he has written have played in Sundance, The Toronto International Film Festival and MOMA. He teaches at Harvard.

JAMIE QUATRO is the author of the short story collection *I Want To Show You More*. A second collection and a novel are forthcoming.

KEITH RATZLAFF's awards include: The Theodore Roethke Award, a Pushcart Prize and inclusion in *Best American Poetry 2009*. He teaches at Central College in Pella, Iowa. He is the author of *Then, A Thousand Crows; Dubious Angels* and *Across the Known World*.

ANNE RAY works on the eighteen floor of an office building in lower Manhattan. She has been a waitress, a gardener, an English teacher, a fishmonger and the author of the libretto for the ten minute opera "Symposium".

GEORGE SAUNDERS teaches at Syracuse University and is the author of several prize winning story collections and the recent novel *Lincoln In the Bardo*.

VALERIE SAYERS last appeared here in *Pushcart Prize XXX*. She teaches at the University of Notre Dame and is the author of several acclaimed novels.

SOLMAZ SHARIF's first collection of poems, *Look*, was recently published by Graywolf Press and was a 2016 National Book Award finalist She teaches at Stanford University.

SUJATA SHEKAR's stories have appeared in *Epoch, StoryQuarterly, The Common* and *Prairie Schooner*. She is a student in the MFA program at Hunter College.

JIM SHEPHARD is the author of seven novels and five story collections, including *Like You'd Understand Anyway*, a finalist for The National Book Award. His most recent collection is *The World To Come* (Knopf, 2017).

SAFIYA SINCLAIR was born and raised in Montego Bay in Jamaica. She is the author of *Cannibal* (University of Nebraska Press 2016).

MAHREEN SOHAIL lives in Islamabad, Pakistan. Her work has appeared in *Post Road, No Tokens,* and *Cosmonauts Avenue*. She is an Emerging Writer Fellow at *A Public Space*.

ANDREW SOLOMON has been recognized with awards from The National Book Critics Circle and The National Book Award. He is active in LGBT rights organizations and lives in New York.

STEVE STERN is the author of several books including *The Wedding Jester*, winner of the National Jewish Book Award. He teaches at Skidmore College.

BEN STROUD is the author of the story collection *Byzantium*, which won the Spotlight Award and the Bakeless Fiction Prize. He lives in Toledo, Ohio

NATASHA TRETHEWEY's most recent book is *Thrall*. She teaches English at Emory University.

CHASE TWICHELL is a past poetry guest editor of the Pushcart Prize, author of several books and lives in upstate New York.

ANTHONY WALLACE is the author of *The Old Priest* winner of the 2013 Drew Heinz Literature Prize and a finalist for the 2014 PEN/Hemmingway Award.

JESS WALTER is the author of six novels including *Beautiful Ruins,* a collection of short stories and a non-fiction book. He was nominated for a National Book Award for Fiction and was granted an Edgar Award for Best Novel. He lives in Spokane, Washington.

CHRISTIAN WIMAN's most recent book is *Hammer Is the Prayer: Selected Poems*. He teaches at Yale Divinity School.

DAVID WOJAHN just published his ninth book of poetry, *The Scribe* (University of Pittsburg Press). He teaches at Virginia Commonwealth University.

CECELIA WOLOCH's most recent poetry collections are: *Earth* (Two Sylvia's Press) and *Carpathia* (BOA Editions). Quale Press published her first novel, *Sur La Route*, in 2015.

JANE WONG is the author of three chapbooks and *Overpour* (Action Books 2016). She teaches at Western Washington University.

PUI YING WONG was born in Hong Kong and is the author of two books of poetry as well as two chapbooks. She lives in Cambridge, Massachusetts with her husband Tim Suermondt

KEITH WOODUFF lives in Akron, Ohio with his wife and son, Witt. "Elegy" is dedicated to his first son, Rainer. His writing has appeared in *Poetry East, Painted Bride Quarterly, The Journal* and elsewhere.

JASON ZENCKA has worked as a newspaper reporter, criminal defense investigator and a high school English teacher. He lives in Delmar, New York.

INDEX

The following is a listing in alphabetical order by author's last name of works reprinted in the *Pushcart Prize* editions since 1976.

588

591

594

598

601

603

604

605

608

610

611

617

618

621